'That thing in the van,' he stuttered, 'it was the same as whatever we saw under the bridge. Not the same one, though. So there's more of—'

'They can put on human faces,' the hippie interrupted from the back seat.

'They'd taken the place of all the staff there!' Church said, finally accepting what he'd seen.

'Waiting for you,' he continued. 'I think, if we took the time to investigate, we would find something similar at the airport and at other sites on all the arterial routes out of the capital.'

Church felt queasily like things were running out of control. 'They're after us?' he said dumbfoundedly.

Also by Mark Chadbourn

FICTION

Underground

Nocturne

The Eternal

Scissorman

Darkest Hour
Book Two of the Age of Misrule

NON FICTION

Testimony

WORLD'S END

BOOK ONE OF THE AGE OF MISRULE

MARK
CHADBOURN

Lines from 'Little Gidding', *Four Quarters*, by T. S. Eliot are
reproduced by kind permission of Faber & Faber Ltd.

This edition published in Great Britain in 2000 by
Millennium
An imprint of Victor Gollancz
Orion House, 5 Upper St Martin's Lane, London WC2H 9EA

To receive information on the Millennium list, e-mail us at:
smy@orionbooks.co.uk

A CIP catalogue record for this book
is available from the British Library.

ISBN 1 85798 980 5

Typeset by Rowland Phototypesetting Ltd,
Bury St Edmunds, Suffolk
Printed in Great Britain by
Cox & Wyman Ltd, Reading, Berkshire

For Elizabeth, Betsy and Joe

Acknowledgements

Bob Rickard and the Gang of Fort;
John Charlick and Sean Devlin at Trebrea Lodge;
Coach and Horses, Salisbury;
White Hart Hotel, Okehampton

For information about the author and his work:
http://www.markchadbourn.com/

Contents

PROLOGUE   1

ONE   Misty Morning, Albert Bridge   3

TWO   Different Views from the Same Window   24

THREE   On the Road   53

FOUR   The Purifying Fire   73

FIVE   Where the Black Dog Runs   102

SIX   A View into the Dark   131

SEVEN   Here Be Dragons   156

EIGHT   The Light That Never Goes Out   180

NINE   At the Heart of the Storm   209

TEN   The Hunt   239

ELEVEN   Away from the Light   256

TWELVE   Mi Vida Loca   287

THIRTEEN   The Hidden Path   316

FOURTEEN   A Murder of Crows   341

FIFTEEN   A Day as Still as Heaven   362

SIXTEEN   The Harrowing   379

SEVENTEEN   Hanging Heads   408

EIGHTEEN   The Shark has Pretty Teeth   443

NINETEEN   Flight   469

TWENTY   Revelations   494

TWENTY-ONE Last Stand 521
TWENTY-TWO Beltane 549

BIBLIOGRAPHY 556

PROLOGUE

And now the world turns slowly from the light. Not with the cymbal clash of guns and tanks, but with the gently plucked harp of shifting moods and oddly lengthening shadows, the soft tread of a subtle invasion, not here, then here, and none the wiser. Each morning the sun still rises on supermarket worlds of plastic and glass, on industrial estates where slow trucks lumber in belches of diesel, on cities lulled by the whirring of disk drives breaking existence down into digitised order. People still move through their lives with the arrogance of rulers who know their realms will never fall. Several weeks into the new Dark Age, life goes on as it always has, oblivious to the passing of the Age of Reason, of Socratic thought and Apollonian logic.

No one had noticed. But they would. And soon.

CHAPTER ONE

Misty Morning, Albert Bridge

It was just before dawn, when the darkness was most oppressive. London was blanketed by an icy, impenetrable, February mist that rolled off the Thames, distorting the gurgle and lap of the water and the first tentative calls of the birds in the trees along the embankment as they sensed the impending sunrise. The hour and atmosphere were unfriendly, but Church was oblivious to both as he wandered, directionless, lost to thoughts that had turned from discomfort to an obsession, and had soured him in the process. If anyone had been there to see his passing, they might have thought him a ghost: tall and slim, with too-pale skin emphasised by the blackness of his hair and a dark expression which added to the air of disquieting sadness which surrounded him. The night-time walks had become increasingly regular over the past two years. During the routines of the day he could lose himself, but when evening fell the memories returned in force, too realistic by far, forcing him out on to the streets in the futile hope he could walk them off, leave them behind. It was as futile as any childhood wish; when he returned home he could never escape her things or her empty space. The conundrum was almost more than he could bear: to recover meant he would have to forget her, but the mystery and confusion made it impossible to forget; it seemed he was condemned to live in that dank, misty world of not-knowing. And until he did know he felt he would not be whole again.

But that night the routine had been different. It wasn't just the memories that had driven him out, but a dream that God had decided His work, the world, had gone irrevocably

3

wrong and He had decided to wipe it away and start again. Inexplicably, it had disturbed Church immeasurably.

There was a clatter of dustbins nearby, some dog scavenging for food. But just to be sure, he paused, tense and alert, until a russet shape padded soundlessly out of the fog. The fox stopped in its tracks when it saw him, eyed him warily for a second, until it seemed to recognise some similar trait, and then continued across the road until it was lost again. Church felt a *frisson* of some barely remembered emotion that he gradually recognised as a sense of wonder. Something wild and untamed in a place shackled by concrete and tarmac, pollution and regulations. Yet after the initial excitement it served only to emphasise the bleak view of the world he had established since Marianne. Perhaps his dream had been right. He had never really been enticed by the modern world. Perhaps that was why he was so drawn to archaeology as a child. But now everything seemed so much worse. If there *was* a God, what would he want with a world where such a vital force as a sense of wonder was so hard to come by? Although most people seemed to hark back to some golden age where things were *felt* so much more vibrantly, it seemed to Church, with his new eyes, that they didn't even seem to have the passion to hate the world they lived in; they were simply bowed by the boredom of it: a place of routine and rules, where daily toil was the most important thing and the only rewards that really counted were the ones that came in currency. There wasn't anything to get excited about any more; nothing to believe in. You couldn't even count on God. Churches of all denominations seemed to be in decline, desperately stripping out the supernatural wonder for some modernist sense of *community* that made them seem like dull Oxfam working parties. But he had no time for God anyway. And that brought him in an ironic full circle: God was preparing to wipe the world clean and God didn't exist.

He snorted a bitter laugh. Away in the mist he could hear the fox's eerie barking howl and for a hopeful second he considered pursuing it to a better place. But he knew in his heart he wasn't nimble enough; his legs felt leaden and there seemed to be an unbearable weight crushing down on his shoulders.

And then all the thoughts of God got him thinking about himself and his miserable life, as if there were any other subject. Was he a good person? Optimistic? Passionate? He had been once, he was sure of it, but that was before Marianne had turned everything on its head. How could one event sour a life so completely?

It wasn't the damp that drew his shiver, but he pulled his overcoat tighter nonetheless. Sometimes he wondered what the future held for him. Two years ago there had been so much hope stitched into the direction he had planned for his life: more articles for the learned magazines, a book, something witty and incisive about the human condition, which also instigated a quiet revolution in archaeological thinking, building on the promise he had shown at Oxford when he had become the first member of his family to attain a degree. At twenty-six, he had known everything about himself. Now, at twenty-eight, he knew nothing. He was flailing around, lost in a strange world where nothing made sense. Any insight he thought he might have had into the human condition had been expunged, and poking about in long-dead things suddenly hadn't seemed as attractive as it had when he'd been the leading light of his archaeology course. It sounded pathetic to consider it in such bald terms, and that made it even more painful. He had never been pathetic. He had been strong, funny, smart, confident. But never pathetic. He had potential, ambitions, dreams, things that he thought were such a vital part of him he would never be able to lose them, yet there he was without any sign of them at all. Where had they all gone?

The only work of which he had felt capable was hack journalism, turning technical manuals into plain English and writing PR copy, bill-paying rather than future-building. And all because of Marianne. Sometimes he wished he could channel his feelings into bitterness, maybe even hate, anything that would allow him to move on, but he just wasn't capable of it. She'd dragged him out of life and left him on a mountaintop, and he felt he would never be able to climb down again.

With a relief that was almost childlike in its intensity, his thoughts were disturbed by a splashing of water which jarred against the sinuous sounds of the river. At first Church thought it might have been a gull at the river's edge, another sign of raw nature intruding on his life, but the intermittent noise suggested something larger. Leaning on the cold, wet wall, he waited patiently for the folds of mist to part as the splashing ebbed and flowed.

For several minutes he couldn't see anything, but as he was about to leave, the mist unfurled in a manner that reminded him of a theatre curtain rolling back. Framed in the white clouds at the river's edge was a hunched black shape, like an enormous crow. As it dipped into the eddies, then rose shakily, Church glimpsed a white, bony hand. An old woman, in a long, black dress and a black shawl, was washing something he couldn't see; it made him think of pictures of peasants in the Middle East doing their laundry in muddy rivers. The strangeness of a woman in the freezing water before dawn didn't strike him at first, which was odd in itself, but the more he watched, the more he started to feel disturbed by the way she dipped and washed, dipped and washed. Finally the jangling in his mind began to turn to panic and he started to pull away from the sight. At that moment the woman stopped her washing and turned, as if she had suddenly sensed his presence. Church glimpsed a terrible face, white and gaunt, and black, piercing eyes, but it was what she held that filled his thoughts as he ran away along the footpath towards Albert Bridge. For the briefest instant it appeared to be a human head, dripping blood from the severed neck into the cold Thames. And it had his face.

* * *

6

Ruth Gallagher had a song in her head that she couldn't quite place; something by The Pogues, she thought. Then she considered the holiday she hoped to take in the South of France that summer, before admiring the pearly luminescence of the mist as it rolled across the surface of the Thames. And when she opened her ears again Clive was still whining irritatedly.

'And another thing, why do you always have to act so superior?'

Clive gesticulated like he was berating a small child. He didn't even look at her; he had been lost in his rant for so long that she was no longer needed in the conversation.

'I don't act superior, I am.' It was the wrong thing to say, but Ruth couldn't resist it. She had to stifle a smile when a sound like a boiler venting steam erupted from his throat. It didn't help that at nearly six foot, she towered above him. Such nastiness wasn't normally in her nature, but he had treated her so badly throughout the evening she felt justified, while still acknowledging the whiff of childishness in her response.

When they had met at the Law Society dinner six weeks earlier, she went into the relationship with the same hope and optimism as always; it wasn't her fault that it hadn't worked out. In fact, after so many previous failed relationships, she had tried especially hard, but Clive was like so many other men she had met in recent times: self-obsessed, nervous of her intellect and wit while professing the opposite, quickly becoming insecure when they realised she wasn't so desperate to hold on to them that she'd kowtow to their every whim and turn a blind eye to their many insufferable qualities. It didn't take her long to see that Clive equated long, dark, curly hair and refined, attractive features with some pre-war view of femininity which he could easily control.

That sort of attitude could have made her blood boil, but the simple truth was she had realised that night that she felt so far removed from him it was hardly worth losing sleep over.

But Clive was just symptomatic of a wider malaise. Nothing in her life seemed fixed down, as she had expected it would be by the time she approached thirty; the job, her great ambition since her father had instilled it in her at thirteen, left her feeling empty and weary, but it was too late to go back and start over; she was ambivalent about London; the best word she could find for her friends and social life was *pleasant*. It was as if she was holding her breath, waiting for something to happen.

She hummed The Pogues' song in her head, trying to recall the chorus, then turned her attention once more to the marvellous way the mist smothered the echoes of their footsteps. Not far to go until she was home, she thought with relief.

'And another thing—'

'If you say that one more time, Clive,' Ruth interjected calmly, 'I'll be forced to perform an emergency tracheotomy on you with my fountain pen.'

Clive threw his arms in the air. 'That's it! I've had enough! You can make your way home alone.'

He spun on his heels and Ruth watched him march off into the fog with his head thrust down like some spurned, spoiled child. 'The perfect gentleman,' she muttered ironically.

As his footsteps faded away, Ruth became acutely aware of the stifling silence. She wished she'd left the club earlier, or at least countermanded Clive's order for the cab to pull over so they could have a 'quiet chat' as they walked the last few hundred yards to her flat. London wasn't a safe place for a woman alone. Her heels click-clacked on the slick pavement as she speeded up a little. The rhythm was soothing in the unnerving quiet, but as she approached Albert Bridge other sounds broke through: scuffles, gasps, the smack of flesh on flesh.

Ruth paused. Her every instinct told her to hurry home, but if someone was in trouble she knew her conscience wouldn't allow her to ignore it. She was spurred into life by a brief cry, quickly strangled, that seemed to come from the river's edge in the lonely darkness beneath the bridge. Two itinerants fighting over the remnants of a cheap bottle of wine, she supposed, but she had seen too many police reports to know the other possibilities were both many and disturbing. She located the steps to the river and moved cautiously down until the mist had swallowed up the street lights behind her.

When he heard the same struggle, Church's heartrate had just about returned to normal, but his nerves still jangled alarmingly. The image of the woman's terrible face wouldn't go, but he had almost managed to convince himself he had been mistaken in his view of what she was holding. Just a bundle of dirty clothes, a trick of the light and the fog. That was all.

He had been approaching Albert Bridge from the opposite direction to Ruth when the scuffling sounds provided a welcome distraction. Negotiating the treacherously slick steps down to the river, he found himself on a rough stone path that ran next to the slim, muddy beach at the water's edge, where an oppressive smell of rotting vegetation filled the dank air. A slight change in the quality of light signalled that somewhere above the mist, dawn was finally beginning to break, but the gloom beneath the bridge was impenetrable.

With only the soothing lapping of the Thames around him, he wondered if he had misheard the source of the fight. He paused, listening intently, and then a muffled cry broke and was instantly stifled. Cautiously he advanced towards the dark.

Keeping close to the wall so he wouldn't be seen, odd sounds gradually emerged: heavy boots on stones, a grunt, a choke. Finally, at the edge of the darkness, his eyes adjusted enough to see what lay beneath the bridge.

A giant of a man with his back to Church grasped a smaller man by the lapels. The victim looked mousily weak, with tiny, wire-framed spectacles on a grey face, his frame slight beneath a dark suit. There was a briefcase lying on the ground nearby.

The taller man, who must have been at least 7 ft 6 ins tall, turned suddenly, although Church was sure he hadn't made a sound. The giant had a bald head and long, animalistic features contorted by a snarl of rage. In the shadows, his pale, hooded eyes seemed to glow with a cold, grey fire. Church shivered unconsciously at the aura of menace that washed off him in a black wave.

'Put him down.'

Church started at the female voice. A woman with long dark hair and a beautiful, pale face was standing on the other side of the bridge, framed against the background of milky mist.

The tall man's breath erupted in a plume of white as it hit the cold; there was a sound like a horse snorting. He looked slowly from Church to the woman and back, effortlessly holding his victim like a rag doll, his gaze heavy and hateful. Church felt his heart begin to pound again; something in the scene was frightening beyond reason.

'If you don't put him down, I'm going for the police,' the woman continued in a calm, firm voice.

For a moment Church thought the victim was dead, but then his head lolled and he muttered something deliriously. There was contempt in the attacker's face as he glanced once more at Church and the woman, and then he hauled the smaller man off the ground with unnatural ease. Transferring his left hand to his victim's chin, he braced himself, ready to snap the neck.

'Don't!' Church yelled, moving forward.

In that instant, for no reason he could pinpoint, Church felt fear explode in every fibre of his being. The giant glared at him and Church had the disorienting sensation that the mugger's face was shifting like oil poured on water. He flashed back to the old woman at the water and what she was holding, and then his thoughts devolved into an incomprehensible jumble. His brain desperately tried to comprehend the retinal image of the giant's face becoming something else, and for a moment he almost grasped it, but the merest touch of the sight was like staring into the heart of the sun. His mind flared white, then shut down in shock, and he slumped to the ground unconscious.

Dawn had finally come when Church woke to the sensation of hands pulling him into a sitting position. There was a spinning moment of horror when he thought he was still staring at the changing face, and then he became dimly aware of the dampness of his clothes from the wet ground and a flurry of movement and sound around him. He grappled for some kind of understanding, but there was a yawning hole in his memory from the moment of his collapse, as raw as if he had been slashed with a razor.

'Are you okay?' A paramedic crouched in front of him, shining a light into his eyes. When the flare cleared, Church saw uniformed police and what were obviously plain-clothes detectives hovering near the river's edge.

Church remembered the mugger and his victim and suddenly lurched forward. The paramedic held him back with a steady hand. 'Did you see what happened?' he asked.

Church struggled for the words. 'Some kind of fight. Then . . .' He glanced around him curiously. 'I suppose I fainted. Pathetic, isn't it?'

The paramedic nodded. 'She said the same thing.'

Nearby was the woman Church had seen earlier. A blanket was draped around her shoulders; a medic checked her over while a detective tried to make sense of her replies. As Church watched, she looked up at him. In the second when their eyes met, Church had a sudden sensation of connection that went beyond the shared experience: a recognition of a similar soul. It was so intimate that it made him uncomfortable, and he looked away.

'Do you feel up to a few questions, sir?' The detective offered a hand and Church allowed himself to be hauled to his feet. The CID man seemed unnaturally calm for the activity going on around them, but there was an intensity in his eyes that was disturbing. As they headed towards the water's edge, Church saw the body in the glare of a camera flash; the neck had been broken.

'How long was I out?' Church asked.

The detective shrugged. 'Can't have been long. Some postman on his bike heard the commotion and we had a car here within five minutes of his call. What did you see?'

Church described hearing the noise of the fight and then seeing the tall man mugging his victim. The detective eyed him askance, a hint of suspicion in his face. 'And then he attacked you?'

Church shook his head. 'I don't think so.'

'So what happened to you and the young lady?'

There was an insectile skittering deep in his head as he fought to recall what he had seen; he was almost relieved when the memory refused to surface. 'I was tired, the ground looked so comforting...' The detective gave him the cold eye. 'How should I know?' Church looked round for a way to change the subject. 'Where's his briefcase?'

'We didn't find one.' The detective scribbled a line in his notebook and seemed brighter, as if the disappearance of the briefcase explained everything; a simple mugging after all.

Church spent the next hour at the station, growing increasingly disturbed as he futilely struggled to express his fears in some form the police could understand. In reception, he bumped into his fellow witness, whose expression suggested she had had a similar experience.

'Look, can we go and grab a coffee? I need to talk about this,' she said without any preamble. She ran her fingers through her hair, then lightened. 'Sorry. Ruth Gallagher.' She stuck out a hand.

Church took it; her grip was strong and confident. 'Jack Churchill. Church. They weren't having any of it, were they?'

Ruth sighed wearily. 'No surprise there. I'm a solicitor, in court every day. I found out pretty early on that once the police have discovered the most simplistic idea out there, they're like a dog with a bone. If they want to file this under M for Mugging, by God they're going to, and nothing I'm going to say will change their minds.'

'A mugging. Right. And JFK got roughed up that day in Dallas.' Church watched her features intently, trying to discern her true thoughts.

She looked away uncomfortably, disorientation and worry reflected in her face.

There was an intensity about her that Church found impossible to resist. They went to a little place on St John's Hill at Clapham Junction, filled with hissing steam from the cappuccino machine, the sizzle of frying food and the hubbub of local workers taking an early breakfast. They sat opposite each other at a table in the window and within seconds all the noise had faded into the background.

Sipping her coffee hesitantly, Ruth began. 'What did we see?'

Church chewed on his lip, trying to find the words that would tie down the errant memory. 'It seemed to me that his face began to change.'

'Impossible, of course,' Ruth said unconvincingly. 'So there has to be a rational explanation.'

'For a changing face?'

'A mask?'

'Did it look like a mask to you?' He tapped his spoon in his saucer. The merest attempt at recollection made him uncomfortable. 'This is what I saw: a man, much bigger than average, picked up someone with a strength he shouldn't have had, even at that size. Then he turned to us and his

13

features started to flow away like they were melting. And what lay beneath—' He swallowed. '—I have no idea.'

'And then we both went out at exactly the same time.'

'Because of what we saw next.'

Ruth gave an uncomfortable smile. 'I'm not the kind of person who has hallucinations in a moment of tension.'

Church glanced out of the window, as if an answer would somehow present itself to him, but all he could see was a tramp on the opposite side of the road watching them intently. There was something about the unflinching stare that disturbed him. He turned back to his coffee and when he looked again the tramp was gone.

'This whole business is making me paranoid,' he said. 'Maybe we should leave it at that. We're not going to discover what happened. Just put it down to one of those inexplicable things that happen in life.'

'How can you say that?' Ruth exclaimed. 'This was real! We were right at the heart of it. We can't just dismiss it.' She leaned forward with such passion Church thought she was going to grab his jacket. 'You must have some intellectual curiosity.'

'I find it difficult to get curious about anything these days.' There was a hint of surgical dissection in the way she eyed him; he almost felt his ego unpeeling.

'At least give me your number in case one of us remembers any more details,' she said. It was too firm to be a request. Church scribbled the digits on a paper serviette and then took Ruth's business card for her practice in Lincoln's Inn Fields with her home number on the back.

As he rose, she said, in a quiet voice that demanded reassurance, 'Were you frightened?'

He smiled falsely, said nothing.

The days passed bleakly. Winter receded a little more, but there was still an uncomfortable chill in the air that even the suffocating central heating of Church's flat seemed unable to dispel. Once spring was just around the corner, he always used to feel an urge to get his hands dirty in some dig or other, grubbing around for flaking bits of pottery or corroded nails which used to instil in some people a depression for the fleeting nature of life, but always filled him with a profound sense of the strength of humanity. At that moment, as he dredged deeply for any remaining vestige of enthusiasm to help him complete a manual for spreadsheet software, the feeling seemed further away than ever. It was compounded by a terrible uneasiness brought on by what he now called *that night*; whatever secret his mind held pressed at the back of his head like a tumour, sometimes feeling so malign it unleashed a black depression of such strength he found himself considering suicide, a feeling he had never countenanced before, even in the worst days after Marianne had left.

Dale, one of his few friends from before (he always saw his life as two distinct units, Before Marianne and After Marianne), was so shocked by his latest state of mind he almost attempted to pressgang Church into getting some kind of medical help. After a wearying struggle, Church had convinced him it was simply a passing phase, while secretly knowing neither Prozac nor EST could put him back on the road to wellbeing. The only option was to lance the boil, unleash the memory, and how could he do that when it was so unbearable in the first place?

'You've got to start getting out, you know.' Dale, always the most irresponsible of his friends, suddenly sounded like some geriatric relative. Church, seeing how he was infecting others, winced with guilt.

'It's not as simple as that.'

'I know it's not as simple as that. I'm not stupid,' Dale bristled. He swigged from his beer bottle, then suddenly flicked it in a loop in the air and caught it without spilling a drop. 'Hey! That was good, wasn't it?'

'Marvellous.'

'Okay. This weekend. We get a bootful of cans and take

15

off for Brighton. Drink them all under the pier, a few burgers, a mountain of candy floss, then off to the pleasure beach and see who's first to vomit on the rides. You know it has to be done.'

Church smiled wanly; two years ago he would never have guessed Dale would have been the one to stick around. 'It's a good idea, but I've got too much work on. Financial planning software, for my sins. It's got to be in by Monday.'

Dale said, resignedly, 'You remember the time you cancelled your holiday in Cyprus and bundled us all into the car for a week in Devon to cheer up Louise after her dad died? That was spontaneous fun.'

Church shrugged. 'Cyprus would have been too hot that time of year, anyway.'

'You don't fool me. You'd been planning for that holiday for months. Years probably, knowing you. And you gave it up in an instant.'

'I'm so selfless,' Church said sarcastically. He caught Dale examining him as if searching for the person he remembered. 'Of course, I've still got the photo of you at that gig we drove up to in Oxford.'

Dale blanched. 'Not the one where I lost my trousers when I was stage-diving?'

'Boxers too. Jesus, that was a horrible sight.'

'I was expecting you to catch me, not take photos!' Dale said indignantly. 'If I ever find out who pulled my keks down—'

'Serves you right for stage-diving. The rest of us were respectfully enjoying the music,' Church mocked.

'Yeah, you were a real muso, weren't you? You were like the bleedin' HMV computer. Name a CD and you'd list every track on it. And you could play the guitar *and* the drums. Bloody show-off.'

'You know you needed me. I provided the intellectual conversation while the rest of you were drinking your own weight in alcohol.'

Dale chuckled at the memories. 'We had some laughs too, right? You, me, Pete, Kate, Louise, Billy . . .'

And Marianne.

'That was a long time ago,' Church said.

Dale visibly winced at his *faux pas*. 'Listen to me. I sound like some old git reminiscing about the war.' His voice trailed off, and he looked Church in the eye a little uncomfortably. 'We can't keep talking around it, you know.'

'I'm okay,' Church protested. Here it was, as he feared, coming up on him from his blindside. 'I'm not some sap mooning around who can't accept his girlfriend's gone. It's been two years!'

'Bollocks. We both know it's not about the fact she's not here. It's the *way* it happened. And what you saw. That would be enough to screw anybody up.'

'Are you saying I'm screwed up?'

'Are you telling me you're not?' Dale dropped his bottle and the contents flooded out. 'Shit. Now look what you've made me do.'

'Forget it.'

Dale scrubbed the beer into the carpet with his boot. 'You shouldn't tear yourself apart. It wasn't your fault, you know.'

'You think she'd have gone like that for no reason? Of course it was my fault.'

'Listen, you're a good bloke. I'll never repeat this in company, but you're probably the most decent bloke I've ever met.' He paused thoughtfully. 'I know about your doctorate, you know.'

'What are you talking about?' Church looked away.

'Billy's a screw-up – he always was. But you gave him that money you'd been working round the clock for a year to save so you could go back and get that qualification you'd been dreaming about ever since you were a kid. Don't deny it, Church – he told me, even though you tried to keep it a secret. I know your family never had much and you had to get a job to send some cash back to them. And then you saved Billy from all that disgrace and now look at him – the fattest of fat-cat accountants in the West End. Thanks to you. And all it cost you was your life's dream – to be a doctor of digging-up-crap. Not much to anybody else, but I know how much it meant to you. So don't go beating yourself up thinking you're some little shit because of Marianne.'

Church shook his head dismissively. Dale didn't understand – how could he?

'I'm only saying these things because I'm a mate.' Dale was on a roll now; Church recognised the gleam in his eye. 'I remember what you used to be like. You used to enjoy yourself, all the time, even when the rest of us were miserable and it was pissing down with rain and some club wouldn't let us in because Billy was dressed like a stiff again. When Louise and Pete had one of their irritating arguments, you'd always find something positive to get them back together. You used to read more books and see more films and hear more music than anybody I knew. And now—'

'I don't.'

'Exactly. Now you don't do anything. You've lost all focus. What's done is done. You've got to start living again.'

Church made some concilatory sounds, but it didn't convince Dale; he'd heard it all before. In the end he departed in irritation, but Church knew he'd be back to try again. He was good like that. But Dale couldn't be expected to understand the depth of the problem, how many futile hours had been spent looking at it from every angle; if there was an easy solution he would have found it long ago. The worst thing was he felt so bad about how he'd made Dale feel over the months, he couldn't bring himself to talk about the experience under Albert Bridge.

For the rest of the evening he kept flashing back to the moment before he fainted that night, interspersed with too many memories of Marianne: on the banks of Loch Ness, at her birthday in Covent Garden, the Sunday morning she brought him a champagne breakfast in bed for no reason apart from the fact that she loved him. Finally sleep crept up on him.

'Ruth. My office. Now!'

Ruth dropped the pile of files at Milton's barked order and then cursed under her breath as she scrambled to collect them. What was wrong with her? She wasn't the nervous type, but since that morning by the river she had been permanently on edge, jumping at shadows, snapping at colleagues. Her work had always been the calm centre of her life where she could do no wrong, but now it seemed dangerously askew.

Dumping the files on her desk, she marched into Milton's glass-walled office, sensing the atmosphere before she had crossed the threshold. The senior partner glowered behind his desk.

'Close the door,' he growled, his repressed anger bringing out his Highland brogue. That was always a bad sign. Ruth waited for the fireworks.

'What's wrong with you, Ruth?' he asked. 'Is it drugs? Drink?'

'I don't know what you mean, Ben.'

He tapped a letter that was placed precisely in the centre of his blotter. 'Sir Anthony is absolutely livid. He says you hung up on him yesterday.'

'It was an accident,' she lied. She'd always been able to cope with the peer's toffee-nosed pomposity and condescension, but, for some reason, yesterday she'd had enough. She knew at the time she should have called him back, but she couldn't bear to listen to any more of his bluster.

'He's our top client, for God's sake! Do you know how much money he brings into this firm? And he was *your* client because you were the best and you could be trusted.'

Ruth didn't like the sound of the past tense. 'It won't happen again, Ben.'

'It's not the only thing, Ruth. Not by a long shot.' He

angrily flicked open a thin file. 'During the last two weeks you've overcharged three clients, undercharged two. Your brief to the barrister in the Mendeka case was so incompetent it's possibly actionable. You were so late in court on Friday the case had to be rescheduled. Two weeks for at least three sackable offences. Jesus Christ, what kind of a firm do you think this is?' Her ears burned. 'To be honest, I don't want to know what's wrong,' he continued. 'I just want it sorted out. Anybody else would have been out on their ear by now, but your past record has been exemplary, Ruth. I hope you've not simply become aware of that and you're resting on your laurels.'

'No, Ben—'

'—Because even our best man can't go about pissing off the clients who make this a premier league firm thanks to their patronage and their money. At your best you're still an asset to us. I want you to find out where that best has gone.'

'Ben?'

'You've got some time off, unpaid of course. The next time you're here I want it to be the old Ruth.'

He lowered his attention to the paper on the desk in a manner that was both irritating and insulting. Ruth had never liked him, but at that moment she wanted to grab him by the lapels and punch him in the face. The only thing that stopped her was that every word had been true.

In the toilet, she blinked away tears of frustration and rage and kicked the cubicle door so hard it almost burst off its hinges; her hatred for the job made her feel even worse. It had never been what she wanted to do, but her father had been so keen she hadn't been able to refuse him. But that wasn't the real cause of her sudden bout of incompetence; it was the scurrying, black lizard-thing that had taken up residence in her head.

For the first time she had an inkling how the victims of abuse suffered in later life from the hideous repressed memories that manipulated their subconscious. Whatever had truly happened that early morning beneath Albert Bridge had turned her into a different person: depressive, anxious, underconfident, hesitant, pathetic.

She put her hands over her eyes and tried to hold the emotions back.

Church was spending too long surfing the web and he knew his phone bill would be horrendous, but there was something almost soothing in the crashing waves of information. It was zen mediation for the new age; every time he felt an independent thought enter his head he would click on the hotlink and jump to a new site with new images and words to hypnotise him. He had been around a score of different subjects – cult TV, music, new science, even delving into some of the archaeology sites, but somehow he had found himself at www.forteantimes.com – and everything had gone horribly wrong.

He knew vaguely of the magazine the website represented. The journal of strange phenomena, *Fortean Times* it called itself, an erudite publication which examined every odd happening, from crop circles and UFOs to contemporary folklore, bizarre deaths to crazy coincidences, with a ready wit and a sharp intellect. He always flicked through copies in Smiths, but he'd never gone so far as buying one.

On the lead page was a brief story:

In the last few weeks the world has gone totally weird! As you know, we continually compile all reports of strange phenomena from around the globe for an annual index to show if the world is getting weirder. Since Christmas the number of reports has increased twentyfold. Postings on the Fortean newsgroup {alt.misc.forteana} indicate an astonishing increase in *all* categories, from electronic voice phenomena and hauntings via amazing cryptozoological sightings to UFOs and accounts of more big cats in the wilderness. What's going on!?!

Church went through the report twice, feeling increasingly unnerved for reasons he couldn't explain. Briefly he considered how he should have read it – as cranky but fun – but it sparked disturbing connections in his mind. He clicked on the hotlink to Usenet. When alt.misc.forteana appeared, he scrolled slowly through the postings. In Nottingham, a sound engineer for Central TV had recorded strange giggling voices when his microphone should have been picking up white noise from a radio. A rain of fish had fallen on Struy in the Scottish Highlands. Mysterious lights had been seen moving slowly far beneath the surface of Ennerdale Water in the Lake District. A postmistress from Norwich wrote passionately about a conversation with her dead father late one evening. Unconnected incidents, but as he worked his way down the neverending list of messages he was staggered by the breathtaking diversity of unbelievable things happening around the country, to people from all walks of life, in all areas. The accounts were heartfelt, which made them even more disturbing. It put his own odd experience into some kind of context.

One posting leapt out at him from LauraDuS@legion.com. It said simply:

All this is linked. And I have proof.
Email me if you want to know more.

He vacillated for a moment or two, then rattled off a quick reply requesting more information.

Further down the list there was a message from one of the *Fortean Times* editors, Bob Rickard, talking in general terms about the magazine's philosophy. With a certain apprehension, Church typed out the details of his experience at Albert Bridge and sent it off for Rickard's views. Then he returned to the list and immersed himself in the tidal wave of weirdness.

With bleary eyes and a dry mouth, he eventually came offline at 1 a.m. feeling an odd mixture of excitement, agitation, concern, and curiosity that left his head spinning. It was a pleasure to feel anything after two years of hermetically sealed life.

Away from the computer, he became aware once again of the hidden memory's horrible presence at the back of his head; his mood dampened instantly and he knew there would be no relief for him until that desperate event was put into some kind of perspective. He was so lost in his introspection that at first he didn't notice the figure outside as he began to draw the curtains. But a passing car disturbed him and within seconds he had grown rigid and cold. From his first-floor vantage point, the figure was half-hidden by the over-hanging branches of the tree across the road, but the subtle way the body was held was as unmistakable to him as his own reflection.

And a second later he was running through the flat and down the stairs, feeling the first tremors of shock ripple through his body, wincing as the cold night air froze the sweat that seemed to be seeping from every pore. Desperation and disbelief propelled him out into the road, but the figure was gone, and although he went a hundred yards in both directions, there was no sign of the person who had been watching his window. Finally he sagged to his knees at the front gate and held his head, wondering if he had gone insane, feeling his thoughts stumble out of control. There were tears where he thought he had exhausted the well. It had been Marianne, as surely as the sun came up at dawn.

And Marianne had been dead for two years.

CHAPTER TWO

Different Views from the Same Window

Inactivity did not sit well with Ruth and it seemed only right that her enforced absence from work should be put to good use. Although she knew the buried trauma of Albert Bridge was responsible for her daytime confusions, black moods and constantly disturbed nights, she was determined she would not be paralysed by it; practicality was one of the strengths which had seen her rise so rapidly in the firm.

No one had been arrested for the Albert Bridge murder, although photofits based on Ruth and Church's descriptions had been given wide circulation throughout the media; the suspect had appeared so grotesque that Ruth found it hard to believe he hadn't been picked up within hours. Yet the investigation had drawn repeated blanks and as the days turned to weeks it became increasingly apparent it wasn't going anywhere. One advantage of Ruth's position with Cooper, Sedgwick & Tides was her direct access to the Met, where she found plenty of contacts who weren't averse to allowing her a glimpse into a restricted file or digging up some particular snippet of information. So it was relatively easy to find herself that morning in an empty room, bare apart from a rickety table, with the murder file.

The victim was a low-grade Ministry of Defence civil servant named Maurice Gibbons, a fact which had at first raised suspicion of some shadier motive beyond a simple mugging. When it became apparent the only secrets Gibbons had access to centred on the acquisition of furniture for MoD property, all conspiracy scenarios were quickly discarded. He was forty-eight and lived with his wife in Crouch End; both their children had left home. The only gap in the information was exactly what he was doing at Albert Bridge at that time of night. He had told his wife he was calling in at his local for a pint and she had gone to bed early, not realising he hadn't returned home. She didn't remember him leaving with his briefcase, although it was possible he had picked it up from the hall on the way out; why he had felt the need to take a briefcase to the pub was not discussed. And that was about it. He had no enemies; everything pointed to a random killing. Ruth jotted down Gibbons' address, phone number and his wife's name and slipped out, pausing to flash a thankful smile at the detective lounging by the coffee machine.

While there could be a completely reasonable explanation for his appearance at Albert Bridge – an illicit liaison, hetero or homo – to ignore it wasn't the correct way to conduct an investigation. Ruth knew she would have to interview the wife.

Her decision to take action had raised her mood slightly, but it seemed morbidity and depression were still waiting at the flat door, emotions so unnatural to her she had no idea how to cope. Bitterly, she set off for the kitchen to make a strong coffee in the hope that a shock of caffeine would sluice it from her system. As she passed the answer machine, the red light was flashing and she flicked it to play.

It was Church. 'We need to talk,' he said.

They met in the Nag's Head pub in Covent Garden just before the lunchtime rush. Church had a pint of Winter Warmer and Ruth a mineral water, which they took to a table at the back where they wouldn't be disturbed. Church felt in turmoil; he had barely slept since the shock of seeing – or thinking he had seen – Marianne outside the flat. He had tried to convince himself it was a hallucination brought on by all the turbulence in his subconscious, but it added to the queasy unreality that had infected his life. It had had one good effect, though: it had shocked him so severely that he could no longer passively accept what had happened to him.

'I didn't think I'd be hearing from you again. The last time we spoke you didn't sound too enthusiastic about opening this can of worms any further,' Ruth said.

'You can only bury your head in the sand for so long. That is, if it's been affecting you the same way it's affected me,' Church began cautiously. He tapped the side of his head. 'I can't remember a thing about what happened, but my subconscious can see it in full, glorious Technicolor, and that little bastard at the back of my head won't let me rest until I sort it out.' Ruth nodded. 'So,' he added, almost dismissively, 'what I'm saying is, you were right.'

'I do love to hear people say that.' Ruth appraised Church carefully behind her smile. She instinctively felt he was a man she could trust; more than that, she felt he was someone she could actually like, although she couldn't put her finger on exactly what it was that attracted her. There was an intensity about him that hinted at great depths, but an intriguing darkness too. 'So what do you suggest?'

Church took out a folded printout of the email he had received from Bob Rickard, the *Fortean Times* editor. 'I made a few enquiries online about what options are available for people with repressed memories.'

'This happens all the time, does it?'

'You'd be surprised. Apparently, it's *de rigueur* if you've been abducted by aliens. You thought that aching rectum was just haemorrhoids? Here's how you find out you've really had a nocturnal anal probe. Regression hypnosis. To be honest, the expert I contacted wasn't, let's say, *enthusiastic* about its effectiveness. Some people think it can screw you up even more. There's something called False Memory Syndrome where your memory's been polluted by stuff that's leaked in from your imagination, things you've read, other memories, so your mind actually creates a fantasy that it believes is real. The Royal College of Psychiatrists has banned its members from using any hypnotic method to recover memories, so this guy says. But then there're a whole bunch of other experts who claim it does work.'

'And the alternative?'

'Years, maybe decades, of therapy.'

Ruth sighed. 'I'm not too sure I'm comfortable with someone stomping around with hobnail boots in the depths of my mind.'

'So we'd only do it if we were desperate, right?' Church's statement hung in the air for a moment before he turned over the printout to reveal several scrawled names and numbers. 'I've got a list of qualified people here.'

Ruth closed her eyes and jabbed her finger down at random. 'They say a leap of faith can cause miracles.'

'Don't go getting all religious on me,' Church said as he circled the name. 'I have enough trouble sleeping as it is. The last thing I need is you telling me it was the Devil we saw.'

The appointment was fixed for three days hence. As the time grew closer, Church and Ruth found themselves growing increasingly anxious, as if whatever lay deep in their heads sensed its imminent removal and fought to stay in the comforting dark. Church received his first email from LauraDuS-@legion.com. She was Laura DuSantiago, a software designer at a computer games company in Bristol. She didn't actually say how the strange phenomena were connected, but she dropped some broad hints of a personal experience which had given her a unique insight. The ever more disturbing aspects of his own life had left Church oddly intrigued by what she had to say and he fired back an email straight away.

The day was bleakly cold, with depressing sheets of rain sweeping along Kensington High Street as Church and Ruth made their way west from the tube. There was no hint of spring around the corner. The street scene was a muddy mess of browns and greys, with the occasional red plastic sign

27

adding a garish dash of colour. A heavy smog of car fumes had been dampened down to pavement level by the continuous downpour.

'When you're a kid the world never looks like this. What happened to all the magic?' Church said as they negotiated the honking, steaming traffic which was backed up in both directions for no apparent reason.

'Didn't they pass a law or something? It was putting the workers off their toil.' Ruth led them to shelter in W. H. Smiths' doorway for a while in the hope that the cloudburst would blow over, but their anxiety to reach the therapist's office soon drove them out again with Ruth holding a copy of *Marie Claire* over her head.

Their destination lay up a side road just off the High Street. They buzzed the entryphone and dashed in out of the rain. 'The pubs are open now,' Church suggested. Ruth smiled wanly; for a second she almost turned back.

The reception smelled of new carpets and polished furniture. It was functional and blandly decorated, with a blonde Sloane smiling behind a low desk. Stephen Delano, the therapist, stepped out of the back room the moment they entered, as if they had tripped some silent alarm. He was in his forties, with light brown hair that had been blow-dried back from a high forehead and a smile that wasn't exactly insincere, but which made Church uneasy nonetheless. He strode over and shook their hands forcefully.

'Good to see you. Come on through.' He led them into the rear office which was dark, warm and filled with several deep, comfortable chairs. The blinds were down and it was lit ambiently by a couple of small, well-placed lamps. Several pieces of recording equipment were sitting near the chairs. 'Welcome to the womb,' Delano said. 'I think you'll feel comfortable and secure here. You need to feel at ease.'

Ruth slipped into one of the chairs, put her head back and closed her eyes. 'Wake me when it's over.'

'You're absolutely sure you want to go through this

together?' Delano continued. 'I think it would be more effective to do it separately, if only to prevent what one is saying influencing the other. This isn't like surgery. Memories are delicate, easily corrupted by outside sources.'

'We do it together,' Church said firmly. When they had discussed it earlier, they both instinctively felt it was something they could only face up to together.

'Well, you're the bosses.' Delano clapped his hands, then ushered Church into a chair next to Ruth's and manoeuvred a reel-to-reel recorder between them. 'So we have a good record of what you say,' he explained. 'I can transfer it to a cassette for you to take away, and I'll store the master here.'

After a brief explanation of the principle, he dimmed the lights even further with a hand-held remote control. Church expected to feel sleepy in the gloomy warmth, but the anxiety had set an uncomfortable resonance which seemed to be buzzing around his body. He turned to look at Ruth, her face pale in the dark. She smiled at him, but the unease was apparent in her eyes. Delano pulled up a chair opposite and began to talk in measured tones that were so low Church occasionally had trouble hearing him. After a minute or two, the words were rolling in and out of his consciousness like distant thunder and he was suspended in time.

For what could have been one minute or ten, the sensation was pleasurable, but then Church began to get an odd feeling of disquiet. On a level he couldn't quite grasp, he was sensing they were not alone in the room. He wanted to shout out a warning to Ruth and Delano, but his mouth wouldn't respond, nor would his neck muscles when he tried to turn his head so he could look around. He was convinced there was a presence somewhere in the shadows in the corner of the room, malign, watching them balefully, waiting for the right moment to make its move. When the sensation faded a moment later, Church convinced himself it was just a by-product of Delano's hypnosis, but it didn't go away completely.

'It is the morning of February 7,' Delano intoned calmly. 'Where are you, Jack?'

Church found himself talking even though he wasn't consciously aware of moving his mouth. 'I can't sleep. I've gone out for a walk to wear myself out so I'll drop off quickly. I have bad dreams.' He swallowed; his throat felt like it was closing up. 'It's foggy, a real pea-souper. I've never seen it like that before, like something out of Dickens. I see a woman washing something in the river . . .' A spasm convulsed him. 'No . . .'

'It's okay, Jack. You rest a moment,' Delano said quickly. 'Ruth, where are you?'

Ruth's chest grew tighter; she sucked in a deep breath until her lungs burned. 'I've been to The Fridge. Clive is whining on. He realises we've got nothing in common.' Her voice turned spontaneously singsong: '"Why don't you do this? Why don't you do that?" He doesn't really want me, just the woman he thinks I am. He gets wound up . . . blows his top . . . walks off. I'm a bit frightened – it's so quiet, so still – but I try not to show it. I can make it home in a few minutes if I walk quickly. Then I hear the sound of . . . a fight? . . . coming from under the bridge.' Her breath became more laboured. She wondered obliquely if she was having a heart attack.

'Jack, do you hear the fight now?' Delano's voice seemed to be floating away from both of them.

'Yes. I was frightened by the old woman, but when I hear them fighting I forget her. I could walk on . . . ignore it . . . but that's not right. I've got to try to help. Somebody might be in trouble.'

'Are you afraid for yourself?'

'A little. But if I could do something to help I've got to try. Too many people walk by. I find the steps down to the river. They're wet . . . I go down slowly. There're more scuffling noises. A grunt. I wonder if there's an animal down there. Maybe a dog or . . . something. I can smell the river.

30

Everywhere's so damp. My heart's beating so loud. I edge along the wall.' Another spasm. He thought he almost saw something; was it in the room or in his head?

'Take a rest, Jack. Ruth?'

'I go down the steps. I'm ready to run at any moment, but I'm aware I've got heels on. If the worst comes to the worst I'll have to kick them off. They're expensive though . . . I don't want to lose them. It's dark under the bridge. I can't see anything. I move closer. I think I've bitten my lip . . . I can taste blood.' She heaved in another juddering breath; each one was getting harder and harder. 'There're two men. They just look like shadows at first. One of them big, the biggest man I've ever seen. He's shaking the smaller one. I look over and there's another man there watching the fight. I can see he's come from the other side. I'm relieved . . . I'm not alone.'

'Is it Jack?' Delano asked quietly.

'Yes, yes, it's Church. He's got a strong face. He looks decent. He makes me feel safer. We both look at the two men—'

'Is he dead?' Church suddenly interjected, his voice too loud. 'Christ, I think he's dead! No . . . he's moving. But the giant's picking him up. How can he be so strong? Just one arm . . . what's going on? . . . he's going to break his neck!'

'Calm down,' Delano hushed.

'Don't do it or I'm going to call the police!' Ruth yelled. She snapped forward in her seat, then slumped back.

'Take it easy now,' Delano said soothingly. 'Be peacef—'

'Stop!' Church thrashed to one side. Delano placed a comforting hand on Church's forearm, but Church knocked it away wildly.

'He's looking—' Ruth was wheezing, but she couldn't seem to draw any breath into her lungs.

'—at us!' Church continued.

Delano was alarmed at the paleness of her face. 'I think

that's enough now,' he began. 'It's time to take a break. We can come back to this.'

'My God! Look at—' Church gasped.

'—his face! It's changing—'

'—melting—'

They were convulsing in their seats. Delano grabbed both their wrists, gripped by anxiety that he was losing control; they were all losing control. He stood up so he could place his head between them. 'On the count of three . . .'

'Not human!'

'His eyes—'

'—red—'

'—a demon!' Ruth gasped. 'Twisted . . . monstrous . . .' She leaned to one side and vomited on to the carpet.

'One . . .'

'Evil!' Jack cried. 'I feel evil coming off it! It's looking at me!'

'Two . . .'

Ruth vomited again, then stumbled off the chair to her knees.

'I can't bear to look at its face!'

'Three . . .'

For a second, Delano was terrified he wouldn't be able to bring them out of it, but gradually they seemed to come together, as if he were watching them swim up from deep water. Church bobbed forward and put his face in his hands. He felt like he was burning up, his hair slick with sweat. Ruth levered herself back into the chair and sat there with her eyes shut.

Delano was visibly shaken. There was sweat on his own brow and his hands were trembling as he switched off the tape recorder. Frantically he thumbed the remote control until the light flared up too bright and drove the shadows from the room. 'Well that was an unusual experience,' he mumbled bathetically. He fetched them both water, which they sipped in silence. Then called in his assistant to clean up the carpet. It was a full ten minutes until they had recovered.

'That was unbelievable,' Church said eventually. His voice was like sandpaper in the arid stillness of the room.

'You're right,' Ruth responded, 'because it's not true.'

'What do you mean?' Church eyed her curiously. 'We saw the same thing.'

Ruth shook her head emphatically. 'Think about it, Church. There must be a rational explanation. We have to use a little intellectual rigour here – the first answer isn't always the right one. We were talking about how memories can be corrupted by other aspects of the mind's working. That can happen, can't it?' she said to Delano. He nodded. 'Remember in the pub you made some throwaway comment about us seeing the Devil, so that's exactly what we did see. You placed that thought in both our heads and our subconscious turned it into reality. It was self-fulfilling.' She looked to Delano for support.

'Your reactions were very extreme, which suggests a serious trauma buried away, but if you witnessed a particularly brutal murder, as you told me on the phone, that would explain it,' the therapist said. 'What you recalled today is known as a screen memory. You create it yourself to protect your own mind from further trauma. Yes, it was quite horrible, but the unbelievable elements allow you to dismiss it within the context of reality as you perceive it so it's not as threatening as it first appears. The *true* memory that lies beneath is much more of a threat to you. I think we'll need a few more sessions to get to it, to be honest.' Delano's smile suggested he was relieved by his own explanation. 'I must admit, I was a little worried. I've never come across anything quite like that before.'

Church wasn't convinced. 'It was pretty real.'

'Sorry about the carpet,' Ruth said sheepishly. Church thought she was going to burst into a fit of embarrassed giggles.

'Don't worry,' Delano said. 'Let me just check the recording and I'll make arrangements to get your cassette copy.'

He knelt down and rewound the tape. When he pressed play there was a blast of white noise and what sounded like an ear-splitting shriek of hysterical laughter. Delano's brow furrowed. He ran the tape forward a little and tried again. The white noise hissed from the speakers. A second later the giggling started, fading in and out as if it was a badly tuned radio signal, the laughter growing louder and louder until Church's ears hurt; it made him feel sick and uncomfortable. Delano snapped off the recorder in dismay.

'I'm terribly sorry. That's never happened before,' he said in bafflement. 'It must have picked up some stray signal.'

'Remind me not to book with that mini-cab service,' Church said.

Outside, the rain had stopped briefly to allow a burst of insipid sunlight, but the oppressive experience with Delano clung to them. Their reclaimed memories, even if false, were now free, scurrying round, insect-like, in the back of their heads, making them feel queasy and disoriented.

'I feel much better after that, even if we didn't find out exactly what happened,' Ruth said, trying to put a brave face on it. She gave Church a comforting pat on the back. 'Come on, don't let it get to you. It was a bad dream, that's all.'

Church looked round at the black office windows above the shops, unable to shake the feeling they were being watched. 'I need a drink.'

'Let's see what we can do about that.'

She took him for lunch to Wodka, a Polish restaurant nestling in the hinterland of well-heeled apartment blocks on Kensington High Street's south side. Over blinis and cream and ice-cold honey vodka, they discussed the morning's events and what lay ahead. Church was taken by Ruth's brightly efficient manner and sharp sense of humour which helped her see the inherent farce in even the bleakest moment.

'You always seem like you've got something on your mind,'

Ruth said when she felt comfortable enough to talk a little more personally.

'You know how it is.' Church sipped at the strong Polish coffee, but if Ruth noticed his discomfort she didn't pay it any heed.

'Anything you want to talk about?'

'Nothing I should burden you with.'

'Go on, I'm a good listener. Besides, after an experience like that we're a minority of two. We have to stick together.'

It would have been easy to bat her questions away, but there was something in her which made him feel like unburdening himself; a warmth, an *understanding*. He took a deep breath, surprised he even *felt* like talking about it. 'I had a girlfriend. Marianne Leedham. She was a graphic designer – magazine work, some book covers, that kind of thing. We met soon after I'd left university. I had a seedy flat in Battersea, just off Lavender Hill, and Marianne lived round the corner. We'd see each other in the local Spar or in the newsagents. You know how it is when you see someone and you know it's inevitable that sooner or later you're going to get together, even if you haven't spoken?' Ruth nodded, her eyes bright. 'I felt like that, and I could tell she did too. The local pub, the Beaufoy Arms, used to hire a boat to go along the Thames each year. It was an overnight thing, lots of Red Stripe, jerk pork and dancing, up to the Thames Barrier and then back again for dawn. I went with my mates and Marianne was there with hers. We both knew something was going to happen. Then just before sunrise we found ourselves on deck alone.' He smiled. 'Not by chance. We talked a little. We kissed a lot. It was like some stupid romantic film.'

Ruth watched his smile grow sad. 'What happened, Church?'

His sigh seemed like the essence of him rushing out. 'It was all a blur after that. We saw each other, moved in together. You know, people think I'm lying when I say this, but we never argued. Not once. It was just the best. It was

35

so serious for both of us we never even thought about getting married, but Marianne's mum was getting a bit antsy, as they do, so we started muttering about getting engaged. Everything was fine, and then—' His voice drifted away; the words felt like heavy stones at the back of his throat, but somehow he forced them out. 'Two years ago, it was. I'd been out for the night. When I came back the flat was so silent, I knew there was something wrong. Marianne always had some kind of music on. And there was this odd smell. To this day I don't know what it was. I called out for her – there was nowhere else she could have been at that time of night – and my heart started beating like it was going to explode. I knew, you see. I knew. I found her face down in a pool of blood on the bathroom floor. She'd slashed her wrists.'

'Oh, God, I'm sorry,' Ruth said in dismay. 'I shouldn't have pried.'

'Don't worry, it's okay. It doesn't hurt me to think about her any more. I've got over all that grief thing, although sometimes I feel a little . . .' His voice trailed off, but her smile told him she understood what he was trying to say. 'It's how she died that I can't cope with. There hasn't been a single day gone by since then when I haven't tried to make sense of it. There was no reason for it. She hadn't been depressed. We'd never, ever argued. As far as I was concerned, everything in our lives was perfect. Can you imagine what that's like? To discover your partner had this whole secret world of despair that you never knew existed? Enough despair to kill herself. How could I have been so wrapped up in myself not to have even the slightest inkling?' He couldn't find the words to tell her what it was that had soured his life since that night: not grief, but guilt; the only possible explanation was that he, in some way, was complicit.

But Ruth seemed to know exactly what he was thinking. She leaned across the table and said softly, 'There could be a hundred and one explanations. A sudden chemical inbalance in her brain—'

'I've been through them all. I've weighed it up and turned it inside out and investigated every possibility, so much that I can't think of anything else. To answer your original question, that's why I always seem so preoccupied. Nothing else seems important beside that.'

'I'm sorry—'

'No, *I'm* sorry. It's selfish of me to be so wrapped up in myself. We've all got problems.' He looked out into the puddled street. Briefly he considered telling Ruth about Marianne's appearance outside his home, but to give voice to it would mean he would have to face up to the reality of the experience and everything that came with it; besides, it was too close to his heart right now. 'I wish I could put it all behind me, but there are so many things about it that don't make sense. Only hours before, she'd been making plans for the wedding.' Church grew silent as the waitress came over to pour more coffee; it broke his introspective mood and when she left it was obvious he didn't want to talk about it any more. 'This is a good lunch. Thanks.'

Ruth smiled affectionately. 'My philosophy is eat yourself out of a crisis.'

'Yet you stay so thin!' he said theatrically. They laughed together, but gradually the conversation turned to what they had seen beneath the bridge, as they had known it would. 'So whose face lies behind the Devil?' he asked.

Ruth's expression darkened. 'I don't know. Why should our reactions in the trance have been so extreme, and identical?' Church understood her confusion. 'But it's strange. For the first time in months, I feel like I've got some kind of direction. I really want to keep going until we get to the heart of it.'

Church was surprised to realise he felt the same way. 'How ironic can you get? It takes a brutal murder to give us some purpose in life.'

'Of course, there's also the danger that if we let it drop now that awful memory will start its destabilisation again, and I could really do without wrecking my career at this stage in my life.' She called for the bill and paid it with a gold Amex.

'So where do we go from here?' Church asked.

Ruth smiled. 'Elementary, my dear Watson.'

Maurice Gibbons had lived in a three-storey terrace in a tree-lined avenue; not too imposing, but certainly comfortable; it looked like it could have done with a lick of paint and a touch of repointing here and there. The lights were already ablaze in the twilight as Church and Ruth opened the front gate and walked up to the door, shivering from the chill; the night was going to be icy. They'd spent the afternoon quietly at Ruth's flat, drinking coffee, talking about comfortingly bland topics, but now they were both feeling apprehensive. Susan Gibbons was a quiet woman who looked older than her years. Her grief still lay heavy on her, evident in the puffiness of her eyes, her pallor and her timidity as she led them into the lounge where condolence cards still gathered dust on the mantelpiece. She accepted at face value Ruth's statement that they were looking into her husband's murder and sat perched on an armchair listening to their questions with a blankness which Church found unnerving, if only because he recognised something of himself in her.

'I know you've probably been through all this before, Mrs Gibbons, but we have to go over old ground in case there's anything we've missed,' Ruth began.

Mrs Gibbons smiled without a hint of lightness or humour. 'I understand.'

'Your husband had no enemies?'

'None at all. Maurice wasn't what you would call a passionate man. He enjoyed his job and he did it well, but he didn't really have any ambition to move on, and everyone recognised that and accepted it. No one felt threatened by him.' Her hands clutched at each other in her lap every time she mentioned her husband's name.

'I know he told you he was going to the pub. Do you have

any idea how or why he ended up south of the river?'

'No.'

A look of panic crossed her face, and Church moved quickly to change the subject. 'Had your husband been acting any differently in the days or weeks leading up to his death?'

There was a long pause when Mrs Gibbons appeared to have drifted off into a reverie, but then she said quietly, 'Now that you mention it, Maurice was a little . . . skittish, perhaps. He was jumping at the slightest thing.'

'He was frightened of something?' Church pressed.

'Oh, I wouldn't go that far. Not frightened, just . . . uneasy.' She let out a deep sigh that seemed to fill the room. 'He went to church on the Sunday before he passed on. That was so unlike Maurice. Do you think he might have sensed something, wanted to make his peace with God?'

'Perhaps he did,' Ruth said soothingly. Church was impressed with her manner; her caring was from the heart, and he could see Mrs Gibbons being visibly calmed.

'Would you like to see his room?' Mrs Gibbons asked. 'Maurice had so many interests and he had a room where he could be alone to think and read. That's where he kept all his things. You might find something of interest there. Lord knows, there's nothing *I* can tell you.'

She led them up two flights to a little box room lit by a bare bulb. It was quite tidy, uncluttered by any kind of decoration; just a cheap desk and chair, a filing cabinet and a bookshelf. A pair of plaid slippers were tucked in the corner.

'I'll leave you to it. Make a cup of tea, how about that?' Mrs Gibbons slipped out, closing the door behind them.

'Why do you think he was *uneasy* just before he was killed?' Church said as he sank on to the chair and opened the desk.

'Don't start extrapolating. You'll end up with all sorts of hideous conspiracy theories.'

'"Just the facts, ma'am."'

'Exactly.' Ruth crouched down to examine the bookshelf. 'I think one of us should pay a visit to the local vicar. You never know, Maurice might have seen fit to bare his soul.'

'Wouldn't that be nice and simple. He fingers his murderer to the vicar and everything falls into place.' He started to go through the sparse contents of the desk aloud. 'Pens, envelopes, writing paper. Look at this, typical anally retentive civil servant – a big pile of receipts, most of them for cabs.'

'Nothing wrong with being anal retentive,' Ruth said tartly.

'Hoping for some tax deduction, I suppose,' Church continued. 'A notebook—'

'A lot of these books are new,' Ruth mused. 'UFOs, Von Daniken, *The Occult* by Colin Wilson, *Messages from the Dead: A Spiritualists' Guide*. Looks like he's been reading that magazine you were rambling on about.'

'That's a bit of a coincidence.'

'Sure. Life's full of them. Anything in the notebook?'

'The first few pages have been torn out. There's only one thing in it: a phone number. Barry Riggs. Crouch End UFO Association.'

'Great. Little Green Men got him,' Ruth said wryly. 'We should check it out anyway. You never know.'

They caught a cab back to South London and dropped Ruth off first. Church felt chastened by Mrs Gibbons' grief. Afraid that the depression would come back to ruin the first halfway-normal mood he had felt in a long time, he quickly switched on the computer and went online. There was an email waiting for him from Laura DuSantiago.

Greetings, Churchill-Dude (No relation, I hope. I don't want to picture you with a big, fat cigar.)

I get the impression from your last email that you think I'm full of hot air, but you're too polite to say so. Well, I'll stop teasing, big boy – I wouldn't want a *premature* withdrawal on your behalf. Everyone else who emailed me has scarpered before I had the chance to get down to the *meat*. And I better stop now before this becomes a bad Carry On film . . .

Here's the dope: the increase in paranormal activity that all the net-nerds noticed started on the same day. Coincidence? I don't think so. There's stuff happening around the globe, but the epi-centre is the UK – and most of it is happening around places of significance to our pagan/Celtic ancestors. Now, statistically, I know that's not difficult in an island like ours, but look at the big picture, not the details. I'm not going too fast for you, am I?

And here's the big story, Morning Glory. I saw something that changed my life. Me, technohead, feet-on-the-ground Laura DuS. Something that all the crazies and geeks of the UFO/Spirit World would give their right arms to see. And losing their right arms would really hamper those types. This was a drug-free, alcohol-free experience, and it talked to me. You want to know what it said, you'll have to meet me on my own turf. I'm not spreading this stuff around online so I can be branded as another nut.

But here's a tip: don't go making plans for the next millennium . . .

Your new best friend, Laura.

And there, at the end, was the thing that hooked him and made his blood run cold.

PS Before we meet I need to know if this name means anything to you: Marianne.

Church read the line three times, trying to work out if he was going insane, then wondering if someone was playing a nasty trick on him. It could have been another coincidence, but the way they were piling up gave him an eerie feeling of some power behind the scenes manipulating his life. He turned off the computer and busied himself with mundane tasks for the better part of an hour, but it wouldn't leave him alone and it was only a matter of time before he returned to the keyboard to type out his reply. Then he retired to bed without once looking out of the window into the dark, quiet street.

* * *

Ruth reached the church shortly after 9 a.m. It was a bracing morning, with the wind sending the clouds streaking across the blue sky. Standing in the sun, peering at the skeletal trees through screwed-up eyes that cropped out the buildings, Ruth could almost believe she wasn't in London, away from the smog and the traffic noise and the omnipresent background threat. Sometimes she hated the modern world with a vengeance.

The vicar was in the churchyard, in his shirt-sleeves despite the chill, trimming the hedge with an electric cutter. He was tall with a red face – although that might have been from the exertion – and a balding head with white hair swept back around his ears. The drone of the cutter drowned out Ruth's first attempt at an introduction, but she eventually caught his eye.

'I said, shouldn't you have a gardener to do that?' she said.

'Oh, I like to get my hands dirty every now and then. What can I do for you?'

'My name's Ruth Gallagher. A solicitor. I'm looking into the death of Maurice Gibbons. I was told you knew him.' She was still surprised how quickly people parted with information once she announced her legal background; it was almost as if they considered her a policewoman-in-waiting.

The vicar nodded ruefully. 'Poor Maurice. Still no suspect, I suppose.'

'Not yet, but no one's giving up. There was one particular line of enquiry I wanted to discuss with you. It might be nothing, but Mrs Gibbons mentioned he came to church the week before his death which was unusual—'

'He was a very troubled man,' the vicar interjected. 'He came round to the rectory after the service for a chat. I can't betray the confidences of the people who come to me . . .' He paused, weighing up his options. 'But with Maurice dead, I don't see the harm, especially if it gives an insight into his state of mind.' Folding his arms, he stared up at the steeple. 'Maurice was concerned about spiritual matters. We discussed, amongst other things, the return of the spirits of the dead, ghosts, you know, and possession by demonic entities. He wanted to know how easy it would be to arrange an exorcism if necessary, and I told him something of that magnitude would have to be sanctioned by the bishop.'

'He thought he was possessed!' Ruth said incredulously.

'No, I didn't feel that. It was more as if he was talking in general terms, but he was certainly very anxious. He seemed to fear being tormented by the more malignant aspects of the spiritual realm.'

The memory unleashed by the therapist returned in force, and Ruth stifled a shudder.

'Are you feeling all right?' the vicar asked, concerned.

'Fine. Just a chill.' She forced a smile. She didn't believe in those kind of things, but the coincidence was hard to ignore.

The Victorian house could have been stately, but it had been indelibly scarred by thoughtless *improvement*: cheap, UPVC window frames and door, grey plastic guttering, an obtrusive aluminium flue for a gas boiler. Barry Riggs smiled broadly when he answered the door to Church, but it seemed forced, almost gritted. He was around forty, slightly overweight, with a doughy face and glasses that were a little too large. He smelled of cheap aftershave fighting to mask body odour. Inside, he seemed to have the builders in. Planks leaned against the stairs, an empty paint can stood in the hall, there were dust sheets everywhere and a pristine toilet bowl stood in the lounge, but he made no mention of the mess and there was no sound from anywhere else in the house.

'I know why you're here,' Riggs said conspiratorially as Church was ushered on to the sheet that covered the sofa.

'I did tell you on the phone,' Church replied dryly.

'No, the *real* reason. Something much bigger than Maurice Gibbons.' He nodded knowingly.

'You better fill me in from the beginning, Barry.' Church

was already harbouring doubts about the validity of his visit. As 'chief investigator' of the Crouch End UFO Association, Riggs had sounded more authoritative on the phone than he appeared in his natural habitat.

'Maurice heard of my investigations on the grapevine,' Riggs began, sitting a little too close to Church for comfort. 'People talk. There's never any coverage in the media, but you talk to people in the street and they know of the importance of my work. It's the future, isn't it? Anyway, I digress. Maurice knew I'd uncovered some unarguable evidence about Government knowledge of the UFO threat. I'm not going to go into details now, but let me just say *secret base* and *St Albans*. We can talk about that later if you want.'

'Why did Maurice come to you, Barry?'

'Alien infiltration, Jack. Plain and simple. Maurice was a Government employee. He knew he was a target. He was frightened, Jack, very frightened, and he came to me looking for any information that might protect him. "They walk among us," he said. I remember it well. He was sitting just where you are, with his little briefcase. He'd got classified information in it, but he wasn't ready to show me just then. It was a matter of building trust, but they got to him before he could divulge what he knew.'

'Who got to him?'

'The aliens! In the future, Maurice will be seen as a hero. He was a whistleblower, ready to open up the whole can of worms about the Government selling us down the line for alien experiments.'

Church stared out of the window at the sinking afternoon sun, wishing he had opted for the vicar. 'And he told you this? That aliens were after him?'

Riggs paused. 'Not in so many words. But he wanted to know everything about my investigations. We ran through the dates and times of sightings, witness reports, everything. He was particularly interested in the descriptions of different races, the Greys and the Nordics and all that. And alien abduction scenarios. What the abductees experienced in real detail. What they heard, lights in the sky. I tell you, Jack, he was here for hours.'

Church stood up quickly before he was overpowered by Riggs' body odour. 'Thank you, Barry. You've been very helpful.'

Riggs grinned. 'You know, that's just what Maurice said. "People need to know what's out there, Barry. They're sleep-walking into a disaster."'

'So here are the options. Maurice was crazy. Maurice was overworked and suffering from stress-induced psychosis. Or Maurice was crazy. Either way, it's a good explanation for why he was wandering along by the river at the crack of dawn.' Church sprawled on the sofa in Ruth's lounge, looking out at the city lights against the early evening sky.

'Do you think you could possibly be a little more glib?' Ruth said ironically.

Over a take-out curry and a bottle of Chilean red, they had spent half an hour trading information and finding there was no common ground whatsoever.

'You were the sceptical one,' Church replied. 'This was supposed to be taking us away from the Devil living under Albert Bridge. Now we have one man thinking Gibbons is being hunted by aliens, another convinced our man is being haunted by ghosts and demons.'

'You're still skating on the surface, Church. Dig a little deeper.'

'Do you think you can patronise me a little more? I haven't had my fill yet.'

She laughed and topped up his glass. 'The important fact is that Maurice Gibbons was a frightened man. Something was disturbing him enough to seek out the vicar and your UFO loon for information. He knew something.'

'Or he was crazy.'

'He was a civil servant, down-to-earth. If he was frightened,

45

why was he keeping it to himself? There must have been hundreds of people he could have discussed it with, not least his wife.'

'Perhaps he was waiting until he was sure.' Church took a deep swig of his wine and then said out of the blue, 'Do you believe in ghosts?'

Ruth looked at him in surprise. 'Why do you ask?'

'It doesn't matter. So where do we go from here? I can't think of any other lines of enquiry . . . hang on a minute.' He suddenly stared into the middle distance, ordering his thoughts, then he snapped his fingers. 'There's something we've missed.'

Susan Gibbons welcomed them in forty-five minutes later after Church's phone call had convinced her their visit would only take a few minutes. In Maurice's room, he went straight to the desk and pulled out the pile of taxi receipts, riffling through them quickly. They were all for a Monday evening and for the same amount.

'So where was he going on a regular basis?' Church asked pointedly. Mrs Gibbons had no idea. 'I think the police looked into this, but didn't get anywhere,' she said. Church wasn't deterred. He called the minicab firm. The receptionist asked around in the office and a few minutes later came back with an address.

The house was a small semi in High Barnet; half-rendered, with more UPVC windows and a paved-over front garden where a few yellow weeds forced their way among the cracks. The light that glared through the glass of the front door seemed unpleasantly bright. They rang the bell and it was answered immediately by a woman with dyed black hair and sallow skin. She dragged on a cigarette, eyeing them suspiciously while Ruth ran through her patter. She reluctantly allowed them into the hall, which smelled of cigarettes and bacon fat.

'He came round to see my uncle every week,' she said, glancing at a photo of Gibbons which his wife had lent them. 'Queer duck, but he used to perk the old man up. He's not well, you know. Hasn't left his bed in weeks. I got lumbered looking after him.' She wrinkled her nose in what could have been disgust or irritation.

'Can we see him?' Church asked.

The woman nodded, then added combatively, 'I'm going out soon.'

'Don't worry, we can let ourselves out,' Ruth said disarmingly. 'What's your uncle's name?'

'Kraicow,' the woman snapped as if that was all she knew.

She led the way up the stairs and swung open a bedroom door on to a painfully thin old man, his limbs just bone draped in skin. He lay on the top of his bed in striped pyjamas with one arm thrown across his eyes. His hair was merely tufts of silver on his pillow.

'Is it okay if we talk to him?' Church said.

'Just one of you,' the woman said. 'He gets very confused if there's more than one person speaking.' She added obliquely, 'He's an artist, you know. Used to be quite well known.'

The woman left them alone, and Church went to sit by the bed while Ruth watched from the door. Church remained quiet as Kraicow twitched and moaned beneath his arm, but eventually the old man removed it from his face and looked at Church with clear grey eyes, as if he had known he had a visitor all along.

'Hello, I'm Jack Churchill,' Church said quietly. 'I hope you don't mind me coming to see you.'

Kraicow looked away and mumbled something; Church wondered if he'd be able to get any sense out of him at all. But when Kraicow looked back he spoke in a clear, deep voice. 'I'm pleased to see any human face after looking at that miserable bitch all day long. She never leaves me alone.'

'You don't know me,' Church continued, 'but I wanted to talk to you about Maurice Gibbons.'

47

Church wondered how he would be able to discuss the matter without upsetting Kraicow about Gibbons' death, but the old man said simply, 'He's dead, isn't he?'

Church nodded.

'I warned him.'

A hush seemed to descend on the house. 'Warned him about what?'

Kraicow levered himself up on his elbows so he could look Church in the face. For a moment the old man's eyes ranged across Church's features as if he was searching for something he could trust, before slowly lowering himself down with a wheeze. 'Maurice saw my breakdown . . . what the bastards at the health centre call my breakdown,' he began in a voice so low Church had to bend forward to hear him. 'It was in the street, in Clerkenwell – where I work. I was making too much noise. Ranting, I suppose. Not surprising under the circumstances. Maurice overheard some of the things I said, and he knew straight away I was telling the truth because he'd seen the same thing too.'

'What had you seen?' Church whispered.

Kraicow licked his dry lips. 'You know much about the old myths and legends?'

'It depends which ones.'

'The final battle between Good and Evil. The end of this cycle and the start of something new.' The front door slammed loudly; Kraicow's niece had gone. 'The legend is the same all over the world. The End-Time.' Kraicow grabbed Church's wrist with fingers which seemed too strong for his feeble state. 'They're coming back.'

'Who are?' Church's mood dampened; more craziness. 'Aliens? Demons?'

'No!' Kraicow said emphatically. 'I told you, the old myths. Not fairytales, no, no, not folklore!' His eyes rolled back until all Church could see were the whites. 'The legends are true.'

'Are you okay?'

Kraicow threw his arm across his face again. 'The legends

48

said they'd be back for the final battle and they were right! Do you think we stand a chance against them?'

'Take it easy,' Church said calmly. 'Why did Maurice come to see you?'

'He knew they were back! He'd seen them too. He knew they were biding their time, but they'll be making their move soon – they won't wait long. The doors are open!'

'Did Maurice say—'

'He wanted to know what to do! He was so frightened. So frightened. He knew they wouldn't let him have the knowledge for long . . . they'd get to him. But who could he tell? The bastards put me in here!'

Church sat back in his chair in disappointment; he was getting nowhere. Was Gibbons as crazed as Kraicow, or were his visits some kind of altruistic act? He glanced at Ruth, about to take his leave, but Kraicow grabbed his shirt and dragged him forward.

'Remember the old legend: *In England's darkest hour, a hero shall arise.* It's there. It's been written.' He took a deep breath and some degree of normalcy returned to him. 'You don't believe me, do you?'

'I'm sorry—'

'No, no, it's crazy talk. I've spent too long breathing in those paint fumes.' He chuckled throatily. 'Look in the top drawer.'

Curiously Church followed his nod to the bedside cabinet. In the drawer was an envelope; an address was scribbled on the front. 'That's my studio. You go there, you'll see.'

'I can't—'

'You'll find what you're looking for. Peace of mind. Direction. You'll know what happened to Maurice. It's up to you now.' He pushed Church away roughly and rolled over. 'Go!'

Church glanced at the envelope one more time, then reluctantly took it. At the door, he silenced Ruth's questions with a simple, 'Later.' Downstairs was in darkness. In the gloom, Church felt eyes on his back although he knew the place was empty, and he didn't feel safe until they were outside, dialling a cab on Ruth's mobile.

Kraicow's studio was at the top of a Victorian warehouse in one of the many unredeemed backstreets that formed the heart of Clerkenwell. From the outside it seemed almost derelict: smashed windows filthy with dust, graffiti and posters for bands that had long since split up. Unidentified hulks of machinery were scattered around the ground floor, which stank of engine oil and dirt. But when they climbed out of the service lift at the summit, Kraicow's room presented itself to them in a burst of colour and a smell of oil paint and solvent. An enormous, half-completed canvas was suspended over the centre of the floor, but it was impossible to tell from the splashes of colour exactly what it would eventually be. Other canvases of all sizes were stacked against various walls. The floor was bare boards, but clean, and there was a small camp bed in one corner where the artist obviously snatched a rest during his more intense periods of work. On an uneven table was a collection of tubes of oil, dirty rags, a palette and a jar filled with brushes.

'Do you ever get the feeling you're wasting your time?' Ruth said as she looked around at the disarray.

'You were the one who insisted we go down every avenue, however ridiculous,' Church replied. 'Personally, I think you've been reading way too much Sherlock Holmes.'

Ruth began to search through the stacked canvases. 'What are we looking for?'

'God knows.' Church busied himself with an investigation of a pile of rags and empty paint pots near the window. On the top was a sheet of sketch paper where Kraicow had written *El sueño de la razón produce monstruos.* Church read it aloud, then asked, 'What does that mean?'

Ruth paused in her search and dredged her memory for a translation. ' "The sleep of reason brings forth monsters." It's the title of—'

'—a painting by Goya. Yes, I remember.'

Ruth leaned on the canvases and mused, 'It's strange, isn't it? We go about our lives thinking the world is normal and then we stumble across all these people who obviously have a completely different view of reality, indulging in their paranoid fantasies.'

'Are you including the vicar in that?'

Ruth laughed. 'The UFO guy and Kraicow and obviously Gibbons, all feeding each other. And obviously Mrs Gibbons had no idea what was going on in her husband's head.'

Church moved on to another collection of canvases, older, judging by the thick layer of dust that lay on the top. 'Well, paranoia's like a fire. It quickly gets out of control and suddenly the norm looks weird and the weird becomes perfectly acceptable.'

'You'd know, would you?' Ruth jibed. Church didn't respond.

Their search continued for fifteen minutes more, becoming increasingly aimless as the futility of the task overcame them. Church, for his part, was afraid to stop; he didn't want to return to his empty flat with its bleak memories. Their hunt for meaning in their experience had released a whole host of emotions with which he hadn't had time to come to terms.

Ruth let the final canvas drop back with a clatter. 'We should call it a day,' she said. Church noted a hint of gloom in her voice. After a second she added morosely, 'I don't think we're getting anywhere and I'm afraid if we don't sort out what happened I'm never going to get back to who I was. That morning was so destabilising I feel like every support for my life has been kicked away.' She wandered over to the window and hauled up the blind to look out over the city.

'I know exactly what you mean,' Church said, remembering the morning after Marianne's terrible death with an awful intensity. 'Sometimes you never get straight again.' He checked the final canvas, a surreal landscape with hints of Dali. 'Nothing here. I don't know what Kraicow was talking about. Serves us right for listening to the views of a mental patient. So what do we do next?'

There was no reply. Church turned slowly. Ruth was standing at the window with her back to him, so immobile she could have been a statue. 'Did you hear me?'

Still no answer. He could tell from her frozen body something was wrong. A hum of anxiety rose at the back of his head, growing louder as he moved towards her. Before he had crossed the floor, her voice came up small, still and frightened. 'He was right.'

Church felt his heart begin to pound; somewhere, doors were opening.

When he came up behind her, he could see what it was that had caught her attention. On the window ledge was a small sculpture in clay, rough and unfinished, but detailed in the upper part. It was a figure with a face so hideous in its deformity and evil they could barely bring themselves to look at it.

And it was the perfect representation of the *devil* they had recalled during Delano's therapy session. Kraicow had seen it too.

It existed.

CHAPTER THREE

On the Road

For the rest of the night they sat in Ruth's lounge, talking in the quiet, clipped tones of people who had suffered the massive shock of a sudden bereavement. The discovery of the desperately crafted statue left them with nowhere to turn. Suddenly the shadows were alive, and life had taken on the perspective of a bottle-glass window.

'What the hell's going on?' Ruth looked deep into the dregs of her wine. She had drunk too much too quickly, but however much she told herself it was an immature reaction, she couldn't face up to the immensity of what the statue meant and what they had truly seen that night. For someone immersed on a daily basis in the logic and reason of the law, it was both too hard to believe and impossible to deny; the conflict made her feel queasy.

Church rubbed his tired eyes, at once deflated and lost. 'We can't walk away from it—'

'I know that.' There was an edge to her voice. 'I never thought one moment could change your life so fundamentally.' She walked over to the window and looked out at the lights of the city in the pre-dawn dark. 'We're so alone now – nobody knows what we know. It's a joke! How can we tell anybody? We'll end up getting treated like Kraicow.'

'And what do we know? That there's some kind of supernatural creature out there that looks like a man one moment and something too hideous to look at the next?'

'We know,' she said dismally, 'that nothing is how we imagined it. That if something like that can exist, anything is possible. What are the rules now, Church? What's going on?'

Church paused; he had no idea how to answer her question. He drained the remainder of his wine, then played with the glass thoughtfully. 'At least we've got each other,' he said finally.

Ruth looked round suddenly, a faint smile sweeping away the darkness in her face. 'That's right. You and me against the world, kid.'

Church mused for a moment. 'Kraicow must know more. He'd seen something, the same as Gibbons.'

'Then,' Ruth said pointedly, 'we should pay him another visit.'

Unable to sleep, they arrived at Kraicow's house at first light and sat outside in Church's old Nissan Bluebird until a reasonable hour, dozing fitfully. His niece answered the door, her recognition giving way instantly to anger.

'Did you two have something to do with it?' she barked. Church and Ruth were taken aback by her fury, their speechlessness answering the woman's question. 'He's gone,' she snapped.

Church's puzzlement showed on his face; Kraicow had seemed too weak to move. 'Where—'

'I don't know where, that's the problem!' Anxiously, she looked past them into the empty street. 'They came for him in the night. I had the fright of my life when I opened the door.'

'Who was it?' Church asked.

'I don't know! They didn't tell me!' She back-pedalled, suddenly aware they might judge her for not questioning the men further. 'They were coppers,' she said unconvincingly. 'Looked like a bloody funeral party, all dressed in smart suits and ties. I don't know what the old man's done. He never tells me anything.'

Church and Ruth looked at each other uneasily. 'Do you know where they took him?' Ruth said.

The woman shook her head. 'They said they'd let me know.

54

They told me it was in his best interests!' she protested pathetically before slamming the door.

'What was that all about?' Ruth asked once they were comfortably in heavy traffic heading back into town.

'Could be the murder squad. They might have linked Kraicow to Maurice Gibbons.'

'Could be.' Her voice suggested she didn't believe it. 'Seems more like the kind of thing Special Branch would do. Or the security services.'

'What would they want with Kraicow?' The question hung uncomfortably in the air for a moment until Church added, 'Let's not get paranoid about this.'

'If this whole episode isn't a case for paranoia, I don't know what is. We haven't got any more leads now. Where do we go from here?'

They crawled forward through the traffic for another fifteen minutes before Church found an answer. 'There's a lot of weird stuff going on around the country just like this. I mean, not people turning into devils, but things that shouldn't be happening.' Church explained to her at length about the massive upsurge in supposed paranormal events he had read about on the net. 'I don't know . . .' He shrugged. 'It may be nothing. All the nuts coming out of the woodwork at once. But it seems to me too much of a coincidence.'

Ruth sighed heavily and stared out of the passenger window at the dismal street scene; no one seemed happy, their shoulders bowed beneath an invisible weight as they headed to the tube for another dreary day at work. It depressed her even more. 'I can't get my head round this at all.'

'Let's just pretend it's not happening,' Church snapped, then instantly regretted it; he was tired and sick of nothing in his life making sense.

Ruth glared at him, then looked back out of the window. 'Sorry.'

She ignored his apology frostily; Church could see she was tired herself. 'Gibbons was killed to prevent him telling what he'd seen,' she mused almost to herself. 'But what did he see?'

'I've had some emails from a woman who says she saw something which could throw some light on what's going on,' Church ventured. He considered telling her about Laura's mention of Marianne, but thought better of it; he could barely handle the implications himself.

'You really think all that stuff's linked to what we're dealing with?'

'Who knows?' he said wearily. 'These days, everything's a leap in the dark.'

'So is she going to tell you what she knows?'

'She wants to do it face to face. I was going to see her anyway, you know, just out of curiosity.' He winced inwardly at the lie about his motivations. Ruth didn't deserve it, but how could he tell her he wanted to find out how this woman knew about his dead girlfriend? It sounded a little pathetic, worse, like an obsession.

'Why the hell not. Where is she?'

'Bristol.'

Ruth moaned. 'Oh well, I've got no job to keep me here. Just give me a couple of hours to pack. Looks like we've got us a road trip.'

Although it had been two years since he had last felt the warmth of her skin, Marianne's presence still reverberated throughout the flat. On the wall of the hall hung the grainy black and white photo of the two of them staggering out of the sea at Bournemouth, fully clothed, laughing; Marianne had had it framed to remind them both how carefree life could be if they ever faced any hardship. In the kitchen, in the glass-fronted cabinet, stood her blue-and-white-hooped mug with the chip out of the side. Church couldn't bear to throw it away. He saw it every day when he made his first cup of tea, and his last. The dog-eared copy of *Foucault's Pendulum* which they had both read and argued about intensely sat on the shelf in the lounge, next to the pristine edition of *Walking on Glass* which Marianne had given him and which he had promised her he would read and had never got round to. The paperweight of a plastic heart frozen in glass which they had bought together in Portobello. The indelible stain of Marianne's coffee on the carpet next to her seat. A hundred tiny lies ready to deceive him in every corner of his home. Sometimes he even thought he could smell her perfume.

With the TV droning in the background and the holdall still half-packed on the bed, Church suddenly found himself taking stock of it all in a way he had not done since the immediate aftermath of her death. For months the reminders had simply been there, like the drip of a distant tap, but as he trailed around the flat, they seemed acute and painfully lucid once more. Perhaps it was the bizarre, disturbing mention of her name in the email, or what he thought he had seen in the street, but he had to visit each one in turn with an imperative which he found disturbing.

But he was sure he could give it all up, turn back to the future, if he could somehow understand what had driven her to suicide and how he had been so blind to the deep undercurrents that must have been in place months before. He had played over every aspect of their relationship in minute detail until he was sick of it, but the mystery held as strong as ever, trapping him in the misery of not-knowing, a limbo where he could not put the past and all its withered, desperate emotions to rest. No wonder he was seeing her ghost; he was surprised it hadn't come sooner, lurching out of his subconscious to drive him completely insane.

In the lounge, the TV news had made an incongruous link from an account of a bizarre multiple slasher murder in Liverpool to details of a religious fervour which seemed to be sweeping the country; the Blessed Virgin Mary had allegedly appeared to three young children on wasteland in Huddersfield; a statue of the Hindu god Ganesh had given forth milk in Wolverhampton, and there were numerous reports of the name of Allah spelled out in the seeds of tomatoes and aubergines when they were cut open in Bradford, Bristol and West London. Church watched the item to the end, then switched off the TV and put on a CD. The jaunty sound of Johnny Mercer singing Ac-cent-tchu-ate the Positive filled the flat as he returned to his packing.

He picked up Laura's email confirming the details of their meeting and then checked the road atlas. Church hoped his car would make the trip to Bristol. It had seen better days and very few long journeys, but he had bought it with Marianne and hadn't been able to give it up.

A haze of chill drizzle had descended on the city just after he had dropped Ruth off and by the time he began to load up the car, it seemed to have settled in for the day. The world appeared different somehow; there was a smell in the air which he didn't recognise and the quality of light seemed weird as if it was filtering through glass. Even the people passing by looked subtly changed, in their expressions or the strange, furtive glances which he occasionally glimpsed. He felt oddly out of sorts and apprehensive about what lay ahead.

When he stepped out of the front gate, a group of children splashing in the gutter across the road stopped instantly and turned to face him as one, their eyes glassy and unfocused. Slowly, eerily, they each raised their left arm and held up the index finger. 'One!' they shouted together. Then they splayed out their fingers and thumb. 'Of five!' Some stupid catchphrase from a kids' cartoon, Church thought, but he still felt a shiver run down his spine as he hurried up the street to the car.

As he threw his bag into the boot, he heard the shuffle of feet on the pavement behind him. He whirled, expecting to catch the children preparing to play a prank, only to see a homeless man in a filthy black suit, his long hair and beard flattened by the rain. He walked up to Church, shaking as if he had an ague, and then he leaned forward and snapped his fingers an inch away from Church's face.

'You have no head,' he said. Church felt an icy shadow fall over him, an image of the woman at the riverside; by the time he had recovered the man had wandered away, humming some sixties tune as if he hadn't seen Church at all.

On his way to Ruth's, Church passed through five green lights and halted at one red. Nearby was a poster of a man selling mobile phones; the top of the poster was torn off and the man's head was missing. Further down the road, he glanced in a clothes shop to see five mannequins; four were fine, one was headless.

And as he rounded the corner into Ruth's street, a woman looked into the car, caught his eye, then suddenly and inexplicably burst into tears.

He finally reached Ruth's flat just before 1 p.m. She was ready, with a smart leather holdall and Mulberry rucksack. 'I can't help believing all this will have a perfectly reasonable explanation and we'll both end up with egg on our faces. God help me if the people at work find out,' she said.

'Let's hope, eh.'

Church drummed his fingers anxiously on the steering wheel as they sat in the steaming traffic in the bottleneck of Wandsworth High Street. Ruth looked out at the rain-swept street where a man in a business suit hurried, head bent, into the storm with a copy of the *FT* over his head – as if it could possibly offer any protection. 'You know,' she mused, 'I have the strangest feeling. Like we're leaving one life behind and moving into a different phase.'

'Too much Jack Kerouac.' Church's attention was focused on the rearview mirror; he had the sudden, uncomfortable feeling they were being followed.

'It's frightening, but it's liberating too,' Ruth continued.

'Everything was set in stone before – my job, where I was going. Now it feels like anything is possible. Isn't that weird? The world has turned on its head and I feel like I'm going on holiday.'

'Sunny Bristol, paradise playground of the beautiful people. I hope you packed your string bikini.'

'Have you got any music in this heap?' Ruth flicked open the glove compartment and ferreted among the tapes, screwing up her nose as she inspected each item. 'Sinatra. Crosby. Louis Armstrong. Billie Holiday. Anything from this century?'

'Old music makes me feel secure.' He snatched *Come Fly With Me* out of her fingers and slipped it into the machine. Sinatra began to sing the title track. 'And old films and old books. *Top Hat*, now there's a great movie. Astaire and Rogers, the perfect partnership, elegance and sexuality. Or *A Night At The Opera*—'

'The Marx Brothers. Yeuckk!' Ruth mimed sticking her fingers down her throat.

'Or *It Happened One Night*. Clark Gable and Claudette Colbert. Romance, passion, excitement, great clothes, great cars. You can't get better than that.'

Ruth smiled secretly when she saw Church's grin; he didn't do it enough.

'Life was great back then.' He waved his hand dismissively at the jumble of shops on Upper Richmond Road. 'Where did it all go wrong? When did style get banned from life?'

'When they decided big money and vacuous consumption were much more important.'

'We need more magic. That's what life is all about.'

Ruth flicked her seat into the reclining position and closed her eyes while Sinatra serenaded the joys of Moonlight in Vermont. The traffic crept forward.

The journey through south-west London was long and laborious. In rain, the capital's archaic transport system ground to a halt, raising clouds of exhaust, steam from hissing engines and tempers. By the time they reached the M4 more than an hour later, Church and Ruth were already tired of travelling. As the planes swooped down in a neverending procession to Healthrow, they agreed to pull in at Heston Services for a coffee before embarking on the monotonous drag along the motorway. By the time they rolled into the near-empty car park, Church's paranoia had reached fever pitch; at various stages on the journey he had been convinced that several different cars had been following them, and when a grey Transit that had been behind them since Barnes proceeded on to the services too, it had taken all of Ruth's calm rationality to keep him from driving off.

Beneath the miserable grey skies, the services seemed a bleak place. Pools of water puddled near the doors and slickly followed the tramp of feet to the newsagents or toilets where the few travellers who hung around had a uniform expression of irritation; at the weather, at travelling, at life in general.

As Church and Ruth entered, they could see through the glass wall on their right that the restaurant was nearly empty. They proceeded round to the serving area where a couple of bored assistants waited for custom and bought coffee and Danishes before taking a seat near the window where they could see the spray flying up from the speeding traffic. Through the glass, distant factory towers lay against the grey sheet of sky, while beneath the fluorescent lighting the cafeteria had a listless, melancholy air. Despite the constant drone from the motorway which thrummed like the bleak soundtrack to some French arthouse film, they spoke quietly, although there were only three other travellers in the room and none of them close enough to hear.

'This is killing me,' Church mused. 'Every time I look behind I think someone's following us.'

Ruth warmed her hands around her coffee mug; she didn't meet his eyes. 'A natural reaction.'

Near the door, a tall, thin man was casting furtive glances

in their direction, the hood of his plastic waterproof pulled so tightly around his face that the drawstrings were biting into the flesh. At a table on the other side of the room, an old hippie with wiry, grey hair fastened in a ponytail was also watching them. Church fought his anxiety and turned his attention back to Ruth.

'When I was a boy this would all have seemed perfectly normal,' he said. 'You know how it is – you're always convinced the world is stranger than it seems.'

'That just goes to show we *lose* wisdom as we get older, doesn't it,' Ruth replied edgily. 'We've obviously been spending all our adult lives lying to ourselves.'

'When I was seven or eight I had these bizarre dreams, really colourful and realistic,' Church began. 'There was a woman in them, and this strange world. They were so powerful I think I had trouble distinguishing between the dreams and reality, and it worried my mother: she dragged me off to the doctor at one point. They faded after I reached puberty, but I know they affected the way I looked at the world. And I'm getting the same kind of feeling now – that all we see around us is some kind of cheap scenery and that the real business is happening behind it.' He glanced around; the man in the waterproof had gone, but the hippie was still watching them.

'I'm finding it hard to deal with, to be honest,' Ruth said. 'I've always believed this is all there is. I've never had much time for ghosts or God.'

Church nodded. 'I always thought there was something there. An instinct, really. You know, you'd look around ... sometimes it's hard to believe there's not something behind it all. But these days ... I don't have much time for the Church ... any churches. After Marianne died, they weren't much help, to say the least.'

Ruth sipped her coffee thoughtfully. 'My dad was a member of the Communist Party and a committed atheist. I remember him saying one day, "The Bible's a pack of lies,

62

written by a bunch of power-hungry men who wanted their own religion."'

'Christmas must have been a bundle of fun in your house.'

'No, it was great. It was a really happy, loving home.' She smiled wistfully. 'He died a couple of years ago.'

'I'm sorry.'

'It was sudden, a heart attack. His brother, my uncle, was murdered and it just destroyed my dad. It was the unfairness of it ... the complete randomness. Uncle Jim was in the wrong place at the wrong time, and some desperate, pathetic idiot killed him. You know, I work in the law and I see all the motivations for crime, but if I came across that bastard today I'd probably kill him with my bare hands. No jury, no legal arguments.' She bit her lip. 'Dad just couldn't cope with it. It didn't fit in with the ordered world view, you see. He tore himself apart for a couple of days and then his heart gave out. And in one instant I could understand the need for religion.' Emotions flickered across her face. 'Of course, by that stage it was too late to suddenly start believing.'

Church felt an urge to comfort her, but he didn't know how. 'The time when the Church had any relevance to people's lives is long gone, yet we all still have these spiritual needs. So where do we turn when things get dark?'

'We look into ourselves, I suppose,' Ruth said quietly.

The hippie's unwavering stare was beginning to unnerve Church; behind his wire-rimmed spectacles, his eyes were cold and grey, sharply intelligent and incisive. One hand rested protectively on a faded, olive-coloured haversack bearing a large peace symbol and a CND badge.

Ruth drained her coffee and stood up. 'I had better go to the toilet or we'll be stopping all the way to Bristol.'

As she wandered out, the hippie watched her intently. Church gnawed on his Danish while keeping one eye out to make sure Ruth wasn't followed. The man didn't have an unpleasant face; the skin was the kind of brown that only came from an outdoor life, the lines around the mouth

63

suggested more smiles than tears or rage. But there was a world-weariness to him that had added a touch of bitterness or cynicism around the eyes. A large gold ring hung in his left ear and he wore a tie-dyed and faded pink T-shirt, old army fatigues and a pair of rugged walking boots.

He did nothing further to arouse suspicion and after a while Church's attention wandered, but when ten minutes had passed he began to grow anxious. He finished his coffee and went to stand outside the toilets, but although he tried to wait patiently, alarm bells were ringing in his head. He swung open the door and called Ruth's name. When there was no reply, he headed to the newsagents, but she wasn't there either. The car park was deserted. She hadn't slipped by him and returned to the cafeteria. Suddenly his heart was pounding as his uneasiness worried into a pearl of panic in his gut.

He decided the best option was to get security to put out an announcement, or at the very worst he could check to see if they had seen her on the surveillance cameras. The office lay at the furthest point of the thoroughfare, through a windowless door and up a short flight of stairs. Church stepped on to the stairs, desperately trying not to think the worst. But he had barely climbed three steps when he became starkly aware the temperature was dropping rapidly. By the time he reached the top, his breath was pluming and shivers rippled through him. The main office door creaked open noisily. Against one wall there was a curved desk with a bank of black-and-white monitors showing scenes from the car park, the Travelodge, the cafeteria and others. An uncomfortable silence lay heavy over everything, punctuated occasionally by sudden bursts of static from the radio speaker on the desk. But what caught Church's eye first was the glittering cobweb of frost that dappled everything – the desk, the equipment, the walls and floor. His head was spinning as he advanced slowly; it didn't make sense. A high-backed leather chair was turned away from him at the desk; he could just make out the tip of the head of a man sitting in it.

'Hello?' he said hesitantly.

His voice echoed hollowly; all remained still and quiet. He stared at the man's unmoving head, hoping the guard hadn't heard him, knowing in his heart that wasn't the answer. And suddenly he wanted to run out of there, not turn the chair around, not find any answers at all, but he forced himself to move forward. His footsteps sounded crisp, his breath was clouds of white. He spun the chair round in one movement and his stomach contracted instantly. The guard was frozen as solidly as if he had been left out in an Antarctic night; frost rimed his eyebrows and hair. His stare was glassy, his bloodless skin blueish beneath the unforgiving striplight. Church backed away, unable to come to terms with a situation that both terrified and baffled him. But as he turned, another shock brought him up sharp. Behind the door, hidden from his initial view, several bodies had been stacked. He recognised one of the women he had seen working in the cafeteria; the others also seemed to be staff from the services. Church felt like his head was fizzing as ideas banged into one another without forming one coherent thought. He rushed through the door and down the stairs two steps at a time.

When he crashed through the door into the main thoroughfare, the hippie from the cafeteria was waiting for him. 'They've taken her,' he said, with a faint Scottish brogue. He glanced around furtively. 'Outside. Don't draw attention from any of the staff.'

'Who's got her?' Church snapped, the anxiety cracking his voice.

'Quiet,' the man said sharply. 'They want you both dead. They already know who you are.'

'Ruth—'

'—is not dead yet. But she will be soon and you'll be next. Now, come.' He led the way to the car park, Church following like a sheep, confused, but slowly regaining his equilibrium. The hippie gazed around the bleak, puddled car park until his eyes settled on the grey Transit Church had earlier believed was following them. 'There,' he said.

Church looked into the man's face, wondering if he should trust him, and then he threw caution to the wind and set off weaving among the parked cars. As he neared the Transit, he could see it shift slightly on its suspension, although the windows were too dirty to see who was in the back. Without a second thought, Church grabbed the handle and yanked the rear door open.

There was a roar that wasn't human and a stink that reminded him of the monkey house at the zoo. Ruth was unconscious on the floor of the van. Standing over her, his face wild with rage, was the man in the waterproof Church had seen at the door of the café, his beady, darting eyes like an ape's behind the mask of his face, which had a strange waxy sheen. The man snarled and lashed out. Church caught a glimpse of a silver-bright knife that almost curved into a crescent near the end, and then he was yanked back suddenly.

Church's new associate stepped to his side. 'Stay out of his reach. He's too strong for you.'

Church was overwhelmed with sensations; the stench coming off the man making his head spin; the way the black-pebble eyes were filled with a monstrous anger Church couldn't begin to comprehend; the rasp of breath deep in the man's throat; the flash and glimmer as the blade danced in the air between them; and then the instinctive knowledge that *this* was what he had seen under the bridge. Ruth's captor jabbed the knife at Church and said what sounded like, 'Arith Urkolim.'

'What did he say?' Church snapped.

At Church's voice, Ruth stirred slightly, and his relief that she was okay surprised Church with its force. He edged to one side, looking for an opening, but there didn't seem any way he could get past the knife, and Ruth's captor was already trying to manoeuvre into a position to close the rear doors; strangely, he seemed wary of Church, ensuring the knife was always between the two of them, when he could probably have snapped Church's neck with one flex of his fingers. At the same time, he was changing; his skin seemed milky, then translucent and Church thought he could glimpse scales glistening just below the surface, while his tongue had grown forked at the tip like a snake's; when it wriggled out over his thin, dry lips it was accompanied by that deep, disturbing rasp from the back of his throat.

Ruth's eyes flickered open and briefly met his. Church saw a brief instant of panic as she took in the surroundings and then her natural control reasserted itself. At that moment her attacker lunged forward to grab the door handle. Knowing all would be lost if it shut, Church fumbled, then grasped the edge, feeling his knuckles pop and his tendons stretch to breaking as, effortlessly, Ruth's captor began to drag it closed.

'Get away!' the hippie barked. 'He's going to use the knife!'

Church looked up to see the blade at throat level, drawn back to strike. The snake-man said something in the same guttural language, his eyes now black with a red-slit pupil.

Suddenly Ruth's boot struck her attacker's calf with such force he overbalanced. Before he could recover, she had tangled both her feet among his legs. Church seized the moment, shifting his weight to fling the door shut so that with the force of the snake-man's pull it slammed into his face like a hammer. The dirty window glass exploded in a shower of crystals as the attacker crashed backwards over Ruth. In a sudden burst, Ruth scrambled out from under him, kicked open the door and tumbled out on to the wet tarmac, but Church's attention was still focused on the knife. He half thought about grabbing it when it clattered on to the floor of the van, but before his eyes it shimmered, then changed shape into something that resembled a silver spider which scurried away into the shadows.

'Let's get away from here,' the hippie hissed, dragging them both by their jackets. 'Where's your car?' The snake-man was already pulling himself to his feet, his face a mess of blood and torn flesh. An ear-splitting, inhuman roar erupted from its throat as they ran to the Nissan, and for a second of pure terror, Church thought it was coming after them. As he pushed the key in the lock, Church couldn't help glancing back, and instantly wished he hadn't; framed in the open van doors, he saw the snake-man howling terrible monkey cries as he tore at his clothes and face which was transforming, melting, shifting into something so awful Church gagged and turned away.

When they were safely inside, he fired up the engine, gunning the accelerator, and then they were lurching forward in a screech of tyres.

Only when they had pulled off the slip road into traffic did Church's heart start to return to normal. He turned to Ruth in the passenger seat. 'Are you okay?'

She nodded, her face pale and drawn.

'That thing in the van,' he stuttered, 'it was the same as whatever we saw under the bridge. Not the same one, though. So there's more of—'

'They can put on human faces,' the hippie interrupted from the back seat.

'They'd taken the place of all the staff there!' Church said, finally accepting what he'd seen.

'Waiting for you,' he continued. 'I think, if we took the time to investigate, we would find something similar at the airport and at other sites on all the arterial routes out of the capital.'

Church felt queasily like things were running out of control. 'They're after us?' he said dumbfoundedly.

'I was in one of the cubicles when I heard someone else come into the toilet and hang around outside. When I started to come out, the door burst in. Caught me a right one.' Ruth tenderly touched the ripening bruise on her temple. 'The first thing I thought was, "What a geek", because he had that hood pulled so tightly round his face you could only see the little circle of his features. He looked like a mental patient. And then I thought, "You'd better make some noise because this bastard is going to try to rape you." And then his face changed. Just a bit, like a flicker in transmission or something, but I got a hint of what was behind it.'

Church shook his head in disbelief. 'They're after us?' he repeated stupidly. 'I thought we were after them?' Gradually his thoughts started to come together and he turned and briefly examined the hippie before returning his gaze to the road. 'And who are *you*?' he asked then. The man's cold eyes had been impossible to read; Church thought he might have done too many drugs, something to take him one step away from normal human experience.

'Tom,' he replied. 'I've never had much need for any other name. But Learmont is my family name.'

'That wasn't what I meant. You'd better start explaining.'

Tom removed his glasses and cleaned them, then checked through the window at the quality of light; although it was mid-afternoon, night did not seem far away. He smiled inscrutably. 'Life is a poem and a new verse is about to start.'

Ruth saw the anger flare in Church's face and calmed him with a hand on his forearm. She turned round in her seat and stared at the hippie coldly. 'You've been speaking like you know what's happening. You've been acting like you were waiting for us, even though we didn't even know we were going to stop here. I've just had the most frightening experience of my life. Don't play games with us.'

Tom removed a small tin from his haversack and began to roll himself a thin cigarette. To Church's irritation, he remained silent until the blue smoke clouded his face, and then he said, 'The world you grew up in is dead. It simply doesn't know it yet. This society is like some dumb animal that's had its throat cut and is still wandering around as if nothing has happened. You see, the most enormous conceit of this time is that the rules of the game are known. The scientists have fooled the populace – and themselves – that

69

the universe is like clockwork, and that grand lie will cost everyone dearly. The universe is not like clockwork. The universe is like stoats fighting in a sack, bloody and chaotic, and any rules there might be could never be glimpsed by you or I.'

He sucked on his cigarette, choked a cough in his throat. Church felt odd licks of anxiety, while Ruth waited for the punchline.

'The one true law of the universe is duality,' Tom continued. 'You would think even the most confused of philosophers would see that, but it seems to have eluded all the apologists for this so-called Age of Reason. Hot and cold. Life and death. Good and evil. And what would be the flipside of science?'

He addressed the question to Ruth, but it was Church who answered: 'Magic?'

Tom smiled slyly. 'The seasons have turned. The Age of Reason has passed. We're on the cusp of a new age.'

Church laughed dismissively. 'I thought all that Age of Aquarius rubbish went out with flower children and love-ins.'

'The Age of Aquarius is one way of making sense of it, but it isn't the whole of it. Yes, we are entering an era of spirituality, wisdom and magic. But there will also be blood and brutality. All I'm saying is you must let go of old certitudes, keep an open mind. That's the only way you'll be able to face the trials that lie ahead.'

'You're not telling us anything,' Church protested.

'This isn't the time or the place. We need to move quickly. What happened back there wasn't the end of it. They won't be happy till you're both dead.'

When Church looked in the rearview mirror he could tell from Tom's set face that he was not about to reveal any more. A small nugget of anger made him want to drop the man off at the next services in retaliation, but he knew he couldn't dismiss the one person who seemed to know something about what was happening in his suddenly chaotic life.

He glanced at Ruth, who smiled back as warmly as she could muster, but her eyes were still terribly scared.

They hadn't gone much further when Ruth's mobile phone rang. She answered it, then said to Church, 'It's someone called Dale for you.'

'He's a friend. I gave him your number for emergencies.' He nursed the phone against his shoulder as he drove. 'What's wrong, Dale?'

'You tell me.' Dale's voice was drawn and worried. There was a long pause, then he said, 'You've had some trouble at your flat.'

'What do you mean?'

Dale sighed. 'Well, there's no easy way to say this . . . It's been burnt out.'

'What?' Church almost dropped the phone.

'Someone broke down the door, then set fire to it. The fire brigade got there before it took out the rest of the house, but . . . well, I'm sorry, Church, everything's a write-off.' Another pause. 'That's not all. I've had the cops round here asking after you. I don't know how they found out where I worked, how they even knew we were friends . . .' Dale's voice faded; he sounded disorientated, worried. 'They wanted to know where you were. I got the feeling it was about more than the fire.'

'What did you tell them?'

'Nothing, honest. Listen, if you're in any trouble—'

'Don't worry, Dale. It's probably just a mix-up. But I'd appreciate it if you didn't tell them where we are.'

'I don't know where you are!'

'Then you won't have to lie.'

After he'd switched off the phone, he told Ruth what Dale had told him. 'They have probably done the same to your home too,' Tom said to Ruth. 'And if either of you had been there you would be lying in the ashes now.'

'Who are *they*?' Church snapped; he felt at breaking point.

71

Tom sniffed at Church's tone, then lay across the seat and closed his eyes. 'Later,' he said dismissively. However much Church protested, he wouldn't respond, and in the end Church and Ruth were forced into a desperate silence as the sun slipped towards the horizon.

CHAPTER FOUR

the purifying fire

Twilight was upon them. The traffic was growing heavier as the weekend rush from London to country homes in the west gathered force. The lights of Reading were now behind and the featureless landscape they had been passing through since they left the capital had given way to more wooded country-side, the trees eventually pressing in so that at times it was impossible to see beyond the edges of the motorway. Church adjusted the rearview mirror to check on Tom, who was still asleep on the back seat.

'Perfect. He sleeps, we worry.'

Ruth glanced at him askance. They had barely spoken since they had restarted the journey, lost in their own thoughts. 'Patience is a virtue,' she said.

'I don't trust him,' Church said quietly. 'I don't like being manipulated and that's what he's doing with all his talk that says nothing.' When he glanced at Ruth for a response, he saw how exhausted she looked; her experience at the service station was taking its toll. 'Why don't you close your eyes for a while?' he suggested.

She shook her head. 'Every time I do that, all I can see is that bastard coming at me in the toilets.'

'You'll get over it. I've seen you in action – you can cope with anything.'

'Is that what it looks like? In my head I feel like I've fought every step of the way through my life to keep it all from falling apart.' She watched the grey light disappearing over the horizon ahead. 'My dad always expected great things from me. He was the one who pushed me into the law. I think he had this idea I'd be some bigshot barrister.'

'Don't you like the job?'

'There were other things I could have done,' she said non-committally. 'But I suppose my dad's attitude made me focused. Now I don't think I could loosen up if I tried.'

'You can never shake off those chains that keep you tied to the past, can you?' He thought of Marianne and the night swept in.

The driving was hard. There were too many lorries winding their way to Bristol, too many coaches with weekend trippers, cars bumper-to-bumper, filled with anxious, irritable people desperate to get out of the city for a breath of fresh air, even though they were destroying it with each piston pump and exhaust belch. Drivers threw themselves in front of Church in suicidal bids to win the race, forcing him to slam on the brakes, cursing through gritted teeth. There were a thousand accidents waiting to happen in sleepy eye and stressed hand; the desire to escape was voracious, coloured by all sorts of ancient impulses. Church put on *London Calling* by The Clash to drown out the noise of the traffic, but Ruth had turned it down before Strummer had barely started to sing so as not to wake Tom; Church couldn't tell if it was through kindness or because she was afraid of what their new companion might have to say.

Newbury and Hungerford were long gone and they were on the flat, unspoiled stretch of countryside somewhere near the Ridgway. Swindon's lights burned orange in the sky ahead. Church flexed his aching fingers off the steering wheel. It would be late by the time they reached Bristol and they still had to find somewhere to stay. In the back seat, Tom stirred, mumbled something, then hauled himself upright to lean on Church and Ruth's seats. 'We need to find something to eat,' he said bluntly.

'Right away, Tom,' Church replied acidly. 'Have to keep you well-fed after your long sleep.'

'Can we try to get along?' Ruth asked. 'This is a very small car for—' She paused suddenly.

'What's wrong?' Church asked.

Ruth leaned forward to peer through the windscreen. 'What's that?'

'What's what?' The traffic was too heavy for Church to take his eyes off the road.

'A flash of light in the sky over to the south-west.'

'A UFO? I can give you Barry Riggs' number if you like. I'm sure he'd like to take you to his secret base.'

'Maybe it was lightning,' Ruth mused, still searching the skies.

'Actually, Salisbury Plain's over there somewhere,' Church continued. 'They had a big UFO flap down near Warminster in the sixties when all the believers and hippies used to gather on the hilltops to wait for the mothership to come.' He glanced in the mirror to see if Tom would rise to the bait, but the man ignored his gaze.

There was another flash and this time they all saw it: among the clouds, lighting them in an orange burst like a firework. 'That's not lightning,' Church said. 'It's more like a flare.' His attention had wavered from the road and he had to brake sharply to avoid hitting the car in front, which had slowed down as the driver also saw the lights.

'How long until you can get off this road?' Tom asked sharply.

'We don't need to get off this road.'

'How long?'

The tone of his voice snapped Church alert. 'Not long. I remember a junction somewhere on the outskirts of Swindon. Why?' Church glanced in the mirror, but Tom had his face pressed against the passenger window scanning the night sky.

There was another burst of light somewhere above them, so bright that Church saw the ruddy glare reflected on the roofs of the cars around. Ruth gasped in shock.

'What's going on?' Church thumped the horn as another

distracted driver strayed across the line into his lane. 'There's going to be a pile-up in a minute!'

Ruth tried to crane her neck to see upwards through the windscreen. 'I think there's something up there,' she said.

'Probably the army on helicopter manoeuvres with no thought for anyone else as usual,' Church said. 'Jesus Christ!' He swung the wheel to avoid hitting a motorbike weaving in and out of the traffic. The rider kept glancing up at the sky in panic as he gunned the machine. Cold water washed up Church's spine. The traffic had become more dense, with no space to overtake. He was glad he was in the slow lane, with the hard shoulder available for any drastic evasive action.

Tom was becoming more anxious by the second. 'We must leave this traffic as soon as possible,' he stressed.

'I'm doing the best I can,' Church snapped. 'Do you think I can pick up the car and run with it?'

Ahead of them something big swept across the motorway about thirty feet off the ground. It was just a blur, a block of darkness against the lighter night sky, but its size and speed made Church catch his breath.

'What the hell was that?' he exclaimed.

'My God,' Ruth whispered in awe. 'Was that alive?'

The shock rippled back through the vehicles in a slewing of wheels and a sparking of brake lights. A red Fiesta gouged a furrow along the side of a Beetle before righting itself. There was a burst of exploding glass as a car in the centre lane clipped the one in front. Both cars fishtailed, but miraculously kept going.

Church was afraid to take his eyes off the road, but he had the awful feeling that something terrible was about to happen. He wound down the window; above the rumble of the traffic he could hear an odd noise, rhythmic, loud, like the rending of thick cloth. After a second or two he suddenly realised what it sounded like: the beating of enormous wings.

He shifted the rearview mirror. Reflected in it was Tom's

troubled face, his jaw set hard. 'What's going on?' Church barked. 'You know, don't you?'

Before Tom could answer, a column of fire blazed from the black sky on to a blue Orion, shattering all the windows with one tremendous blast and, a split second later, igniting the petrol tank. The car went up like it had been bombed. And then all hell erupted.

A shockwave exploded out, driving chunks of twisted metal and burning plastic like guided missiles, shattering wind-screens, careening off roofs and bonnets, imbedding in doors and wings. The vehicles closest to the blast were the first to go. Some were travelling too fast and simply ploughed into the inferno. Others, attempting to avoid it, swerved, clipped other vehicles and set off a complex pattern of ricochets that rippled across the motorway. A lorry, its windscreen a mass of frosted glass, crushed a Peugeot before slamming into the side of a coach. The coach driver fought with the wheel as his vehicle went over on two wheels, then back on the other two, before toppling over completely in a bone-juddering impact that crushed two more cars. Church caught sight of terrified white faces through glass and felt his stomach churn.

And then there was chaos as vehicles thundered into each other, smashing through the central reservation, piling up twisted wreckage in a deafening Wagnerian cacophony of exploding glass, screeching tyres and rending metal, until it seemed all six lanes were filled with death and destruction. The flames leapt from collision to collision, feeding on rup-tured petrol tanks, until a wall of fire blazed across the whole of the motorway. Another column of fire lanced down from the heavens, blowing up a living fountain of flame that soared high above their heads.

Their ears rang from the noise, and the sudden, awful smell of thick smoke and petrol engulfed them as Church threw the car on to the hard shoulder; the accident had happened too fast for the vehicles ahead to attempt the same route. Behind them and to the side, cars were still smashing into the carnage. Ruth thought she could hear terrible screams buried in the sounds of wreckage, but she convinced herself it was just an illusion. A juggernaut jackknifed and was lost to the fire. A motorcyclist skidded along at ground level, his arms raised in a futile attempt to ward off the inevitable. And more, and more, too much to bear. They turned their heads away as one, and Church hit the accelerator, launching the car forward. The nearside wheels churned up mud and grass on the bank; the rear end skidded wildly, but he kept his foot to the floor. As they approached the inferno at breakneck speed, Ruth screamed and threw her arms across her face, Tom dropped flat on the seat and Church closed his eyes and whispered a prayer.

The heat made his skin bloom and he half-expected the glass to implode, but then they were through it and racing across the empty motorway ahead.

'God,' Ruth said in shock. She clasped her hands together in her lap to stop them shaking.

Church slowed down and headed towards one of the emergency phones on the hard shoulder.

'Don't stop!' Tom yelled. 'The worm will still be here. It doesn't give up easily!' Then he added with exasperation, 'Don't you see? It's after us.'

Church swung the car in a wide arc until they faced the wall of fire. Vehicles had backed up on the other side of the central barrier. In the distance came the sound of sirens.

'What are you doing?' Tom snapped.

'I have to see for myself.' Church leaned forward over the wheel and searched the skies. He and Ruth saw it at the same moment, just a glimmer at first, high above the billowing grey smoke. But as it came lower it fell into focus and they both froze in their seats. They saw glints of copper and gold and green as the red glare of the fire burnished its scales. A scarlet eye as bright as a brake light. Enormous, leathery wings that beat the air with a slow, heavy rhythm, and a long tail that writhed and twisted behind it as if it had a separate

78

existence. As it swooped low, it opened its mouth wide and belched a gush of golden-orange fire that sprayed into the inferno and sent another torrent of flames spouting high. Its movements were fluid as it soared on the air currents, terrifying and majestic at the same time.

'I don't believe it,' Ruth said in hushed, incredulous tones. Church's head was spinning.

'They have been away too long, excluded against their will. They miss their old places,' said Tom.

'I don't believe it,' Church echoed in a mix of wonder and fear.

Tom rested a hand on his shoulder. 'We have to be away. It will soon realise we've escaped its first strike.'

'What the hell's going on?' Church spun round in a rage. 'You know. Tell us!'

'I told you.' Tom's tone was darker than he intended. 'They've recognised you. They won't let you live.'

'Stop procrastinating—'

Ruth caught his arm, signalling that it wasn't the time or the place. 'Where will we go?' she said in dismay. 'Look at the speed of it. It won't take long to catch us, however fast we're driving.'

'There's only one place we can be assured of safety until dawn comes,' Tom replied. 'But it's still a long journey from here. We have to get the wind behind us and pray to God we reach there first.'

Following Tom's directions, Church put the pedal to the floor until they reached the next exit, where they took the A346 south. An oppressive silence lay on them as they each struggled with the terrible sights they had witnessed. Even with the window down, Church couldn't clear the stink of burning from his nose, and when he glanced at Ruth, he saw in the flicker of the street lamps her cheeks were wet. Behind all the churning emotions was an incomprehension at how they had suddenly found themselves in a situation where terrible, unbelievable forces had emerged from the shadows to target them alone. There seemed no reason for the magnitude of the power ranged against them, or for the unflinching focus of its cold eye.

Tom barely removed his head from the rear window shelf, where he was pressing his face against the glass in numerous contortions to search the skies. The thick cloud cover made it impossible to get a clear view, but the wind had blown the rain away and the driving was easier.

'I don't believe what we saw there,' Church said quietly. 'What's going on?' He glanced in the mirror at Tom. 'I said, what's going on? You weren't surprised by that thing—'

'I've seen one before,' Tom replied. 'And I'll tell you all about it when we get where we're going. If we get there.'

Church shook his head incredulously, then glanced at Ruth for support. She caught his eye for a second, then looked away.

The road was straight, but slow after the motorway, and seemed very old. Grassy banks and ancient wire fences lined it, punctuated at intervals by bursts of elder and bushy hawthorn. There seemed little habitation on either side away in the dark where fields stretched up to the downy hills. The route dipped and rose so it was always hard to see too far ahead and Church had to temper his speed accordingly. They eventually passed a golf club and two large thatched cottages with lights burning brightly in the windows; Church felt oddly warmed by the sight.

After a while they burst from the dark, worrying countryside into Marlborough, the road sweeping down through its age-old buildings, jumbled topsy-turvy in a mix of pastel shades.

'Have we lost it?' Church asked anxiously. 'We must have by now.'

'We won't be able to evade it,' Tom said distractedly. 'All we can hope is we reach our destination before it.'

'You're telling me it can recognise the make and model of a dark-coloured car at night, from hundreds of feet overhead?' Church said.

'She isn't *looking*,' Tom replied obliquely. 'The Fabulous Beasts are highly sensitive. She knows our signature. She can locate us from miles distant.'

'*She?*' Church said incredulously. 'How do you know so much about something that shouldn't exist? Christ, tell me something! This is driving me insane!'

There was a long silence until Ruth said, 'You're wasting your breath, Church. Just keep your eyes on the road.'

Still heading south, Tom directed them through Pewsey alongside the Avon, guarded by the stone bulk of its twelfth century church. In the countryside beyond, the road was so dark the driving became even more difficult. Trees clustered in tightly, with only the occasional light of a farm off in the distance breaking through the branches. But through Upavon they became aware of a change in the countryside as Salisbury Plain rolled in, bleak and uncompromising. The military presence was unmissable, with signs for armoured vehicle crossings and tank tracks tearing up the landscape on both sides. There were high, chainlink fences topped with barbed wire and a checkpoint for the forces off to the left.

The sight sparked an idea in Church. 'Why haven't the RAF scrambled to shoot it down? There's an early warning base at Lyneham.'

Tom was distracted and nervous, glancing repeatedly out of the window to ascertain their relative position. 'They won't know it's there unless they happen to glance up to see it. And then they wouldn't believe their eyes.'

'It must register on radar at that size.'

'It belongs to the old world. Technology can't comprehend it.' As they passed Figheldean in a blur of sodium glare, he said darkly, 'I see her. She is circling up high, trying to find us.'

For a while the trees offered some cover, but then Tom caught his breath. 'She's seen us. Drive faster!'

'I'm just about blowing a piston now!' Church grunted.

Ruth wound down the window and hung her head out, fighting against the buffeting slipstream. At first she could see nothing, but then the clouds parted to reveal the moon and the Fabulous Beast caught in its milky luminescence, its scales glinting like polished metal; for the briefest instant, it appeared to be made out of silver. Its wings, at full stretch, could span a football pitch. They looked like dark leather which at times seemed scarlet, and then emerald, sparkling as if dusted with gold. Occasionally Ruth could make out its eyes glowing like the landing lights of a plane. She pulled her head in and said in hushed awe, 'It's magnificent.'

'What's it doing now?' Church felt the sweat pooling in the small of his back.

'Circling like a bird of prey.' Ruth turned to Tom. 'If we could get off the open road, under cover somewhere—'

There was a roar like a jet taking off, a concentrated burst of orange-yellow light that illuminated the interior of the car as brightly as day, and then the hedge on their side of the road disintegrated in a firestorm. Church fought to keep the car on the road against the sudden shockwave of superheated air.

They crashed across a roundabout, narrowly avoiding another car, and then Tom ordered Church to take the next right. For the first stretch it was a dual carriageway, allowing Church to floor the accelerator; the car complained under the sudden pull. But then the road narrowed to a single carriageway and Church feared the worst. At Tom's instruction he took a right fork on the wrong side of the road, his shirt wet with sweat.

'Turn right when I say!' Tom yelled. Church's eyes were constantly drawn to the sky, but he steeled himself for the order. 'Now!'

Church swung the wheel, clipping the kerb as another

pillar of fire erupted from the heavens. Behind them the tarmac exploded in molten gouts. They swung round in a massive car park, the plain rolling off flatly ahead of them.

'Where do we go from here?' Church shouted, suddenly confronted by a huddle of low buildings and a barrier with a turnstile.

'Out of the car,' Tom ordered, wrenching the door open.

Before Church could protest, Tom was moving rapidly for someone in his late fifties. He vaulted the barrier, and by the time they had caught up with him he was turning into a tunnel which cut back under the road. Overhead, the slow beat of the creature's wings was almost deafening. They felt the surge of air currents as it swooped by, but by the time it had rounded to emit another blast of fire they were already deep in the tunnel.

Ruth slumped against the wall to catch her breath. 'Thank God,' she gasped.

'Not here,' Tom stressed, grabbing her arm and pulling her on. A few seconds later, a wall of flame roared along the tunnel to the point where she had been standing, the wave of scorching air knocking them to the ground.

Coughing and choking, with lungs that seemed to burn from the inside, they scrambled forward and emerged into the cool night. Church was instantly transfixed by a view of black megaliths crowded squat and ancient beneath the light of the moon.

'Stonehenge?' Ruth gasped.

They ran forward and clawed their way over the perimeter fence, only pausing once they were amongst the stones.

'It can see us here as easily as anywhere else,' Ruth protested as she watched the creature soar and turn high overhead, a black shape blocking out the stars as it passed.

'I told you, she senses.' Tom knelt and patted the scrubby grass affectionately. 'The land is filled with power. Earth Magic. Tremendous alchemical energy that flows among the old places and sacred spots. The Fabulous Beasts feed on it, use the lines for guidance when they are flying. We can't see it, but to them it appears like a network of blue fire on the land. And here, in a powerful nexus of that energy, we're lost in the glare.'

There was a moment of silence as Ruth gaped at Tom, then she turned to Church; he shook his head dismissively.

Tom shrugged and turned away. 'Believe what you will. You have seen one of the Fabulous Beasts. You cannot wish your way back to your old life.' He wandered off amongst the stones and was soon lost in the shadows.

Ruth and Church watched the sky, ready to run at any second.

'Well, he's right about one thing,' Ruth said after a tense few moments. 'It's not attacking.' She watched it circling, the arc growing wider and wider.

Church followed her gaze. 'What the hell's going on?'

Gradually the creature disappeared from view. The wind picked up, blustering over the sweeping plain, driving the few remaining clouds ahead of it until the night sky was clear and burning with the beacons of a thousand stars. Church couldn't remember the last time he had seen the sweep of the heavens in such a virginal, breathtaking state.

'Beautiful,' Ruth whispered in a state of dazed incomprehension. 'I knew there was a reason to move out of the city.'

The enormity of their experience made it almost impossible to consider so Church focused on the mundane. 'What do you make of him?'

Ruth thought for a while, her face hidden in shadows. 'I think he could help us.'

'But you don't trust him.'

'No.' She chewed on her lip thoughtfully, then said, 'I don't like the way he's not telling us what's happening. You can see he knows more. But it's like he's using it to control us.'

The wind that had been rushing around the henge died

down and for a second there was just peace and quiet. 'Who is he, Church? How can he know these things?'

'I've given up trying to make any sense of it,' he replied morosely. 'I'll just be happy getting out the other end in one piece.'

They found a spot on one of the fallen stones where they could lie without getting damp and simply watched the stars, almost touching, aware only of their presence in the universe, the noise of their chaotic thoughts shut down for a brief moment of tranquillity. A shooting star streaked brightly across the arc of the sky, and the last thought Church remembered having was, 'That's an omen.'

The tramp of Tom's boots disturbed them some time later as they floated half in and out of sleep.

'I feel like I've slept for hours,' Church said, scrubbing his face to wake himself. 'Must be the stress.'

'The blue fire,' Tom corrected. 'It heals and invigorates if you open yourself up to it.' Something landed on the ground before them. 'Dinner,' he said. A rabbit lay there, its tufts of white fur ghostly in the dark.

'How did you catch that?' Ruth asked.

'You pick up a few tricks when you're hungry on the road.'

'We're going to eat it raw?' Church said in disgust.

'You can if you like. *I'm* lighting a fire.'

'And have every security guard in the county here in five minutes. I'm surprised they haven't picked us up already,' Church said.

'Their technology is blind to us. And there's no need to worry about the fire, either. I'll make sure of that.'

Church lay back and closed his eyes again. 'I'm not even going to ask.'

Tom looked around for some fuel; the land was just grassy scrub in all directions so he tore up a walkway of wooden

85

pallets that kept the tourists out of the mud in wet weather. It was enough to build a decent fire, and even though the kindling was damp he was able to get it alight with relative ease. He skinned, gutted, trimmed and jointed the rabbit with a Swiss Army knife, then stuffed the various pieces in packets of turf and placed them in the embers around the edge of the fire.

'It will not be long,' he said when he'd finished. 'A hedge-hog would have been quicker, but I could not find one.'

'Mmmm,' Church said acidly. 'Vermin.'

'It's a tasty dish. You're soft.'

'That's why God invented pizza parlours.'

Tom smiled wryly. 'And what will you do when all the pizza parlours have gone?'

'More doom and gloom. The end of the world is nigh.'

'You're starting to sound like an idiot who can't count the fingers held in front of his face,' Tom countered.

Tom and Church glared at each other until Ruth inter-jected. 'Don't argue – I haven't got the energy.' Her face seemed too pale in the firelight and her eyes brimmed with tears. 'I keep thinking of all those people who died on the motorway. Everywhere there was something horrible – some-body's face screaming. I can't get it out of my head.'

Compassion lit Tom's face, softening the lines and the set of his jaw that gave a hardness to his appearance.

'And we caused it!' Ruth continued.

'You didn't cause it,' Tom said flatly. 'What you saw this evening is just the first of many outrages. Some you will be at the heart of, many will happen without your involvement.'

Church had reached his limit. 'You're driving me mad, saying things like, "Oh, that's because of the blue fire", what-ever *that* means, or pretending you have intimate knowledge of the habits of mythical creatures. Why should we believe anything you say?'

There was no outburst in response. Tom merely stared into the middle distance thoughtfully as he gently rubbed his chin. 'How can I explain things to you when you have no frame of reference to understand them?' Then: 'Unfortunately I don't have any credentials to show you. All I can say is that I've seen unmistakable evidence of what's occurring. You'll have to accept me on trust until we know each other well enough to discuss the past.' He held up his hand to silence Church's protests. 'But if you're looking for some kind of proof, there is something I *can* show you.' He dipped into a hidden pocket and pulled out his tobacco tin and a small block of hash which he used to roll a joint.

'I don't think this is the time to get off your face,' Church said.

'This isn't for pleasure,' Tom replied. He lit the joint and inhaled deeply. 'Before the Christian era, psychoactive substances were used by most cultures to put them in touch with the sacred. And that's what I'm about to do now, to show you so you understand what lies behind it all.' He closed his eyes in meditation for a short while, then said, in a gentle voice barely audible over the wind and the fire, 'The people who put up these stones were smoking as they sat here, looking at the stars. In the fougous and under the barrows, beneath the cromlechs, in the circles and the chambered cairns, they were eating sacred mushrooms and ingesting hallucinogens thousands of years before the so-called Summer of Love. It helped man touch the heart of the universe.' He blew a fragrant cloud into the breeze. Then he said in a strong, powerful voice: 'You have to understand that magic works.'

'Magic as in spells and funny hand movements and all that mumbo jumbo,' Church said tartly. 'Sure, why not? A few hits on that and I'll believe in anything.'

'Magic as in influencing people and events without having any obvious direct contact with them,' Tom said, calmly but forcefully. 'Magic as in beings with abilities you can only dream of. An old word for something that may lie just beyond science, that has its own strict rules, that operates with subtle energy flows and fields. A completely different way of looking at how the world works.' Church's expression remained unchanged, so Tom walked over to the nearest standing stone. 'Science says this is just a lump of rock stuck in the earth. Magic says it's something more. Look at it closely, along the edge silhouetted against the sky.'

'What am I supposed to be looking for?' Church said.

'Look close and look hard. Dismiss nothing as a trick of your eyes. Believe.'

Ruth and Church stared at the point Tom was indicating and after a few minutes Ruth said, 'I think I can see a light.'

'Keep looking,' Tom pressed.

Church shook his head dismissively, but then he squinted and after a second or two he seemed to make out a faint blue glow limning the edge of the menhir. The more he stared, the more it came into focus, until tiny azure flames appeared to be flickering all around the ancient stone. 'What is that?' he asked in amazement.

'Magic,' Tom replied softly. He slowly held out his right index finger to the stone and an enormous blue spark jumped from the rock to his hand; a second later the force, whatever it was, was running to him directly, infusing him with a soft sapphire glow. Still smiling, he raised his left hand palm upwards; shimmering shapes danced in the air above it. Church thought he glimpsed faces and bodies, but nothing stayed in focus.

'Static electricity,' Church ventured without believing it himself. 'An electromagnetic field given off by geological stresses.'

Tom simply smiled.

'Does it hurt?' Ruth asked.

'I feel like I could run a hundred miles.' He drew in a deep, peaceful breath. 'This is the power in the land. Earth Magic. The Fiery Network. Science can't measure it so science says it doesn't exist. But you see it.'

Church felt his mood altering in proximity to the crackling

88

display; he was overcome with an exuberation that made him want to shout and jump around. Negative thoughts sloughed off him like mud in the rain; he couldn't stop himself grinning like an idiot.

Tom broke off the display and returned to his seat by the fire. 'Belief in a new way – the true way – won't happen in a night, but all things flow from this and once you accept it you'll truly understand.'

'But what is it exactly?' Church's intellectual curiosity had been piqued alongside the buzz his emotions had received.

'The vital force of the world, the thing that binds humanity and the planet together. An energy unlike any other, spiritual in essence. If you look closely enough you'll find it within you as well as within the earth.'

'The New Agers always said there was something like this.' Church felt a shiver wash through him; he felt deeply affected in a way he couldn't understand.

'The ancients knew about it. The Chinese call it *chi*, the dragon energy, for it's always been linked with the Fabulous Beasts who are both its symbol and its guardians. That's why the standing stones were raised, the old stone chambers, the earliest churches. To mark the sacred sites where the energy was strongest, to channel it, to keep it flowing freely. But when the so-called Age of Reason came, it was discounted by the new generation of thinkers – it couldn't be quantified, bottled, replicated in a laboratory. And as that new way of seeing the world took hold, the people forgot it too. Over time it became dormant. For centuries no one could have stirred it, however hard they tried. But with the change that came over the world at the turn of the year, it awoke again. Now a few of us know how to raise it briefly, but it still needs to be woken completely, to become the vital force once more. And this,' he added, 'is the first sign that the world is now a very different place.'

'How do you know all this?' Ruth asked.

'I was called. Informed—'

'Called by whom?'

He smiled at the insistence in her voice. 'If you must know, by a gentleman called the Bone Inspector. Any the wiser?'

'That's an odd name.'

'He's an odd man. His people have been linked to the land for millennia, the custodians of secret knowledge and ancient ritual. He guards the old places where the blue fire burns the brightest. He felt the changes first. Perhaps you'll meet him one day and then you can ask him all these questions yourself.'

'This is making my head hurt,' Church said. 'People who guard the old places?'

'The best way to approach this is to forget everything you thought you knew,' Tom said bluntly.

'Okay,' Church said, 'you've convinced me you've got some sort of insight, but there are still a lot of questions to be answered—'

'At least I have your attention now,' Tom said acidly.

'Then what is going on?' Ruth asked. Beyond the ruddy glow cast by the fire, the night seemed too dark; past the comforting bulk of the stones the shadows seemed to rise up from the plain. 'Why are all these things happening now?'

Tom crimped out the joint. 'Everything changed, suddenly, dramatically, sometime around the New Year.' He prodded the fire with a broken branch, sending a shower of sparks skyward. 'The world's turning away from the light. History is cyclical, you should know that. Empires rise and fall, knowledge is learned then lost, and sometimes things that seem gone for ever return unannounced. There's a basis for all legends, folklore, fairytales—'

'Symbolism, rites of passage, religion,' Church interrupted. 'A way to pass important wisdom down the generations so it can be easily understood by those learning it.'

'All true, of course. How very erudite of you. But some of it is *literal*. As I understand it, the world used to be a very different place. You saw the Fabulous Beast so this is unde-

90

niable – creatures of myth once walked this land, old gods, ancient races, things you would think existed only in the imagination. And the old stories are our way of remembering this time of wonder and miracles.'

Church glanced at Ruth; Tom's words were an echo of what Kraicow had begun to say. 'There's no archaeological record—' he began, but Tom waved him silent.

'Somehow, for some reason, all these things were swept away to' – he made an expansive gesture – 'some other place. But now—'

'They're back.' Ruth shivered. Somewhere nearby an owl's forlorn hoot keened over the wind. She searched the darkness, but it was impossible to see anything beyond the circle of the fire. 'And this man you called the Bone Inspector told you all this?'

'Some of it.'

'And you believed him straight away?' Church put his head in his hands and closed his eyes for a moment. But having seen what Tom called the Fabulous Beast, he knew there was no rational explanation for it. 'So where did all these creatures of myth go for the last millennia or so?'

Church couldn't tell if Tom's silence was because he didn't know or because he didn't want to tell them.

'And what we saw under the bridge and at the service station were some of the things from those days?' Ruth asked hesitantly.

Tom searched for the right words. 'This is how it was told to me: long ago, long before mankind had established itself, there were old races. Beings of tremendous power, under-standing of all the secret forces in the universe. They were so incomprehensible to us in their appearance and their actions they could have been gods. They were the source of all our legends. In the Celtic stories, in the sacred traditions of other races and cultures. Even in the Christian heritage.'

'Demons,' Ruth ventured.

'And angels,' Tom continued. 'Folklore is the secret history

91

of this land. There's a bright truth in every story. Look at mediaeval wood carvings. Illustrated religious texts. The stone creatures on some of the churches. Once seen, never forgotten. Over time the old races went into decline and soon the season came for them to move on. They disappeared beyond the veil, supposedly for ever. There have been echoes of them down the years – some of the old gods could not leave well alone. Other times their power leaked through, into the ancient places, the sacred places. In all but that they were gone, and the world breathed again, and mankind prospered.' He stared deep into the heart of the flames. 'But now their season has come round again.'

The wind picked up as if in response to his words; Church shivered and pulled his jacket tightly around him. 'If what you're saying is true, and I'm not saying it is, why have they returned now?'

Tom shrugged. 'As I said, everything is cyclical. Perhaps it is simply their time. And perhaps the time of mankind has now passed. Who knows? The rules remain hidden; life is a mystery.'

Church tried to read Tom's face in the hope that he could see the lie, any sign that it was all just a fantasy made up to frighten them; he looked away a moment later in failure.

'But how many of them are there?' Ruth asked.

Tom shrugged. 'Of the larger creatures, the Fabulous Beasts, a handful, I would guess. Many of the wilder mythical creatures, probably the same. I haven't seen an outcry in the media over the last few weeks, so they must be so few as to be able to find hiding places in this over-populated island.'

'And the things that are after us?'

Tom looked down. 'They seem to be everywhere. You saw them – they're shapeshifters. They hide in plain sight. But their skills aren't perfect. If you look close enough, you can see.'

'The skin was too waxy,' Church noted. 'The face looked like a mask.'

'And Gibbons and Kraicow stumbled across them among us,' Ruth said. 'And they both paid the price.'

'They seem to be going to any lengths to prevent themselves being discovered.'

'Like setting a fire-breathing monster on us just because we went to see Kraicow. With that kind of overreaction they must be scared of being uncovered. What are they planning to do?' Church asked. 'Stay in hiding?'

'I don't think,' Tom mused, 'it's in their nature to stay hidden for long.'

'Then what?' Church said insistently.

'Your guess is as good as mine. But I think there will be some kind of conflict. They appear more powerful than us.'

'Even so,' Church said dismissively, 'what could they do?'

'There's one thing I don't understand,' Ruth said. 'You seemed to be waiting for us at the services, yet we didn't even know we were going to be stopping there ourselves until the last minute.'

'I had a feeling I had to be there.'

'What? You're psychic now?' Church shook his head dismissively.

'Things have changed more than you think,' Tom said coldly. 'How can the rigid laws of physics exist after what we've discussed this evening? Science and magic are incompatible. When the doors opened, it wasn't just the stuff of legends that flooded back into our world – it was a new way of thinking, of existing.'

Ruth looked particularly uncomfortable at that prospect. 'What do you mean?'

'There are some Eastern religions that believe the world is the way it is because we wish it that way,' Tom continued. 'In this new age it will be wished another way. Do you think there will be a place for the old, masculine, ultra-logical, highly-structured way of thinking that has dominated for so long? This will be a time of instinct, of the feminine aspect,

93

of wonder and awe. Science and technology, certainly, will suffer.'

Tom's voice was lulling, hypnotic. In the crackle of the flames, Church could almost hear whispers echoing down the centuries, in their dance he seemed to see faces, dark and alien. It disturbed him too much and he looked back into the impenetrable night.

'You're saying it could be the end of the world as we know it?' Ruth said fearfully.

'It will be a time of change, certainly.' He didn't sound very reassuring.

A cold wind blasted into the clearing, making the fire roar, showering a cascade of sparks upwards. Church had the sudden impression they were being watched. He looked round quickly, trying to see beyond the pathetic circle of light, but the darkness was too dense. Tom threw some more wood on the fire and listened to it sputter and sizzle for a while.

Church eyed Tom suspiciously. 'Sitting here, having seen what we've seen, this all makes a stupid kind of sense. But there's still a part of me that says—'

'That I'm lying? I never lie.' He poked the fire. 'The food should be ready now. Let's eat.'

'It hasn't been in long enough,' Ruth said.

'I think it will be ready.'

'More magic?' Church said.

'That, or good cooking technique.' Tom's smile was inscrutable, and Church was instantly aware he had no idea what was going on behind the man's eyes.

The rabbit was steaming hot, fragrant and tender. They gnawed the meat off the bone with the fire hot on their faces and the chill of the night at their backs. Although it may have been the aftermath of the strange energy, Church was convinced it was one of the best meals he had ever eaten.

Afterwards, as the night grew colder, they huddled closer

to the fire, relaxed and replete, the uneasiness forgotten, at least for the moment. Tom picked the remaining meat from his teeth with a twig while he surveyed the position of the stars.

Eventually, he said, 'Everything is changing. You have to be prepared for the new ways ... the new, *old* ways ... if you're to be of any use in the coming struggle.'

'But what could we possibly do,' Ruth began, 'if things are as dire as you say? We could try to warn the Government, the police, the army, but I think we'd pretty much be laughed out and locked up.'

'They will not be able to do anything anyway,' Tom said. 'This is a time for individuals, not institutions, for passion not planning.'

'Very poetic,' Church noted. 'But, with all due respect to Ruth ... look at us. We're not exactly people of action.'

'Adaptation is the key, and people adapt quicker than groups. If you can learn to work within the new rules, then ... perhaps something can be done.' Tom eyed them both with a dissecting look which made Church feel uncomfortable.

Ruth wasn't convinced. 'Two people against the sort of powers that you're talking about? Get real.'

'But we have to do something,' Church said passionately. 'We have a responsibility—'

'A good word,' Tom interjected.

'Don't be so patronising!' Church felt his emotions were on the edge of swinging out of control.

'I apologise,' Tom said, without seeming in the least contrite.

Church grunted with irritation and marched over to lean on the great trilithon. Ruth watched him affectionately as he gazed up at the stars.

'It would help if you were a little less smug,' she said to Tom diplomatically. 'He's a good man. He wants to do something. You shouldn't be so hard on him.'

He shrugged. 'We all have our flaws.'

'There's so much more we need to know—'

'We can discuss it tomorrow, when we're all a little more receptive. I've given you plenty to chew over – a whole new way of looking at life, a new belief system, things that at first glance seem impossible. Isn't that enough to be going on with?'

'How much more is there?'

'There's always more.' He yawned and stretched. 'It's late. We need to sleep. We've got a great deal ahead of us, and we may not always have such a fortuitous place to rest our heads.'

'You expect me to sleep after all this?'

'You will sleep.' Tom brushed her forehead with his finger-tips and she went out as if he had flicked a switch. He caught her and laid her down next to the fire, removing her coat and pulling it over her like a blanket.

'It is a magnificent place, isn't it?'

Church hadn't heard Tom approach behind him. 'I wish I'd seen it under other circumstances.'

'You should see it on June 21, at the solstice at sunrise. If you stand at the centre of the circle, there comes a moment when the sun appears to be suspended on the heel stone and the whole place is painted gold. Beautiful.'

'I wish I hadn't got dragged into all this. Life was compli-cated enough as it was.'

'It's too late for that.'

'Yes. I know.'

Tom lit another joint, took the smoke down deep, then exhaled into the wind. 'There are journeys without and within to make,' he said softly, 'and many mysteries to be uncovered before the end of the road. We are surrounded by them, all the time, every day, and when we think we are trying to expose one, it often turns out we are delving into another. Take this place. They *think* Neolithic man dug the outer circle more than four and a half thousand years ago. They *think* the Beaker People erected the bluestones eight hundred years later and the Wessex People put in the sarsen blocks in 1,500 BC. But who did it is not as important as why. Why did different peoples value this place so highly they returned to it over all those years? Simply because it aligned with the sun, moon and stars? Would they have put so much effort into it if it was simply a tool? Or a metaphor for some religious experience?'

Church drew his fingers across the surface of the stone, feeling the years heavy under his touch. 'They were searching for some meaning,' he said.

'That's right. They were trying to find the magic at the heart of reality. And they found it, the most valuable thing mankind could ever possess. But somehow we lost it again, and during the twentieth century it got as far away from us as it could possibly get. But if one good thing can come out of all the terrible things that lie ahead, it will be that we, as a race, will get back in touch with it again.'

Church scanned the dark horizon. 'That's tomorrow taken care of. What do we do on the day after?'

'You're no longer the person you used to be.' Church couldn't tell if it were an admonition or a pep talk. 'The path away from that person began with your alchemical experience under the bridge, and there are plenty of changes on the road ahead, for you and Ruth.' Tom rested one hand on Church's shoulder and pointed towards the heel stone. 'You see that star there? Wait five minutes until it touches the stone.'

They stood in silence watching the gradual descent until, at the exact moment of alignment, Church felt a tingling at the base of his spine. A second later it felt like heaven had exploded around him. The blue energy Tom had summoned earlier erupted upwards from the top of the stones, forming a structure that soared at least a hundred feet above their heads. The lines of force met at the pinnacle and sheets of paler blue, shifting between opaque and clear, crackled among them. Church had the sudden sensation of standing in a cathedral, magnified by a feeling of overwhelming transcendental awe and mystery that left him trembling. Ahead, lines of azure fire raced out across the land, criss-crossing into a network as they reached other ancient sites, where they exploded upwards in glory. To Church, it seemed like the whole of Britain was coming alive with magnificence and wonder. Tears of emotion stung his eyes and there was a yearning in his heart that he hadn't experienced since childhood.

After five minutes the flames shimmered then dwindled until all was as it had been, but Church knew he would keep the moment with him for the rest of his days.

Still lost in the spell, he started suddenly when Tom touched his hand. 'Before you passed under the bridge that night, you would never have seen that. It's a mark of how much you have already changed, and a hint of the potential ahead.'

As they wandered back to the fire, Church felt calm and energised by the experience. 'Make the most of this night,' Tom said as they lay down and looked up at the stars. 'This is a safe place, but from here on, things are going to get wild and dangerous.'

'We'll cope,' Church said, surprising himself at his confidence.

The last words of Tom's he heard were almost lost on the edge of sleep: 'One more thing – do not leave the circle before sunrise.'

Church awoke some time in the early hours. Tom and Ruth were still sleeping, cast in the faintest reddish glow from the embers of the fire. His soft back muscles ached from the hard ground, but as he rolled around trying to get comfortable, he became aware of an uneasy feeling in the pit of his stomach and the sensation that he was being watched. Over the next five minutes it grew gradually stronger until he had to stand up to look warily around. Beyond the small circle lit by the dim mantle of the fire, the night seemed uncommonly dark.

He waited for a minute or two, but when the sensation didn't diminish he cautiously edged towards the shadows. Beyond the reach of the fire's luminescence, his eyes grew accustomed to the dark and he began to make out the shapes of hedges and trees on the plains that rolled away from the henge. There was no sign of movement and his ears, tuned for the tramp of a foot, could only pick up the bleak moan of the wind as it swept across the lowlands.

When he reached the outer stones, Church paused, his heart thumping madly from the discomfort of invisible eyes. 'Who's there?' he hissed.

There was a lull, as if the night were waiting for him to progress further, then he heard what appeared to be the faintest reply on the edge of his hearing, barely more than a rustle of grass.

After a few seconds he caught a glimpse of movement, like a dark shape separating itself from the lighter dark of the night. His skin seemed to grow taut across his body. A figure, slim and tall, moved towards him, gradually developing an inner light as if tiny fireflies were buzzing around within it. Long before it had coalesced into any recognisable form, Church was overcome. And when it finally halted twenty feet away from him, his eyes burned with tears and his trembling knees threatened to buckle.

'Marianne,' he whispered.

She was pale and fragile, her eyes dark and hollow, as if she had gone days without sleep; Church couldn't bear to look into their depths. Her skin had an opaque quality that seemed to shimmer and for the briefest instant become transparent. Her arms hung limply at her sides, her shoulders slouched from an unseen burden. Church felt an overwhelming wave of despair and longing washing off her, sluicing away the *frisson* of fear he felt at her terrible appearance.

And all he could remember was that moment when the last dregs of life drained away and the intelligence died in her eyes, leaving him with just an armful of hope and chattering images of promised futures now lost and, worse, the certain knowledge he would never know why everything he ever needed or believed in had been taken away from him.

He thought he might die if he heard the truth, but he asked anyway, in a hoarse voice that didn't sound like his own: 'Just tell me why.'

If she heard, she gave no sign; her blank features still radiated that sense of terrible loss. Church couldn't bear to look at her; he closed his burning eyes and stifled the sobs that threatened to rack him.

When he did finally look again, she had raised her arms, beckoning.

His breath froze in his throat. Tom's warning flickered for an instant, then was driven away. He took a step and passed the edge of the stones.

But as he moved forward, Marianne began to recede, still holding her arms in front of her, faster and faster, however quickly he advanced, eerily gliding an inch or two above the ground. And then he was running madly down the slope and Marianne was whisking away from him, growing smaller until she was just a glowing spot on the horizon that eventually winked out.

Heartbroken, Church fell to his knees, his loss as raw as in the days just after her death. Somehow he managed to compose himself enough to trudge back to the stones, but as he passed the spot where she had waited he noticed something unusual. On the ground lay a rose, its petals as black as the night, perfectly formed, with a stem that had been neatly clipped. As he picked it up, he felt a whisper in his head that said *Roisin Dubh*, and he knew in a way he couldn't explain that it was the flower's name; and that it was a gift from Marianne.

Although he couldn't fathom its meaning, he felt a rush of elation. He tucked the flower secretly into his jacket and made his way back to the dying fire.

CHAPTER FIVE

Where the Black Dog Runs

They woke early with the sun heavy and red on the horizon. A thick dew sparkled on the ground and on their jackets and there was a chill in the air that made their bones ache, but they soon stamped the warmth back into their limbs. As soon as they had properly woken, Church and Ruth realised they felt strangely refreshed; new and clean like they had been reborn; Church could not remember having slept so deeply in the last two years.

'It's the healing and energising effect of the earth energy,' Tom told them as they made their way back to the car.

'The NHS should get a franchise,' Ruth replied with a relaxed smile. Church was pleased to see her face clear of the anxiety and worry that had transformed her the previous evening.

In the tunnel they stopped to examine the black crust scorching the concrete and were instantly reminded of how close their escape had been. And before they could depart, Church had to scrape the car windows free of a thick layer of ash made tacky by the dew; the air smelled like the aftermath of a house fire.

'I still do not understand how the Fabulous Beast was marshalled in our pursuit,' Tom mused as Church cursed quietly in his labour. 'They are supposed to be wildly independent, uncontrollable.'

'Maybe that's one bit of your lore that's wrong,' Church said sourly. 'A good council Fabulous Beast training course ... sit ... beg ... roll over. They'll do anything for a treat.'

Tom muttered something under his breath and wandered

off to take the air while Church finished the windows.

'Doesn't he speak funny?' Ruth found a clean part of the wing to perch on. 'Like some bad historical novel.'

'He's a strange fish all round. I still don't trust him. It feels like he's just throwing out enough titbits to keep us interested while he works on his own agenda.'

'As long as we're aware of it.' Ruth closed her eyes and put her head back to feel the sun on her face.

Church was glad of the silence that followed. He could barely contain the emotional upheaval he felt after his encounter with Marianne; it resonated confusingly through every thought. Why was she visiting him – to torment him further or to pass on some message? Was it linked to all the other high strangenesses that had descended on the country? And what was the significance of the Black Rose which was secreted in the inside pocket of his jacket close to his heart? Instinctively, he felt he ought to tell Ruth about it, but there was a niggling part of his mind that forced him to hold back. *Maybe later*, he promised himself.

Their first aim was to find somewhere to eat. At the A345 they came across a Little Chef surrounded by trees and were the first inside once the doors opened. Over full English breakfasts and tea looking out over the sun-drenched car park, they tried to make some sense of what was happening.

'I still don't see what we can possibly do,' Ruth said as she dunked her toast into her egg.

'Probably nothing apart from find some way to raise the alarm. But we do have a responsibility to do *something*.' Still distracted, Church sipped on his tea; he knew *exactly* what he wanted to do: discovering what the mysterious email woman knew about Marianne was still the driving force. At the moment that dovetailed with their search for more information about the imminent crisis Tom had described, but if he ever had to make a choice between the two, he didn't know how he would react.

Ruth suddenly glanced down at her hand in surprise. 'Look at this: I cut my hand scrambling through the fence last night, and this morning there's no sign of it. It's completely healed.'

'Make the most of it,' Tom mumbled grumpily. He seemed preoccupied, constantly glancing around the room.

'Expecting guests?' Church said.

'Just because we survived last night doesn't mean it's the end of it.'

'There's a cheery thought,' Ruth said breezily, but Church could see she was disturbed by it.

'So now we're on the run,' he said. Tom didn't answer.

They went to the checkout, but as the waitress totted up their bill the till suddenly started spewing out reams of receipt paper. Her eyes flashed irritation while she attempted to maintain a pleasant smile as she wrestled with the snaking roll. Eventually the register jammed and she tore off the streamer with restrained anger. On it was the same thing printed over and over again:

1 OF 5

It bore no relation to what she had keyed in. When Church noticed it, he felt strangely uneasy. He was immediately thrown back to his journey to collect Ruth and the odd sequence of coincidences.

Church leaned on the car bonnet in the sun with Ruth's mobile phone after struggling for ten minutes to find a signal. Laura's sleepy voice told him he'd woken her.

'It's Jack Churchill. I'm sorry we didn't make the meeting with you last night. We got delayed in Wiltshire.'

There was a long pause, then: 'It's Sunday. Mornings have been banned. What's the matter? The missus thrown you out of bed?'

'I'm sorry.'

'Yeah, yeah.' She yawned. 'So what's the score? You still want to meet?'

'Yes, and soon. We can get up to Bristol by—'

'Don't worry, I'll come to you. If you're in Wiltshire then you might as well head to Salisbury. That's where it happened. You can take the ghost train with me, see if you get the full Fright Night treatment too. Or maybe I really have done too many drugs.' The line threatened to break up, but then her voice came through clear once more. '—king mobiles! I'll meet you tomorrow at Poultry Cross in the city centre. 10 a.m. You'll find it.'

'What about your work?'

'Yeah, like it matters any more.'

They reached Salisbury just after 10.30 a.m. The March sun was strong enough to catch the historic cathedral town in an unseasonable light, bright and buzzing with tourists through the main shopping area and Market Square. Ruth used her credit card to check them into a hotel in the centre of town, selected by Tom for its olde worlde appeal: a thirteenth century coaching inn, half-timbered in black on white, with hanging eaves, high chimneys and diamond window panes which, from the pavement, made the interior seem mysteriously murky. They managed to get rooms side by side. They were fitted with all mod cons, but the sloping floors and oddly angled ceilings still gave them a time-lost feeling.

With the threat of so much darkness looming on the horizon, they agreed to take a break, from each other and, hopefully, from the stresses of the events sweeping in around them, until early evening. Ruth and Church both felt they needed time to assimilate all that Tom had shown and told them at Stonehenge.

In the sun outside the hotel, amongst the bustle of everyday life, they could easily have pretended nothing had changed. But as they walked away, Tom called out, 'Be on your guard.'

For some reason he couldn't quite explain, Church found himself drawn to the cathedral which stood on the south of the city, an imposing vision of majesterial white stone in acres of greenery bounded by the River Avon. As he stood in The Close looking up at the soaring spire, he had a sudden impression of it as a symbol of all that was under threat. Seven hundred years of British history, built on solid foundations that not even an earthquake could throw down. It had overseen the coming of the Age of Enlightenment, of the establishment of a civilisation based on science, reason and logic. And more than that, it represented the glory of a God who had created that world; a religion which allowed no space for the truth that was slowly being unpeeled before their eyes. The magnitude of what could be swept away dwarfed him.

It was too much. He hurried in through the south-west entrance as if he were seeking sanctuary and walked slowly up the nave to take a seat in the pews. For long minutes, he couldn't bear to think, instead losing himself in the quiet beauty of the surroundings. Organ music played gently in the background, adding to the air of reverent tranquillity which soothed him a little, and eventually his attention fell upon the altar and its intricately worked cloth. The central image showed a crown of thorns in gold and red surrounding the Holy Grail. There was something about the image which seemed to speak to him, whispering insistently at the back of his head until he became disturbed by the suggestion of a subconscious connection which he couldn't make. In the end he had to force himself to look away.

Then there was no other choice but to let his mind turn to Marianne, as he knew it would. Carefully, as if he were handling a fragile piece of pottery, he drew out the Roisin Dubh, wondering how he knew what he guessed was the Gaelic, marvelling at how the rose had survived so immaculately. The petals were like velvet, the black so rich it seemed to have numerous depths. He lifted it to his nose, but surprisingly it had no fragrance at all. Was it, as he hoped, a sign from her of their enduring love?

The thought filled him with such a swell of desperate emotion he had to close his eyes, and in that instant he almost prayed. But since Marianne's death, nothing any religion preached made sense any more; however much he hoped her essence lived on in some kind of afterlife, the mundanity of everyday life had almost convinced him that death was an end. Now he couldn't even wallow in that existentialist purgatory. Two years of weighing up every option, trying to find some common ground between hope and reality, had left him sick and mentally worn down. He was too tired to have faith. He just wanted to *know*.

His sense of alienation on the sacred ground drove him to his feet, but as he turned to go he glimpsed someone watching him from across the nave. The figure seemed unreal, oddly proportioned and hazy. It darted behind a pillar when it saw him look, but it left him with a sudden chill, as if its gaze had transmitted a hoarfrost. Suddenly he had to see who it was.

Cautiously, he made his way along the pews to the pillar. His footsteps sounded uncommonly loud, although an elderly couple passed by immersed in their guidebook, oblivious to him. The space behind the pillar was empty, but in the corner of his eye he saw a shimmer away to the right; someone was moving unfeasibly quickly along the south aisle. Church had an impression of a man, yet he was almost mist, as if he were radiating a grey light. In his trail there was a claustrophobic sense of threat.

Get out of here, he told himself. But running away seemed a weak thing to do, and after Marianne's death he didn't want to be pathetic again. He moved quickly in pursuit.

He slipped through an exit near the refectory and found himself in the cloisters, a square of wide corridors with low, vaulted ceilings surrounding a brightly sunlit lawned area which only served to make the other legs of the cloisters seem impenetrably shadowed. His first impression was that it was eerily still, as if he had stepped through time into after-hours.

There were no tourists, even near the entrance to the Magna Carta exhibition in the Chapter House, and the sound of the organ had mysteriously disappeared. His skin prickled as he watched for any sign of movement. Gradually he became aware of an atmosphere of disquiet lying across the area. A cloying scent of lavender hovered in the air.

Slowly Church left the protection of the door. He hadn't progressed far when the stillness was broken by a deep, guttural growling that raised the hairs on the back of his neck. He froze, then turned slowly in a circle. Still nothing. It was impossible to see through the sunlight of the square into the darkness beyond.

The growl rang off the stone once more, filled with menace, hinting at some enormous beast. He glanced down one corridor, then another, unable to tell from where it was coming. There was no sign of the shadowy figure either. Slowly he advanced along the north corridor, but with each step the sensation of unease grew more intense until he felt an unbearable urge to get out of that lonely place.

But as he rounded the corner into the east corridor, it was there, waiting for him, halfway along: a black dog, bigger than any he had ever seen before; it was only when it took a step forward on its heavy, sinewy limbs that he realised it was the size of a small pony. And then Church noticed its eyes, red as blood, with an inner light that burned with a cruel, demonic intelligence. A long strand of saliva drooled from its yellow fangs to splatter on the stone flags, where it sizzled like acid. It was so monstrous he knew it was no earthly creature.

The dog growled once more, rumbling menacingly deep in its throat. Then it lowered its head and took a slow step forward. Church knew if he turned it would be on him in a second. He noted the power in its jaws; he would have no protection if they were tearing at his throat. He took a tentative step backwards.

Deep in his head he felt a buzzing like a swarm of flies,

sickening in its intensity, and he knew that in some way it was the creature's alien, terrible thoughts interfering with his own; there was nothing there he could make sense of, just a primal feeling of threat and devouring. His stomach churned at the contact. *What is it doing?* he thought.

Slowly it moved forwards, each heavy paw echoing as it thudded on the stone. Powerful muscles rippled beneath the sleek black fur. Its eyes ranged across his face with a terrible, malign force, scarlet pools surrounding a circle of black like the drop into the abyss; the buzz of its thoughts crackled louder in his head. And in that moment he knew this was no chance encounter; it wanted him.

Church backed away a little further, but he realised the door was too far away to run. Slowly the muscles on the dog's back began to pull together as it lowered its enormous head. The deep, rattling growl dropped a notch into its throat. It was preparing to attack.

Church felt the cold wash of fear. He had an instant to decide what to do, but there were no options. Hopelessly, he decided he should turn and run. The dog's nails clicked loudly on the stone.

This is it, he thought.

But just as he was about to launch himself, the door into the cloisters crashed open and a guide leading a column of tourists marched in, his voice echoing out with the history of the site. Church was about to yell out for them to flee when he noticed a sudden, subtle change in the atmosphere. Out of the corner of his eye he saw the beast pause on the cusp of its attack, its eyes falling sullenly in the direction of the tourists. Briefly, it seemed to consider whether to continue its assault, but then it closed its jaws with a faint snick and padded away with a heavy step. Church remained frozen, unable to tear his eyes from it. When it was twenty feet from him, it turned its head and surveyed him balefully before losing itself in the shadows.

The column of tourists trooped past him, clicking their

109

cameras, muttering in foreign languages. Church rested back against the stone wall in relief, his heart pounding madly, the stink of the dog all around. 'Are you all right?' the guide asked in concern.

Church smiled weakly, but he couldn't bring himself to reply. He had the sudden feeling that events were closing in around them.

Ruth wandered through the city, staring into shop windows without really seeing, her head swimming with the bizarre experiences that had impacted on her life. She felt completely at odds with herself. Everything she had seen and heard filled her with a feeling of dread for what might lie ahead, yet at the same time she was overcome with a sense of freedom that was remarkably uplifting; the office was just a bad dream; from a distance the career seemed like shackles preventing her living her life. Now she was able to do what her heart told her. At the same time, these feelings ignited a tinge of guilt, as if she was betraying the memory of her father. He had always dreamed of her establishing a great career in law and he had been so happy when she was offered her job. It was all a mess of conflicting emotions and for the first time she felt she didn't know herself at all.

But she had been intrigued by Tom's manipulation of the blue fire; more than that, she decided, she wanted to be able to do it for herself. Now *there* was freedom. The thought of it raised her spirits enough that with the sun and the crowds she finally began to feel optimistic, for the first time since she had left her flat.

After a while she found herself crossing a gushing stretch of the Avon to The Maltings shopping centre, a modernist slab of brown brick at odds with the age of the rest of the city. As she mused whether there would be anything in it worth her attention, she suddenly caught sight of an old woman watching her intently. She had a sun-browned, wizened face with diamond-sparkle eyes and tight grey curls, and although she was slightly hunched with age, she was still tall and slim. Her smile reminded Ruth of the richness of autumn, while the crisp, golden-brown of her long dress was like fallen leaves. Ruth smiled in return, but the way the woman was focusing on her alone unnerved her and she hurried quickly by.

She picked up an alley that took her around the squat, grey mound of St Thomas's Church, but as she glanced over into the churchyard, she felt a sudden tingling deep in her belly. A woman was standing amongst the stones watching her. If Ruth didn't know better she would have sworn it was the woman she had just seen; the same proud line to her jaw, the same sparkling eyes, the same body shape. Only this woman was years younger; the face had no wrinkles and was rounder, with the apple cheeks of middle age. The dress was the same design too, but the colour was the deep, dark green of summer vegetation. And then she smiled and Ruth felt the tingling turn into a cold shiver; it was the same smile.

Suddenly it was as if her eyes had opened. She felt an odd, unearthly atmosphere around the woman, as if the air was shifting between opaque and translucent. And no one else passing by seemed to notice the woman standing there, staring at Ruth with such eerie intensity. Fearing the worst, Ruth hurried on aimlessly, following the crowds back to the city centre before somehow turning back on herself to arrive at the gently undulating greenery of Queen Elizabeth Gardens along the banks of the Avon.

She glanced around anxiously before flopping on to a bench, where she rested for a moment with her head in her hands, trying to understand what she had experienced. She hadn't felt any sense of threat from the woman; if anything, she was warm and comforting, almost motherly. But how could she know that was not a deception? Everything was wild and unfamiliar; there was nothing to get a handle on.

After a while Ruth began to relax and watch the children laughing and running in the play area while their mothers chatted secretively nearby. Ducks splashed in the river, then waddled over to sun themselves on the grass, while the air was filled with the intoxicating scents of spring wafting in from the woods and hills that lay just beyond the river's floodplain. Everything seemed so incongruously peaceful and normal, it was hard even to begin to grasp what was happening.

Then, inexplicably, her left hand began to shake uncontrollably. She gripped the wrist with her right hand to steady it, and when she looked up and around she gasped in shock. The woman now stood directly behind her, her hands resting on the back of the bench. Ruth leapt to her feet, her heart thundering; she hadn't heard even the slightest sound of the stranger's approach. And it was the same woman, except now she was in her teens, her face beautiful and pale like the moon, her long, lustrous hair glinting in the sun. The familiar dress was now the bright green of early spring shoots. Her eyes, though, still sparkled with great age and unnerving mystery, and there was a terrible aspect to her face that made Ruth shiver in fear, although there was no malice that she could see; she felt in the presence of something so inhuman, she couldn't begin to comprehend what it was that stood before her.

'He is missing. The night to my day, the winter to my summer. We must be joined and then you must join us, daughter.' The tone of her voice was eerie, part rustle of wind in the branches, part splash of water on rock.

Ruth backed away slowly, that awful, unblinking stare heavy upon her. 'Leave me alone,' she said hoarsely.

Slowly the girl who was not a girl raised her arms in a beckoning gesture. It was too much for Ruth. She turned and hurried away several yards. But when she glanced back, confused and troubled, the girl had gone and in her place was an odd effect, as if gold dust had been sprinkled in a sunbeam. After a few seconds something began to form in the glimmering; light shifted and blazed from nowhere, forming an intense halo around a dark figure which gradually became the Virgin Mary.

Someone called out, 'Look! It's a miracle!' and then people were running from all over the park to the bench where the vision was already beginning to fade. Ruth watched the joy and amazement infuse the crowd for a while longer before walking slowly back to the city centre, the burden of her thoughts heavy upon her.

The Haunch of Venison was almost empty at 7 p.m. when Church and Ruth arrived within minutes of each other. The pub had all the twisty-turny nooks and crannies one would expect of fourteenth century architecture and it took them a while to locate Tom at a table in a shadowy corner. He appeared tired and irritable, nodding emotionlessly when they sat down with their drinks.

Church looked from Ruth to Tom. 'I saw something this afternoon.'

'So did I.' Ruth shifted in her seat uncomfortably. She had spent the rest of the day walking, but she still hadn't been able to escape the memory of what she had seen in the woman's eyes.

Tom made sure no one was watching, then folded down the upright collar of his jacket to reveal four livid scars on the soft flesh of his neck.

Ruth stared in horror. 'My God, what happened?'

'The Baobhan Sith.' Tom winced as he gingerly raised his collar.

'What's that?' Church asked although he wasn't sure he wanted to hear the answer.

'In the old tales, they are the sentries of the night. Terrible things that take on the shape of beautiful women to lure passers-by. Get too close and they'll tear out your throat and drink your blood.'

'And now they're here too,' Church said, before adding, 'You seem to have a good knowledge of folklore.'

113

'I thought, if the worst came to the worst, we might be able to go back to Stonehenge for the night,' Tom continued. 'But I wanted to be sure the road would be open to us so I went out on foot for a couple of miles to check the route. I presumed they would have moved to bar our retreat in some way, but not . . .' He paused to touch his neck tenderly. 'One of the Baobhan Sith was lying in a ditch, waiting. She rose up when I passed.' His face seemed to drain in the halflight. 'There were more, I'm sure. We would never get past them.'

'They're bad, then?' Church asked facetiously. Tom's expression gave him all the answer he needed.

'How many more things are there going to be?' Ruth fidgeted with her glass, slopping vodka and tonic on to the table. 'This afternoon I was followed by a woman, only she wasn't, she was something more, pretending to be a woman. She kept changing age. There was no sense of threat, but . . . It was me she wanted. To do something for her. What's that all about?'

Church took a long draught of his Guinness while he thought. 'Is this how it's going to be from now on?'

'I think it probably is,' Tom replied dismally.

'I suppose only a few people have seen them so far,' Ruth mused. 'But what will the response be when it becomes so widespread that everyone realises what's going on?'

'Chaos. The kind of supernatural fear you used to get in mediaeval times,' Church said.

'What bothers me is the intelligence behind it,' Ruth said. 'What do these things want?'

'At the moment most of them seem to want you and me wiped off the face of the earth,' Church said. 'And that's another thing. A lot of effort is being expended on two people who aren't very much of a threat. Why should they be even bothering to hunt us down because we know something – and not much at that – when it's bound to become common knowledge sooner or later? Christ, I'm surprised it's not all over the media now after a big, scaly monster blitzed the M4!'

'It's not – I checked,' Ruth said. 'I can't understand why nothing's appeared – you'd have thought the *Sun* at least would have gone for dragons tearing up the motorway, wouldn't you?'

Church turned to Tom. 'Well? You're the man with all the answers.'

'I wish I *was* the man with all the answers.' Tom cupped his cider with both hands and stared into its depths.

The pub had started to fill up quickly, but they still felt alone in their gloomy corner. 'Should we be sitting here?' Ruth asked. 'If those bloodsuckers that took a bite out of you are on their way, shouldn't we be hitting the road again?'

'We haven't heard what Laura has to say yet!' Church protested. 'We can't just keep running until we hit the sea.'

'The Baobhan Sith are supposed to have little intelligence or guile. They're more like animals, I suppose . . . hunting dogs . . . point them in the right direction and they'll bring you down. But it's possible to hide from them.'

'And you're basing this knowledge on, what?' Church said sharply. 'Some old fairytale you read? There might be some truths in the folklore and legends and myths, but we can't take them as gospel. People add bits to spice them up. Take things out. Mis-tell them.'

'And what do *you* suggest we do?' Tom snapped.

'Okay, we should calm down.' Ruth raised her hands between them. 'Same team and all that. I vote we sleep together tonight and take it in turns to keep watch. You're right, we need to check out what that Laura woman has to say and we've only got to get through the night.'

They agreed, but before they could return to their drinks, Ruth turned to Church and asked, 'And what did you see?'

'A black dog, but like no—'

Tom froze with his glass halfway to his lips. 'My God,' he said in a thin voice.

As Church related what had happened that afternoon in the cathedral cloisters, Tom's face grew darker. 'Black Shuck,' he said when Church had finished. 'The Devil Dog. I hoped it would just be the Baobhan Sith—'

'What is it?' Ruth said.

'A demon, some claim. And the precursor of something far worse. It was here long before the first settlement was hacked out, trailing disaster in its wake. I remember once, in Scotland, lying awake one night listening to its awful howling above the raging of the worst storm of the year, and I knew some poor bastard was about to die horribly.' Tom took a deep swig of his cider. 'Before you encountered it, or just after, did you see something – like a shadow flitting across your vision, or a misty figure passing nearby?'

Church nodded. 'In the cathedral. It seemed to be watching.'

Tom took a breath and said, 'Black Shuck marks the way for the Grey Walker. The Erl-King, the leader of the Wild Hunt.'

Church stared into his Guinness, recalling a snippet from the reading he had done for a strand of his degree. 'The hunt that hounds lost souls to damnation.'

There was a commotion at the bar as a tall, thin man with swept-back silver hair and a hollow face was berated by a group of drinkers. He was smiling obsequiously, but one woman seemed on the verge of attacking him.

Ruth raised her glass. 'Here's to the end of the world.'

'Now there's a toast to which one can really drink.' The silver-haired man had slid up behind her, clutching the dregs of a half-pint. His broad smile revealed a gap between his middle teeth, which were stained with nicotine. His black suit had the grey sheen of overuse, but it was offset with a red brocade waistcoat. His boots were dusty and worn; the smell of the road came off him, of muddy verges and damp hedges, a hint of sweat and the bloom of being caught in too many downpours. Despite the colour of his hair, he couldn't

116

have been more than forty-five. Tom eyed him suspiciously; Church finished his drink.

'Knock it all down and start again, I say. Deconstruction before reconstruction.' He raised his glass heartily. 'Cheers!' Ruth smiled in return, and the man gave her a wink.

Church picked up his empty glass and offered the others a refill with a nod. As he turned towards the bar, the silver-haired man quickly drained his glass and held it out. 'As you're going, old boy, do me a favour and fill this up. I'll get the next one in.'

A sarcastic comment at the stranger's audacity sprang to Church's lips, but it seemed more trouble than it was worth. Grudgingly, he snatched the glass as he passed.

'Cider, please,' the man said, slipping into Church's seat. 'And thank you kindly.' He turned to Ruth and took her hand. 'Charmed to meet you, my dear. I have many names, though the one I like the most is Callow. I hope you don't mind me resting my old bones. It's been a long day's travelling. The romance of the open road is a fine thing, but no one talks about the exhaustion at the end of the day.'

'Where are you going?' Ruth asked politely.

Callow laughed. 'Oh, from here to there and back again. There's too much to see on this beautiful, beautiful island of ours to be resting in one place for too long. I've done all that, you see. Worn a strangling tie in an office prison, filed the papers, counted the paper clips, watched the clock mark the passing of my life. Slow death for a poor wage. But how much could they pay you to make it worth dying? One needs to hear oneself think. In the words of Longfellow, "Not in the clamour of the crowded street, Not in the shouts and plaudits of the throng, But in ourselves, are triumph and defeat." And if you can't find a reason for being in one place, or even for being, then you have to look elsewhere.'

'I know what you're saying.' Ruth was entertained by his attitude. It was an act he had obviously perfected over time, a mix of music hall comedian and slightly fey theatre ham.

If it managed to get him a few free drinks, who was she to judge?

'Ah, a kindred spirit. And have you broken the shackles of mundanity for the life of quicksilver heels?'

'We're just touring around,' Tom interjected coldly before Ruth could answer.

Callow reached across the table. 'Pleased to meet you.' He nodded towards the badges on Tom's holdall at the edge of the table. 'A veteran of the road too, I see. Ah, the Isle of Wight Festival. I remember it well. Hendrix played guitar like an angel. And Glastonbury, so many weeks there in the summer. The mud! You must remember the mud! Terrible. But fun. If you know what I mean. The Stonehenge Free Festivals too! Ah, how I miss them. The Battle of the Beanfield. I was there, I was there. Took a truncheon from a stormtrooper in blue. Saved some poor young girl from getting her head stove in.' He shook his head sadly. 'Ah me, the end of the world. And not a day too soon.'

Church placed the others' drinks before them, then pointedly held Callow's cider up high for him to vacate his seat. Callow stood up to take it, then sat down quickly and snatched a thirsty sip. 'And cheers to all of you!'

'That's my seat,' Church snapped.

'There's one over there, old boy.' Callow waved his hand dismissively to a stool next to Tom. 'Don't interrupt us now. We're reminiscing about the good old days.'

Ruth couldn't help a giggle at the irritation on Church's face. It deflated the moment, making it churlish for him to have stood his ground. With obvious annoyance, he took up his new position.

Callow didn't leave a gap in the conversation long enough for the others to throw him out, and soon his constant spiel mingling with the effects of the alcohol had almost lulled them into a hypnotic acceptance. As their guards dropped, they loosened up and the conversation became fourway.

There was no doubting that Callow was entertaining, with a knowledge of every subject, it seemed, and a colourful use of language that was bizarrely at odds with his lifestyle, although, if they had been sober, they would have admitted to themselves he was accepted more because he was a distraction from the worries that lay heavily upon them.

When Callow finally felt comfortable enough to go to the toilet, Church said, 'How did we get lumbered with that freak?'

'Oh, he's harmless,' Ruth said, 'and entertaining, which is a relief after listening to you and Tom go at each other with knives.'

'I'd be happier if he stood his round,' Church said. 'He's freeloading his way to getting well and truly pissed.'

Ruth punched him on the shoulder a little harder than she intended. 'Don't be so miserable. You can afford it – spread a little happiness.'

As the night progressed, the pub became more and more crowded, the air filling with smoke, shouts and laughter. Ruth surprised them all with a tale of her engagement to a political activist whom her father had admired and whom she had jilted on her wedding day after a panic attack that had almost resulted in a call for an ambulance. Church related the story of his brief, aborted career as a guitarist in a band which ended at his debut gig in a pub backroom when he vomited on stage through a mixture of nerves and too much drink. And Tom, loosened by several pints of cider, had several outlandish tales of his wanderings, most of them involving drug abuse: to Goa, and a frantic escape from the local police; to California, and a trip over the border to Mexico in search of the fabled hallucinogenic cactus; how he had raised the alarm about the brown acid at Woodstock; and his brief time as a 'spiritual advisor' to The Grateful Dead which seemed to involve little more than handing out vast quantities of drugs.

As drinking-up time rolled around, Church leaned across the table to Tom and said drunkenly, 'So when will we get the Wild Hunt knocking at our door?'

Tom waved him away with a dismissive snort, but Callow's eyes sparkled and his brow furrowed curiously. 'The Wild Hunt?'

'Don't you know?' Church slurred. 'Every fairytale you ever heard is true! Bloody goblins and bogles and beasties are real – they've just been hiding away! And now they've come back!'

Callow laughed, although he didn't get the joke, but when he looked around the table he saw there was obviously some truth in what Church was saying. 'What do you mean, old boy?'

'It's the end of the world, right. That's why we're all sitting here drinking. For tomorrow we may die.'

'Don't mind him,' Ruth said, who was nowhere near as inebriated as Church. 'He talks rubbish when he's drunk.'

'No, no, please tell me. I love a good tale,' Callow said. 'I once met a man in a pub in Greenock who swore the fairies were real. He claimed he'd seen them one Midsummer's Eve.'

Tom finished his drink. 'It's late. We better be on our way.' He added pointedly, 'We've got an early start in the morning.'

'Oh? A little sightseeing?'

'We're meeting a woman who's going to tell us about it,' Church said. Tom helped him to his feet a little too roughly.

'If you don't mind, I'll walk with you a while. It's a nice night,' Callow said. He sidled up next to Church. 'So tell me all about it, old boy.'

The evening was surprisingly mild. As they walked, Church poured out everything he knew, not caring if Callow believed him or not, while Ruth chipped in wry comments every now and then. Tom trailed behind, cautiously watching the shadows off the main road.

'Why, it seems to me that this could be a time of great opportunity for people like us,' Callow said in a tone which suggested he didn't entirely believe them, but was going along with the joke anyway. 'Forward thinkers and dazzling iconoclasts who have shaken off the shackles of a society which only wants to keep us locked away! *We* are free to adapt while the sheep mutate into lemmings and rush towards the cliff! Magic – now there is a great leveller. Power on tap for all! Raising the lowly up to the level of the great and good!' He paused thoughtfully. 'If one doesn't get eaten first, of course.'

Church and Ruth both laughed at this, the first time they had found humour in anything for too long, and, coupled with the act of unburdening, it provided a greater release than they could have imagined.

'Where are you staying?' Ruth asked Callow. Unselfconsciously, she slipped her arm through Church's and leaned against him.

'Here and there,' the stranger replied. 'A different night, a different billet. But enough of that. Look at the sky! Look at the stars! What a world we live in, eh? We are all in the gutter, but not enough of us look at the stars, to paraphrase Wilde. And where are you staying, my dear?' Ruth told him and he smiled broadly. 'A fine establishment. I could tell you appreciated quality and I am rarely wrong when it comes to character. Let's be off, then!'

'Be off where?' Church asked.

'Surely you're not going to abandon me now?' the stranger asked with a hurt expression. 'On such a fine night, and with it being so early and all. We still have stories to tell, experiences to share! The end of the world is nigh! We must make the most of what we have left. There must be a bar in your hotel that serves libations after hours to guests?'

'No—' Church began to protest.

'Go on,' Ruth laughed. 'Let him get another drink. We don't have to stay up.'

Callow took her hand and kissed it. 'You are a lifesaver, my dear, and I am eternally in your debt!'

In the bar, Ruth set Callow up with a pint of cider and a whisky. He wrung her hand, praised her to the roof and tried to entreat all three of them to stay with him drinking.

Finally retreating to a table in the corner, he called out jovially, 'Remember the words of T. S. Eliot, fellow travellers: "We shall not cease from exploration, And the end of all our exploring Will be to arrive where we started And know the place for the first time." Philosophy does not come easily at this time of the night and that, unfortunately, is the best I can do.'

They left him there, attacking his drinks with a gusto that suggested not a drop had passed his lips all night.

'I shouldn't have got drunk,' Church groaned. He was slumped in a chair in a corner. 'Bloody stupid!'

'We did it to forget. Don't criticise yourself for being human.' Ruth sprawled on the bed against the plumped-up pillows, her eyes closed, while Tom leaned against the wall near the window, occasionally peeking out behind the curtains. 'You know, I'm not a wilting flower. I don't *have* to have the bed just because I'm a woman,' she continued. They had chosen Church's room to spend the night; it was slightly bigger and it had a better view of the street.

'Indulge us.' Tom nodded towards Church. 'I wouldn't want him to have the bed if I have to sleep on the floor, and I'm sure he would feel the same about me. You're the compromise candidate.'

'In that case, you won't catch me arguing.' Ruth's laugh faded quickly. 'Do you think we're going to be safe?'

'We can hope.' Tom glanced outside again. 'No sign of anything yet.'

'Do you think they'll keep sending bigger and bigger things after us until they get us?'

'The Wild Hunt is coming,' he replied darkly. 'There *is* nothing after that.'

'Yeah, but we'll be safe tonight,' Church mumbled. He crawled on to the mat at the side of the bed, threw his coat over him and was asleep within seconds.

When he awoke in the deep still of the night, Church at first wondered if Marianne had come to him again. His head was thick with the alcohol, but he soon realised he had been disturbed by a strange grating noise, faint yet insistent. It seemed to be coming from the window. And it sounded like fingernails on glass.

'What's that?' he hissed to himself.

'Be still.' Church started at Tom's strained whisper; Church hadn't noticed Tom was awake, but he was sitting up, staring at the drawn curtains. 'The Baobhan Sith are here.'

'But we're on the first floor.'

Suddenly Church was filled with an overwhelming desire to see what was on the other side of the thick drapes, high above the ground; the fingernails scraped gently, chinking on the glass, calling to whoever was inside. He began to crawl towards the window. He could just peek through the gap, get some final proof that he'd left one world behind and entered another one which had no rules he could grasp. And what would he see? he wondered. What would he feel finally looking into the face of the unknown? He reached out to peel the curtains aside.

Tom's arm crashed on to his shoulder and thrust him to the floor, his nails biting almost to the bone. Tom's breath was hot in his ear. 'Don't,' he hissed, 'if you want to live a second longer.'

There was a pause in the scratching, as if whatever was outside had heard them. Tom and Church froze, their breath hard in their chests. Church half-expected the glass suddenly to burst inward, but then the scratching resumed and they both exhaled slowly and painfully. Tom gripped Church's upper arm relentlessly and dragged him back to the other side of the bed.

'They only know we're *somewhere* in the vicinity, but they can't pinpoint us, or they would have had us in our sleep,' Tom whispered. 'The scratching is to draw the occupant of the room. If you had pulled back the curtains, you wouldn't have seen anything, but they would have seen you.'

'Sorry,' Church said, 'I don't know what came over me.'

A noise in the corridor outside made them both catch their breath again. Tom's face was pale in the dark, his cold eyes fearful. 'I think they're coming in,' he said.

Before Church could speak, he had leapt across the room and was kneeling next to the bed where Ruth was still sleeping soundly. He roused her gently, then clasped a hand across her mouth before she could speak; her eyes grew wide and frightened, but Tom silenced her with a finger to his lips.

He summoned Church to his side, then said, 'Hide under the sheets with Ruth. I'll get into the wardrobe. When they come into the room, don't make a sound. Don't move a muscle.'

'But they'll see us under the covers,' Church protested.

'If they don't see you move or hear you they won't investigate further. They have little intellect. They simply respond,' Tom said. 'Trust me. Now, quickly.'

He held up the sheets so Church could wriggle down next to Ruth, then pulled them over their heads. It was hot and stifling, emphasising the swirl of alcohol in Church's head and the steadily increasing rumble of his heart; for the first time in his life, he had a sudden twist of claustrophobia. The wardrobe door clicked and then there was silence. In the dark he couldn't see Ruth's face, but he could feel the bloom of her breath. Her fingers found his hand and gave it a confident squeeze.

They didn't have to wait long. A dim clunk echoed hollowly; the tumblers of the lock turning although Church had sealed it on the inside. The faint creak of the hinges as the door swung open. A soft tread on the carpet, deceptively light as if it was a child, moving to the foot of the bed.

Church held his breath; Ruth's stopped too. Her fingers around his hand were rigid. Together they listened. It seemed the intruder was watching the heap of covers on the bed for any movement, listening for a barely audible rustle. Suddenly every nerve on Church's body came alive. A tic was developing in his calf, a spasm in his forearm; he didn't know how much longer he could hold it. Somehow Ruth seemed to sense his discomfort for her fingernails started to bite into the soft flesh at the base of his thumb, drawing his attention to the pain.

After what seemed like a lifetime, they heard movement again. The quiet tread progressed around the bed to the head and with his blood ringing in his ears, Church waited for the sheets to be snatched back. Instead, the tread continued to the wardrobe door, where it waited again, then to the window and finally back to the door. Even when they'd heard the click of the door closing, they remained in hiding for five more minutes, not daring to move.

Finally they heard the wardrobe door open tentatively and Tom stepped out. 'Gone,' he whispered.

Church threw back the covers and sucked in a breath of cool air. Ruth rolled over and gave him a hug in relief and he was surprised at how comforting it felt; he responded, and she nestled her head into the crook of his neck briefly before getting up.

'Will they be back?' she said.

'I doubt it. They'll continue to search the area until dawn, but we should be out of here before sunset tomorrow.' Tom stretched and cracked his knuckles.

Despite Tom's earlier warning, Church couldn't resist peeking behind the curtains. All along the street shadows flitted in and out of doorways or shimmered in the streetlights like ghosts. It wasn't as if they were insubstantial; Church had the feeling they simply didn't want to be seen. And high over the rooftops there were others, floating like leaves caught in the wind. It was an alien infestation that made him shudder and he returned to the others dreading what the forthcoming days would bring.

They slept fitfully, but awoke with a sense of purpose driven as much by what was at their backs as what lay ahead. They made the most of a heavy breakfast of bacon, sausages and eggs and tea, not knowing when the next meal would be, and then went to check out. Church carried out the formalities and got the credit card slip for Ruth to sign, while Ruth and Tom watched the street outside, but when he came back over to them there was anger in his face.

'What's wrong?' Ruth asked.

He waved the bill at them. 'That sneaky bastard from the pub stiffed us! It looks like he was drinking till sun-up, plus food from the kitchen, and he signed it all on to our bill! I knew he was a conman the moment I laid eyes on him!'

'He was quite sweet in his own way.' Ruth laughed. 'He stopped us wallowing in our misery so we owe him something for that.'

'Fifty quid! That's Harley Street rates!' He screwed up the bill angrily. 'If I see him again I'm going to take this out of his hide.'

At first there was a shock of colour glimpsed through the throng; white-blonde hair, short at the sides, spiky on top, expensively cut to look like a mess. Then there were the sunglasses, round, hi-tech and, again, expensive, on a morning when the sun was as pallid as a watercolour; the clothes, shabby, long overcoat, jeans and engineer boots, designed to look hard and uncompromising; the portable computer tucked under her arm; and finally the air of confidence that seemed, at least to Ruth, to border on arrogance. They knew it was Laura DuSantiago long before she spoke. She looked as out of place in the crowd of shoppers and business people as if she had beamed down from another planet.

'You brought the posse,' she said to Church after they'd exchanged introductions.

'They're both trustworthy. Within reason.'

'They better be. I don't want my insanity made public. I have enough trouble getting a loan as it is. So, you fancy something hot, wet and sweet?' The sunglasses prevented Church reading her eyes to tell how he should take the innuendo so he simply nodded. 'Yeah, I bet you do. Face it, tiger, you just hit the jackpot.'

She led them down a side street off the main drag to a café called Mr C's Brasserie that was quiet enough to talk and not too empty to be overheard. They took a seat in the window and once the espressos and cappuccinos had arrived, Laura plugged her computer into a mobile phone and logged on to the net. The forteana newsgroup was so jammed with postings it seemed to take forever to load.

'It's getting worse,' she said. 'All over the country, an epidemic of bozo-ness. Claims of alien abductions, hauntings, UFOs, sightings of the Loch Ness Monster, even fairies, for God's sake. Now don't get me wrong, not so long ago I wouldn't have acknowledged these geeks if they'd painted themselves red and were doing naked handstands in Cross Keys Shopping Centre. Anybody who believed in the supernatural was dead between the ears. But we're talking smoke and fire here, if you know what I mean.'

'You said something happened to you.' Church had to restrain himself not to ask her about Marianne.

'I'm getting to that. Slowly. Because I don't want to talk about it, but I do.' Her confidence seemed to waver for a moment. 'Listen to me. I sound like I've got Alzheimer's.'

'If it makes you feel better, we've seen things too—' Ruth began.

'Does one crazy make another seem better? Look, I'm doing this because somebody has to, because there's something important going down, but all I see is dull sheep going about their lives either blind to it or pretending things are just how they were. And I'm doing it for me. To make sense of my experience before it eats its way out of my head.' She sipped her espresso, watching Church over the top of her sunglasses with eyes that were cold and unreadable. 'So, you ready to get screwed in the head?'

He met her eyes without flinching. 'Tell us what you know.'

'It happened back here in Salisbury, the city that made me into the woman I am today. I was staying with friends for the weekend and we went out to a party on the Saturday night. Talk about dull. I thought I'd gone into the Incontinence Home for the Elderly. But I made sure I enjoyed myself, even if *they* didn't know how to, and the next morning I needed to chill out so I took a walk. Ended up on this industrial estate. Right in the middle there's a depot for something or other – cogs or shit, I don't know. Anyway, it's pretty rundown, grass pushing up through the tarmac, the odd broken window, you know what I mean. I was standing outside looking at it thinking it would be a good place to hold a party when I heard . . . I mean, I thought I heard . . . it could have been the wind . . . I heard my name. Now I don't want you thinking I'm the kind of person who always follows imaginary voices, but I thought I ought to check it out. I've seen enough slasher flicks to be on my guard in that kind of situation, but, you know, it bothered me. I had to see.'

She looked from one face to the other as if searching for validation, but not wanting them to think she needed it.

'You don't have to explain yourself,' Church said. 'We've been through the same thing – trying to deal with something your head tells you can't be true, but your heart tells you is.'

'Sorry? Do you think I'm interested? Quiet, bud, this is my story.' Her attitude was antagonistic, but there was something, a flicker of a facial muscle, perhaps, that told Church his words had given her some comfort. 'So, I went through the wire and had a look around. It was deserted, Sunday morning, but I still thought there might be some social inadequate with a uniform and a dog so I moved out of the open sharpish. Then I heard it again. Laura. Definitely, Laura. It seemed to be coming from this route between two buildings where lots of yellow oil drums had been stacked. By that time even I was thinking I was crazy – there could have been any psycho down there – but it was like I was being *pulled* in by something. I picked my way through the drums, and then ... Can I get another coffee?'

Church could tell she'd done it for effect. Even though her face remained impassive, she seemed pleased at the grumble she'd elicited from Tom; Church could see Ruth wasn't wholly warming to her either, but there was something in her obviously *faux* obnoxiousness that he quite liked. Tom ordered her another espresso which she took without thanks, and then she continued.

'I walked past the last heap of oil drums and it was like the air opened up in front of me.' She fumbled for the right words. 'Like the depot and everything around was some kind of stage scenery and somebody had peeled it back to show what really lay behind. I tried to back off, until I realised it was coming towards me quicker than I could move. And then it swallowed me up.'

Ruth looked at her incredulously. 'It was alive?'

'No, it was like some *Star Trek* effect – with no Scotty to pull me out at the last minute. There was this weird, spangly shit like I was having beads of oil sprayed on me, and then it was like I was tripping. I'm not going to start to describe the sensations – I don't want to sound like some burnt out acid case.' She nodded to Tom. 'No offence, space cadet. And then I saw things, heard things—'

'What kind of things?' Church interjected.

'Images. Sounds. It was a trip. And a half.'

'But what did you *see*?' Church stressed.

129

'Enough to know that this whole world's in deep trouble. And I was told—'

'Who told you?'

'—I was told that all this strange, supernatural shit that's been going on all over the country is tied into it. The basic message was: don't go getting any longterm mortgages.' Before Church could complain about her reticence, she added, 'Anything I say won't do it justice. But I can show you.'

CHAPTER SIX

A View into the Dark

Churchfields Industrial Estate lay on the western outskirts of the city. It was a maze of low, flat buildings in bleak, sixties design, each enclosed by chainlink fence or barbed wire. The entrance was through a dark, long tunnel under a railway bridge, which added to the sense of grim isolation. There was a constant smell of petrol fumes and engine oil, claustrophobic in the growing heat of the day, but despite the many builders' merchants and car lots, there was no sign of life.

Church parked the car round the corner and they sauntered up to the depot on foot. It comprised a large warehouse surrounded by smaller units, with a wide turning area for lorries at the front; the tarmac was cracked and tufts of yellowing grass poked through. As they neared, a fork-lift truck whizzed by carrying a pallet full of yellow oil drums, and through an open slide-door they could see movement deep within the building. Twelve-foot-high gates barred the way; they seemed to be opened electronically.

'We've got no chance of getting in there unseen,' Church said.

'Don't be defeatist, Church-dude. Where's your ninja training?' Laura waited patiently and when a lorry pulled up at the gate five minutes later, she slipped through in its wake and motioned for the others to follow. The rumble of the lorry's engines drowned their footsteps as they sprinted across the wide open space to the shelter of the depot. Laura led the way along the wall and then dived down the alley she had described. Once they were out of sight of the main entrance, they rested briefly behind a pile of oil drums while Laura checked her bearings.

'This is the place.' She turned back to the others. 'I hope you're set. There's no turning back now.'

'We're set.' Church steeled himself, but the apprehension he felt was increasing with each moment.

Laura picked her way among the oil drums with the others close behind, the air thick with the stink of chemicals. Finally they came to a clearing among the stacks.

'Here we are,' she said.

'What do we do? Say abracadabra?' Church could see nothing out of the ordinary.

'This is the place,' Laura repeated defiantly, but there was a note of anxiety in her voice, as if she were afraid it really had all been in her mind.

Tom and Ruth hung back, keeping watch as Laura and Church investigated, but the moment they stepped into the clearing there was a sudden drop in temperature and a rushing sound like water cascading over rapids. Tom and Ruth turned in time to see the air opening, not like a door as Laura had described it, but like someone slashing silk with a razor blade. They moved forward together, but they were too slow. The gap in the air folded around Church and Laura then sealed, leaving only a faint aroma of pine forests and lemon.

Ruth and Tom had just a second to wonder what had happened. There was movement at the end of the alley; an oil drum clanged, then rolled over noisily. Three depot workers appeared, moving menacingly towards them. At first Ruth thought they would be able to talk their way out of the corner until she saw the wild look in their eyes and smelled the choking stench of animals' cages. Their faces began to move like oil on water.

Tom put an arm across Ruth's chest, forcing her to back away, but another sound from the other end of the alley brought them to a halt. More were coming from the other direction. Tom cursed under his breath. 'She's led us into a trap.'

There was a brief sensation of floating in water and then Church was suddenly somewhere else. The odour of chemicals and diesel fumes was replaced by more natural smells, of clean, fresh air and damp stone. He was standing in a corridor with a flagged floor and rough-hewn stone walls. Torches burned at intervals, but they didn't cast enough light to dispel the gloom. It was too sudden a transition to comprehend and for a second he felt as if the ground was violently moving under his feet; desperately he flailed around until he found a wall on which to cling. With his eyes clamped shut and his chest feeling as if it were being crushed by an anvil, his mind screamed out for some kind of explanation. Feebly, he tried to tell himself he had fallen through a hole in the ground into some structure beneath; it was such a ridiculous assertion it didn't hold for a second. He hadn't fallen at all. Beyond the floating, he couldn't describe what *had* happened to him. With dread acceptance, he opened his eyes and looked around. It was true; somehow he had gone from there to here – wherever here was – in the blink of an eye. All at once his gorge rose and he turned to one side and vomited.

It took him several minutes to reach some kind of equilibrium, but he knew there was no point pathetically trying to deny the truth; and after all, over the past five weeks he had seen enough impossible things simply to start to accept without trying to understand.

His initial worry was what had happened to Laura. She had been at his side when the strange effect had begun to happen in front of them, but there was no sign of her along the stretch of corridor. Briefly he considered calling her name; but who knew what else might answer?

Certainly there was no point staying where he was. He was about to choose a direction at random when he heard someone singing, though faintly, as if it were filtered through numerous layers of stone. It hadn't just started, he was sure of it, but neither had he been aware of it before. It had a quality that made the hairs on his neck prickle. He weighed his options for a moment, decided he had none, and then started to move towards the music.

His footsteps echoed louder than he would have liked, and he remained permanently alert for any sound of someone approaching, but at the same time his mind was working overtime: where was he? There were few clues in his surroundings, but his deliberations took a new turn as he rounded a corner into another branch of the corridor.

On his right was a window, the first he had seen. He approached it in hope that it would allow him to get his bearings, but the moment he glanced out, an icy cold rushed through him. The view was of an infinite black void where occasional flashes of fire like distant explosions flared then subsided. There was no sign of surrounding land; whatever building he was in seemed to be floating in space.

Panic came first, like spiders in his mind; it was worse than he had feared. But somehow he managed to damp it down and continue on his way with a stoic acceptance; there would be time enough for explanations. He hoped. Tom had been right when he suggested Church's experiences had changed him; certainly if he had been presented with the same situation a few months ago he would not have remained so calm.

Although the singing didn't grow any louder, he found it increasingly entrancing, soothing even. Round another bend, he came to an oaken door, studded with black iron. It didn't seem particularly special, but after what he had seen he was filled with apprehension at what might lie behind; still, the safe option would get him nowhere. Throwing caution to the wind, he grasped the iron handle and threw the door open.

Church didn't know what he had expected, but it certainly wasn't the bedroom he had occupied as a seven-year-old. It was there in detail, down to the blue bedspread adorned with a picture of a cowboy on horseback, the annuals and comics, the lamp with the mosaic base on the bedside table: everything he could remember, and some things he couldn't. And there he was, asleep in his cowboy pyjamas, his pale face so innocent and untroubled it made him feel like crying; he could barely remember being that way. It seemed almost like he was watching the scene through glass. When he reached out, his hand came up against resistance and the air sparkled and shimmered around it.

The sparkling continued after he removed his hand until he realised that now it was coming from within the room. Something was gradually coalescing out of the glimmering at the foot of the bed. Eventually he saw it was a woman with long auburn hair and a beautiful, fine-boned face that reminded him of the idealised females in classical paintings. Her dress was long and of the darkest green, and it was embroidered with the finest filigree of gold in an astonishingly intricate pattern which, disturbingly, seemed to be moving as if it had a life of its own. Church had a sudden sense of majesty that took his breath away. Slowly she raised her arms and the sleeping Church woke as if she had called his name. He blinked once, twice, then a broad smile of wonder crept across his face. The woman smiled in return, then said three words softly.

In that instant, Church knew the scene that was happening *had* happened. The memory clawed its way from the back of his head where it had been dismissed as a dream and buried by reality; and it had happened not once, but several times over a short period.

The tableau slowly grew dark and then disappeared into inky blackness. Church closed the door and turned back to the corridor, trying to understand the tears that had sprung to his eyes. There was one other thing he did remember; the phrase she had uttered as a greeting:

This time Laura managed to control the nausea. As the stone corridor settled into focus, her biggest fear returned in force: that she would be compelled to look once again upon the things she had faced during her previous visit. Of all she had seen then, it was not the glimpses into her past that had been the worst, although that had been bad enough, but what she had to accept was a vista on to her future. It had been more than anyone should be expected to bear.

For a moment she wondered what had happened to Church, but in that place nothing was a surprise. The ethereal singing filtered through the walls; at least this time she knew what to expect. She set off purposefully, wishing there was some direct route, recalling how the maze had changed, even when she had tried carefully retracing her steps. She guessed it wasn't even as simple as stumbling across the right path; she felt instinctively that the maze *allowed* her through when she was ready.

The windows tempted her to peer out, but she resisted; it disturbed her too much. Instead she turned her thoughts to Church and the others. She hadn't made up her mind about them yet. Church was impossible to read at first glance; he was all dark water moving deeply, but she liked that in people. Superficiality was boring; the fun came in stripping away the layers, like unwrapping a surprise birthday present, until the real person was revealed, good or bad. Ruth seemed a little too nicey-nice, and, if she admitted it to herself, Ruth's easy confidence made her uncomfortable. The hippie disturbed her on some deeper level. When he looked at her she felt like squirming, as if he were mentally dissecting her with a cold contempt.

Deep in the building a rumbling began which sounded like the breathing of some mighty beast. Laura picked up her step, hoping against hope that Church and the others were the right ones and she wouldn't have to come here again.

* * *

'Follow me,' Tom urged, clambering on to a heap of oil drums. He held out a hand and hauled Ruth behind him and then he was scrambling to the top of the precarious pile like a monkey. Ruth was more cautious, but the sight of the approaching men-who-weren't-men spurred her on.

The top of the heap was level with a dusty window which Tom smashed with his elbow, turning away to shield his face from the flying glass. Beneath them, their pursuers were already tearing at the drums in an attempt to unbalance them, roaring in the guttural language Ruth had first heard in the service station car park. Out of the corner of her eye she caught the merest glimpse of their true faces before she had snapped her attention away, but it was enough to make her head swim to the verge of blacking out.

Tom grabbed her as he knocked out the remaining shards of glass from the frame before hauling her through on to a metal walkway. 'Sorry, I couldn't help looking,' she gasped as she slowly regained control.

'Their faces are too much to bear until you're used to it.' Ruth had an instant to wonder how Tom knew this before he grabbed her arm and pressed his palm against her forehead. At first it was cool, but then she felt a warmth spread out into her brain. 'There. It won't be pleasant, but at least you'll be able to deal with them now.'

Ruth glanced down and felt her gorge rise, but she didn't black out. It was still too much for her mind to register, as if she were looking at a TV where the signal was distorting and breaking up; misshapen bone and scales, things writhing both on the skin and underneath it. But the horror that assailed her didn't even come from the appearance; it was as if it were part of their existence, radiating out from deep within them. She turned quickly and pushed Tom away from the window.

'What's happened to Church?' she cried. Her heart jumped when she thought of him.

'I don't know where the door leads. We can come back for him later. First we have to save ourselves.'

The walkway overlooked the depot's loading bay. A lorry had its rear door down and had been half-filled with the oil drums. A fork-lift truck was abandoned nearby. There was no one around, but they could hear an insane cacophany of roars drawing closer.

'They've been put here to guard the door. They let us in, knowing we wouldn't get out again. They'll tear us apart if they catch us.' Tom stopped suddenly, then climbed on to the walkway's railing. 'Come on.'

His leap carried him on to the roof of the lorry, where he landed awkwardly. Ruth moaned when she saw him lie there for a second or two, but then he was up and limping along to the cab. She swayed on the railings for an instant, afraid to follow, but then she saw the creatures swarming in through the main door like insects, their forms thankfully blurred into grey shadows by her mind. Her landing was graceless, but she managed only to wind herself and then she was scrambling and sliding behind Tom, who was already lowering himself over the side through the cab's open window.

The creatures were moving astonishingly quickly for their size. One of them picked up an oil drum as easily as if it had been a paper cup and hurled it at the truck which Tom was already gunning into life. It smashed against the front just below the windscreen and bounced off to one side where it leaked foul-smelling chemicals.

The lorry was already moving forward jerkily so she lay flat on the cab roof, gripping the edge tightly, her eyes closed, praying she wouldn't fall off. It built up speed rapidly. There was a loud bump as it hit one of the creatures and then it was rolling out of the doors.

She heard Tom shout a warning and looked up to see a long, sinewy arm reaching out for her ankle from the side of the cab where one of the things was clinging on. She snatched her foot away at the last moment and the talons dug into the metal, tearing furrows through it like paper.

Before it could have another go, Ruth kicked out wildly.

Her boot slammed against the creature's head with a jarring impact that felt like she had kicked granite, but it did enough to loosen its grip. It fell away and a second later the lorry jumped as the wheels went over it. The sound behind them was awful to hear, a screeching chorus of animal noises filled with threat.

Suddenly Ruth could smell smoke. The chemicals in the drum must have been highly volatile because the heat from the engine had ignited the residue on the front of the lorry and flames were licking up the windscreen. It wouldn't be long before the whole thing was alight.

Tom headed for the chainlink fence, then slammed on the brakes at the last moment. Ruth desperately tried to hold on, but the momentum was too great; it propelled her over the top. She hit the pavement hard, the shock winding her, bringing tears to her eyes. When she looked up, Tom had slammed the lorry into reverse and was heading back into the depot at speed.

At the last moment, he threw open the door and leapt out. She saw his head hit the tarmac, but somehow he rolled over and came to his feet, and then he was limping as fast as he could towards her with blood streaming down his face.

The lorry careered into the depot, showering sparks as it passed too close to the door, and then it hit the piles of oil drums waiting to be loaded. For the briefest instant there was a sound like a huge inhalation of breath and then the whole place went up, a rapid series of firecracker bursts as each drum exploded, merging into a gigantic conflagration. The depot was ripped apart, debris erupting like missiles as a tempest of heat-blasted air roared out. Ruth's head rang with the furious noise. An enormous piece of roofing narrowly missed her, embedding itself in the tarmac. The rest of the building rained down in fiery chunks for what seemed like an age as Ruth rolled up into a foetal ball.

When it subsided, she jumped to her feet, unable to believe her luck. Where the depot had stood, an inferno blazed up so high she could feel the heat on her face from fifty feet away, blackening the midday sky. Nothing could have survived.

Relief mingled with worry about what had happened to Church, but then another realisation surfaced. Slowly she scanned around the blasted site: Tom was nowhere to be seen.

Church no longer had any idea which way he was going. The corridor twisted and turned, often folding back on itself as if it had been designed by some insane architect. Nor was he helped by the unending array of stone walls, flickering torches, occasional windows on to nothing and, every now and then, a door, although most of them had been locked. Of the two that had been open, he had received more startlingly clear visions, seemingly of his life. The first showed him sitting on a hill watching the burning of a city which looked disturbingly like London. Billowing clouds of black smoke turned the sky almost as dark as night, although somehow he was sure it was daytime. Yet it was the way he looked that affected him the most: though he didn't appear much older, his face was burdened with trouble and suffering that made him seem closer to forty. He was hunched over as he scanned the horizon, clutching an ornate sword to his chest like one of those characters who spent their weekends re-enacting ancient battles. His hair was longer and he had a tightly clipped goatee; there were tears in his eyes at what he saw.

The second door showed him pale and broken, alone in the flat the day after Marianne had died. Seeing the terrible torment frozen in a face that had never experienced such depths before brought back the intensity of the emotions and he slammed the door and ran down the corridor before any more of the tableau could present itself to him.

What could it all mean? He suspected that wherever he was lay outside of the existence he knew; time seemed to flow back and forth randomly and he wondered if it were possible to see any point in the past or the future. If he opened a door at the exact right moment, would he see Marianne in the weeks or days or hours that led up to her making her tragic decision to take her life? The thought brought with it a blast of such hope it made his head spin.

As if in answer, he rounded a corner and came upon another door. Nervously he stood before it for a full minute until he found the courage, and then he swung it open.

He was instantly deflated when the scene was unfamiliar: a green bank running down to a fast-flowing stream that passed under a stone bridge. Someone lay on his back in its shadow, the head and shoulders submerged in the foam, unmistakably dead. Church knew who it was before the white water cleared for a second to allow him to see the pale skin and staring eyes.

This was how he would die.

He threw the door shut and pressed his back against it, his head in his hands. He hadn't looked much older than he was now.

How he kept going he didn't know; his head was spinning and his emotions were so raw he wondered if he were having a breakdown. Nothing made sense. There was just a queasy disorientation and a sense of growing despair.

He wandered on in a daze until he realised something had changed: there was a faint trail of incense in the air, like the hint of a lover's perfume in an empty room. Then, as he progressed, the music grew noticeably louder – for the first time since he had been in that place. The melody was power-fully evocative, of warm summer nights beneath a full moon, of the smell of pine forests and the taste of a cool mountain stream; yet despite the images that flashed through his mind the words seemed to be in some alien language, so exquisitely formed they wove in and out of the music to create something greater than the sum.

It made Church's heart quicken until a sudden joy over-came all the negative thoughts that had been consuming him.

He broke into a jog and then a sprint, any reticence left behind in the rush.

When the corridor opened into a wide, lofty room he almost tumbled into it. Ahead of him, windows twice as tall as a man ranged in a semi-circle, offering a prospect out into the void. An ornate, gold telescope stood in front of them. On either side of the hemisphere, braziers burned, filling the air with the sweet, soothing incense. Intricately designed tapestries hung on the walls showing a vast range of scenes like a more exquisite Bayeux Tapestry, while thick rugs lay on the stone flags. And looking through the telescope with her back to him was the woman who had appeared in his childhood bedroom.

She turned as he entered and her beautiful face was even more potent than in the vision through the door. Her cheekbones were high, her lips full and her skin seemed to glow with an inner, golden light that mesmerised him; her cool, blue eyes, filled with wisdom and passion, were so deep he felt he could never reach the bottom of them.

'Who are you?' In his head his voice sounded weak and pathetic.

She smiled and he instantly felt like his veins had been flooded with honey. 'A friend.'

'Was that you singing?'

She nodded gently. 'It is a song from the old world, from the time before times, about two star-crossed lovers capturing one night for themselves before they are torn apart. It is sad but beautiful, like all things that move the soul. Come closer.'

She held out one delicate hand and Church descended the three steps into the room. 'You came to me when I was a boy.'

'Many times, always on the edge of dreams.'

'Why?'

'To convince myself you are who you are.'

'Which is what?'

'A Brother of Dragons.' She looked at him with a faint, curious smile, as if it was the most obvious thing in the world.

Church shrugged. 'I don't know what that means.' But at that moment it didn't seem important. What mattered was the tint of her skin, the faint emotion that flickered around the edges of her mouth, the musical timbre of her voice, the smell of her, like lemongrass and cardamon, so seductive he was mesmerised. Right then she could have said anything of importance to him and it wouldn't have registered. Finally he became aware that he was staring and he blushed, looking around uncomfortably. 'Where is this place?'

'It is called the Watchtower. A place between the worlds, neither human nor faery, neither sun nor moon, neither sand nor water. Time flows around it.'

'Is it your home?'

Her laugh was as musical as her voice. 'It is a refuge for now. And, if you like, it is an adequate stepping stone for someone from your land. I would not wish to present the majesty of my true home to you until you were fully adjusted.'

'I'm sorry. I shouldn't be here. I was curious—'

She took his hand and her fingers were as cool as a stream in summer. 'You *should* be here,' she said forcefully, leading him to two carved wooden chairs, between which was a table on which was a jug with a thin neck and twin pewter goblets. 'I have been waiting for you.'

Church looked at her curiously. 'I didn't know I was coming here until today.'

'*I* knew you were coming here.' She sat him down and poured him a drink from the tall jug. 'Do not worry. The laws of my home do not apply here. You are free to take of this place what you will.' It looked like water, but the taste was heavenly, so complex on the palate that Church experienced a new flavour every instant until he gave up and just let it slip down his throat; it felt like liquid gold, glowing bright as it infused him.

'That's amazing,' he said.

She nodded. Then her face slowly darkened. 'There are

143

many things of which we must talk, and time is growing rare. Your world is turning from the light.' Church felt a sudden *frisson*; Tom had used the same phrase. 'The old Covenant has been broken and now the Night Walkers have returned to the land of man to shape it to their own way. They must not be allowed to succeed. In the time before time they defeated my people and brought in the Season of Eternal Night, a rule so bitterly malign the Filid's lays can bring tears from the coldest heart. The land was blighted, the people lived in permanent shadow and no corner of the world was free from suffering and despair. Never again.'

'The Night Walkers.' He knew whom she meant without questioning her further.

'They have always existed in darkness, crawling along the edge of the light, envying it and fearing it.' She looked down so Church couldn't see her eyes. 'They were the worst of the old races. The Great Destroyers, leeching the heat of life, leaving only the cold of the void. Their corrupt power laid waste to all before them.'

There was an odd tone in her voice that filled him with a creeping dread. If the creatures were as powerful as she intimated, it didn't sound like all the military might of humanity stood a chance against them. 'Then who are your people?' he asked.

When she looked up her face was filled with such sadness he winced. 'Most Glorious of the old races, known as the Golden Ones, Shining People of the Light, raised above all others.'

Suddenly Church could feel some of the pieces falling into place. 'Your people and the Night Walkers were on our world sometime in the distant past? And you interracted with humanity in some way—'

'We ruled peacefully until the Night Walkers came,' she said proudly. 'They defeated my people through trickery, not power, but only for a while. And when we struck back they fell before us and were made to pay for their deception.' Her flashing eyes were frightening in their intensity. Church knew he would not want to have her as an enemy.

But here was something that made Church give pause: an age-old story stitched into the very fabric of human understanding. Two immensely powerful races, one of the light, the other of the dark, opposing each other in a war that shook the world while humanity trembled beneath them. He wondered how this woman and the terrible creatures they had seen under the bridge and at the services must have seemed to the ancient people who first encountered them. It was hardly surprising they had resonated down the millennia in legends and race memories, spawning the archetypes that were buried deep in the human subconscious. Suddenly he felt on the edge of something monumental, transcendental; the source of everything that mattered to mankind. He felt humbled by it all. 'But where did you come from? Some other galaxy? A different planet?'

Her expression suggested she didn't seem able to comprehend what he was saying. 'We came from the Far Lands.'

'The Far Lands?'

She nodded. 'And after the Covenant was forged, in the days of sorrow and joy that followed the second great battle, we returned to the Far Lands once more. The Night Walkers accepted their bleak purgatories beneath the lakes and seas. As victors, we occupied all that remained, the cloud-topped mountains, the thick, dark forests, the lush fields. We returned to our courts glittering with wonders.'

'And you left our world behind?'

'That was the Covenant.'

'And now it's been broken. But then your people could help us! You have the power to—'

'The Night Walkers unleashed the Wish-Hex.' There was fire in her voice. 'My brethren were swept away. A few of us escaped, to places like this, or to your world. Some were tainted by the Night Walkers.' Whatever this meant, it seemed to fill her with horror.

145

'And the rest?'

'In some empty place beyond the land, hidden from all our searching, prisoners—'

'Isn't there anything that can be done?' he asked passionately.

She smiled at his display of emotion. 'That is why you are here, Jack Churchill.'

'What can *I* do?' It seemed such a ridiculous question he had trouble restraining the self-contempt in his voice, but he instinctively knew she would not accept any disrespect.

'You are not yet in tune with your heritage. When you find your true heart, the strength to act will come with it. Yet it is true, even then the Brothers and Sisters of Dragons would not have the power to defeat the Night Walkers alone. Yet you do have the power to free my people—'

'How?'

'—given the right calling, given the correct conjunction of important things. And that is your task, Jack Churchill, should you accept my patronage. Indeed, it is your destiny, and if truth be told, you have little choice in the matter. Assemble the five Brothers and Sisters of Dragons who are one in spirit, the quincunx that make the hero foretold by the Faithi, who will save the Age of Man from the final threat. Locate the objects of power that will make the summoning.'

'This is all moving too fast. I don't understand—' Church's right hand began to shake uncontrollably and he had to replace the goblet on the table; he couldn't tell if it was the weight of her words that had triggered the violent tremor or his subconscious rebellion at the threat of what lay ahead if he did as she said.

'Tell me,' he said, staring off into space, 'those things I saw in the rooms—'

'They will come to pass.'

'Even if I refuse to take part in this?'

'They will come to pass.'

Church could still see his pale, dead face submerged in the water, his torment as he watched the burning city, and it seemed whatever life stretched ahead was bleak and despairing; but then, was that any different to the days since Marianne had died? Deep within him, something stirred; if he knew his burden, he would shoulder it as best he could, and if he could do some good for others then that would be enough. The woman was smiling as if she could sense his thoughts. 'I'll do what I can,' he said.

'The fire burns strong within you, Jack Churchill, though you cannot see it yourself.'

He sighed. 'I wish I could say that gave me some comfort.'

He was surprised when the woman took his hand and wrapped her own around it, even more surprised when he felt some strange succour from the act; his heartbeat subsided, the stress seeped from his muscles, his shoulders relaxed gradually. Her voice, when she began speaking, was quieter than before, as if she were afraid the walls would overhear the secrets she was about to reveal. Church looked into her eyes, entranced.

'When my people first came to your land, they brought with them four objects of the most remarkable strangeness and power. They were touchstones for my people, prized above all else, celebrating our origins and our power, the culmination of our great tradition. Though our beginnings are lost to time, for we are an ancient race, the Filid tell of our days in four marvellous cities of the northland: Falias, Gorias, Finias and Murias. There, buildings of glass and gold soared to the clouds; the days were filled with glory, the nights with wonder. There, we learned magic, craft and knowledge, became aware of the weft and weave of nature and, eventually, transcended our humble beginnings to become gods. When we ventured abroad, we took a talisman from each of the magical cities so we would never forget our transformation and grow arrogant in our power. And finally, for we are a nomadic people, our journeying brought us to your land.'

147

There was a sadness in her smile as she recounted her tale; the heart of her melancholy, Church guessed, lay in whatever had encouraged her people to leave paradise, for having seen heaven, how could they truly know peace again? 'And you want me to find these four talismans?'

She nodded slowly. 'They will be like a candle in the night, leading my people across the void.'

'What are they?' Church asked.

'There is a stone which can recognise the true king of your land. The sword of our great war leader, which inflicts only a fatal blow. The Spear of the Lord of the Sun, for ever exalted as the slayer of the Adversary, bringer of victory over the Night Walkers. And finally, and most importantly, the Cauldron of our Allfather, an object filled with such power to heal or destroy that few can survive in its presence.

'When we left your land for our new home, the talismans were hidden, for we knew the Night Walkers envied them and we could not risk them falling into their hands. And by then the talismens were too tied to the land to take with us,' she continued. 'The Night Walkers would never have been able to use them, for they would have been consumed by the light the talismans contained, but they were such a vital part of my people's tradition and pride that they *were* my people. And to see them in the hands of the enemy would have been more than we could bear.'

Something stirred deep in Church's memory at her description of the artefacts, but the details wouldn't come forth. 'A stone, a sword, a spear and a cauldron. They seem familiar.'

'They have played important roles in the history of your land. Found, then lost again, they have been used to shape momentous events by some of the most consequential mortals to walk your world. Indeed, they are now as much a part of your tradition and pride as mine. They have become infused with the very essence of your world. And that is why only the Brothers and Sisters of Dragons can find them.' She paused as a shadow flickered across her face; in that moment, Church had the sense that she was something more than just the woman he saw before him, something alien and terrifying. 'These are the forms you can understand. They are objects of pure power, their shapes defined by the stories. They have existed under other names, but at their heart, in your terms, this is what they are: a stone, a sword, a spear and a cauldron. But they have been missing for an age and though many have searched, none have found.'

'Then how will I find them? You said time is short, so surely you can't expect me to spend years wandering the country, digging holes.'

She led him to a large oak chest in one corner which he hadn't noticed before. The hinges creaked as if it hadn't been opened for centuries, and from within came a strong azure light which he recognised from Stonehenge. Carefully she removed an iron lantern on a short chain with a hook on the end. The light glowed from a blue flame which flickered through the tiny bottle-glass panes on the lamp's four sides. She held it out to Church, who took it gingerly.

'You must take this back with you. It will light the way.'

'How?'

'Follow the flame. It is the essence of your world and is drawn to the talismans. Trust your instinct.'

A feeling of wellbeing flowed up the arm that was holding the lantern aloft. 'Thank you,' Church said honestly. 'I'll do what I can.'

'Now—' she began.

'Wait,' Church said anxiously. 'There's so much more I need to know. Who are the five?'

'You will know them when they come together.'

At that moment, Laura emerged cautiously from the shadows of the doorway. She looked from Church to the woman.

'You did well,' the woman said to her. 'He is the one.'

149

Church eyed Laura suspiciously. 'Wait a minute, you were *supposed* to bring me here?'

'Don't get antsy, Church-dude. I couldn't take the chance you were going to get all yellow-bellied on me.' She seemed to be shying away from the woman as if she was afraid of her.

Church felt a bolt of awareness that made his palms sweat. 'When you mentioned Marianne—'

'She told me the one I had to bring here would know the name and it would be reason enough to make him come.' Laura glanced at the woman, unsure she had said the right thing.

The woman's expression was impassive. 'You would have been drawn here in time—'

'But you knew that would get me here quickly.' Church felt his hands shaking and he hid them behind his back; he was almost afraid to ask the question. 'This place looks out over all time, you said.' He swallowed; his mouth was too dry. 'Do you know—' There was a flicker across the woman's face that told him he didn't have to continue the question; he could see she knew something.

'Once you have done as I asked, all will be revealed to you.'

The lack of emotion in her face disturbed him; it was a mask to hide the truth, but he couldn't tell if it was because it would destroy him, or because she felt suspending the answer would drive him on to succeed. 'You must tell me now,' he pleaded. He hated the desperation in his voice – it seemed so weak ‐ but he couldn't control it.

She shook her head, said nothing. But for the first time he had real hope of finding out what really drove Marianne to take her own life; real hope of ending his own purgatory. If it was all he could take away with him, it would be enough.

The woman motioned for Church to move towards Laura. 'You must locate my people before the Beltane fires light the land or they will be lost to you for another year, and by then . . .' Her voice trailed away.

Church felt a surprising twinge of sadness that he was leaving the mysterious woman behind. 'You still haven't told me your name.'

She smiled. 'When we become friends, then we will know each other.' She touched his shoulder so briefly he barely felt it, but in that instant energy crackled between them. He thought he glimpsed something in her face then, but before he could be sure, she had turned away, by chance or on purpose. Then she made an odd, convoluted movement with her hand and the next second the woman, and the Watchtower, were gone.

The air was foul with the stink of burning, melted plastics and charred metal. Where the depot had stood was a broken outline, blackened and dripping water on the sodden, scorched ground; trails of smoke drifted up into the twilight sky from the twisted girder framework that was still too hot to touch. Three fire engines were parked in what had been the forecourt, their firemen, exhausted and sooty, standing around in small gaggles surveying the wreckage or spraying bursts of water on to pockets that were still burning.

'My God!' Church said, turning slowly to examine the carnage; the shock on their re-entry had taken any conscious thought away for a moment. Then: 'We couldn't have been gone for more than a couple of hours.'

'Time's different over there,' Laura said distractedly.

They both stood for five minutes trying to come to terms with the upheaval until Church noticed a group of men in suits standing among the wreckage examining something on the ground before them. He squinted, but the haze made the object difficult to discern. Then a gust of wind cleared the smoke away and he saw it was a skeleton charred by the fire. But it was clearly not human; the bones were enormous, twisted into such monstrous forms he couldn't imagine what it would have looked like when it was alive.

Laura saw where he was staring. 'What is that?' There was a note of sick disbelief in her voice.

'A Night Walker,' he said quietly.

Suddenly one of the men spotted them and said something hurriedly to his colleagues. They looked towards Church and Ruth, their faces cold and serious, and then they started to advance. They weren't police, Church was sure; something in their manner suggested a higher authority.

'We had better get out of here,' he said.

As one of the men called out harshly for them to stop, they turned and ran through the smouldering wreckage towards the gates which had been blown down. As they crossed the forecourt, they heard a cry and then saw Ruth waving from the other side of the fence.

'What in heaven happened to you?' she said; the strain was evident on her pale face.

There wasn't time to answer. The men were yelling furiously, but the three of them had enough of a head start. By the time their pursuers had reached the gates, Church was already behind the wheel of the car, the engine roaring.

'Who the hell were they?' Laura said as they pulled away at speed.

Ruth ignored her and turned towards Church. 'We should dump her now,' she said. 'She led us into a trap. And now Tom's missing.'

In the rearview mirror, Church watched the smoke obscure the angry red glare of the sunset. Laura spent several minutes denying trying to cause them harm, but her ironic manner made it difficult for them to accept anything she said at face value.

'Look, I tumbled through that hole to God knows where by accident,' she said to Church. 'I spent hours wandering around those corridors getting my head well and truly screwed, and then I met Lady Freakzone who insisted I'd be contacted by some Brother of Dragons and I had to bring him straight to her. She didn't have to say *or else* – I'm not stupid, and I'm not about to mess with someone who lives on a big floating castle in space. I had no idea if you were the right one. I hoped, because I didn't want to keep jumping on the Nightmare Shuttle. But I didn't *know*. And I certainly didn't have any idea about whoever those geeks were who jumped the old guy and Miss Smarty Pants here.'

Ruth glanced at her coldly, then said, 'The point's moot now. We need to find what's happened to Tom and move on.'

'You're not leaving me behind,' Laura said. 'I'm in on this now.'

Ruth turned to Church. 'We can't take someone with us we can't trust. And she's just excess baggage—'

'Who made you—'

Church silenced Laura with his hand. 'The woman on the Watchtower told me there had to be five of us – the right five, the chosen ones, I suppose – involved in this mess and I don't reckon she would have involved Laura if she wasn't one of us.'

Ruth chewed on her lip. Reluctantly she said, 'You had better tell me what else you were told.'

For the next fifteen minutes, Church related everything that had happened to him on the Watchtower, detailing the four items they needed to find and showing them both the lantern with the blue flame.

'This is getting crazier by the minute,' Ruth said. 'Soon we aren't going to have any frames of reference at all. But in our current insane world I suppose it makes a certain kind of sense. So we have a deadline? What's this Beltane?'

'A Celtic festival,' Church said. 'It falls on May 1 and celebrates the onset of summer.'

'Barely two months! How the hell are we supposed to find things that have been missing for eons in that short time? And why is it down to us?' Ruth seemed irritable and exhausted after the shock of her experiences. 'And what's happened to Tom?'

Church recalled the blasted site; if Tom had been caught in the explosion there wouldn't have been much hope for him.

'The last thing I saw he was running away from the depot, then the explosion hit,' Ruth continued. 'I searched everywhere. Questioned the firemen . . .' Her voice trailed away dismally.

Only a sliver of red sun was visible on the horizon, painting Salisbury scarlet and ruddy browns. With the flakes of soot whisked up by the wind and the choking smell of burning, it felt like a scene from hell.

'We can't wait here for him,' Church said eventually. 'You heard what he said about the Baobhan Sith. They'll be hunting tonight.'

'But we can't just abandon him,' Ruth protested.

'He's smart enough to lie low if he's okay.' Church felt a tinge of guilt at not discovering what had happened to Tom, but they had no other choice but to press on. 'We need to get out of town by dark, see where this takes us. The roads might not be safe at night, but we don't have much choice, do we?' He turned to Laura. 'What about an overnight bag—'

'I travel light. I'll pick up some things along the way – that's the wonder of credit cards. And the way things are going, I'll never have to pay them back.'

The lantern flame was already leaning heavily in one direction, as if it was caught in an air current. With a certain apprehension, Church eased the car through the winding streets until they were heading the same way: north.

Yet his emotions were in such turmoil it was almost impossible to concentrate on the driving. Now he knew what the old woman on the banks of the Thames had meant: it was a premonition of his death. He would have thought the knowledge would have destroyed him, but he couldn't quite work out what he felt: disbelief, despite what the woman had said, hope that it would all work out differently, even some relief that the tiring struggle of the last two years was coming to an end. But it was too soon to consider that. In the brief time he had spoken to the woman she had given him so much information his head was spinning. What did it all mean, and why was he involved? And was he finally going to find out the answer to the only question that mattered to him: why Marianne had taken her life? He switched on the radio in the hope that it would drown out his chattering thoughts.

As the music filled the car, he knew it would prevent Laura hearing any conversation, so he said quietly to Ruth, 'Do you ever think about dying?'

She looked at him suspiciously, as if she could see right through his question. 'Not if I can help it.'

'But you never know how much time you've got, do you?'

'Did something happen to you in that place that you're not telling me?'

He kept his eyes firmly on the road ahead. 'I think if I knew I was going to die, I'd like to do something good, something unselfish for once.'

Ruth could see the heaviness of his thoughts echoed on his face and it upset her that he didn't feel he could open up to her.

Suddenly it didn't seem right to talk any more. The sun slid beneath the horizon and they fell into an uneasy silence as the car headed out into the night.

hERE BE dRAGONS

Church wanted to keep to the well-lit roads while following the lantern's general direction, but that would have meant heading back towards Stonehenge, where Tom had said the Baobhan Sith had posted sentries. Instead he had to follow a looping route which took them on to an unlit road across Salisbury Plain. As they left the sodium haze behind and the night closed around them, they all thought they could see strange things moving off across the plain; odd lights flickered intermittently, will o' the wisps trying to draw their attention, and at one point a large shadow loomed at the side of the road. Church floored the accelerator to get past it and didn't look in the rearview mirror until they were far away.

It was a disturbing journey; they all felt the countryside had somehow become a no-man's land filled with peril. At first, hedges were high and trees clustered against the road oppressively, but as they moved on to the plain it opened out and they were depressed to see there were no welcoming lights anywhere. They passed a sign for Ministry of Defence land where a red flag warned of military manoeuvres; Church wondered briefly if they were already having to cope with things that shouldn't exist; whether they *could* cope.

They felt relief when they reached the outskirts of Devizes. The lantern pointed them towards the north-east as they passed through the town and they found themselves on another quieter road, although there was not the same sense of foreboding they felt on Salisbury Plain. The landscape on either side was ancient, dotted with hill figures and prehistoric mounds. By 10 p.m. they had wound through numerous tiny villages and eventually found themselves in Avebury, where the lantern flame relaxed into an upright position. The village was protectively encircled by the famous stone circle, its lights seeming a pitiful defence against the encroaching night. Church pulled into the car park in the centre where they could see a handful of the rocks silhouetted against the night sky; he felt oddly unnerved by the synchronicity of long lost times shouting down the years.

'More standing stones,' Ruth said, peering through the windscreen at the squat, irregular shapes. 'What are we supposed to do now?'

'It's too late to do anything now.' Church stretched out the kinks in his back.

Laura leaned forward between the two of them. 'Looks like we've just driven into the dead zone. Any danger this place has a pub?'

'We're not here for the night life,' Ruth said sourly.

'No reason why we can't enjoy ourselves while we're waiting for the world to end.' Laura picked up her computer and mobile phone and climbed out.

Although it was only just March, the night was not unduly cold. An occasional breeze blew from the Downs, filled with numerous subtle fragrances, and the lack of any traffic noise added to the time-lost feeling which was, oddly, both comforting and disconcerting. The Red Lion pub lay only a short walk along the road, an enormous, many-roomed inn whose black timbers creaked beneath the weight of a thatched roof.

'I can't help feeling we should be digging out a foxhole instead of sitting down for a quiet drink like nothing was wrong,' Ruth said as they settled at a table.

'When everything is going insane, it's reassuring to do normal things,' Church replied. 'Pubs have a lot of power in situations like this. It's all about humanity coming together, celebrating in the face of—'

'Do you two always talk bollocks like this?' Laura took a swig of her beer from the bottle, then leaned back in her chair. 'Because, you know, I'm starting to see an upside to Armageddon.'

Ruth bristled. 'You're still on probation. It would be a shame if you made us dump you here in the dead zone.'

Laura smiled mockingly which irritated Ruth even more, then directed her comments at Church. 'Mystic Meg wouldn't have told you all that information if she didn't think you could do something with it.'

Church nodded. 'You're right. *She* thought we were capable of it.' He took a long draught of his beer, then looked at Laura curiously. 'You've got a good job, a life. Why did you decide to come with us?'

Laura shrugged, then glanced around the bar with studied distraction. 'I can't go back to my life and wait for the world to go to hell in a handcart.'

'No, you want to give it a helping hand down the slope,' Ruth said acidly.

'And let's face it, I'm a different person now,' Laura continued. 'I've done a few drugs in my time. It's not big or clever, but, hey, I enjoyed myself. And if you've done drugs you know they change you. Suddenly you find yourself apart from all your old friends who haven't done them. They couldn't ever understand what you've been through without experiencing it themselves. After crossing over to that castle, that's how I feel now. It was such a big thing, such a life-changing experience, bigger than the wildest trip, there isn't a single person on earth who understands me now. Except you. We've got an affinity, Church-dude. We're beyond everyone else. Could you go back to your life after that?'

Church felt Ruth stiffen beside him. He couldn't tell if Laura was specifically trying to annoy her by making her feel excluded, but he guessed she was. 'We've all experienced weird things,' he said. 'I suppose that puts us on common ground.'

'But we don't have to like each other,' Ruth said coldly.

Laura looked away; nothing seemed to concern her.

'So what's all this nonsense about Brothers and Sisters of Dragons?' Ruth said directly to Church. 'It sounds like some ridiculous secret society.'

'She was implying we were important somehow. Different. Special.' He wrinkled his nose; it didn't make sense to him either.

Ruth snorted ironically. 'The way you told it suggested it was some kind of destiny thing. But we wouldn't be here now if we hadn't been under Albert Bridge at that particular moment in time, and that was chance. A big coincidence. If I hadn't had that row with Clive and got out of the taxi, if you'd stayed in bed for five minutes longer, none of this would have happened to us. So how can it be destiny?'

Church shrugged. 'Well, she wasn't *lying* to me – at least it didn't seem that she was. Maybe she was mistaken.'

'She wasn't lying,' Laura said emphatically.

'How do you know?'

'I just feel it.'

'But maybe that explains why those things have been going for the nuclear option in trying to stop us,' Church mused. 'It would have helped if the mystery woman had told us exactly what our little dragon group is supposed to do. Something about our *heritage*, she said—'

'If Tom were here I bet he'd have something to say about it,' Ruth mused.

'Yeah, he'd be sitting back dispensing enigmatic wisdom like Yoda,' Church said. 'He was obviously keeping stuff from us – we couldn't trust him. Maybe we're better off without him.'

'Do you reckon he's scattered in bits and pieces across Salisbury?' Laura stared out some elderly local who was watching her curiously.

'Who knows where he is. Maybe he fell through another of those holes in the air. Maybe he's hiding out and doing this just to wind us up.'

'Oh, he helped us out, Church. He was just selective in

159

what he said.' Ruth pondered for a moment, before adding, 'He seemed a little scared when you told him about that black dog.'

'You should have seen it.'

Ruth glanced out of the window, but the lights were too bright within to see anything clearly. 'I wonder how much longer we've got?'

'What do you mean?'

'Before the next thing comes after us. The Wild Hunt, Tom said. The worst thing we could expect.'

Outside the pub, while they waited for Church to return from the toilet, Ruth could no longer contain herself. Laura was chewing on some gum and kicking stones at the parked cars.

'You ought to know I don't trust you,' Ruth said, 'and I'm going to be keeping an eye on you.'

'Ask me if I'm bothered.' Laura continued to boot the stones; one rattled on the side of a brand new BMW.

'You should be.'

'What do you want me to do, cry myself to sleep because you don't like me? Wake up, it's never going to happen.'

Ruth wanted to slap her, but she controlled herself. 'What's wrong with you? This is a nightmare. We could die at any moment. You could at least make the effort to get on.'

'I am who I am, Miss Boring Pants. Like it or lump it.'

'Really? You expect me to believe DuSantiago is your real name? Lots of South Americans in Salisbury, I suppose. And you really haven't tried hard to build up that cool, hard exterior? Yeah, right.'

'Nice sermon. Pity you're talking out of your arse. You don't know anything about me.'

'That's the problem. If you opened up, we could start trusting you . . . if you really want to help.'

'Don't go getting all touchy-feely, New Agey on me. I'm not one for hugs and baring my soul.' A stone bounced off the bonnet of a Volvo and set the car alarm blaring. Laura turned back to Ruth, her face lit by the flashing indicator lights. 'I'm as committed to this as you are. That's all you need to know.'

'No, it's—' Ruth caught her tongue as Church emerged from the pub.

'So . . . a night in the car. Should be very restful,' he said ironically.

'Lucky me. I get the bijou back seat.' When Laura dropped into step next to Church, Ruth felt an odd twinge of loneliness, as if she were slowly being cut out.

'You think we'll be safe there?' she said.

'As safe as anywhere. At least we'll be able to drive off if anything happens.' He laughed quietly to himself.

Ruth trailed behind them, overcome by the sudden knowledge that her friendship with Church had become deeper than she realised. How had that happened? she wondered. Their situation was complicated enough without bringing emotions into the fray, but somehow the whole stupid mess had blindsided her. She looked at Laura and hated herself for feeling a twinge of jealousy that the cosy relationship she had with Church was being interrupted. She just hoped she was level-headed enough to prevent her feelings getting in the way during the difficult times ahead.

Church woke at first light. His joints ached, his feet felt like ice and there was a band of pain across his thigh where his leg had been jammed under the steering wheel. Sleep had been intermittent, troubled by the discomfort of his quarters, nightmares and fears of things off in the dark. He resolved to buy a tent for any future emergencies. But the moment he wiped the condensation from the window with the back of his hand, any grumbles were swept away by the beauty of the early spring day. The sun was just breaking above the horizon, painting the few clouds golden beneath a sky that was slowly turning blue. Among the stones a faint mist rose and drifted, and a stillness lay across the whole area. From his viewpoint, there was no sign of the twentieth century; it could have been anytime. The thought sent prickles down his spine, adding to the haunting quality of the moment that left him feeling like he had been cut adrift from the life he once knew.

Ruth and Laura were still sleeping. He was instantly struck by how beautiful they both looked, in their own ways, once the troubles of the day were stripped from their faces.

But as he wondered if he should wake them, he caught sight of something out of the corner of his eye that jolted him alert. A man was perched on a fencepost next to a hawthorn hedge, eyeing the car intently. Church had to look twice to convince himself it was what he had seen; the watcher was old, thin and angular with skin so sun-browned he seemed almost like a spindly tree growing out of the hedge. He was holding a long, gnarled wooden staff that must have been at least six feet tall, and his grey-black hair hung lank and loose around his shoulders. Apart from his clothes — mud-spattered sandals, well-worn, baggy brown trousers and a white cheesecloth shirt open to the waist — he resembled nothing so much as the pictures Church had seen of the men who helped raise the stones and build the longbarrows that were scattered across the landscape.

'Who is that?' Ruth's voice was sleepy. She rubbed her bleary eyes as she leaned close to Church to peer at the onlooker.

Laura stirred and after a few seconds she too was up, resting her elbows on the backs of their seats. She already had on her sunglasses. 'Probably just a peeping tom,' she said throatily. 'Thought we'd been having a little three-way here in the car. Let's put on a show — see if he goes blind.'

'Just some local,' Church muttered. He opened the door and climbed out. The air was chilly despite the sun, and he couldn't prevent a convulsive shiver. The only sound was that of the birds in chorus. Ruth and Laura joined him, pulling their coats tight about them, stamping their feet to start their circulation.

The old man's eyes never left them as they walked the short distance to the fencepost. Up close, the most startling quality was the colour of his eyes, which were as blue as a summer sky, and given more power by the brownness of his skin. Church couldn't tell his exact age, although he guessed from the wrinkles on the man's face that he was in his sixties.

'Morning,' Church said.

'Morning,' the man replied impassively.

'Early start,' Church noted.

'Aye. Same as you.'

Church wished he had some idea of exactly what they were trying to unearth. Although the lantern had brought them to Avebury, it didn't seem to be much help in establishing an exact location. 'Seen anything strange going on round here recently?'

'Depends what you mean,' the old man said slyly. 'I see lots of strange things in my travels. I've covered the country from Orkney to Scilly a hundred times in my life and every place I've stopped there's been something strange.'

'You're not a local?' Church gave the man a renewed examination; there were none of the slightly odd features or waxy skin that disguised what the woman in the Watchtower had called the Night Walkers, but Church felt suspicious nonetheless.

'I'm local wherever I go.'

Church was starting to feel distinctly uncomfortable in the old man's presence. There was a faintly threatening air about him and his gaze was becoming more dissecting, as if he knew exactly who Church was.

The old man glanced away across the stones and when he looked back, his eyes were cold and hard. 'You cause any trouble here and there'll be hell to pay.'

'Who are you?' Ruth asked.

'I guard the old places. Keep an eye on the hidden treasures,

163

the undisturbed burials, the sacred spots. From the Scottish Isles to the South Downs, Land's End to the Fens.' He grabbed his staff tightly with hands that looked much stronger than his years suggested. 'Sleeping under the stars, watching out for the grave robbers and the sackers and the vandals. Tending to the land, you might say. Some call me the Stone Shepherd—'

'The Bone Inspector.' Ruth recalled Tom's account of the man who had first alerted him to the crisis. 'Tom mentioned your name.'

'And where is he?' he said gruffly.

Church and Ruth glanced at each other uncomfortably.

'He's fallen already, has he? And you are the ones he was looking for?' His expression suggested he wasn't impressed.

'Who are you exactly, and what do you know about what's going on?' Church insisted.

'And who are you to ask questions of me?' As Church began to answer, the old man waved him silent dismissively. 'There's been a Bone Inspector since these stones were put up. When one dies, there's always another ready and waiting to take over. In the old days there were lots of us. The keepers of wisdom, we were, worshipping in the groves, tutoring the people. Now there's just me.'

In his eyes, Church saw the flat, grey sky over Callanish and the green fields around the Rollrights. In his voice there were echoes of the solemn chant of ancient rituals. But there was the hardness of nature in him too, and Church knew he would be a fool to cross him. The old man held the staff more like a weapon than a walking aid, and his lean limbs were sinewy and powerful.

'How did you find out that everything had changed?' Church asked.

'I felt it in the land. In the force that sings to you if you're of a mind to listen.'

'The blue fire?'

'Aye, that's one way of seeing it.' He banged his staff gently on the turf. 'It's all changing, going back to the way it was.

164

The cities haven't felt it yet, but out in the country they're starting to know. People are keeping clear of the quiet places, specially after dark. There've been a load of disappearances and a few deaths, all put down to accidents so far. They'll know the truth soon enough. I was up at Arbor Low in the Peaks the other day and I saw a wolf that walks like a man. Just a glimpse, mind you, away in the wild. But when I went to look I found an arm. Or what was left of it.'

'Gross!' Laura made a face.

'That's when I knew for sure, even though I'd felt the change long before. Soon they're going to have to redraw all the maps. No one will know this land, see. It will be all new, and terrible. Even some of the lost places are coming back. I saw . . .' He caught himself and looked into the middle distance. 'Well, there'll be time enough for that later.'

There was an uneasy note in his voice that made them all feel uncomfortable. They shifted from foot to foot, not really knowing what to say.

Eventually he broke his reverie and turned back to them, his face dark. 'And now you three rabbits are here. You look like troublemakers to me. Maybe I should be seeing you off.' He raised his staff menacingly. Church held up his arm in instinctive protection and instantly the staff was performing a deft, twisting manoeuvre that was so fast it was almost a blur. It flicked Church's arm to one side, then cracked him obliquely on the elbow, too gently to hurt. But in an instant fiery lances of pain ran up to his shoulder and he crumpled at the waist in agony. Ruth stepped in to help, but the Bone Inspector thrust the staff between her calves and twisted, knocking her to the floor. In one fluid movement, the staff came up to point directly at Laura's throat. 'Now you better be telling me what you're doing here,' he said in a voice like flint.

Church drew himself upright, rubbing his elbow furiously, and then took a sudden step back when the staff was levelled at him. 'Take it easy,' he said as calmly as he could muster. 'We're not here to cause any trouble for you.'

165

'We're looking for something,' Ruth added hastily. 'One of the four talismans.'

The Bone Inspector knew exactly what she meant. 'You'll never find them.'

'We have to,' Church said. 'Or else— Well, you tell me the *or else* bit.'

The Bone Inspector lowered the staff and looked at them slyly again. 'Who are you to think you can do something about it?'

A thought jumped in Church's mind. 'We're the Brothers and Sisters of Dragons,' he said.

It was the confirmation for which he was obviously waiting. 'So Thomas did find you,' he said thoughtfully. 'You don't look like much. How do I know you're who you say you are?'

'Wait here.' Church returned to the car and came back with the lantern. 'Would I have this if I wasn't?'

The Bone Inspector laid down his staff and approached, almost deferentially. Gently, he reached out his hands until they were on either side of the lantern, though being careful not to touch it. The flame flared brightly, painting his skin blue. 'The Wayfinder,' he said in awe. 'I'd heard it was no longer of the land.'

'It wasn't,' Church said. 'I brought it back.'

The Bone Inspector cursed under his breath. 'And you don't know what you've got, do you? Leaving it in the bloody car! Are you mad, man?' Church shifted uncomfortably. 'Keep it with you at all times,' the Bone Inspector said with irritation. 'Don't ever let it fall into the wrong hands.'

Now it was out in the open, close to the circle they could see the flame was gradually rotating. 'That must mean we're in the right place,' Ruth said. 'But where do we start looking? And what exactly are we looking *for*?' she added with exasperation.

'And why here?' Church said.

The Bone Inspector shook his head, contemptuous of their

166

lack of knowledge. 'Stonehenge may be better known, but this is *the* place. It doesn't look much now, thanks to those Bible-obsessed fools in the last century who pulled all the stones down because they thought they were the Devil's work. But it's the most important place in the land, the source of all the power. That's why I'm here, now, to be in the most important place at the time when I'm most likely to be needed.' He knelt down and marked out a wide arc with his arm. 'Imagine it getting on for five thousand years ago – a sacred site stretching three miles. Here was the main temple, two stone circles surrounded by a circular ditch twenty-five feet deep with a bank fifteen feet high. And approaching it from either side were two gently curving avenues, a mile and a half long, each of them, marked out by ten-foot-high stones. Can you imagine the work that went into that? And they wouldn't have done it if they didn't have a reason.'

'This is the source of the blue energy?' Church asked. 'The Earth Magic?'

'This is the place where it's strongest. It's a Dracontium, a Serpent Temple, so called because of the way the avenues snaked. There were no straight lines back then – we have the bloody Romans to thank for that. But that's not the only reason – the dragon is the symbol of the Earth's power.'

'And the Fabulous Beasts are drawn to it too,' Ruth said thoughtfully as she tried to imagine the scene without any of the houses cluttering up the line of sight.

'You've heard of them, have you?' Ruth could tell from his expression that he suddenly saw her in a different light. 'Well, that's another reason why this is the Serpent Temple.'

'What do you mean?' Ruth said.

'Sometimes,' he said with a sly smile, 'when you put your ear to the ground you can hear it roar.'

Church, Ruth and Laura looked at each other, unable to tell if he was joking. Before they could ask him further, he stiffened and turned suddenly in the direction of Windmill Hill, the ancient site which looked over the village a few miles away. His brow furrowing, he stared hard, although none of them could tell what he was seeing. After a moment, he said, 'We're being watched.'

They followed his gaze, but could see nothing across the countryside. 'Where?' Ruth asked.

'Up there. On top of the hill.'

'Right,' Laura mocked, sneering at the distance that turned the hill to a blur of green beneath the blue. 'Tell me what's happening in Birmingham while you're at it.'

The Bone Inspector ignored her, squinted, concentrated. 'I see a tight flurry of crows, swirling madly like a black cloud. And at their heart is a man. Not a man, a monster. And with him are more monsters.'

'Monsters.' The breath caught in Church's throat.

'They're here for us,' Ruth said. 'You have to help us.' He stared at her coldly. '*Please* help us.'

'How should I know what to do?' he replied sourly. 'I know as much about the resting place of the talismans as the next man, and it's something I wouldn't *want* to know.'

'But one of the talismans is here somewhere. The lantern is telling us that,' Ruth continued. 'You know the place better than anyone. Where do you *think* it would be?'

He stared at her for a long moment, weighing up her worth, then he said, 'In a hidden place.' His pause carried his doubt about revealing too much, but something in Ruth's face prompted him to continue. 'All the old sites have hidden places. It's part of my job to make sure they stay hidden, away from prying fingers that might destroy them, and by doing so destroy the land itself.'

'You have to show us,' Ruth said with passion. 'If we don't find the talismans the land will be destroyed anyway.'

'You better not be making an idiot of me.' He made a clicking sound at the back of his throat, then whirled on his heel and strode out powerfully across the grass. He came to a stop five minutes later beside a large megalith which cast an imposing shadow across the land in the dawn sunlight.

'The Devil's Chair,' he said, nodding to it. 'The villagers here say if you run around it a hundred times you'll hear the voice of the Devil. But it isn't the Devil they hear.'

'If I ran around it a hundred times I'd hear the sound of my stomach coming out through my mouth,' Laura said.

'Three times widdershins will do,' the Bone Inspector said, leading them around the stone. They felt stupid, traipsing in line like primary school children, but by the third revolution they experienced the buzz of the earth energy in the air, creating a resonance which began to creep along the meridians of their bodies from the base of their spines. 'Now, quickly, along West Kennet Avenue,' the old man said.

He hurried up a steep embankment and skidded down the other side before crossing a road and darting through a gate. Two rows of concrete markers led to the largest group of megaliths they had seen, stretching out in an avenue across the fields. As they moved forward, shimmers of blue shot out from beneath their soles and the tingling in their spines had now reached the base of their skulls. Church felt like he was hallucinating; the dappled patterns of light and shadow across the landscape seemed to move fluidly and unusual bursts of sound kept breaking through into his ears. When the ground began to open up in the centre of the avenue ahead of them, he at first thought it was a vision. But the Bone Inspector hurried them along and then they were scrambling down into the dark as the turf and soil closed behind them with a rumble.

As the Bone Inspector had seen them, the creatures on Windmill Hill had seen the strange ritual that opened the secret way to the hidden place. They were prevented from venturing into the station of light and life, but when the earth spewed out the Brothers and Sisters of Dragons, they would be waiting. Rapidly they moved towards Avebury, keeping to the hedges and ditches and whatever feeble shadows the landscape offered. But the occasional villager who glanced out of their window at that early hour would have seen only one thing: a cloud of crows churning so tightly, it was impossible to tell how they could keep aloft: a vortex of black, beak and talon, man-shaped and moving with resolute power.

'Where are we?' Church asked, blinking in the gloom. He held up the lantern, which provided enough eerie blue light to see. The air was dank and filled with the odour of loam. The hollow echo of dripping water resounded from some-where nearby.

'The heart of the mystery,' the Bone Inspector said icily. 'Don't betray my faith in you. Or you won't be in a position to tell of this experience to anyone.' His bald threat unnerved them and they refused to meet his piercing stare. Instead, they turned their gaze ahead where a low tunnel dipped down gradually into the depths of the earth. The Bone Inspector led the way with Church at his shoulder, holding the lantern aloft, all of them maintaining an anxious silence.

They walked for about fifteen minutes, the tunnel widening almost without them noticing it; the light no longer played on the walls, merely faded into the oppressive dark, and the quality of the echoes of their footsteps became duller. It was getting brighter; the lantern's light was being dwarfed by another, more fulsome blue glow from further ahead. With a jarring mixture of wonder and apprehension, they crept forward until they stood on the lip of a ledge overlooking a lake of the blue energy, churning and roiling as if it was boiling water. Ruth began to ask what it was, but the Bone Inspector shushed her with an impatient wave of his hand. Resting his hands on his knees, he peered into the depths of the blue lake and, as they followed his gaze, they gradually saw a dark shape deep in the azure depths. It was rising; slowly at first, but then with increasing speed, churning the energy even more, until suddenly it broke the surface with its long, serpentine neck before dipping back down below. It was only the briefest glimpse, but they had a sense of something magnificent, of scales gleaming gold and green on a body filled with elegant power.

'This Fabulous Beast never left,' the Bone Inspector said. 'It merely slept.'

The others cautiously drew themselves upright, listening to the unnatural echoes that bounced around the cavern. 'Are you sure it's safe?' Ruth asked. 'It could fry us in a second here.'

'It could if it wished,' the Bone Inspector said, offering no comfort.

'It's the king of them all,' Laura said in a tone which surprised them; it was something she felt instinctively. She pushed her way past them to the edge, but the creature was lost beneath the blue waves.

'It is the oldest,' the Bone Inspector agreed. 'When all the creatures of imagination departed in the Sundering, this one stayed behind to protect the land, keeping the fire alive here in the furnace of the planet. Ready for the time when the power would flow freely again.' He looked at Church knowingly.

'Is that one of the things we're supposed to do?' Church asked. The Bone Inspector shook his head contemptuously.

'We don't know what we're supposed to be doing!' Ruth protested. 'We have no idea what a Brother or Sister of Dragons is. Why everyone thinks we're one. What's going on at all!' The stress brought a snap to the end of the sentence.

'Don't lose it,' Laura chided.

'I'm not your teacher.' The Bone Inspector walked to the edge and began to scan around the cavern. 'I'm giving you a helping hand here, but after this you're on your own. To be honest, I don't think you're up to the job.'

'What do you know,' Laura muttered.

When he turned she thought he was going to hit her with the staff, but instead he used it to point to the wall of the cavern nearest to them. 'There's a path that goes right round the edge of the lake to the far side. You might find what you're looking for there. Or you might not.'

Church squinted to see where he was pointing. 'It looks a bit precarious. It's only about a foot across.'

'Better not look down then,' Ruth said.

The Bone Inspector caught her arm before she could walk away. 'Just one of you.'

'Why?'

'Because the one whose home this is will only *let* one of you go.'

They stared into the blue depths for a moment, considering this, and then Church said, 'I suppose we have to trust you. But how can we be sure it won't attack even one of us?'

'It senses the dragon-spirit,' the Bone Inspector said. 'One of you will be safe.'

'What are you saying? We're family?'

'Not in any way you'd understand,' the Bone Inspector replied curtly.

Church sighed. 'Looks like—'

'Not so fast, leader-man,' Laura said. 'I admire your chivalry and all that, but I want to do this one.'

'No way!' Ruth was shaking her head forcefully. 'She's probably after the talisman for herself—'

'So you don't trust me,' Laura snapped. 'But you had better start doing so, because this is a partnership and I have an equal say. If you believe what Mystic Meg said and you believe I'm one of the five big cheeses, then you have to at least listen to me.'

'I don't know . . .' Church chewed on a knuckle.

'I say no,' Ruth said firmly.

The Bone Inspector snorted with derision. 'There isn't a hope.'

'He's right.' Church scrubbed a hand over his face, hoping he was making the right decision. 'We can't start off this way. We have to have some kind of faith in ourselves.'

'I appreciate the vote of confidence,' Laura said with a broad grin.

'I still say no,' Ruth added a little childishly.

Without a backward glance, Laura headed over to the path. She caught her breath when she saw it. Church had been right: barely a foot wide, with a precipitous drop into the roiling blue energy. Without showing her nervousness, she pressed her back against the rock wall and confidently stepped out on to the ledge.

Anxiety had turned Laura's shoulders and stomach into knots of steel cable, but she had been unable to resist the pull that had forced her to look down at the surface of the lake. The sinuous body of the Fabulous Beast occasionally broke the surface, as if it were shadowing her progress, but even the slightest glimpse filled her with excitement; she felt like a child again.

The inside of her mouth tasted metallic from the blue energy which spouted up from the surface in an effect which reminded her of a lava lamp; every tiny sound she made was strangely distorted by the cavern and the energy into something that was almost hallucinatory. She had to keep clinging on to the wall, feeling with her foot as she took each step. It was laborious and terrifying, but she was making good progress. Church and the others were lost to the blue haze and now the cavern walls had started to close in on both sides, allowing her to see things which both chilled and intrigued her. Human bones protruded from the rock, as well as the remnants of other skeletons which were not remotely human, nor animal either; they were yellowed and pitted with great age. Corroded helmets, swords and chain mail hung from ledges, next to axes and rougher tools from older times. And there was treasure, jewels beyond imagining, gold artefacts which still gleamed, mysterious objects: it was like a magpie's nest of historical plunder, all scattered on rocky outcroppings or lower ledges.

The cavern grew smaller and smaller until the walls were less than fifteen feet apart and Laura feared she would eventually become trapped. Then, as she made her way into what appeared to be a separate cavern, they widened out once more. This cave was much smaller than the other, and the ledge opened on to what Laura could only describe as a beach, where the blue energy lapped like surf.

Cautiously, she explored towards the rear wall of the cavern. As she neared, she saw the sheer face was intricately carved with symbols and shapes that were unmistakably Celtic: spirals, circles interlocking, infinite lines, faces, stylised animals, a dragon. It seemed to have some sort of meaning beyond simple design, but she had no idea what it was. Further along the wall was an alcove framed by two carved trees forming an arch with their intertwined branches. At the foot were severed heads, hollow-eyed with bared teeth; peering through the branches was a face made out of leaves.

Although the alcove appeared to be shallow, it was heavily shadowed and she couldn't tell what lay within its depths. There seemed little else of note around, so she stepped in for a better look and instantly realised her mistake.

With a deep rumble, some hitherto hidden door slammed behind her, shutting her in utter dark. A second later there was movement, a tremor of a touch at her ankle, her back, her neck. Something like bony fingers closed tightly around her wrists, yanking her arms up and to the side, caught in her hair, pinched her waist. Laura couldn't help herself, she opened her mouth and screamed.

The sound stifled in her throat as, with a brutality that surprised even her cruelly disciplined, modern, mature self, she forced calm on the frightened little girl struggling to escape. *Don't be pathetic*, she thought furiously. But it was so dark, and so claustrophobic, and she had no idea what was gripping her: things that felt like fingers, felt like bone, felt alive yet dead.

The door at her back was solid rock; no amount of pushing would budge it at all. She estimated a gap of six inches in front of her face, and if she moved from side to side her shoulders brushed the walls. It was a tomb. She choked back panic again. *Stay calm, stay calm*. Surely the Fabulous Beast wouldn't have allowed her to this secret spot just to have her sealed in a stone wall. Frantically, she tried to remember the carvings on the wall in case they had offered any instructions to escape the trap. Steel bands seemed to be closing across her chest and she was sure it was getting harder to breathe. Was the alcove airtight? She struggled against whatever was gripping her, but that only made it tighter. The panic started to come again, black waves that threatened to drown her, until she was gasping, feeling everything fall apart. And then, suddenly, a moment of lucidity that she clung to with the desperation of a drowning woman. She suddenly went limp, relaxing every muscle as she slumped forward. In response, the hands loosened their grip and, as she continued to play dead, they eventually fell away: the trap was for a threat who would fight, not for a friend who would offer themselves supinely. Or perhaps it was more than that, she thought. Perhaps it was a test of some kind.

'Abracadabra,' she said hopefully. She ran her fingers over the wall in front of her. It was uniformly smooth, except for one area where there were faint indentations. In the impenetrable dark, she could focus on her sense of touch without any distractions: a circle, and within it two smaller circles. On the left, a line snaked out and ended in a hole as big as her fingertip. On the right, another line started to snake out, but was abruptly curtailed. Laura pictured the outline in her mind, and after a moment of deliberation she realised what it was: a map of the Avebury Dracontium; except the curving right hand line should have extended, mirroring the one on the other side. She continued tracing it to where it should have ended and felt a small lump.

Suddenly she knew what she had to do. She pressed hard and the raised area sank in. A second later, there was a corresponding click and a small hatch opened at head height, flooding the alcove with a diffuse blue light. In the newly exposed area lay a shiny black stone as big as the palm of her hand. When Laura plucked it out, she was surprised, and a little disturbed, that it felt like skin, warm and soft. As she slipped it into her pocket, the doors slid back and, with a relieved gulp of dank air, she stepped back out into the cavern.

'This waiting is terrible.' Church sat with his legs dangling over the edge above the lake of blue energy; he had the disturbing feeling that if he pushed himself off he would be able to walk across its surface.

'Now you know how I felt in Salisbury.' Ruth was still annoyed he had allowed Laura to go on such an important mission; she was more angry at herself for feeling that way. The Bone Inspector had left them alone and was waiting silently in the shadows near the tunnel through which they entered.

Church stared into the blue depths, his hand unconsciously going to the Black Rose in his jacket; since they had gone underground it had felt horribly cold, like a block of ice burning his skin, and now the discomfort was starting to make him a little queasy. 'Brother of Dragons. What does that mean exactly? I wish somebody would give us a look at the script. Why are we so special?'

'Don't you feel special?' She controlled an urge to slip an arm around his shoulders and hug him. Since he had returned from the Watchtower, he seemed different; darker somehow, more intense, if that were possible. That odd conjunction of emotional fragility and strength of character moved her on some deep level so acutely, at times she wondered if she was falling ill, although she knew the truth, and that was just as bad.

'Not in the way all these weird people are intimating,' he said. 'I've always felt *different*. Even at school I knew I wasn't like other kids. She came to me, you know? When I was a boy.'

'Who?'

'The woman in the Watchtower.'

'There you are, then. You were different right from the start.'

'But I don't feel it inside me. I feel normal, like I always have done.'

'I don't know if anybody does feel different until they're called upon to—' She was interrupted by a call from Laura, who was edging her way along the last stretch of the ledge.

They ran to meet her as she stepped back on to the rock shelf. 'We'd just about given up on you,' Church said.

'Bad pennies always turn up. You should know that.' She dipped into her pocket and pulled out the stone; it seemed to glow with an inner light. 'Look what I found.'

Church and Ruth gathered round. 'Is that it? Wow! I expected a lump of rock or something,' Ruth said.

Church looked at her curiously. 'It is a lump of rock.'

'No, it's not. It's a diamond,' Ruth said incredulously.

'Are you both insane? It's a black stone, like polished obsidian.'

They looked from one to the other in disbelief until the Bone Inspector stepped up. 'Save your breath. It has no true shape in this world. It's fluid, like everything from the Other Place. Our tiny little minds can't grasp it, so we give it some kind of shape to make sense of it.'

'That's crazy,' Ruth said. 'How are we—'

'It doesn't matter what things look like,' the old man said with exasperation, 'just as long as *you* know what they are.'

Church peered at the stone in Laura's hands. 'The first of the four talismans. What does it do?'

Laura held it out to the Bone Inspector for advice, but the old man backed away hastily. 'Don't bring it near me! It's too powerful. It's your burden now.'

'But what does it do?'

'It doesn't *do* anything,' the Bone Inspector snapped. 'It's not a toy! It has a purpose which I'm sure you'll find out

177

sooner or later. Now enough of the fool questions. Let's get back to the light. And not the way we came either. I have no doubt our friends from Windmill Hill will be waiting for us on West Kennet Avenue.'

He led them to another tunnel off to one side. As they made their way uphill by the light of the lantern, Church said to Laura, 'So did you have any trouble getting it?'

'Easy as pie,' she replied.

They emerged blinking into the warm morning light on Beckhampton Avenue, the snaking route on the other side of Avebury. After the dank passages, the air was fragrant with spring flowers and the verdant aromas of the countryside.

'You leave here quickly now and don't look back,' the Bone Inspector said gruffly. 'Dawdle too much and you'll find the Devil at your heels.'

'Where are you going now?' Ruth asked.

'I've got a country full of ancient places to tend, graves to visit, old bones to check, and in these times I think they'll need me more than ever.'

'Thanks for your help,' Church said, stretching out a hand which the old man ignored. 'We couldn't have done it without you.'

'Aye. And don't you forget it. I bloody well hope I've done the right thing. Don't go and ruin it all.'

Then he turned and was loping away, over a gate and into the fields, faster than they would have believed, almost dropping to all fours at times so that he seemed more animal than man as he disappeared into the countryside.

'We could have used his help,' Ruth said regretfully.

'We don't need any crumbly old folk.' Laura replaced her sunglasses after the dark of the cavern. 'We've got youth, good looks and sex on our side.'

'Look at this.' Church held up the lantern; the flame was now flickering towards the south-west.

They hurried through the quiet streets until they reached

the car, and then they were speeding out of the village before anyone noticed.

On West Kennet Avenue, the cloud of whirling, flapping crows suddenly turned towards the south-west. A guttural voice filled with the grunts of beasts rolled out from the heart of it, and four shadows seemed to separate from the base of the hedges. The voice barked and snorted again, incomprehensible to human ears, and all the birds, and the cows lowing in the fields fell silent.

the light that never Goes out

'You want to push me completely over the edge, you go ahead and play Sinatra one more time.' Laura gave the back of Church's seat a sharp kick. 'Because we've only heard "Come Fly With Me", like, what, a thousand times? Music-induced psychosis is not a pretty thing to see.'

Church ejected the tape with irritation. 'What do you want, then?'

'Somebody who's not dead would be nice.'

'I hate to say it, but I'm with her on this one,' Ruth chipped in.

'Fine. Gang up on me.'

Laura rested her arms on the back of his seat, her breath bringing a bloom to his neck. 'Have you got anything that makes your ears bleed?'

'An icepick?'

'How about some golden oldies, like, say, The Chemical Brothers?'

'No.'

'What's the matter? Don't you like music that makes your blood boil?'

His first reaction was to say *I used to*, but he realised how pathetic it sounded. If truth be told, his irritation with Laura came more from how she pointed up the parts of his character that he had lost than from her forthright manner.

'How about the radio?' he snapped, feeling the first bite of self-loathing. He switched it on and tuned across the band until he heard music.

'It'll do, I guess.' Laura slumped back into her seat, successful.

The music gave way to the syrupy voice of a local DJ who rambled aimlessly for a minute or two before another fizzy, optimistic Top Ten hit came on. Outside the car the windswept uplands had given way to sun-drenched green fields, trees on the verge of bursting with new life, sparkling streams and little stone bridges. The road behind was comfortingly empty and, despite everything, Church was feeling remarkably at ease in the light of their success at Avebury. The lantern had directed them on to the A4 towards Bath where they were able to build up some speed and put some distance between them and whatever the Bone Inspector had feared was waiting for them on West Kennet Avenue. They felt confident enough to pause briefly at Chippenham, where they bought a couple of tents, cooking equipment and other camping gear for emergencies. Laura protested she wasn't the outdoor type, but, as usual, it seemed to be more for effect.

Bath was choked with traffic, the winter season already forgotten as tourists flocked to the Roman baths or to gawp at the Georgian architecture. Ruth muttered something about the bliss of ignorance, and for a brief while a maudlin mood fell across the car as they all became acutely aware of what was at risk.

But by the time they had passed through Bath into the more sparsely populated countryside beyond, their mood had buoyed as they focused on the task ahead. They were making good time and the lantern seemed to be taking them into the deep south-west, far away from the troubled areas of the previous few days.

As they travelled through tiny, picture-postcard villages south of Bristol, with the undulating slopes of the Mendips away to their left, they were shocked by a sharp, ear-splitting burst of static on the radio. When it faded, the DJ's voice was replaced by giggling, mocking laughter fading in and out of white noise, growing louder, then softer; there was something inhuman about it. It was the same mysterious sound Ruth and Church had heard on the tape in the therapist's office when they had first discovered what they had seen under Albert Bridge. Church hastily ran the tuner across the band, but the laughter remained the same, and even when he switched the radio off, it continued to come out of the speakers for a full minute. Ruth and Church shot an uneasy glance of recognition at each other.

Five miles further on, all the electrics failed.

'I'll have a look, but there's no chance I can do anything today.' The mechanic glanced at a dusty clock above the door of the repair bay; it said 3 p.m. He was unusually tall and massive-boned, with a solid beer belly kept in check by his grease-stained blue overalls. His face was ruddy and his unruly black hair was peppered with grey. 'Everything's going bloody crazy at the moment.'

Church sat wearily on the Nissan's wing. He'd spent an hour searching for a garage with a towtruck. This one had only relented and agreed to come out after he had virtually begged.

'It's these modern cars, you see,' the mechanic continued. 'They build 'em to break down. Though this last week I've never seen anything like it. The place has been full every day, most of it electrical stuff, though I've had a fair share of busted alternators. I tell you, you need a bloody degree to sort out these electrics. This week I've worked on some all day long and then, just like that, they've been fine again. No explanation for it. Couldn't find any fault at all, yet they were dead as a dodo when they were brought in.' He shook his head at this great mystery, then added, 'Still, bloody good for business.'

Church got his assurances that the car would be looked at first thing the following day, then wandered out to Ruth and Laura who sat with the camping equipment on the dusty forecourt. The garage was well off the beaten track, a run-down affair that seemed to have been barely updated since the fifties, down to the period petrol pumps that stood dry like museum pieces at the front. Only farms lay scattered around the surrounding countryside, and there was no sound of traffic, just the song of birds in the clustering trees.

'What did he say?' Ruth asked anxiously.

'Tomorrow. I think we can risk giving it a shot before we start looking around for the local Avis.'

'Yeah, there'll really be one round here,' Laura said sarcastically.

Ruth noticed Church's concerned expression and asked him what was wrong. He repeated the mechanic's tale of mysterious breakdowns. 'I think things are starting to go wrong, just like Tom predicted. It's as if the rules of science are falling apart in the face of all these things that shouldn't exist.'

Laura looked at him curiously. 'What do you mean?'

'I mean,' he said, nodding to the computer in the bag on her arm, 'that pretty soon that will be as much use to us as it would be to some lost Amazon tribe, along with every other technological gadget. New rules are falling into place. Science is dying.'

'Unless we can do something about it,' Ruth said hopefully, but Church merely shouldered the tents and rucksack and began to trudge along the lane.

They found a good campsite in a secluded grove out of sight of the road. They didn't ask permission, preferring anonymity. The trees were thick enough to prevent the tents being seen by the casual passer-by, and there was a natural clearing shielded by a tangle of brambles where they could light a fire. Ruth seemed uncomfortable at the prospect of sharing with Laura, but they reached some kind of unspoken agreement, and Church slipped off to collect firewood.

Lost in thought as he scoured the edge of the copse, he

failed to see the figure until it was upon him. He whirled in shock, ready to fight or run, and was then suffused with embarrassment when he saw it was just a girl of about ten, pretty, with long blonde hair and a creamy complexion. She was wearing a tight T-shirt with a sunburst motif and baggy, faded jeans.

'Hello,' she said in a thick West Country accent. 'Are you looking for something?'

'Just sightseeing,' he replied ridiculously.

'Not much to see round here.' She laughed disarmingly.

Relaxing his guard, Church returned her smile. 'Not really my cup of tea.'

'Where you from then?'

'London.'

'I'd love to live in London.' She looked dreamily into the middle distance. 'It'd be great to be somewhere where there's a buzz.'

'Nothing to stop you when you're older.'

Her smile became slightly more enigmatic. 'My name's Marianne. What's yours?'

'Jack.' Although he knew nothing about her, the simple matter of her name suddenly made him warm to her. 'That's a nice name,' he continued. 'I used to know someone called Marianne.'

'A girlfriend?'

'She was.'

'Did you split up?'

He thought twice, then said honestly, 'She died.'

Marianne nodded ruefully. 'It figures.' Church looked at her curiously, but she'd already danced ahead of him. Noticing the wood he'd piled nearby, she grinned and said, 'Sightseeing, eh? Looks to me like you're going to have a little fire.' She looked around. 'Where's the camp?'

Church's shoulders sagged. 'Blimey. Rumbled. Look, we're trying to keep a low profile. I'd appreciate it if you didn't tell anyone.'

Her laughter at Church's obvious dismay was innocent and infectious. 'Don't worry, I'm not going to rat on you. But if my dad finds out it'll be a different matter. He farms on this land and he's always going mad about *bloody trespassers*. Threatened to set the dogs on the last lot he caught. We're close enough to Glastonbury to get those scruffy New Age types passing through. Some of them leave the place in a right mess, but most of them seem okay to me. My dad thinks they're all scroungers and vandals, though.'

'Well, I'm neither.'

'I can see that. Come on, I'll help you collect some wood.' She walked at his side for a minute or two, then said, 'Do you miss her?'

'Marianne? Yes. A lot.'

'I thought you looked sad. I could see it in your eyes.' Church winced at the thought that it was so obvious. There was a long, thoughtful pause and then she said, 'Do you think people die for a reason?'

He shrugged. 'I don't know—'

'Yes, but do you *think*?'

'I'd like to believe that, but it's not always easy to see.' The maturity of her conversation surprised him, and made him feel a little uncomfortable. 'This is heavy stuff for someone your age.'

'Just because you're young doesn't mean you have to fill your head with rubbish,' she said tartly. 'Anyway, I do like a lot of *rubbish*. It's just I like to think about other stuff too.'

'I stand corrected.'

'Apology accepted,' she laughed, picking up a rotten tree branch and tossing it to Church. 'Why are you so bothered about dying? Don't argue – I can see you are! It's just another part of life, isn't it? The only thing worth bothering about is what we do *before* we pop our clogs.'

'It's not as simple as that—'

'Why not? I want to do exciting stuff every day, learn new things, see life. I want to pack a week into a day, a month

185

into a week and a year into a month. Don't you think that's a good philosophy? Why doesn't everybody do that?'

Church pretended to scour the grass for wood while he attempted to think of an answer, but he couldn't summon anything that didn't sound pathetic. Her victorious grin forced him to laugh. 'I think I should be Prime Minister,' she said triumphantly, sashaying theatrically ahead of him.

When she turned back to him, she'd pulled out a locket from under her T-shirt. With a dexterous flick, she opened it and held it up to show him the tiny picture squeezed inside.

'Princess Diana,' he noted. 'Did you like her?'

'I loved her. That's why I asked you about dying. She did so much good with her life. I think *she* died for a reason.'

'Oh?'

'To make us see how bad we were all living our lives. So that we could learn from her and live more like her, you know, doing good, helping the world.'

Her tone was so adamant it would have been reprehensible to sour her views with adult cynicism. 'She seemed very decent. All that campaigning for land mines. And all that.'

Marianne looked up at him with a faintly pitying smile. 'I can see you're not a believer.'

'I'm sorry. I'm just . . . an old grouch.'

'I've got pictures of her all over my bedroom. And in one corner I've got a little table with the best photo I could find in a frame. You'd know it if you saw it. It's famous. She's looking at the camera really thoughtful, and when you look right into her eyes you can see so much goodness it almost makes you cry.' She lowered her voice conspiratorially. 'Before bed, I kneel down in front of it and pray to her.'

Church lowered his eyes, trying to remember the last time he felt such an innocent belief. 'What do you pray for?'

'For Diana to make me a better person. For me to do some good, like her, before I die.'

'Well, of all the things to pray for, that sounds like one of the best.'

'You should try it some time.'

He laughed. 'Maybe I should.'

'No, I mean it.' She undid the locket and offered it to him. 'Not to keep. Just try it tonight and I'll get it back off you tomorrow.'

'No, I couldn't—'

'Don't be silly!' She grabbed his hand and forced it into his fingers, laughing. 'She's a saint, you know. She'll listen to you.'

He felt uncomfortable taking it from her, and that made him wonder why: perhaps it *was* the cynicism – Diana, Patron Saint of Bulimics and Damaged Women Everywhere. But then maybe Marianne was right. Perhaps blind faith was what was needed. It certainly seemed to make her happy.

'Okay,' he said finally. 'Maybe you'll make a convert of me.' That seemed to please her.

They spent the next hour trailing through the trees and along the hedgerows, doing more talking than wood collecting. Church found himself enjoying Marianne's company; she was funny and passionate, filled with questions about every subject that entered the conversation, and possessed of a generosity of spirit that made him feel good to be around her, and a little humbled. She was an only child, yet quite unspoilt, with a love of music that reminded Church of his younger days. They argued about the strengths and weaknesses of a few pop icons, then listed their top ten songs, which ended in uncontrollable laughter when she made Church sing the chorus of all his selections.

Finally they'd located enough firewood and Marianne helped Church carry it back to the camp. Ruth and Laura weren't anywhere to be seen so they lit the fire together and made some tea. Oddly, Church found himself talking about his own Marianne with an openness that he hadn't managed since her death. The young girl was an easy listener and she seemed to have a handle on his emotions that belied her years. When she said goodbye, with a promise to bring them milk at breakfast, he was sorry to see her go.

Night still fell quickly at that time of year, and there was a chill to it which made a mockery of the warmth of the day. Ruth and Laura had reached an uneasy, unspoken truce; enough to follow directions from the garage to a local shop where they had bought enough provisions for the evening meal and breakfast: some vegetables for a stew, rice, bacon, eggs and bread, although Laura revealed she was a strict vegetarian. They cooked around 7.30 p.m., keeping close to the fire for warmth, speaking in voices that were subconsciously low. The conversation was muted. The darkness among the trees seemed deep and disturbing; none of them would admit how scary the quiet countryside had become.

While the food bubbled over the fire, Laura plugged her computer into her mobile. 'Thought it would be worthwhile to check up on some of those lines the old guy had been spinning you before he caught his ticket to Neverland.'

When she booted the computer up, Church noticed her desktop wallpaper was a strange design of interlinking trees. 'What does that mean?' he asked.

'It's a design. It means I like looking at it,' she sneered. 'Shit. The battery's getting low. I'll need to find somewhere to charge it soon. Anyway, earlier I found this site called the Charles Fort Institute, which is like this massive online reference library and archive for all sorts of bizarre shit. They've got lots of links to folklore sites. So why don't we start with the pooch.' The screen jumped to *The Black Dog Reporter*. 'Here we are: Black Shuck. Shuck comes from *scucca*, the Anglo-Saxon for demon.' She scrolled quickly down the page. 'There's an account of a great storm in East Anglia in 1577 when a black demon dog "or the Devil in such a likeness" appeared in Bungay Church, leaving two parishioners dead at their prayers and another "as shrunken as a piece of leather scorched in a hot fire". Loads of tales from all over the country, but he's usually described as big as a calf with saucer-sized eyes that weep green or red fire, and he only comes from his secret lair at dusk. In East Anglia when someone is dying they still say "The Black Dog is at his heels." Generally seen as a portent of something much worse, death or disaster.'

'Hang on, if it only comes out at dusk, how come you saw it in daylight in Salisbury?' Ruth asked.

'Maybe he's found a good sunscreen,' Laura said.

'The tales might simply have it wrong. Because he was only seen at night, the people thought he could only come out then,' Church suggested.

Ruth sighed. 'Some come out by day, some are nocturnal. This is all too confusing.'

'Nothing about how to drive it away?' Church asked hopelessly.

'Well, being as how this stuff is generally regarded as not *real*, there's not much of a user's guide,' she replied tartly. 'Nothing in the folklore to link him to the Wild Hunt either. But I guess we're in uncharted territory here.'

'What have you got on the Hunt?'

After she'd jumped to the next site, Church tried to read her screen, but she moved it so he couldn't see. 'Lots of conflicting stories. It comes from the Norse tradition, long before the Vikings or Christianity came to Britain.' She scanned down to the relevant section. 'Odin was supposed to race across the sky on stormy winter evenings with a pack of baying hounds. Anyone who saw the Hunt could be carried off to a distant land, while anyone who spoke to the Huntsman died. Later, Odin's place was taken by the Devil, but the Wild Huntsman has also been seen as Herne the Hunter or Sir Francis Drake, who used to ride in a black coach led by headless horses across Dartmoor. The pack is called Yeth Hounds or Wish Hounds, another bunch of demon dogs, and they say you can hear their screams on the wind as they

189

hunt down the souls of unbaptised babies. Cute. The Wild Huntsman's also known as the Erl-King, which is some mis-translation of an old Danish legend about the King of the Elves leading the Wild Hunt.'

'We've got to remember the legends aren't the truth,' Church cautioned. 'They're just stories twisted from the few facts people recall—'

'And isn't that a relief,' Laura interrupted. 'Demon hounds whisking poor bastards off to some kind of Purgatory. Portents of death and destruction. We're still not in line for Big Fun, are we?'

'Can't you find anything useful?' Ruth said with irritation.

'Sorry, I forgot you're a completely useless waste of space. It really is all down to me.' She logged off the net and clicked off her computer.

Ruth didn't bite. 'Okay, we've suddenly been swamped with every supernatural creature known to man, but what do you think is really going on?' she said to Church. 'These Night Walkers are obviously manoeuvring in the shadows. I mean, why were they all at that depot? Are they all getting regular jobs? I don't think so.'

Church nodded in agreement. 'Exactly. If they're so power-ful, why haven't they made any move yet?'

'Maybe they're planning a first strike that will wipe us off the board in one fell swoop,' Laura noted.

'Whatever they're planning, it's something so important they can't risk us messing it up.'

Ruth looked out into the encroaching dark. 'They could be all over the country, just mixing with people, and nobody any the wiser. That funny-looking bloke you always think is a bit odd at the bus stop. The weirdo staring at you in the supermarket. Everywhere.'

'That's a good recipe for paranoia.' Laura lay back so she could see the moon coming up through the trees. 'There's going to be the war to end all wars and nobody knows.'

* * *

After dinner, Laura handed out the beers she had bought and they discussed what lay ahead. Church was surprised how optimistic the other two seemed, despite everything, although he knew his view had been coloured by his vision of his own death in the Watchtower. Laura had been entrusted with the stone, although they had never discussed it; it just seemed natural as she had been the one to find it. As their conversation turned to the possible locations of the other talismans, she pulled the stone out from the small rucksack where she had decided to keep it.

'It's a weird thing,' she said. 'I still can't get over the feel of it. It's kind of creepy.'

'What do you mean?'

'You'll know if you touch it. Here, cop a feel.'

She handed it over to Church for the first time. But as his fingers brushed it, an ear-splitting shriek burst from the stone and he dropped it like a hot coal. 'What the hell was that?' he asked in shock.

They all looked at it for a moment before Laura picked it up. 'Care to try that again?' Laura held it out to him again.

Church hesitated, then gingerly brushed his fingers over the stone's surface. The shriek erupted immediately.

'Jesus, why don't you set off a flare so everyone knows where we are!' Ruth protested.

'What does it mean?' Church said curiously. 'You try it,' he said to Ruth.

She took it from Laura, passed it from hand to hand, then gave it back. 'Looks like it doesn't like men,' Laura said to Church. 'Or maybe you've just got clammy palms.'

Church felt suddenly cold. 'The woman in the Watchtower said it had the power to recognise the true king of the land.'

Laura burst out laughing. 'King Church the First! That's a good one!'

Church shook his head. 'Don't be ridiculous.'

'You can't get away from the fact it only reacts to you,' Ruth said.

'I don't want to think about that. With this kind of stuff we can spend forever guessing. Who knows what any of it means?'

Laura was still laughing like a drain. 'The king! With his royal carriage, the Nissan Bluebird!'

Her mockery was so sharp they couldn't help joining in the laughter. It eased some of the tension which had been collecting around them.

They spent the next couple of hours drinking beer, talking quietly and feeding the fire from the rapidly diminishing woodpile; a cold wind threatened a storm. The conversation never strayed far from their mission, as they called it (ironically at first, but with increasing seriousness); even Laura's attempts to keep the chat superficial failed.

Shortly after 9 p.m., Ruth felt a change come over her. It started as a simple shiver that reached from deep within her, followed by a prickling of the skin that suggested the onset of some virus; a moment or two later she heard, or thought she did, her name whispered somewhere among the trees. Church and Laura continued to talk in hushed voices, oblivious to whatever had alerted her. Yet despite their situation, she didn't feel frightened. The pull was too strong to resist; she told the others she was going to stretch her legs and slipped off into the trees.

As she walked, she realised she couldn't turn back, even though some distant part of her was warning of the dangers of straying too far from the fire; obliquely, she recognised something was in her head, dragging her on and calming her at the same time.

She had wandered barely a few yards when she regretted it. The light from the fire faded quickly, as if it were being leached by the dark which quickly enfolded her. The noises seemed unnatural and disturbing; the creak of the branches above her head too loud, out of time with the gusts of the wind, as if they had a life of their own, the arms of living

192

tree-gods reaching down to her; crunches in the under-growth, near then far, which could have been small animals but sounded like footsteps circling her; whispers scarcely reaching her ears, dispossessed words fading out before she could make sense of them. Within moments she felt Church, Laura and all of civilisation were lost to her; she was in a dark, elemental world that considered her an interloper.

The flap of large wings made her jump and a second later an owl swooped close to her head, its face ghostly white against the dark. The owl shrieked once, sounding more human than bird, and a second later the trees were alive with light. Tiny white flames flickered as if myriad candles had been placed among the branches and for an instant Ruth had a breathtaking vision, as if the stars had been brought down to earth.

A figure stood next to an ancient, twisted hawthorn bush, its shape distorting amongst the shadows. As Ruth drew closer, she saw it was the young girl she had seen in the park in Salisbury – although she knew in her heart it was neither young nor girl – a cloak of what appeared to be thousands of interlocking leaves billowing in the wind around her.

Ruth felt drawn to the apparition as if she were in some hypnotic state, yet at the same time she was consumed by fear and awe: the figure was so alien. She knew, on some level she couldn't understand, that the girl had some specific interest in her; she could feel the subtle strands of manipu-lation in her head, the sense that the girl was trying to com-municate something important.

'He is missing. The night to my day, the winter to my summer.' The words came out without her mouth moving; it was the same thing she had said in the park in Salisbury.

Who is missing? Ruth thought. *And what has it got to do with me?*

As if in answer, the quality of the light changed and Ruth could see something large crashing and stumbling among the undergrowth behind the girl. It was a vision, not reality, primal and terrifying. Ruth caught a glimpse of powerful muscles, and a shape slightly larger than a man, but with antlers curving wickedly from his head. Beyond him the small grove of trees went on for ever.

Whatever moved through the trees made snorting noises and began to circle closer, but still beyond the circle of light thrown by the flames in the branches, so it was impossible to see it fully. As the vision disappeared, the girl's flowing dress seemed to fade beneath her cloak, leaving her naked. Her skin was almost translucent, milky like the moon, her breasts small, her belly rounded, hips shapely. Ruth felt an incipient sexuality in the air, as if it were electricity and the girl a generator.

'Find him and then you must join us. Become our daughter. Our champion.'

Ruth stared into her mesmerising eyes, trying to comprehend. The girl reached out to Ruth, but the thought of touching those alien hands filled her with such dread, the spell was broken. She started to back away.

The owl that had startled her earlier suddenly swept down into the space between them and stared at Ruth with eyes that were unnervingly intelligent; it made her shudder.

'A companion,' the girl continued, 'a familiar, to guide you through the dark. When you see him, remember me.'

She began to say something else, but Ruth couldn't bear to stay any longer. And then she was running wildly through the trees, terrified by the knowledge that she had been recognised by something unknowable, and filled with the awful belief that she would never be allowed to return to the life she once knew.

'Are you making any sense of this?' Laura lounged back against the twisted trunk of an old ash tree, supping on the last of the beers. In her eyes, Church saw a sharp wit, incisive, and dark things moved beneath it.

'I try not to make sense of anything any more. If you

thought about all the things happening to us in any kind of rational way, you'd go mad. The only way is to just deal with it as it happens.'

She shrugged, looked away into the dark. Since Ruth had gone for her walk, she seemed to have sloughed off some of the superficiality and mocking humour; for the first time Church felt a glimmer of the real Laura. 'Sort of screws up the belief system, doesn't it?'

'Belief,' Church said with surprise. 'What do you mean?'

'You know, God and all that. Not much in the Bible about this.'

'You believe the Bible then?' Church asked cautiously.

'I've got no time for any religious dickheads,' she said brutally. In that simple sentence, Church sensed dark currents running, but she made it clear it was something she wasn't going to discuss further.

'When you get into the historical truth of that whole Bible thing, it's hard to keep any faith,' he said.

'What do you mean?'

'Well, you know, how the Bible was put together by a council of the religious establishment from all the various texts lying around. Some got put in, some got left out – the Apocrypha – so it presented a simple, uncomplicated teaching guide for the masses, and a unifying cosmology. Politics. So even if the Bible is God's word, it was edited by men. How reliable does that make it?'

She shrugged. 'Maybe it's just like all these legends you keep pontificating about – some truth, lots of crazy stories trying to explain it.' She drained her can, carefully slipping it into the rubbish sack. 'Or maybe there's nothing out there at all. The No-Point Law – the perfect justification for staying in bed every day until we finally fade out.'

'That sounds a little bleak.'

'You think there's a meaning to it all? To all this we're going through?' Church was surprised; she sounded almost desperate.

'I don't know. A few weeks back, I thought there was no meaning to anything. Now I'm not so sure. We're suddenly living in a world where anything can happen. These days it's impossible to be sure, full stop.' He paused thoughtfully. 'Maybe we just think too much.'

The hoot of an owl made them both jump and they laughed nervously. Although he knew Laura irritated the hell out of Ruth, he felt remarkably comfortable with her. He enjoyed the spikiness of her character, and there was something oddly moving about the vulnerability he sensed beneath the patina of hardness; he was surprised Ruth couldn't see it too.

Laura cracked her knuckles, then seemed to become aware of the night's cold. With a shiver she moved closer to the fire, sitting crosslegged next to Church. 'So tell me,' she said, the faint mocking smile returning once more, 'have you and Miss Goody Two-Shoes done the monkey dance yet?'

Church looked at her in bafflement at the sudden switch in conversation. 'It's not like that. We're friends.'

'Come on! Don't tell me you don't realise she's desperate to get into your Calvins?'

Church shook his head forcibly. 'She's never shown any sign—'

'What do you expect? A big, flashing neon heart? Believe me, she's yearning to get to your loins, boy. So what are you going to do about it?'

Church shifted uncomfortably. 'There are things you don't know—'

'Well, tell me then.'

It was obvious she wasn't going to back down, so he reluctantly told her about Marianne. Yet as he spoke he became aware that something had changed; the rawness he felt inside whenever he discussed Marianne was gone. He felt sad, but not devastated – for the first time since her death. His hand went to the Black Rose in his pocket, gently caressing the petals, closing around the stem. Had the rose freed him from the despair, or was it because he knew some part of Marianne still existed in whatever place the dead dwelled? A sign that the new Dark Age was not all bad.

'So you haven't had sex for two years?' Laura said insensitively when he'd finished. 'What's the matter? You've got a phobia about it now?'

He felt his cheeks redden, with irritation rather than embarrassment. 'When you've been in love you don't automatically jump to someone new once a vacancy arises.'

'Look, I'm sure she was a nice girl and all that, but she's dead. Get over it. What are you going to do? Spend the rest of your days living in the past while life passes you by? I'm sure all this moping around was touching and romantic in the first few months after she died. But let's face it, it's pretty pathetic at this stage. And not a very attractive quality for the chicks.'

He snorted in exasperation.

'Ooh. Have I touched a nerve?' Her triumphant grin made him fume, but it was instantly tempered and once again he caught a glimpse of some honest emotion moving behind. 'You don't want to cut yourself off too much. In these days, with everything falling apart, you need to have someone close to you, know what I mean?'

'Yes. I know.' He looked her in the eye. She didn't smile, but there was a faint shift of something in her face that suggested they both recognised the subtext of their conversation.

Ruth saw it too. She was standing in the shadows amongst the trees after trying to find her way back to the camp. She had been desperate to tell them of her unsettling experience, but her emotions had diffused after hearing Church speak about her in terms that suggested little more than acquaintanceship and seeing Laura's obvious – at least to her – attempt at seduction. She felt more excluded than ever as she watched them looking deep into each other's eyes, locked in their own world. She hovered, undecided, for a moment, then hugged her arms around her and turned to walk back into the night.

She halted when a distant whirring sound broke through the stillness, and when she glanced back she noticed Church and Laura had seen her as they searched the sky for the origin of the noise.

'Sounds like helicopters,' Church called to her. 'Several of them.'

They walked to the edge of the glade, where they had a better view. Four searchlights played across the fields and hills as the choppers circled, searching the landscape.

'What are they looking for?' Ruth asked.

'Some crook on the run,' Laura said.

'You won't find many forces with the resources for four 'copters,' Church noted. They watched the lights for ten minutes more until they eventually drifted away. There was no evidence, but they all felt, instinctively, that it had something to do with the growing shadow that was falling across the country.

The morning was chill and grey, with heavy clouds banked up to the horizon, and there was rain in the wind. They waited patiently for Marianne to arrive with the milk, as she had promised, but when she didn't turn up, Church rekindled the fire and cooked bacon and eggs for him and Ruth while Laura simply had some black coffee. They were keen to move on as soon as possible. Church visited the garage the moment it opened, but the mechanic had made no progress and told him to come back after lunch. The breakdowns seemed to be continuing at an unaccountable pace; cars were starting to back up on the forecourt waiting for repair and the phone in the cluttered, nicotine-smelling office rang continuously.

The rain started to fall heavily by midmorning and Church, Laura and Ruth huddled morosely in their tents, one of them continuously watching the landscape for signs of movement. The conversation was muted and at times fell to silence as they struggled with their own thoughts. Church feared the worst when he returned to the garage, but the Nissan was waiting for him. The mechanic was apologetic; all the diagnostic tests on his equipment had found nothing wrong; it had started mysteriously an hour earlier as if it had suddenly decided the time was right. Church drove quickly back to the campsite where Laura had organised a methodical clean-up, insisting nothing was left behind which would damage the environment.

As they loaded their tents and bags into the boot, they were disturbed by the sound of crying caught on the wind, fearful and despairing, lost then as the gusts twisted among the trees. Soon after they caught sight of a red-cheeked man, his face distorted by grief, running wildly along the road nearby. Church's first thought was to ignore the distraught passer-by, but some instinct had him pounding through the trees to hurdle a fence and intercept the sobbing man further along the road.

'What's wrong?' Church asked, catching at his arm.

The man, who was in his late forties, grey hair plastered over his balding head by the rain, was startled by Church's intervention and for a second he seemed to be in such a state of shock he didn't know where he was. Then he said, 'My daughter—' before he was wracked by a juddering sob that crumpled his body. He came to his senses and roughly grabbed Church's shoulders. 'Have you got a car? I need a car!' Church nodded and hurriedly led him to where the Nissan was parked. 'My daughter's sick. Dying. Bloody car won't start. Only had it serviced the other week. Too far for an ambulance to get here and back to Bristol—' Another sob engulfed him.

Ruth and Laura wanted to know what was wrong, but the man made it plain there was no time to talk. They piled in the back and Church followed the man's directions up a long, winding lane to a neatly tended farmhouse. He scrambled out of the car and ran inside and before Church could follow he was out again carrying a young girl, with his hysterical wife close behind. It was Marianne.

* * *

Suddenly all her questions about death made sense. For nearly three years she had been living with a blood clot in her brain after a fall at the farm. It was in a position which made it too dangerous to operate, unless it moved or spread to become life-threatening, which, the doctors had warned her parents, it could at any time, without warning. When that happened, there was so little to lose that an operation became feasible. And the clot had chosen that day to strike her down.

'Her mother found her out cold on the kitchen floor with a bottle of milk smashed beside her,' her father said.

The one she'd been on her way to bring to us, Church thought.

As her father recounted the details, her upbeat, optimistic character took on a sharp poignancy; Church marvelled at how she had managed to remain so unspoilt while living permanently in the shadow of death. And it made his own doubts and fears seem so insignificant; he felt weak and pathetic in comparison.

The drive to Bristol passed in a flash of recklessly taken corners and jumped red lights. Each time Church glanced at Marianne in the rearview mirror, his heart rattled and his stomach knotted. Her face was impossibly pale. She was still out cold and he couldn't tell if she was suffering. He couldn't believe how acutely he felt for someone he barely knew; perhaps it was just the name creating echoes in his subconscious – maybe this Marianne he could save! – but whatever it was, she had touched him on some deep level. More than anything else in the world, he didn't want this Marianne to die.

Laura warned the hospital of their approach with the last gasp of life in her mobile phone and when they arrived at Frenchay the staff were waiting for her. As Marianne was rushed on a trolley up to the operating theatre, the farmer paused briefly to offer thanks for their help before chasing after his daughter.

'Poor girl. I hope there's something they can do,' Ruth

said softly. Seeing the concern on Church's face, she touched his arm gently and said, 'At least we were around to get her here quickly.'

After occasional bouts of drizzle, the gathering storm clouds finally broke in a downpour that hammered against the reception doors. Bursts of lightning crackled overhead. 'We should be hitting the road,' Laura said as she watched the fading light.

'I can't go until I know how she's going to be.' Church silenced Laura's protests with a shake of the head before wandering slowly to the lift doors through which Marianne had disappeared.

Like most hospitals, the layout of Frenchay was labyrinthine. Church thought he was following the numerous signs, but he must have missed one at some point, for he found himself in a quiet ward with no sign of any operating theatres. Looking for directions, he stepped inside. Unlike the rest of the hospital, it was so still his footsteps on the creaking, sticky linoleum sounded like he was wearing hobnailed boots. There was the unmistakable smell of antiseptic that he always associated with sickness. Small rooms lay on either side of the corridor at the start, but further on he could see double doors through which he could just glimpse a large, open ward filled with beds. The room to his right had a big viewing window like a storefront. Inside, a sickly boy lay on his bed staring blankly at a TV set which featured US cartoons that were cut so fast it made Church feel nauseous. Numerous tubes snaked from his arms and his nose and there was a bank of monitors to each side of his bed. From the intricate locking system and the red light above the door, Church guessed it was some kind of isolation unit.

The door on the room to his left was slightly ajar and as he approached it Church could hear voices whispering a mantra over and over again. Through the glass panel he could just see a middle-aged woman in the bed, her arms so thin they looked like sticks. Her eyes were closed and she had on a black wig. A man with grey hair and a face lined by grief sat on one side of her, his hand resting gently on her forearm; his fingers trembled intermittently. On the other side a younger man, in his twenties, his face flushed from crying, held her hand loosely. They were both repeating the words 'I love you' in quiet, strained voices.

'Are you a relative?' The voice made him start. A black nurse, short and dumpy with a pleasant face, was at his side.

'No. I'm sorry, I didn't mean to intrude. I just ...' His eyes returned unbidden to the painful tableau. 'What's wrong with her?'

The nurse smiled, but she wasn't going to give much away. 'She hasn't got long. She's been in a coma for the last day. But she can still hear, we think, so they're just saying what they feel, trying to show her she's loved.'

Before the end, Church thought. He looked on to the double doors where he could now see people of all ages lying in the beds. 'Them too?'

'Leukaemia mainly. Some others. The boy in the room behind's just had a bone marrow transplant. We need to keep him isolated because he's susceptible to infection.'

'Looks like some people's worlds are ending ahead of schedule.' Laura had walked up unseen and had been watching the two men whispering to their wife and mother. Church rounded on her to berate her for her callousness until he saw her eyes were brimming with tears.

The nurse glanced at them both, then said questioningly. 'Is there someone—?'

'No,' Church apologised. 'A friend's just been rushed into an operating theatre. I got lost.'

'Easily done,' she smiled. 'This place is a rabbit warren. The next floor up.'

'Where's Ruth?' Church asked as he led the way up the stairs.

'In reception, sulking.'

202

Church guessed that wasn't the case, but said nothing. When they reached the next floor, he held open the door and said, 'I never thought about the repercussions.'

'What do you mean?'

'How many people rely on technology. That boy in the isolation unit, all those monitors and electronically regulated drips—' He broke off when he saw Marianne's father sitting on a chair with his head in his hands. 'How is she?' Church asked cautiously.

'They're just prepping her now. The op should take about five hours, they reckon. They think we got here in time. If all goes well—' He swallowed, grasped Church's hand again. 'Thank God you were there.' Church sat next to him, listening to the clinical sounds of the hospital, the rat-chat of swing doors, the measured step of soles on lino, the clink of trolleys, the whir of lifts. 'I've spent years preparing myself for this moment and it hasn't done one bloody bit of good,' the farmer continued. 'I should've just pretended she wasn't ill and dealt with this when it happened.' He added bleakly, 'I hope I haven't wasted the time I've had with her.'

'No point thinking about the past,' Church said calmly but forcefully.

'Do you believe in God?' The farmer's hands were shaking. He caught his wrist, then buried his hands in the folds of his jacket.

'I'd like to,' Church replied guiltily.

'And so would I. I used to pray, when we first found out about Marianne. I stopped after a while. I couldn't really see the good of it, you know? It didn't seem like the kind of thing grown-ups should be doing. The wife kept at it, though. Down the church every Sunday. I should have carried on. That was me being selfish.' Church politely disagreed, but the farmer waved him quiet. 'She's the only one we've got. We never seemed to get round to having any more, but she got lots more love because of it. You couldn't have wanted for a better child. Never been any trouble. Always done her schoolwork, passed her exams. Never been lippy to me or the wife. Helped out around the farm, even when I didn't want her to because she was going through one of her bad periods. She's a bit of a dreamer, I suppose. Used to read books all the time. Not like me. I like to be out there, bloody well doing stuff with my hands. But Marianne, she liked to think.' He paused reflectively. 'I always hoped she'd take over the farm one day.'

'She still might.'

The farmer nodded, tight-lipped, refusing to tempt fate. For a long period they sat in silence, listening to their thoughts. Laura seemed to grow uncomfortable at the inactivity and after a while muttered something about going off to find the canteen.

Through the windows at the end of the corridor Church watched the night draw in, wrapping itself around the storm that still buffeted the building. Flashes of lightning flared briefly like the distant fires in the void he had witnessed through the windows of the Watchtower.

When four hours had elapsed, a nurse emerged from the theatre, her expression closed. The farmer caught her arm as she passed and pleaded for some information.

'I can't really say. Mr Persaud will be out as soon as he knows the situation,' she began, but looking at his face, she relented a little. 'It looks like it's going well,' she said with a comforting smile. 'Barring anything unforeseen—'

As if her comment had been heard by the gods, in that instant all the lights went out. The farmer cried out in shock as the darkness swallowed them. 'Just a power cut,' the nurse said reassuringly, before muttering, 'Bloody storm.' The lack of illumination through the window suggested it had hit most of the city. 'Don't worry. We're well prepared for things like this,' she continued. 'We've got an emergency generator that will kick in any second.'

Like statues, they waited in the claustrophobic dark, their heavy breath kept tight in their lungs.

'Any moment now,' the nurse repeated. There was an edge in her voice that hadn't been there before.

It was as if the entire hospital had been held in stasis, but then the dam broke and the cries started far off, rippling towards them in a wave of despair and anxiety. Church heard the rattle of the nurse's feet as she ran from their side and then the bang of the swing door as she disappeared back towards the operating theatre. The cry that squeezed out from the farmer's throat was filled with such devastation that Church felt tears sting his eyes. A man calling out, 'They're dying! They're dying!' reverberated up the stairwell, followed by the jarring punch of a woman screaming, 'Do something!'

The movement came out of nowhere; people rushing by in the dark, what could have been a hair's breadth away, or several feet. Church tried to remember where the wall was for safety, but before he could move someone clipped him hard and he slammed against it with such force he lost consciousness.

When he recovered, the chaos had reached a crescendo. He didn't know how long he had been out, but screams and shouts punctuated the gloom, along with the sound of running feet like machine-gun fire. Church called out for the farmer, but there was no reply. He felt a sudden wave of despair when he realised there was no way the surgeons would be able to finish the operation; Marianne would be dying, if she wasn't already dead.

Before he could dwell on it, someone came hurrying along the corridor and knocked him over again.

The intense confusion and claustrophobia left his thoughts in a whirl, but he know he ought to get to the ground floor as soon as possible. He found the stairwell easily enough by scrambling along the wall. Negotiating the descent was trickier; he clung to the railing and felt for each step like a blind man.

As he reached the next floor, a burst of the purest white

light suddenly flared through the glass panel in the door, so bright it lit the entire stairwell. It faded just as quickly, leaving flashes of purple dancing across his retinas. It had been far too dazzling for a torch, and without electricity nothing else could have explained the quality or the intensity of the illumination. He fumbled for the door handle and stepped out into the hall.

Oddly, the screams and cries on that ward had died away, leaving an incongruous atmosphere of tranquillity. The stillness was broken a second or two later by the sound of a man crying, only the sobbing didn't seem despairing. Then there was laughter, tinged with an obvious note of disbelief, and someone whispering, 'Thank God!' over and over again.

Another flash of the burning white light erupted through the double doors that led to the wider ward and in its glare Church caught a glimpse of a scene he would never forget. The woman the nurse had told him was in a coma and dying of leukaemia stood in the doorway of her room, tubes trailing from her arms and nose like decorations. She was staring at her hands in incomprehension, a smile of amazement drawn across her face. Her husband and son had their arms around her, burying their faces into her neck, their bodies racked with sobs of joy. And then the darkness returned again.

Desperate to understand, Church propelled himself through the double doors. As he crossed the threshold into the larger ward the power came back on. The patients, many of whom had seemed close to death, were sitting up in their beds, examining themselves with new eyes, smiling, chatting to those around them. Some were clambering out, testing legs that hadn't walked with strength for weeks, pulling out chemotherapy drips with distaste.

One tall man, his skin sun-browned but his body wasted by the illness, smiled broadly at Church. 'What ho! I feel like I could run a marathon!' He pulled back the sheets to reveal a long scar on his lower belly. 'Cancer. They said the op hadn't worked.' He held out his hands in joyous disbelief.

Moving through the wave of uplifting emotion, Church looked for some clue to what had happened. Then, when he reached the far wall, he noticed a small figure slumped on the floor like a bundle of dirty clothes. With shock, he realised it was Marianne. Before he had even knelt at her side, he could tell she was dead; she was covered in blood which had poured from the open incision on her shaved head. The wound seemed to have partly sealed itself – there was no evidence of stitching – but it was still impossible to believe she could have made it even a few feet from the operating table. Inexplicably, there was faint charring of the skin around her eyes so that it appeared she was wearing a black mask; despite that, her pale face was composed.

Church took her hand, marvelling at the softness of her skin as stinging tears sprang to his eyes.

'She did it.' A short, dumpy man with chemo-baldness stood behind him. 'At first I thought she was a ghost walking through the ward. After the lights went, I thought it was the end – I was a bit delirious, I think. And then there she was.' He raised his hands in awe. 'Suddenly she burned with the brightest white light. It was the most amazing thing. I thought, "She's an angel come for me." And when the light fell on me I suddenly felt better.' The tears were streaming down his cheeks at the memory. 'She carried on through the ward and did it again. She made everybody better. And then she just fell down here like she'd burned herself out.'

Church brushed a stray hair from her forehead, touched her cheek with his fingertips, as if the contact would in some way impart an awareness of what had truly happened. He took out the locket she had lent him – only the previous day – and considered fastening it around her neck; let Princess Diana guide her into the light. But then he hesitated, before slipping it back into his pocket. Even though their meeting had been brief, Marianne had been inspirational to him and he wanted something to remind him of her. Perhaps the new saint for the new age really would do him good too. All he could think was that in that terrible, awesome new world, belief and faith really could move mountains. Magic was alive, and it wasn't just the providence of the dark side; good people could make a difference too, lighting a beacon that would shine out in the coming night.

CHAPTER NINE

At the Heart of the Storm

Ruth and Laura were waiting anxiously for Church in reception. They were surrounded by a chaotic mass of distraught relatives, bewildered patients and hard-pressed hospital staff, their faces uniformly etched with painful disbelief. Church felt sick from the piercing noise; alarms were ringing throughout the building, mingling with the terrible sounds of grief and the barking of orders. Occasionally he caught a whiff of smoke carried on draughts from the heart of the hospital.

His journey from the cancer ward had been one of the most painful he had ever made. All the nurses had been caught up in the crisis, so he carried Marianne to a bed and drew a sheet over her before setting off in search of her father to break the news. Church found him in a state of near breakdown, running frantically around outside the operating theatre, desperately begging any passing hospital employee for information on his daughter's whereabouts. When he read Church's face he crumpled like a sick child, lost in tearing sobs that seemed to suck the breath from him. Church felt broken inside; it was even more unfair than the farmer realised: two months ago, a week ago, perhaps only a day earlier, the power cut would not have happened and Marianne might have lived.

Her father was immune to any attempts to comfort him and Church could do nothing but leave him there. As he hurried down through the floors, all his own painful thoughts about Marianne were lost as he became aware of the true devastation the power cut had wrought. On each floor the victims of failed life support systems were laid out on trolleys with sheets thrown over them. The hospital staff seemed to be wandering around dumbly. One nurse was in tears as she demanded answers from a colleague; not only had the power supply failed to a regulated drip, but the back-up battery had also ceased to work. 'How do you explain that?' she pleaded. By the time Church reached reception, he felt nauseous. He couldn't bring himself to answer Ruth and Laura's questions, and headed out to the car in silence, head bowed into the raging storm.

They picked up the M5 in the city and followed the lantern's flame back south. High winds buffeted the car and the rain lashed the windscreen with such force the wipers could barely function.

'Think of those cancer patients – *they*'ve survived. *Some* good has come of it,' Ruth said hopefully. 'Marianne did that. She achieved something wonderful with her life, gave hope ... magic ... to people lost in despair. That's more than most could ever dream of doing. It made her life mean something.'

'I can see that,' Church replied darkly, 'but it doesn't make it better.' He smiled bitterly as a flash of lightning glared off the roof of a Porsche going too fast for the weather, the driver unaware that his gleaming status symbol would soon be going the way of the dinosaurs. 'That scene at the hospital was like something out of the Middle Ages. And it's going to be like that all over the country ... all over the world ... before too long. I understood what was happening in an abstract way, but *that*'s the true cost of the upheaval that's being inflicted on us. It's not about TVs breaking down and cars working randomly. It's about human suffering on an unimaginable scale. It's about the end of our entire way of life.'

'So it's not about Marianne, then?' Laura chipped in pointedly from the back seat.

Church didn't respond.

The storm didn't seem to be abating. Muscles aching from being hunched over the wheel trying to peer through the driving rain, Church eventually drew off the motorway into the Taunton Deane services. He stretched out the stress knots in his back, then turned on the radio and searched for some report about the crisis at the hospital; he wanted to know how they were going to explain it. But the Radio 4 news only carried a couple of dull political stories, one about a sharp dip on the FTSE and a report about the police investigation into the horrific knife murders in the north-west; even the local stations made no mention of it.

'There's something wrong here,' he said. 'The news must have got out by now.'

'Maybe they're covering it up,' Ruth suggested.

They went to the restaurant for a drink and an attempt to plan their next step. It was empty, apart from one bored youth on the checkout, and with the storm blasting in the dark night, it felt like they had been marooned on a comfort-less island.

While Ruth and Laura went to the toilet, Church brooded over his coffee. Although there were three of them, he felt the responsibility for success or failure was increasingly being heaped on his shoulders. For some reason he had been singled out – by Tom, by the woman in the Watchtower – and he really didn't know if he were up to what was expected of him. But he accepted, whatever the outcome, that he couldn't turn his back on the responsibility; he had always firmly believed in facing up to obligation.

Carefully, he drew out the Black Rose and examined it closely; it hadn't wilted in the slightest. The petals were warm and silky, almost luxurious to the touch, and the scent, if anything, was even more heady. He hadn't questioned the gift of the flower before, but if he heeded the young Mari-anne's advice about forgetting the past and enjoying the present, he knew he should throw it away; no good could possibly come of it. He brought it up to his lips, kissed it absently, traced it across his cheek as he weighed up his choice. Then he slipped it back into his pocket.

Church sipped his coffee, listening to the hiss of cars speeding by outside. Perhaps it was just the weather, but there seemed to be less traffic using the motorway than he would have expected for the time of year. He wondered if the change coming over the country was starting to affect people subconsciously, an unspecified unease that nagged away at them constantly. Lightning flashed, a clap of thunder rumbled loudly; the storm was directly overhead.

But as the peal died away, Church thought he heard something else, mingling with the noise, continuing for just a split second longer. It left the hairs on the back of his neck standing erect. He stood up and walked over to the window; beyond the dismal lights of the car park, the wooded hillsides clustered darkly.

He returned to his table, but couldn't settle. It bothered him that he was jumping at the slightest sound. When the rumbling thunder made the windows boom once more, he listened carefully, but there was no subsequent sound. Yet he was sure he had heard it before. And it had sounded like the howl of a dog.

'So do you think he's going to lose it?' Laura said above the whir of the hand-drier.

Ruth leaned against the wash basins, her arms folded. 'He's got his problems, but nothing he can't handle.'

'You saw him when he came out of the hospital—'

'Hardly surprising after seeing all that suffering. If you had any kind of heart you'd understand—'

'I understand all right. But it wasn't just those people dying. It was the girl. He's got her all mixed up in his head with that dead girlfriend of his.' The drier died and suddenly the toilet seemed unnervingly lonely, trapped in the uncomfortable glare of the artificial lights. 'This isn't some nice jaunt to see the sights. It's life or death and a hundred other clichés. We can't afford someone tripping us up because they're too lost in their head.'

'What do you suggest? We dump him?' Ruth led the way out into the main corridor. There were a few travellers, but no one was hanging around; they all seemed eager to get back to their cars, back to their homes.

'Aren't we Frosty the Snowman? Bothered that I'm attacking your boyfriend?' Ruth flinched at the lash of Laura's mockery. 'I'm saying we keep an eye on him. Rein him in if he gets too freaky.'

'He'll be fine,' Ruth said coldly. 'You just worry about yourself. For a change.'

Lightning lit up the car park like a searchlight. Ruth had gone on several steps before she noticed she was walking alone. Behind her, Laura was peering out into the night. 'I saw something,' she said. Ruth could tell it had unnerved her.

Cautiously they approached the electronic doors, which hummed open like magic. Stepping out into the area where the overhang of the roof protected them from the rain, they searched the car park. There seemed more cars than there were travellers in the services, but the night made it impossible to see if there was anyone inside them. Parts of the car park were already flooded and water was bubbling up out of the drains. Rain gusted across the open areas in sheets and overhead a rumble of thunder barely died away before another started. It was a bleakly unfriendly scene.

'Doesn't seem to be anyone out there,' Ruth ventured.

'It was big, on all fours. Like a shadow, shifting quickly.'

'You're sure it wasn't a trick of the lightning?'

Laura stepped out into the full force of the rain. It plastered her blonde hair on to her head within seconds. 'There's something moving. Out among the cars.'

'How can you see? It's so dark.' Ruth joined her in the

213

rain. The pounding droplets were heavy and icy, forcing their way down the back of her neck, soaking her jeans. 'I don't think we should—'

'You scurry back to be with your boyfriend if you like.'

Ruth felt like punching her. 'Oh yes. Real smart to put ourselves at risk when we could be the only ones with a chance to stop the world going to hell.'

'You do what you want. I'm not hiding away.'

An incongruous note in Laura's voice made Ruth suddenly aware there was more at play than mere bravado. 'And what are you planning to do when you discover what's out there?'

Without answering, Laura set off with Ruth close behind, regretting every step, but unable to let Laura go into the dark alone. She felt a spark of primal fear. Amidst the pounding of the rain, the wild gusting of the wind and the susurration of car wheels on the motorway, any sound of movement in the car park was drowned out; the lights seemed too dim to dispel the deeper shadows.

There were some twenty cars which could provide a hiding place for whatever Laura had seen. A few were scattered at random around the car park, but most were clustered together in the centre. By the time they reached the first one, their clinging clothes were hampering them. As they passed some of the vehicles they glimpsed an occasional pale face staring out, hands gripping steering wheels as if the drivers were afraid to move away from the oasis of light offered by the service station.

'I still don't see anything,' Ruth said, but almost as soon as her words were lost to the wind and rain they heard a low, rumbling growl, like distant thunder. Ruth clutched at Laura's arm and they both froze, unable to tell the direction of the noise. 'An animal,' Ruth said.

'You're so sharp you'll cut yourself.' Laura's mockery was drained of its usual acid.

'I think we should get back,' Ruth said. Laura hesitated, then nodded, but as they turned, a shape flashed between them and the building. Ruth caught a glimpse of something burning red, like hot coals.

Moving quickly over to one side, they tried for an elliptical route back to the light. Another growl, closer at hand this time, turned into a chilling howl.

'Shit!' Laura hissed.

Ruth thought: *It's hunting*.

And then they were running, the splashing of their feet accompanied by the thunder of powerful paws. Whatever it was crashed into a car in front with such force the side crumpled and it spun into their path. Ruth stifled a scream. They darted sideways between two other cars, no longer knowing in which direction they were running. Along the way, Laura slammed into a wing mirror and careened into the other vehicle. Ruth was already several feet away before she realised Laura had slipped to her knees.

As she turned she caught sight of the black shape, as big as a small pony; it shifted its bulk and started to run. If it hit the nearest car, Laura would be crushed between them. Without thinking, Ruth sprinted back as Laura hauled herself to her feet. At the moment Ruth yanked on Laura's jacket, there was the sledgehammer sound of buckling metal and a crash as the windscreen exploded. The impact hurled them backwards into a deep puddle.

The beast leapt and slammed on to the bonnet where it poised over them. Their minds locked in fear at the first clear sight of it. It was the dog that had attacked Church in Salisbury. Black Shuck. The horribly intelligent eyes burned crimson as its hot breath steamed in the chill night. The rain was running in rivulets off its black velvet hide, mingling with the sizzling drool that dripped from its fangs. Unable to move, Ruth and Laura watched as its muscles bunched. Slowly, it raised its haunches to attack.

Then, from out of the swirling rain, there was a penetrating screech as an owl swooped down, claws raised at the dog's eyes. It soared away just as the beast snapped its enormous head round. But it was enough of a distraction; Ruth and Laura were already moving as the dog's jaws gnashed on empty air.

The services seemed to be at the distant end of a dark tunnel. Their lungs burned from exertion, but they closed the gap quickly as they heard the beast leap from the bonnet and start to pound the tarmac behind them. *We're not going to make it,* Ruth thought. The sound of its feet thundered closer. But then, miraculously, the doors were opening and they were slipping and sliding on the floor in the glaring lights.

Any thoughts they had reached sanctuary were dispelled a moment later. The dog was travelling with such speed the doors didn't have time to open again. They burst inwards, showering glass and twisted metal across the floor as the dog skidded, then righted itself. Two women emerging from the toilets shrieked and darted back inside. Another man chose that unfortunate moment to wander haphazardly out of the shop. The dog turned its head and in one fluid movement of its jaws, took his arm off at the shoulder. It was too quick for him to scream; he blacked out from the shock and collapsed into a growing pool of blood. Ruth and Laura scrambled away again, their eyes burning with tears of fear.

They could hear the rasping breath of the dog echoing along the corridor as they sprinted to the restaurant, a rough, traction engine sound filled with power and menace. As they burst in, Church's face registered momentary shock at their bedraggled appearance, but then he was moving without asking any questions.

'Into the kitchen,' he hissed, hauling them towards the hot food counter. They scrambled over it, burning themselves on the hot metal. When the dog entered a second later, the youth on the checkout took one look at it and slipped under his till, either in a faint or in fear. In the kitchen, two bored cooks waited patiently for orders. Their sudden flurry of protests were silenced by the roar of the dog.

'My God, what's that?' one of the women cried, eyes wide.

'Can you lock this door?' Church demanded. It was of a reinforced design to contain a fire.

The woman nodded in confusion, fumbling for a bunch of keys in her pockets. Through the door, the beast's rasping breath drew closer. There was a clang as it jumped on the hot food counter and then a dull thud as it landed on the other side. As the woman located the key, Church snatched it from her hands and secured the door. They retreated to the other side of the room and ducked down behind a stainless steel unit just as the dog thundered against it.

'What's out there?' the other woman whimpered.

Church looked to Ruth. 'Black Shuck,' she said in a small, cracking voice. She suddenly started to shake from the cold and the shock. Church slid his arms around her shoulders and pulled her close to him. 'Is it going to be like this all the way?' she said weakly. 'Never being able to rest?'

There was another crash against the door and they all jumped.

'What's going on?' one of the cooks screamed. She crawled away with the other woman, casting angry, frightened glances at Church, Ruth and Laura.

'How can we hold off something like that?' Ruth said. 'It's going to get us sooner or later.'

'The dog isn't the worst of it,' Church replied fatalistically. 'You heard what Tom said. It's a precursor, a portent.'

'For what?' Laura asked. As if in answer, there came a mighty clattering on the roof far above them, rumbling from one side of the building to the other; like hoofbeats. The dog howled, in warning or welcome.

Ruth saw the vaguest shadow pass across Laura's features; in the imposing edifice of her confidence it was as if the foundations had shattered. Cautiously, Ruth reached out a comforting hand to Laura's arm; Laura flinched, didn't look at her, but nor did she knock it away.

* * *

217

They stayed huddled there for the rest of the night, listening to the sounds beyond the door; the grunts and growls, snufflings and crashings that couldn't have come from any beast born on earth. On one occasion, after a forty-five-minute gulf of silence, they thought it had finally departed, but just as Church was about to turn the key in the lock it crashed against the door, almost bursting it inwards. It was a warning that they heeded.

When the faintest glimmer of dawn first brushed the clouds, Church ventured to the slatted glass windows and opened them just enough to look out. The motorway was empty, the storm blown out, although the clouds still roiled above them. And in that surging vapour he had the uneasy feeling he could glimpse dark figures on horseback, riding the clouds, lost among them; seeking refuge from the light, ready to return another night.

He turned to the others. 'Let's go,' he said.

The restaurant was empty, the dog gone, as Church knew it would be. The two cooks ran out, crying with relief, to greet the checkout youth who emerged from beneath the till looking like he'd been sedated; he hadn't come between the monstrous dog and its prey, so it had left him alone. The reinforced kitchen door was gouged and splintered.

The rest of the services seemed deserted, but Church eventually located some members of staff in the management office. In a room beyond they could see the covered body of the man who lost his arm to the dog. Phone lines had been down throughout the night, so no emergency services could have been called; even mobiles hadn't worked. Some kind of electrical disturbance caused by the storm, the staff said, but that didn't explain what had happened to those who had gone off in their cars to fetch help and had not been heard from since. No one seemed quite able to believe that what had taken place had actually happened. They talked of wild dogs, as if there had been a pack, and seemed oblivious to

218

anything uncanny. Church, Ruth and Laura returned to the car park, leaving them trying to impose some order on an event that wouldn't accept it.

As they approached the car they noticed the interior light was on and one door was slightly ajar. They circled the Nissan cautiously, suddenly on guard, until they noticed the boot was open too, the contents of their bags strewn around the interior. A knife or screwdriver had been crudely forced into the keyhole.

'Bastards!' Laura said. 'We've really been hit with the bad luck stick.'

'I don't think it's a coincidence,' Church said as he sifted through their possessions.

'You think they were looking for the stone?' Laura asked, her hand automatically going to the rucksack.

He nodded. 'But whatever was here last night wouldn't have jimmied open the boot.'

They repacked their possessions in silence, filled up with petrol and returned to the motorway, haunted by too many unanswered questions.

After the storm, the day turned bright and clear. At that early hour the motorway was eerily devoid of even the slow caravans of lorries lumbering towards Exeter and Torbay. The scenery gradually changed as they crossed the county line, the tranquil green fields of Somerset giving way to Devon's wilder landscape of hills, rocky outcroppings and impenetrable, dark woods, filled with romance in the glimmering post-dawn light. At Exeter, the lantern, which Ruth held in her lap like a baby, began to tug westwards. The motorway died just south of the city anyway, so they picked up the A30 which ran all the way down to the end of the world along the spine of Cornwall. They were only on it for a short while as the lantern suddenly flickered with irritation and guided them on to a tiny B road which spiked into the heart of Dartmoor.

'I don't like it when we get too far away from civilisation.' Ruth glanced uncomfortably out of the window at the disappearing habitation as they moved toward the looming expanse of Dartmoor on the horizon.

'You should see the map,' Laura said, poring over Church's *AA Book of the Road*. 'The roads around here look about good enough for pig-droving, and there're only a handful of villages, all with about three houses in them. Welcome to Nowhere.'

As the fields became scrubby uplands and windswept rocks, Ruth said uneasily, 'I wonder what's out there.' Then, after a moment or two when neither of them answered, 'I want tall buildings, cars, pollution—'

'I don't think that would be any safer,' Church said. 'It's just an illusion.'

Laura suddenly craned her neck to peer through the side window up into the blue sky. 'Hey! There's another one! I thought they slept during the day?'

Ruth followed her gaze. An enormous owl swooped on the air currents, dipped low, then soared again, but it seemed to have no trouble keeping up with them. Ruth squinted, trying to pluck details from the silhouette; she knew instinctively it was her *familiar*, the same one that had attacked the beast in the car park.

For some reason she didn't quite understand, Ruth still hadn't got around to telling them about her meeting with the mysterious girl in the glade. Although she had been disturbed by it, in some way it had seemed intensely private and to talk about it felt instinctively like a betrayal of trust; which was a strange way to think about it. Besides, in the cold light of day it hadn't seemed frightening at all.

'That one at the services saved our lives,' Laura continued.

'It doesn't make sense,' Church said. 'Why would a bird do something like that? They're normally smart.'

Ruth didn't answer. Now she was speculating on why the girl had particularly used that word *familiar*, with all its connotations. She followed the owl's progress carefully, and wondered.

Soon the last signs of civilisation disappeared. As if on cue, another storm blew up from nowhere. It swamped the blue sky with slate-coloured clouds that billowed and twisted in high winds like the smoke from some conflagration, and drew a line of shadow across the land. Lightning flashed on the horizon and thunder boomed out dully. Church flicked on the wipers a second after the first drops hit, but it was like someone had thrown a bucket of water at the windscreen. He pulled the car over to the side of the road in the hope that it would pass and instantly felt exhaustion overcome him. Reluctantly he suggested they find somewhere to rest.

When the rain lessened slightly, they continued slowly on their way, but there was little to see. They passed through a place called Two Bridges right in the centre of Dartmoor which seemed to consist of just one house and a sprawling, white-painted pub tucked away in a hollow. And then, as they crested the ridge beyond, they came across an ancient inn made of Devonshire stone with a half-timbered upper storey; squat and heavy, it looked as if it had been thrown up out of the ground by some force of nature. The Elizabethan windows were a mass of tiny panes, too dark to see through, although Church did catch sight of the welcoming flicker of an open fire. An old wooden sign swung in the gale featuring a hand-painted design of a vaguely human face made out of leaves and the legend The Green Man, the ancient title which offered a particular welcome to travellers. A small note in the window said *Accommodation*.

Church pulled the car on to the tiny pockmarked car park and they sprinted through the rain to the stone porch. The door was locked – it was well before opening time – but Church hammered on a brass knocker until they heard movement within. The door swung open to reveal a thin man in tight blue jeans and a white T-shirt that flapped on his bony frame. He was severely balding, with just tufts of black hair curling back over his ears. A thick moustache hung like a brush over his top lip. He had eyes like a rodent, darting and curious, and a scar curved over the right one, but his smile was pleasant enough.

'Waifs and strays from the storm?' he enquired in a fey, accentless voice.

'We could do with some rooms if you've got any spare,' Church said.

'As you can see, it's not exactly Piccadilly Circus round here at this time of year so I think you might be in luck.' He stepped back and swept his arm theatrically to invite them in. The tasteful décor of the pub reflected the building's great age: stone flags, dark wood tables, benches and stools, a few line drawings and old photographs on the stone walls. The fire Church had seen earlier burned heartily in a fireplace big enough to have two small bench seats inside the chimney breast. The landlord saw Church looking at it. 'Nice, isn't it? I have to keep it going, even in summer, though. There's a superstition in these parts that if the fire ever goes out the landlord will meet a terrible death. I don't believe it myself, naturally, being a sophisticated urbanite, but then again I'm not about to take unnecessary risks.'

There were only three guest bedrooms, none of them taken, huddled up where the sloping roof made Church stoop; the tiny windows were low down so he had to bend even further to look out. The rooms were cosy with brass beds, old-fashioned bedspreads and an open grate in every room. The landlord, who introduced himself as Simon, busied himself lighting a fire in each of them, 'to take the damp out of the air.' He seemed to enjoy the company and within minutes his non-stop chat had given them the abridged version of his life story. He used to run a bar in Leeds with his partner Stuart, but after a holiday in Devon they'd decided to buy The Green Man, which was then ramshackle and in danger of being pulled down. 'We're missionaries,' he said sardonically.

'We're here to bring wit and sophistication to a backward culture which doesn't realise the importance of good food, good wine and perfect interior design.'

'Leeds to Dartmoor is a dramatic move,' Church said.

Simon shrugged. 'It felt right, that's all I can say. Too many people expect you to follow the unwritten rules, but sometimes it's better just to go with what you feel inside. So I can't buy a good shirt or a decent pair of shoes round here – but at least I'm queen of all she surveys. Just call me a drop-out.'

There was something he wasn't telling them and when Ruth asked him about the jagged scar above his right eye he shifted uncomfortably. 'Small minds don't know much, but they know how to aim well.' It seemed he would leave it there, but the issue obviously still burned. 'We had a nice house in a nice suburb, but gradually we noticed the ambience of the area changing. Normally you expect a drug gang or some criminal layabouts to change the mood of a neighbourhood, but in this case it was the God Squad.' He sucked on his lip angrily. 'Born Agains. Fundamentalists. All those racist comments about ethnic groups colonising an area, well, no one is a patch on them. They were some particular sect based at an academy they'd had built in the area. I don't know what stripe – they're all the same to me. *He* didn't die for me.'

His eyes narrowed as he searched their faces for any anger at his comments, then he continued: 'They snapped up a house for sale in the street at well over the asking price. Then, whenever one came on the market, they were always first in the queue. It didn't take long before we were infested.' He sighed. 'You know, I'm an easy-going person – it takes a lot to rattle my cage. But it soon became obvious they didn't want people like Stuart and I in the area. Their Rule Book sees us as the spawn of Satan or something. I mean, so much for the Christian hand of fellowship. We used to know everyone in the street and we all looked out for each other.

Suddenly we couldn't find anyone to talk to us. There were little things . . . constant calls to the police complaining that our car was double-parked. Then I got a call from the local paper. I used to help out at a nursery in my spare time, just organising parties, entertaining the kiddies, that sort of thing. I'd done it for years. But suddenly there'd been complaints that I wasn't a *fit and proper person*, whatever that means. It was after that that things started getting mean.'

'How awful,' Ruth said with honest concern.

He shrugged dismissively. 'Oh, it's one of our burdens in life. Anyway, one thing led to another and then one night when we were walking home some sneaky little coward threw a half-brick out of the shadows. It caught me just here.' He traced the scar, then snapped his hand into a fist. 'I wouldn't have minded, but they got blood all over my favourite shirt,' he said with a bitter smile.

'And that's why you moved?' Ruth asked.

'Actually, no. I've never run from things that threaten my way of life. But then there were so many of them they started standing for the council, elbowing their way on to school boards, anywhere where they could have influence. Once values like that get a political platform you know the apocalypse is on the horizon. Agents of the Devil, all of them. Stuart and I were on the next train out.'

He seemed filled with a terrible rage at the injustice of it all, but he moved on to enthusing with passion about his plans for the pub. It seemed obvious from his comments that he had found some kind of acceptance in the small, rural community not normally noted for an outward-looking attitude; the irony was not lost on them.

He would have talked all afternoon if they'd let him, but eventually he wandered off to let them settle in. They chose their rooms and went straight to bed, listening to the rain gust against the windows, straining to hear the howl of a dog away in the wind, afraid to close their eyes.

* * *

Church's dreams were tumultuous and disturbing. The woman from the Watchtower was there, beseeching him to do something, but he couldn't hear her words, just see her troubled expression and her outstretched arms. And then there were things circling him, drawing closer: low, bestial shapes that at times moved on four legs, then on two. Behind him he felt eyes boring into his head and an overwhelming feeling of dread, but his legs were stone and he couldn't turn to see who or what was waiting there. A sudden pain stabbed into his hand and he looked down to behold the Black Rose. A thorn had protruded mysteriously from the stem and had pierced the fleshy part of his palm. The blood fell like rain, splashing his clothes, staining the ground beneath his feet, running away in a trickle that turned into a torrent.

He woke with a start. Twilight had fallen and the fire had been reduced to a few raw embers in the grate: the faint red glow was strangely comforting. He couldn't believe he had slept so long. Remembering the fading remnants of his dream, he pulled the Black Rose from his pocket and examined it cautiously. There was no sign of any thorn. He stroked it lovingly, then glanced into the shadows in the corners of the room.

'Marianne? Can you hear me?' His voice rustled like paper in the still air. He waited hopefully for a moment and then swung his legs off the bed and rested his head in his hands.

Through the window, Dartmoor looked cold and menacing, a muddy smear of charcoal and grey and brown beneath a churning sky. At least the rain had stopped.

There was faint music coming through the floorboards, the Pet Shop Boys singing 'Being Boring' so he made his way downstairs to the bar to see Simon dancing alone in front of the roaring fire. He squealed when Church spoke.

'Lordy, you gave me a start! Do you always creep around like a thief in the night?'

Church shrugged. 'I didn't know I was creeping.'

'Well you were!' Simon flounced to the bar, then did another little dance and finished with a forgiving smile. 'Enjoy your beauty sleep?'

Church nodded. 'Any chance of something to eat?'

'You're a lucky boy. Stuart's a gourmet chef and when I say gourmet, I mean to die for. He was out all day buying some goodies in Plymouth, so we have some mouth-watering delights for tonight's menu. Salmon, John Dory, lamb in a redcurrant sauce, something very delicious with pasta and squid ink. You'll think you've died and gone to heaven. They've started to come from all over to sample his wares, so to speak.'

He disappeared behind the bar and returned with a hand-written menu. 'I hope you'll be staying around later. It's entertainment night. A little spot of glamour in a bleak landscape.'

Church smiled falsely, but his mind was elsewhere: Marianne, dead on the floor; the young Marianne, dead in his arms; his own body lying in a stream. Sometimes he wondered how he managed to keep going.

His food arrived quickly, and the pan-roasted chicken and spring onions was as good as Simon had promised. It seemed forever since he'd eaten, and as he was tucking into it hungrily Ruth emerged, her hair still wet from the shower. She looked fully refreshed, untroubled even, and flashed him a warm smile as she slipped in opposite him.

'Thinking of your stomach again,' she said, leaning over to pluck a piece of chicken from his plate.

'You seem different.' He searched her face, which seemed to glow with an inner light.

'What do you mean?'

'I don't know.' He shrugged. 'I've only noticed it since the other night when we camped out. You seem stronger somehow.'

She laughed easily and snatched up the menu. 'I didn't feel it last night with that dog chasing me.'

'At least you kept going. Most people would have keeled over faced with something like that.' He paused, averting his gaze to toy with his food. 'I'm glad you're on board.'

Ruth's eyes sparkled, but she restrained a broad smile. 'That's the closest thing to a compliment I've heard from your lips.'

'Make the most of it. That's as good as it gets.' He finished off the last of the chicken and pushed the plate away. 'I guess it would help if we knew exactly where we were going and what we were supposed to do when we got there.'

Simon lurched out from behind the bar humping a machine which he placed on a table. Sweating and cursing under his breath, he proceeded to drag tables and chairs around noisily until he had cleared a space in one corner. A young black man emerged from the bar area wearing an irritated expression. He was astonishingly attractive, with perfect cheekbones, well-defined muscles beneath his silk shirt and a faintly feminine turn to his features. They guessed he was Simon's partner. There was engine oil on his hands and he was brandishing a spanner. He was obviously about to launch into some tirade when he spotted Church and Ruth and smiled with embarrassment.

'He's tinkering with his motorbike while I'm breaking my back,' Simon said with theatrical haughtiness; it was clearly the source of their disagreement.

Ruth glanced anxiously at the windows, where a gust brought a splatter of rain as if someone had thrown it; it was too dark to see beyond the circle of light cast by the porch lamps.

'You think Black Shuck will come tonight?' Her eyes grew fearful.

'We're doing the best we can, Ruth,' he said firmly. 'We're out of our depth here. We have no defence against these things. You can't plan for it. I think we just have to face up to crises when they materialise, like anything else in life. What do you suggest?'

'I don't know.' She looked into the fire, wishing they were sitting closer together. 'Do you think we can trust Laura?' she asked incongruously.

'Don't you?'

'I don't know. Sometimes. I don't like her attitude, and I'm not convinced she always tells the truth, like she's got some secret agenda.'

'She's not going to win any good personality awards, but she seems okay so far.'

Ruth tried to read any more in his comments than there appeared. She was convinced he was attracted to Laura, whether he knew it or not, and she hoped her suspicions weren't born out of jealousy because of it. For someone who had always maintained emotional equilibrium, her latest predicament unnerved Ruth with its unpredictability. Her feelings for Church had crept up on her, forged through their harrowing experiences, yet she couldn't see a glimmer of a response in him. She didn't know if that was because he was still trapped in his feelings for Marianne, or if he simply didn't care, but she knew, deep inside, she felt like she'd finally found something for which she'd been waiting all her life.

'If you have any doubts you should say.' Church looked her in the eye. 'I'm not always the most perceptive of people.'

'Not yet. When I'm sure.' Ruth made her selection from the menu and caught Simon's eye as he pushed the makeshift sections of a stage into the recently cleared space. She didn't have to wait long for her seared salmon and grilled vegetables, which was as succulent as Church's meal.

Simon made a face at Laura when she came out of the door to the bedrooms at the foot of the stairs, her computer clutched under her arm. She glared in return and said, 'Get many guests here? Didn't think so.'

'Ooh, listen to her,' Simon said before returning to his work.

Laura glanced at Ruth and Church's plates and said grumpily, 'I hope they do vegetarian.'

'What are you in such a bad mood about?' Ruth asked.

'It's not working.' She slid the computer on the table in front of them. 'I charged up the battery fine, and then I booted it up to do some more research. The moment I got online I got some of that screeching laughter, some of the freakiest images I've ever seen, and then it just died on me.'

There was a crash as Simon dropped a microphone on the stage, which made them all jump. He smiled apologetically, then cursed under his breath as he attempted to untangle the coiling lead.

Church examined the computer briefly, then shook his head. 'I wonder if it will carry on intermittently like this – some days everything works properly, some days it doesn't – or if we'll just lose technology overnight and wake up in the stone age.'

They wrestled with their thoughts in silence for a while until Laura decided to call Simon and harangue him until Stuart could come up with a vegetarian dish that matched her unreasonably detailed recipe. When it arrived, Ruth and Laura ordered some red wine and Church had a beer. The alcohol seemed a comfort in the face of the storm lashing the building, and after Laura had finished eating they moved closer to the fire which Simon had just loaded up with cracking and sputtering logs. The warmth and the drink made them feel a little easier, although they knew it was an illusion.

Eventually Church glanced up at Simon's stage, which now had a microphone, a monitor and a strange-looking machine. 'What *is* he planning?'

'Karaoke,' Laura replied distractedly. She was stabbing her boot on to one of the new logs in the fire to make sparks shoot up the chimney. 'That man is the definition of desperate. As if all the sheep-shaggers and inter-breeders of Dartmoor are going to come to his poxy pub to lose what little dignity they have by performing a Celine Dion cover.'

'You know you'll be up there with the best of them,' Ruth gently mocked.

'Yeah, like I'm so perverse I need to debase myself before lower life forms.'

They spent the next couple of hours drinking slowly, talking little, listening to the rain patter like ghostly fingers at the window and the wind moan in the chimney. They were as close to the fire as they could get to dispel the March chill; it made them feel secure, as it had done for travellers on such a night down the long years.

Much to their surprise, the drinkers continued to arrive in dribs and drabs until the pub was full. There were bedraggled old men in beaten windcheaters with rain in their beards and cheeks flushed from the wind as though they'd walked miles across the moor, young couples holding hands and laughing at every opportunity, husbands and wives in matching Barbours and wellies, with the occasional wet Labrador, sullen teenagers, women in pearls, men in dole-cheque faded shirts and patched trousers. The moment they entered, their shoulder muscles seemed to relax and their conversation sparkled. The mood was infectious and it wasn't long before Church, Ruth and Laura found their spirits rising. In the chatter and laughter of humanity, fired by beer and wine, it seemed possible to hold the darkness at bay.

As Simon collected glasses from a nearby table, he bent down near Laura and said, 'What's it like to be wrong, Missy Sharp Tongue?'

'It's a first for me. Give me some time to assimilate the experience.'

'You seem *very* experienced already,' he said pointedly, but beneath the mock-frostiness there was a certain regard.

When he'd gone, Ruth leaned over and said with a tight grin, 'Queens always like bitches, don't they?'

'Queens are renowned for having excellent taste, which is why he didn't waste any breath on you.'

The karaoke started soon after, with Simon taking the spotlight as if he was born to it. The regulars seemed to love him, and responded to his barbs with obviously well-repeated heckles, applauding his every tart comment, forcing him to be even more outrageous. There was no shortage of people ready to take the microphone, and while their voices were rarely good, they made up for it with the gusto of their performance. The most popular was a farmer with a red face and haystack grey hair who didn't appear ever to have crossed the borders of Devon, yet who managed a rendition of *Shaft* as if he'd been born in Brooklyn South. He finished with a clenched fist salute and a shout of 'Yo!' which brought a burst of feedback.

When he'd finished, Simon took the mike once more and said, 'We've got three guests in tonight and you know The Green Man tradition for newbies.'

A chant and a clap started as Church, Ruth and Laura looked around, taking a second or two to realise they were suddenly the centre of attention.

'You have *got* to be joking,' Laura protested.

Ruth hid her head in embarrassment. 'Oh God, I can't hold a tune!'

Church took a long drink of his beer and then made up his mind. 'Come on,' he said, standing up to a loud cheer. 'We've been entertained by them.'

Laura looked away uncomfortably, muttering something under her breath, but Church took her hand and her face lightened, although her expression remained grudging; she followed him to the stage like some spoilt child. Ruth trailed behind, her cheeks stinging pink.

As Church took the spotlight, he had a sudden flashback to the first gig he had ever done. It had been at Leeds University, in the Student Union, on a similarly rain-swept November night when only a few hardened drinkers had turned out. He'd always been a quiet, introspective person, but that began to change when he bought his first guitar. And that first time on stage had been an epiphany – after he had recovered from his terrifying stage fright, his shame about the vomit; heart pounding, nerves afire with adrenalin buzz, his conscious mind slipping away as he merged with the music, a bundle of notes dressed up as a scrawny kid with a too-big leather jacket. It wasn't an ego thing; it was the sense of giving, of being a part of something bigger, of feeling the music in his arteries. It was about celebrating life. He didn't attempt to make a career of it because he knew the joy of performing wasn't backed up with any ambition, and over time the purity of the experience would have been eroded.

But there on the little makeshift stage, even though he would only be singing, he felt it as acutely as that first time, and for one fleeting instant everything else in his life fell into relief: what was right and what was wrong, the terrible mistakes he was making and the path he knew he should be taking. And even as they selected their song and the first bars eased out of the speakers, he had the awful knowledge that the insight would be lost to him the moment he walked away from the stage.

There was no doubt in his mind when he saw the song in the list, but Laura jammed her fingers in her mouth and made vomit noises while Ruth rolled her eyes heavenwards. Their protests were only for his sake, though, and the moment he took the microphone, they slipped in close to him, his two backing singers. He glanced down at the monitor, but he knew the lyrics by heart:

Fly me to the moon
And let me play among the stars . . .

When he glanced back at Laura he saw she was maintaining her expression of sullen disinterest, but her eyes were sparkling with enjoyment; she looked away when she realised he'd glimpsed behind her façade. And Ruth made up for her technical flaws with a passion that surprised him. Soon she even had Laura performing a pastiche of a backing singers' dance while Church fell to his knees and hammed up his Sinatra impression.

At any other time they probably wouldn't have been able to do it, but the anxiety and the danger drove them to seek some kind of release in an act that was simple, mindless and fun, away from thoughts of black dogs, wild hunts, and the debilitating stress of fear. The crowd loved it. Each time Church executed a few steps, or skidded across the stage on his knees while holding the microphone stand across his chest, they cheered and applauded. Laura and Ruth found their own fans among many of the men who hollered out to them in the lulls between verse and chorus. While the music was playing, for the first time in weeks, everything was right.

The storm buffeted and howled against the walls, but within, with the fire roaring and the drink flowing, everyone felt secure. The singing continued until well after last orders, with few people drifting away early. But just before midnight Simon stepped on stage to draw the proceedings to a close with a cheery thank-you and a sharp putdown to the few grumblers who wanted to keep things going. Church could understand the feeling; he didn't want the night to end either.

'We could always stay here,' Laura said bluntly, as if she could read his thoughts. She tried to pass it off as sarcasm, but there was a brief flash of brittle vulnerability in her face before she stifled it.

As the drinkers filed out to the car park or prepared for the terrible journey on foot, the storm seemed to crash even louder overhead; it felt like the very walls were rattling with the thunder. Bursts of lightning flashed through the bottle-glass windows.

'I'll never be able to sleep in this,' Ruth said quietly. Then: 'Do you think one of us should keep watch?'

'Wouldn't hurt,' Church replied.

It sounded like the storm had come down right into the car park now. The noise was unbearable and, with the wind screaming, they could barely hear themselves talk. It seemed nearer to a hurricane than a gale.

In the glare of another flash of lightning, Ruth saw one of the drinkers run past the window. She flinched; her subconscious had caught some detail which jarred. The wind crashed against the door so hard she thought it was bursting inwards.

'We should start at first light,' Church was saying. 'It seems the only way. Travel by day, find somewhere secure to shelter by night.'

Laura swigged down the last of her wine. 'Bank vaults, that's what we need. Check ourselves into safe deposit boxes every night.'

Ruth tried to peer through the nearest window, but she was too far away to see anything. She returned her attention to the conversation, only to jump again at the next flash of lightning.

'What's wrong?' Church asked.

Her heart was beating double-time. Out of the corner of her eye she thought she'd seen a white face contorted with fear pressed up against the window, hands hammering to get in. There was nothing there now, but her heartbeat didn't subside.

Another clap of thunder burst overhead, followed by the shriek of the wind, which went on and on until they realised it wasn't the wind at all. As the gale died briefly, a keening cry of fear rang out. They jumped to their feet as one, suddenly noticing other sounds that the storm was masking: a peal of thunder that had a metallic rending beneath the bass echo, a clatter of hoofbeats merging with the spatter of rain at the window, another scream, definitely not the wind this time. They ran to the window and peered out.

Intermittent flashes of lightning revealed the scene in oddly frozen tableaux. The car park was a scene of carnage. People were frantically running for cover like frightened rabbits from a group of men on horseback who were filled with the dangerous majesty of the storm. At least Church thought they were men; their faces were swathed in shadows. They wore furs and armour like barbarians from the steppes and brandished long poles with cruel sickles at the end, which they used to herd and hook the terrified, fleeing people. And at their heart was one larger and more terrifying than all the others. Church knew he would see him in his nightmares for the rest of his life: the Erl-King.

Their horses' eyes glowed red, like the eyes of Black Shuck, and the breath vented from their nostrils in gusts of steaming vapour. And around their hooves ran a pack of alien dogs with strange red and white fur, long and lean, with glittering yellow eyes, harrying the prey with snapping jaws.

There was too much blood. Church, Ruth and Laura watched in horror as the strange sickle implements tore at flesh, severed joints, sliced into muscle. In each flash they could see more bodies piling up. One horse clattered on to the roof of a car, caving it in before smashing down on to the bonnet without losing its footing. A sickle ripped open a wing, flicked out a door, like it was gutting some beast. No one could escape the hunting men. Soon there would be no one left.

An exclamation made Church, Ruth and Laura turn. Simon was behind them, watching the monstrous butchery over their shoulders. 'My God! My God!' His voice rose to a whine of shock and horror. He grabbed Church's arm in desperation. 'What's going on?'

Church's head was spinning. He'd thought they could hide away. He should have known they wouldn't be allowed, and now others were paying the awful price for his mistake.

Simon ran around shrieking until Stuart emerged to see what was wrong. When he followed Simon's pointing to the window, he suddenly bolted towards the door. Church caught the movement out of the corner of his eye and intercepted him. 'Don't go out there,' he pleaded. 'You won't stand a chance.'

'But someone's got to help them!' he said desperately.

Simon was on his knees in front of the window, sobbing uncontrollably at the horror. 'What's happening?' he whined.

Church looked from Stuart to Simon and then at the others. 'We've got to do something,' he said hollowly. 'It's our fault.'

Laura glanced out at the wild scene; it made her think of a film she'd seen of piranhas feeding on a carcass. 'If we go out there, they'll kill us.'

There was a brief instant when they all felt ice in their hearts and then Ruth said bluntly, 'He's right.' There was no fear in her face; just a blind acceptance of their fate. 'It's our responsibility.'

Church nodded in agreement, but Laura whirled, her equanimity stripped away by fear. 'You're crazy! I'm not walking out there to be butchered!' She sucked in a deep gulp of air. 'We can't sacrifice ourselves! We're the only ones who can stop all this. We're important! That's what they all say, right?'

Church snatched up her hand; time was running out. 'We can't let those people die. I wouldn't be able to live with myself. And neither would you.' There was an instant when another outburst seemed likely, but then her face, her whole body sagged, as if his words had reached the rational part of her mind closed off by terror. With a despairing acceptance that pained Church, she pulled back her hand and turned away from him, saying nothing.

'We can still make this work,' Church said, turning to Ruth, the adrenalin suddenly thumping through his system. 'We split up. You and Laura run for the car. You've got the Stone. Try to get as far away from here as you can. I'll go in the other direction. I'm betting they'll follow me. In fact, I know they will.'

'You're crazy,' Laura muttered. 'You won't get twenty feet on foot. Look at those horses, you idiot.' There were tears in her eyes.

'I've got a bike out back,' Stuart interjected. 'A scrambler. It will get you over rough ground.' You ridden one before?'

'A long time ago.' Church glanced out of the window one final time and then he was racing off with Stuart.

They hauled the bike through in seconds. Church threw

Ruth the car keys before he jumped on, fired it up and positioned it in front of the door.

The desperation in their shared glance masked their emotions, and then Ruth said quietly, 'You can count on us. Take care.'

Church smiled, lowered his head and nodded to Stuart. There was a freezing gust as the storm blasted in, then Church popped the clutch. He had to fight to keep it upright in the wind and for a second he thought he'd lost control as the bike bounced down the steps of the porch. But then he righted himself on the puddled road, snatched on the accelerator and roared off without glancing back.

He didn't need to check if the Huntsmen had seen him. From his back came a roar of jubilation that rose above the noise of the storm; the hunt was on. Hooves clattered like gunshots. The horses shrieked like banshees and the dogs howled as one, ready to be loosed on the prey.

Church was shaking with terror. The only conscious thoughts that flared in his mind were images of him being torn apart by savage jaws, but his motor instinct took over, guiding the scrambler along the road at full speed.

No horse should have been able to keep up with such a powerful bike, but he could hear the thunder of the hooves and the wild whoops of the riders drawing closer. He allowed himself one glance back, but the image of the Satanic Hunt bearing down on him was so terrible he knew he would not be able to look again.

He swung the bike off the road in the futile hope that the rough ground might slow the riders, but he knew in his heart it was only a matter of time. The wheels chewed up grass and mud as he roared out into the heart of the moor. While the storm whipped him from side to side, the bike sloughed around as it countered the dips and hollows that made the going so treacherous. Even with the headlamps on full beam, Church could barely see the outcroppings of rock which he knew could be the end of him.

The hollers and whoops of the riders became almost sounds of nature, caught on the wind, soaring up to the clouds, filled with the passion of the hunt, the lust for blood. And then, from the midst of them, came a low, mournful sound that seemed to suck all other noise out of the air. Church shivered. It was the hunting horn of the Erl-King.

Church gunned the bike over a rise so fast both wheels left the ground. Somehow he kept it upright when it landed. The countryside had grown even wilder, and just as he started to wonder how many miles he had put between himself and the pub, the ground suddenly disappeared beneath his feet and he was falling in darkness. He had only a few seconds to question what was happening as the engine roared out of control, and then his head hit something and he plunged into unconsciousness.

the hunt

Ruth and Laura choked back their emotions as they sprinted across The Green Man's car park, which now resembled an abattoir among the burning wreckage of several cars and a minibus. The few survivors were slowly beginning to stumble out from underneath vehicles or the deep shadows where they had been hiding, transformed by the shock and horror into scurrying animals, wide-eyed and dumb.

They were relieved to find the Nissan had not been harmed during the Hunt's attack. Ruth jumped into the driver's seat and sparked the ignition, releasing the clutch before Laura had time to settle in. She was thrown back into her seat as the tyres screamed and whirled on the spot, sloughing the car around the park before it roared on to the road.

'Yee haw,' Laura said mutedly.

Heading in the opposite direction to Church and the Hunt, Ruth found the road signposted for Buckfastleigh, ten miles away. She was surprised she didn't feel more scared. Instead, she felt a cold determination to do the right thing, and an awareness for the first time that what they had to achieve was more important than everything; even her own life.

She glanced secretively at Laura who was slumped silently, half-turned to look out of the passenger window. Ruth was surprised to see she wasn't taking it well at all. Her face was white and strained, turned even ghostlier by the bleached blondeness of her hair, and her cheeks were streaked with tears. A tremor ran through her body and Ruth noticed she had her hands tucked between her thighs to stop them shaking.

'We're going to get out of this,' Ruth said supportively.

'Sorry, you must be thinking I care about your opinions,' Laura replied without turning her head.

Ruth returned her attention to the dark road ahead; if Laura felt she was better internalising her fears, there was no point wasting her breath.

Two miles further on, Laura broke her silence. 'What's going to happen now?'

'We meet up with Church—'

'We're not going to meet up with Church, you stupid bitch. It was a suicide run. You know that.'

Ruth did know it, but she hadn't allowed herself to think about it. Now the idea that Church might be dead made her feel like she had a cold, hard rock lying on her chest. 'There still might be a chance. He said it himself: these days we live in a world where anything can happen.'

There was a hopeful hush and then Laura said, 'Okay. But say he *doesn't* make it back. What then?'

'Then we carry on with what we have to do. Find the remaining talismans—'

'Smart plan. Except for one thing. Church took the Wayfinder with him when he left. It was stuffed in his jacket.'

Ruth dropped her head briefly in despair. She couldn't believe how stupid they'd been. Without the lantern, they'd never find the talismans. And without the talismans, everything was lost.

'So we better hope he does get back to us,' Laura said emotionlessly.

For ten minutes they drove in silence, wondering how the fate of the world had come to be placed on their shoulders, filled with despair at the mess they had made of it, when Ruth said suddenly, 'I feel strange.'

'You've only just noticed?'

Ruth focused on the unnerving sensation which seemed to be buzzing underneath her skin. A second later she saw something red glowing nearby and froze in fear, instantly thinking it was the eye of some lurking beast. When she realised it was a vehicle's rear light she laughed nervously at how the mundane was now the last thing she considered.

A large white Transit van was pulled up on to the verge. One of the rear lights was broken and it seemed to have a flat; someone was hunkering down trying to change the wheel by torchlight in the driving rain.

Ruth's heart told her to stop to help, but her head warned her it was too much of a risk. But as she drove by, the buzzing under her skin grew unbearable, as if an infestation of insects were burrowing there; she could tell from Laura's sudden jerk and expression of discomfort that she was feeling it too. Then, without warning, the lights went off. Ruth slammed on the brakes, her heart pounding.

'What's going on?' Laura hissed fearfully.

The lights came on after a long beat, but just as Ruth was about to engage the gears once more, they flashed off and on five times in quick succession.

'The electrics are going crazy,' Laura said. 'Just drive. We can't risk sitting here. Or maybe I should get out and paint red and white circles on the roof?'

Something nagged at Ruth's mind. The headlights were fine now. She glanced in the rearview mirror to see whoever had been changing the tyre was now standing in the road, silhouetted against the van's lights, staring at them. All she could tell was that it was a man. She listened to the rhythmic clack of the windscreen wipers, hit the accelerator, but the car didn't move.

'Come on,' Laura said anxiously. 'You're too young to have Alzheimer's.'

'No,' Ruth said thoughtfully. 'There are new rules now. We have to start operating by them.'

'What do you mean?' Laura glanced over her shoulder to

241

see if the van's driver was approaching. 'He's just standing there,' she said with obvious relief.

'Instinct. Coincidence,' Ruth continued. 'We have to listen to things talking to us.'

'What kind of things?'

'*Unseen* things.' She caught her breath, hoping she was right. 'That strange sensation we both felt – that was our instinct telling us to be aware, not to miss something important. And the lights. One long flash, five short. Not an accident. A message.'

'A message,' Laura repeated with a sneer. 'The car's talking to us. Shall we give it a name?'

'Not the car. Life. The world. Whatever makes all this tick. The player behind the scenes.' Thunder rumbled ominously and lightning danced across the horizon in a breathtaking light show that beat anything created by technology. This time Laura stared at her curiously, without mocking. 'There are supposed to be five of us who make a stand,' Ruth continued. 'Five who become one, something greater than the sum of the parts.' She turned to look at the figure in the road who was stock-still despite the storm, staring at their car.

Laura followed her gaze. 'Or he might just spout hair and fangs and tear us apart the moment we get out of the car.'

Ruth shivered; Laura had instantly lanced the doubts she had tried to put to one side. Every rational thought told her not to get out of the car; it was hard to fight years of conditioning for something so intangible as a whim.

'So do you have enough faith in yourself?' Laura said. 'Or is there still some sense in your head?'

'Look at him – he feels it too,' Ruth said, trying to convince herself.

'Or else he just smells meat.'

'Stop it.' Ruth rested her hand on the gear stick, tightened her grip. *Just drive*, she told herself. *Don't be crazy. Laura's right – you can't risk everything on a notion.*

242

She glanced back once more, then turned quickly and flung open the door. Laura's protests were lost as she threw herself out into the wind and rain, shielding her eyes with her arm. She took a few steps to the rear of the car. The man still wasn't moving.

'Do you need any help?' she called out.

In the long moment when she thought he wasn't going to answer, the anxiety returned in force. But just as she was on the verge of leaping back in the car and driving off, he called out, 'Please.'

Ruth steeled herself and walked forward as confidently as she could manage. With the storm raging around her, it was difficult to see or hear any warning signs; she would be close enough to grab by the time she knew if she had made the right decision.

Gradually his features coalesced out of the stark shadows and light thrown by the headlights. He was Asian, about 5 ft 10 ins, with shoulder-length black hair plastered to his head by the rain. As she closed on him, Ruth guessed he was probably of Indian blood; he had the most beautiful face she had seen on any man. His bone-structure was so finely cut, his eyes so wide and dark, his lips so full, that there was a hint of androgyny. When she was near enough he unveiled a smile of perfect white teeth which was so open she instantly felt at ease.

'Thank you,' he said in a soft, tranquil voice. 'On a night like this I would not expect anyone to stop to help.' He took her hand in both of his in greeting, as if she were a long lost friend; his fingers were long, slim and warm. 'My name is Shavi.'

Ruth introduced herself and Laura, who had just climbed out of the car, casting a suspicious glance in their direction. 'Let's get this tyre changed before we all catch pneumonia.'

As they eased the wheel off the axle, Ruth asked him what he was doing driving across the bleak moor in a terrible storm at that time of night. 'Searching,' he said enigmatically.

There was a glimmer in his eye that made Ruth feel he knew everything going through her head.

Laura peered over their shoulders, her arms folded. 'So are you one of us?' she said bluntly.

Shavi flashed her another smile and Ruth was surprised to see a faint warm response on Laura's face. 'Perhaps,' he said.

'You're not going to wear out that word, are you?'

'What caused the broken light and the flat?' Ruth asked.

Shavi grunted as the wheel came free and rolled to one side. 'Something came across the road in front of me, fast, just a shadow. At first it was on four legs, then two, then four again. You know?' Anyone else wouldn't have understood the meaning of the question, but Ruth nodded; they had all seen the strange shapes lurking off in the dark country night. 'I felt the van hit it, but there was no body, no blood. Perhaps it was thrown off the road.'

Ruth and Laura both glanced off into the night uncomfortably. 'We should finish up here as quickly as we can,' Ruth said redundantly.

'I'll keep watch.' Laura scanned around, but it was hopeless; the night was so dark and the rain so heavy that they wouldn't see anything until it was upon them.

Although they tried to work fast, the cold drove the feeling from their fingers and the simple act of screwing on the wheelnuts became torturous; there was repeated scrabbling in icy pools under the van for ones that had been dropped. And the more anxious Ruth got about what might be prowling in the dark, the more clumsy she became. But finally, with all of them shivering and sodden, the wheel was changed and Shavi lowered the jack.

There was such a potent inner peace about Shavi that he looked almost beatific, soaked to the skin and battered by the wind. Ruth was convinced her instinct about him was right, but what could she say – *we're trying to stop the end of the world; want to come along for the ride*?

At that moment Laura suddenly tensed. She was peering back the way they had come.

'What is it?' Ruth asked.

'Can't you see it?' Laura's voice was almost lost in the wind.

And then she could. There was something moving on the horizon, roiling and churning as if the storm clouds were folding in upon themselves; it was flickeringly illuminated by an odd, inner light as if coloured lightning were crackling within it. The billowing clouds moved towards them. Ruth felt a cold that went beyond the chill of the rain.

'What is it?' Laura asked.

A second later they heard the sound that others could have mistaken for thunder: the clattering of iron-shod hooves. And then they saw the figures among those swirling clouds, lost then revealed, distant, but bearing down on them.

Ruth whirled and made to run towards the Nissan. 'We've got to move. We might still be able to—'

Shavi caught her arm and gently but forcibly held her back. 'Take the van with me. It is fast. Turbo-charged.'

Ruth glanced at Laura who nodded; there were flashes of wild fear in her eyes. Shavi leapt into the driver's seat and the engine roared into life while Laura hauled herself through the rear doors. The bag with the stone in never left her grasp. Ruth began to follow her, but then shouted, 'Wait!' She turned and ran for the Nissan. Shavi had pulled up beside her by the time she had found what she wanted and she jumped into the passenger seat.

'The water's warped your brain,' Laura said sharply. 'What are you doing?'

Ruth held up a handful of cassettes. 'Church's music. I didn't want to leave it there.'

Laura eyed her as if she was crazy, but she said nothing; they both knew why she had done it. It might be the only thing they had to remember him by.

And then Shavi slammed the van into gear, hit the accelerator and the van hurtled forward so fast Laura was thrown across the back amidst a hail of cursing. Ruth gripped for support as she was pressed into the seat. She glanced over at Shavi who was as placid as if he were out on a Sunday drive. *Of course*, Ruth thought. *He doesn't understand what's behind us.*

'You've got to keep your foot down,' she said. 'If we're caught, we're dead. Literally.'

'I know.' He flashed her a smile. 'What is it exactly?'

Laura scrambled to the rear doors and pressed her face against the window. 'They're getting closer.'

'Something that will tear us apart if it catches us.' She glanced at him, unsure. 'Something supernatural.'

He nodded as if what she had said was the most normal thing in the world. 'The van should be fast enough.'

The engine had the throaty rumble of a big cat and the acceleration was breathtaking, although the ride was as smooth as silk. But Ruth found it impossible to put her faith in anything technological after seeing science fail so easily.

'Worry more that we should run out of road,' Shavi said. 'Do you have any direction in mind?'

'Just keep driving until the sun comes up. The Hunt seem to go at first light.'

'Definition of an optimist,' Laura chimed from the back. 'Someone who thinks they can keep ahead of the Hounds of Hell for four or five hours with just a crappy van.'

'What would you rather we do? Throw ourselves to the dogs?' Ruth snapped. She looked back anxiously. The figures in the swirling clouds were more starkly defined now, the odd lighting diminishing as they moved closer. There was a flurry of movement around the horses' legs which Ruth guessed was the pack; distantly she could hear their howling breaking through the storm.

'I'm sorry you got dragged into this,' she said to Shavi.

He shook his head dismissively. 'I was meant to be here.'

246

Ruth eyed him curiously. 'Meant how?'

'I was guided here by my dreams.'

A snorting noise echoed from the back, followed by some muttering which Ruth couldn't decipher.

'All my life I have had vibrant, colourful dreams,' Shavi continued. 'Sometimes they were like trips. Certainly not like the kind of dreams other people told me about. I had no idea what they meant, but I always knew in my heart they meant *something*. And then, a few weeks ago, I began to have the same dream night after night. It was about a dragon, landing on the ground, becoming part of the ground, and lines of blue light spreading out from it in all directions. And then I was following one of the lines to the place where the sun sets. To a big moor.' There was a screech of tyres as the van slid around a sharp bend, which Shavi accelerated out of like a professional rally driver. 'Somehow I found myself on the road where we met and I knew at once it was the right place.'

'How did you know?'

'I just felt it.'

Ruth couldn't concentrate on talking further; her muscles felt like steel knots and her chest hurt from breathing too hard. Looking back once more, she saw the Hunt had drawn only slightly closer. The speedo said they were doing sixty-plus on the treacherous moorland road, which was a risk in itself, but if they could maintain that speed there was a chance they could keep ahead.

In the back, Laura attempted to hold herself fast, but the cornering was so intense she was bouncing off the walls, being slammed by Shavi's holdall, narrowly avoiding a sliding tool box; she was already covered in bruises and there was blood leaking into her left eye from a cut on her temple. But the pain was the least of the things concerning her. She couldn't believe how fearful she was becoming. Each glimpse of some terrible thing that shouldn't exist made it seem her life was spinning away from her, when she really needed to keep it under tight control. The only way she could deal with it was to damp it down into the hard, cold space deep inside her where she kept every other negative experience. Only that space was full to bursting and Laura knew it was just a matter of time before everything started to eat its way out.

'Where did you learn to drive?' she vented. 'Some school for the blind?' She slammed into another wall before rolling back, her head ringing.

Shavi apologised, but Ruth said, 'Ignore her. All she does is moan. Just focus on the driving.'

Somewhere along the way the road had dropped a grade. The straight-as-a-die, well-surfaced tarmac had given way to something that was little more than a country lane, throwing twists and turns so regularly they either had to cut their speed or risk a wipe-out. Shavi shifted gear rapidly, using them to complement the brakes, but they all knew he was living on borrowed time. On one corner, the nearside rear wheel skidded on to a grass verge, churning up mud and vegetation so violently they thought the tyre was going to burst or the van roll over. Although the storm seemed to be receding with the last flicker of lightning over Rippon Tor in the north, huge pools of water still covered the road at irregular intervals, threatening to throw the van into the moorland whenever it ploughed into them at speed.

'They've got closer,' Laura said as she managed to claw her way up to look through the rear windows once more. 'These country roads are slowing us down too much.'

'Yes, but what happens when we hit an urban area?' Ruth said. 'We can't keep going at this speed.'

'We will simply have to do the best we can,' Shavi said as he hunched over the wheel, trying to concentrate on the road; Ruth marvelled that there was still no strain showing on his face. 'We should avoid the smallest country roads, the bigger roads that might be too busy, the heavily built up areas where we could be stopped by traffic lights—'

Laura began to make some sneering comment, but Ruth

threw herself round and glared at her. She turned back to Shavi. 'Just do what you have to.'

He pointed to a book of maps in the pocket on the door. 'Select a route.'

Anxiously Ruth riffled through the pages until she found the correct map. It was difficult to read when she was being thrown from side to side as the van rolled around the corners, but she eventually managed to focus on the broken capillaries of roads that filled the countryside between Buckfastleigh and the motorway at Exeter. 'We've got a choice: A38 or country lanes,' she said dispiritedly. Neither were right; one prone to obstructions and police patrols, the other too small.

Buckfastleigh slowed them down; the roads were narrow and even at that time of night they had to watch out for pedestrians and other vehicles. As they picked up the dual carriageway, the Hunt closed on them. Ruth wondered how it must have looked to anyone peeking out of their windows to investigate the noise; a van roaring way over the speed limit, being pursued by a nightmarish vision of riders in furs and armour surrounded by a pack of spectral hounds howling hellishly. No one would believe it, she thought; she barely did herself. It was only the fear, sharp like a knife, that made her aware it was bitter reality; that if the engine blew a gasket or the van clipped a kerb and ran out of control she would be torn apart by dogs that had no business existing.

At least the A38 was faster. They sped through Ashburton, feeling more positive that they at least stood a chance. 'We're not pulling away from them,' Laura said in one of her regular reports, 'but at least they're not getting any closer.'

But as they passed Bickington their hearts fell as they saw a red light glowing in the distance. Major road works blocked one carriageway where the dark hulk of a steamroller loomed.

'Change,' Shavi willed the light aloud.

'You can't stop,' Ruth said redundantly. 'They'll be on us in no time.'

'What's going on?' Laura called from the back.

Shavi and Ruth focused their attention on the light. 'On a busy road like this, there's bound to be something coming if we jump it,' she said.

'We have no choice,' Shavi said grimly.

When they reached the stop light, it still hadn't changed. Shavi pulled out without braking, put the lights on full beam and accelerated. Every muscle in Ruth's body was tense. They passed the steamroller. The other carriageway had been stripped of tarmac and was a mass of broken hardcore. They travelled fifty yards in a blur, but the end of the roadworks was still hidden around a bend. A second later the trees clustering around the road lit up from as-yet-unseen headlights.

She yelled in shock as the juggernaut hauled around the bend, but Shavi was already reacting. The trees on Shavi's side were too close; if he tried to pull off it would be the end of them. The lorry's horn blared a frantic warning. Even if Shavi hit the brakes, they wouldn't stop in time. Thoughts were piling up in Ruth's mind as the lorry bore down on them. She could see the animated, terrified face of the driver in the cab, flooded sickly white in their headlights as he waved his arm at them as if he were swatting away a wasp.

This is it, Ruth thought. She threw her arms across her face.

She didn't see what happened next, but she felt the surge of forces pulling at her body as Shavi dragged the wheel to one side. There was a rhythmic rumbling and the van bounced around crazily as it ploughed through the bollards. The screaming of the juggernaut's brakes merged with the strangled sounds coming from Ruth's throat, punctuated by Laura's yells. When they hit the hardcore Ruth waited for the tyres to burst, flinging the vehicle on a wild roll into the trees. But somehow they held. The van slewed crazily as Shavi fought to regain control, tipping up on two wheels before bouncing on to the other two. Shavi managed to keep it upright, but it spun round in an arc until it was facing in the opposite direction.

Ruth could barely bring herself to look. The muscles of her neck and shoulders ached from the strain of being thrown around. As she lowered her arms, she saw with horror that Shavi was slumped across the wheel, a trickle of blood running down his cheek. But then he sucked in a huge gulp of air and raised his head, his expression as calm as it had been when they met. When he flashed her a smile she almost cried.

The juggernaut had come to a rest across both carriageways. The driver was already clambering out of the cab, an expression of fury replacing one of relief.

But their attention was drawn past him to an eerie light in the sky just beyond the silhouetted bulk of the lorry. When Shavi scrambled to start the stalled vehicle, the engine rumbled without firing.

'Flooded,' he said.

The light in the sky was growing more intense as the Hunt neared, a swirling, uncomfortable mix of greens and reds. Ruth stared wide-eyed at Shavi's hand as he turned the ignition key again.

Laura hauled herself up between their seats. Her face was streaked with blood from numerous cuts and her skin was darkening in anticipation of several bruises. 'Good driving,' she said sardonically.

As the juggernaut driver marched towards them angrily, Ruth realised she ought to call out a warning. She was too late. Transfixed, she watched the Hunt rise up above the lorry in all its awful majesty. The horses were black and sleek with sweat, but they were like no horses she had seen before: larger, more muscular, there was something almost serpentine about them; their eyes glowed as red as coals in the gloom. The riders exuded power from their large frames, but their faces were still hidden in shadow. At the head of them was the Erl-King, wearing a helmet made from the bleached bones of their prey. As they moved over the lorry, the roof of the vehicle was torn apart by their cruel weapons, showering shards of metal over a wide area as if a grenade had exploded.

The driver whirled, seeing the Hunt for the first time, and as he did so, the strange red and white dogs surged over the top of his rig. Snapping and whirling in a way that made Ruth think they were one creature, they speedily hurtled towards their target. In horror, she saw him start to run one way, then another, and then scream in fear, and then the dogs were upon him, their needle-sharp teeth rending and tearing; his frail human body was dismantled in seconds as a red mist filled the air.

Finally the engine fired and caught. Shavi popped the clutch and hauled the van back on the road, the tyres complaining loudly, but miraculously holding. As they sped past the other end of the roadworks, the silence in the van was palpable; they were jointly overcome with loathing at what had happened to the driver – another death they could mark up to their actions – and a sodden feeling that their situation was hopeless. They had lost too much time. Ruth didn't have to turn to ask Laura how they were doing; she could hear the thunder of hooves drowning out even the sound of the engine.

Shavi put his foot to the floor as often as he could, but there were too many twists and turns along the road, forcing him to brake sharply then accelerate again, and on several occasions he had to put their lives on the line to overtake cars that were already speeding. Ruth was relieved the Wild Hunt paid the other travellers no heed this time, but it was a small success as the riders spurred on their mounts to close on the van.

The villages went by in a blur: Coldeast, Heathfield, Chud-leigh Knighton; when they saw the sign for the motorway just four miles away they had a brief moment of hope. It was killed in the instant it was born by a startled cry from Laura. The stink of horses, musky and oppressive, had grown stronger, even through the door and over the exhaust fumes, and it had prompted her to peer once more out of the rear windows.

The Hunt was almost within reach of the van. Laura could see the muscles rippling on the arms of the riders, the delicate ornamentation on the clasps and buckles which held their furs tight, the shining leather and metal of the bridles, and then she made the mistake of looking into their faces. They were all terrible in aspect, but the worst was the Erl-King leading the charge. His face seemed to have exposed bone breaking through on the cheeks, brow and jaw, so that when the streetlights caught him it glistened like a death-mask. And where there was skin, it had the faintest green hue and appeared to be scaled like a lizard. But it was the eyes that made her sick and terrified. Red-rimmed beneath a lowering brow, they glowed with an inner yellow light, the pupils slashed like a serpent. When he saw her frozen stare, he grinned malevolently, revealing a menacing row of stained, pointed teeth. Laura had a sudden vision of herself as a terrified rabbit before a predator and then she thrust herself backwards as the Erl-King lashed out with the spear-sickle.

There was a deafening rending as it shredded the door like paper, and then, with a tremendous heave, he tore it from its hinges. It flew up high and landed with a crash far behind them. The van was filled with the searing sound of the road and the horses. Too frightened to speak, Laura scrabbled backwards until her back pressed into Ruth's seat. Ruth's hand snaked down and caught hers, holding it firmly, squeezing for comfort; Laura squeezed back.

Framed in the hole where the door had been, the Wild Hunt drew ever closer. Ruth thought she was going to be sick when she looked at them – it was as if she was queasily drunk and everything was distorted – and she couldn't bear to look into their faces, although she was sure they were mouthing hypnotic words that hissed in the back of her head: to give herself up, to throw herself to the pack. She placed her hands on her ears and yelled.

Shavi looked at her with concern. 'We are nearly there.'

The dual carriageway gave way to the motorway outside

Exeter just as the other rear door was torn free. Laura's nails were biting into Ruth's hands so hard they drew blood. With the extra lane, the traffic thinned enough for Shavi to slam his foot on to the accelerator. The turbo kicked in, propelling the van forward violently until they were hitting 85 m.p.h.

'We're doing it!' Laura gasped. The Hunt had dropped back several yards and were falling further behind as Shavi continued to accelerate. Cars swerved to avoid them as the horses pounded along the motorway, the hounds spreading out to fill all three lanes. A Lotus ploughed into the central reservation, showering sparks, glass and metal up into the air.

'God,' Ruth whispered hoarsely, looking at the vehicles driving ahead of them. 'Have we consigned all these poor bastards to death?'

'Casualties of war,' Laura said.

'I wish I could be that cold.'

'Better get used to it.' Laura tapped Shavi on the shoulder. 'Have we got enough petrol, hero?'

There was a long silence before he replied, 'Let us hope.'

'Great.' Laura's hand went limp and slipped out of Ruth's grip. 'Knock me down when I'm on a high, why don't you?'

'I am not saying we have not . . .' His voice trailed off.

'Just put some miles between us.'

The Hunt was a half-mile behind now, but they all knew the distance would be covered in no time if they had to stop. Secretly, they each checked their watch, wishing dawn upon them.

They lost sight of the Hunt somewhere past Bristol, but although his eyes were tired and burning, Shavi continued to drive. And when first light broke Ruth found herself crying uncontrollably, making no attempt to hide her tears. If Laura saw, she said nothing. They pulled off the motorway at the first junction and sat quietly watching the dark sky turn purple then gold and finally powder blue. It was going to be a fine day.

Ruth was the first one to see the owl hovering over a field nearby. When she'd finally recovered enough to talk, she convinced the others to follow it, without giving them any explanation; none of them questioned her anyway. Slowly it began to head back south at the side of the motorway. Laura took over from Shavi at the wheel, allowing him and Ruth to sleep if they wanted, although neither of them felt able. And at Junction 23 the owl veered off to the east. Half an hour later they found themselves at Glastonbury.

away from the light

The first thing Church sensed as he surfaced from a world of tormented images was a miasma of aches and pains that made him agonisingly aware of what seemed like every nerve in his body. He felt like he'd been thrown down a flight of concrete stairs. Then came the odours: dank air, stale and unpleasant, mildew, straw, the musky stink of animals, and beneath it all the sickening smell of an open sewer. Dully, he forced himself to open his eyes, then realised they *were* open; the place was so dark he seemed to be drifting in space. And then the sensations came thick and fast: the sound of dripping water creating echoes that testified to some kind of confined space with bare, hard walls; nausea; a burning sensation in his arms, which were hauled up above his head. He yanked at them and heard the clang of metal on rock. Chains. Manacles around his wrists, biting into the flesh. Panic swept through him as he desperately fought to recall where he was and what was happening to him. Slowly chunks of memory floated up like wreckage bobbing to the surface of a stormy sea. The Wild Hunt. The race across the moor. That awful awareness that his life was on the brink of being snuffed out. And then ... what? A brief sensation of falling.

The cotton wool that clogged his head gradually began to clear. He must have tumbled into some kind of shaft. He knew the moor was littered with all sorts of old mine workings, but he was sure a fall of that kind would have killed him. And then how did he end up wherever he was?

At least he was alive. With a twist of anxiety he prayed Ruth and Laura had got away too. Cautiously he stretched various muscles to try and ease some of the tension in his hanging body, but the stabbing pain that followed made him stop with a groan. The fall might not have killed him, but it felt like it had been close to it. He sucked in a deep breath and that was a mistake too; fire spread out across his ribcage. He prayed it was just bad bruising and not broken ribs.

When the agony subsided, he listened for any sign of his captors, but it was as still as the grave. Steeling himself for further pain, Church checked the chains, but they seemed solid; he wouldn't be able to pull them out of the wall, even if he were fit. Morosely he leaned back against the wall and desperately tried to think of a way out of his predicament.

The total darkness tricked his mind into hallucinating that he was floating, and in that strange state he lost all track of time as his thoughts constantly drifted in and out of day-dreams. For a while he thought Marianne was there with him. He could smell her perfume, hear the soft whisper of her voice on the periphery of his senses; once he thought he saw her, pale and disturbing like the time she had come to him at Stonehenge.

'Don't worry,' he muttered. 'Soon I'm going to find out why you did it. And I'll make amends to you somehow for whatever I did. Then I can die in peace.'

She didn't reply, if she was there at all, and then his thoughts tumbled back into darkness.

Sometime later he was startled out of his deeply drifting thoughts by the noise of heavy footsteps and a muffled, hectoring voice that sounded agitated. They drew closer until a door opened, and although the light without was only a lantern, it was so blinding after the dark that Church wrenched his head away. But in that briefest instant, he got a sense of his surroundings. He was in a place which seemed to have been cut from the bedrock. A low ceiling hung only a few inches above his head and straw had been scattered across the ground. A row of rusty bars lay a few feet away; beyond them was a small passageway, before more bars for another cell which was still swathed in shadows. He heard laboured breathing and smelled the animal stink of a Night Walker. He closed his eyes so he wouldn't have to see it.

'Who's that?' The voice made him jump and for a second he did look, before screwing his eyes shut again. A man was being hauled into his cell. Church heard the jangle of the door opening and the man protesting before he was shackled to the wall. He spat noisily – obviously at his captor – and an instant later there was the sound of something heavy striking him, then silence. Church heard shuffling, sensed a disturbing presence hovering over him. It made a guttural noise deep in its throat and then moved off, pausing briefly to do something in the passageway. Church waited until he heard the main door close before looking round.

A lantern had been hung on the wall outside his cell, its flickering light casting bizarre, distorted shadows around the rough room. The man hanging from the wall nearby was around thirty, with straight, dark brown hair that fell around his slumped head. He was goodlooking, with a square jaw and sharp cheekbones, but there was a granite hardness in his features that suggested a tough upbringing. The most striking thing about him was the mass of tattoos that covered his naked, muscular torso, a swirling, iridescent panorama of odd pictures, strange images and symbols which Church had never seen before, but which affected him deeply on some subterranean level. At that distance, and in the gloom, it was impossible to make out the detail, but the more he looked, the more he felt even the pictures were speaking to his subconscious, stimulating half-remembered memories, faded dreams. In the end, he had to force himself to look away.

Church was thankful for the light, but its illumination didn't provide him with much hope. Even if he could get out of the manacles, there was no chance he would be able to break through the iron bars, and even then he would have to face whatever lurked without. But he refused to give in to despair and he steeled himself until his fellow prisoner recovered from the blow.

On awakening, his companion shook his head a few times as if being buzzed by an angry wasp and then he cursed under his breath. Looking round sullenly, he spied Church, remembering him from before the blow. 'Who the hell are you?' he asked a little suspiciously, in the hard tones of working class south-east London.

'Jack Churchill. Who the hell are you?'

Silence. Then: 'Ryan Veitch.' He continued to look around furtively. 'They pick you up too?'

Church shrugged. 'Can't remember. I was riding across the moor on a bike and fell down some kind of hole. Where is this place?'

'Some abandoned mine. The place is swarming with them.' Veitch yanked at his chain angrily, but it held fast. 'Bastards.' He took a deep breath, then said, 'What are they?'

'Our worst nightmares.' Now it was Church's turn to be suspicious. 'You seem to be taking this pretty well, being confronted by something that shouldn't exist.'

'I've had plenty of time to get used to it, haven't I? About a bleedin' week since the bastards dragged me down here. I was hitchin' across the moor. The first time I saw them I threw up, then blacked out. I tell you, it was a stomach-full, projectile. The second time wasn't so bad. Half a stomach and three hours unconscious. Now I've just about got used to them, and that's a horrible bleedin' thought in itself.'

'Even so,' Church pressed, 'you're pretty much on top of it.'

Veitch hung his head so his hair obscured his face. Church thought he was being cold-shouldered, but his companion was obviously thinking, for a moment later he looked up and said bluntly, 'I've been dreaming about these sorts of things all my life. It's like I knew they were out there. The biggest surprise was that I wasn't surprised when I saw them. It was almost like I expected to meet them.'

'Dreams?' Church felt a tingle of recognition.

'Yeah. You see these tattoos? They're my dreams. When I was a kid they used to make me miserable. I couldn't get them out of my head. I screwed up school, had trouble making friends, couldn't keep any bird on the go for too long – anti-social tendencies, they said. Attention deficit. Half a dozen other excuses. But it was the bastard dreams. I think I'd probably have topped myself by now if I hadn't found some way to get them out of my head.' He nodded to the tattoos. 'Every time one came into my head and wouldn't leave I went to this place in Greenwich and had a picture of it done somewhere or other. That night it'd be gone. I tell you, this body is a picture book of my screwed-up head.'

Church peered hard through the gloom and saw what seemed to be a tower floating in space. 'I had dreams too,' he began. 'Nothing like yours, but—'

Veitch flashed him a strange, intense look that stopped him dead. 'Dragons?' Veitch said, his eyes searching Church's face. 'Brother of Dragons?' Church nodded. 'Those words've been doin' my head in for weeks now. Just floating there. In fire, on a black background. What do they mean?'

Church shrugged.

Veitch looked truly disconcerted. 'I jacked in my job to come here. Didn't mind that too much. Renovating houses near the Dome for some tight landlord to make a mint on. I just thought I'd get some bleedin' answers—'

'But what made you come here?'

'A little bird told me.' His crooked grin was enigmatic but disarming.

'What do you mean?'

'I thought it was a dream at first, but now I'm not so sure. Some Judy turned up in my room one night and told me to head out west if I wanted to find what I'd spent all my life looking for.' He laughed sourly.

A shiver ran through Church's body. Cautiously he described the woman he had met in the Watchtower. 'Yeah, that's the one,' Veitch said. 'So she *is* real. How'd she get in my gaff then?'

Before Church could answer there came a sound like a tolling bell, echoing dully through the walls from somewhere distant. The reverberations continued for a full minute and then slowly died away, leaving a strange, tense atmosphere.

'What's that about?' Church asked.

Veitch looked uncomfortable. 'Something's going on down here. I've seen things. There's a big cave full of oil drums. Some other place that looks like a church, only not one you've ever seen before. And those things . . . what do you call them?'

'The woman in the Watchtower called them Night Walkers. God knows what they really are.'

'Right. Well, I don't know what they're eating, but I've seen bones . . .' His voice trailed off; Church didn't press him further.

They fell silent for a while, then Church asked, 'So how did you see the place? They don't let you out for a walk, I presume.'

'Every now and then they take me out for a good kicking. My exercise, I suppose. Beats walking round in circles.' He winced, then masked it with a smile. 'It's like they expect me to tell them something. They keep grunting at me in those gorilla-voices, but I can't understand a bleedin' word they're saying. Not very bloody smart, are they?' A shadow passed across his face and he added, 'There's one of them who can speak English, though. He's scary. Doesn't look like the others. He's almost . . . beautiful.' The word seemed to catch in his teeth. 'Until you look in his eyes. The others make me feel like my head's bein' pulled inside out, but he's scary in a different way.' Veitch glanced at Church curiously. 'If

261

he talks to you, just give him what he wants, all right?'

At that moment, the lantern guttered and died.

In the dark it seemed harder to talk. But the bond Church felt with Veitch was unmistakable, even though it was operating on some deeply subconscious level; they were both Brothers of Dragons, after all.

Their distracted, mumbled conversation turned to the past. Veitch told of his childhood in south-east London, the youngest of six children struggling in a household where their mother had died when he was just a baby. His father had fallen to pieces in the aftermath and the boys had been left to keep the household running, cooking and cleaning, trying to scrape together a meagre living in any way possible. Now three of his brothers were in prison, one for drug dealing, the other two for a bungled armed raid on a building society in Kilburn. Veitch's life sounded harrowing, punctuated by brutal explosions of mindless violence, but he had a tremendous affection for his home and upbringing which Church found incongruous. The hardness of his environment had shaped his character into what seemed a mixture of knotted muscle and scar tissue, but beneath it Church sensed a basic decency with which he could connect. He could do worse than having someone like Veitch along for the ride – if they ever got out of there.

For his part, he told Veitch very little about himself – even in those extreme circumstances he couldn't bypass his overwhelming need for privacy – but he did fill him in on everything that had happened to them since that night beneath Albert Bridge.

As they began to exchange theories about what was really going on, the sound of heavy footsteps echoed loudly once again and then the door was flung roughly open. Church snapped his eyelids shut as the silhouette appeared in the doorway, his gorge rising even at that brief glimpse. The beast's voice was guttural, vibrating on bass notes so low

Church could sense them in the pit of his stomach rather than hear them; the tone was insistent and grew noticeably angrier as the cell was opened. Church felt the presence approach him like a cold shadow until he caught that deep, nauseating stench. Crushing, bony fingers snapped around his jaw, digging into the soft flesh of his cheeks until they burned like hot pokers and slowly Church's head was forced round. The pressure was so great he felt his face was on the verge of disintegrating; he had no choice but to open his eyes.

He looked into deepset eyes with red slit pupils, something that could have been scales or a hideous skin deformity, monstrous bone formations, but the overwhelming terror he felt didn't come from the hellish appearance; in some uncanny way it was like he was looking deep within the creature, and what he saw there was too terrible to bear.

His mind screamed for an instant and then flickered out.

Church woke on the floor in the stinking straw, vomit splattered all around. His wrists ached as if they had been plugged with nails, but the sudden knowledge that he was no longer manacled came like a reviving draught. Although his head thundered, he sat bolt upright and glanced hastily around, ready to dart for any opening that presented itself.

'Save it.' Veitch sat in the corner, spooning something grey and watery from a rough wooden bowl. 'The cage is still locked – there's no way out.' He slurped the soup and grimaced. 'Now I know how those people in the plane crash in the Andes could eat their dead mates. You'll force down any old shit if you're hungry enough.'

Church noticed another bowl nearby. 'What is it?'

'Don't know. Don't want to know. Don't even want to think about it, so don't mention it again.'

Church slid over and picked up the spoon and bowl, his stomach contracting with hunger. Circles of translucent grease floated on the top of the grey liquid; the smell was like sour milk. Dunking the spoon in, he swirled it around, but there was no substance in it at all. He half-raised the spoon to his mouth, thought for a moment, then let it drop. 'Obviously I'm not hungry enough.'

'You will be, mate,' Veitch said ominously. He drained the bowl and threw it to one side in the straw.

'I don't intend being in here that long.'

'What's your plan?'

'I'll know it when I see it.'

Veitch laughed. 'Bleedin' hell! An optimist!'

Church hauled himself to his feet and tested the cell door. The bars were iron, solid and unshakable, the lock enormous, looking impossible to pick, even if he had the faintest idea how to go about it.

'I haven't worked out yet if this is the larder,' Veitch said darkly.

Church followed the bars along to where they were held fast in the slick, living rock. 'That might be the end of the line, but right now we're too important to be an appetiser. We're the key to stopping them and they know that. I think they're a little scared of us. Well, not of us exactly, but of what we represent, what we can do.'

'And what's that exactly?' Veitch tried to mask his incredulity, but it broke through nonetheless. Church wasn't offended; he knew exactly how Veitch felt. He lived a normal life, thought normal thoughts; there was nothing that set him apart from the ordinary. The suggestion that he was destined to become some kind of hero of mythic proportions, foretold in prophecies millennia ago, diverged from his own reality so much that it seemed laughable. But all the evidence seemed to be guiding him in that direction: the magical coincidences, the dreams, the talk of *Brothers of Dragons* which suggested some aspect of him that he hadn't seen.

'*Brothers of Dragons*,' he muttered.

'What is it? Like the Masons?'

'I think it's a catch-all for five of us who are supposed to come together *in Britain's darkest hour*. Or, more rightly, something that binds us together.' He cast his mind back to the carnage on the M4 and told Veitch about their encounter with the Fabulous Beast.

'Maybe it means we can talk to them, like Doctor bleedin' Doolittle.'

Church rested his back against the hard bars and slid to the ground. 'I think it's something more symbolic. The dragons are linked to the earth energy, the magic that we were shown at Stonehenge. They feed off it, swim in it, follow it. I can't explain it, but the energy seemed to be a part of nature. Almost a living part.'

'Its blood.'

'In a way. And dragons have always been used to represent the power in the earth, going back to the ancient Chinese. Maybe it means we're supposed to be defenders of that energy. No, of the planet itself. We're the brothers of the dragon-energy, the blood of the world.' Church surprised himself by his logical progression; even in that environment he was still capable of it.

'That's a big job,' Veitch said dismissively. 'Don't you think they'd have chosen somebody up to it?'

'I don't think choice came into it,' Church replied. 'I think this was something laid out years ago, long before any of us were born. The onus is on us to live up to that responsibility.'

'And here we are stuck in a bleedin' hole in the ground, waiting to die. I can't stand it in here!' he yelled as the repressed anger at his captivity finally bubbled to the surface. 'You bastards!'

Church was shocked to see the rage transform his face; there was so much of it within him, so close to the surface, that Church knew he was dangerous. 'Calm down,' he said. 'You don't want to bring them in here.'

But it was too late. The noise coming towards the door suggested several beasts were on their way. Church moved to a corner, bowing his head so he wouldn't have to look

265

into their faces. When the door burst open with a crash, Veitch cursed quietly under his breath. There was something almost terrified in that small sound and Church couldn't help a brief glance up. Several of the creatures hung back in the shadows, but Church was shocked to see the one at the front was not monstrous. He presumed it was the one Veitch had mentioned before, for his face would have been beautiful if it had not been spoiled by a veneer of cruelty. Church forced himself to focus on the strange creature so he did not have to look into the terrible faces of the others: his skin was faintly golden, his face oval and delicate. The eyes were almost like a cat's, with purple irises, and his silver hair was long and lustrous; there was something about him which reminded Church vaguely of the woman in the Watchtower. And where the other beasts had bodies which were huge, misshapen and filled with an inhuman power, his was almost weak and effeminate, slim-hipped, small-waisted, with thin legs and arms that hung loosely from his joints. But although he didn't resemble them, the foul animal stink that came off him still marked him out as one of them. He wore what appeared to be a silk blouson and strange, heavily stained breeches, like some pastiche of a human. For the briefest instant, Church thought he was no threat, but then his eyes came back to the creature's face and he felt a chill run through him.

Slowly the visitor turned towards Veitch and said softly and with a faint sibilance, 'You are making too much noise again, little dear.' Church expected Veitch to unleash some of his pent-up fury, but instead he simply looked away.

The creature turned his attention back to Church. 'My name is Calatin. Among the tribes so many tales had been told about you, Brother of Dragons, or, as you are known to us, *Arith Urkolim*.'

Church felt a sudden *frisson*. That was the same phrase the creature at Heston Services had used when it had tried to abduct Ruth.

'So many prophecies and portents delivered by our fathers' fathers' fathers, but here before me you are diminished. I see you are as weak and frail as all your kind.' He stroked his chin elegantly with a long, slim finger that ended in a dirty, broken nail. 'A cautionary tale about the validity of myths.'

Church couldn't understand the disparity in appearance nor his grasp of English when the others had only ever spoken in that incomprehensible mix of shrieks and roars.

Calatin moved forward until the reek of him was almost overpowering. 'All that energy expended in clearing you from the board. The Fabulous Beast, I must admit, was draining in the extreme to bridle. They are so independent, it takes an exhaustive ritual to direct the will necessary to control them. And the Wild Hunt demanded a price that was almost too high to pay. But pay it we did. And then you deliver yourself to our door.' He shook his head in mock disbelief. 'I still cannot decide which would have been the best outcome for you. To be cut down by the Hunt, brutal but mercifully swift. Or to end up here, with us.' He smiled coldly.

Church's head buzzed; Calatin seemed to be radiating some kind of energy field that made him uncomfortable. 'And now you have me the Hunt can go back to wherever it came from?' He hoped Calatin didn't recognise his concern for Ruth and Laura.

'Oh, there is no way to call off the Hunt until they have been sated,' Calatin replied with obvious cruelty. 'Wild magic, once unleashed, cannot be controlled.'

'But—'

'And now we have to decide what to do with you,' Calatin continued. 'There are those who feel your head will provide powerful magic if it is built into the walls of our citadel once all our plans have been achieved. Others believe a choice meal of your brains would allow your prowess, however well hidden it might be, to be passed on to the Cadrii, our greatest warriors. We can afford to take our time in deciding. In the meanwhile, there are certain matters which need to be resolved.'

He nodded, and the others moved out of the shadows to grasp Church's arms. He tried to hide from their faces, but it was impossible and within a second or two he plunged into unconsciousness once more.

The smell of some indescribable meat cooking to the point of burning filled his nose. Wherever he was, the suffocating heat was so overpowering Church almost blacked out again the moment he regained consciousness. Leather straps held him fast to some rough wooden bench, but he could lift his head enough to look around, and instantly wished he hadn't. The room had been hacked out of the bedrock like his cell, and was lit by a red glow that emanated from a furnace roaring away in one corner. One of the hideous creatures tended it with his back to Church, moving what looked like blacksmith's tools around in the blazing scarlet heart of the fire. In another corner a large black cauldron boiled away over an open fire. It was stained by thick, brown juice which slopped over the side with each viscous, bursting bubble and it was from here the heavy meat smell emanated. Next to it was a heavily discoloured bench with a variety of cleavers embedded in it, obviously where whatever food was in the cauldron had been prepared. His eyes were drawn back to the cauldron by something he hadn't first noticed. Church squinted, then looked away in disgust from the torso and head hooked over one side by a trailing arm.

Fighting back the nausea, he continued to scan the room as best he could. It quickly became apparent what its use was. Various torture instruments he had only ever seen on display in mediaeval castles hung in the half-light between the outer shadows and the furnace's ruddy glow: an iron cage, a large studded wheel, a rack of cruelly tipped tools whose uses he could only guess at, a curtain of hooked chains that hung from the ceiling, and more that he couldn't bring himself to examine.

Before his terror had chance to take root, a heavy door in

front of him ground open, framing Calatin and two other beasts in the outer light. Although Church couldn't bear to look at them, he didn't feel so close to blacking out; he could only imagine he was growing numb to their horrors which upset him more than he could have believed.

Calatin glanced at him in a manner that suggested Church was almost beneath his notice before turning his attention to the creature at the furnace. They spoke briefly in that yelping, bizarre language, and from the body language and tone Church guessed Calatin was in some position of power. But as he advanced, Church saw he was shaking as if he had an ague and his face had the drawn, wearied expression of someone battling against illness. When he reached the table where Church was strapped, Calatin allowed himself one brief look which was filled with such contempt it was as if all the sourness brought on by that inner struggle had been flushed out in Church's direction.

'What now?' Church said. The two words were all he could manage without the knot of fear in his stomach breaking his voice and cracking the mask he had drawn on to protect his dignity; he had to fight to prevent his eyes being drawn to the cruel tools hanging on the wall, to prevent the images of blood and suffering flooding his mind. But deep inside him there was a place that the fear couldn't reach, where he was calmly aware of his responsibilities and of keeping his humanity intact in the face of an evil that wanted to see it broken and debased. The essence of the hero he had denied was in there too, and it startled him to recognize it, as if someone had shone a searchlight to reveal a new, pristine room in his flat.

Calatin ignored his question. He turned sharply and summoned one of the creatures who had accompanied him. The beast was carrying one of the tools he had selected from the rack, a long, sharp spike like a knitting needle which ended with a short corkscrew. Compared with the other implements on show, it was one of the mildest, but Church knew it was only the start.

269

'We have the Wayfinder,' Calatin began in a whining, reedy voice. 'I am astonished you would allow such a valuable and powerful tool to slip so easily from your grasp. And now you have frittered it away as if it meant no more to you than a passing fancy.'

Church stared him in the eye, but said nothing. Calatin's words were too close to the bone.

'We cannot use it, nor bear too long to be in its presence, but with it secured here your feeble compatriots should be blind to the locations of the Quadrillax,' Calatin continued. He sucked in a deep breath and said, 'We know you have the stone. Where is it?'

Church looked at him, straight through him, preparing his mind for what lay ahead.

The pain that lanced through his leg was excrutiating, and although he had hoped he could survive a while without calling out, it was impossible; his yell burned his throat. The beast removed the bloodstained corkscrew from Church's thigh and held it up so the scarlet droplets splattered his shirt. Church could feel his jeans growing wet around his wound.

'I know you're going to kill me,' he gasped, 'so there's no point me telling you anything.'

'It will be many days before we kill you, and plenty of roads of pain to explore before then.' Calatin leaned over until Church could smell the foul reek of his breath. 'But this is the beginning and all roads lead from here. I will ask you again: where is the stone?'

Church closed his eyes, muttered a prayer, and then screamed and screamed.

Calatin's voice floated to him through the waves of pain, fading in and out with the susurration of the tides.

'. . . citadels are hidden in the dark places beneath the earth. We are scattered to the four winds. No point on this island is free from us. And we wait and we wait, for we have

270

waited for so long, until the stars are aligned, the seasons are ready, until the gates fall open for ever and we can see to eternity. The end ...'

Fading in and fading out. Calatin standing nearby, talking as if to himself, his eyes fixed firmly on some inner horizon, painting a picture of future terror.

'... your land will be transformed. The eternal night will be drawn across the fields and hills, the moors and rivers, and not even the brightest light will pierce the gloom. Blood will flow through the streets of your cities like rivers and we will have fresh meat on our plates at every meal. Madness will strike you down when you look upon the face of the returned ones and know no prayer will deter them, no god will be listening. Your voice will have no authority in the face of powers you thought impossible. Your people will be herded, screaming, desperate, alone ...'

Darkness and pain. Hiding in the hole of his head, digging down deep until he could find that spot where the hero lay sleeping, waiting to be wakened to defend the island once more. But the road to the cave was long and filled with unquiet spirits. Marianne was there, repeatedly. She blew him a kiss as she jumped off the tube on her way to her interview in Wardour Street. She paddled in the warm waters of Ganavan, splashing him with her feet before they rushed to the dunes to make love. And she stood on the deck of a boat as the rising sun painted the Thames red, offering a kiss that transformed his life. Then she was speaking the words of the young Marianne, about life and death, the two of them merging into one. Here there was meaning and that gave him the strength to continue.

He awoke on the straw of the cell once more, his body afire with agony, his clothes soaked with blood.

'I thought you were dead,' Veitch's voice floated over him. He tried to speak, but the words were strangled in his throat. Rough hands grabbed his head and levered it up so he could take some stagnant water on his tongue from a wooden bowl. Veitch's face fell in and out of focus, concerned, yet also filled with the fear of his own memories. 'You look like shit. And I thought I had it bad when that bastard got me in his little playpen.' He heaped some straw with one hand, then lowered Church's head gently on to it. 'If it's any consolation, I don't think you told them anything. He was in a foul mood when they threw you in here. You're a better man than me. I'd have given up my nan if they'd asked me.'

Church closed his eyes and felt a wave of relief settle through him like mist. He feared he might have said something and forgotten it in his pain-induced delirium, but he had come through. Ironically, the suffering had driven him so far inside himself he had found what he had been looking for all along: the sleeping hero. And now he *did* feel different: stronger, more confident, less concerned by the petty fears and mundane terrors which had been undermining him for so long. Not even the thought of more torture could bring him down. He felt reborn.

'We find strength in hardship,' he croaked deliriously. Veitch saw the smile on his face and asked him if he were going mad from the pain, but Church was already drifting off into a recuperative sleep.

He didn't know how long he had been out, but he felt much better when the sound of the door disturbed him. He managed to lever himself on to his side to see two shadowy forms dragging what appeared to be a shapeless sack before throwing it into the other cell. When they had left he watched it closer. After a while it moved, then groaned.

'Are you okay?' His voice still sounded tissue-paper thin.

There was silence for a minute, and then the new arrival pulled himself weakly across the floor and used the bars to haul himself into a half-sitting, half-leaning position. In the flickering torchlight, Church saw an old man, his face haggard from suffering, his grey hair dirty and matted. He looked about a hundred. But then, gradually, Church saw through the mask crafted by pain and a wave of horror swept over him.

'Tom?' he hissed. Nearby, Veitch stirred and looked up.

The man looked across at Church, his piercing grey eyes now dull and flat. 'I never thought they would do it.' His voice was frailer than Church's, rustling on the edge of hearing, so weak it seemed he was only a step away from death. 'The old ways do not matter to them any more. They are so sure of their power, of victory, they feel able to ignore everything that has been established. I never thought . . .'

Veitch knelt down next to Church. 'Who's that?'

Church explained briefly, then said to Tom, 'Did Calatin do this to you?'

'He wanted to know if the others still had the power without you.' Tom's Scottish brogue was stronger in his weakness. He sucked in a deep, juddering breath and seemed to find a little strength from somewhere. 'They don't want to divert their attention from whatever it is they are doing, but they know you are all a threat.'

'What are they doing?'

Tom shook his head. 'Waiting. Making preparations.'

'Can the others stop them without me?' He glanced at Veitch. 'And Ryan?'

Tom seemed to see Church's cellmate for the first time. 'I don't know. I know some things, enough to help, but not everything. The legends of the Brothers and Sisters of Dragons have always talked about them as a unit, greater than the sum of its parts. The power you represent is heightened and focused when you are all brought together. Individually, you have some particular strengths, but—'

'Not enough,' Church finished bleakly.

Somewhere far off through the rock the tolling bell started once again, striking its long dismal notes that seemed to mark the end of them all.

* * *

273

The blast in Salisbury had left Tom weak and disoriented. As he staggered around attempting to find Ruth, the few remaining creatures had attacked him mercilessly. And when he came around, he was in the dark and in the hands of Calatin. The tortures inflicted on him had been intense. It seemed the Night Walkers' plan was in effect, but many elements were finely balanced and the timing was crucial; they could not afford any disruption. Although their infiltration of society was overwhelming, it appeared they feared Church and the others intensely; or rather, feared what Church and the others could do if they were allowed to reach their potential.

'But did you find out anything we could use?' Church said hopelessly.

'I do not know. It is so hard to remember.' Tom seemed disoriented, older than his years. Tenderly he touched the side of his head, where Church could make out the dark smear of encrusted blood.

'Are you okay?' Church enquired; it seemed a serious wound. Tom didn't seem to want to talk about it so Church pressed him again for information. 'At Stonehenge it was obvious you knew more than you were saying. You've got to tell me everything, Tom.'

'Sometimes there's so much in my head,' he said deliriously. 'All those years of thoughts piling up . . .' Suddenly he seemed to lock on to a random memory. 'Do you want to know how it started?'

'Yes, I'd like that.'

'No, not how it really started. No one knows that. But how it started here. I can tell you that.'

'Go on.'

Tom shifted awkwardly until he found himself a relatively comfortable position. 'You're an educated man. You know about the Celtic myth cycle?'

'A little. Some reading at university—'

'That's where it began. The secret history, locked in a few

274

stories and passed down the years so mankind would never forget the suffering and the terror.'

Church struggled to remember, but it had seemed such an insignificant part of his studies that the details had not remained. 'There was the Tuatha Dé Danann,' he began hesitantly.

'The name the Celts gave to them. The people of the Goddess Dana, the last generation of gods to rule before mankind's ascendence. When they arrived in our world, they brought with them great knowledge and magic from four marvellous cities – Falias, Gorias, Finias and Murias – as well as four talismans: the Stone of Fal, which screamed aloud when touched by the rightful king; the Sword of Nuada, their High King, which inflicted only fatal blows; the Spear of Lugh, the sun god; and above all else, the Cauldron of Dagda, the Allfather of the gods, source of life and death and healing.'

'Yes! Those are the things we're searching for—'

'People have always been searching for them. No one ever finds them.'

'But we have to. To free the . . . the Golden Ones.' He told Tom about the woman in the Watchtower.

Tom snorted. 'She is of the Danann. Of course she wants her people freed. But to find the talismans . . . They are more than they appear to be to human eyes, powerful symbols that . . .' His voice trailed off. 'Listen to me. These gods and everything they deal with are so alien they are unknowable. Their appearances, their motivations . . . the best our minds can do is give them some shape that's recognisable to us. Some are closer to us, like the woman you encountered between the worlds. Some are so incomprehensible we cannot even begin to give them form.'

'The creatures here—?'

Tom nodded. 'Too terrible for your mind to bear, but it can be taught to give them shape. The Celts called them the Formorii. Misshapen, violent, they were supposed to have come from the waters to invade this world. They were, to all intents and purposes, the manifestation of evil, a corruption, perhaps, or an infestation. The embodiment of negativity, constantly striving to drag the cosmos into chaos and darkness. And they were led by the most devastating, destructive force of all – the Celts called him Balor, the one-eyed god of death. The legends claimed he was so dreadful that whoever he turned his eye upon was destroyed.'

Tom's description was so desolate Church felt a blanket of hopelessness descend on him. He couldn't tell if Veitch felt it too; his head was lowered, his expression hidden by his hair.

'The Fomorii came like a tidal wave,' Tom continued. 'The Tuatha Dé Danann were unprepared. They were enslaved and the Fomorii established a reign of terror that became known as the Eternal Night.'

'But the Danann struck back.' Church recalled the woman in the Watchtower's account. 'They had the power to defeat the Fomorii.'

Tom nodded. 'The war leader Nuada led the Danann in a counterstrike, but he seemed doomed to defeat until he was joined by Lugh, the sun god, who was part Fomorii. In the stories, his grandfather was Balor. At the second battle of Magh Tuireadh, Lugh plunged his spear into Balor's eye, killing him instantly. The Fomorii were demoralised; the Danann easily regained power. But there had been too much destruction and suffering – even for gods – for things to return to the way they had been before. To preserve some kind of order, a truce was reached – the Covenant. Both the Danann and the Fomorii would leave earth to man and return for ever to the Danann homeland which the Celts called Otherworld. And they took with them almost every magical creature, everything which couldn't abide by the strict laws that would remain in their passing. That exodus was known as the Sundering and it was the end of the Age of Wonders, known also as the Age of Terror.'

'You're just talking about bleedin' stories!' Veitch said suddenly with exasperation.

Tom closed his eyes and laid his head back wearily. 'The stories can only begin to hint at the truths of those days – they are coded messages from the distant past. There have been other legends in other cultures attempting to make sense of what happened, but the Celts came the closest in their descriptions, which is why they have been the most enduring. The stories are confused – the gods were given different names by the different Celtic tribes across Europe – but in essence they were all talking about the same thing.'

'So they left us behind for good—'

'Not wholly. The boundaries between Otherworld and here were supposed to be sealed, but there were weak spots, the mounds, the lakes and rivers – the liminal zones.' Tom's voice continually faded away, then grew stronger, so Church had to strain to hear what he was saying. 'Some of the gods crossed back over for brief excursions or exerted their influence from Otherworld. Some of the magical creatures too. And sometimes people from here found their way over there.'

'I remember now,' Church interjected. 'The Celtic gods slowly metamorphosed into our faery myths and Otherworld became Faeryland. The keepers of treasure and secrets, mischiefmakers—'

'Mischief!' Church was taken aback by the venom in Tom's voice. 'They interfered with us down the years, tormenting people, tricking people. Yes, sometimes it was just lights in the sky, strange sightings of lake monsters, nocturnal manifestations. And sometimes it was slaughter.'

'That's all very interesting,' Veitch said sarcastically, 'but it doesn't exactly help us, does it?'

'Any information helps you,' Tom replied.

'It tells us the Danann have defeated the Fomorii before and they can do it again,' Church said. 'It tells us there's hope.'

'It doesn't tell us how to get out of this bleedin' cage!'

'You could have mentioned all this before,' Church said sharply.

'I could have.'

'How do you know all this? Did the Bone Inspector tell you?'

'Some of it.' There was a long silence in which he seemed to be wrestling with his thoughts, and then he said, 'I have been to Otherworld.'

Church at first wondered if it were some kind of stupid attempt at humour, but he had never heard Tom joke before. 'You're lying.'

He sighed. 'I never lie.'

'Then how?'

'Through one of those weak spots I mentioned. In Scotland, on a hillside.'

Veitch seemed excited by this turn in the conversation. He crawled to the front of the cage and gripped the bars. 'What was it like?'

'So many wonders.' Tom's voice was oddly strained. 'I was changed, immeasurably. I learned things there, wisdom, certain skills, the ability to manipulate subtle energies—'

'Magic,' Church said.

'If you like. Though I'm not adept, I achieve some little things.'

'Like getting us out of here?' Veitch said hopefully.

Tom shook his head and they all fell silent for a long minute.

'You're not lying to us?' Church stressed.

'I said, I never lie.'

Veitch hammered a fist against the bars angrily, then crawled back to the corner of the cage.

'Then you know at first hand what all these so-called gods can do,' Church continued. 'Is there hope?'

'There's always hope.'

'What about Calatin and the Fomorii?'

'The Fomorii are a race made up of tribes, some large, some small, all vying for power. Since Balor died they have been on the verge of civil war. Although Calatin is the

278

nominal leader, his halfbreed status has not endeared him to the others. But that's by the by. Their return to our world has reunited them to a degree, but the power struggle has simply moved into the background.' He coughed fitfully, then spat through the bars. 'You and the others are a fine trophy, the symbol of everything the Fomorii wish to eradicate. Whomsoever holds you captive, or eliminates you, is advanced in the eyes of all the tribes.'

'What are you saying?' Church gripped the bars to lever himself up; although the pain had receded a little, he felt like nails were being driven into his flesh.

'Were you to escape,' Tom continued weakly, 'there would be others at your back apart from Calatin. He is dangerous . . .' He paused, moistened his lips. 'But there is one much worse. He controls dark power to a degree which Calatin can only dream of, but it has consumed him physically. Now his presence can only be contained by a murder of crows, swirling tightly together in a proscribed pattern that prevents his life energy seeping out. His name is Mollecht.'

Church remembered the description the Bone Inspector had given of their pursuers at Avebury. 'So Calatin set the Fabulous Beast and the Wild Hunt after us, but this Mollecht is hunting us too?'

'Christ, it sounds like we're wasting our time,' Veitch groaned.

'No,' Church said adamantly. 'If we can get out of here and find the four talismans by Beltane then we can free the Danann—'

'Beltane?' Veitch looked at Church in bafflement.

'May Day.'

'Shit.' He slumped down in the straw, his head in his hands.

'—and they can do all the dirty work for us,' Church finished, ignoring Veitch's despondency.

'Best be careful what you wish for,' Tom croaked. His head

279

was nodding; he was on the verge of either sleeping or blacking out.

'Tom!' Church called. 'Stay focused. We need some answers. You've been out of this cell a lot. Did you see any chance of a way out of here?'

There was a long pause, then: 'No. No way out.'

Occasionally noises would filter through the walls, their source impossible to discern, but disturbing nonetheless; Church tried his best to ignore them. Instead, he turned his thoughts to Tom and his outrageous assertion that he had visited the home of the gods. Church had noticed a single expression that had convinced him; it was so fleeting, it had probably only been there for an instant, but it had been so stark and filled with terror Church had almost flinched.

He and Veitch spent what seemed like hours turning over every possibility that might lead to escape, but their talk only increased their sense of hopelessness. Yet as they crawled off to their separate corners to sleep, Church's mind was still turning, refusing to give up. Whatever had been released from deep within during his agonies on the torture table still fired him, refusing to allow him to drift into despair.

He awoke suddenly, aware that there was someone standing near him. With a start, he threw himself up and back against the cold, slick stone wall, ready to defend himself. But instead of a threat, there was a moment of shock while he struggled to comprehend what he was actually seeing. Before him, wrapped in a thick, dark green cloak with a hood thrown over her head, was the woman from the Watchtower. She raised a hand quickly to silence him before he could cry out. Quickly he glanced around to get his bearings; both Veitch and Tom appeared to be sleeping.

'How did you get in here?' he hissed.

Her face peered from the dark depths of her hood, pale and beautiful like the moon. 'I am here to help,' she said in that soft, musical voice that had so entranced him before. 'I am your patron, Jack. I am guiding you to a greater destiny. In the current climate, it is dangerous for me to leave the Watchtower, but you need my aid to leave this foul place. Do you know what the Night Walkers plan to do with you?'

'I can guess.'

'No,' she said darkly, 'you cannot. It was foolish of you to allow yourself to fall into their hands.' There was an edge to her voice he hadn't heard before; it suggested darker emotions lying just beneath the surface. 'It was even more foolish to let them take hold of the Wayfinder. You must not leave here without it. Should they ever utilise the secrets it represents, it would be the end of everything. Do you understand?'

Church nodded dumbly.

Gold flecks seemed to flicker in the depths of her eyes. 'When next you try the cell door, it will be open. And all the doors before you this night will be open. That is my help, the rest you must do yourself. You are a Brother of Dragons, and perhaps you need to earn that title for yourself.'

'Deus ex machina,' he muttered.

She held up a hand sharply. 'Do not disappoint my faith in you again.' Her cloak seemed to shimmer and then fold in on itself. There was the strange sucking noise he had first heard outside the Salisbury depot as the air collapsed, and then she was gone.

Church stared blankly into the vacated space, trying to come to terms with what he had heard, and then he launched himself across the cell. His rough shaking woke Veitch, but Church didn't wait to explain. He was already at the cell door, almost afraid to try it, but it swung open with a loud creak at just the touch of a finger.

'How'd you manage that?' Veitch said incredulously.

'I'll tell you later.' Church propelled himself across the gap to Tom's cell; the door opened just as easily. It was a little harder to stir the exhausted man, who was mumbling and twitching in the throes of nightmare. Up close Church could see the bloody scar on Tom's temple; he wondered how much damage had been done to him.

Veitch helped Church get him to his feet, but it didn't take Tom long to fight through his daze. He seemed sharper than the last time they had spoken. 'Stop manhandling me!' he snapped. They let him go, and although he wavered slightly, he seemed able to walk unaccompanied. Cautiously they pulled open the main door.

The corridor without was shored up by rough timbers in parts. It was lit intermittently by torches, but the gloom was pervasive. As they moved out, anxiously glancing around, they became aware of vile smells awash in the air, the foetid stink of the Fomorii, the dampness of the underground atmosphere, and beneath it all the stench of cooking that Church had experienced in the torture chamber.

Their bodies were clenched, their eyes darting anxiously; Church didn't think he had ever felt so much fearful apprehension. It seemed it would only be a matter of time before they stumbled across one of the dark creatures, but the winding corridors were as silent as the grave, almost as if the Fomorii had deserted the mine.

When they reached a junction in the tunnels, Tom paused to lean against the wall. Church thought he was fading again, but Tom waved him away furiously when he went to help. Eventually he pointed along the tunnel which sloped deeper into the ground. 'That way.'

Veitch glanced in the opposite direction. 'You sure? It looks—'

'That way,' Tom snapped. 'We cannot leave until we have the Wayfinder.'

Church concurred, then led the way along the tunnel which grew steeper and steeper with each step. Soon they were almost slipping and sliding down an incline, desperately trying not to make any noise, but the sound of their shoes on the rough surface echoed crazily. The tunnel came to an abrupt halt in a cavern so large the roof was lost in shadows. After the grey and black of the corridors, Church was shocked to see the gleaming, manmade yellow of the drums he had first come across at the depot in Salisbury; they were piled across the expanse of the cavern.

Alarm bells started ringing in Church's mind. 'What's going on?' he whispered. 'I thought this chemical delivery was just a front for whatever the Fomorii were doing in Salisbury.'

'They are not chemicals,' Tom said darkly. 'Not in any sense you mean.'

Veitch prised off the lid of one of the drums and peered inside, snatching his head back suddenly as the foul stink of the contents hit him. 'Shit! That's bleedin' disgusting!' he hissed. Inside a viscous black solution like crude oil reflected their faces.

'What is it then?' Church searched Tom's face for any sign.

'A ritual potion of some kind.'

Church looked around dumbly at the stacked drums. 'What could they use all this for? And why are they transporting it?'

Veitch cocked his head and listened carefully. 'We can't hang around here gassing all day. Let's sort this out later. Where do we find that Wayfinder thing?'

Tom pointed across the cavern. 'Over there somewhere.'

Veitch shook his head. 'If you say so, mate. Lead the way.'

Their footsteps echoed hollowly off the stacks of drums as they wove their way among them; it almost seemed like they were in a maze. At any moment he expected the Fomorii to fall upon them from all directions. But though he strained to hear a sound, there was nothing, and that was just as unnerving.

It took them fifteen minutes to reach the other side, tension growing with every step. Tom led them to an upward-sloping tunnel, and five minutes later they came upon a rough-hewn door. There was a large padlock on it, but when Church

283

touched it, it fell open in his hands and the door swung in. It led on to a small room cast in blue from the flickering flame of the Wayfinder, which stood on a bench against the far wall. Next to it, on a velvet cloth, was the Black Rose, and beside that was a handgun and some boxes of ammunition. Church stepped in ahead of the others, snatched up the rose and slipped it into his pocket.

'What was that?' Tom asked.

'Just something they took from me when I got here,' Church said dismissively. He examined the Wayfinder carefully and then hid it under his jacket.

'Is that what everybody's so worked up about?' Veitch said. 'A bleedin' lantern?' He picked up the gun and slugs.

Church eyed him suspiciously. 'Are those yours?'

Veitch shrugged. 'For self-defence.'

They hurried back into the tunnel, but Church felt increasingly uncomfortable. 'This doesn't make any sense. Surely they wouldn't leave the Wayfinder here without any guards if it's supposed to be so important to them.'

'Perhaps they didn't expect us to be wandering freely out of our cells,' Tom said sarcastically.

'Even so—' Before he could finish his sentence, the mine reverberated with the chilling sound of the tolling bell they had heard before. It seemed close at hand, but still muffled, as if behind thick walls of stone.

'Shit,' Veitch muttered. His face looked drained of blood in the flickering torchlight.

'Which way?' Church prompted. Tom was expressionless; Veitch merely shrugged. On a hunch, Church left them and sprinted back down the tunnel to the cavern. Through the gloom on the other side, he could see movement. It was hard to make out at first, just oddly shifting patterns of shadows like running water in the dark, but as his eyes focused he had the disturbing impression of insects swarming from a nest, an impossible multitude sweeping out amongst the yellow drums. The image was almost hypnotic, but it filled him

284

with dread. He sprinted back up the tunnel, not even pausing as he reached the other two. 'This way,' he yelled as he passed.

The tunnels were low, dark and slick, and numerous times they slipped or cracked their heads against low roofs, but they were driven on by the noise growing behind them; it sounded at first like the low, deep rasp of an enormous beast, then it began to fragment into a mix of individual sounds, of rumbling, bestial voices and thundering feet.

Their breath burned in their throats and sweat stung their eyes, but they knew they couldn't slow for a moment. The tunnel rose upwards relentlessly, but Church couldn't shake the terrible feeling that it would suddenly start dipping down again, leaving them nowhere to run but round in circles. As they passed another junction, Church felt a blast of chill air. Scrambling to a halt, he herded the others up the branch tunnel. A minute later they hit a dead end.

'Shit!' Veitch's eyes blazed like a cornered animal.

The thunderous sound of pursuit was growing louder; the Fomorii couldn't be far off the tunnel junction.

'Up,' Church gasped; it was all he could force out.

Veitch and Tom raised their heads, but all they could see was darkness. Then another gust of fresh air hit them in their faces and they realised what he meant. Fastened to one wall was a rusty iron ladder. Although Church wasn't convinced it would hold, he forced Tom up first and then Veitch made him follow before taking up the rear. Tom was starting to fade, but Church egged him on insistently. The ladder was cold and wet to the touch and once or twice Church's foot slipped off it, almost hitting Veitch in the face; a flurry of cursing followed. Their muscles ached almost too much to hold on, but the threat of what lay below was enough to free any last reserves of strength they had. It wasn't long until they felt the vibrations in the ladder that signalled the Fomorii were behind them.

Church was just beginning to fear that the climb was too high for them when Tom suddenly hauled himself over the top. Church launched himself out, rolling on to scrubby grass and Dartmoor granite. It was night, cold but clear, the sky sprinkled with stars. Veitch landed on top of him, winding him.

'They're right behind,' Church gasped unnecessarily. 'We'll never get away—'

'Give me a hand.' Veitch was at the shaft entrance. For a second, Church couldn't understand what he was doing, but then it clicked. Together they gripped the top of the ladder and strained. Church thought he could see movement in the dark just below and wondered briefly if they had made the right decision. But then there was a deep rending noise as the rusty supports pulled free from the wall of the shaft. The weight of whatever was ascending continued the movement and with a loud crash the ladder tore away and plummeted into the depths.

Veitch clapped Church on the shoulder jubilantly. 'Bloody hell. We did it!'

But Tom was insisting there was no time for celebration, and soon they were stumbling across the moorland in the moonlight.

The land rose and fell, but they kept to the hollows, crawling on their bellies when they had to mount a ridge, and eventually they made their way to a windswept copse which allowed them some shelter. Church leaned against a tree and looked back, but he could see no indication of pursuit. Suddenly Church was filled with all the pain and exhaustion inflicted upon him by Calatin's torture. It had somehow been suppressed by the urgency of their flight. As he began to pitch forward, Veitch caught him and supported him to the ground.

They allowed themselves only ten minutes to rest, just in case, then Church pulled out the Wayfinder and, with Veitch's help, he wearily began to follow its flame westwards across the moor.

CHAPTER TWELVE

Mi Vida Loca

Sunlight drenched the streets of Glastonbury and the air was filled with the sweet aroma of honeysuckle and lemon. The sky overhead had been as blue as the brightest summer day since Ruth, Laura and Shavi had nursed the van into town, shattered by the rigours of their pursuit by the Wild Hunt. The temperature had remained unseasonably balmy, without the briefest hint of rain or a chill on the wind.

'It doesn't seem right,' Ruth said, trying on the cheap sunglasses she had bought after browsing in the proliferation of New Age shops. She glanced up, trying to reconcile the weather with the time of year.

'Don't knock it.' Laura was impassive behind her own sunglasses.

'It's more than just the weather,' Ruth continued. 'There's something in the air. Can't you feel it?'

'Peace,' Shavi interjected.

'For the first time since we set off from London, I feel safe. It's like there's a bubble over the place, protecting it from everything that's out there. Smell all those scents! There doesn't seem to be any pollution at all. And the air almost seems to . . . sparkle? Like there's gold dust in it.'

The mood was reflected in the open, smiling faces of the people who passed by, nodding to the three of them as if they had always lived there. The residents moved slowly, lazily, gazing into the shop windows, ambling across the road, heedless of the slow-moving traffic.

'Glastonbury has always been seen as one of the most magically powerful places in the country,' Shavi noted. 'For hundreds, perhaps thousands of years, people have been drawn here by the supposed power in the land. Celts and Christians, hippies and New Age Travellers. It is supposed to be on one of the longest ley lines in the country, running from St Michael's Mount in Cornwall, through Glastonbury, Avebury and on across the country to East Anglia.'

'You seem to know a lot about all this.'

He smiled curiously. 'When I was six years old I had a map on my wall with all the ley lines drawn on in red felt tip. When I was ten I had read every book ever written about the subject, from Alfred Watkins' *The Old Straight Track* to the latest scholarly journal. I branched out from that into reading about Buddhism, Taoism, Islam. In my head it all seemed linked.' He shrugged. 'Where does all that come from in a child?' He already seemed to know the answer to his question.

Ruth had a sudden sense of great wisdom in his eyes. 'So you think there's something in all this ley line stuff?' she ventured.

'There are plenty of people ready to pour scorn on it, as there are for anything which is difficult to categorise, compartmentalise, measure and define. But you have seen the blue fire.' Ruth nodded. She remembered the look of almost childlike wonder on his face when she described it to him as they dropped off the van at the garage for repairs. 'If only I could have seen it too,' he continued dreamily.

'You will. The visible evidence of it is all part of this new age, so it seems.'

'Did you know,' he said thoughtfully, 'that ley is an old Anglo-Saxon word, but it has an older, obsolete meaning, of *flame* or *fire*? Our ancient peoples knew more than we give them credit for. Interestingly, there is also a well-established ley linking Stonehenge and Glastonbury—'

'Yes, very interesting,' Laura interjected, 'now how about getting some food? At least with a full stomach I can sleep through all your ramblings.'

Ruth refrained from making any comment; there was plenty of time for Shavi to reach his own judgment about Laura.

They had pitched camp in a copse on the outskirts, but they needn't have worried about secrecy. They had been discovered by the farmer who owned the land within the hour, but he cheerily wished them well and continued on his way. The feel of the sun on their faces was a relief after the endless storm and the terrifying night and they had lain outside their new tents against a fallen tree, trying to come to terms with what had happened. It soon became apparent they had no idea what they were going to do next. Ruth wanted to head back to Dartmoor to search for Church, but while Laura didn't want to abandon him, she felt it was both futile and dangerous. Ruth tried to call the pub from her mobile, but the line was dead. In the end, they resolved to rest a while in Glastonbury while they recovered, hoping that some plan would present itself to them.

They wandered around until they found a café, the Excalibur, where Shavi and Laura had the vegetarian option of tomatoes on toast and Ruth opted for bacon and eggs. They felt more refreshed than they had any right to; whatever strange atmosphere now permeated Glastonbury seemed to be healing both their psychological scars and their exhaustion.

Afterwards, they dozed for a while in the sun, catching up on the previous night's deprivation, and then they explored the town, drinking in the unique atmosphere of ancient history that seemed to permeate every street. It didn't take Ruth and Laura long to get to know Shavi. He was unguarded in a way few others were, answering every question they had for him without a hint of embarrassment or reticence; his openness seemed to make Laura particularly uneasy, and she spent the first two hours trying to catch him out, to prove he was lying to them.

He was brought up in a tight-knit family in west London, and although his father had adopted most western ways since he came to the UK to study medicine in his twenties, Shavi had still had a strict upbringing when it came to the traditions and religion of his family. Shavi's interests had soon taken him well away from his heritage, throwing him into conflict with his father almost daily. As he progressed into his teens, his father's fury at his rebellious ways had threatened the stability of the family and, once he turned sixteen, he was forced to leave home.

Ruth was aghast at the blasé way he mentioned such a period of upheaval. 'Didn't it bother you at all?' she asked.

'I shed tears for my family every day,' he replied, 'but what could I do? Remain in a life I had no empathy for, pretending to be someone else? The only option was to be true to myself, whatever price I had to pay.'

His life after leaving his family seemed to have been an odd mix of hedonism and spiritual questing. He freely acknowledged experimenting with various drugs, and, at Laura's prompting, admitted a healthy sex life fired by curiosity. Yet at the same time he had an insatiable thirst for knowledge, particularly of a spiritual and philosophical kind. 'If I indulged in self-analysis I would admit to trying to fill some kind of void,' he said, 'but it is more important to me to follow my instincts to see where they take me.'

Laura was curious about a small scar above his top lip, the only blemish on his perfect features; they were both surprised at the downcast expression her question elicited.

'It happened two years ago. I was with a boy in a club in Clapham,' he began. 'The Two Brewers. It was quite renowned in London as one of the top gay clubs—'

'You're gay?' Ruth instantly regretted her exclamation; it sounded faintly bigoted, the way she said it, although she certainly hadn't meant it that way. 'It's just, you don't seem gay.'

'I put no boundaries around my life. I have had men and

I have had women.' He smiled forgivingly. 'Anyway, the Two Brewers had a reputation as the kind of place you could go without encountering any of the trouble you would find in the more unenlightened parts of the capital. The boy I was with – Lee was his name – had been a very close friend for many years. We had a good night, got a little high, plenty of dancing. When we left in the early hours we thought we'd go for a walk on Clapham Common to look at the stars. It was a beautiful night. We were walking down one of the side streets towards the common when the mood took us to stop and kiss.' He closed his eyes, remembering; at first his face was tranquil, but then a shadow flickered across it. 'Somebody hit me, hard.' He tapped the scar. 'I think it was a gun, or perhaps a piece of piping – it is very hard to remember. I think I blacked out for a while. When I came to, Lee was struggling with someone further down the street. I called out, tried to get to him, but I was so dazed.'

When he opened his eyes, they were wet, but he made no attempt to hide the emotion. 'My vision was fractured – I had concussion – but I could see the man attacking Lee. He was swinging something down on his head. The crack sounded like a piece of wood snapping in two. But even then he did not stop. He kept hitting, and hitting.' He closed his eyes once more. 'Lee died. His murderer got away. I cannot even remember what he looked like.'

'I'm so sorry.' Ruth rested a comforting hand on his forearm.

Laura was just as moved by the story. 'What a homophobic bastard! If I found out who it was, I'd cut off his dick and shove it down his throat.'

Shavi raised his hands and shrugged. 'I have done my best not to let it scar me emotionally as well as physically, but it has been difficult. I try to tell myself there is enough hatred in the world without me adding to it.'

His honesty created a bond with them both; it was imposs-ible not to trust him completely. Ruth found herself almost hypnotised by him. His voice was so calm, it made her feel tranquil, and his eyes were both mischievous and intensely sexual. His body had a graceful power, like a ballet dancer, compact, with muscles she had not expected to see in someone so cerebral. She had watched him performing his t'ai chi after they had awoken from their nap and she had almost cried to see him so at peace with himself. She was glad he was with them.

Despite herself, Laura felt the same way. Shavi's confidence in his abilities and direction in life was reassuring to someone who felt as if her own existence had been spinning off its axis for most of her adult life. In the disparate crew so far assembled, Shavi felt like the cement that would hold them all together. It gave her secret hope that it might, after all, turn out okay.

'We need to get you some clothes,' Church noted as they rested in the wan sunlight on the lea of an outcropping of grey Dartmoor granite. He felt much better. Tom had found some foul-tasting roots and leaves which had taken the edge off much of the pain and tiredness he had felt following his ordeal in Calatin's torture chamber. Ahead of them, a large fox picked its way cautiously across the scrubland, its russet fur a splash of colour against the grubby green. Church had a sudden flashback to the one he had seen in the street near Albert Bridge on the night his life changed for ever. Oddly, he did not have the same sense of wonder.

'No hurry. It's not like it's winter.' Veitch did seem oblivious to the elements, despite his naked torso. In daylight, Church couldn't stop looking at the startling, colourful pictures tattooed on his flesh. Some were scenes of remarkable beauty, but others were almost too disturbing to consider: deformed faces that looked out at the viewer with a palpable sense of threat; odd, surreal shapes that seemed alien and unrecognisable, but touched disturbing notes in his subconscious; creatures that seemed half-animal, half-human.

Tom scanned the sky thoughtfully where a little blue was breaking through the heavy cloud. 'The weather should be fine,' he noted almost to himself before adding to the others, 'It will make travel a little easier. We may have a long way to go before we can rest.'

'We need to find Ruth and Laura.' Church fought back any thoughts suggesting they might not have survived the raid on the pub.

'Have you not learned anything yet?' Tom glared at Church through his spectacles, which, against all the odds, he had somehow managed to hang on to throughout the time in the mine. 'Time is of the essence! Your world is winding down and you want to dally searching for your friends? You are Brothers and Sisters of Dragons. You will find each other when the time is right.'

Veitch bristled at the man's tone. 'Oi. Nobody made you the gaffer. Keep a civil tongue in your head.'

Tom held his gaze for a minute, then looked to the horizon. Finally he hauled himself unsteadily to his feet and said, 'There are many miles ahead of us.'

They set off slowly across the moorland, enveloped by the moan of the wind and the plaintive cries of birds. The going was hard; the ground was uneven and marshy after the rains, while hidden hollows and boulders forced them to be cautious. The lamp was still flickering westwards, and Church wondered how far they could be expected to travel without a car. At the rate they were moving, Beltane would come and go before they left Dartmoor.

'Any idea what the date is?' he asked. 'I can't work out how long we were in that place. The lack of daylight plays havoc with your body clock.' No one had any idea.

Church noticed Tom was eyeing him strangely and asked what was wrong. 'You seem different to the last time I saw you,' he said. 'More in control of who you are. You might actually be able to live up to what's expected of you.'

'Thanks,' Church said sarcastically. He even felt different;

the vision in the Watchtower, the death of the young Mari-anne, his terrible experiences at the hands of Calatin, all had altered him on some fundamental level. He himself was still coming to terms with who he now was.

'So, you still haven't told us what it was like in that Otherworld place,' Veitch said to Tom.

'No, and I'm not about to.'

'Why not?' Veitch said with irritation; Church was a little concerned at how close to the surface his temper lay.

'Because it would be like describing an impressionist paint-ing to a blind man.'

'Are you saying I'm stupid?' Veitch's fists bunched subcon-sciously.

'No, I'm saying you're blind. But perhaps you'll see it for yourself one day, and then you'll understand.'

That thought seemed to cheer Veitch immensely. 'That would be bleedin' great! I bet it's better than this shitty little world.'

'Different,' Tom replied sourly.

Amidst regular ribald humour from Veitch, their step picked up and as the sky turned blue and the sun grew stronger, the miles fell behind them. After the disgusting food in the mine, they were all consumed with hunger and by midmorn-ing they broke off their travelling to hunt for food. Tom did one of his tricks and returned with a couple of rabbits, and while they were cooking over a spit on the fire he pointed out various herbs for Church to collect and had Veitch grub-bing for tubers and mushrooms. It was a bizarre meal, half of which Church couldn't begin to recognise, but it tasted remarkable and they finished every scrap. After a brief nap in the shade of an ancient hawthorn tree, they continued on their way and soon the grim, bleak expanse of the moor gave way to budding trees and hedgerows and, eventually, a tiny, winding lane. With sore feet and aching muscles, they moved slowly, searching for any signs of civilisation.

* * *

An hour or so later they found a small farm surrounded by a thick wall of trees. At first glance it seemed deserted; a tractor and equipment sat idle in the yard at the back of the house and there was no sound apart from the mewling of a litter of kittens underneath a broken old cart. After hammering futilely on the door, Church and Veitch searched the outbuildings until Tom's cry called them back to the farmhouse. A ruddy-faced man with wiry, grey hair was pointing a shotgun at Tom's head.

'We're just looking for a place to stay for the night,' Church protested.

The farmer eyed them suspiciously, but didn't lower his weapon.

'Bloody hell, it's *Deliverance*,' Veitch hissed under his breath.

'Okay, we'll go!' Church said. 'So much for West Country hospitality.'

'Christ, a night sleeping under a hedge,' Veitch moaned as they turned away.

The farmer brought the shotgun to his side. 'You can't be staying out there at night,' he said, hesitantly. Church saw fear in his eyes. 'Don't you know what's happening?'

'What do you mean?' Church asked.

'It's changed. It's all bloody well changed.' He looked away uncomfortably.

'What's troubling you?' Tom attempted a note of concern which came across as insincere, but it didn't seem to trouble the farmer.

'Don't tell me you don't bloody see it. Everybody in the countryside knows it's different now, only nobody talks about it!' His voice rose, then cracked, on the edge of hysteria. He looked from one to the other frantically. 'You can't bloody go out at night! You take your life in your hands if you go into the wilder places! There're all sorts of things out there—'

'You've seen them?' Church asked.

The farmer's mouth clamped shut as his eyes narrowed

suspiciously. 'Oh, ah, I'm not bloody mad, you know.'

'We've seen them too.' The farmer looked at Church with such sudden hope it was almost childlike. 'Things *have* changed.'

'What's gone wrong?' the farmer pleaded. 'What are they?' There were tears of relief moistening his eyes; Church thought he was going to hug them. 'You better come inside.'

The kitchen was dark despite the sunlight outside; it didn't look like it had been modernised in years. There was a large, heavily scored wooden table in the centre of the room, and a stove on the far wall over which hung a line of fading clothes drying in the dull heat. The floor was tiled and muddy and the kitchen was filled with old cooking smells and the underlying aroma of wet dogs. The farmer introduced himself as Daniel Marsh. He'd worked the land since he was a boy, as had generations of his family before him, but Church couldn't see any signs of other family members. He put a battered kettle on the stove and boiled up the water for an enormous pot of tea, which he served in chipped mugs. It soon become apparent to Church and the others that some heavy burden was lying on his shoulders beyond his obvious fear of the change in the countryside. After half an hour of small talk, he couldn't stop himself any more.

'When the sun goes down, I'm never the same,' he began cautiously. His eyes looked hollow from too little sleep and his face muscles had sagged under the weight of an array of dismal emotions. 'One of those things out there, it comes here.' He motioned to the house. 'Not every night, but enough so I can't rest.'

'What sort of thing?' Veitch eyed the farmer askance.

'A devil. A little devil, 'bout as high as this here table.' His head fell until his face was hidden and he was racked by a juddering sob. 'I don't know how I'm going to go on. I thought about taking that' – he waved towards the shotgun – 'and blowing my bloody head off, but I don't know, I don't know . . .'

'What does it do?' Church asked anxiously.

'It talks to me, pinches me. Hurts me. I know that doesn't sound much, but the things it says!' He covered his face for a moment, then seemed to catch himself. 'You can stay here tonight if you like,' he said, unable to hide his desperation.

'Sure. You've sold it to us so well,' Veitch said.

Marsh acted as if a weight had been taken off his shoulders. He promised them good food for dinner, then left them alone while he headed out to do some work in the fields.

'Do you think it's happening like this all over?' Veitch asked as they sat around the table gorging themselves on the farmer's bread and cheese.

'What do you mean?' Church was looking at deep score marks in the kitchen walls, as if they had been swiped by razor-sharp nails.

'People all around the country dealing with this weird shit, but too scared or too worried their neighbours will think them crazy to talk about it. So they just keep it all to themselves and nobody knows what's going down.'

Church shrugged. 'It can't stay bottled up for much longer. Sooner or later it's going to blow up and the Government is going to have to do something about it. It'll be on the front page of the *Sun*—'

'Unless things reach a head before then.' Tom pushed his chair away from the table and rested his hands on his belly. 'By the time anyone really realises what's happening, there might not be any Government, or newspapers. Just people running for their lives with nowhere to go.'

There was a long moment of silence and then Veitch said, 'You're a bundle of laughs, aren't you. I'm surprised the army or MI5 or some of those bastards aren't on to it already.'

Church considered the lack of media coverage about what events they had witnessed, and then thought about the stone-faced men clustered around the charred skeletons at the Salisbury depot and the helicopters they had seen scouring the landscape. 'Maybe they already are. Maybe they don't know what to do either.'

The evening was so balmy it could have been summer, and it was filled with the kind of perfumes that shouldn't have been expected for several weeks: rose, jasmine, clematis and the sweet bloom of night-scented stock. Overhead the clear sky sparkled with an array of stars that had Ruth, Laura and Shavi gazing up in awe.

'You never see that in the city.' Laura was unable to hide the wonder in her voice.

'I can't believe this place. It's almost magical.' Ruth felt a shiver run through her. 'If this is part of the New Age too then it can't all be bad.'

'A time of terrors and wonders,' Shavi agreed. 'Perhaps all the other focal points for the power in the earth are like this – a sanctuary, a place to rest and recharge your own energy where the Evil outside cannot touch you.'

'I feel like staying here for ever,' Ruth said regretfully.

'Somewhere safe.' Laura glanced from Ruth to Shavi.

His faint smile suggested he knew what they were feeling, but that it could never be. 'Let us make the most of this time,' he added, leading the way along the street to the pub. But his unspoken words lay heavy on all of them.

In the King William pub next to the Market Cross they ordered three pints of potent scrumpy. The cloudy drink had a rough quality and a powerful aroma of apples that was completely dissimilar to the mass-produced cider they had all tried before, but whether it was the invigorating, dreamlike atmosphere that pervaded the town or the sudden infusion of alcohol, within moments it felt like the best drink they had ever had.

Shavi nodded. 'This is what our ancestors used to feel. The body, mind and soul need to be in perfect balance. The trinity leading to enlightenment represented by the eye opening in the pyramid. Knowledge is fine, but the Age of Reason's focus upon it above all else threw us out of balance. Our souls became weakened. Instinctively, we all recognised it – that feeling of discontent with our lives and our jobs that has pervaded us all for the last few decades. You must have noticed it?' They nodded, entranced by his voice. 'We need to learn to feel again.'

'Well, aren't you the guru.' Laura grinned at him, but there was none of the spite that usually infused her comments; Ruth wondered if the magic was working on her character too.

'Perhaps that is part of this quest we are all on,' Shavi mused. 'Not merely to find physical objects of power to defend ourselves, but in some way to discover and unlock the truly alchemical part of our souls that will make us whole and more able to cope with the trials ahead. A quest for the spiritual rather than the physical, a search that goes inward—'

'Why don't you shut up and do a quest to the bar,' Laura jibed.

His smile warmed them both. 'I talk too much,' he apologised, 'or perhaps I think too much. Either way, now is the time for enjoyment.'

At the end of the evening they made their way back to the camp in a drunken haze of laughter and joking. But the first thing they saw when they reached the tents was clothes scattered across their sleeping bags and their possessions ransacked. Nothing seemed to have been taken.

'This is weird,' Ruth said. 'Just like the car at the service station. It feels like someone's following us.'

Even that didn't dampen their spirits, nor remove their feeling that Glastonbury was an oasis of safety for them that night. Ruth and Laura tidied up while Shavi lit a fire, and once it was roaring, they lazed around it. The atmosphere felt so relaxing and secure, Ruth only managed ten minutes before her eyes started to close. She crawled into her tent, leaving Laura and Shavi to talk dreamily into the night.

After a while he dipped into his pocket and pulled out a plastic bag filled with mushrooms. 'The sacrament,' he said with a smile. 'Care for some?'

Laura pulled out a handful and examined them in the firelight. 'Magic shrooms? Where'd you get these?'

'I brought them with me. Since the change, they have become even more powerful, almost shamanistic in effect. Taken in quantity, I find my spirit—' A smile sprang to his lips as he caught himself. 'I am talking too much again.'

'Before I hooked up with this weird crew I used to be blasted on Es and trips all the time in the clubs. Dust, even. God knows what I was doing to my body.' There was a note in her voice that suggested her experiences hadn't all been pleasurable.

'I have a feeling the lab drugs will lose their potency,' he mused. 'All part of the blight on our technological world. Natural things seem to be coming into their own.'

Laura peered into the bag. 'Been a while since I've been on mushrooms,' she said thoughtfully. She popped a few into her mouth. 'How many do we take?'

'Not many,' he said. 'This can be a ritual of awareness and bonding, not a trip.'

'Nothing's simple with you, is it?'

'You can look at things in different ways without harming the experience. There are some who think drug-taking is inherently immoral without considering that psychedelics have been a part of some cultures' religious experience for centuries. Other people's wine and wafer, if you will, transubstantiating into the body and blood of nature.'

Laura snorted, but didn't comment further. She chewed the rubbery mushrooms, trying to ignore the metallic taste, then swallowed with a wince. Shavi followed suit and they lay next to the fire watching the flames, waiting for the drug to kick in.

It didn't take Laura long to notice the familiar fuzziness on the edge of her vision. It was followed by the faint auditory hallucinations in the crisp crackle of the fire or the rustle of the breeze in the branches, and then the growing sense of wellbeing that made her laugh for no reason apart from the joy of being alive. They chatted amiably for a while as Laura felt the layers of her defences slowly being stripped away. *Don't make a fool of yourself,* she thought, but after so long honesty was pressing hard against her throat.

'This may sound weird,' she began, 'but despite all the shit flying around I really feel like I've found some purpose in my life. I wouldn't tell them to their faces, and I wouldn't have believed it myself if someone had told me a few weeks ago, but I feel like I belong with Church and Ruth. For all their faults. And you. Like we're coming from the same place.' She turned her head away, suddenly aware of her words.

'You do not have to be embarrassed by your feelings,' Shavi said gently.

'Yeah, I do, because if I let my real feelings out I'll tear myself apart.'

'Is that what you believe?'

'It's what I know. Blame my parents.' Her voice trailed off morosely. She expected Shavi to question her further, but when he didn't she couldn't contain herself. 'My loving mother and father have really screwed me up and I hate them for it.'

'Talk about it if you like.'

'I don't know if I can.'

'Then ignore it.'

'I can't.' She lay on her back and watched Ruth's owl swoop and soar in the sable sky, feeling the currents beneath its wings as if she were flying alongside it. And then she closed her eyes and she was there, in the dark, nursing the welts, smelling the iron tang of blood, too sore even to move. 'You know, religion is a dangerous thing. For strong people, it's just teaching, guidance, a few rules to keep them on the

301

path for good. But weak people let it eat them up. There's so little inside them they can trust, they allow it to control them, like some devil on their backs, following what it whispers to them even when it's obviously wrong. Which is about as ironic as it gets. For them it's a class A drug and they should be treated like addicts, put on some religious methadone treatment. Yeah, religion-lite. Wonder what that would be? The Church of the Soap Opera?' She laughed at the ridiculousness of the image. 'Anyway, guess which category my darling folks fell into.'

'Some people draw strength from it—'

'I have no problem with that,' she snapped. She sighed and added, 'Sorry. Raw nerves-a-go-go. My parents were Catholics gone mad. And like all fundamentalists, they believed absolute discipline was the only way. You know, you allow a little weakness in and suddenly the cracks are shooting up the wall. They were terrified of the chaos of life and they had to lock themselves away in their little religious fortress to stop them going mad. But of course I was in that fortress with them. A sneaky little spy who couldn't be trusted not to let the enemy past the gates, so I had to be *convinced* to be a true patriot. The slightest misdemeanour and my mum would go crazy. It started off with just the back of the hand, but as I got older it developed to a rolled-up newspaper, belts, table tennis bats, just about anything she could pick up and thrash about with. And after she'd finished and got it all out of her system she used to lock me in the airing cupboard. Pitch black. So hot I was almost choking. I cried myself out pretty young.'

'Did you tell anyone?'

'It was all I knew from when I was a tiny kid. I thought it was normal, for God's sake. Stupid bitch. Now I know my mum wasn't wired up right. Yeah, crazy as a loon.'

Shavi examined her face carefully; her words were glib, almost dismissive, but her experiences were etched harshly in her features. 'Did your father—'

'My dad never laid a finger on me. He just condoned it when *she* did. He'd crawl away like some weak little mouse and read the paper, and for that I almost hate him more.' She closed her eyes and after a while Shavi thought she had fallen asleep, but then she said, 'I killed her, you know.'

Shavi waited for her to continue.

She laughed, her hand going to her mouth like a young girl. 'Nothing fazes you, does it?'

'Go on.'

'I realised my mum was going nuts when I was in my teens. I could see it in her eyes. Whenever she looked at me, they went all starey, like she hated me. I could see the whites all around them.' Her voice had grown more serious. 'And the more funny she went in the head, the worse she got with me. Somewhere down the line it went beyond punishment. I used to get burnt, cut. Once I spent a whole weekend in the airing cupboard listening to her say her Hail Marys outside the door. What do you expect? – I rebelled. I was drinking like some rum-sodden old sailor before I was sixteen, hoovering up any drugs that came near me. I wasn't exactly an angel when it came to boys. And the worse I got, the worse my mum got. Luckily I'd an aptitude for technology. Somehow I winged it through my exams and got a place at university. She didn't want me to go, the witch, but I was old enough to do what I wanted then so I just legged it. Of course, by that time they'd decided I was the Devil himself. I was no longer part of the family, as simple as that. Which, by me, was great. It was like getting let out of jail. Just call me Papillon.'

Shavi reached over and rested his hand on the back of hers. She didn't flinch.

'A couple of years ago I must have had a brainstorm or something,' she continued. 'I had a dream about her and thought maybe it was time I made my peace with her. Yeah, right. Like some stupid, gullible idiot I turned up at the old homestead. My dad was out. She answered the door and I

303

knew straight away she'd fallen out of the crazy tree and hit every branch on the way down. I was surprised she was still walking around. But she just smiled and invited me in like it was only yesterday she'd seen me. I had a cup of tea, tried to make small talk, but then she started spouting all that Bible crap, saying she'd been praying for my salvation. I thought, *Here we go again*. I got up to go and as I was walking through the kitchen she came up behind me and hit me with a fucking iron. Clunk. Big comedy moment, no laughs unfortunately. And when I woke up she'd done this.'

She rolled on to her side so her back was towards him and pulled her T-shirt up to her neck. In red scar tissue across her pale skin were the words *Jesus loves you*.

Shavi was overcome with such a deep pity for her he couldn't find any words to say. He reached out to trace the scars gently with his fingertips and this time she did flinch. But then she reached out behind her, caught his hand and held it against her side.

The psychedelics were swirling through her system now, releasing terrible memories, freeing the awful thoughts she had attempted to contain for so long. Under usual circumstances she would have expected the experience to induce levels of paranoia and terror that would have left her crumpled in a ball on the ground, but in that strange, charged environment all she felt was an immense sadness which she knew she had to expunge from her system.

'There's a place where you go when life's threatening to destroy you,' she continued in a small voice, without turning over to face him. 'Some kind of sanctuary in your head, and thank God it's there because right then I don't think I'd have carried on without it. She'd used one of my dad's razors. My back was in agony and I was covered in blood, vomiting from the shock. And she was still spouting Bible stuff and waving the razor around in this kind of dance. A stupid, childish dance. And at that moment I knew what a complete moron I was. I hated her and wanted her dead for everything she'd done to me in my life, but I loved her as well and I just kept asking her to hug me and make it all right. But she wouldn't listen.' A shiver ran through her, and Shavi squeezed her side supportively. 'A stupid fucking moron. Sometimes I hate myself.'

'You were just being human.'

'And then she came at me again. I tried to get out of the way, but she was crazy, thrashing around with the razor. I've got a great scar on my scalp under this perfectly styled hair. I was flailing around and somehow I grabbed this big wooden crucifix they'd always had hanging on the wall next to the fridge. I lashed out with it and it caught her on the temple. She must have hit me with something at the same time, or maybe it was just the shock of what I'd done, but I blacked out too. And when I woke up she was dead. I don't know if it was from me hitting her or where she'd gone down hard against the edge of the cooker, but whichever way you slice it, I killed her. There was blood everywhere—' The words choked in her throat.

Shavi moved in close to her, sliding his arm around her waist, pulling her into him. She went rigid at first, resisting the human contact, but then she relaxed against him, crossing her arms over his in a desperate yearning for comfort.

'My dad came back soon after and found me still sitting there. All I wanted was for him to hold me, but it was like I wasn't there. He started mumbling, "We must call the police", detached, emotionless things like that, and I was screaming, "Dad, Mum's dead" over and over. I just wanted some reaction from him. Then he turned to me and said really coldly, "If the police find you here they'll arrest you for what you've done. Get out." It was like a slap in the face. I got up, washed the blood off and walked out. Later I found out he'd told the police he'd done it. Can you believe that?'

'He was trying to save you,' Shavi suggested.

Laura laughed hollowly. 'You'd think, wouldn't you? But it wasn't about me, it was about the sacrifice. By giving himself up instead of me, he felt he'd done the right thing, the Godly thing. It was his big chance. In his eyes it made him a better person: God would smile on him and throw wide the gates of heaven. Hallelujah! There wasn't a single thought for me and I have never heard him from him since. I don't even know what happened to him – he could be rotting inside the squirrel house, or still living in the house basking in his own glory for all I know. For all I care. Whenever I go back to Salisbury to see my mates I never go anywhere near the place, and I make sure they don't tell me anything about him.'

'You could be wrong about him.'

'No, I could see it in his eyes when he walked into the kitchen and took in the situation. He was already thinking about it then.' She let out a deep breath of air that seemed to drain her. 'What a crazy life, eh? And now the world's ending. That big old Catholic God must really be despairing of everything that's been done in his name.'

Shavi hugged her tightly, nuzzling his face into her neck so he could speak softly into her ear. 'You have suffered terribly—'

'I don't want pity! That's not why—'

'And I am not giving you any. I want to show you respect for the success you have made of your life—'

'Success! I feel like a loser! Fucked in the head, washed up in drugs, lonely, bitter . . . Funny choice of words you have there, pal.'

'But you have overcome such a terrible experience. You are carrying on, and that is all we can really hope for. In the end, we have to make our own way, without our parents, without our loved ones, using our own strength. And what you are doing now shows your worth.'

'Well, that's one way of looking at it. If you're a nut.' She laughed lightly; oddly, she felt better than she had done in years. 'You're a strange dude, Shavi. I don't know why the hell I'm talking to you.'

'We are all strangers, but we have connections that go much deeper than conscious thought.'

'You could be right. Everything is insane enough now for that to be true.' She paused, suddenly aware of his hands on her skin. At the thought, a tingle ran through her groin, heightened by the drugs. 'You can't beat talking about misery for making you feel sexy,' she said.

He was silent for a long minute, as if shocked by her comment, but then he said calmly, 'Do you want to make love?'

'Sure, why not? There's nothing like gratuitous, no-strings-attached sex with a stranger to make a girl feel good. But you better have some protection, big boy.'

She could sense his smile behind her. 'I always come prepared,' he said.

Whether it was the magical atmosphere or the drugs, her nerves seemed charged. When he ran his fingertips up from her belly to the soft curve of her breast, it felt like a web of electricity crackled across her body, and when he lightly touched the end of her hard nipple she jolted with a spasm of delight. She turned her head so he could reach her mouth. The kiss was moist and supple and filled with passion. The excitement of the moment took control of her mind, and she gave herself up to it hungrily. Snaking her hand behind her, she slid it over his clothes until she felt the hard, hot mound in his trousers, which she kneaded gently. Then he was undoing her jeans, slipping his hand over her belly and under her knickers to her pubic hair and beyond, where he began to stimulate her with soft, subtle movements of his fingertips. There was something so expert in his action she had to fight to prevent herself coming in an instant. And then they were both overwhelmed, rolling over, kissing each other hard, pulling their clothes off hastily. In the heightened atmosphere, Laura could barely believe how every sensation was so charged; she felt permanently on the point of orgasm. When he flicked a tongue over her nipple, she had to clench to control herself. And when she slid her naked body up and down his before taking his erection and lowering herself on to it, she thought her senses were going to crash through the overload of excitement. She moved on top of him for a while, before they rolled over, slick with sweat, and he started to thrust into her. His body was hard muscle under her hands, his face darkly handsome in the firelight, and all she could think was he was the best lover in the world.

For a while she gave herself up to the waves of sensation, losing all sense of time, but later she did remember one moment, when she looked past him, up into the sky, and saw what seemed to be scores of golden lights swirling around in the currents from the fire. They were bigger than sparks, almost the size of fireflies, and for the briefest instant she had the oddest feeling that they were tiny, beautiful people with shimmering skin, dipping and diving around them on gossamer wings. It was a moment of pure, undefinable wonder, but later, when they rolled off each other sweat-streaked and exhausted, the night air was clear and she couldn't bring herself to mention it. The image stayed in her heart, though, adding to the feeling of transcendental joy that infused her.

The power was off and the darkness that filled the farmhouse seemed almost to have substance, refusing to retreat in the flickering light of the candles Marsh had hastily placed around the room. But the roaring fire provided some stronger illumination and warmth, although it still didn't seem to penetrate beyond their tight circle of chairs pulled close to it.

Their conversation had all but dried up long ago. Despite cooking them a fine meal which went some way to make up for the privations they had experienced underground, Marsh had been reticent for most of the evening. Church didn't get the impression he had anything to hide; more that his lonely existence had made him taciturn, and that his fear had added to his normal withdrawn state.

The grandmother clock had chimed midnight half an hour earlier, but no one seemed to want to retire; its tick was low and sonorous, like an insistent warning. Marsh had his loaded shotgun across his lap, which made Church feel nervous, but Veitch also kept reaching to the bulge of the gun in his jacket for comfort. Just as Church wondered how much longer they should sit up, the room was suddenly pervaded by a foul smell, a mix of sulphur and human excrement. When it reached Marsh's nostrils, a faint tremor ran across his face and he made an odd mewling sound in the depths of his throat.

'Is this the start of it?' Tom asked.

Marsh's terrified expression had already given away the answer. The whole room held its breath as they cast glances to the darkened corners. It began like the distant rustling of dry paper, eventually becoming something like the sound of rats' claws on wood, but it felt as if it were inside their heads. Marsh raised the shotgun and began to aim it around the room. Veitch was on tenterhooks, his eyes darting while his hand stayed firmly inside his jacket. He'd had the gun out once already, but Church had complained that he felt like he was sitting in some Wild West Saloon. 'What's coming?' he whispered redundantly. Church watched them both warily. They were in the wrong place at the wrong time.

Overhead, there came the abrupt sound of clattering across the roof tiles and then a shower of soot billowed out from the whooshing fire. They all leapt back at once, their chairs flying. When the soot had cleared, a small figure lay huddled on the hearth. Marsh blasted both barrels of the shotgun; it sounded like a thunderclap in the room and they jumped out of their skins.

'You stupid bastard!' Veitch cursed.

But the thing had already moved like lightning into the shadowed corners before the buckshot hit. Burbling, throaty laughter floated back to them.

Church had caught the merest glimpse of the creature, but

it was enough. Though as small as a child, it had the proportions of a man, with an oversized head like a baby. Black,
shiny scales covered the skin and its eyes were large, red and
serpent-slitted. A pointed tail snaked out behind it, seemingly
with a life of its own. In mediaeval times a witness would
certainly have branded it a devil, and Church wondered if
he should see it that way too.

'Daniel Marsh, you are so harsh, all the things you said,
soon you will end up dead.' The hideous, old man's voice
ended in chittering laughter.

Tom stepped forward. 'Show yourself,' he said authoritat-
ively, unruffled by the creature's appearance.

'Oh Daniel, you have some friends!' it replied in a sneering
singsong. There was a moment when it seemed to be considering its response, and then it sashayed into the centre of
the room in an odd, jerky motion which Church would have
put down to poor stop-go animation if he had seen it in a
film. 'What, no holy water? No crucifixes, no *in spirito sancto*
or crossing hand movements and mumbled prayers? You
have changed!' He held out his arms like some penitent Jewish
tailor.

Marsh chewed on the back of his hand, moaning pathetically while Veitch stared unsurely. But Tom confronted the
creature head-on. 'You are a foul thing, tormenting this poor
man. And so much to do on your return. Why waste time
here?'

'Why, good sport, coz!' The devil did a little flip back into
the shadows as Veitch advanced on it menacingly. A second
later it was back, like a tame monkey sensing food.

'Let's kill it!' Veitch snapped.

'If only you could, little brothers, but you have not grown
up that much in time passing!' It moved suddenly, so fast it
was almost a blur, bouncing on the sofa across the room
towards Marsh before disappearing back into the shadows.
The farmer howled in pain. Four streaks of red appeared
on his cheek. 'First blood to me, I think!' the devil said

triumphantly; the voice came from nowhere in particular.

'Why are you here?' Tom continued calmly. He seemed familiar with the creature.

'Here to fill a void,' it replied. Somehow it was back on the hearth.

'I don't deserve it! I weren't doing anything!' Marsh howled pitifully.

'Nothing apart from living!' the devil cautioned.

'My wife left me a year ago, the farm's going bust, I feel sick all the time! I've suffered enough! There's no reason for this! It's not fair!'

'But that is the reason, Daniel. I am here because you have suffered. I am making you suffer more because I can, for no other reason than that. And if you seek meaning in life, perhaps you will see it there.'

'Do not listen to him,' Tom said. 'Lies spring easily to him and his kind. His only desire is to torment.'

'You wound me!' The devil clutched his heart theatrically. 'But because I can lie does not mean that I always lie. In a field of ordure a single pearl of truth shines brighter.'

Veitch pulled out his gun and rattled off a couple of shots. 'Don't!' Church yelled too late as the bullets zinged off the stone hearth. One shattered what appeared to be an antique plate on the wall while the other burst through the window. But Veitch's attack seemed to have got closer than Marsh's shotgun blast. The devil backed up against the wall, flaring its nostrils and baring its teeth at him. Veitch moved faster than Church could ever have imagined. He launched himself forward, swinging his foot and catching the creature full in the stomach. It squealed like a pig, arcing up, head over heels, to crash against the far wall.

It bounced back like a rubber ball, ricocheting off the floor towards Veitch, a flailing mass of claws and scales. Effortlessly it clamped itself on his head and neck, then threw back its head, opening its jaw so unnaturally wide its head seemed almost to disappear. Veitch had a view of row upon row of

311

razor sharp teeth about to tear his face from his skull.

Tom moved quickly. Snatching up the coal pincers from next to the fire, he gripped the devil firmly about the neck and hauled it off Veitch; it yelled as if it had been branded.

'You and your brethren still do not like cold iron, I see,' he said snidely.

The thing wriggled like a snake in his grasp, but Tom heaved it forward and plunged it into the depths of the fire. It howled wildly until it managed to free itself from the pincers. Then it scurried off to the shadows to compose itself. 'Not fair,' it hissed like a spoiled child. 'You know us too well.'

'Quick,' Tom said, but it was too late. It rolled itself into a ball, then fired itself out of the shadows fully into Marsh's face. The farmer went over backwards, his nose exploding in a shower of blood. As he lay on his back screaming, the devil sat on his chest, ripping and tearing at Marsh's face. It managed to get in only a couple of swipes before Church took a swing at its head with the poker. The blow sent the devil rolling across the floor. Veitch fired another shot, this time blowing the leg off an armchair. And then it was away, tearing out the stuffing of the sofa, streaking up the wall, ripping up the paper as it passed, shattering a mirror with a cry of 'Seven years' bad luck!' before settling on a sideboard where it proceeded to fire crockery at them.

Veitch and Marsh fired off random shots, while Tom and Church dived for cover. Clouds of plaster dust erupted from the walls; the light fitting came down with a crash; the sideboard burst open, showering glassware across the floor.

While they stopped to reload, Tom scurried forward and whispered, 'We will never kill it like that. Trickery is the only way.'

'Let me address you as an equal,' he said loudly to the devil. 'What should I call you?'

'You may call me "master",' the creature said slyly. 'If you

312

wish to uncover my true naming word, you will have to do better than that. But I know your name, do I not, Long Tom? Your silver tongue seems to have forsaken its poetry for threats. And how is your Royal gift? More curse than gift, I would think.' Tom ignored him, pulling Church close to whisper in his ear. Then he turned back to the devil and said, 'Would you like me to see your future, little one?'

The creature squirmed. 'Thank you for your kind offer, Long Tom, but I prefer to live in the here and now.'

'Come, now!' Tom said with a broad grin.

The creature was so concerned at Tom's words that he failed to see Church circling round to his blind spot. Church felt a cold sweat break out on his back. The devil had shown he was terrifyingly fast and vicious; one wrong move and he could lose an arm, or worse. Tom was doing his best to distract the creature, but the things he was saying hinted at a hidden side of him which made Church feel uncomfortable.

'Perhaps I should compose an epic poem to your grandeur, little brother,' Tom continued.

'Indeed, that would be a deep honour from a bard so renowned.' The devil was not so arrogant now and he was watching Tom suspiciously, as if they were long-standing enemies who knew each other's strengths and weaknesses.

'But then what would I call it?' Tom said. 'Ode to a Nocturnal Visitor is so vague. Ode to—?' He held out his hands, suggesting the devil should give him his name.

For a second it almost worked, but then the devil caught himself and simply smiled. 'I am sure a rhymer of your great skill could imagine a fitting title. I—'

Church moved quickly, pulling out the Wayfinder from his jacket and holding it in front of him like a weapon, as Tom had instructed. The blue flame flared and licked towards the devil, who caught sight of it out of the corner of his eye and squealed. At the same time, Tom clamped the coal pincers on the devil once more. He howled as he futilely attempted to wriggle free.

'Now,' Tom said, suddenly threatening, 'we shall have some plain speaking.'

The flame sizzled like an acetylene torch as Church held the Wayfinder close. The devil tried to tug its head away, its eyes wide with fear, but it had nowhere to turn. 'Keep it away from me!' it hissed.

'The flame will consume you if we allow it – you know that,' Tom said bluntly.

'What do you require, masters?' the devil replied obsequiously.

'Just burn him!' Veitch snapped.

'No!' the devil cried. 'Anything!'

'This, then.' Tom's eyes blazed. 'You will leave Daniel Marsh alone for the rest of his days. And,' he added, 'you will do nothing to bring about that end earlier than fate decrees. Do you so swear?'

'On the warp and weft!' the devil screamed frantically. 'Now let me go!'

Tom nodded to Church, who retreated a few feet with the Wayfinder; the flame flickered back to normal and the devil bounded free to the hearth. When it turned, its face was filled with malice and it spat like a cornered cat. It turned to Church first: 'You will never find out why she died.' Then Veitch: 'There is no redemption for murder.' And finally to Tom: '*You* carry your suffering with you.'

Then it pointed a finger at the three of them. 'Thrice damned,' it said coldly before bounding back up the chimney.

Marsh stared for a moment in shock, before falling to his knees in front of the fire, tears flooding down his cheeks. He looked at them incredulously, then said simply, 'Thank you.'

Church turned to Tom. 'Is that it? Will it be back?'

'Not here. But we will have to be on our guard from now on. Word will spread quickly through the brethren, and they hate more then anything else to be humbled by mortals.'

Veitch collapsed on to the sofa. 'Blimey. What's going on?'

He looked at Tom. 'What's this brethren, then? They're not Fomorii.'

'There are many things that come with the night.' Tom poked the fire, sending sparks shooting up the chimney. 'Every creature of myth and folklore has its roots in Otherworld. And they're all coming back.'

Veitch looked puzzled. 'So it's like if London Zoo opened up all its cages at once.'

Tom nodded. 'One way of looking at it.'

Church rested wearily on the mantelpiece. The room looked like it had been attacked by a wrecking crew. 'That thing thought you were someone important.'

Tom stared into the depths of the fire, saying nothing.

Marsh jumped up, trembling with relief. 'That were fine – you bloody well did it! You saved me!' He shook all their hands forcefully, unable to contain himself. 'I'll tell you what, the only thing I've ever loved in my life was the land. Then when farming went through all those rough years, I felt like I'd got nothing. But when something like this happens, it makes you think, don't it? About what's important an' all.'

Veitch watched the farmer like he'd gone insane. 'I reckon you need a bloody good sleep, mate.'

'Oh, ah, I'll tell everyone about what you bloody did,' Marsh said adamantly.

Church turned to Tom. 'And that little devil's going to be spreading the word too. Looks like we're going to get us a reputation.'

the hidden path

They ate at first light while Marsh slumbered heavily in what must have been his first good rest for weeks. After Veitch had collected eggs from some chickens roosting just off the yard, Tom plucked some new nettle shoots out of an overgrown patch that had obviously once been the garden and scrambled them all up. He claimed it had been a popular Anglo-Saxon dish, and although Veitch ate suspiciously, it tasted remarkably good. They left Marsh enjoying his sleep and were out of the house by 7 a.m.

Church suggested their first aim should be to find some transportation. With technology unreliable, Tom didn't want to risk trains, and buying another car was out of the question.

'Looks like we'll have to rely on the comfort of strangers,' Church said. 'Hope you're all good at thumbing.'

Their first ride took them into Tavistock where they convinced a farmer collecting supplies to let them travel on the back of his truck. He was just trundling west past Liskeard when Church noticed the direction of the lamp flame had turned to the north-west. Angry with himself for not paying more attention, he forced the others to jump off the truck as it slowed at a crossroads. By the time it was out of sight they were already regretting their decision. Ahead of them lay the bleak expanse of Bodmin Moor, rising up in sludgey browns and grey-greens beneath a lowering sky.

'How bad can it be?' Veitch said. 'It's half the size of Dartmoor and we're already bang in the middle of it.'

'Bad enough if the weather changes,' Church said, checking

the slate clouds that were backed up over the moor. 'And the weather out here can change in a minute.'

'Oh, you're a bleedin' wilderness expert are you now?' Veitch said. 'The sooner we start, the sooner we finish.'

Church grinned at Veitch's bluntness – he had already warmed to their new companion. They chatted aimably for a while, but their conversation faded the further they got out into the moor. The higher the land, the stronger the wind, and although they were in the first burgeoning days of spring, it had a bite to it that reminded him of winter. At least there was a single-track road they could follow which made the going much easier than stumbling across the uneven turf and gorse. Half an hour after leaving the main road they might have been in a different world; there was no sound of civilisation, just the howl of the wind, no stink of car fumes, just the damp, cloying smells of nature.

'How are you doing, city boy?' Church said with a grin.

'Sorry, mate,' Veitch deadpanned, 'I'm too soft. I should live in a rough place like you to harden myself up.'

'What you need is a few archaeological digs on the North Yorkshire moors. That'd put hairs on your chest.'

They continued a little way and then a thought came to Church that he had wanted to mention the previous night. 'You handled that gun pretty well at the farm.'

'I told you I was a bit of a villain. I'm not proud of it.' There was a long pause before he added, 'There's lots I'm not proud of.'

'Last night, that devil—'

'I knew you'd ask sooner or later. He called me a murderer.'

'Are you?'

Veitch looked away. 'Bang to rights.'

'Do you want to talk about it?'

'I haven't so far, not to anyone outside the family.' He thought for a moment, then said, 'Fuck it, you might as well know what you're getting in with. You know that building society raid where my brothers got arrested? Well I was in

317

on it too. We knew it was a bleedin' mistake before we set out, but once you start thinking about something like that, it's like it's got a weight of its own – it just carries you along. There were lots of times we could have pulled out, but we'd go to bed and when we got up in the morning it was still on. We were desperate, you know. We'd been listening to all those politicians who told us we could have anything, only we didn't have anything. We had nothing. And just like we thought, it started going wrong from the moment we went in there. But we could have got out, you know, if I hadn't screwed up. We'd all got masks on. Brendan was up there at the counter, Mitch was covering him with his shotgun. I'd got a gun too and then it was like I heard this voice in my head, or just behind me or some shit. It said, "He's going to get you" or something like that.

'Anyway, I turned round and I caught this bloke moving out of the corner of my eye. And I just let him have it. Don't ask me why. I've thought about it a million times and I can't explain it. It wasn't like me at all. But there it was. Blam. Blood, guts and some poor bastard dead. I ran like hell – Brendan and Mitch took the rap. My own brothers banged up because of me! I wanted to give myself up, but they wouldn't let me. Said it'd make it even worse for them if they knew I was inside too.' The weight of emotion in his voice made Church regret bringing the subject up. 'They didn't blame me for a minute and that just killed me! I wished they'd made me suffer for being such a fuck-up, like they should've done. So they go inside, and I'm just eaten up by what I did to that poor bloke and my own family. And I wasn't even allowed to pay my dues for it.'

Church clapped a supportive hand on his shoulder. 'It sounds like you're paying for it now.'

'But it's not enough, is it?'

'I reckon what lies ahead for us, Ryan, will give you plenty of opportunity for payback.'

'I've never done the right thing in my life, ever, even when

I tried to. But I'm going to make up for that somehow.'

Church decided to turn the conversation to Tom so Veitch could have a break. He was amazed at how quickly the man had recovered; even the scars on his temple had healed. 'What about you, Tom? Are you going to break the habit of a lifetime and tell us what that devil's message meant to you?'

There was a long silence, and when Church glanced up he saw the strangest thing: Tom was trying to speak, but it was as if he couldn't control his jaw. No words would come out, and in the end he turned away in frustration.

'Are you okay?' Church asked, concerned. But Tom dismissed him with a wave of his hand, his eyes focused on the road ahead.

In the cold dark before dawn, Shavi slipped away from the camp and lost himself among the trees. He could sense the sun coming in a way that still surprised him, although he had discovered his odd sensitivity a few months earlier. It was just one of several subtle changes which, inexplicably, had been thrust upon him overnight at the same time that the change came upon the world, a transformation that was so distinct at first he thought he was suffering some sudden, debilitating brain ailment. There were the psychic flashes which he initially thought were hallucinations, but which he came to recognise as precognitive, or visions of distant events. The odd sensations he received when he handled objects were as if he could *feel* what had happened to them in the past. And he seemed to understand what animals were thinking, although he didn't know if it was an increased awareness of their rituals and routines, or if he were actually picking up what was passing through their heads. It was all still quite unfocused, but all his abilities were growing much sharper, as if his mind were learning to use them now he had them at his disposal. He accepted it without question as a gift from some higher authority, and he was determined to use it as best he could.

Shavi found a clearing in the most thickly wooded area and stripped off his clothes, shivering from the chill on his skin. For twenty minutes he worked through his t'ai chi routine to clear his mind and then followed it with twenty minutes of yoga, by which time the sun was beginning to break through the branches. His studies had showed him that ritual and drugs made his abilities considerably more effective, and he had worked hard to develop a shamanistic framework to enable them.

With his mind wiped free of thoughts, his breathing regulated, he stood and raised his arms to the coming sun; the heat from the first rays licked over him in greeting. He slipped the Mexican mushroom on to his tongue, feeling the bitter taste spread, and then chewed slowly. When he finally swallowed, he lowered himself slowly and took up the full lotus, closing his eyes so the only sensations were the sun on his feet and the gentle breeze breathing on his naked skin.

'Come to me, spirits,' he whispered. 'Show me the path.'

Ruth was already up cooking breakfast when Laura emerged from the tent, bleary-eyed and puffy-faced. 'Stay up late?' Ruth asked as she flipped the sizzling bacon in the pan.

'No,' Laura lied, slipping on her sunglasses in the bright morning light. 'I'm just not a morning person like you, Miss Perky.'

Ruth served up a mug of tea which Laura took with a nod and then proceeded to sip halfheartedly.

'Shavi must have been up early,' Ruth continued; Laura grunted noncommittally. Ruth carried on serving up her breakfast, then suddenly threw the plastic plate down in irritation. 'I don't know how much longer we can carry on doing this!'

Laura looked up in surprise at the outburst. 'What do you mean?'

'Church could be dead! Time is running out! And we're just sitting here!'

'Okay, don't blow a gasket.' Laura took another sip of her tea, then added, 'Shavi's going to try something.'

'What?'

Laura shrugged. 'He reckons he can do stuff. You know, spooky stuff. When the world changed, he got super-charged . . . seeing things, hearing things. He's trying to find a way we can carry on without Church and his little blue lamp.'

'You seem to know a lot about him and what he's thinking,' Ruth said suspiciously.

'That's what talking to a person gets you. You should try it sometime.'

Ruth picked up her plate and took out her frustration on her bacon and beans. She had just decided to have another go at Laura when Shavi emerged from the trees looking tired and haggard. He flopped down next to them, rolled on his back and closed his eyes.

'That's what comes of taking exercise before breakfast,' Laura said.

'There is something here, in Glastonbury,' Shavi muttered.

'What do you mean?' Ruth asked.

'One of the talismans. The energy here is so vital it acts as an ultimate defence. None of the dark creatures can enter the Isle of Avalon, so it was the perfect place to locate one of the most powerful objects.'

'Where is it?' Ruth felt a sudden surge of hope that they weren't as powerless as she'd feared.

'I do not . . . It would not . . .' Shavi's eyes suddenly rolled up until all they could see were the whites, and for an instant they thought he was going to have a fit. In his head he flashed back to the ritual in the trees, the moment of awe and terror when the air appeared to fold in on itself and the amorphous cloud which seemed to contain both eyes and teeth suddenly manifested. Somehow he dragged himself back and focused on Ruth's concerned face. 'The abbey,' he croaked. 'There is a sign in the abbey. "Where feet in ancient times walked," it said.' He closed his eyes and rested as best he could.

By midmorning Shavi had recovered enough to walk with Ruth and Laura into town. The abbey lay just off Magdalene Street, its ruined stone lying at peace amidst acres of well-tended lawns in a tranquil setting that was at odds with its location so near to the bustle of the shops. Despite the bare bones of its once powerful form, it was still easy to see how it had once been the greatest monastic foundation in all of Britain, second only in wealth and size to Westminster. Pilgrims still wandered beatifically along its winding paths as they had done since the Middle Ages, when it had been one of the most important shrines in Europe; even, some said, on a par with Rome itself.

The sun was bright and hot, but a cool breeze made their wanderings easy; the birdsong within the high walls drowned out the traffic beyond.

'It's so peaceful here,' Ruth remarked as she stood in what had been the nave and looked towards the choir. 'No, more than that,' she added thoughtfully. 'It's spiritual.'

'You notice that too?' Shavi replied. 'I wondered if it was a by-product of this new age which seems, to me, to be an age of the spirit after one of materialism. Can we now *feel* the energy of sacred sites, the cumulative outpourings of generations of the faithful? Or was it always like this?'

'Perhaps it was like this, just muted.' Ruth ignored Laura, who was faintly but obviously sneering at their intellectualising. 'You know, some of the things that have come with the change have actually been good. Perhaps this whole new age isn't as bad as it's made out to be,' she continued.

'Yeah, right,' Laura said, wandering away from them. 'Tell that to the Wild Hunt.'

While Shavi and Ruth mulled over the abbey's uncommon atmosphere, Laura picked her way amongst the stonework until she discovered a sign which made her call the others. It said:

> Site of King Arthur's Tomb. In the year 1191 the bodies of King Arthur and his queen were said to have been found on the south side of the Lady Chapel. On 10th April 1278 their remains were removed in the presence of King Edward I and Queen Eleanor to a black marble tomb on this site. This tomb survived until the dissolution of the abbey in 1539.

'I thought he was just made up,' Laura said.

'He was,' Ruth agreed. 'A conglomeration of old heroes that a succession of writers have used to create this romantic myth.'

'Some say,' Shavi added, 'the monks invented this because it would bring in some funds at a time when they were particularly hard-pressed.'

'I've always said you can't trust the religious,' Laura sniffed, before turning away again.

But Ruth felt a strange *frisson* tingle along her spine. She recalled Tom talking about the sleeping king who needed to be awakened; the king who, in legend, had been Arthur.

Shavi noticed her expression. 'What is wrong?'

'It's nothing,' she said, before adding, 'Coincidences always spook me. I'm starting to see strange connections in all this, recurring themes about legends and religions, Celts and Christianity. But I can't quite fit it all together.'

'These things happen in the subconscious,' Shavi advised. 'Let it come naturally.'

Taking his own advice, he led her among the ruins, hoping inspiration would come to illuminate the cryptic hints he had received in the ritual; as they walked, they mused over the words.

'It reminds me of a line from "Jerusalem",' Ruth noted. '"And did those feet in ancient times . . ."'

'And that, of course, is tied in to Glastonbury,' Shavi said.

'It relates to the legend of the young Jesus, who is supposed to have come here to Glastonbury with his uncle Joseph of Arimathea. The stories say they built the first Christian church out of wattle and daub, somewhere in the abbey's grounds, I think. After Jesus was crucified, Joseph gave up his tomb to house the body. It is said he took the Grail which caught some of Christ's blood at the crucifixion and brought it here where he buried it, possibly on Chalice Hill. According to legend, that is.'

'"Folklore is the secret history",' Ruth muttered distractedly.

'What is that?'

'Something Tom said. That myths, legends and folklore reflected what really happened, although not accurately, or as metaphors. And of course the Grail is part of the Arthurian tales.' She felt oddly uneasy. 'What does it mean? Anything?'

Before he could answer, Laura ambled over lazily. 'Before you two burst your brains with all that heavy thinking, you should see this.' She took them to a wooden cover in the ground in what had been the north transept. Underneath were perfectly preserved mediaeval floor tiles still in situ where they had been unearthed by archaeologists. 'This is "where feet in ancient times walked", right?'

Shavi smiled at the difference in their approach, then ducked down to examine the tiles. Although they had faded with time and the pressure of numerous soles, the intricate design was still clear and the colours shone, but there seemed nothing out of the ordinary.

Ruth knelt down next to Shavi. 'Perhaps there's something hidden in the pattern.'

'Or perhaps it's nothing to do with this at all,' Laura added. 'Why don't we talk about needles and haystacks instead.'

For the next fifteen minutes they looked at the tiles from every angle, so close their noses were almost brushing the surface, then far away, much to the irritation of the tourists who jostled to see. Eventually Laura wandered off in boredom to throw stones at the fish in the abbey pool while Shavi and Ruth lay on their backs on the grass, desperately trying to solve the conundrum.

'We must be looking in the wrong place,' Ruth said.

Shavi disagreed. 'I feel instinctively that this is it. We simply need to look at it in the correct way.'

'But can you trust the information you were given?'

'According to tradition, sometimes the spirits lie, dissemble, obscure the truth. Again, I intuitively believe that it was the correct guidance. The problem lies with us and our vision.'

'Okay,' Ruth sighed, 'lateral thinking time.'

As they lay in silence, Ruth's mind gradually turned to her surroundings. Even in ruins there was a majesty to the abbey, the cumulative power of centuries of faith and worship; she felt dwarfed in its presence, and at the same time, adrift in her inability to *feel* what generations had obviously found so comforting.

'I wish I had something to believe in,' she said, almost to herself.

'You are not alone.' Shavi's voice floated to her dreamily. 'That is the only true quest that we all find ourselves on.'

'When my father died I wished . . . I wished like a child . . . that there was a God to give some reason to his passing. And at the same time I hated myself for being so weak that I needed a crutch to help me through life. It's all so pointless.' There was a note of self-loathing in her voice. She looked over at him. 'What is your religion, anyway?'

There was a faint smile on his lips. 'My religion? Spirituality. A belief that there are foundations and walls and a roof encapsulating this life of ours. A belief in a reason. In a force for overwhelming good that all religions touch.'

'Why should there be some higher power? There's no sign when you look around. Just people fooling themselves.'

'It is important to—' He paused, then sat up suddenly and stared at the tiles. 'To ignore the noise of everyday life and focus on the signal that lies behind it.' He scrambled on his hands and knees to the tiles excitedly.

'What is it? What have you thought of?'

Ruth crawled next to him; she still couldn't see anything in the patterns. Shavi leaned forward and gently traced his finger on the glass that covered the tiles. 'Here,' he said triumphantly.

'I can't see anything,' she said in frustration.

'It is all a matter of perspective. Look past the colour and design. Look past all the noise to find the signal. It is a lesson. For life.'

Ruth followed the tracing of his finger. There was a faint indentation in the baked clay of the tile, partially obscured by the design painted over it. It was an arrow. They both looked up to follow its direction. It pointed straight at the remains of the wall in the choir and through it to the tor rising high up above the town with the remaining tower of St Michael's Chapel perched on top.

'The tor,' she said. 'Of course. With all the legends tied to it, it had to be the key.'

'Not just the tor,' Shavi corrected. 'The wall too. Both of them.'

'What do you mean?'

He wandered forward, his eyes fixed on the crumbling stonework. 'So much of this new age seems to be about duality – the light and the dark, the two forces opposing each other. And there have been dual meanings so far today. The link to "Jerusalem", Joseph and the Grail *and* to the tiles. Now this dual meaning – the wall and the tor. It makes sense.'

'What can the wall have to do with it?' Then she realised what he had said. 'You think this is about the Grail!'

'I do not know.' He turned and smiled so she wouldn't be offended by his words. 'Let me concentrate.'

She backed away and sat down; Laura joined her a moment later. After she had watched Shavi staring up at the stonework for five minutes, she said, 'He's done too many drugs, hasn't he?'

'He's a smart guy,' Ruth replied. 'I wish he'd been with us from the start.'

'Don't tell me you've got damp knickers for him as well.'

'I admire him, that's all,' Ruth said tartly. 'And what do you mean *as well*?'

Laura smiled and looked away, her sunglasses somehow adding to her supercilious expression. Ruth bit her tongue and simmered silently.

Half an hour later he called them over excitedly. 'Look! The sun is in the right position now. You can see it clearly.'

'Yeah, right,' Laura said sarcastically. 'It says, "Shavi, you are a big dickhead."'

'No, he's right,' Ruth corrected, adding in as superior manner as she could muster, 'You have to look for the signal, not the noise, Laura.'

'Do not look at the stonework,' Shavi explained. 'Look at the shadows cast by the lumps and indentations in the stone.'

And then, when they squinted and focused, they could both see exactly what he meant: the shadows spelled out words in thin, spidery writing that would not have been visible to the casual observer, nor from any other perspective. Some of it, however, seemed to be missing where the wall had crumbled.

'Aqua something,' Ruth said.

'Aqua fortis,' Laura corrected sharply. 'That's nitric acid.'

'Nitric acid?' Ruth asked.

'I know my chemistry—'

'I do not think that is the context here,' Shavi corrected gently. 'The literal translation is something like *strong water*.'

'That's right,' Ruth said.

'Oh, yeah, that really makes sense,' Laura huffed.

They continued to study the wall intently and eventually

they decided the rest of the remaining message read *sic itur ad astra*.

'Astra is "stars",' Ruth said. 'I studied Latin before I did my law degree, but I can't remember much . . .' She paused thoughtfully. 'Something like "such is the way to the stars."' That's it.'

'It doesn't make much sense without the rest of the message,' Laura complained.

'There doesn't seem to be a great deal missing,' Shavi said.

'Perhaps, then,' Ruth said quietly, 'we just have to make a leap of faith.'

The wind somehow seemed to find its way through their jackets and shirts as Church, Veitch and Tom worked their way across the moor. Although the sky regularly threatened rain, the gale managed to keep the clouds scudding along so that patches of blue and bursts of sunshine occasionally broke through. Away from the main road however, the atmosphere became almost as bleak as the landscape. Strange shapes moved ominously across the scrubland in the distance and every now and then flocks of birds would soar up into the sky, suddenly disturbed by something none of them could see. The sense of threat was palpable and growing.

'It's getting worse, isn't it?' Church said, shielding his eyes to peer at the horizon.

Tom nodded. 'These places where man has a feeble hold were always going to be the first to go. The old things can re-establish themselves without much confrontation. I think it will not be long before they move in towards the centres of population.'

'And then the shit really hits the fan,' Veitch said morosely.

In the late afternoon, they wearily mounted a ridge to look down on a wide expanse of water, grey and somehow threatening in its isolation. The wind howled around them as they moved down the slope; even when it dropped there was still the eerie sound of waves rippling across the lake, giving the uneasy sensation that something was emerging from the depths. Church felt his fear grow as they neared; he could tell from Tom's face that he felt it too.

'It's just the spooky atmosphere,' Church said hopefully.

Tom's face remained dark and troubled. 'I would have thought by now you would have learned to trust your instincts. In this new age, what you sense is as important as what you see.' He stretched out his arm, bringing them up sharply.

Veitch squinted at the murky surface of the water. 'What's that moving? Is it the shadows of clouds? Or is there something in there?'

'This is Dozmary Pool, a place of legend.' Tom said. 'Local stories claim it is the lake where Sir Bedivere threw Excalibur after Arthur's death. A hand rose from the water to pluck the sword and take it down beneath the waves.'

Church tried to read his face. 'None of that Arthurian stuff is true,' he ventured.

'Not literally, no. But all legends reflect some aspect of a greater truth. I told you before – lakes and hills are liminal zones, the boundaries between this world and the place where the old races went after they retreated from the land. There are doors in all of them. Some of them have remained closed tight down the years. But not here.'

He wouldn't venture any closer to the lakeshore, so they took a long, circuitous journey along the ridge, their eyes constantly drawn to the lapping waves. It wasn't until the lake had long disappeared from view that the sense of brooding and menace slowly started to fade.

A mile and a half further down a tiny, winding lane they reached the village of Bolventor, little more than a small group of houses huddling together for shelter. And just beyond it was Jamaica Inn, its lamps already burning in the growing gloom. It had been heavily commercialised since the days when Daphne du Maurier had used its heritage of smugglers and violence as the basis for her story, yet it still retained an atmosphere that transcended the trappings of the late twentieth century. History lived on in its aged timbers, brooding slate and heavy stone walls which kept out the harsh Bodmin weather. Exhausted, and with little sign of welcome in the surrounding moorland, they were drawn to its cheer and decided to take a room for the night. As they crossed the cobbled yard where stagecoaches once clattered and heard the inn-sign creaking in the breeze, Church felt he had been flung back hundreds of years. A few months earlier, it would have been romantic; now it seemed like a warning of what lay ahead.

They ate steak in the restaurant and drank a little too heavily in the bar before settling into their room. The wind rattled the windows and thumped against the walls and they were thankful they were secure indoors. But Church knew that however sturdy the building, it wouldn't amount to anything if the things that ranged through the night decided they wanted to break inside.

At the window he tried to pierce the darkness, but beyond the lights of the car park there was nothing but a sea of black; they could have been alone in the void, and for an instant he was disturbed by a memory of his view into the abyss from the Watchtower window.

'I hope Ruth and Laura are okay,' he said; then, to Tom, 'Do you think the Wild Hunt will be back?'

'Devon and Cornwall is their favourite hunting ground. I have tried to mask our presence as much as possible, but they will not leave until the blood of their prey has been spilled. It is only a matter of time.'

'"Mask our presence"?' Veitch repeated. 'Is that one of your little *tricks*?' Tom ignored him.

Outside, the gale clattered like iron horseshoes on stone and howled in the eaves like the baying of hounds. Church drew the curtains tightly and retired to his bed.

* * *

The stark red digits of the clock radio displayed 3 a.m. when Church woke with a start from nightmares of a pursuer that snapped relentlessly at his heels. Tom and Veitch both slept deeply, although Tom occasionally twitched and mumbled deliriously. Church stumbled out of bed and headed to the bathroom for a glass of water. On his return he had the odd sensation someone was standing outside the door, although he could hear nothing. He dismissed it as another by-product of the nightmare, but after he had slid back under the sheets it didn't diminish and he knew he wouldn't be able to sleep until he had investigated.

Sleepily cursing his own obsessive tendencies, he unlocked the door carefully so as not to wake the others, his natural caution blanked out by his half-awake state. As he had thought, there was no one without. But if anything, his uneasiness had grown stronger now the door was open. Cautiously, he leaned out and looked up and down the corridor. For the briefest instant he thought he glimpsed a figure disappearing round the corner at the far end. He weighed up his options and then closed the door behind him and hurried in pursuit.

The gale was still in full force and the creak of the inn-sign echoed ominously throughout the building; there was no other sign of life at all. But as he rounded the corner he was brought up sharply, his breath catching in his throat. Facing him twenty feet away was Marianne, as pale and dark-eyed as the last time he had seen her at Stonehenge.

This time he was more ready to confront her. 'What do you want, Marianne?' he asked softly.

There was a ripple like a sigh that seemed to run through her whole body. Church felt the shiver echo within him, filled with the terrible ache of loss that he was convinced he would never lose. He tried to look in her eyes, but couldn't; the things he glimpsed there were too awful. But her face held the same delicate combination of beauty and sensitivity with which he had fallen in love. He bit his lip to prevent the tears.

She didn't reply, although he hadn't expected it; he had come to believe speech was no longer within her power. Instead she stretched out her right arm and gently touched the wall. Where her pale fingertips brushed the plaster a spot of red bubbled out, like a thumb that had been pricked by a rose. Gradually she began to retreat, in that same unmoving, horrible way he had witnessed at Stonehenge, her fearful aspect turned upon him like the light of a beacon. And as she receded, the blood spread out from her fingertip as if it had a mind of its own, tracing words that sprang to life like a speeded-up film of flowers bursting in the sun.

Somehow Church managed to draw himself from her face to look at the message, and in that instant he felt as if he had been blasted with an arctic wind. It said:

Murder. Avenge my death.

Church thought for a moment his legs were going to buckle. Marianne had reached the far end of the corridor and was now fading into the wall as if she were slipping below waves. And in the last instant he thought he saw her expression change. The look that frightened him so much became, briefly, tender and sad and if he had had any doubt this was truly Marianne it was gone then. But it was too quick, and he was left with an aching emptiness that made him feel sick.

Back in the room he couldn't sleep. Suddenly his whole life felt like it had been turned on its head; his guilt that he had been somehow complicit in Marianne's suicide had been a part of him for so long, he could barely consider the prospect that she had been murdered. It was such an upheaval that he considered whether it had been some instance of supernatural trickery designed to destabilise him. If that were true, it had worked well. But he knew it was Marianne as well as he knew himself and instinctively he felt her message was genuine. He was shaking so much he could barely consider what that meant for him. To calm himself, he took out the locket the young Marianne had given him and rested it in the palm of his hand. Although he couldn't explain why, it seemed to do the trick.

At that moment he became aware of a strange, unearthly cold that washed out from his jacket on the chair next to him. Anxiously he pulled the Roisin Dubh from the inside pocket and examined it secretively. All of the shining black petals were spotted with droplets of blood.

Ruth, Shavi and Laura spent the next morning studying information about Glastonbury in the local bookshop *Gothic Image*. A mountain of words had been written about the town, more than any other place they had visited, and most of it formed an intricate tapestry of tradition, fact and romance, with little sign where one ended and another began. But after wading through numerous books, they stumbled across a locally printed pamphlet which gave them their breakthrough: the translation of the Latin phrase.

The Chalice Well lay at the foot of Chalice Hill, the third and gentlest of the three hills that surrounded Glastonbury; of all the many mystical sites in the Isle of Avalon, it was the most revered, and the most ancient. The well was fed by a spring rising on the slopes of the hill which provided water so iron-impregnated it flowed red. That had earned it the alternative name of Blood Spring, adding to the ancient legend that the Grail was hidden somewhere near.

Following its centuries-long veneration by pilgrims from around the world, a garden had been established to create a tranquil atmosphere for contemplation and prayer. Shavi, Ruth and Laura entered it just before noon, in the bright of the sun beneath clear blue skies. They recognised the same rare, sanctified atmosphere they had experienced at the abbey.

'In Celtic and pre-Christian cultures, springs were renowned for their magical, life-giving properties,' Shavi noted. 'They were sites of worship, the homes of fertility spirits. *Genius Locii*. Sacred groves often grew up around them. And Christianity has always followed in the footsteps of pagan worship. At all the most important sites, the old religion was there first. Who is to say,' he mused, 'that they were not worshipping the same power?'

The path to the well wound around the outskirts of the garden like a route of pilgrimage, twisting through clumps of trees and bushes where hidden seats surrounded by fragrant flowers were placed for meditation. Eventually it folded back on itself and they found themselves at the wellhead, set against mediaeval stone beneath the hanging branches of ancient trees; the light in that one spot seemed to have an unusual quality; an uncommon calm lay over everything. The well itself was covered with a lid of wood and fine wrought-iron which showed two interlocking circles revealing at their centre the ancient symbol of a fish. The pamphlet they had been given at the entrance called it the *Vesica Pisces*. The design pre-dated Christianity and represented the overlapping of the visible and invisible worlds, yin and yang, the conscious and the unconscious, masculine and feminine natures. *More duality*, Ruth thought.

Shavi noticed the troubled expression on her face. 'Are you okay?'

'That design is similar to the layouts of some of the stone circles. I think it has something to do with the earth power, the Blue Fire.' She chewed on a nail. 'Everywhere I look I see hidden knowledge, signs, portents, things that point to something unimaginably big. It makes me feel so . . . uneasy.'

'We always feel that way when we glimpse movement behind the curtain,' he replied. 'And, as you rightly point out, the signs are everywhere if you only look.'

'More signals behind the noise,' she said wearily. 'I don't think I can cope with it all.' Ruth half-expected Laura to make some sarcastic comment, but she stayed staring at the well, her face impassive behind her sunglasses.

They were about to return to the path when Ruth became

aware someone was behind them. She spun round with a start. In the shadows under the trees stood a man in his late forties, his pate balding, but his greying hair bushy at the back. He was wearing the dog collar of a cleric, a black jacket and trousers, and around his neck hung a gold crucifix, glinting in the morning light.

'I'm sorry,' he said. He smiled gently; his face was honest and open. 'I didn't mean to startle you.' There was a long pause while he looked into all their faces, then he said, 'I saw you at the abbey yesterday. You discovered the message, didn't you?'

'Yes, and it said *Don't talk to strangers*,' Laura blurted defensively.

He laughed bashfully, his hands rubbing together in faint embarrassment. 'I suppose I deserved that, sneaking up on you this way.'

'Are you going to try to stop us?' Ruth asked combatively.

He shook his head, still smiling. 'The path is there for everyone who has the patience and insight to look for it. If not, do you think we would have kept those particular tiles there in that particular position? Hundreds more were unearthed and discarded. I simply wanted to be sure you were aware of the risks.' The others eyed him cautiously. 'Shall we sit?' he said, motioning towards a seat near the wellhead.

Shavi nodded and joined him on the bench, but Laura hung well back, with Ruth hovering somewhere between the two.

Once they had settled, the cleric said, 'My name is Father James, or Jim if you like. I must apologise for approaching you like this, but it seemed the best time and the surroundings are certainly conducive to contemplation.' He paused, as if to search for the correct words, then continued, 'We keep watch on the tiles in the abbey, just in case, but I don't think any of us ever expected the secret to be discovered.'

'Who's we?' Ruth asked.

'A few of us, chosen every ten years from the local parishes and abbey establishment. People who can be trusted to keep the secret. We're known as the Watchmen.' He laughed. 'I know what you're thinking: *Quis custodiet ipsos custodes!*'

'Yeah. That's just what I was thinking,' Laura said sourly.

'A vast amount of knowledge has always been stored at the abbey,' he continued. 'In the early days, the library had a collection of ancient manuscripts that was unmatched in all Christendom. Great wisdom. And much secret knowledge handed down the years. It was all supposedly destroyed in a great fire, and any manuscripts that escaped were lost during the dissolution.'

'But it was not all lost,' Shavi mused.

'Typical double-dealing Christians,' Laura said spitefully.

James didn't seem offended by her words. 'The great twelfth century historian William of Malmesbury was allowed to study some of those manuscripts before he wrote his *Antiquities of Glaston*. He quotes the story of Joseph of Arimathea's arrival at Glastonbury, and his burial here, recounted in several manuscripts. And although his reading was heavily censored, he dropped broad hints about a "sacred mystery" encrypted in the mosaic of the church floor. William had no idea what that mystery was. But we, as I'm sure you can see, had every idea and it has been passed down among a select few of us throughout the centuries. That, and another . . . prophecy? . . . legend? I'm not quite sure of the right word. Of a saviour rising in the world's darkest hour. Although the word is in the singular, in context it seems to be plural. Curious.' He eyed them thoughtfully. 'And these are certainly dark times.'

Shavi nodded. 'We are aware of these things.'

'Excellent. I am particularly interested to find out what this has to do with King Arthur. William speaks of reading a connected manuscript referring to him, but that knowledge *has* been lost to us.' Jim nodded excitedly and clapped his hands. 'This is like being at the end of history. So many different threads leading to this point. You know what you are to do next?'

Shavi stroked his chin thoughtfully. 'Take some of the water from the well—'

'Yes, yes, the *strong water*,' Jim interjected.

'—up to the top of the tor.'

'After that we get a bit vague,' Ruth added.

'Of course, part of the guidance is lost. And do you know what this all leads to?' To Ruth's surprise, Jim actually seemed pleased with their discovery. She had warmed to his pleasant, optimistic manner very quickly; and more, she trusted him, which surprised her even more.

'I would guess,' Shavi answered, 'the Grail.'

'Of course. All the legends, all the mythology, centuries of stories would suggest that is the only answer. But do you know what the Grail is?' He seemed to be enjoying the intellectual game he was playing with them.

Ruth glanced at Shavi, but he didn't respond so she said, 'Everyone knows the Grail is the cup that was supposed to have been used to catch Christ's blood at the crucifixion. It had amazing magical powers, and in the romances the Knights of the Round Table spent their time searching for it.'

'To heal the land. To bring purity to the world,' Shavi interposed.

'But we're actually looking for a Celtic artefact,' Ruth added. She turned to Shavi once again. 'I suppose, of the four, the nearest to a cup would be the cauldron?'

This time Jim laughed aloud. 'We live in a universe where the language is one of symbols. Through it, the cosmos speaks directly to our subconscious, the symbols and messages repeating across the millennia. Words written by man are only interpretations of those symbols, so it's never wise to trust them implicitly—'

'Does that include the Bible?' Laura said pointedly.

The cleric ignored her. 'Grails and cauldrons. Same thing,

337

different names. A vessel of great power. Do you feel comfortable enough for a little instructional dialogue?'

'I suppose you're not going to let us go until you do it,' Ruth sighed.

'Officially, the Church doesn't believe that Joseph brought the Chalice of the Last Supper to Britain,' he began. 'Our scholars recognise that the myth surrounding it goes back much further than Christ's death. Back, in fact, to the pagan cup of plenty, the Graal, which had power over life and death, healing and riches. But somehow the Graal became the sangreal or the *sang real* – Holy Blood. You can see the connection. The Church has always been very good at using the religions of other cultures to further its own ends – and I don't mean that in any disrespectful way. But the Graal is one of those symbols I spoke about, representing the ultimate prize, only attainable by the most pure. Something that we constantly strive for, but can never reach. And in all the stories about it, there are always the same elements: the King, a Good Knight, a Maiden, the powers of Life and Death, a Hermit. What is the universe trying to say to us? Well, I could spend ages discussing that with you, but there's no way of truly knowing. It is simply a matter of faith.'

'So it's a big prize – how come you and your crew haven't cherry-picked it?' Laura asked.

'More than anyone, I would say, we're aware of responsibilities. It isn't meant for us.'

'For something that's so unattainable we seem to have broken into the mystery remarkably easily,' Ruth said.

'You haven't got it yet.' There was some quality to his reply that made Ruth shiver. 'Come, let us collect your water.'

He led them from the wellhead along a path to a partly walled area where the water tumbled from a lion-headed fountain. Shavi filled one of the two goblets that stood nearby and tasted it.

'Amazing!' he said. 'I can actually feel it lifting my spirits.'

338

'I bet you love it when the doc gives you a placebo.' Laura still refused to stand with them.

'Doubting Thomas,' Jim said with a laugh. 'Did you know the Elizabethan magician John Dee announced that he had discovered the *elixir vitae* – the water of life – at Glastonbury?'

'You seem remarkably at ease with the fact that so much of your religion is based on older beliefs,' Ruth said as Shavi filled a plastic water bottle from the spring. 'Don't you feel it undermines your faith?'

Jim shrugged. 'I can be very pragmatic. But Christianity still speaks to me more clearly than anything else; I can't ignore that. And I suppose, in my heart, I don't see a conflict between the Old Ways and the new. There are always higher levels.'

Once Shavi had taken enough water, they continued along the path past two yew trees to another decorative pool in a sun-drenched lawn area.

'I'm very happy to be here,' Jim continued. 'Glastonbury has always been somewhere special, sacred even, right back to neolithic times. The druids set up a college here to pass on their beliefs and wisdom. What is it about Glastonbury? You see, I believe the power of Christ is here, in the land itself. And I'm sure the pagans recognised the same thing, although they called it something different.'

Ruth wondered how much he knew about the Blue Fire, but she didn't raise the point. 'You said you wanted us to be aware of the risks.'

He nodded, suddenly serious. 'No one has ever followed this to its conclusion, the Grail itself. But we know enough. We know it isn't buried in any physical sense; it's in some place that lies alongside our own world. I can't really explain it any better than that. The ritual you're about to embark on will unlock the door – that has been done before, once, long ago. But after that . . . Well, we only have the stories to go on.'

'What stories?' Ruth asked. Shavi was listening intently, as if there was no one in the world apart from Jim.

The cleric wandered over to the shade beneath a tree and leaned against the trunk. 'In the third century BC the Celts established a lake village near here. In those days all the lowlands around here were underwater – there really was an Isle of Avalon. One reading has that name coming from the Celtic legend of the demi-god Avalloc or Avallach who ruled the underworld, and this was supposed to be the meeting place of the dead where they passed over to the next level of existence. Our knowledge of the Celtic tradition is limited and confusing – characters were called by different names in different parts of the Celtic world. Others said the subterranean kingdom of Annwn exists beneath the tor, ruled over by Arawn, the lord of the dead, and anyone who ventures into it encounters demons rather than the land of bliss that greeted those who were invited. Others said the place was the home of Gwynn ap Nud, Lord of the Wild Hunt, which local stories say haunts the hills around Glastonbury.'

Ruth went pale at this information, but he didn't seem to notice.

'The names don't matter. The common thread is that the place you will visit is terribly dangerous. And,' he continued darkly, 'we discovered that for ourselves when we opened the door long ago on that one occasion I mentioned. Never again. So I will ask you now to consider carefully before you continue.'

Shavi stepped forward deferentially. 'I feel we have no choice,' he said gently.

Jim nodded. 'I guessed that would be your answer. Then know this: the part of the message that is missing would have told you the timing is vital. You must take the water up on the tor at first light. And then God help you.'

a Murder of Crows

Church, Veitch and Tom left Jamaica Inn after an early break-fast. The day was bright, with cloud shadows sweeping across the moor beneath the imposing background of Brown Willy, the highest point. But the light had that strained spring qual-ity which threatened inclement weather at the drop of a hat. They could continue their trek, but there were no roads in the direction indicated by the lamp and they knew the going would be treacherous. Instead, they found a local woman who allowed them to cram into her carefully preserved Morris Minor on a shopping trip to Launceston, where they hoped they would be able to pick up another lift.

Although Tom and Veitch could both sense something was wrong, Church hadn't spoken about his encounter in the night. Marianne's revelation had tormented his sleep and on waking he wondered if he would ever sleep peacefully again. On the one hand he felt a great relief from the burden of responsibility in her death; yet the new mysteries that arose in its place were just as frightening in their implications. Who could possibly have killed her?

Despite Launceston buzzing with all the life of a healthy market town, they had to wait until midafternoon before they could find someone who could take them on the next leg of their journey. They bought some heavy Cornish pasties, which they ate in the back of a painter and decorator's van while they made their way slowly through North Cornwall villages which didn't seem to have changed since the fifties; the only sign of modernity was a huge battery of wind turbines, turning eerily in the sea breeze. 'We like the old ways round here,' the driver said between drags on a cigarette. The countryside was green and leafy after the desolation of Bodmin Moor and the closer they got to the coast the stronger the sun became, until it was beating down with all the force of a summer afternoon. Eventually they crested a ridge to see the deep blue sea ahead of them. The road wound down to the coast through an avenue of gnarled, ancient trees where the breeze smelled of salty, wet vegetation. They were dropped off in Boscastle outside the sun-drenched white walls of the Museum of Witchcraft, and although the lantern was still flickering towards the south-west, Church sensed they were near to their destination.

They set off walking along the road which clung precariously to the craggy coast, heavy with the history of smugglers and shipwreckers, and three miles later, as the sun slipped towards the horizon, they found themselves in Tintagel.

'I really should have guessed,' Church said as they rested in the village at the top of the steep track that dropped down to the ancient monument. 'Arthur again. All those references don't make sense.'

Veitch stuffed the last of his bag of chips into his mouth. 'What's this place got to do with King Arthur?'

'Just stupid legends. There was some writer in the twelfth century, Geoffrey of Monmouth, who made these outrageous claims that Tintagel was the birthplace of Arthur and that Merlin took him from here to be fostered in secret. Good for the local tourist trade, not much good for actual history.'

'There are no such things as stupid legends,' Tom interjected coldly.

'I know what you're saying, Tom, but when people believe this kind of stuff it makes an archaeologist's job so much harder.'

'*The Folie Tristan* said the castle was built by giants and

342

that it used to vanish twice a year, at midsummer and mid-winter,' Tom said with a strange smile.

'Exactly.' But Church had the uncomfortable feeling that Tom's comments weren't in support of his own argument; the man continued to smile until Church looked away.

'So was he real or not?' Veitch said looking from one to the other. 'Excalibur! Lancelot! Bleedin' great stories.'

'I don't deny they're great stories,' Church said, 'but that's all they are. Archaeologists recently dug up a piece of slate or something here with part of the name *Arthur* scrawled on it, and suddenly all the thick bastards on the national papers were saying it was proof he lived here. But Arthur and all the derivations were common names, meaning bear-like—'

'Old stories do not always tell the truth in a literal sense,' Tom said directly to Veitch, 'but sometimes they tell the truth in their hidden meaning.'

Veitch seemed quite satisfied by this, but, wearied by the travelling, Church had little patience for Tom's obfuscations. 'So what are the hidden meanings?' he snapped. 'I know this was an important place to the Celts, like all the other places we've trawled through, but I can't see what any of it has to do with a character who didn't exist, or at least not in the form everyone's talking about.'

Tom glanced up at the darkening sky, then turned to the track down to the castle. 'Come on. We must be there before nightfall.'

Church thought it was another attempt to divert his questions, but as they trudged down the steep incline, Tom said, 'When the Celts ruled Britain was the last time the land was truly alive.'

'You're talking about the Blue Fire – the earth energy?'

He nodded slowly, thoughtfully, his eyes fixed firmly on the sea in the distance. 'When the gods departed, the people were freed from the yoke of terror, but they lost something too. The people and the land are linked; like a mother and the baby in the womb, the blood that flows through one

343

nourishes the other. But more than that, what you call the Blue Fire is also a powerful force for offence – for the defence of the land and the people. But like any weapon it needs to be nurtured to prevent it falling into disrepair. With the gods gone, there was no longer the immediate need for the people to unite and stay strong, with the force of the land at their backs. The mundane, day-to-day struggle of survival in a difficult environment took over and they forgot the importance of caring for the land through ritual at its sacred sites. The power dimmed, then grew dormant, and the people continued happily in their ignorant belief that all they needed was what their hands could grasp. But the Blue Fire is the spirit of the land *and* the people, inextricably linked for all time.'

The track grew less steep as a small valley opened beside them with a tiny stream winding among wildly overgrown nettles and brambles. To their left, the side of the valley soared up high above their heads where part of the ruined castle lay. No tourists ventured down at that time, and the only sound was that of the sea crashing against the crags.

'So now the Fomorii are back we need to awaken that power again? To help us get the strength to defend ourselves?' Church searched Tom's face for answers, but his features were unreadable.

'It's all talk with you two, isn't it.' Veitch seemed uncomfortable. He was continually scanning the thick vegetation away to their left and the growing shadows behind them.

'And Arthur?' Church continued.

'The Celts used their stories to pass vital information down the generations. Nobody can be bothered to remember facts, but if they are stitched into the fabric of an exciting tale . . .' Now *he* was distracted by the landscape. Perhaps it was the way the valley's steep slopes made them feel insignificant and trapped, or perhaps Veitch's obvious uneasiness was catching, but Tom seemed to be growing increasingly wary.

'And?' Church said with frustration.

'And all myths and legends are the same. Arthur is not a man. He is the embodiment of the spirit of man and the spirit of the land.'

Church suddenly saw what Tom was suggesting. 'The legend of Arthur sleeping under a hill to be woken in Britain's darkest hour . . . That's a coded message to awaken the power in the land.'

'Finally,' Tom said wearily.

'And all the sites linked to Arthur are ones that are important to the earth energy! But I don't understand—'

'No more talk,' Tom snapped. He stopped suddenly and glanced back up the sweeping track, as if he had heard something. Church listened intently, but the only sound was of the faint breeze rustling the bushes. 'Let us get to our destination. At least we should be safe there.'

'Safe from what?' Veitch said. Church saw his hand go unconsciously to the gun hidden in his jacket.

They speeded their step along the gravel track, falling into an uncomfortable silence. Above, the sky had turned deep blue and they could make out the diamond stars; it made Church feel very alone. The English Heritage building was locked and dark at the point where the valley opened out at the coast. The stream plunged into an impressive white waterfall cascading down on to the pebbled beach. The tide was out, the sea dark and powerful, licked with creamy surf where the waves broke powerfully.

And high up on their left were the ruins of the twelfth century castle like jagged teeth on a broken jaw. 'We go up there, I suppose,' Church said hesitantly.

'No,' Tom corrected. 'Down. To the beach.'

Church looked at him curiously, but he gave no hint of how he knew the direction.

They clambered across the culverted stream and along a path that ran over treacherous, slick rocks where signs warned of the dangers of the crumbling cliff face. In the growing gloom, it was difficult to haul their way over the jumbled boulders to the crunching pebbles, but they managed it with only a few knocked bones. The beach had the thick, fishy smell of seaweed and the thunder of the waves was almost deafening.

Tom led them across the stones to a gash of impenetrable black in the soaring cliffs beneath the castle. 'Merlin's Cave,' he noted.

Veitch laughed. 'Merlin! That's not you, is it? You've got that look about you.'

'No, it is not,' Tom said indignantly.

'We're going to do ourselves some damage in there,' Church said, trying to pierce the darkness. 'We won't be able to see our hands in front of our faces.'

Tom marched past him into the shadows. Church cursed and glanced at Veitch, who circled his finger at the side of his head. But a second later they were slipping and sliding over seaweed and rocks, splashing into pools and stubbing their toes, while desperately trying to keep up with him; in the end they were gripping on to each other's jackets so they didn't become separated. They seemed to hang suspended in the dark where the echoing sound of the sea was almost unbearable until Church cursed, irritated with himself for not thinking, and pulled out the Wayfinder. In its shimmering blue light he could see the cave actually went right through the thin promontory that joined the mainland to the bulk of the island where the oldest part of the castle stood.

'What the hell are we looking for in here?' Veitch yelled above the roar.

'A door of some kind, I suppose.' Church told him how the ground had opened magically at Avebury. Veitch shook his head in disbelief.

Tom's frustration was obvious as he stood on an enormous boulder and scanned the shadows that scurried across the walls away from the lamp's light. 'Where is it?' he muttered.

Veitch glanced back to the cave entrance nervously.

'There's something out there.' He looked back at Church for some kind of comfort. 'I must be going mad. I can't see anything, hear anything, but I feel like my heart's going to burst. I can't shake the feeling there's something bad coming for us.'

Church nodded as supportively as he could muster, then returned his attention to washing the lantern's light across the rock. 'We've all got to learn to trust our feelings,' he said distractedly.

'Thanks a bunch,' Veitch replied moodily.

And then Church did hear something, in the slight lull between the breaking of the waves. It sounded like a wild rustling or fluttering, but he couldn't think of anything that might have caused it. He looked to Tom, who was searching the walls with renewed, almost frantic energy. 'Just keep looking,' he said before Church could speak.

'There!' Veitch exclaimed suddenly. He pointed to a part of the wall that was now in darkness. 'Bring the lamp back!'

Church slowly swung the Wayfinder round until the section was illuminated. The shadows ebbed and flowed and then, for the briefest instant, a shape appeared. Church adjusted the lamp gently until the faint outline of a broadsword materialised out of a chaotic jumble of cracks that would not have been visible in any other light. Tom bounded from the boulder with a sprightliness that belied his age and slammed his palm against the symbol; blue sparks burst from his fingertips.

At that moment the pounding of the surf died again and the mysterious sound filled the cavern, throwing them all into a state of anxiety. Church looked back towards the entrance and saw some kind of whirling movement, darker even than the shadows. He thought he was going to be sick.

His attention was snapped back by a sudden rending sound from deep within the rock wall. A crevice mysteriously grew until it was wide enough for them to slip through. They hung back for just a second while the disturbing sound from the

347

entrance seemed to rush towards them, then they dived in without a backward glance.

Although they weren't immediately aware of it, the wall closed behind them, trapping them in a tunnel in the rock barely big enough to stand upright. Their feet kicked up sand and seashells, and the deep, salty smell of the sea was everywhere.

'This place floods with the tide,' Church noted ominously.

'How can rock open up like that?' Veitch asked.

'It didn't. It simply appeared as if it did,' Tom replied obliquely.

'What was that outside, Tom?' Church asked.

'No point talking about that now. The tide is coming in. We do not have much time.' He pushed past them and led the way along the tunnel which opened up into a cave the size of Church's now burnt-out lounge. In the wall opposite were three holes set out at intervals along a line at waist-height.

'What are we supposed to do?' Veitch asked.

Tom dropped down on his haunches to peer into the holes. 'I can see something . . .' A shrug. 'I would expect the objects of power wouldn't be lying around for just anyone to pick up.'

Veitch inspected the rest of the chamber, but there were no other distinguishing marks. 'So, what? We have to find the combination?'

'Something like that.'

'Good job there's not a lot riding on it,' Veitch noted bitterly.

'You know,' Church said, 'there might be a switch in one of those holes.' He tapped his fingers gently at the entrance to the middle one.

'That's not much of a security system.'

'Here,' Tom said sharply. Church and Veitch turned to where he was pointing. A trickle of frothy sea water had washed up the tunnel to the mouth of the chamber.

'The tide must sweep in quickly through the other entrance to the cave.' Church handed Tom the Wayfinder, then turned back to the holes. 'Bloody hell. We haven't got much time. What do we do?' Steeling himself, he rammed his hand into the middle hole. It went in up to the middle of his forearm and at the far end there were two loops of metal which his fingers slipped through easily. 'I think there is a switch here!'

'Well, pull the bleedin' thing then and let's get the hell out.' Veitch eyed the advancing water nervously; it was already another six inches into the chamber.

Tom and Veitch both realised something was wrong from the sudden, bloodless expression on Church's face. 'Something's closed around my wrist. I can't get my hand out.' He tugged frantically, but his arm wouldn't retract at all.

The sea water washed around their shoes, which were sinking into the sandy floor. Veitch leapt into action. He put his arms around Church's waist, braced himself with one foot against the chamber wall and heaved. Church yelled in pain. 'You'll pull my bloody hand off!' Veitch released his grip with a curse.

'Relax your muscles,' Tom ordered. 'It might be like one of those oriental finger locks – the harder you pull, the more you are held tight.'

'I don't feel in a particularly relaxed frame of mind,' Church hissed. His socks and the bottoms of his Levis were already wet. He closed his eyes and attempted to calm himself with pleasant thoughts from his past, then felt a dismal wash of emotion when he realised they all contained Marianne. But it did the trick. Yet even when he let his hand go limp, the bond around his wrist remained as tight as ever. His shoulders slumped and he shook his head desolately.

'This water's flooding in!' Veitch barked. It was up to their calves, and when he paced anxiously it splashed dark stains up the legs of his trousers.

'That's not doing any good!' Church snapped.

'Calm down,' Tom said. 'It won't do any good to panic.'

'That's easy for you to say.' Church could feel his heart beating like a trip-hammer, his back and shoulder muscles knotting tightly. Although he tried not to think about it, images flashed through his mind of the water flooding into his mouth and nose, filling his throat, his lungs. 'You two should get out of here while you still can,' he said as calmly as he could muster.

'Don't be stupid! We can't leave you here – you're the important one!' Veitch's face was filled with the anger of frustration.

'Just get out!' Church shouted, his eyes blazing.

'He's right,' Tom said, his voice almost lost beneath the echoes of lapping water. 'Someone has to be left to try again, or everything—'

'Shut up, you coldhearted bastard,' Veitch growled. 'You're talking bollocks.' He splashed around the cave like a trapped animal, his fists bunching, then opening. 'I told you, he's the important one. We're just a couple of losers.'

'Get out,' Church repeated, gentler now he had seen the dismay in Veitch's face.

'There's got to be an answer!' Veitch exploded. 'Whoever did this wouldn't just leave it so everybody died!'

The water surged in, lapping up the walls, tugging at their legs. It appeared to be coming faster and faster. When it hit Church's waist, it seemed to flush the panic from him briefly. Suddenly, on a whim, he pushed his free hand into the left hole. There was a click and his trapped hand came free, but as he withdrew it jubilantly a bond snapped around his other wrist. He cursed loudly, waving the now-free hand to stimulate the blood supply.

'So triggering one switch frees the other one,' Tom said.

'That's a lot of use!' Church said. 'There's always got to be one hand in there.'

'But still. . .' Tom mused, wiping the splashes of water off his glasses.

'How can you be so calm?' Veitch bellowed at him. Tom

replaced his glasses as if he hadn't heard a sound, and for a second Church thought Veitch was going to punch him.

'Take it easy, Ryan,' he said.

Church's calmness had an odd effect on Veitch. For a second his eyes ranged over Church's face, then he turned away as if he suddenly couldn't understand what was happening in the world.

The sea water continued to rush in, splashing up high, throwing them around. It had reached their chests in just a couple of minutes; desperation gripped them all. Tom held the Wayfinder up high, its light painting the water azure, but even when the tide splashed over the flame it didn't extinguish it. Church wondered if it would still be burning away beneath the water at the side of his drowned, bloated body.

Tom placed one hand on Veitch's shoulder. 'We need to leave,' he said quietly.

The water whooshed in, the current almost too much to bear. Church thought it was going to tear his hand off at the wrist. He had to fight to keep his head above the swell. Now he could feel the panic surging.

There were tears in Veitch's eyes as he looked from Tom to Church, then he ducked his face in the water. When he threw his head back, the shock of the cold had sluiced off his emotion and he seemed to have a renewed purpose.

Church took a mouthful of salty water. He choked, tried to kick upwards, sucked in a huge gulp of air.

Veitch half-swam over to the holes and paused while he looked deeply into Church's eyes. Through his panic, Church could see Veitch weighing something up. Then the Londoner moved, suddenly forcing both his hands into the remaining holes.

'No!' Church yelled, but it was too late. He felt the bond around his wrist release and his hand shot free.

Before Church could vent his anger at Veitch for his sacrifice, there came a rumble from deep within the cavern wall and gradually a dark space appeared at head height above the holes. Within it Church could see blue sparks flashing, and an aged iron sword lying on a stone shelf. At the same time, Veitch's hands came free and another space opened – a doorway this time – on the other side of the chamber. Veitch whooped triumphantly as Church grabbed the sword and then they were all swimming frantically to the doorway. On the other side was a tight spiral of stairs rising steeply. They scrambled up high above the water level and crashed down on to the steps in exhaustion.

'I don't believe it,' Church gasped. 'I don't bloody believe it!'

Tom removed his glasses and rubbed a hand over his weary eyes. 'There was another dimension to the puzzle,' he said. 'The key was sacrifice. It would not give up the sword until we showed we understood *sacrifice.*'

'You're talking like it knew what we were doing.' Veitch had a satisfied, slightly amazed smile on his face. He closed his eyes and lay back on the steps until his breathing returned to normal. Then he sat up and said, 'Let's have a look at it, then.'

Church laid the sword on the steps and held the Wayfinder over it so they could examine it. Few would have given it a second glance. It was of a bare, basic design and appeared to be made of iron which had corroded badly; there were no distinguishing marks or aesthetic elements at all.

But it was obvious from Veitch's face that he was seeing something different. 'Excalibur?' he asked reverentially.

'The Sword of Nuada Airgetlámh,' Church corrected. He glanced at Tom, who had a flicker of a knowing smile on his lips. 'Or perhaps they're different names for the same thing, for something that can't be defined.'

'That is the problem with legends,' Tom said wryly. 'They are imprecise ways of defining the indefinable.'

'You two bastards should never be allowed to talk to each other,' Veitch grumbled, pulling himself to his feet. 'Let's get out of here before the water finds us.'

As Church rose, he turned to Veitch and said awkwardly, 'Thanks. You know, for what you did—'

Veitch shifted uncomfortably. 'No problem.' Then, 'You're not going to bloody hug me, are you?'

'No, I'm not!' Church said indignantly. 'Come on. Let's climb.'

The steps ascended steeply in a spiral so tight it made them dizzy; they had to rest at regular intervals. Yet their success had left them with a strange euphoria, as if they had started living only at that moment; the sharp, salty tang in the air, the touch of the hard, cold rock, the echoes of their feet, the shimmering blue light reflected off the wet walls, all seemed heightened to such a degree they almost seemed like new experiences. The sword was strangely warm against Church's back as they scrambled up the rough-hewn steps; if he allowed himself to think about it, he would have noted it almost felt alive, like some unseen friend was resting an arm against him.

The steps ended suddenly at a stone ceiling on which was carved a stylised image of a dragon with a serpent-like body. There was another brief flurry of blue sparks when Church placed both hands on it and heaved, and then, with a loud creak, a square trapdoor eased open, revealing a patch of star-sprinkled sky. Church hauled himself out on to clipped grass and then offered a hand to Veitch and Tom.

They were on the windswept top of the island where the oldest part of the castle stood. All around, Church could see the broken foundations and rough outlines of buildings that dated back to the Celts.

'We did it!' Veitch said with a broad grin. Even Tom allowed himself a tight smile of triumph.

'If Laura and Ruth got away, we're two artefacts down and only two to go,' Church noted with a grin. 'You know, I think we're going to do it.'

'That was a buzz and a half!' Veitch continued exuberantly. 'Better than drugs. This is what life's about!'

The small island was just a high mound of rock covered by scrubby grass and the ruins. From their vantage point they could look down on the surrounding coastline where the sea crashed in eruptions of white foam, and in the distance the lights of the village of Tintagel blazed like a beacon.

'You reckon we can get a room for the night? I don't fancy kipping in a ditch,' Veitch asked as they headed in the direction of the bridge over the thin neck of rock that joined the island to the mainland.

Before Church could answer, the wind died briefly and they heard the unnerving fluttering sound that had pursued them into the cave earlier. Tom's face grew taut; in the excitement he had obviously forgotten about it too.

'What *is* that?' Veitch asked anxiously. They stood stock-still, listening intently; it seemed to be coming from the direction of the bridge. As it grew louder it sounded like a sheet flapping in the wind, but there were other disturbing notes which they couldn't place.

Church looked behind him. The land fell away sharply into treacherously steep, crumbling cliffs. 'There's no other way out, is there?'

'I said, what is it?' This time Veitch gripped Tom's arm, who shook it off roughly, then started to cast around for some place to turn.

While the others held back, Church ran to the ruins of a chapel and peered down the bank to the Inner Ward, fifty yards away from where the noise seemed to be emanating. He saw several dark shapes moving cautiously through the castle and, at the head of them, a strange disturbance in the air; he could see movement, but the shadows prevented him picking out any detail. Two of the shapes waited at the top of the steps which were the only exit from the island.

'Fomorii?' Tom asked him when he ran back to them.

'I think. And something else too, but I can't make it out. There's no way past them.'

'Then we fight the bastards here.' Veitch's bravado belied

the fear in his eyes. He pulled out his gun and examined it – they all knew it would do no good – before returning it to his pocket and removing a long hunting knife from a sheath he had hidden under his jacket.

'I got it while you two were buying the food in Launceston,' he said.

'I didn't think you had any cash,' Church noted.

'I don't.' He looked away uncomfortably, then pointed to a small jumble of foundations near where the land fell away on to the cliffs. 'If we make a stand there, they won't be able to come up behind us.'

As they hurried towards the spot, Church pulled out the sword; Tom shied away from it instantly. It seemed to shift slightly in Church's hand, as if it were settling into his grip. The warmth he had noted earlier flowed up his tendons into his forearm.

'That thing looks like it'll fall apart if you clout anything with it,' Veitch said.

'It's got power inside it, I can feel it. I reckon I can do a bit of damage.'

They were aware of the Fomorii approaching before the dark shapes had separated from the shadows; the attackers were preceded by an unpleasant feeling that operated beyond the five senses, churning the stomach and making their throats constrict. Tom brushed Church's and Veitch's temple briefly. 'You will keep your senses when you see them,' he said quietly.

'Magic?' Veitch grunted. 'You bloody well are Merlin.'

'Shut up,' Tom snapped.

The fluttering sound grew much louder as the hideously misshapen figures gradually took form. They crested the summit of the island and began to move forward, powerfully and relentlessly. In the centre of the approaching force was an intense, tightly constrained mass of whirling shapes.

As it drew nearer, Church picked details out of the gloom, until he said querulously, 'Birds?'

355

'Crows,' Tom corrected.

'Mollecht.' Church winced at the memory of Tom's description.

The crows were swirling around, wings flapping madly yet seeming never to collide with each other. Their incredibly complex pattern suggested the shape of a man at their core, but it was impossible to see any sign of him.

Veitch gasped as the birds swept across the grass towards them with an eerie, unnatural speed; it was such a terrifying sight that the other Fomorii seemed insignificant.

Tom was muttering something under his breath, prayers or protective incantations, Church couldn't tell which. Veitch kept glancing down at the hunting knife in his hand, now made pathetic and useless. He went to throw it away, then clutched it tight for security.

Church took a deep breath and cleared all thoughts from his head. Ignoring the fear, he stepped in front of the other two and held the sword up with both hands. He moved it awkwardly, but somehow it seemed to correct its balance itself. From the corner of his eye, he thought he glimpsed a crackle of blue fire along its edge.

It had an immediate effect. The crows came to a sudden halt about twenty feet away and began to shift back and forth along a wide arc. The night was suddenly torn by the monkey screeches and guttural roars of the Fomorii. Church moved the sword around, hoping it would be enough to frighten them off, but the attackers held their ground.

Before he could make another move, the crows emitted a fierce cawing and their swirling became even more frenzied. A second later a hole opened up in the heart of them. Church glimpsed an entity inside that made his eyes sting and his gorge rise, and then something dark and translucent erupted out of it and burst over their heads. The shockwave threw them to their knees and an awful sulphurous smell filled the air. Church felt his skin crawling, as if insects were swarming all over him. He glanced down to see pinpricks of blood bursting from his pores. Tom was screaming something, but Church's ears were still ringing from the explosion, and when he glanced to one side Veitch was yelling too. His face was covered with blood.

In that instant the other Fomorii surged forward. Tom grabbed Church's shirt and yanked, a signal to retreat. The three of them backed away hurriedly, but within seconds the ground was falling away beneath their feet and they were desperately trying to right themselves on the steep incline towards the cliffs. Church brandished the sword before him, but the Fomorii seemed quite content to herd the three of them where there was nowhere else to go. The buffeting wind at his back and the roaring of the sea as it crashed against the cliffs told him when they had run out of land, and time. He glanced back briefly. They were a foot away from the precipice; far beneath, the white water sucked and thrashed menacingly against the rocks. There was no way they could survive a plunge.

His skin was slick with blood from head to toe, but the only thought that dominated his mind was that he had wasted too long worrying about the Watchtower's untrue premonition of his death.

The first of the Fomorii moved forward with a roar and, despite Tom's spell, Church could still not look it full in the face. He closed his eyes and lashed out blindly with the sword. The impact made his bones ache, forcing his eyes open. He was shocked to see the sword had sliced through whatever the creature had instead of a collar bone and had imbedded itself in its skeleton. It was howling wildly and flailing its limbs as it died; Church almost vomited from the foul stench that was emanating from the wound. With an immense effort, he wrenched out the sword and swung it in an arc, cleaving off the beast's head.

He didn't have time to celebrate, for at that moment the screeching of the remaining Fomorii reached a crescendo and they moved forward as one. Out of the corner of his eye, he glimpsed Tom hunched over, muttering to himself, his hands and arms twitching as if he had an ague. Then Veitch was at his side, shouting obscenities as he waved the hunting knife so violently it no longer seemed as feeble as it had before.

The Fomorii bore down on them in a wave of deformed bodies, radiating a dark, terrifying power that made him sick to his stomach. Feeling the fear and despair surge through him, Church swung the sword back and closed his eyes. He thought, *This is*—

Something grasped the collar of his jacket and hauled him backwards. His heels kicked grass, rock and then nothing, and he was falling so fast the wind tore his breath from his mouth. There was no time to think of anything before he hit the waves hard. An instant later he blacked out as the water surged into his mouth and nose and pulled him far beneath the swell.

Shavi, Ruth and Laura sat on the cold stone bench in the tiny tower that was all that remained of St Michael's Church, perched high on top of the tor. Through the open arch where the wind blew mercilessly they could see the lights of Glastonbury spread out comfortingly in the intense dark just before dawn. On the cracked stone floor before them stood the plastic bottle which contained the water they had brought from the Chalice Well.

'I don't feel ready for this,' Ruth said. 'It would have been a little easier if Jim hadn't gone on at length about all the dangers.'

'That's God people for you,' Laura noted. 'They're never happy unless someone's worried or scared.'

Ruth watched the stars for a long moment, remembering a similar night in Stonehenge, and then said almost to herself, 'I wish Church was here.' She realised what she had said and glanced at Laura. 'I don't mean because I'm not up to it myself—'

Laura didn't look at her. 'I know what you mean.'

Shavi rose and went through a series of yoga movements to stretch the ache of the night chill from his muscles. It felt like they had been sitting in the tower for hours, although it had only been about forty-five minutes.

'So what do we do now? Do you think Mister Dog Collar could have been any more vague?' Laura asked gloomily.

'It is all about ritual,' Shavi explained, 'and part of the ritual is finding the path ourselves. He gave us *some* guidance – the time of the ritual – and I think the rest of it is pretty obvious.'

'To you, maybe, but then you're some big shaman-type.' Laura stood up and leaned in the arch, looking down at the town.

Shavi moved in beside her and pointed to the faint terraces cut into the hill centuries ago, visible by their moon-shadows even in the dark. 'You see those? What use are they? They are patently not fields, nor could they be the kind of defences thrown up on some earthworks from neolithic times. Yet it would take a tremendous amount of effort to level out those terraces, so they must be of some significance to whatever culture invested all that manpower and time hundreds or thousands of years ago.'

Ruth joined them in the archway, tracing the path of the terraces with her fingertip. 'They're like steps.'

'Exactly,' Shavi nodded. 'A path to the top, but not in the manner you suggest. A labyrinth, a three-dimensional one. You can walk a route back and forth around the tor to the summit.'

'Why do that when it's easier to go in a straight line?' Laura said.

'The labyrinth is a classical design found in rock carvings, coins, turf mazes around the world. It has more than one meaning, like everything else we have encountered, but at its heart it represents a journey to and from the land of the dead. Birth, death and rebirth.'

'I really don't like all this talk of death,' Ruth murmured.

'And what happens when we get to the end?' Laura stamped her feet to boost the blood circulation.

Shavi shrugged.

'And the water?'

'An oblation to be offered at the point where we find ourselves.'

'You call it ritual, but it sounds like magic to me,' Ruth noted.

'Perhaps.' Shavi put an arm around both their shoulders, an act that would have seemed too familiar from any other man they had just met, yet from him it simply suggested friendship and security. 'We think of magic as something from children's stories, but it may simply be a word for describing that activation of the earth force you have seen. New knowledge which we have no frame of reference to understand. Magic is as good a word as any.'

'Sometimes you sound just like that old hippie,' Laura said with an acidity that was transparent to both Shavi and Ruth.

They continued to discuss the tor and the mysteries they had uncovered for the next half hour, yet none of them touched on the matter that was most important in all their hearts; the sense that they were on the verge of something profound, a turning point which would finally reveal the truth about the events that were shaping the world, about the forgotten past and the hidden future, and, above all, about themselves.

The closer the sunrise drew, the more they seemed to feel an electric quality in the air which resonated deep within them. Barely able to contain their anticipation, they sat against a wall and watched the eastern sky for its lightening. It was a magical moment that stilled conversation, of stars, and wind and the sound of the trees at the foot of the tor, and for a while they seemed to feel the axis of the heavens turning, as they knew their ancestors would have done millennia ago.

It was during one such lull in the conversation that they were startled by the noise of something heavy hitting the ground and a strange liquid, flopping sound. It was incongruous enough to set their hearts racing, and they hurried around the tower to search for its origin.

But as they rounded the western flank of the tower, they were brought up sharp by a bizarre sight that sent their heads spinning: three figures floundered like fish on the slopes of the tor, soaked to the skin and retching up sea water.

'Oh great,' Laura said sourly. 'The old git's back.'

a Day as Still as heaven

Ruth reached Church first. 'We're on the highest spot in the area and they're drowning,' she said incredulously. Without giving it a second thought, she jumped astride him and began massaging his chest to free the water trapped in his lungs.

The others reacted slightly slower – Laura gave the kiss of life to Veitch while Shavi administered to Tom – but within five minutes the three new arrivals were sitting up, gasping and wringing out their sodden clothes.

Bafflement at the bizarre situation was washed aside in a rush of emotion. Ruth threw her arms round Church and hugged him tightly. 'God, I'm so glad you're alive!'

Although still dazed by the situation, his relief at seeing her was palpable. He kissed her affectionately on the cheek, then glanced up at Laura who was standing uncomfortably a few feet away.

'I knew you were too stupid to get yourself killed,' she said.

He smiled; the message between the lines was obvious. 'I missed you too.'

Their brief introductions dissolved into a mess of garbled comments as they struggled to understand what had happened. Church described the confrontation at Tintagel and their plunge into the ocean, while glancing at Glastonbury's lights. Then he caught Tom's eye. 'What do you know about it?'

Tom's grey, drawn face suggested the experience had affected him more than the others. 'I moved us along the lines of power.' He sucked in a deep, juddering breath.

'You *transported* us here?' Church said incredulously.

'It was always theoretically possible. A matter of shaping the energy to do your bidding, forcing a connection between two nodes. I'd been taught the ritual movements, the correct vibrational sounds to make—'

'Magic!' Shavi said, his face alight with excitement.

'—but I'd never achieved anything like this before. Desperation must have focused my mind.'

'Who taught you?' Church asked. 'You owe us a lot of explanations—'

'There is no time now,' Shavi interrupted. He explained the impending sunrise ritual and the events that had led them to it.

'Don't we get a bleedin' rest?' Veitch flopped back on the grass.

'We can rest later.' Church retrieved the sword from where it lay and made a tear in his jacket, slipping it in between the lining; the handle protruded above his right shoulder where he could reach it easily. 'Two down,' he said, 'and two to go.'

Huddled in the tower away from the wind, they made hasty introductions and exchanged fuller details of their experiences, but any excitement they may have felt at their reunion was muted by the apprehension of what lay ahead. Twenty minutes later the first faint silvering in the sky brought with it an oppressive silence. Shavi rose and led the way to the Living Rock, a standing stone that marked the entrance to the labyrinth. While the others waited uncomfortably behind him, he bowed his head silently in meditation. Then, when the first rays of dawn crept across the grass to hit the stone, it seemed to ignite with blue fire. A gasp of amazement rippled through the others, but Shavi simply rested his hand upon it for a moment before setting off along the first terrace; the others followed in a solemn procession.

The going was not easy. They weaved back and forth in

363

horseshoe patterns around the tor, slowly rising through the terraces as the sky exploded in gold, purple and powder blue. Though none of them spoke, the dawn chorus soaring from the trees at the base of the hill provided an epic soundtrack. Whatever power lay in the ground reinvigorated Church, Veitch and Tom, but there was still a hard lump of fear in all their hearts.

It took them nearly two hours to complete the serpentine route. At the final turn, the path seemed to disappear, leaving a precipitous, near-impassable way to the summit. Veitch opened his mouth to question, but Church silenced him with a wave of his finger. At that spot, the underlying rock broke through the short grass to reveal a large boulder.

The others waited patiently while Shavi produced the plastic bottle containing the Chalice Well water and, after another moment of meditation, he poured the oblation upon the boulder. A strange dual tone emerged from deep within the tor, like falsetto singing merging with a bass rumble. Tiny threads of blue fire spread out across the boulder and then into the other exposed rock. It fizzed and licked for a moment while the noise grew in intensity and then, with a sudden roaring, the rock drew aside to reveal a dark tunnel winding down into the black depths.

They could remember nothing about that journey through the dark. Sometime later, they found themselves in a place that took their breath away; not some dingy cavern lying inside the tor, but green fields and thick woods, rustled by a slight breeze in the heat of a summer's day. Nearby they could hear the faint babbling of a brook. The air smelled sweeter than anything they had experienced before; to breathe it in was so fulfilling it was almost as if they had eaten a hearty meal. Ruth caught a fleeting glimpse of her owl soaring high above and wondered how it had got there.

'Where are we?' Veitch said in bewilderment. 'We should be underground. I can see sky.'

Tom knelt down and gently kissed the green sward. 'Tir na n'Og,' he muttered.

Ruth looked round in confusion. 'We're not in Somerset any more, Toto.'

'The Land of Youth, or Always Summer.' This Church did remember from his studies. 'The Celtic heaven. The Otherworld where all the gods were supposed to have gone to after they left Earth in the hands of man.'

'That's one aspect of it.' Tom rose and stretched; he looked revitalised. 'Like everything else, it has a dual aspect. It is also The Land of Ever Winter, or hell, by any other name, depending how you come to it.'

'I don't understand.' Veitch looked from one face to the other.

'This place is not fixed,' Tom said, 'like all the things that originate here. You are all seeing something slightly different, depending on your perception. What is within, is without.'

'Listen to the voice of Buddha,' Laura sighed.

But now he had mentioned it, they could all see it. The edges of each blade of grass, tree branches, even the horizon, seemed vaguely fluid, as if they could change at a moment's notice; they seemed to radiate a subtle, inner light, creating a distorted sense of unreality.

'But we should be underground,' Veitch protested.

'Hey, new boy, when you find your brain, let us know.' Laura kicked up a few sods of turf. 'We've crossed over. We're in Never land now.' Veitch returned a combative scowl.

'Look at it!' Shavi said. 'It is amazing. Everything is so vital.' He whirled round to take in the landscape. 'Even the quality of the air, the sounds—'

'Don't be mistaken,' Tom interjected. 'There's danger here too.'

'It looks deserted,' Ruth said.

'The Danann are missing. Everything else is in our world,' Church said.

The Wayfinder's flame pointed them down the gentle slope of the meadow to a wood that lay beyond the brook. As they walked, Church caught up with Tom. 'So this is where you stayed for all those years. Is it good to be back?'

'You misunderstand.' Tom didn't take his eyes off the path. 'I miss this place like a murderer who has spent his entire life in solitary confinement misses his cell. Familiarity forces you to love the things you hate.'

'You were a prisoner here?'

'A prisoner, a plaything, something to be tormented by the gods, torn inside out and reshaped for their enjoyment.'

Church eyed him askance. 'I hope that's a metaphor.'

'I told you – they are alien, unknowable. We cannot begin to grasp the power at their disposal. Do not be fooled because we view them in vaguely human form. They are beyond most of our emotions – love, hate—'

'Cruelty?'

He paused. 'No. Not beyond that.'

Tom was interrupted by a cry from Veitch, who had moved into lead position along the path which was skirting a thick wood. They hurried through the meadow flowers until they saw what had alerted him: an odd circular structure of timber and stone with a tower at its centre. The Wayfinder flame flickered enticingly towards it.

'Before this land was deserted you wouldn't have been able to get within an arrow's fall of this place. Even the Danann revered it and what it contained,' Tom said.

'The bloody Grail!' Veitch said enthusiastically.

They walked slowly until they were in the shadow of the building; an odd atmosphere hung heavily around it that invoked both awe and fear. Church pointed out five doors around its walls, without needing to explain what that meant. Shavi and Ruth were keen to enter, but after their experiences with the first two talismans Church, Veitch and Laura were more hesitant.

Tom wandered back into the sun and took up a position

on one of the grassy slopes overlooking the building. 'You're not coming?' Church asked.

'I would be torn apart by all the power in there. This isn't for me. It's about you, all of you.'

There was something in his words that made Church feel uncomfortable, but he turned back to the others, readying himself for what lay ahead. After fifteen minutes boosting each other's confidence, they each took up a spot in front of one of the doors and on the count of three they swung them open and stepped in.

The corridor was long, pitch-black and oppressively warm. Shavi edged down it cautiously, trailing his fingertips along the rough walls for guidance. His footsteps echoed strangely, as if the size of the space were far greater than it appeared to be, and after he had been walking for ten minutes he realised that must certainly have been the case, for he could have circumnavigated the building five times in that period. By then, the faint light from the door had disappeared completely, the impenetrable darkness closing around so tightly he felt like he was floating in space. His progress slowed even further as he felt each step with his foot in case the floor fell away suddenly.

But after a short while he got a sense of diffuse illumination ahead, like candlelight. To his surprise, he found himself in what appeared to be a funfair hall of mirrors, the polished glass lined up in continuously branching avenues like a maze. After the dark it was destabilising and he had to close his eyes for a moment while he steadied himself.

It was impossible to guess where the source of the light was in the myriad subtle reflections, but it allowed him to move more freely. He chose his path at random.

For what seemed like an hour, he wandered among the images of himself, most of them normal, some grotesquely distorted. It seemed to him it was simply a trap to drive intruders insane. He could have been going round in circles for all he knew; there was nothing to distinguish the routes among the mirrors.

But as he rounded a sharp bend in the maze, he came upon a mirror which was unlike any of the others. It was larger, with a bevelled edge to the glass, and a frame of what appeared to be silver, designed with the spiral paths and interlinking patterns of Celtic art. Shavi felt drawn towards it as if it were radiating some dark power. And once he stood before it he could see it was unusual in other ways, too; at first glance, his reflection seemed perfectly normal, but the more he looked, the more he could see a difference that was so subtle it was almost a variation of mood. There was a darkness to the features, the merest tinge of cruelty around the mouth, a sense of bitter loss in the eyes, a resentment in the way the head was held.

Shavi examined it for a long moment, and then its mouth moved in no reflection of his own.

'Why do you do this to yourself, Shavi? Searching for meaning in all these silly places? All these religions that have nothing to do with you? The meaning is here, with your family and the way you were raised. It will destroy you, Shavi.' It was his father's voice. A chill crept through him. He recalled the rest of that conversation, the anger, the terrible things that were said.

The mouth on the reflection became faintly sneering. 'You are a selfish man, Shavi.' This time it was his own voice, though harder, more contemptuous. 'You destroyed your family with your actions. Think of your father and your mother – the effort they expended raising you in the correct Muslim way. Think how they must feel to see you abandon every principle which has been the bedrock of their lives. They see themselves as failures in the thing that is most important to them. You destroyed them, Shavi.'

'I did not—'

The image spoke more forcefully to block his protestations. 'Lies. Your only motivation was your own selfish spiritual advancement, your own intellectual curiosity, and you had no concern how many people were hurt as you walked your road of excess to your own personal palace of wisdom. Life is about community, Shavi. About society. Helping others achieve their own nirvana—'

'I am helping others now.'

'Because it coincides with your own desires. You are revelling in the light these experiences shine on the dark of the greater reality.'

'True.' Shavi felt more confident after his initial shock. Once he had realised it was the test they had all expected it became easy to detach himself. The mirror was reflecting back at him his own doubts and fears about his choices in life. But there was nothing it could show him that he hadn't weighed and discarded, or had accepted in order to change himself.

The mirror suddenly took on a milky sheen and when it cleared he was looking out on a Clapham street late one night. Several yards away, Lee was being bludgeoned to death. The blood splashed high with each thunderous blow. The attacker was like a smear on the surface of the glass, but Lee's expression was in stark relief; his eyes were turned towards Shavi, pleading for help, his mouth was an O of horror and desperation of a life about to be eradicated.

'You could have saved him, Shavi. You had the strength inside you to stand up, to fight. But you were afraid for your own safety. The haziness from the blow was just as an excuse. You gave in to it easily so you would not have to risk yourself. And Lee died because of your cowardice.'

Shavi felt the emotion well up in him uncontrollably until tears sprang from his eyes like they had been pricked by needles. There was such a rush of loss and guilt he thought he was going to break down.

'You're a bitch, Laura, and you deserve everything you get.' The face in the mirror, her face, spat the words with venom.

'Let's face it, you killed your mum! On a scale of one to ten that's off the Sick Bastardometer. What do you think that did to your dad? Well, it probably wasn't what was crossing his mind when he held you in that little girlie white dress at your Christening. He probably thought you'd turn out to be a vet or a nurse. You know, something *useful*. Hell, maybe even a dutiful daughter – some stupid fantasy like that. No wonder he opted for a life of shrinks and cells instead of giving you a big soppy hug.

'So now you think you're going to find some kind of salvation with Mr Brooding-and-Soulful Churchill. Think again. You'll just screw up his life like you have everybody else's. You couldn't feel anything as selfless as love if it walked up and bit you on your bony arse. You're just sucking out of him anything you can find that will make you feel, Vampire-Girl. Get real. If you wanted to do something worthwhile you'd top yourself. Save the rest of the world any more heartache.'

Veitch felt his finger close on the trigger, felt the kick from the ejaculation of the bullet, saw it embed itself in the man's body, burst through it, spraying the bone and the blood, saw the terrible pain on his victim's face; felt the faintly perverse pleasure rise through him, like a hard porn orgasm, the kick of having ultimate power and dispensing it with the merest thought. Nothing could control him; *he* could control everything.

'That was how it was, wasn't it, Ryan?'

'No! I've been living with that every day of my life since!'

'Because you enjoyed it.'

'No—!'

'Yes. Secretly. In your quiet moments. Lying in bed when everyone else was asleep. When your other poor bastard brothers were doing time for you. You thought, "Yeah! That was what it was like to be a top man!"'

'You lying fucking bastard! I'm gonna make up for that if

it's the last thing I do. That's right. Even if I have to die, I'm gonna pay it back. I learned a big lesson—'

'No, you didn't. You'd kill again at the drop of a hat.'

'You bastard! You might look like me, but you don't know me! I've never done anything right in my life and I'm sick of it! I want to be a good bloke! I want people to look at me like they do Churchill—'

'Yeah, it's all about self, isn't it, Ryan? You don't want to do good because it makes other people feel good. You want to do it because it makes *you* feel good.'

'Fuck you!'

'I loved my father!' The tears seared down Ruth's cheeks.

'You hated him. He dominated you from when you were young. He forced you into a career you didn't want to do—'

'He didn't force me! I did it because I wanted to make him happy! So it was the wrong career for me. It's not Dad's fault. He didn't—'

'What? He didn't know his own daughter? No, he was a typical working class bloke who wanted a bit of respectability for his family. A lawyer! That'd be something to tell them all down at the union meetings and in the labour club. His daughter had worked hard and made something of herself, despite starting with nothing. And he didn't care a thing about what you wanted—'

'That's not true! Dad didn't think like that!' The next few lines out of the mirror were drowned out by Ruth's racking sobs. She had not felt so raw since the day her father had dropped dead of a heart attack, in that fleeting moment when she thought time had stopped and the whole world was coming to an end. Somehow the magic surrounding the mirror had pushed all the right buttons to bring the emotions rushing out of her.

'He knew you were unhappy in your work. That's what killed him.'

'Not true! It was the shock of Uncle Jim's murder—'

The mirror went milky and when it cleared Ruth was looking on the interior of a building society. A tall man with greying hair and a pleasant face that was locked in anxiety stared out at her; he looked remarkably like her father.

'That's Uncle Jim,' she said curiously. Suddenly she realised what was coming next. 'Oh no—'

The blast of a gun made her jump with shock. Her uncle was flung back against the counter, clutching at his stomach as a large red patch began to spread across his sweater.

'Oh, Uncle Jim—'

Somebody ran forward to inspect the body. He was cursing and waving his gun at Uncle Jim, as if he had done something to provoke his own murder. Ruth was transfixed in horror. The killer had on a mask, but Ruth recognised the shape of his muscular body, the long hair that flapped around as he shook his head wildly, in anger it seemed. But most of all she recognised the garish tattoo she could see snaking out from under his sleeve.

'That's the man Church brought with him.' Even as she said it Ruth couldn't believe it; but it was true. 'That's Veitch.'

Church stared impassively at the scene of Marianne lying on the floor, her skin so pale she looked like a statue. 'You're wasting your time,' he said coldly. 'I've lived with that image for so long now I'm immune to it. When I thought I was responsible . . . when I thought I was some kind of terrible person who could live with someone yet be so self-centred they had no idea of the torment their partner was going through . . . then it might have hurt me. But now I know she was murdered.'

'You're still responsible,' his voice said as the image faded and his dark, bitter reflection returned. At first he had thought it resembled him exactly; it seemed just like the face he had seen in the mirror so many times over the last two years. But now he wasn't so sure. It didn't feel like him. He felt better than that; and that thought surprised him.

'How can that be? Someone else killed her and pretty soon, with any luck, I'm going to find out who did it. That was the promise made to me, and that's the only thing driving me forward. You see, I'm going to die soon. I've seen my own death. Can you believe that? So nothing else matters, apart from finding out what happened to Marianne and getting some kind of peace before the end. Some might call it fatalistic. But if it's going to happen it's going to happen – you've just got to make the best of it. That's a big lesson I've learned recently. It's the quality of the life up to the big peg-out that matters.' The reflection went to speak, but Church wouldn't let it. 'Shut up. And here's something that has to be said, just for the sake of getting it out in the open, really. Once I find out who killed Marianne, if I get the chance before I die myself, I'm going to take the bastard with me. That's a promise.'

The reflection opened its mouth once more, but Church had had enough. He turned his back on it and prepared to return to the maze in search of the way to the talisman. And as he did so there was a sudden shattering as shards of the big ornate mirror exploded out. Miraculously, none of them touched him. As he glanced back he noticed that behind the broken mirror there was another tunnel, this time lit by the flickering blue light of the earth energy.

Church found himself in a circular, domed room cast in sapphire by the light of four braziers burning brightly with the blue fire. There was a sense of serenity that sluiced all the negative emotions from him. In the centre was a raised marble dais bearing an object which he couldn't quite make out; the air seemed to shimmer and fold around an image which constantly changed. Church saw a construct of light with strange, unnerving angles, a robust cauldron blackened by fire, a crystal goblet, an ornate gold vase studded with jewels. As he approached, the object seemed to freeze, the air cleared and he was looking at a chipped bowl of heavily aged wood that most wouldn't have given a second glance.

He stood before it, overwhelmed by the weight of myth and symbolism; here was the dream of generations.

It was too much. Afraid to even touch it, he rested his hands on the marble top. Instantly, the bowl slid towards him of its own accord and came to a stop between his fingers, offering itself up to him. Steeling himself, he grasped it firmly, and at that moment he heard the distant sound of fracturing glass. Within minutes the other four had made their way to the chamber; Church was shocked to see their shattered expressions.

Shavi's face brightened the moment he saw what Church was holding. 'The Grail!' His voice was filled with awe and wonder.

'And the cauldron, one and the same. It—'

They were interrupted by a sudden commotion. In a fury, Ruth had propelled herself towards Veitch and slammed a fist into his face. He pitched backwards, blood spouting from his nose, and now she was raining blows upon him which Veitch batted away as best he could.

'You bastard!' she screamed. 'You killed him!'

Shavi and Laura managed to pull her off with great difficulty; she was transformed by rage, swearing and spitting. Veitch pulled himself into a sitting position, dabbing at his bloody nose. 'Stupid bitch,' he hissed, but Church could see the anger in his face was purely defensive.

Laura looked at Ruth in disbelief. 'Take a stress pill. What's wrong with you – something finally popped?'

'He killed my father.' She shook Laura and Shavi off, consumed by the coldness of her words, which brought back the terrible ache of futility and emptiness she had felt just after her father's death, and she hated Veitch as much for making her feel it again as for his original crime.

'He killed your dad?' Laura looked from Ruth to Veitch. None of them could comprehend what she was saying.

'He was some stupid, petty bigmouth with a gun trying to

get rich quick by robbing a building society.' The contempt in Ruth's voice hissed acidly. 'My uncle was in there and that bastard shot him dead, then ran away. And when my father found out what had happened, it killed him.'

They stared at Veitch for some sort of denial, but he couldn't look at any of them.

'He was just an old man!' Ruth cried. 'He couldn't have done anything to you!' She swallowed noisily. 'He was going down to Brighton with my aunt to celebrate their silver wedding anniversary. We were going to have a party...' She swallowed again. 'What you did that day destroyed our family!'

Veitch bit his lip, said nothing.

Ruth glared at him, but her eyes were already filling with tears. She turned away and Church stepped in and put his arms around her. There was resistance at first, then she folded against him, although her body still felt rigid and cold, as if made of compacted ice.

'I didn't mean to do it,' Veitch protested. 'I know it's no fucking excuse, but I just... I was frightened. I knew I shouldn't have been there. And then I turned round and I thought he was coming for me...' He stared blankly at the ground. 'If it means anything, I've never had a minute's peace since that day.'

'It doesn't mean anything,' Ruth said coldly.

The others shifted uncomfortably in the blast of raw emotions. Eventually Church said, 'I know how you feel. Exactly how you feel. And that's why I'd never ask you to forgive him. But what's at stake in the world is more important than everything that's happening in our lives. If you break us up now—'

'I'm not going to break anything.' Ruth pulled away from Church and looked him full in the face. 'I'm not some stupid bimbo. I know what's at stake. I know what my responsibilities are. And I'll be there to the end.' She stared hard at Veitch and what Church saw in that look unnerved him. 'But don't expect me to be friends with that bastard. Don't expect me to pass the time of day with him. And if we get to the end of this alive I'm going to make sure he faces up to *his* responsibility. And see he gets put away for his crime.'

They emerged from the Temple of Mirrors to a balmy summer night alight with thousands of stars. Only the faintest breeze stirred the treetops. Church staggered up the grassy bank with the Grail held before him so Tom could see what they had achieved. Tom was already on his feet, and Church was shocked to see his face was glowing with respect.

As they walked back across the meadows, Shavi and Laura talked quietly with Ruth while Veitch trailed along behind, lonely and isolated.

Tom caught up with Church at the front and grabbed his arm. 'I'm worried we'll lose the boy.'

'I'll have a word with Ryan,' Church said wearily; the emotional distractions were a blow too much. 'I don't want us pulled apart from within. If we can't count on each other—'

'Remain focused,' Tom said. 'You've done a remarkable job so far. Better than I expected on our first meeting.'

'Is that a note of support?'

'Make the most of it. They're few and far between.'

Was that a glimmer of humour? Church wondered. He glanced surreptitiously at Tom, but his face was as implacable as ever; all his emotions were locked so tightly inside they seemed almost separate from him. Church had the impression he hadn't always been like that, that his experiences at the hands of the gods had been so terrible that emotional detachment was the only way he could have survived.

'Are you ever going to let us into all your secrets?' Church asked.

'When the time's right.'

'We're not children, you know.'

'You are children, in the ways of the gods and in the true

376

mysteries of the universe. You're learning how to see things truly after a lifetime of being blinkered. And like any learning process, too much too soon would be detrimental.'

'And you're our teacher.' Church sighed.

'For my sins.'

'Can't you at least tell me what lies ahead?'

'That's the last thing I'd tell you.'

Church glanced back at the rag-tag bunch following and felt a sweep of pessimism. There was no one he would describe as a hero. In fact, most of them seemed damaged to the point of uselessness.

Tom seemed to sense his thoughts. 'People are forged by hardship,' he said simply.

Church shook his head, stared at the ground.

'It's a terrible fact of life that nobody has wisdom until they've tasted bereavement,' he continued. 'Of all life's experiences, that's the sole one with truly alchemical power. Knowing that, given a choice, we would all stay ignorant. Yet, ironically, we're better people for having gone through it. Bereavement is the key to meaning, and you all have that wisdom within you. The building blocks are there—'

'And you expect damaged goods to pile them into some sort of structure?'

Tom shrugged and looked away; Church couldn't tell if Tom was annoyed by his defeatism or acknowledging it.

They reached the tunnel back to the world soon after. At the entrance they all turned and looked back over the idyllic landscape, glistening in the moonlight, breathing deeply of the sweet, scented air; there was true magic in every aspect of it.

'I could stay here for ever,' Ruth said.

Tom nodded. 'Yes. That's the danger.'

When they emerged on the tor, it was the dark just before dawn, yet they all felt that only an hour or more had passed since they had first entered the tunnel. They immediately noticed a subtle difference: the night was significantly warmer.

'It's like summer,' Ruth said curiously.

They made their way down the winding path to the town as dawn broke, golden and comforting. But as they killed time on the high street waiting for the café to open for breakfast, a delivery van dropped off a bundle of papers outside the newsagents. Church wandered over to glance at the headlines.

'Look at this,' he said in an uneasy voice.

The others gathered round as he pointed out the date beneath the masthead. During their brief stay in Otherworld, two weeks had passed. It was April 1.

the harrowing

'You lot have got it all wrong. This is the key to eternal youth. You spend a couple of weeks in that place and when you get home, everyone goes, "How do you stay so young? What are your beauty secrets?" Then you go round to all your old boyfriends and point out their wrinkles.' Laura sat with her feet on the dashboard between Veitch and Shavi, who was driving. Church, Tom and Ruth sat in the back amidst the camping equipment and what clothes and supplies they could afford. The discovery of the time differential had left them feeling uncomfortable.

'You're missing the point,' Church said irritably. 'We can't afford to lose two weeks. We've still got one more of these damned talismans to recover—'

'Stop moaning.' Laura swivelled to flash him a challenging smile. 'There's nearly a month to the deadline. That's enough time to do this walking backwards.' She turned to Tom. 'Anyway, Grandad, you must have known about this before we crossed over.'

'Yes,' Ruth said. 'Why didn't you say anything? I'm sick of you not telling us things before they happen.'

Tom took off his glasses and cleaned them on his shirt. 'No point. We had to go. You would have found out sooner or later.'

'You mean you didn't want to take the chance some of us wouldn't cross over.' He didn't return Ruth's pointed stare.

'It's a good thing this mission is based on trust,' Laura said ironically before slipping off her boots and planting her feet on the windscreen.

'Bet that position feels familiar,' Ruth said sharply. Laura showed her middle finger over her shoulder.

Church rested one hand on the crate they'd picked up from the grocer's to store the stone, the sword and the cauldron; it seemed faintly sacrilegious, but the need for easy, well-disguised transport was more pressing. He could almost feel the power of the talismans through his fingertips. And sometimes it was like he could feel them talking to him, incomprehensible whispers curling like smoky tendrils around his mind. Part of it made him tremble with awe; another part of it made his skin crawl. 'I feel nervous carrying these things around with us.'

'The Fomorii can't touch them,' Tom noted.

'They'll just get somebody else to do their dirty work.' He paused. 'Now we're out of Glastonbury, does that mean we're meat for the Wild Hunt again?'

Tom nodded.

'We'd better make sure we're somewhere secure by nightfall,' Ruth said.

'How about some music?' Laura went to turn on the radio. Ruth told her to wait while she pulled a cassette out of her bag and threw it up front. Laura made a face, but put it in the machine anyway. A second later Sinatra began to sing about flying off to foreign climes for excitement and romance.

Church's face brightened with surprise. 'I thought we'd lost this!'

'Even the Wild Hunt didn't want it,' Laura said sulkily.

Ruth flashed him a grin and he smiled thankfully; he found real comfort in the way she seemed instinctively to know him. If nothing else, the previous few weeks had given him a true friend.

The Wayfinder led them back to the M5 motorway and then north in the bright, warm sunshine. The van ran as good as new after the repairs, but the cost had made them worry about their funds. They all had credit cards and made their monthly payments by phone transfer from their savings accounts, but their reserves weren't endless.

Shavi was talkative on a range of subjects and Laura kept the banter going, but Veitch hardly said a word. His confrontation with the results of his actions seemed to have had a profound effect on him; above all, it appeared to have confirmed his own worst fears about himself. Church began to worry that Tom's assessment of Veitch had been correct and he resolved to talk to him as soon as he could get him alone.

They picked up the M4 and headed west into Wales, which, as Shavi noted, was an obvious destination, with its rich Celtic history and links to Arthurian legend.

'So, we're talking themes here,' Laura noted. 'Church has got his sword, so that makes him the big, fat king. I guess the tattooed boy here is Lancelot, the old hippie would be Merlin, Miss Gallagher back there acts like Queen Bee so I suppose she's Guinevere.' She slapped a hand hard on Shavi's thigh. 'Don't know what that makes you and me, though.'

'Is that it?' Ruth said with the excitement of someone who's just seen the light. 'We're, like, some kind of reincarnation—'

'No, that's too literal,' Church said insistently. 'And I keep saying this, but those are just stories. There was no Round Table or chivalrous knights. Arthur, if he existed at all, was a Celtic warlord—'

'So the *historians* say.' Tom pronounced the word with faint contempt.

'I'm not even going to begin talking to you about it.' Church waved his hand dismissively. 'You'll keep us talking round in circles and then tell us nothing new.'

Laura grabbed the rag Shavi used to wipe the windows and threw it hard at Tom's head. 'Come on, you old git. Spill the beans or we're going to tie you up and drag you along behind the van.'

He glared at her and readjusted his glasses.

'Brothers and Sisters of Dragons,' Shavi mused. 'Could

that have something to do with *Pendragon*, Arthur's family name?'

Church shook his head. 'Pendragon is a mixture of Celtic and old Welsh meaning Chief Leader. The word root has nothing to do with dragons.'

'Or perhaps,' Tom said, as if he were dealing with idiots, 'it's simply another manifestation of the duality which is at the heart of everything.'

'That means double meanings, Laura,' Ruth called out.

'Come on, Tom, you can't do this to us,' Church protested.

'Yeah, come on, *Tom*.' Laura looked around the dashboard for something else to throw.

Tom noticed her and said hastily, 'I suppose it wouldn't hurt to tell you now. You're almost there anyway. You're not reincarnations in the literal sense that you mean, but you do carry within you the essence that the legends speak of. The Pendragon Spirit. It is a subtle power, a state of mind, an ability which is gifted to some to defend the land. That's the true meaning of the legend.'

'So Arthur and the knights are also a metaphor for this Pendragon spirit?' Church said.

'So we're descendants or something?' Laura said quizzically.

Tom shook his head. 'The land gifts it to the most deserving. It chooses the ones who'll defend it the best.'

'It screwed up this time, didn't it.' Veitch continued to stare out of the passenger window.

'That is . . . a tremendous burden,' Church said.

'Yeah, if you believe this,' Laura said.

'You're still at the start of your journey.' Tom delved into his knapsack for the tin where he kept his drugs. 'The journey that the Tarot delineates. At the moment you're all the Fool. When you come out at the other end, you'll be aware of the true meaning of the Pendragon Spirit.'

'The ones who survive,' Church said. He fought to damp down a sudden flash of the portent of his death.

'The ones who survive,' Tom agreed.

'There is something happening here,' Shavi interrupted. They felt the van slow down sharply and Ruth, Church and Tom clambered forward to peer through the windscreen. The motorway ahead was blocked by a row of emergency vehicles. Police were directing traffic up the slipway at the next exit. Ominously, Church could see army trucks on the deserted road ahead and some troops with guns discreetly positioned near the central reservation and the opposite bank. 'Where are we?'

'Just past Cardiff,' Shavi said.

As they pulled off slowly, Shavi wound down the window and asked a policeman what was wrong. 'An accident,' he said with a face like stone. 'Now be on your way. And keep to the diversions.'

'I've never seen the army brought in for an accident,' Veitch said.

'They're covering it up, aren't they?' Ruth sat down behind Shavi's seat. 'They know what's going on. Or if they don't know exactly what's happening, they know something out of the ordinary has hit the country. They'd have to know. And they're trying to stop everyone finding out so there isn't a panic.'

'Like holding back the waves.' Tom's voice was quiet, but the words fell like stones.

'What do you think's happened down there, then?' Laura seemed suddenly uneasy.

'Must be something bad to close off the whole motorway,' Veitch said. 'It'll be causing chaos on all the roads around.'

'It seems like a great deal has happened during the two weeks we were away,' Shavi said darkly.

An uncomfortable silence filled the van as they joined the queues of traffic.

Although the Wayfinder continued to point west, they found it hard to follow its direction; a whole section of the country seemed to have been closed off with police and army barricades. But although they constantly checked the radio news broadcasts, there was no information about what was happening.

Just as they were considering abandoning the van and setting off on foot, they finally managed to break away from the main route and weave along deserted country roads through the soaring Welsh hills and mountains. There was an unearthly desolation to the countryside; no tractors in the fields, no pedestrians, although they could see lights in houses and smoke curling from chimneys.

Eventually they started to swing south-westwards until they hit one of the main tourist drags to the coast. Their speedy journey marked how effective the authorities had been at driving traffic away. Veitch, who was in charge of mapreading, pointed out a small town, Builth Wells, which lay ahead of a long stretch of open countryside. They all agreed it would be a good place to stop for food, rest, and to see if any of the locals had any idea what was happening nearby.

But the closer they got to the town, the more they realised something was wrong. Even on the main road in there was no traffic, while the only sign of movement was a flurry of newspaper pages caught in the wind sweeping across the huge showground where the Welsh agricultural fair was held each year. They all fell silent as they crossed the old stone bridge over the River Wye that marked the entrance to the town proper, faces held rigid as they scanned the area.

'It's a ghost town,' Veitch said in a voice that was almost a whisper.

The van swung on to the one-way system that took them up the High Street where shops which should have been bustling at that time of day stood eerily empty. Cars were parked on the right, but they could have been left there days ago for all they knew. Nothing moved anywhere. Shavi wound down the window in the hope of hearing something they were missing, but the silence was so intense it made them feel queasy.

'Do you think they've been evacuated?' Ruth asked.

Church didn't give voice to what his instincts were telling him.

They followed the one-way system round to a nearly full car park alongside the river where Shavi pulled into a bay and switched off the engine.

'What are you doing?' Veitch said. 'You could have left it anywhere.'

Shavi shrugged. 'What can I say? In situations like this, I find comfort in following old routines.'

'Head-in-the-sand dude,' Laura chided, but they were all reluctant to get out.

Eventually Church led them from the car park up a side road to the High Street, where they argued about what to do.

'Wake up,' Laura said. 'It's deserted. Looting is an option.'

'That's just what I'd expect from someone with your easy morals,' Ruth snapped. 'It's still stealing.'

Veitch emerged from a health food store chewing on a cheese and onion pastie. 'It's still fresh,' he said. 'Wherever they've gone, it's only just happened.'

Shavi looked up and down the street, noting the open doors. 'If they were evacuated, they would have locked up at least.'

Despite Ruth's initial opposition, they agreed to take some of the fresh food which would spoil quickly. Veitch and Laura picked up a couple of bags and headed into the health food store, the baker's and the butcher's with what Ruth noted as undue glee.

'Least you won't need your gun this time,' she said sourly to Veitch as he passed.

Church and Shavi left her with Tom while they explored further up the street. Church had quickly learned to value the Asian's quick insight and measured views; Shavi's obvious intelligence and ability to keep a cool head under pressure made Church feel some of the weight had been taken off his shoulders.

'What do you think, then?' Church turned and looked back down the length of the High Street and beyond to the dangerous face of nature rising up in thickly wooded hills all around.

'I think everything out there is getting braver. Villages, small towns . . . they do not seem concerned by them any more. The problem is, the enemy is not one group – it is a complete existence that is so alien to us any contact is destructive.'

'So can we hold back the new Dark Age?'

'This is a world of the subconscious, of nightmares and shadows. Those things are always more powerful than their opposites.'

'So we're wasting our time?'

'We are doing the best we can.' Shavi smiled wanly.

They were both suddenly alerted by a faint sound which seemed to emanate from a tiny cobbled alley which ran at breathtaking steepness upwards between two shops; it sounded like a firecracker in the silence.

'What was that?' Church asked.

They both moved forward to the foot of the alley. At the top they could see a parked car, a house, blue sky; no movement. Church put one foot on the cobbles, but Shavi placed a restraining hand on his arm. They stood motionless for a minute until they heard the noise again; the inhuman sound was like an insectile chittering laid over the cry of a baby. A second later a grey shape flitted across the other end of the alleyway, too quick to make out its true form.

'We should get out of here,' Church said.

Another movement; there seemed to be more than one of them.

They sprinted back down the High Street, where Ruth was leaning against the wing of a car. She caught their expressions and asked what was wrong.

'Where are the others?' Church snapped.

'The criminal fraternity are back in the health food store. Tom's gone into that clothing store.' She pointed across the street. 'Are you going to tell me what's happening? Is there something here?' She jumped off the car, glancing around anxiously.

'You two get Veitch and Laura and head back to the van. I'll find Tom.' He sprinted into the clothing store, past racks of waterproofs and outdoor wear. Tom was in the back, trying on a pair of walking boots.

'Come on,' Church said. 'We don't have time for that. Bring them with you if you want.'

Tom stood up instantly at the insistence in Church's voice. 'Fomorii?'

'I don't think so.'

Tom didn't need any more prompting. He hurried behind Church to the entrance, but as they stepped out into the street they both saw movement at the top end of the High Street: fleeting shapes that looked almost ghostly flashed back and forth across the road.

'You're the expert,' Church said. 'What are they?'

Tom stared for a second, then shook his head. 'I have no idea. The twilight lands were filled with all manner of things. I had more to do than study them all.'

As they ran across the road, movement erupted in the shops all around. The shapes seemed to be emerging from the back-rooms as if they had awakened from their rest in the shadowy interiors and were now intent on seeking out the trespassers on their property. Church caught a glimpse of green eyes and gnashing teeth. A sudden wash of fear spurred him on.

With Tom close behind, he ran down the side road to where Shavi had the van warmed up and waiting. They piled in the back and the van took off with a screech of tyres, going the wrong way through the one-way system.

'Changed your mind about sticking to routine, I see,' Veitch said to Shavi. The Asian smiled tightly.

As they careered out of town, Church, Tom and Ruth glanced back through the rear windows to see the High Street now swarming with the grey shapes in a manner that reminded them of a disturbed ant hill. It was a scene that filled them all with the utmost terror.

'Where do you think the residents have gone?' Ruth asked feebly.

Church and Tom took up their seats without answering. The atmosphere had become even more dark and oppressive.

When eventually they reached Carmarthen, they were relieved to see the town buzzing as if nothing were wrong. 'It shows the size of habitation that is safe,' Shavi noted. They followed the Wayfinder along the side of the river and then on the main dual carriageway to the coast, through green fields, past caravan parks, and by 4 p.m. they had reached the palm trees that marked the entrance to the holiday resort of Tenby.

The mediaeval walled town lay perched on cliffs of brown shale and hard grey limestone, offering panoramic views along the rugged Pembrokeshire coastline. Amongst its twisty-turny streets, pastel-painted bed and breakfasts slumbered beneath a powder-blue sky in which seagulls soared and turned lazily. Looking up, Ruth also fleetingly spotted her owl companion skimming the ancient tiled rooftops, although she found it hard to believe it had followed the van from Glastonbury, or even that it had got out of Tir n'a n'Og unseen.

The streets were too small to negotiate effectively in the van, so they parked at the South Beach and returned through the five arches that formed a gateway in the soaring stone walls. Veitch and Shavi carried the talisman crate between them while Church went in front with the Wayfinder held within the fold of his jacket where it couldn't be seen by passers-by. It took them down Tudor Square, bustling despite the unseasonal time of year, and along a winding road to a picturesque harbour where rows of boats bobbed gently on the outgoing tide. At the harbour wall, Church halted, puzzled. The lantern's flame seemed to be pointing out to sea.

After a brief discussion, Veitch set off to scout the area, returning only five minutes later to herd them along a path past a tiny, white-walled museum to a bandstand on the headland overlooking the beach and the brilliant blue sea.

'There,' he said. Basking in the sun in the bay was a large island.

Caldey Island was home to an order of Cistercian monks. Regular boat trips were despatched from the mainland several times a day so tourists could experience the isolation – and contribute to the monastery's upkeep – but they had missed the last boat of the afternoon. Their only option seemed to be to find somewhere to hole up until morning and hope they could stay safe through the night.

They checked into one of the pretty bed and breakfasts in the backstreets of the old town, not too far from the front, relishing the opportunity to have a shower and sleep in a bed for a change. After an early dinner, Tom retired to his room where he agreed to oversee the talismans, although he wouldn't go near the crate. The others opted to look around the town while daylight was still with them. Church took the opportunity to steer Veitch away for a heart-to-heart, leaving Shavi, Ruth and Laura to pick their way through the streets dominated by pristine ice cream parlours and restaurants. After all they had witnessed, the place seemed uncommonly happy, untouched by the dark shadow that had fallen across the land. It both raised their spirits and made them feel uncomfortable, for they knew it couldn't last.

'I can't believe we've got this far.' Church closed his eyes so he could appreciate the early evening sun on his face as he inhaled the salty aroma of the sea caught in the cooling breeze. There on the beach, he could almost forget everything. The sensations reminded him of childhood holidays before the burdens of responsibility had been thrust on his shoulders, and happy summer days with Marianne before life had truly soured. The womb noises of the ocean and the breaking surf calmed him enough to realise how stressed he had become, his shoulders hunched, neck muscles knotted. Opening his eyes, he watched Veitch trudging beside him, oblivious to the seaside joys. 'When I went to the Watchtower and heard about the four talismans, I thought it was only a matter of time before it went pear-shaped. But finding them has been easy,' he continued, and, after a pause, 'Relatively easy.'

'That's because they were waiting for us, so Tom says,' Veitch said unenthusiastically. 'We were meant to get them, at this time, and we did. No mystery there.'

Church shook his head. 'I don't believe it works like that. Even if the stars were aligned, it wasn't fated that these things would fall into our hands. *We* did this and I'm not going to have it taken away from us.' Caldey Island caught his eye and he brought himself up sharp. 'But we haven't got them all yet. There's still time for things to go wrong.'

'Now you're talking my kind of language.'

Church stopped and rounded on him. 'Come on, Veitch, stop being so bloody pessimistic. You're not the only one who's had a miserable time—'

'Miserable time! I killed somebody! That's not miserable, that's a fucking catastrophe! I have to live with it every bleedin' day and now I can't forget it for a minute because I'm spending time with the poor bastard's niece, just so I can see on a regular basis how my stupidity fucked up a whole family's life!'

He made to walk on, but Church grabbed at his shoulder roughly. Instinctively Veitch's fists bunched and he adopted a threatening posture. 'So you screwed up and you're feeling guilty about it. Fine. That's how it should be. But self-pity is just you being selfish. You've got a job to do now that's more important than your feelings. If you want to tear your-self apart, you can do it after this is over.'

'Fuck off.' Veitch made another attempt to walk off and Church grabbed him roughly once more. This time Veitch's response was instant. He swung his fist hard into Church's jaw, knocking him to the sand.

For a moment, Church was dazzled by flashes of black and purple. Then he jumped up, lowered his head and rammed Veitch in the stomach. They both fell, rolling around in the sand, wrestling and punching. Eventually Church hauled himself on top and locked his arms on Veitch's shoulders so the Londoner couldn't move.

'I'm no hero,' Church said through gritted teeth. 'I didn't choose to be here. I've got my own agenda going on too. But I know I can't let all this misery and suffering happen if I can do something about it. I mean, who could?'

Veitch's eyes narrowed. 'Lots of people could.' He searched Church's face for a moment longer, then threw him off with an easy shrug. After he'd dusted himself down, he said, 'Don't worry, I'm not giving up on my bleedin' responsibilities. But I want to do something to make it up to Ruth. I know I'll never actually make amends, but I've got to try.' He paused. 'I'm not a bad bloke, you know. Just stupid.'

Church rubbed his jaw, which ached mercilessly, but he'd known what he was doing. 'Ruth's a smart person. If you've got any good in you, she'll see it eventually. You've just got to give it time.'

'Yeah, best behaviour and all that. Listen, sorry about smacking you. I've got a bleedin' awful temper.'

'Don't worry. I'll point you in the right direction before I activate you next time.' He shook sand out of his hair and added, 'Come on, let's find a pub. It's ages since I've had a pint.'

'What a great place.' Ruth sat on the steps of a statue of Prince Albert and looked out across the harbour. 'Everybody

391

here's on holiday, so happy . . . I can't believe it might all get swept away.'

Laura crawled out to the end of the barrel of a cannon and sat back, basking in the sun. 'Talk about something important for a change. Like isn't our working class London boy a babe. I wonder how low his tattoos go?'

'If you're trying to wind me up, you've picked the wrong subject,' Ruth snapped.

'What about you, Mr Bi?' Laura said to Shavi. 'Does he get your sap rising?'

'He is not unattractive.' Shavi smiled, but continued to lie on the grass with his eyes closed.

'You know, I'm noticing a distinct pathology to your sexual obsession.' Ruth glared at Laura, who ignored her.

'That's just what I'd expect from you, Frosty. But I'm not a one-obsession woman. I like drugs, music and technology too.'

'Well, I never realised you were so deep.' Ruth stood up and wandered around the base of the statue. 'What do you think we've got to do once we get this last talisman?'

Shavi hauled himself into a sitting position. 'Perhaps everything will become obvious once we have all the pieces together.'

'Having seen just a glimpse of what's out there, it makes me feel what we're doing is so ineffectual. Do you think these other gods can really oppose the Fomorii?'

'For me, there are more profound concerns,' Shavi said. 'The Danann are supposed to look like angels. Was the Christian mythology based upon them? Are all the world's religions a reflection of the time when the Tuatha Dé Danann and the Fomorii ruled over humanity? This may be an opportunity for us all to meet our Maker.'

'*Opportunity*. I like your optimism,' Ruth said sardonically.

'That's too heavy,' Laura noted uneasily. 'It's bad enough as it is without thinking about things like that.'

'But we should think about it,' Shavi pressed. 'For millennia our lives have been based around religion. If our entire system of belief and morality rests upon a lie, we are truly adrift. It would be difficult to comprehend how our society could recover from a blow like that.'

'We lose our faith in science and religion at the same time. That doesn't leave any refuge for most people,' Ruth said thoughtfully.

'Most people don't believe in anything anyway,' Laura said. 'Religion is just a place for sad bastards to go to hide, and scientists can't agree on anything, so why should anyone else believe them?'

'And I thought *I* was cynical.' Ruth looked down at the jumbled streets of the old town; from that vantage point they could almost have been in the Middle Ages. Briefly a cloud shadow swept across the rooftops and she shuddered involuntarily; unconsciously she wrapped her arms tightly around her. From nowhere the thought sprang; a portent: things were going to get worse from that moment on.

Amidst a large group of garrulous tourists, Church and Veitch spent the rest of the evening in a pub on Tudor Square finding the common ground that lay between their different backgrounds. Veitch had a dangerous edge to his character which made Church feel uneasy, but it was tempered by an encouraging sense of loyalty; and for someone who had dabbled for so long in petty crime, he seemed to have a strict moral code. Ultimately it was those contradictions which made his character so winning. Veitch showed a respect for Church which the latter hadn't experienced before.

'I can't get my head round it.' Veitch's brow furrowed as he swigged down a mouthful of lager. 'We were being set up for this from the moment we were born? Those dreams that gave me all that bleedin' misery?'

'I had the dreams too, though not as bad as you. I mean, we call them dreams, but they weren't really. It was the

393

Otherworld contacting us – though that makes it sound like they were getting us on the phone. I think it was more like we were in some way closer to their world, so bits of it kept seeping through when we were most receptive to it.'

'Bastards. I owe them for messin' with my head, whether they did it on purpose or not. But you said that woman from the Watchtower kept visiting you when you were a kid. What was she, your sponsor?'

Church had wrestled with that thought before and he still hadn't reached a satisfactory conclusion. 'I think, maybe, because the Danann knew how important we were supposed to be, they wanted to keep an eye on us.'

'Watched over by angels, eh? You lucky bastard.' Veitch's words gave him pause, and after a moment he said, 'I wonder what they feel about us, really. I know they look like us a bit, the Danann anyway, but they're, like, God, aren't they? God and his angels. And the other lot are the Devil and his crew.'

Church felt uncomfortable at this description; old teachings had dug their way in deep and he couldn't help a shudder at the blasphemy. 'We should be getting back,' he said, draining his pint. It was already closing time and the number of drinkers in the pub had dwindled rapidly. Through the window he could see them making their way across Tudor Square to their hotels and B&Bs, quite a number for out-of-season, but still too few for him. Increasingly, he felt the desire for the security of large numbers. Wide open spaces were simply too dangerous.

They were halfway across the square when Veitch glanced up suddenly and exclaimed, 'What's that?'

Tiny sparks of light darted overhead, accompanied by a flutter of wings which reminded Church of the sound of bats on a summer evening. But as he peered up into the clear night sky he felt a tingle of wonder. Tiny, full-formed figures, neither men nor women but a little of both, flashed around high above on wings that seemed too flimsy to carry even

394

their slight weight; the light was coming from their skin, which had the faint glow of phosphorus.

'What are they?' Veitch asked curiously.

'I would say the analogue of nature spirits. Whatever made our ancestors think the trees and rivers were alive.'

'No trouble, then?' Veitch's hand was inside his jacket where he kept his gun. Church wanted to tell him it would be worthless in what lay ahead, but he supposed if it gave Veitch comfort then it had some use. The hand didn't come out and Church could tell Veitch was weighing up whether he could get away with taking a few potshots.

'They look harmless,' Church warned. 'Leave them be. They might even be helpful to us at some time.'

'I don't want help from any of them,' Veitch said harshly. 'I want things back the way they were.'

'It's not all bad,' Church replied. 'We've got the magic back. We were missing that in all our lives.'

Veitch didn't seem convinced. 'Why are they flying around like that? Most of these things seem to stay out of the way when people are around.'

Now that he mentioned it, Church did think it was curious. He examined the fleeting trails of the creatures once again, and when one swooped low enough so he could see its face, the answer was unmistakable. 'They're frightened,' he said. 'Something has disturbed them.'

Veitch traced their path back across the sky. 'They came from over there,' he said, pointing to Castle Hill, where Shavi, Laura and Ruth had lazed earlier.

'We could go back,' Church mused. He was torn between the knowledge of what terrible things now lurked out in the night and the desire to know what might present a problem to them in the future.

Veitch was already striding down St Julian's Street. 'We'll be fine if we keep on our toes. We've got to check this out.'

The quay was awash with the reflected sodium light from the town dappling the gently lapping waves. Tranquillity lay across the area, in direct opposition to the hubbub of the day. The boat trip booth was shut, as was the ice cream shop and surf store on the ramp down to the beach. A few lights glimmered in the holiday apartments overlooking the harbour, but as they passed the old bath house and joined the path which curved around the headland, all signs of life disappeared. Away to their left, the sea rolled in calmly, the breakers crashing on the rocks under the lifeboat station. On their right the bank rose up, too steep to climb, to the top of Castle Hill.

Church and Veitch advanced along the path cautiously. Although it was a clear night, it was dark away from the town's lights and the susurration of the sea drowned out any nearby sounds.

'What do you reckon?' Veitch asked at a point where the path wound round so it was impossible to see far ahead or back.

'Doesn't seem—' The words were barely out of Church's lips when the night was disturbed by a throaty bass rumble, deep and powerful, rolling out from somewhere close by.

'What was that?' Veitch hissed.

Church felt the now-familiar shiver of fear ripple down his back. He glanced down the path behind them, then ahead, and finally up the steep bank. Another sound echoed out. 'Up there,' he whispered.

They stood stock-still, trying to peer through the gorse and willowherb, their breath burning in their throats. Finally they caught a glimpse of a black bulk moving against the sky on the ridge above them. Veitch went to speak, but Church silenced him with a wave of his hand. The silhouette moved slowly, dangerously, and then it turned its head and Church caught the terrible glitter of red eyes, burning like embers.

'Black Shuck,' he muttered.

He thought his words had been barely more than an exhalation, but the creature suddenly froze. Another throbbing growl rolled out menacingly. Slowly, the eyes moved, searching.

The dog disappeared from view and a second later they heard crashing through the undergrowth as it thundered down the bank to the path.

'Is it in front or behind?' Veitch asked, glancing around anxiously. Church shook his head. They vacillated, desperately hoping for some sign, but they knew once they had one it would be too late.

Finally Church grabbed Veitch and forced him onwards around the corner. They breathed easily when they saw the dog wasn't there, but its growls were still reverberating loudly and seemed to be drawing closer. Church nodded to a point where the bank wasn't so steep. 'If it's down here, we should be up there.'

'Yeah, but we have to come down sooner or later.'

They launched themselves at the bank and scrambled up, digging their nails in the turf and weeds to haul themselves along. At the clipped lawn on the summit, they rolled on to their stomachs and peered back down. Church caught a glimpse of the dog prowling menacingly back and forth along the path.

'It knows we're here,' Veitch noted in a hoarse whisper. 'It can smell us.'

'Something more than that, I think.'

'Okay, but from what you've told me, if the dog's here, the Hunt can't be far behind, right?'

That was the one thing Church had been trying not to consider. 'We have to get back to the others,' he said.

Shavi, Ruth and Laura sat in Tom's top floor room looking out across the rooftops. Tom lay on the bed, his face pale and drawn.

'Where've they got to?' Ruth paced around anxiously. 'You're sure they're going to be all right?'

'I told you. I've done all I can. A simple direction of the

energies, a masking.' The snap of anger in Tom's voice was born of exhaustion. 'If they're not in plain sight, they should be fine.'

'What if they're pissed and lying in a gutter?' Laura asked. 'You know how boys like to play once they get together.'

'You'd think they'd have thought to get back here by nightfall,' Ruth moaned.

'*They never call.*' Laura's singsong voice dripped with mockery. 'Listen to you. You sound like their mother.'

'Why don't you—'

'Listen.' Concern crossed Shavi's face. From the street without came the gentle clip-clop of horses' hooves, an everyday sound, but it made their blood run cold.

'Can you see?' Ruth knew she was whispering unnecessarily, but she couldn't bring herself to raise her voice.

Shavi pressed his face up close to the glass and attempted to look down. He shook his head. 'Only if I open the window.'

'Don't do that!' Laura snapped.

'I was not about to.'

They listened as the sound of the hooves slowly moved away and only when the sound had finally disappeared did they speak again.

'Maybe it wasn't them,' Ruth said hopefully. 'Earlier I saw a guy who takes tourists on tours of the front in a horse-drawn carriage.'

'It was the Hunt.' Tom's voice had an edge of fatalism.

'How fast does it move?' Veitch panted. They slipped and slid down the grassy bank on the other side of the hill until they reached the museum.

'Faster than you could ever run, even on a good day.' Church dropped on to a path and peered over the old castle walls. If the tide had been out, they could have taken a short cut across the beach and up the vertiginous seafront steps to the street where the B&B lay, but the waters crashed against the cliffs on which the town perched.

'Hey, I'm fit. You're the one who spends his time sitting on his arse writing about old bones.'

They hurried under the crumbling stone arches of the castle's defences and quickly arrived back at the quay. Disturbingly, the dog's growls didn't diminish. Church glanced back and thought he could see the eyes burning in the distance.

'It's got our scent,' he said. 'Or whatever. We might lose it up in the town where there are too many other distractions.'

But as they turned to run back up St Julian Street, the threatening blast of a horn echoed out across the quiet town.

Church's heart skipped a beat. 'The Hunt. They're in the old town.'

As they waited uncertainly, with the dog's growls growing louder behind them, they heard a horse approaching slowly down St Julian Street. A streetlight threw an enormous angular shadow across the front of the pastel houses in which Church could make out the cruel pike-weapon he had seen used so effectively on Dartmoor.

'Just one?' Veitch said.

'They're trying to flush us out.'

They turned and ran instead around the harbour, diving into an alley that led up to the Tudor Merchant's House tourist attraction. Church could feel the thundering of his blood in his ears. For a long time there was just the lapping of the waves. They both held their breath, listening. Church glanced at Veitch, both ready to make their move; he held up his hand for one more listen. The faint clip-clop of hooves echoed somewhere nearby.

Church cursed under his breath. 'Good job there're lots of tiny streets and back alleys to hide in.'

'And to get cornered in. Bleedin' hell. How did I get caught up in all this?'

Keeping to the shadows, they crept quietly up some old, weathered steps and headed along another alley. At the end of it Tudor Square lay deserted and brightly lit. They listened again; silence.

'We could make a run for it,' Veitch suggested.

'If they catch you out in the open, you won't stand a chance.' Church edged forward to get a better look, but just as he closed on the light, a horse and rider loomed up in the entryway. He could smell the unearthly, musky stink of the beast's sweat, see the light glint on the rider's metal buckles and arm rings, and the odd, lambent shimmer of his greenish skin.

Just as the rider started to look down the alleyway, Veitch grabbed Church's jacket and dragged him back into the shadows of a doorway. The rider stared for a moment, as if he had seen something, and then, just as Church thought he was going to investigate, he spurred the horse and it trotted away down towards St Julian's Street.

'I thought he'd marked us then,' Veitch whispered.

'There's an alley on the other side of the road next to the bookshop I saw earlier. If we can reach that, we might be able to wend our through the backstreets to base.'

Cautiously, they crept back to the end of the alley to survey the scene. The square was empty once more.

'He's probably waiting just around that corner,' Church noted.

'What we need is a diversion.' Veitch pulled out the gun and held it at his side; he seemed to carry it easily.

'What are you going to do with that?' Church asked uneasily.

Veitch moved in front of Church, raised the gun, pointed it at a shop at the top end of the square and fired, all in one fluid motion. The thunder of the retort merged with the high-pitched shatter as the window caved in and the burglar alarm started to scream. In an instant the clatter of hooves erupted as the Huntsman burst from St Julian Street and spurred his horse towards the shop, his sickle-pike glinting in the street light.

Once he'd passed by, they ran. Veitch had been cunning; the noise of the burglar alarm masked the sound of their running feet.

But just as they'd stepped into the road, a car sped up in the trail of the rider, so fast it almost ploughed into them. There were four youths inside, faces flushed from too much beer. The driver swerved at the last moment, screaming his rage through the open window, then hammered the horn. Church knew instantly that stroke of bad luck had ruined them. From the corner of his eye, he saw the Huntsman rein up his horse and turn it on the spot. Veitch must have seen it too, for he didn't slow for a moment; instead he powered up on to the car's bonnet and launched himself off to the other side.

Church was too near to the rear of the car to follow suit, but Veitch's actions were too much for the beer boys inside. They burst from the doors, their faces contorted with anger, fists bulging, mouthing post-pub threats in broad Welsh accents. One of them took a swing at Church and he had to throw himself back to avoid the blow.

'Come on!' Veitch yelled, as if it were in Church's power to respond.

The rider was almost upon him. Acting purely on instinct, Church propelled himself forward, past his assailant and behind one of the doors, surprising the beer boys with his tactics. The Huntsman's pike raised a shower of fizzing sparks as it ripped along the car's wing.

That resulted in another predictable outburst from the four youths. The driver stepped forward and hurled a near-full beer can. It bounced off the rider's shoulder, spraying cheap lager across the road.

He was already advancing, fists raised, when Church yelled, 'No! He'll kill you!' Another of the youths stepped in and kicked Church violently on the leg. More from shock than the agony that lanced up to his waist, Church pitched backwards, half-in and half-out of the car.

401

He tried to call out again, but it was too late. The driver rode forward, stabbing his pike and ripping suddenly upwards as he passed. A fountain of blood spurted, then showered down to mingle with the lager in the gutter.

The shouts were stifled in the other three youths' throats. But a second later, to Church's disbelief, they resumed their assault on the rider with force, hurling anything at him that came to hand, trying to kick out at the ghostly horse as it passed. Church didn't wait to see any more. He scrambled right through the car, rolled out on to the tarmac and was then up and running to join Veitch at the alleyway.

Overcome by despair and guilt, he glanced back and immediately wished he hadn't. The rider tore through the youths like a storm of knives, shredding and dismembering in a manner that suggested he had only contempt for humanity. The horse that was more than a horse jumped on to the car's roof, crumpling it, and then Veitch and Church were running as fast as they could along the alley.

They rounded into Cresswell Street, hoping to make their way along the front where they could lose themselves amongst the mediaeval streets before reaching the B&B, but the futility of their plan became immediately apparent. One rider cantered from the seafront, blocking the bottom end of the street, while another appeared at the top, their pikes raised, ready to harry them like foxes.

'Up,' Veitch croaked.

It took Church a split-second to comprehend what he was saying, and then he was running behind him and getting a leg-up on to a garage roof. He leaned over and hauled Veitch up behind him just as one of the pikes smashed into the brick with a force that belied even the formidable strength of both rider and weapon. The old buildings made it easy for them to find footholds until they could reach the bottom rungs of a fire escape, where they could scramble up to the roof. Crawling over the lip of the gutter was a terrifying experience, and once Church thought the whole frame was about to give way and plunge him to the hard pavement far below.

But eventually they were lying back on the dark slate tiles, staring at the sky as they desperately tried to catch their breath; beneath them the horses' hooves clattered insistently.

'They're not going to go away,' Veitch said redundantly.

'We could stay up here till dawn. They'll leave with the daylight.'

'You think they're just going to let us sit here? Anyway, didn't you say you'd seen them up in the *sky*?'

Church remembered viewing the eerie shapes among the clouds after Black Shuck's attack at the service station, but it was almost as if they had been in some *transitional* phase brought on by the sun's first rays. He shook his head. 'If they could, they'd have done it by now.'

He peeked over the edge. The rest of the Hunt had gathered there now, the imposing figure of the Erl-King at the heart of them. The horses snorted like traction engines as they jostled for space. A few curtains flickered in the apartments overlooking the street, but wisely, no one pursued their investigations.

'If they could rise up here in some way, I think they would have done it by now,' he said, but that didn't give him much comfort.

He had good reason to feel that way. The Erl-King raised his horn to his misshapen mouth and blew a long, aching blast. A second later it was answered by the mournful howl of a dog; not Black Shuck, Church noted – it was too thin and reedy – and then more joined in, yelping ferociously. The sound was so eerie; it almost sounded like human voices.

Within a minute, the pack arrived, surging through the alleyway that led to Tudor Square from wherever they had been sequestered, ready for the final stage of the Hunt. Church's heart froze at the sight of the demonic, red and white hounds; they were almost insect-like in the way they swarmed amongst the horses at the foot of the building.

The Erl-King gave them some silent order, and the sight that followed made Church's breath catch in his throat. The dogs were mounting the building; making inhuman leaps on to the garage roof, on to the window ledges; some even appeared to be climbing sheer faces.

'Jesus Christ!' Veitch's face was as milky-white as the dogs' hindquarters. As they advanced, their snapping needle teeth glinted menacingly.

Church and Veitch pushed their way back from the edge in shock and then stood up, frantically looking around for an escape route. The jumbled slate roofs stretched out all around them in a mix of angles and pitches that befitted the buildings' age, but there seemed only one way: further into the mediaeval quarter where the streets were narrow enough to leap across.

Veitch led the way, slipping and sliding on the tiles. Church was relieved the day had been dry, otherwise they would easily have skidded over the edge. Even so, the gutters remained unnervingly close. Church had never had a problem with heights, but he felt a tight band form across his chest as he glimpsed the street far below during their progress from house to house; and his head was spinning so much he was afraid he might black out or make a mis-step.

At ground level the Hunt was following their progress, ready to catch their prey if either of them plummeted. And behind, Church could hear the clicking of the dogs' nails as they clambered over the guttering on to the slates. He told himself not to look back, but he couldn't resist. The dogs were mounting the roofs in force, their white patches glowing in the moonlight like small spectres. They snapped and snarled venomously.

Church was amazed at how Veitch kept his attention singlemindedly on their escape. When a street opened up ahead of them, he paused, took a few steps back, then launched himself across the gulf, clattering on the tiles ahead and somehow clinging on.

He turned and beckoned to Church. 'Come on! They're almost on you!'

Church looked down at the dizzying drop and knew at once that was a mistake. The only way he could control himself was to close his eyes and jump blind. Suddenly there was a wild snapping at his heels and he threw himself across the gap. The wind whistled past his ears and his heart rammed up into his throat until he felt his feet touch down on the opposite roof. But his relief vanished when he realised he had mistimed his leap; he was toppling backwards, his arms cartwheeling.

Veitch reached out to grab his jacket and pull him forwards at the last moment and they tumbled together on to the slates.

'Try keeping your eyes open next time,' he snapped.

Out of the corner of his eye, Church saw the dogs leap the gap. He scrambled up the pitch after Veitch. The first few missed and fell howling to the street below, but others caught on to the guttering and somehow managed to pull their way up.

Church was breathless from exertion and anxiety. The dogs were relentless. He could hear the gnashing of their teeth so close behind that if he paused for a second they'd have him. At the next street, Veitch cleared the gap easily, but he still had trouble clinging on to the opposite roof's steep pitch. Church felt a brief flurry of relief when he recognised the block where their B&B was situated.

He couldn't stop to time his jump. A dog had almost sunk its teeth into his trousers, the teeth clacking so close he felt the vibration. But at the moment he launched himself, his foot skidded on the slate and he lost his momentum. He clamped his eyes shut again, and somehow his fingers clasped on to the guttering, which creaked ominously.

Veitch desperately tried to reach him, but before he could get within a foot, the guttering's supports wrenched out of the brick and Church was falling, still clinging on to the fragile metal.

That act saved his life. The guttering broke his fall enough so that he blacked out for only a second when he slammed into the road. But when he opened his eyes the Hunt had him surrounded.

The horses dragged at him roughly with their hooves, and when he saw the sharp teeth in their mouths he wondered briefly if the Huntsmen were going to allow their mounts to eat him alive. Then the Erl-King dismounted and strode over to Church, his terrible face emotionless, his red eyes gleaming. He stood astride Church and pressed the sickle end of the pike against Church's chest; the blade felt hard and icy-cold even through his jacket.

Slowly he bent forward until Church could see the scales of his skin and the bony protrusions which reminded him of the Fomorii, but were somehow very different. In his eyes, there was nothing Church could comprehend; they were alien, heartless.

Just as he had in Calatin's torture chamber, Church felt an uncanny peace come over him as he felt death near. He closed his eyes, and an instant later there was a brief flurry of movement as the pike slashed through his jacket and skin.

It took him a moment to realise he wasn't dead. When he opened his eyes he saw his jacket and shirt had been torn open and a stinging cross had been marked in the flesh of his chest. But astonishingly, that was the extent of his injuries.

Pushing himself up on his elbows, he watched in incomprehension as the Erl-King mounted his horse and led the riders to the end of the street. He gave another blast of his horn, and the dogs swarmed from the rooftops, down the side of the buildings, to gather behind the Hunt.

For one second, the Erl-King glanced at Church with a look that made his blood run cold, and then he spurred his horse and the Hunt galloped away with the hounds howling behind. A minute later, a silence fell on the deserted street as if the Hunt had never been there. With the threat gone, the shock and the pain proved too much and Church crashed back on the road in a daze.

CHAPTER SEVENTEEN

hanging heads

Veitch clambered down from the roof, unable to grasp exactly what had happened. The moment he'd seen Church slip he'd been convinced his friend's life was over; if not the fall, then the hounds or the Huntsmen themselves would dispatch him in an instant. But there Church lay in the deserted street, dazed but alive. It made no sense.

Still half-thinking the Hunt might return, Veitch quickly checked Church for any serious injuries, then supported him back to the B&B. The owner eyed them suspiciously as they made their way up the stairs, but said nothing; he'd seen worse.

The others were waiting in Tom's room, both relieved that Church and Veitch were back safely and irritated that they hadn't returned earlier. 'Typical testosterone-addled minds,' Laura sneered. ' "Let's stay out late and show how brave we are." '

While Shavi tended to the wound on Church's chest, Veitch attempted to explain what had happened. Tom watched the scenario from his bed, saying nothing.

'Were they afraid of you?' Ruth looked exhausted, on the verge of breaking down.

'They wanted to terrify you,' Shavi suggested. 'It was a power game.'

'Partly that.' Church tried to ignore the pain lancing through his ribs. 'But more, I think it was because they couldn't *afford* to kill me.'

'What do you mean?' Ruth knelt next to him and searched his face.

'Their instinct was to hunt, which is what they were doing,

408

but when they came to the kill they couldn't see it through because the Fomorii want us alive.' He closed his eyes and lay back in the armchair; his head was still swimming. 'The Fomorii can't touch the talismans directly. Unless they're wrapped in something. But they know how dangerous those things are—'

'—so they want us to do all the dirty work finding them, and then they're going to take them off us,' Ruth finished. 'They're just using us.'

'They let us get out of the mine for the same reason,' Church continued. 'I couldn't work out why they hadn't massed their ranks around the stone and the Wayfinder, if they're supposed to be so valuable. But we were allowed to just waltz through, pick them up, and waltz out. Thinking we'd done it ourselves, we carried on our own sweet way while they sat back, laughing.'

'That Crow guy really did try to kill us,' Veitch said, questioningly. 'He wasn't messing around.'

'Yes, but Tom said there was some kind of power struggle going on. Mollecht is probably trying to screw up Calatin's plans and get a few brownie points at the same time for wiping us out.' Church glanced at Tom for some input, but he simply rolled on his back and threw his arm across his eyes. He seemed to be shaking, as if he had a fever.

'So they're tearing themselves apart, like the Borgias or something.' Ruth blinked away a stray tear. Church reached out a hand in support, but she moved away, shaking her head defensively. Then: 'And all those times we'd thought we'd won, all the little victories – they just let us do it. We didn't win anything at all.'

'The illusion of free will.' Shavi's words sounded more sour than he had intended.

'Herded like sheep.' Ruth stared blankly out of the window, her thoughts closed off to them.

'We are still no closer to understanding their eventual aim.' Shavi finished cleaning the blood from Church's chest; the cuts weren't too deep. 'They seem well-established. They are strong. They could have moved at any time.'

'You've seen them,' Veitch said morosely. 'What chance would anyone have? The cops, the army – don't make me laugh. It'd be over in a day.'

Church winced at the pain creeping out from the wound. 'Then let's hope we can call back the Danann to do our dirty work for us.'

Laura made herself a cup of black coffee. 'So the time we really have to worry is when we pick up the last prize. Then we're fair game again.'

No one spoke. The atmosphere in the room had grown leaden with disquiet as they all turned their thoughts to the following day.

When the others crawled off to sleep, Church continued to sit up in the chair near the window, watching the dark waves roll across the surface of the sea. After a while, he took out the Black Rose, searching for some kind of comfort. In his mind, it was a direct channel to Marianne and all that she represented to him, all that she had taken away from him. 'Come on,' he whispered to it. 'You told me your name when I first found you. Tell me something else.'

It was a weak, childish thing to do and he didn't know what he really expected – Marianne hearing his voice, coming to him, making everything all right? – but he felt even more desolate in the ringing silence that followed his words. It was then he noticed a thin layer of white on the edge of one of the petals which, strangely, appeared to be frost. After he brushed it away, the cold seemed to linger unnaturally in the tip of his finger. It disturbed him so that when he fell asleep it infected his dreams with images of people he knew frozen to death in sweeping, pristine dunes of snow.

The morning broke bright and hot. They woke to the sound of cawing gulls, swooping in a clear blue sky, and the soothing

sound of the tide washing against the golden sand. Still sub-
dued, they gathered in Tom's room, where something caught
Church's eye on the TV which had been playing silently in
the background. He snatched the remote to boost the sound
on a local news bulletin. Scenes of the police and army
diverting traffic instantly placed it as the incident they had
encountered on the M4.

'—cloud of toxic chemicals escaping from the Pearson
Solutions plant at Barry Island has now dispersed. The massive operation by the emergency services to ensure thousands
of people stayed in their homes while others in the high
risk area were evacuated has been dubbed an overwhelming
success by—' Church muted the TV and tossed the remote
to one side.

'You believe that?' Veitch asked.

Church suddenly felt too weary to consider any of it any
more. 'Who knows?'

Laura shook her head resolutely. 'How can you tell when
a journalist is lying? Their lips move.'

They all jumped as a blast of insane laughter burst from
the TV speaker, then the set fizzed and went blank. Shavi
noticed the clock radio had gone blank too. 'Technology
crash,' he said.

Ruth cursed under her breath. 'I don't get this,' Veitch
said. 'Are those bastards switching everything on and off just
to wind us up?'

'I think,' Shavi mused, 'it is simply the world finding its
new status quo by trial and error.'

Veitch's face suggested he found this an even more disturbing prospect.

'Time to sell the computer and mobile,' Laura said. 'Beat
that glut on the market.'

The power came back on in time for breakfast, which they
consumed in the restaurant in near silence. Afterwards, they
gathered the talismans in the crate and headed down to the

quay where the first boat to Caldey Island was preparing to sail. They were the first on board, although a couple with pre-school twins joined them soon after. The sea was calm and the boat rolled smoothly. Once they were past the rocky outcropping of St Catherine's Island, topped by its Victorian fort, Caldey Island rose up, sun-drenched and green, three miles away in the bay.

When they were almost halfway there, one of the twins who had been gazing into the chopping waves suddenly called out excitedly, 'Mummy! Somebody's swimming!'

The mother laughed and rubbed his hair affectionately. 'Sometimes dolphins follow the boat, sweetie. Now sit down before you join them in there.' The boy protested until a stern look from his father quietened him.

Veitch glanced surreptitiously over the side, not wishing to show the others he was interested in seeing the wildlife, and was surprised to see the boy had been right – someone *was* swimming. Several people, in fact, their outlines distorted by the water. Veitch counted five alongside the boat, several feet beneath the waves. Yet they didn't appear to be wearing scuba gear, although they had been submerged an unnatural length of time, and they were swimming faster than anyone he had ever seen; they easily kept pace with the boat.

He thought about pointing it out to the others when a couple of the swimmers surfaced and he had another surprise. They were women, unashamedly naked to the waist, but their skin had a translucent greenish quality, almost the colour of the water, and their eyes were bigger than average and slightly slanted. And from the waist down they had scaly tails and long, gossamer fins like angel fish. As they turned and rolled in their undulating swim, their lustrous blue hair floated out behind them. Veitch saw gills slashed into the neck just below the ear.

Despite their outlandish appearance, they were stunningly beautiful. He understood how sailors of old were so transfixed by them that they plunged beneath the waves and drowned. One of the women caught him looking and swam up to just beneath the surface where she rolled on to her back and gave him a smile of such honeyed warmth, he almost felt himself melt. He smiled back, which seemed to please her. In response, she pursed her full lips and blew him a kiss before diving back to join her companions.

'What are you looking at?' Laura said accusingly. 'Thinking about jumping?'

Veitch smiled at her too, which obviously surprised her. He thought about telling the others what he had seen, then decided against it. It was his own small spot of wonder, a brief, private, transcendental moment that he would carry with him always.

After the boat docked alongside an old concrete jetty, the team followed the winding path from the small beach to the parkland that lay before the white walls and sunburnt orange tiled roof of the monastery.

'Whoever hid these talismans liked their religious spots, didn't they?' Ruth mused thoughtfully. 'Pagan. Celtic. Christian. That's quite cross-denominational.'

'You think it means something?' Veitch asked.

'Duh!' Laura mocked. Veitch flashed her a dark look.

They continued along past a roadside shrine and then the Wayfinder signalled a sudden change to the west. The paths in that direction were less well-trodden, the island more overgrown with dense trees and bushes. The heat had become almost claustrophobic and there was an abundance of midges and flies, despite the numerous birds cawing in the trees. Apprehension pressed heavily on them as they walked. The cut in Church's chest left by the Erl-King both stung and itched, while the Roisin Dubh in his inside pocket seemed to be reaching out to his heart with frosty fingers.

The dwindling path eventually brought them to a deserted beach sheltered in a small cove. Shavi stood among the blue-green and yellow banks of gorse and shielded his eyes to peer at the sparkling waves. 'Beautiful,' he said.

'Make the most of it.' Church glanced at Tom, who had stopped to wipe his forehead with a handkerchief. 'You okay?' He nodded, but still seemed uncomfortable, distracted.

Church took the lead, picking a way along the serpentine path that led down to the beach. Halfway there he realised the Wayfinder was pointing to a grove of trees on a ledge that broke the steep slope down to the sea. The thick bracken and brambles surrounding it suggested no one had been there in a long while. He nodded towards it.

'If this spear is such a big deal, how come it's left in a bunch of trees where anyone can find it?' Veitch was already on his guard, scanning the landscape for any sign of danger.

'Not just anyone can find it,' Tom said.

'Well, aren't we the lucky ones.' Church ploughed ahead through the dense fern cover.

About ten feet from the grove, he noticed a sudden change in the air pressure and temperature, as if they had slipped through the skin of an invisible bubble. He could taste metal in his mouth and there was a bizarre aroma of coffee in his nose. As he neared the trees, the hairs on the back of his neck mysteriously stood on end.

'There's something pale there,' Ruth noted apprehensively.

Church peered among the branches, but although he could make out the indistinct shapes Ruth had seen, he couldn't tell what they were.

'I advise caution,' Tom said.

'Why don't you advise us all to breathe at the same time?' Laura took a step forward.

Church crept ahead, keeping his gaze firmly on the dark shadows that clung between the trees. When they were close enough to smell the fragrance of the leaves, he finally made out the faintly luminescent orbs that seemed to be hanging like Chinese lanterns from the branches.

'Oh my God!' Ruth said before he could utter a word.

Human heads, eyes staring, mouths drooping, were draped on twisted vines, some of them as fresh and new as if they had been put there only the day before, others with skin as livid as the leaves that shaded them. Men, women, the old, the very young.

'Mondo disgusto!' Laura pinched her nose tightly.

'The Celts revered human heads. They thought they were a source of magical power. They always kept their enemies' heads on display.' Church paused, unsure whether to continue.

'We have no choice,' Shavi said, as if he could read Church's thoughts.

Church steeled himself and stepped into the shade. The smell of the heads was ripe in the hot morning sun; he coughed, tried to hold his breath. The others covered their mouths; Ruth was on the verge of vomiting.

Church felt like they were in another world; the quality of light was wrong; distorted. The shadows were too deep to see exactly where they were going.

'Marianne was having an affair.'

Church froze. The voice was rough, as if it hadn't spoken for days. He turned slowly, looked into the face of a mottled green head. Dead eyes stared back. But the lips quivered, formed new words to torment him again. 'She killed herself because she could not bear to tell you.'

'Don't listen!' Tom instructed from the back. 'Lies to divert you from the path! Thoughts plucked from your own mind!'

'How come you're never at the front?' Church snapped.

'Your uncle's guts spilled from his body,' another head said as Ruth passed. 'Ryan laughed when he saw it.' Ruth's eyes filled with tears and she turned sharply to Veitch. He shook his head forcefully, but it didn't dispel the hate in her eyes. She put her head down, kept walking.

Other words were spoken. Church heard some, but it made him sick to his stomach and the only way he could progress was to deaden his ears to it. And the heads were everywhere. The grove seemed much bigger than it had appeared from the outside, and those foul decorations looked to be hanging

415

from every branch; he wondered if it were a crop scooped from the remnants of an enormous bloody battle. The more they moved forward, the more the trees, and the heads, pressed together until they were regularly brushing against them, feeling the dead skin, setting them swinging like Christmas tree decorations. And the words continued in hideous whispers from all sides, punctuated by the occasional shriek and howl that made their blood run cold, until it seemed like they were being suffocated by waves of noise that threatened to drown their souls.

But however many emotional blows they took, their determination kept them moving forward. Then something seemed to break, as if the heads, or whatever force controlled them, realised their tactics weren't working. The head nearest to Church moved of its own volition and clamped its jaws on the muscle of his upper arm. He howled in pain and frantically tried to knock it off, but it held fast, increasing the pressure. Just when he thought it was going to rip a chunk from his flesh, Veitch stepped forward, pulled out his gun, put the barrel to the head's temple and pulled the trigger. Bone and brain exploded over Church and the jaw dropped free to the ground.

'Jesus!' Ruth yelled. 'You've still got a fucking gun!'

But there wasn't any time for anyone to answer. As one, all the heads emitted a piercing scream and tore their jaws wide, gnashing their jagged, broken teeth as they tried to bite anything that came near them. That far into the grove they were packed so tightly there was barely any space to squeeze between them; to stand still meant the flesh would be torn from their bones in bloody chunks.

Church put his head down and ploughed forward, with the others following suit, cursing loudly and lashing out as if the heads were punchballs. Within a matter of paces, any area of bare flesh was slick with blood.

Finally, when they all doubted they would be able to get any further, they suddenly broke through to an area of hard-

packed leaf mould and mud, free from any grotesque orna-
ments. The moment they stepped into the wide circle, the
heads instantly lost all animation, as if someone had flicked
a switch.

The sun broke through the verdant canopy to illuminate
a small circle at the heart of the open space, like a spotlight
on a stage. And in the centre of the glowing spot lay what
appeared to be a long stick, intricately carved with a tiny,
strange script.

'That's the spear?' Veitch said. 'Where's the business end?'

Church saw that he was right; at the end of the stick was
a scored area where it obviously fitted to a blade of some
kind. 'I thought it was going to be over,' he said dismally.

'The remainder of the spear will be somewhere in the
surrounding area, but not in the immediate vicinity,' Tom
said. He removed his glasses to wipe away the flecks of blood.
'The spear has great power as a weapon, and the two parts
may have been separated to make it more secure, but they
are bound on some intrinsic level and so cannot lie too far
apart.'

'You have all the answers apart from the ones we really
need,' Church said coolly. He picked up the spear, which
seemed to sing in his hands, and inspected the odd inscrip-
tion. 'Looks like Ogham script.'

'Arabic,' Shavi corrected. 'See the swirls?'

'No, I don't see that,' Church replied.

'Greek,' Laura suggested, pushing her way in next to them.

'No, that's definitely Russian,' Ruth prompted.

Church shook his head, then weighed the spear in his
hands. 'What am I going to do with this? It won't fit in the
crate.'

'Carry it,' Shavi suggested. 'It could easily be a staff.'

'But what if I damage it?'

Tom snorted contemptuously.

'Okay,' Church agreed, 'that was stupid. It looks like
ancient wood, but it's not. It's survived millennia and I

417

suppose it's pretty much indestructible. Let's get out of here.'

They stood on the edge of the circle looking at the gently swaying heads with trepidation, but the way they had come was the only way out; the other side of the grove was barred by an impenetrable mass of bramble and hawthorn. Finally Veitch pushed past the others and plunged among the mass of heads. Church followed swiftly behind. They were in such a state of high alert that they had travelled several paces before they realised the heads were unmoving; as dead as they looked. Nevertheless, they all continued through the stinking atmosphere as fast as they could and didn't look back until they had exited the grove and skidded down the bank, back to the beach in the tiny cove. There, they washed away the blood in the sea and dabbed at their wounds, resting on the sand until their tension eased.

Once he had recovered enough, Church took out the Wayfinder for what he hoped would be the final time. Its flame pointed across the strait to a point slightly along the coast. He checked his watch; it was just past noon. 'If we hurry, we can find it and be prepared to make our stand by nightfall,' he said.

Back on the mainland they hauled their few possessions to the van and set off out of town along a winding coast road that ran through beautiful, unspoilt countryside. After a few miles, the lantern pointed them down a side road which picked its way through the sleepy village of Manorbier, where they bought sandwiches, packets of crisps and Coke. At the end of a steep, tree-lined lane, they found themselves in another secluded cove. They parked in a large but nearly deserted car park near to the stony beach where the flame finally resumed its upright position.

'Where now?' Laura asked.

Shavi pointed to a ruined castle which could just be glimpsed through the trees.

They ate lunch in the van and bantered with new-found

vigour, buoyed by their success on Caldey. Church and Ruth led the way to the twelfth century castle atop a red sandstone spur, still partly occupied by its current owners. Inside the gates it was quite small, a lawned area the size of a football pitch lying at the heart of the crumbling battlements. Tom bought a guidebook from the tiny castle shop for reference, which he read while smoking a joint on a wooden bench. The others wandered around looking for a sign of the way forward.

Half an hour later, having futilely scoured the castle from top to bottom, they met up in the shade of the chapel. 'I knew it was going too well.' Church checked his watch anxiously.

'What do you expect – neon signs?' Laura said. 'These things are supposed to be near-impossible to find.'

'Except for us,' Church stressed. 'We're fated to find them, remember?'

Laura bristled. 'Nice line in patronising. When was your coronation?'

'Sorry.' The tension was making them all irritable; Church could see it in their faces, their body language. Unchecked, he was afraid it might tear them apart. 'We'll start looking again—'

'Maybe we're in the wrong place,' Veitch suggested. 'It could be buried under the car park.'

Church shook his head. 'This place fits the trend. It has to be here.'

Ruth looked to Shavi. 'You could do something. Like you did in Glastonbury.'

Shavi recalled uneasily how much the exercise in Glastonbury had taken out of him; there was one point when he feared he might have been consumed by the powers he was unleashing, but he didn't let the others see his thoughts. 'I seem to have an aptitude for certain shamanistic skills,' he agreed in response to Church's enquiring expression. 'In the right conditions, the right frame of mind, I can communicate with the invisible world.'

Veitch looked at him as if he were speaking a foreign language. 'Talk to ghosts?'

'Everything has a spirit, Ryan. People, animals, ghosts. Throughout history shamans have contacted them in search of knowledge.' Veitch sniffed derisively. 'I have always felt I had certain abilities, though unfocused, raw, but since the change that has come over the world they seem sharper.'

'I think we're all adapting,' Ruth said. There was something in her tone that made them feel uncomfortable.

'You're simply achieving your potential,' Tom said. 'That's why you've all been selected.'

'You have to survive to achieve potential,' Church said with irritation. 'Look, this isn't getting us anywhere. Shavi, if you can do something, anything, do it. If not, let's get searching.'

In the end, Shavi agreed he would find a quiet place to attempt a divination while the others continued the hunt. Accompanied by Church, they settled on an area where they were unlikely to be disturbed, in a secluded corner of the ruined hall where thistles and willowherb grew with abandon. It was a fenced-off, sheltered space under an overhanging stairway that ended in thin air.

'I normally do this alone,' Shavi said, taking a mouthful of mushrooms from a tightly wound plastic bag hidden in his jacket, 'but there is no time to recover from the trip. I fear I will be of little use to you for a while afterwards.'

'I don't care if we have to carry you round on a stretcher as long as you give us something we can use,' Church said. He sat on a lump of masonry while Shavi adopted a cross-legged position against the wall. 'This stuff really works, then?'

'Sometimes. Never quite in the way I hope, but enough to make it worthwhile. It is not scientific. If there are any rules, I have no idea what they might be.'

'That sounds like a mantra for this new age,' Church said wearily.

'It was always that way, Jack. Before, we lied to ourselves

420

or listened to religious leaders and scientists who lied to themselves. Perhaps one of the good things that will come out of all this is that people will start searching for meaning within themselves.'

'You have a very optimistic view of human nature.' Church let his eyes rise up the cracked grey walls to the clear blue sky above. 'Sometimes I think there's no meaning in anything. Just random events impacting on one another. Chaos giving the illusion of a coherent plan.' But his words were lost; Shavi was already immersed in his inner world.

For half an hour, nothing happened. Church became increasingly agitated as Shavi sat stock-still and silent, his eyes closed. But just as Church was about to give in to the futility of the moment, Shavi began to mumble, barely audibly to begin with, but then increasingly louder; Church had the uneasy sensation that he was hearing one side of a conversation.

'Yes.'

'We are searching for something. You know what.'

'That is correct.'

'No. Everyone is to be trusted.'

'Why do you say that?'

'Everyone is to be trusted.'

'Yes, I am sure. Will you guide me to the item we need to find?'

'I will accept responsibility if things go wrong. Of course I will.'

'Yes.'

'And we will find it there?'

'Thank you for your guidance. Now I must—'

'What do you want to show me?'

'Oh.'

There was a long humming silence in which Church realised he was holding his breath waiting for the next part of the unsettling conversation. Shavi's lips seemed to quiver as if he were about to speak; Church leaned forward in anticipation.

Suddenly Shavi's eyes burst wide open and he let out a deep, strangled cry. Church leapt back in shock. 'I see it!' he gasped. Blood bubbled out of one nostril and trickled down to his lip.

Recovering quickly, Church jumped forward and grabbed Shavi by the shoulders, afraid he was about to have some kind of fit. 'Are you okay? I can get help.'

Although Shavi's eyes were open, he was not looking at anything Church could see; his pupils were fixed on a distant horizon. 'I see it!' he repeated. 'Coming across the land, like someone drawing a black sheet. They are here! They are everywhere!' He swallowed noisily. 'The city is burning! We walk over bodies heaped in the road. There is no hope anywhere. Everyone is dead. What did they do? They brought him back. Balor!' He coughed a mouthful of blood on to the stony ground. 'Balor.'

The word sent a shiver through Church. Suddenly he was back in the mine, listening to Tom's croaking voice recounting the terrible history of the Fomorii. 'Balor,' he repeated fearfully. Their long-dead leader, all-powerful, monstrously evil. The one-eyed god of death who almost destroyed the world.

Church prevented Shavi slumping sideways, then, holding him under his arms, dragged him to his feet. He was afraid to take Shavi out into the main part of the castle in case someone saw, but the fear that he might be on the verge of a coma or heart attack drove him on. As he struggled to walk with him, though, Shavi seemed to recognise what he was doing.

'Leave me,' he croaked. 'Fine . . . fine . . . Just need time.'

Church was torn, but when Shavi protested more insistently, Church went along with his wishes. He laid him back down against the wall, on his side in case he vomited. 'I'll get the others,' he whispered.

But as he started to walk off, Shavi grabbed his leg and hissed, 'Under the drawbridge.' He wiped away the blood with the back of his hand, but his eyes were already rolling up. Church left him there with an uncontrollable sense of impending doom.

'You reckon we're on a wild goose chase too?' Veitch caught up with Laura on top of the highest tower, where she leaned on the battlements staring out to sea.

Her ever-present sunglasses made it impossible to read her eyes, but there was the hint of an ironic smile. 'That, and other clichés.'

'We haven't had much of a chance to talk—'

'That's because you're a murderer and everybody hates you.'

Despite himself, Veitch felt his welcoming smile wash away. 'That's a sharp tongue,' he said coldly.

'I like it. I can get olives out of a jar without a fork.'

Veitch shook his head, unsure. 'You ever say anything that isn't smart?'

'Do you ever say anything that is?'

The smile remained; Veitch couldn't tell if it was playful or mocking, but his insecurities made him fear the worst. 'If you don't want to—'

'Stop being so sensitive. You shot some poor bastard. Deal with it and move on. Make amends, ignore it, just don't wallow in a big, slimy pool of guilt.' She turned back to the sea, raising her face slightly to feel the sun.

Her words gave him some comfort, but he still couldn't begin to work her out; she made him feel stupid, uncomfortable, but he couldn't deny being attracted from the first time he had heard her display her savage wit. He leaned on the masonry next to her, fumbling for the right words. 'How do you feel about giving up your life to join this nightmare expedition?'

'It's something to do.'

'What about your friends? Your folks?'

'Friends are those who're around you at the time. My parents died in a car crash.'

'Boyfriend?'

She inclined her face slightly towards him, her smile now sly. Veitch felt his cheeks colour. 'Was that your idea of subtle?'

'Dunno what you mean.' He shifted uncomfortably.

'You've got a pretty face and a good bod, but you're not my type, *comprende*? No offence and all, but I think we ought to nip this in the bud before the conversation gets clogged up with all those stupid manoeuvrings.'

Veitch looked away, unsure what to say.

'Don't get all hurt—'

'I'm not hurt.' He felt a sudden surge of irritation at that supercilious smile.

'If you're looking for a girlie, there's always Gallagher, although you could get a bad case of frostbite. Or,' she chuckled mischievously, 'Shavi.'

Veitch eyed her suspiciously. 'He's a queen?'

'Bi, actually.' His face obviously gave away his prejudices, because her smile drained away. 'You never know,' she said icily, 'it might do you the world of good.'

Before he could reply, she spotted Church walking across the green and hailed him. Veitch saw an obvious enthusiasm in her face that revealed exactly how she felt about their unelected leader; it was the first honest emotion he had seen in her, and after his rejection it made him feel cold inside. As he followed her down the steps to meet the others, his anger was already forming into an impacted lump in his chest.

Church took the others back to where Shavi lay, explaining what had happened as they ran. The bloodflow from his nose had stemmed, but he was still dazed, rambling. Ruth knelt beside him and checked his pulse.

424

'We should get him to a hospital.' The concern was evident on her face. 'He could have had a brain seizure. This is what happens when you mess with drugs.'

'I don't think it was the mushrooms.' Church still couldn't shake the memory of what had happened. 'It began after he had some kind of apocalyptic vision.'

'Did he tell you anything important?' Tom said anxiously.

'Come on,' Ruth protested. 'Shavi needs help!'

'I can do something for him,' Tom snapped. 'Leave him with me while you continue with the search. Now, did he tell you anything important?'

Church tried to remain calm. 'Something about them ... the Fomorii, I suppose ... being everywhere. About bodies in the streets and some city burning.' With a shiver, Church had a sudden flash of his own premonition in the Watch-tower; he hadn't made the connection before. 'And he said they're bringing back Balor.'

Tom blanched.

Ruth saw the expressions on both their faces. 'What does that mean?'

'We can talk about it later,' Church said. 'Finding the spearhead is more pressing. Shavi also said to look under the drawbridge. That makes sense – the first three artefacts were under Avebury, under Tintagel and under Glastonbury Tor.'

He left Tom behind to care for Shavi and led Laura, Ruth and Veitch out of the castle gates. His first thought had been to leave the crate with Tom to free up their hands, but after Shavi's premonition he decided to keep the objects of power as close to him as possible. Through the gatehouse they skid-ded down the grassy bank into the dry moat and walked under the drawbridge. At first nothing caught their eye, but after Church had run his hands over the turf on the castle side, he discovered an odd, raised shape. It seemed to be a protruding lump of masonry, but he scrabbled the grass off with his fingernails and discovered it was in the shape of a spearhead.

After checking they weren't being watched, Church pushed, pulled and twisted the rock in a blind attempt to open it. Eventually something seemed to work, although he wasn't sure what, and there was a burst of blue sparks. An opening grew in the grassy bank, leading under the castle. As they slipped in quickly, they felt the same odd sensation of entering a bubble as they had on Caldey. The moment they were all in, the opening closed silently behind them, leaving them in the oppressive darkness of a tomb.

Church took out the Wayfinder, which gave them enough light to see they were in a tunnel in what appeared to be the bedrock. The walls were wet and shimmering, and the floor sloped slightly downwards.

'If these artefacts were hidden millennia ago, are you telling me it's pure coincidence that structures have been erected over the top of them?' Ruth's whisper was almost reverential, yet it echoed like the tide along the tunnel.

'You've felt their power,' Church replied. 'Who knows what subtle influences they exert? Maybe they drew the builders.'

The tunnel opened out into a stone chamber about the size of the one they had discovered under Tintagel.

'If you see any holes in the wall, don't put your hands in them,' Veitch deadpanned.

'There *are* holes,' Church noted, spraying the light across the chamber. 'Or niches, to be more precise.'

The four openings were of different sizes in a horizontal line on the far wall. Veitch was the first to them, and he investigated cautiously, withdrawing his hand repeatedly in case something shut down on it.

'There's an indentation at the bottom of each one,' he said. 'This one's round.' He moved on. 'Another round one.' The next. 'Long and thin. And this one, not so long and not so thin.'

They mulled over the information briefly, but Ruth was the first with the answer. 'They're for each of the talismans,' she said excitedly. 'It's impossible to solve this one unless you've already got through all the other ones.'

'Big wows. Aren't you smart?' Laura said sarcastically. 'So if we're also supposed to learn something from each of these puzzles, tell me what we've picked up from Caldey and here. Apart from never look a severed head in the eye.'

Church ignored her; he was already unloading the talismans from the packing crate. With Veitch's help, he dropped the stone and the cauldron into the first two holes; they fitted perfectly. The sword went into the fourth. The indentation in the third hole showed the full shape of the spear, including the head. Church carefully positioned the handle of the spear and the moment it lowered into place, the space for the head opened and a blue light flooded up. A second later the actual head rose into place.

'We've done it!' Church said triumphantly.

'You know, I almost expected cheers,' Ruth added with a broad grin.

Veitch didn't seem so jubilant. 'Yeah, great, we've just signed our death warrant.'

'Ah, Mr Glass-Half-Empty,' Laura said coolly. 'Just pick up the damned pieces and let's get out of here.'

They hurriedly gathered up the artefacts, and the moment the last one came out, another door opened up in the wall; they could see blazing sunlight at the end of it.

'How long to sunset?' Veitch asked anxiously.

Church checked his watch. 'Four hours. Lots of time.'

'Depends which way you look at it.' Veitch was already in the tunnel and moving as fast as he could.

Whatever Tom had done, Shavi had recovered slightly when they met up with them, but he was still loose-limbed and dazed. To the curious stares of onlookers, Church and Veitch helped walk him out of the castle and back to the van.

'He's not going to be much use to us tonight,' Church said redundantly.

427

'He wouldn't be much use if he was normal,' Veitch said sourly. 'So, we going to run for it or make a stand?'

'I vote we run and don't spare the horses,' Laura said hastily.

Veitch was obviously ready for a confrontation. 'And I vote we make a stand. Let's face it, they're going to catch us sooner or later. That's their whole reason for existing.'

'Well, aren't *you* the macho man. What are you doing to do – flex you biceps and hope they faint?' Laura jabbed him in the sternum with her fingertips, unbalancing him.

Church held out an arm as Veitch advanced angrily. 'He's right,' he said. 'We wouldn't get far if we ran.'

'Then what do you suggest? Wet towels at dawn?'

Church was encouraged to see some real emotion in Laura's blazing eyes; it seemed to be happening more and more. 'We've got four powerful artefacts here. Surely they've got to be some use.'

'What? Use them ourselves?' Laura said.

'It might work.'

'It might work. If we lived in cloud-cuckoo-land.'

'We are supposed to be some kind of champions,' Ruth said.

'Right.' Laura's voice dripped with sarcasm. 'A screwed-up techno head, an old hippie, a woman with a poker up her arse, a drugged-up fey romantic, a murderer and—' she nodded towards Church '—him. Some big fucking champions.'

'So we roll over and die like good little slaves?' Veitch responded angrily.

Laura pulled a face, then walked off. Church waited a moment before following and found her sitting on the grass on the other side of an ice cream van where the attendant was lazing in the back with a copy of the *Sun*.

'All this is out of our hands now, you know,' he said, sitting down next to her.

Eventually she said, 'I like to have choices.'

428

He nodded, watching the midges dance in the sunlight. 'I know it's a cliché, but this is bigger than anything we feel. This must be how they felt going off to the Great War. Scared, but with a great sense of responsibility, a feeling of being part of some great . . . I don't know, destiny.'

'I'm glad you feel that way, because I'm completely ruled by self-preservation here.'

'You're saying we can't count on you when the chips are down? I don't believe that.'

'You think you know me, do you?' She turned her head away so he couldn't see her expression.

'Yes. I think I know you.'

She thought for a moment, then rolled up her T-shirt so he could see the words scarred into her back.

Church caught his breath, but said nothing for a while. Then, 'Who did that?'

'It doesn't matter who.' She paused. 'Does it make you feel sick to see it?'

'My God, how could someone be so inhuman?' Church said in shocked disbelief.

'There are a lot of sick bastards out there. I said, does it make you feel sick?'

Church gently reached out to touch the scar tissue, then retracted his fingers at the last moment. Laura seemed to sense what he was doing for she leaned in towards him, only slightly, but enough to move into his personal space. Away from the pink cicatrix, her skin seemed unduly soft; he could smell her hair, the faint musk of her sweat from the morning's exertions. And suddenly he had an overwhelming need for physical contact, just to feel humanity and emotion rather than the cold, hard wind of constant threat. He reached out his hand again.

'Stop making goo-goo eyes at each other. We're running out of time.' Veitch was standing at the back of the ice cream van, his expression cold and hard.

Church jumped to his feet. 'Yeah, you're right.' He held

out his hand and hauled Laura up; she held on to it for a moment longer than she needed, then withdrew her fingers so softly it was almost a caress.

Back at the van, they decided to find someplace with strong defences where they at least stood a chance of making a stand; if any of them were feeling fatalistic, it didn't show. But when Veitch went to turn the key, the engine was dead. 'We can't fucking rely on anything!' he said, hammering his fist on the steering wheel.

Time was running away. It was too dangerous to wait for everything to start working again and then find themselves caught out on the open road. Veitch hit the wheel one final time, then said, 'We'll have to hole up round here.'

'The castle would be perfect,' Ruth noted, 'but there's no way we'll be able to get in there after it's shut up for the night.'

Veitch thought briefly before pointing to a Norman church perched on the opposite side of the valley to the castle. It stood isolated amidst a sea of green fern and small bushes. 'We could do it there. Nobody's nearby to get hurt and we'll be able to see them coming from a long way off. Plus, it's got a wall round the churchyard, which may be nothing, but every little helps.'

Church was impressed by Veitch's tactical vision and at how comfortable he seemed making those sorts of decisions quickly. 'Okay. You're the boss.'

Veitch glanced at him as if he thought Church were mocking him. When he saw that wasn't the case, he looked both bewildered and a little pleased. 'Right, then. I'm the boss.'

They left the van sitting useless in the car park and walked up to the church half an hour before twilight fell so as not to draw attention to themselves. They needn't have bothered; there was no one around for as far as the eye could see, and the church noticeboard said the vicar was shared with other parishes, so there was no reason why they should be disturbed. The weather seemed to be changing to complement the approaching conflict; after the heat of the day, a chill had swept in from the sea, with slate-grey clouds which turned the waves an angry dark blue. They crashed on the stony beach with increasing violence; enormous fountains of gleaming surf cascaded high into the air, filling the valley with the deep bass rumble of angry nature.

They erected a tent in the churchyard for shelter in case it rained, and then halfheartedly chewed a few sandwiches left over from lunch. The thunder started just as the half-light of evening turned to the gloom of night. Veitch lit a handful of storm lanterns they'd bought in Glastonbury and positioned them around the tent.

'You don't think this is going to attract attention?' Ruth said as the first fat drops of rain fell. Away in the dark an owl hooted mournfully and Ruth wondered if it was the same mysterious bird which seemed to have befriended her.

'No one's going to see it, and even if they did, they wouldn't turn out on a night like this.' Church opened the packing crate and examined the three talismans inside; the spear had been lashed to it with a rope from the van and an oily rag tied to disguise the head. After a moment's thought he selected the sword, as surprised at how it felt in his hand as the first time he had touched it; sturdier than it appeared, warm, tingling.

'Let me have the spear,' Ruth said.

'You sure? I was going to give it to Ryan.'

'Why? Because he's a big tough boy and I'm a *girl*? Besides, he's got his little gun to keep him happy, for all the good it'll do him.'

Church weighed the spear in his hands, then passed it over. He wondered if it might be more effective with Veitch's strength behind it, but he had no doubts about Ruth's bravery.

'Thanks,' she said. 'I'll take that as a vote of confidence. It means a lot to me.' She took the spear and balanced it on

431

her open palms before taking it firmly with a smile. 'Feels good.'

'Ruth Gallagher, warrior woman.'

She laughed. 'I've got so much pent-up frustration and anger I feel like I could take them all down on my own.' She brandished the spear theatrically, then her face darkened. 'What was it Shavi said that disturbed you and Tom?'

Church thought about not telling her, but decided it wasn't fair. 'Shavi discovered why the Fomorii haven't attacked. They're trying somehow to resurrect the one who used to lead them before he was destroyed by the Danann. At least, that's what he seemed to be suggesting.'

'And that's bad?'

'According to the Celtic myths, Balor was a force of ultimate evil and darkness. Virtually indestructible, terrifying to look upon, so powerful that if he turned his one eye on you, you were instantly annihilated. If the myths have captured even a fraction of the truth, it could be the end of everything.'

'Then we need to free the Danann before they bring him back.'

'But we don't know how close they are. They could be doing it tonight—'

Ruth clapped her hand on his shoulder and gave it a squeeze. 'No point tearing ourselves apart. We just have to do the best we can.'

In her face, Church saw something that brightened his spirit. 'I'm really glad we met under the bridge that night. Sorry. I just felt I had to say that.'

She smiled and gave his cheek a gentle pat. 'You're a man of excellent taste, Jack Churchill.'

He pushed the crate with the remaining talismans into the tent where Laura and Veitch sat in frosty silence, and Shavi dozed with Tom beside him. 'How's sleeping beauty?' he said.

'As well as can be expected, given the psychic shock.' Tom's

Scottish brogue was more pronounced, which Church put down to the tension.

'I don't understand it,' Veitch moaned. 'We've got all the prizes together, like you said, but nothing's happened.'

Church nodded. 'I'm hoping we'll get some kind of sign.' He half-expected the woman from the Watchtower to turn up at any moment with the final piece of the jigsaw.

'I know what we've got to do,' Tom said. Everyone stared at him. 'They have to be brought together in the right place to work.'

'So when were you planning on telling us this?' Church asked with irritation.

'At the last possible moment,' Tom snapped. 'There's too much at stake to start throwing vital information around. You don't know who's listening—'

'There's only us listening!' Veitch said angrily. 'It's about time you got on the team—'

'There's no point arguing about it now,' Church said with exasperation. 'Do you all want to come out and choose your weapons, for what it's worth? We've found some pretty mean lumps of driftwood and an iron bar on the beach.'

Veitch crawled out first, and then Laura more reluctantly. 'I'll stay here,' Tom said. 'Look after Shavi and the other talismans.'

Church was disappointed, but there was no point trying to force him. 'If you've got any more tricks up your sleeve, now's the time to pull them out.'

Tom nodded, but didn't let on if there was anything he could do.

'Look at us!' Laura laughed as they gathered anxiously within the circle of light in the pouring rain. 'The Hunt will probably laugh themselves off their horses. Before they drag us off to hell, that is.'

Ruth and Veitch ignored her; they fixed their eyes on the deep gloom, their ears straining to hear any sound beneath the howl of the wind.

433

'Do you know how to use that sword?' Laura continued to Church, realising he was her only audience. 'It'll be about as effective as a toasting fork. Does she know what to do with that spear? And, hey, do I know what to do with this lump of driftwood? Yep, we are some defenders of the realm. Pathetic.'

The rain had plastered her hair to her head and was running in rivulets down her face. At least in the dark she had forsaken her sunglasses; Church saw the fire in her eyes.

'You'll give them hell,' he stated simply. He considered saying more, about her courage, her spirit, but the low, dolorous sound of a horn suddenly came in on the wind and he felt the blood drain from him. Laura's face, too, was white in the ghostly light of the storm lanterns; her dark eyes darted around fearfully.

As if in response to the horn a peal of thunder rolled out and then lightning streaked the sky. The gale gusted the rain at them like ice bullets.

'Okay,' Veitch said. 'Looks like we have us a situation.'

'Just what we need – a meathead raised on war movies,' Ruth muttered sourly.

Before they could utter another word, they saw the bulk of Black Shuck separate from the darkness and pad towards them. It leapt up and sat on the wall in one corner of the churchyard, where it simply watched balefully, its red eyes glowing. Its silence was eerie. It didn't threaten to attack or make any movement at all; it just stared. And there was something in that which terrified them more than at any other time they had encountered it.

They heard the baying of the hounds rising up before they heard the horses. Their white and red forms undulated like a pack of rats as they surged up the lane towards the church. A moment later the riders loomed behind them, majestic, awe-inspiring and terrible in the heart of the storm. The moment they were caught in the white flash of lightning, a primal vision in metal and fur, Church knew exactly how

Laura felt; before them, he was useless, their weapons children's toys. Nevertheless, he adjusted the sword in his hands and brandished it as threateningly as he could. The others followed suit with their own weapons, as if they had read his mind.

As the Hunt galloped up the lane, it almost seemed like the storm was part of them; the wind howled from within the churning mass of horses and the thunder echoed from their hooves as they clattered on the road. The Erl-King was at the head, his monstrous face garish in the lightning.

Church prepared himself for them to come barrelling straight into the churchyard, but instead they surged around it, circling one way, then another, with the dogs before them so it was impossible to tell from which direction the attack would come.

'They're playing with us,' Church shouted above the wind.

'No, they're being careful,' Veitch replied. 'Looks like you were right about these magic things – they want them, but they're scared of them.'

Church realised Veitch was right and that gave him more confidence; perhaps they weren't as mismatched as he had thought.

'Maybe we could hold them off like this every night.' Ruth moved her weight from one leg to the other, holding the spear out before her.

'And achieve what?' Laura asked savagely.

The Hunt continued its circling for nearly an hour, by which time they were all shivering and soaked to the skin. Their constant concentration and high state of alert was exhausting them.

'I wish they'd just do something!' Ruth yelled above the wind.

As if in answer, the riders suddenly roiled around one section of the wall, then reined their mounts up before backing off slightly to leave the Erl-King standing alone. His horse reared up, its breath steaming from its nostrils, and when it brought its hooves down Church was convinced he saw a burst of sparks.

'Give up your burdens!' His voice boomed out, yet, oddly, seemed to come from somewhere all around him rather than directly from his mouth; there was a strange metallic tinge to it that set their teeth on edge.

'You're not having anything!' Church yelled defiantly.

There was a long pause and when the Erl-King spoke again, it was as if the storm had folded back to allow his words to issue with a focused power and clarity; his accent sounded different from moment to moment, as if their ears were struggling to make sense of what they heard.

'Across the worlds we dance, above the storms, beyond the wind. All barriers crumble at our command. We are like the waves, ever-changing. You can never know us. You can never cup our voices in your ear, nor touch our shells, nor smell our fragrance in the wind. Through time and space we slip and change. There are no absolutes.' His voice drifted away and for a moment there was nothing but ringing silence, as if the whole of the world had stopped.

But when his voice returned, it had the force of a hurricane and they were almost bowed before it. 'And you are feeble sacks of bone and blood and meat! Trapped in form, lost to the universe, always questioning, never knowing! Driven by lusts, chariots of wrath! You may not turn your face toward us! You may not raise your voice to speak! You may not lift a hand to challenge! For in doing so, you challenge the all and above and beyond! And your essences will be swept away and torn into a billion shreds! Hang your heads in shame! Be low before us!'

The tone of his words filled Church with trepidation. He recognised that he was dealing with something so beyond his comprehension it was almost like speaking with God. Yet however fearful he felt, he knew he couldn't back down. 'You may think we're nothing, but we'll fight to the last. And if you believed everything you said, you wouldn't be sitting there talking to us. You'd just have taken it. If you want these things, you come and get them!'

'Nice tactics,' Laura said in a fractured voice. 'Don't just stand there. Go open the gate for him.'

There was another ear-splitting peal of thunder and another blinding flash of lightning, and when it had cleared the Hunt was in motion. They galloped halfway round the churchyard wall, and then, without warning, they suddenly cleared the perimeter with a single bound, the dogs running all around. There was no time to talk or think. A hound launched itself at Church's throat, jaws snapping, needle teeth glinting, its eyes glowing with an inner light. Church swung the sword with such force he cleaved the dog in two. But instead of a shower of blood and entrails, it simply turned black and folded up on itself like a crisp autumn leaf until it disappeared in a shimmer of shadow.

Everything was happening too fast. One dog sank its teeth into Veitch's calf before he bludgeoned it to death with the iron bar. The tent was torn up and disappeared in a flurry, leaving Tom frozen in terror, hunched over Shavi's unmoving form. The hounds circled and attacked, circled and attacked, while the four of them continually lashed out to keep them at bay. But it was like holding back the tide. And out of the corner of his eye Church realised the riders were waiting, letting the hounds do all the work for them.

And then the quality of time seemed to change; images hit his brain one after the other like slides in a projector. Ruth's face, pale and frightened, but ferociously determined, in a flash of lightning. Some kind of comprehension crossing it like a shadow. Her head turning, searching, settling on one spot. The weight of her body shifting, muscles bunching, leaning forward slightly.

And then everything returned to normal like air rushing into a vaccuum. Ruth erupted from the spot, holding the spear above her head. With a tremendous effort, she powered forwards, slammed her foot on a stone cross and launched herself on even faster. Church knew it was a suicide run, but there wasn't even a second to call out. She flew through the air and slammed the spear hard into the Erl-King's chest. There was an explosion of blue fire that lit up the entire churchyard. The Erl-King came free of his saddle, his face transformed by some emotion Church couldn't recognise, and the two of them went over the wall together and rolled down the steep bank into the night.

Ruth woke in the sodden bracken, her head ringing and a smell like a power generator filling the air. Every muscle ached and her skin was sore, as if she had been burned. The rain was still pouring down, pooling in her eye sockets, running into her mouth. With an effort, she lifted herself up on her elbows, and as she fought to recall what had happened, flashes came back: her attack, the impact with the Erl-King, the flash of blue fire and her last thought that she had killed herself but saved the others. With that realisation she allowed herself to focus on the outside world: she wasn't alone.

Something was thrashing around in the undergrowth, snorting like an animal, occasionally releasing a bestial bellow of anger or pain. It sounded so primal she was almost afraid to look, but in some perverse way she was drawn to it, even if it meant she might be discovered. Cautiously she peered above the level of the ferns.

Forty feet away, a dark shape crashed around, pawing the ground, stooping low, then raising its head high to the night sky. Her first instincts had been correct; there was more of the animal about it, yet also something sickeningly human. Her stomach turned at the conflicting signals. And then, in another flash of lightning, she saw what it was: the Erl-King, not wounded as she might have expected, but undergoing some bizarre metamorphosis. His entire body appeared to be fluid, the muscles and bones flowing and bulking, the posture becoming more brutish; the greenish scales and bony

438

ridges on his face ran away as if they were melting in the rain; the nose grew broader, the eyes golden and wide-set; there seemed to be an odd mixture of fur and leaves sprouting all over his body, as if he were becoming a hybrid of flora and fauna. Yet despite its strangeness, Ruth felt the sight was oddly familiar. With each new transformation, he bellowed, and that sound also changed, conversely becoming more mellifluous. And finally twin stalks erupted from his forehead, growing and dividing until they became the proud, dangerous horns of a stag.

The vision was terrifying, yet also transcendental; Ruth felt flooded with an overpowering sense of wonder. She caught her breath; it was a slight sound, hidden by the wind, but whatever the Erl-King had become heard her. It froze, cocked its head, then lurched towards her, its hot breath bursting in twin plumes from its flared nostrils. Ruth shrieked in shock and scrabbled backwards, her heels slipping on the wet vegetation, but it was so quick it was over her before she could stand and run.

Knowing she was trapped, she turned and looked up at its huge silhouette looming over her, waiting for the wild attack that was sure to come. And then the strangest thing happened: in another flash of lightning she caught a glimpse of its expression and she was sure it was smiling.

'Frail creature,' it said in a voice like the wind through autumn trees, 'I see in you the sprouting shoots of one of my servants.'

'What's happened?' she croaked.

The creature made an odd, unnatural gesture with its left hand and then seemed to search for the right words to communicate with her. 'When the barriers collapsed, the Night Walkers were prepared. Deep in the Heart of Shadows, they had formed a Wish-Hex of immense power, forged from the dreams of lost souls. As we readied for our glorious return, it swept out in a whirlwind of vengeance, the like of which had not been seen since the first battle. None escaped its touch. Many of my kin were driven out of the Far Lands, a handful escaped to the world, or the places in-between. And some were cursed to walk the Night Walk. And I was one of them.' He made a strange noise in his throat that was part-growl, part-cry, but then seemed to regain his composure. 'But the Night Walkers' influence was always tainted with weakness. And you, a frail creature, broke its hold!'

The sound he made was not remotely human, but she guessed, in its ringing, howling rhythms, its essence was laughter. 'You have the spear, most glorious and wonderful of the Quadrillax. The eternal bane of the Night Walkers, the source of the sun's light!'

His words were strange, but she was slowly piecing it together. 'It freed you from their control?'

'I have as many faces as the day, yet I was trapped in form like you frail creatures, walking the Night Walk. Damned and tormented!'

She looked deep into his face and was almost overwhelmed by an awe, perhaps inspired by some submerged race memory. 'Who are you?' she whispered.

'Know you not my names? Has it been so long? Of all the Golden Ones, I stayed in the World the longest, dancing through even when the barriers were closed. Yet still forgotten?' His sigh was caught by the wind. 'My names are legion, changing with the season. In the first times, when the World was home, the people of the west knew me as Gwynn ap Nudd, White Son of Night, Lord of the Underworld, leader of the Wild Hunt, master of the Cwm Annwn, a Lord of Faery, a King of Annwn. In the great land, across the waves, I was Cernunnos, the Horned One, Lord of the Dance, Giver of Gifts. In the cold lands I was Woden, leader of the Herlethingus; heroism, victory and spiritual life were my domain. Each new frail creature saw me differently, yet knew my heart. Green Man. Herne the Hunter. Serpent Son. Wish Huntsman. Robin Hood. My home is the Green, my time the dark half of the year. Do you know me now?'

Ruth nodded, terrified yet entranced. Images tumbled across her mind, scenes from childhood stories, ancient myths, all pieces of an archetype that walked the world before history began. Whatever stood before her, it was impossible to grasp him in totality; he had as many aspects as nature, his form depending on the viewer and the occasion. The Erl-King, the dark side in which he had been locked and controlled, was now gone. 'What do I call you?' she whispered.

She trembled as he bent down, but when he brushed her forehead with the side of his thumb, the touch was gentle. 'Call me whichever name comes to your heart.'

She plucked a name from the long list. 'Cernunnos,' she said. His description made it seem a gentler aspect. And then she realised why he had seemed familiar: he was in the vision the mysterious young girl had shown her at the camp outside Bristol; the one for whom the girl had been searching. *The night to my day, the winter to my summer*, the girl had said. Twin aspects of the same powerful force.

He rose to his full height, still looking down on her. 'One face of the Green lives within you, another in one of your companions – their eyes, and yours, will open in time. As a Sister of Dragons, your path will be difficult, but my guidance will be with you until your blossoming. And in the harshest times, you may call for my aid. By this mark will you be known.'

He reached down and took her hand. She shuddered at his touch; his fingers didn't feel like fingers at all. A second later a bolt of searing pain scorched her palm. She screamed, but the agony subsided in an instant. Turning over her hand, she saw burned into it a circle which contained a design of what seemed to be interlocking leaves.

He was already turning away as he said, 'Seek me out in my Green Home.' He smiled and pointed to the owl which was circling majestically over their heads.

'What are you going to do now?' Ruth enquired reverentially.

'Once the Hunt has been summoned, it cannot retire without a soul.'

Ruth shivered at the awful meaning in his words. She began to protest, but his glance was so terrible the words caught in her throat.

He raised his head and sniffed the wind, and then, swifter than she could have imagined for his size, he loped off into the night; she was already forgotten, insignificant. A moment later the rain stopped and the wind fell, and when she looked up in the sky she saw the storm clouds sweeping away unnaturally to reveal a clear, star-speckled sky. She hung her head low, desperately trying to cope with the shock of an encounter with something so awesome it had transformed her entire existence. But when she closed her eyes, she could still see his face, and when she covered her ears, she could still hear his voice, and she feared she would never be the same again.

the Shark has pretty teeth

The moment Ruth disappeared with the Erl-King, Church thought all their lives were about to end. He was hacking blindly with the sword, watching the hounds crisp and fade, but seeing another replace each one he killed, realising Laura and Veitch were within an instant of being overwhelmed. Yet in that instant that the spear pierced the Erl-King, the Hunt seemed to freeze in its attack, and a second later the dogs were milling round in confusion, while the remaining riders were reining their horses back and retreating beyond the churchyard wall.

'She's done it,' he gasped, barely able to believe it.

Laura's eyes were filled with tears of fear and strain and blood was dripping from a score of wounds. 'I thought we were dead,' she moaned.

Veitch, who was just as injured, still held the iron bar high. 'Don't relax! They might just be gearing up for a new attack!' he barked.

Church knew he was right and returned to the alert, but he couldn't help calling out Ruth's name. When there was no reply, his heart sank.

They remained watching the Hunt for what seemed like hours, fighting against the exhaustion that racked them all. And then, as if in answer to a silent call, the riders simply turned their mounts and galloped away, the hounds baying behind them. Church looked to the wall in the corner of the graveyard; the glowering presence of Black Shuck was gone too.

Soon after, they heard a noise in the bracken and Ruth

emerged from the shadows, pale and shaking. As she clambered over the wall awkwardly, Church ran forward and grabbed her.

'You did it!' he said, unable to contain his relief. 'I could kiss you!'

'Well do it now, before I faint,' she gasped. And then she did.

After retrieving the battered tent, they lit a fire on the edge of the beach and enjoyed the calm which had followed the departure of the storm. Though not fully recovered, Shavi seemed well enough to talk, which raised their already high spirits. With the van's minimal medical kit, they tended to their wounds, and by the time the warmth had started to penetrate their bones, Ruth was ready to tell them what she had experienced.

Afterwards, they stared into the heart of the fire, trying to assimilate all the new information. 'So,' Ruth said, summing up, 'the way I see it is this: for some reason we don't yet know, the doors between Otherworld and here were opened. The Danann were preparing to return when the Fomorii launched something called the Wish-Hex, which I imagine as a kind of nuclear bomb in their terms. When the blast swept out, it took the majority of the Danann to some place from where they can't return on their own. But some of the Danann were corrupted by this Wish-Hex radiation and, against their basic nature, fell under the control of the Fomorii. The Erl-King . . . Cernunnos . . . was one of them. And some of the other creatures of Otherworld must have been affected too. I think this explains the Fabulous Beast that attacked Church and I near Stonehenge. Obviously they're linked to the earth spirit, power, whatever, so they wouldn't have done the Fomorii's bidding against us unless they were forced.'

'And a few of the Danann escaped entirely,' Church added. 'Like the woman in the Watchtower. But she didn't tell me the doors between the two worlds were already open and the Danann were planning on coming through. She implied everything happened because the Fomorii broke the *Covenant*.'

'Maybe she was spinning you a line,' Veitch said.

Church shifted uncomfortably. Could they really trust a race that was so far beyond them that their motivations were almost incomprehensible? And what did that mean for the woman in the Watchtower's promise that his prize for success in freeing her people would be knowledge of Marianne's fate? He had a sudden image of cynical, educated western explorers conning indigenous people out of land and resources for a few paltry beads.

'So it was like a first strike,' Veitch continued. 'The Fomorii tried to wipe out all the opposition in one swoop, leaving them free to do whatever horrible stuff they wanted once they got over here.'

'But what was he *like*?' Shavi asked shakily. He was in a sleeping bag, propped up by a pile of rucksacks. 'Did you get a sense of something divine?'

Ruth saw the excitement in his eyes, but it was an issue she didn't really want to face. 'I don't believe in God,' she replied, but her voice wavered enough that she knew he wouldn't let her leave it there. 'Yes, I have tailored my beliefs a little. I couldn't be a humanist in the face of something like that. There is an existence beyond our own, and he was certainly unknowable. But divine? You might consider him a god. Others might call him an alien, or a higher being.' She couldn't tell if it was Shavi's smile or her own unsureness after a lifetime of disbelief that irritated her the most.

'But do you not see? *This* is the question. The thing we spend all our lives searching for—'

'Oh, I don't know,' she snapped.

Church stepped in quickly. 'This isn't the time for intense theological debate—'

'No, it's the time for a party!' Veitch held out his arms in jubilation. 'We won!'

445

'That's poultry you're calculating,' Laura snorted. She finally seemed to be coming out of the fearful mood that had gripped her since the encounter in the graveyard.

'What do you mean?' Veitch threw a box of Elastoplast at her with a little more force than was necessary. 'We've found all the talismans. The Hunt has gone for good. And we're all alive!'

'As much as we ever were,' Laura said coolly.

'But we still don't know what to do with the talismans.' Ruth turned to Tom. 'When are you going to spill the beans?'

'When we're nearly where we need to be and there's no chance of anything going wrong,' he replied gruffly.

'At least we're well under the wire on the deadline,' Church said. 'More than three weeks to go. I never thought we'd do it so quickly.'

Despite their certain knowledge that their trials were not over, they slept more easily than they had done in weeks. When they awoke to the sound of seagulls, the sun was already up and the fire had burned out. They all laughed when a man out walking his dog avoided them by a wide margin, realising they must look like dirty itinerants with their matted hair and crumpled clothes.

The sea air was invigorating and by 8 a.m. they felt fully rested and ravenously hungry. Their supplies were low, so Veitch volunteered to walk up to the village to see if he could find something for breakfast. Church, Shavi and Tom said they wanted to come too, to stretch their legs, and once Ruth saw she would be left alone with Laura she opted to join them.

'You lot are freaks,' Laura gibed. 'Choosing physical exercise when you can lounge around and chill?' Tom convinced her she should sit in the van to guard the talismans so she could drive away at the first sign of trouble. Church borrowed Laura's small knapsack and tucked the Wayfinder inside it.

446

'I'm never letting this out of my sight again, whether we need it or not,' he said with a grin.

They strode up the leafy lane to the village with a lively step, despite the exertions of the night before.

'You know what?' Veitch said to Church ahead of the others. 'I never felt as alive as I do now.'

Church knew what he meant. 'It's like you don't fully appreciate life until you've faced up to death. I know that's a real cliché – all those adrenalin junkies doing dangerous sports say it all the time. But I never thought for a moment it might be true.'

'Makes you think how bad we're leading our lives, with awful office jobs and poxy suburban houses.' Veitch thought for a moment, then glanced at Church. 'Maybe we're on the wrong side.'

'What do you mean?'

'We're fighting to keep the things the way they always have been, right? What happens if that's not the best way? What if all this magic and shit is the way it really should be?'

Church recalled a conversation he had with Ruth soon after they first met about his dismay at the way magic seemed to have drained out of life. 'But what about all the death and suffering? People getting slaughtered, medical technology failing?'

'Maybe that's all part and parcel of having a richer life. What's better – big highs and deep lows or a flatline?'

Church smiled. 'I never took you for a philosopher, Ryan. But it all sounds a little Nietzchean to me.'

'You what?'

At that point Tom and Shavi caught up with them and introduced a vociferous religious debate. Veitch listened for a moment, then dropped back until he was walking just in front of Ruth. She eyed him contemptuously. 'Don't even think of talking to me.'

'I just wanted to say that was a really brave thing you did last night. You saved us all.'

'Do you really think I need your validation?'

Veitch went to reply, but her face was filled with such cold fury he knew it was pointless. He dropped back further and trailed behind them all.

The village shop was just opening up for the morning. Church and Shavi both picked up wire baskets and loaded them up with essentials. Just before they reached the checkout, a short, ruddy-faced man in his fifties with white hair and a checked flat cap rushed in, leaving the door wide open.

'Born in a barn, Rhys?' the woman behind the counter said.

Ruth, who was nearest, saw that he wasn't in the mood to banter. His face was flushed and he was breathless, as if he'd run all the way there. 'Did you hear about Dermott?' he gasped. The woman shook her head, suddenly intrigued. 'Missing, he is. They found his bike and a shoe up near the old Pirate's Lantern. Edith is in a right old state. She expected to find him in bed after the night shift and when he wasn't there she called the police.'

The woman and the man launched into a lurid conversation about what might have happened to their friend, but Ruth was no longer listening. She *knew* what had happened to him. The Hunt had found their sacrificial soul. Feeling suddenly sick, she dashed out of the shop and sat on the pavement, her head in her hands. How many people who had crossed their path had suffered? she wondered.

The others emerged soon after, laughing and joking, but she found it impossible to join in. Even when they won, there was a price to pay.

The knock at the passenger door window came just as Laura had settled out in the back, mulling over whether or not she had fallen for Church, hating herself for it. It was brief, friendly; not at all insistent. Deciding it was kids playing or the part-time car park attendant wanting to check their ticket, she decided she couldn't be bothered to answer it. But when it came again thirty seconds later, she sighed irritably and then scrambled over the back of the passenger seat. She was surprised to see a man who looked like a tramp in his shabby black suit. Yet his red brocade waistcoat added a note of flamboyance, as did his swept-back silver hair and sparkling eyes, which suggested a rich, deep humour. His skin had that weathered, suntanned appearance that only came from a life on the road, but his smile was pleasant enough.

Laura wound down the window. 'I haven't got any spare change. I like to sharpen it to throw at authority figures.'

'An admirable pursuit, my dear,' he said in a rich, theatrical voice. 'But I am not seeking financial remuneration. Although I must say I am a little down on my luck at the moment. Travelling great distances can be an expensive business. But that is by-the-by. In actual fact, I am seeking young Mr Churchill. Is he around, by any chance?'

Laura laughed in surprise. 'You know Church?'

'We had a wonderful evening of great humour, fantastic storytelling and, frankly, serious inebriation at a Salisbury hostel. Why, your generous friend even allowed me to drink his health into the night on his hotel tab. A wonderful fellow, and no mistaking.' Laura laughed at his *faux* dramatic persona, which seemed to have been culled from old films and older books, but his charm was unmistakable. 'And, as is his genial nature, he asked me to look him up the next time I was in the vicinity. And here I am!' He suddenly clapped his hands into a praying posture and half buried his face between them. 'Oh, forgive me! I have forgotten the very basis of good manners – the introduction. My name, my dear, is Callow.'

He held out his hand. Laura hesitated for a moment, then took it. 'Laura DuSantiago,' she said, aping his theatrical style.

'And will you allow me to rest a while in your vehicle until young Mr Churchill's return? I fear my legs are weary.'

Laura began to open the door, but then a thought jarred: Church didn't have the van when Callow would have met him, and there was no way he could have known they'd be there in an obscure Welsh village. She looked into his face suspiciously.

Callow smiled, said nothing. He was still holding on to her hand and his grip was growing tighter. 'Let go.' Her voice was suddenly hard and frosty.

She tried to drag her hand free, but Callow's strength belied his appearance. His smile now seemed grotesque. He forced his head through the open window and she was hit by a blast of foul breath. She realised he was trying to prevent anyone seeing what was happening. 'You bastard—'

Before she could say any more, Callow gently brushed his free hand across the back of her arm. She couldn't understand his action, until she saw a thin red line blossom where his fingers had passed. It seemed almost magical. She watched it in bemusement, trying to work out how he had done it. But the stinging shocked her alert and she caught hold of his wrist, forcing his hand up; a razor blade was surreptitiously lodged between his tightly held fingers. She had only a second to take it in when he suddenly let go of her hand and smashed his fist hard into her face. Laura saw stars, felt the explosion of pain, then pitched backwards across the seats in a daze. When she came around, Callow had the door open and was clambering in over her.

She savagely kicked a foot towards his groin, but instead it slammed into his thigh. He winced, but the smile never left his lips. His eyes, no longer sparkling, were fixed on her face.

Laura began to yell and struggle, but Callow made another pass with his hand, slashing the soft underside of her forearm, dangerously near to the exposed veins at her wrist. Before she could respond, he started sweeping his hand back and forth across her face. She threw her arms up to protect herself, feeling her flesh split and the wet warmth trickle down to her T-shirt. She yelled out, the agony of the moment multiplied by a sudden image of her mother showing her the bloodstained razor blade two years earlier. *Not again*, her mind roared.

The seriousness of her predicament hit her like a train; no one was going to save her; Callow had forced her into a position where she couldn't fight back; and just as she decided her only hope was to scream until someone came running, he hit her in the face again, grabbed her by the hair and bundled her over the back of the seats.

In her daze, she was vaguely aware of him dropping down beside her like a giant spider, and then he had gripped the razor blade between knuckle and thumb and was cutting into her in a frenzy. The last thing Laura saw before she blacked out was so horrible she couldn't tell if it was a hallucination brought on by the pain and the shock of her approaching death: his eyes seemed to be flooded with blood, as if every capillary in them had burst at once, and there was a subsequent movement under the skin around his orbits. As if something was crawling there.

Church was the first to notice the rear doors of the van hanging raggedly open. There was nothing inherently sinister in the image – Laura might simply have opened them to get some air to the suffocating interior – but his intuition sent a flood of icewater through his system. And then he was running, leaving the others chatting obliviously behind him. Bloody footprints led away from the van. Anxiety spurred him on, driving all rational thought from his mind. When he reached the doors and glanced in, his stomach turned.

The inside of the van looked like an abattoir. Blood was splattered up the walls and across the floor where Laura's pale, unmoving form lay. Her T-shirt was in tatters, the taunting legend *Jesus Saves* looming out at him, now appearing as if someone had attempted to scribble it out.

And the crate containing the talismans was gone.

The journey back to Tenby passed in a high-speed blur of madly overtaken vehicles, blaring horns and heart-stoppingly dangerous turns. They screamed into Accident & Emergency at the hospital on Trafalgar Road and Church ran in with Laura in his arms, her blood soaking through his shirt, leaving sickening spatter marks behind them like the spoor of some giant beast; despite his first impression, she was still alive, but in shock. If they had tried to deny it until then, the moment they saw the faces of the team of young doctors and nurses, they were left in no doubt as to the seriousness of her condition. She was whisked off behind flapping curtains, leaving them alone in an empty waiting room.

'But we'd won!' Veitch pleaded, his staring expression revealing the shock that played across all their minds. 'It's not fair.' It sounded pathetic and spoilt, but it was all he could think to say.

Ruth chewed her thumb knuckle. 'God, I hope she's going to be okay.' Church watched the regret and guilt play out on her face.

'But we'd won!' Veitch repeated, as if saying it enough times would make it come true.

'They selected the right time to attack,' Shavi noted, 'when our defences were down. Perfect, really.'

'She was attacked with a knife or a razor – you saw the cuts. That doesn't seem like the Fomorii,' Church said. 'Maybe it's just a random disaster – just some nut who crossed paths with us. The kind of thing that happens in life all the fucking time,' he added bitterly.

'Who specifically took the talismans?' Tom seemed more upset than Church would have expected. His eyes had been filled with tears from the moment they had discovered her; sometimes he could barely talk; at other times he shook with the ague which increasingly seemed to be afflicting him.

'All that bleedin' struggle. For nothing!' Veitch buried his head in his hands.

'This is probably not the best time to discuss it,' Tom began, 'but we need to get on the trail of the talismans. There's much more at stake here than—'

'No!' Church stared at him angrily, but all he could see was Marianne. 'Nothing is bigger than people! Individuals. People you love. They deserve your time and attention and passion. Not a world that couldn't care less if it went to hell in a handcart!'

Tom made as if to argue, then looked away.

'I don't care about anything else right now. I just want to see my friend pull through. If you haven't got friends, if you haven't got people you love, you've got nothing.'

Veitch stared at Church as if he was seeing him in a new light, then nodded thoughtfully.

Just then Tom put his head in his hands and started to sob silently. The others stared at him in surprise. Ruth slid up next to him and put a comforting arm around his shoulders, but he seemed inconsolable.

Veitch's shoulders were weighted with desolation. 'What the hell are we going to do now?'

They were allowed to see her at noon. Against the crisp white sheets of the bed she looked uncommonly frail, like a sickly child; they barely recognised her. Her dyed-blonde hair was matted and unkempt, her skin like frost, her body somehow thinner and more angular than they remembered. Pads had been taped to the left side of her face. A couple of tubes snaked into her; she was dead to the world.

'We sedated her,' the doctor explained. 'It was for the best, after the shock.'

'Is she going to be okay?' Church asked.

The doctor didn't look too sure of his answer. 'Physically, I suppose. We gave her some blood, stitched the deepest wounds, bound the others. But . . .' – he shrugged – 'you know, a razor attack. It's sick, disgusting. When I see the mess it leaves, I can't understand how anybody could be so twisted as to carry it out.' He paused, swallowed. 'And her face . . . she's going to have some bad scarring on that left side. You saw her back, her arms. She looks like a jigsaw. The psychological scars will be the hardest to heal. I noticed the old scar tissue . . .' He looked from one face to the other, hoping for an explanation.

'She's suffered before,' Church said simply.

The doctor nodded as if that was answer enough. 'That makes it worse. She's been bitten twice, as it were.'

'When can we take her with us?' Tom asked tentatively. He succeeded in ignoring the others' annoyed stares.

'Oh, well, a few days. She needs lots of rest, nothing too strenuous. I can put you in touch with the counselling service.'

They thanked him for what he had done, but said nothing further until he had left the room. Then Church turned on Tom. 'Christ, if she were dead you'd have us dumping her at the side of the road!' When Tom didn't seem too shocked by this allegation, Church became even more angry.

'You may not be so outraged when you see the way things will be in a few short months.' He seemed to be struggling with the conversation, dragging up each word individually, but some of his old frostiness had returned. 'If you do not pursue the talismans now, you'll be making the decision to give up the world, civilisation, everything. Is that what you are prepared to do?'

Church looked away, angry that Tom was making him face up to it, when all he wanted to think about was Laura.

'She's going to be fine,' Tom continued. 'You heard the doctor. But we can't afford to leave it another day. The trail could be lost by then.'

The room was filled by a long, hanging silence and then Veitch said, 'I'd really like to find who did this to her.'

'You heard the doctor. She's in no state to be moved,'

Church protested. 'What happens if she gets an infection in the wounds? Tears one of them open? We could be putting her life at risk.'

'A decision needs to be taken now,' Tom said insistently.

Church saw all eyes were on him. 'Why are you looking at me?' he raged. They looked away uncomfortably, but the answer to his question was obvious; no one else was going to speak out.

Tom stepped in front of him and rested a hand on his shoulder; there was an honest paternalism in his face. 'It's your call,' he said softly.

Church had the sudden, terrible feeling that he would be damned whatever he decided.

Veitch managed to find a wheelchair and they lifted Laura into it after a heated discussion about the status of the drips and whether they should remove them; one appeared to be a rehydrating solution, while the other was a painkiller with some kind of electronically timed dose. In the end, they decided to wheel both of the drips out behind her, still attached. A blanket was hastily thrown over her legs to try to hide the fact she obviously wasn't in any condition to be moved. If they were stopped, they would never be allowed to take her out, and would probably pay a heavy price for trying to kidnap a patient, so they hurried through the corridors, desperately following a roundabout route that took them away from the busiest areas. The alarm was raised only at the last minute by a furious nurse, when they were forced to pass through reception to where they had abandoned the van.

They made a makeshift bed of sleeping bags on the floor of the van for Laura and tried to secure the drip trolleys with clothes, but every time Shavi went round a corner they fell over with a clatter.

After the euphoria of the morning, the mood in the van was dismal. Suddenly it seemed like everything was turning sour and whatever they did would not be able to make it right. Church sat on the floor next to Laura, watching her face for any sign of awakening, or of her condition deteriorating. He hated himself for the decision he had had to make, and for the fact that he had no choice. And he wanted to yell at them all that he wasn't up to the job of being leader and making enormous choices that people's lives depended on; he had been so unperceptive that he had allowed his own girlfriend to die, hadn't even realised she had been murdered. Sometimes he wondered if it would be better for all of them if he simply walked away and left them to it.

The Wayfinder pointed them north-east out of Tenby. Shavi kept just within the speed limit in any area where it was likely there might be traffic police and floored the accelerator at all other times. Although the lantern suggested a route which took them across country, after their experience in Builth Wells they agreed it would be best to avoid the open Welsh countryside and instead keep to the main roads. They picked up the busy A40 just outside Carmarthen and followed it all the way to Ross-on-Wye, then cut across to the motorway. There the Wayfinder resumed its northwards pointing.

'Whoever has the talismans is travelling fast,' Shavi noted. 'And they obviously have a definite direction in mind.'

'Here, why don't you do that thing you do? You know, with the mushrooms and the trance and everything? We could find out where they're going and try and head them off at the pass,' Veitch suggested.

Shavi fixed his gaze on the road ahead, his face suddenly emotionless. 'No,' he replied simply.

The sky grew an angry red, then shifted through various shades of purple as they trundled north through the West Midlands conurbation, the flat countryside of Staffordshire and Cheshire and then over the Manchester Ship Canal, where the traffic seemed as busy as if nothing were wrong.

By the time they had passed Lancaster and the proliferation of signs for the Lakes, darkness had fallen.

In the back, Church, Ruth and Tom sat quietly around Laura's unmoving form while Veitch and Shavi found security in a rambling discourse on the mundane, punctuated by long, introspective silences.

'I've never seen this much of the country,' Veitch mused. 'Barely been out of London before. The odd trip to Southend to see me nan. Never north of Watford.'

'Beautiful, is it not?' Shavi noted thoughtfully. 'Every part of it. And not just the parts you expect to be beautiful, like the downs and the heaths. Cooling towers seen in the right light are golden. Once I was on a train coming out of Derby and we passed through a terrible industrial wasteland that they were in the process of turning into some civic site. There were heaps of dirt and weeds and huge pools of polluted water. And then, just for one moment, the quality of the light reflected the grey clouds off the pools and the whole landscape turned silver. It was so wonderful it took my breath away. We have lost sight of that wonder in the every day.'

'Yeah, I suppose. But have you ever been to Becton?' Veitch thought for a moment, then looked at him suspiciously. 'You don't look like a queen.'

Shavi returned his gaze, a faint smile on his lips. 'I do not like labels.'

'Well, you are, aren't you? A shirtlifter?'

'I prefer to consider myself polymorphously perverse.'

'What's that bollocks?'

'It means I take my pleasure from wherever and whatever I please. We have a limited time to indulge ourselves. Why limit yourself to just one sex?'

Veitch snorted, stared out the passenger window.

Shavi stifled a laugh at his Victorian values. 'What is wrong?'

'Makes me sick what you people do.'

'Do not think about it, then. I will not force you.'

'You better not try it on with me.'

'You are not my type.'

Veitch snapped round indignantly. 'Why not?'

'You are just not.'

Veitch turned back to the passenger window, muttering under his breath.

At that moment, Laura stirred in the back. Church leaned forward anxiously and for a moment the tense silence in the van was unbearable. Gradually, her eyes flickered open, burst with momentary panic as they tried to establish her situation, then calmed when they saw Church leaning over her.

'Shit, this hurts,' she said in a fragile voice.

'Take it easy,' Church whispered, 'you've been through a lot.'

His heart ached when he saw the terrible memories suddenly play out across her features. Her hand jerked up to the pads that covered her left side. 'My face,' she said desolately. Her eyes filled with tears that brimmed over on to her cheeks. She clamped her lids shut so they wouldn't see her weakness.

Church took her hand, thinking she would shake it off, but she held on tightly. 'We're here with you,' he said gently.

'God, nobody's going to want to look at me.' Her voice was filled with such awful pain that he felt queasy. In her despair he could see through all her defences and the honesty was almost too much to bear, like someone had opened a door on to a searchlight from a pitch black room.

'Don't be silly. You're with friends here.'

She snorted a bitter laugh. 'Friends? You all hate me.' Church could hear the irrational, overly despairing ring of the drugs in her words.

'We'd stand by you through thick and thin.' Church looked round in surprise as Ruth leaned in next to him.

'Hey. Miss Frosty,' Laura said weakly. 'Do I smell the stink of pity?'

'No. That's Tom.'

Laura lifted her head as much as she could then let it drop

once she had seen his indignant expression. She let out a wheezy laugh. 'Old git. Nice to see you. Bet you thought there was someone actually going to die before you.'

'You need to get some rest,' Tom replied acidly. 'A week or two, maybe. We could turn up the drip—'

'How do you feel?' Church asked. When he looked into her face he felt something flash between them; a brief light in her eyes, the faintest hint of a smile; it sang through the air and he felt a shiver run down his spine.

He could see she felt it too; she smiled at him, then it slipped away uncomfortably, as if she couldn't understand the emotions sweeping through her. 'Like I've been on the bacon slicer,' she said.

'They did quite a number on you. Do you know who it was?'

Her brow furrowed as she struggled to remember. 'Some tramp. He said you knew him.' A long pause as the name surfaced. 'Callow.'

'Callow?' Church and Ruth said in simultaneous surprise.

'He's just a scrounging no-mark!' Church looked at Ruth for some explanation. 'He was in Salisbury. What's he doing here?'

'He knew where we were,' Laura said. 'There's no way he could have found us by accident.'

'Shit! What the hell's going on?' Church felt an impotent rage sweep through him. 'When we find the bastard, I'll kill him.'

'There was something else . . .' Laura's voice almost broke from the strain. 'I remember . . . His eyes turned red, like they were filling with blood. And there was something moving under his skin. He wasn't human . . .'

Her voice trailed away and the van filled with silence until Veitch called back, 'We've got to pull in at the next services for some petrol.'

They swung into the sweeping drive of Tebay Services, past clustering trees that seemed too dense and frightening, but

459

the cafeteria was a welcoming oasis of light blazing in the night. Enormous picture windows looked out over the bleak high country of the northern Lakes, the stark interior lamps casting illumination over a cold duck pond and wind-blasted scrub. Church noticed the breathtaking view and thought briefly how pleasant it must have been in summers past; now it seemed too close to the dangerous, deserted country-side.

'I've got to stretch my legs,' he said. 'Get some tea. We should take ten-minute breaks in twos. Who's with me?' Ruth volunteered, but Tom, who had been poring over the book of maps with a pocket torch, overruled her rudely.

They found a seat in the cafeteria next to the windows looking out over the impenetrably dark landscape. There were a few other travellers, scattered around, as if they didn't dare sit near to anyone else, just in case.

'It's changing quickly now, isn't it?' Church stared out into the night morosely. 'I wonder how long we've got before everything falls apart.'

'Not long.' Tom sipped his hot chocolate thoughtfully. 'But there's still time for you to make a difference.'

'Is that irony? We've lost everything we've fought for, and Laura . . . Christ, I can't believe that.'

Tom looked away for a long moment. When Church glanced up to see why he was so quiet, he saw sweat standing out on Tom's brow and shivers rippling though him, as if someone were shaking his shoulders.

'What is wrong with you?' Church said with a lack of sympathy he instantly regretted. 'Have you got some kind of illness you're not telling us about?'

Tom took a moment to compose himself, then said hoarsely, 'None of your business.' He took another drink of his chocolate and continued as if nothing had happened. 'Callow is obviously working for one or the other of the Fomorii tribes – as a backup to the Wild Hunt for Calatin in case of their failure, or as a chancer for Mollecht, hoping to snatch the talismans during the confusion of any of our conflicts with Calatin's agents.'

'He seemed fine when we met him in Salisbury.'

Tom shrugged. 'Perhaps they got to him after then. That's immaterial. The point is to reach him before he hands over the talismans to whomever controls him. And I believe I know how to do that.'

'How?'

'In the current climate, the Lake District will be one of the most dangerous areas in the country. Lakes are liminal zones, as I told you, doorways between here and there, and with so many lakes the place will be overpopulated with all the misbegotten creatures of Otherworld. Certainly a place where it's too threatening to travel at night.'

Church sipped his tea, wincing at the bitterness. 'Go on.'

'That would also make it a prime spot for the Fomorii. Callow *must* be travelling there. If we knew where he was going we could intercept him.'

'But we don't know where he's going.'

'There's a place called Loadpot Hill overlooking Ullswater. It has always held a peculiar attraction for the Fomorii. They'll make the handover somewhere near there.'

'How do you know that?'

'I just do.'

Church searched his face; as usual, there was something Tom was not telling him, but he had learned to trust Tom's silences, if not to appreciate them.

'There are plenty of other things out there beyond the Fomorii, so it will still be dangerous for Callow to travel over the fells at night. I would guess he will probably take the best-lit route rather than the most obvious. We might be able to beat him to the road to the hill where we can cut him off.'

'By the dangerous, direct route? You expect me to sell that to the others?'

'At this stage we have to take risks.'

Tom headed off to the toilet, leaving Church alone to finish his coffee. For some reason he hadn't been able to get warm for the last couple of days, even though he was wearing a T-shirt, shirt, sweater and jacket buttoned tightly. He hoped he wasn't coming down with something.

Despite Tom's claims, the first mile or so from the motorway into the heart of the Lake District was uneventful. Although they saw no other traffic, they passed houses with lights gleaming through chinks in drawn curtains and caught the occasional whiff of smoke from their hearths. But then it was as if they had passed an invisible boundary. Odd, lambent lights moved across the fells that provided the district with its magnificent backdrop, and as they travelled down from the heights, will o' the wisps danced deep in the thick forests that crowded the road. Things were caught in the corner of their eyes which they never saw full on, but could tell instinctively were inhuman. And at one point something flying that seemed half-bat, half-human baby was caught briefly in the headlights before slamming into the side of the van with a hefty clang and a sickeningly childish shriek.

'Don't stop for anything,' Tom said as if any of them had entertained the idea. 'Keep your foot to the floor.'

They all remained silent, eyes fixed on the scenery flashing past, apart from Laura, who was drifting in and out of consciousness; at times she seemed so delirious Church feared seriously for her wellbeing.

But the short cut Tom suggested seemed to work; when Church next checked the Wayfinder, it was clearly indicating the talismans were behind them. Finally Tom ordered Shavi to pull over on a shadowy layby beside the lonely road which wound its way around a hillside halfway up the slope. 'You sure?' Veitch said, peering into the thick woods on both sides. 'Why is this place any safer than anywhere else we've just driven through?'

Tom shrugged. 'I never said it was. But this will be the

462

best place to wait to intercept him.' He motioned away to the west. 'Loadpot Hill is over there. This is the nearest road to it and it ends a little further up the way.'

Veitch didn't seem convinced. 'We can't see anybody sneaking up on us here.'

'If we keep the doors locked, we can drive off if anything comes near,' Ruth suggested hopefully.

Tom shook his head. 'We need to keep watch at the bend in the road. We can pull the van out to block the road at the last minute before he sees us.'

'And you think somebody's going to volunteer to go out there on look-out?' Veitch said.

'We should all go,' Church said. 'Safety in numbers.'

'I should stay here, ready to pull out when the car comes,' Shavi said.

'There will be plenty of time to get back and behind the wheel when we see the headlights,' Tom replied.

'What about Laura?' Ruth stroked a couple of stray hairs from her forehead.

'She'll be fine here with the doors locked.' Church turned to Tom. 'How will we know his vehicle?'

'It'll be the only one on the road in this place at this time.'

'You have all the answers.' Church became even more aware of the chill once the engine was switched off. He wished he had the sword with him. As he opened the rear doors and jumped out, he felt as defenceless as if he had both hands tied together.

The others followed him silently, with Veitch on his guard at the rear, his eyes constantly searching. They took up position at the bend in the road, although it was impossible to stand still for too long; wherever they were, their backs were to the dark, brooding trees, which made them all feel uncomfortable. Several times they turned with the unmistakable feeling that someone was just behind them.

Tom had been correct; the vantage point allowed them a clear view of anyone approaching. Veitch repeatedly complained they were too far from the van until Ruth threatened to shove him in front of Callow's vehicle if he didn't shut up.

Despite the danger, Church felt a tingle of wonder when he opened himself up to their surroundings. He had never experienced a night so silent – no drone of cars or distant rumble of planes, and the air had the clear, fresh tang of the pine trees, as if all the pollution had been drained from it. It was so intoxicating it seemed unnatural – an irony that was not lost on him – and he wondered if it was another by-product of the change.

Their conversation dried up quickly, until the only sound that punctuated the silence was the stamping of their feet to keep warm. They never lowered their guard for a second, even though they kept watch for the better part of an hour. But instead of getting used to their situation, the atmosphere of menace increased gradually until it became so claustrophobic Ruth complained that she felt like being sick.

'Tell you what, I could shoot his windscreen out,' Veitch suggested. Church could tell from the timbre of his voice that he was only speaking because he couldn't bear the now-unpleasant silence any longer.

'Guns are so symptomatic of the worst of what went before,' Shavi said. 'They do not have a place in this new age. I feel the more we rely on the old ways, the more likely we are to bring something terrible down on our heads.'

'What, *more* terrible?' Church said.

'I'm sick of people moaning about how bad guns are,' Veitch said. 'What, you think we should go back to swords? Have you seen what damage they can do?'

'Have you?' Ruth snapped.

After a pause, Veitch replied, 'No, but I can guess.'

Ruth was about to attack this line of reasoning when she suddenly did a double take at Tom. 'You're bleeding,' she said.

Blood was trickling from both his nostrils. Tom dabbed

at it with his fingertips and then examined them curiously.

'Hang on, can you hear something?' Veitch began to look around anxiously, but the night seemed as silent as ever.

Church became aware of the unpleasant expression on Tom's face. It didn't seem to be a reaction to his nose-bleed; more as if he were struggling with some terribly disconcerting thoughts. 'Are you okay?' he asked. 'Is it the illness again?'

Tom looked at him with an inexplicable expression of such horror Church fell instantly silent.

'There is something,' Veitch said insistently. 'Listen!'

'Will you shut up!' Ruth snapped. 'There's nothing! You're just winding everybody up!'

Tom choked, raised his hand to his mouth. Church noticed with alarm there were now trickles of blood at the corners of his eyes, and another seeping out of his left ear. 'Jesus!' he said. 'What's wrong with you?'

'Wait!' Shavi said. 'Ryan is right. There is something.' The two of them were looking with concern all around.

Ruth glared at both of them, then looked to Church for support. 'Is everybody going mad?'

Church turned to the van, thinking of Laura. It did seem too far away. 'Maybe we should move back that way a little,' he suggested.

Tom pitched forward, clutching his head. Blood spattered on to the road surface. Kneeling like a dog, he retched and hawked as if something was stuck in his throat.

Anxiety transfixed Veitch's face. Ignoring Tom, he gripped Church's shoulders. 'Let's get out of here. Something bad is going to happen.'

'I agree,' Shavi said.

But Church was already crouching down next to Tom, one arm around his shoulders. 'We have to get help for him. This looks serious.'

'Church?'

Ruth's quizzical, faintly unnerved voice caught Church's

attention more than anything the others could have done. He looked up into her face, now pale and troubled.

'I *can* hear it,' she said edgily.

And then he could too. It was reedy, high-pitched, almost beyond the audible range, jarring in its intensity. A queasy sensation bubbled in his stomach. It reminded him of the cry of sea birds, yet continuous, and with a vague, uneasy human quality that was intensely disturbing.

'What *is* that?' he said, rising to his feet, Tom now forgotten.

'Look.' Shavi had walked ahead of them a few paces to peer into the trees on the upward slope. 'Is there something in there?'

'I said let's get out of here!' Veitch snapped.

Shavi was correct; shadows seemed to be flitting amongst the trees, oddly lighter in quality than the surrounding gloom.

Tom made another stomach-churning retching sound deep in his throat. Droplets of blood were flying everywhere.

'Why won't he shut up?' Ruth cried uncharitably. Her fearful thoughts played out on her face.

We should run, Church thought, but the shadows' strange movements and the shrieking sound that was emanating from them were so hypnotic he was rooted to the spot.

The shapes were sweeping down the slope towards them across a wide arc. And as they drew closer they appeared grey and oddly translucent, as if they were filled with smoke, finding consistency only in their proximity to whomever was viewing them. Church caught his breath when he realised there were scores of them. Their movements were strange and jarring, almost a dance amongst the trees, twisting and fluttering like paper in a breeze. Church couldn't understand how they could have substance and no substance at the same time.

And then as they drew closer still, Church could make out their grey faces; they were women, quite beautiful in their way, but with hollow cheeks, eyes staring, unblinking, mouths

466

frozen wide to make that terrible scream. They were wearing billowing shrouds and their wild hair streamed behind them. Church, Ruth, Shavi and Veitch were frozen in horror.

'What are they?' Ruth asked hoarsely.

'The Baobhan Sith.'

Church was shocked to hear the croaking words come from Tom's mouth. He had rolled on to his back and was staring crazily at the sky.

'The Baobhan Sith?' Church recalled the sharp pang of fear he felt as he lay under the quilt in the Salisbury hotel room while the unseen thing prowled around the room. Then he realised Tom had uttered the name without seeing. Terrible understanding gelled in his mind. 'You knew this was going to happen! You led us here on purpose!' he shouted at Tom with dismay.

Tom made to reply, but all that came from his mouth was a gout of blood.

It seemed to break the spell, just as the Baobhan Sith were on the verge of emerging from the trees. As one, Church, Veitch and Shavi turned and bolted towards the van.

Still caught in the horror of the moment, Ruth simply backed across the road. For an instant reality seemed to hang in the air, and then suddenly everything erupted in too-fast speed. The Baobhan Sith burst from the trees, now a monstrous hunting pack. The sharp retort of Veitch's gun came and went ridiculously. Most of the shades swarmed round and descended on the fleeing figures of Church, Shavi and Veitch, screeching with an animal ferocity. Although their forms still seemed insubstantial, Ruth saw them latch on to her friends with hideously cruel fingers. And then they seemed to sweep up, as if they were lighter than air, and their mouths seemed to open wider than was possible, revealing rows of needle-sharp teeth. The last thing she saw before she tore her gaze away were the heads swooping down, jaws about to snap shut on her friends' exposed necks.

The remaining Baobhan Sith were coming for her. They

bypassed Tom as if he were not there and danced across the road. Ruth continued to back away hurriedly until she was moving into the trees on the downward slope; she had to escape so she could find some way to save the others. The ground fell away sharply. Her heels kicked, didn't find any purchase. And then, as the shriek of the Baobhan Sith seemed to fill everything, she was falling, turning over and over as she plummeted down the slope, feeling the branches and brambles tear at her skin, rolling faster and faster until everything became a blur of fear and pain.

flight

Ruth came to a rough halt against a drystone wall, knocking the air from her lungs and stunning her for the briefest moment. She had leaf mould in her nostrils and mouth and myriad scratches across her face and hands. Coughing and spluttering, she scrambled to her feet, the terror rising within her as images of the Baobhan Sith burst like fireworks in her mind. Desperately, she glanced back up the slope. There was no sign of them in pursuit, but she could hear the haunted shrieks floating down through the budding branches. It wouldn't be long before they found her.

The thought of having to flee through the wild countryside filled her with dread. Her best option would be to find somewhere secure to hide, but how easy would that be? Glancing round, she discovered she was resting against the garden wall of a tiny cottage. It appeared ancient; the thatch came down to just above the ground floor windows, which were barely larger than portholes. What walls were visible appeared as thick as the length of her arm, to keep out the bitter winter winds. It was surrounded by a neat garden containing a handful of fruit trees that were so gnarled and twisted with age they looked like old men gossiping on a street corner. But Ruth was warmed to see a golden light glowing behind the curtains and the air was scented with the aroma of woodsmoke rising from the large stone chimney.

The shriek of the Baobhan Sith seemed unpleasantly near – she didn't have time to weigh her options. Cursing as she cracked her knees and shins, she clambered over the wall, dropped into a bed of herbs and ran round the side of the house to the front door. It was oak and so weathered it probably hadn't been replaced since the cottage was built. A cast-iron bootscraper stood next to it, alongside a broom made of a branch with twigs bound for bristles.

Although she felt frantic, Ruth knocked on the door as calmly as she could, so as not to frighten whoever lived there. The inhabitant must have heard her run round the house, for the curtain at the window next to the door twitched in an instant; Ruth caught a glimpse of glittering eyes in a woman's face before the curtains fell back.

But still no one came to the door. The nerve-jangling cry of the Baobhan Sith sounded just beyond the garden wall on the other side of the cottage now. There wasn't time to flee anywhere else.

Ruth hammered on the door with all her strength and this time it did swing open. The woman was in her late fifties, her hair long and silver and tied at the back with a black ribbon. Her cheeks bloomed with the broken capillaries of life in the cold Lake District gales. She stood several inches shorter than Ruth, but she was just as slim and elegant. For a split-second she searched Ruth's face, and what she found there must have been agreeable, for she grabbed Ruth's wrist tightly to drag her inside, slamming the door behind her. Three iron bolts shot across an instant later.

Ruth sucked in a lungful of air. 'There's something out there—'

'I know what's out there,' the woman barked. 'Come away from the door!'

They were inside the woman's sitting room, which was spartanly decorated. It was lusciously warm from a log fire banked up in the wide stone hearth. A cracked and aged dresser stood against one wall and a similarly ancient dining table against the other, on which were arrayed a collection of corked pot containers; the contents of a few – seeds and dried herbs – were scattered around. Other herbs hung in bunches from the rafters creating a heady, perfumed atmosphere. A rush mat lay on the flags near the fire, but the only other item of furniture was a heavy wooden armchair with a floral cushion right next to the hearth. A sandy cat was curled up next to it.

'We could barricade ourselves upstairs. Try to keep them out till dawn—' Ruth began.

'They won't even know we're here if we don't draw attention to ourselves.' The woman watched Ruth suspiciously, her eyes still glittering in the light of the fire. 'What are you doing around these parts at this time? It's no longer safe to travel by night – nor even by day, really.'

'I didn't have any choice,' Ruth replied. The full force of what had happened hit her and she rested against the back of the armchair, placing one hand over her eyes to try to clear the image of the Baobhan Sith attacking Church, Shavi and Veitch. When she'd blinked away the tears a moment later, she brought her hand down and noticed the woman was staring at it intently.

She suddenly lurched forward and grabbed Ruth's wrist, turning her arm over so the palm was uppermost. The mark Cernunnos had scorched into her flesh was revealed in the firelight.

'Goddess!' The suspicion drained from the woman's face and was replaced by awe. When she looked up into Ruth's face, her features were now open and smiling. 'These are very strange times. Sit! I'll brew up a pot.'

'There's no time!' Ruth protested.

'There's always time. I've cast a spell of protection on this place. It's invisible to any of those hideous things crawling around out there these days. But we can't go out until the ones after you have gone or they'll have us in a moment. Times when you can relax are few – grab hold of them!'

Ruth reluctantly allowed herself to be pressed into the armchair, but her thoughts were in chaos and she felt a desperate urge to run away, even though there was nowhere she could go. The heat from the fire was comforting after

471

the attack, but still she felt like crying after the strain of it all; everything seemed to be going wrong; Tom betraying them was one blow too much.

'It's all a bloody awful mess!' she said, her voice breaking. 'No. I've got to help them!' She jumped up and ran to the window. Outside, the Baobhan Sith roamed, their wild eyes ranging over the vicinity. Ruth knew she wouldn't get five yards from the door. Dejectedly, she trudged back to the fireside.

'Cheer up, lovie. It's always darkest.' The woman hung a blackened kettle over the fire, then placed two mugs, a strainer, a tin of tea leaves and some milk and sugar on a tray with the pot. 'I'm Nina, by the way.'

'Ruth.' She rested her head on the back of the chair and closed her eyes. 'What's all this about a *spell of protection*?' she added wearily. 'It seems like everybody can do something they shouldn't these days.'

Nina laughed. 'You're right there. I spent ten years studying the Craft, working on spells and rituals. Sometimes they worked, or seemed to work, in a halfhearted way, but very rarely. It always seemed more like wishful thinking on my part. And then just after Christmas it was like I'd had an electric charge! I could do things I never dreamed of! It was . . .' – she laughed again – '. . . magic!'

'Everything's changed,' Ruth said morosely.

'Oh, indeed. At first I thought it was just me, like after all this time I'd suddenly chanced on the knack. But then I saw what was happening all around and I knew it wasn't me at all. It was the world.' She noticed the gloom in Ruth's face. 'It's not all bad – just different. The magic is back. How it probably was centuries ago. That's a cause for celebration.'

'You really can do stuff?'

'Not great, world-changing things. Just the skills we were always reputed to have. Controlling the weather, communing with the birds and animals, making potions that work. It's

472

the link, you see. With nature. It's solid now.' She pointed at Ruth's hand. 'But you should know. You're one of us. Greater than me, certainly. That's the mark of the Horned Hunter, consort of the Mother Goddess.'

Ruth shook her head. 'I don't know what you're talking about. I've never been into all this.'

There was an unmistakably dismissive note in Ruth's voice, but Nina wasn't offended. 'Your brain may not know, but it's there inside you. Or you wouldn't have received the mark. You're a wisewoman, no mistake. You just need to learn and apply yourself.'

'With all due respect, I can't see myself doing, you know, whatever it is you do. I'm a lawyer.'

Nina laughed. 'What, you think only embittered old crones like me get to learn the Craft?'

'I didn't mean—'

Nina silenced her with a goodnatured wave of her hand. 'The only qualification is being a woman. And probably having a natural aptitude for the necessary skills. Take me – I wasn't always how you see me. I just happened to like the traditional lifestyle.' She motioned around the room. 'I used to be in medical supplies. Worked all the hours given to build up the business. Then my Ralph was taken suddenly. Brain tumour. He didn't suffer long.' She fell silent for a moment, the weight of memories adding age to her face. 'After that, work didn't seem important. There wasn't much of my life that did.' She smiled sadly. 'It's terrible, isn't it, that it takes a tragedy to point out that all the things we trick ourselves into relying on in our lives have no substance? We have to have something to believe in – it's the way we're made. But once work and the family disappear, you start to wonder what there *really* is to have faith in. I fell into the old religion. At first it just made me feel good. Then it started to feel right. Now I can't imagine being without it.'

Ruth watched her as she used a teacloth to lift the hissing kettle from the fire. She warmed the pot, then put in the tea leaves, adding a pinch of spice from a dish on the side. 'My own special recipe,' she said conspiratorially. 'Gives it a little kick. It's how they drink it in the Middle East.'

'What's it like to be able to make things happen?' Ruth asked as she took her mug. 'It's the kind of thing you always dream about as a child.'

'Well, it's not like any of that fairybook stuff,' Nina replied a little brusquely. 'You can't just wish and make things happen. It's all about controlling energy – the invisible energy of the world. I always saw it as a science that the physicists haven't got round to explaining yet.' She smiled at the curiosity in Ruth's face.

As the fire blazed and as they sipped their spiced tea, Nina explained about the Craft while Ruth attempted to batten down her anxiety and desperation; she wanted to be doing something, not listening to old stories. When Nina mentioned the triple deity of mother, maiden, crone, though, Ruth's heart quickened as she connected with her visions of the mysterious girl.

She related her experience to Nina who smiled and said, 'See. You were called long before you realised. And probably a long time before that.'

'There was an owl—'

Nina nodded towards the cat on the hearth. 'We all have our friends.'

Ruth stared into her tea, trying to divine her feelings about what she was hearing. The stubborn streak of scepticism her father had instilled in her as a girl was still there, but her instinct was beginning to shout louder.

'Look, this is all too much to get my head round right now. I can't stay here talking. There's got to be something—'

She made to rise, but Nina stopped her with a hand on her thigh. 'I might be able to help you.'

'How?'

She thought for a moment, then said, 'We can fly up, see what has happened to your friends, get the lie of the land.

Then, once you have the knowledge, you'll be able to decide on your course of action.'

'Fly?' Ruth said incredulously. 'What? On broomsticks?'

'No, no!' Nina said sharply. 'Stop falling for the old propaganda, please! I'm showing you how it really is.' She paused, and added with a smile, 'But actually yes, on broomsticks, only not the way you think!'

Ruth sat back down. She covered her eyes for a moment, suddenly aware she might break down in tears if she allowed herself to think about her situation too closely. 'So you're probably the only person in the area who can help me and I ended up here by chance. I don't like coincidences.'

'There are no coincidences. Once you understand there's an invisible world, you can see that.' Nina took her hand and pulled her to her feet again. 'If you really want this, you will have to do exactly what I say.'

'I'll do anything to save my friends.'

Nina nodded understandingly. 'Come, then. Take off your clothes.'

When Ruth hesitated, Nina made hurrying gestures, then turned to the table and went along the rows of jars until she found the one she wanted. Ruth undressed a little unsurely, but Nina just pulled her dress over her head. She was naked beneath it. Her breasts had long lost their firmness and she had shaved off her pubic hair, but she walked around completely unselfconsciously. She opened a cupboard in one corner and pulled out a broom like the one Ruth had seen outside the front door.

As Ruth stepped out of her knickers, she was shocked to see what appeared to be a tiny little man slowly lowering himself upside down from the chimney to peer at her curiously. Ruth pointed and yelled out, 'What's that?' at which point a look of dismay crossed its face and it disappeared from where it had come.

Nina seemed as unconcerned as if it were the cat who had entered. 'One of the brownies,' she said distractedly. 'They

475

seem to have settled in here. They help me out quite a lot with the cleaning at night.'

While Ruth stared at the chimney unsurely, Nina gently pushed her back into the chair, then sat down before her on the rush mat, the broom and jar beside her.

'As with all these things, you must place your trust in me and always do as I say,' Nina stressed.

Ruth nodded.

Nina opened the jar and dipped in two fingers. When she removed them they were covered in a greenish cream, which she proceeded to smear over the end of the broom handle. 'A little hemlock, some monkshood – sacred to Hecate – a little thornapple and a touch of belladonna.' Then she lay back, opened her legs wide and placed the handle against her vagina. 'It would be easier if you could help me,' she said, 'if you can overcome your embarrassment.'

'I'm not putting *that* inside me!' Ruth said in horror.

Nina sighed and sat up. 'The salve has an antiseptic quality, if that's what you're worried about.'

'That's not all I'm worried about! It's disgusting!'

'Let's not be prudish,' Nina cautioned like a school ma'am. 'This is the way it's been done traditionally. When those who weren't practising heard about us riding our brooms, they got the wrong end of the stick, as it were. The vaginal walls absorb the active drug much more effectively. I could insert it in your anus if that suits you better,' she added acidly.

'I don't need a drug trip! I need help!'

'That's what I'm doing!' Nina said with irritation. 'It's not just a drug trip. The mind and body are separate entities. The drug in the salve enables our brain to free our spirit-selves so we can fly over the countryside, see things, hear things, gain knowledge, then return with it to our bodies. All the shamans and the magicmen and women in the old cultures use it.' She laughed dismissively. 'The scientists said their experiences were just hallucinations because there was no way they could *really happen*. I wish I could take a few of them along with me!'

476

Ruth shook her head, still horrified. *I can't do it,* she thought.

Nina seemed to read her mind. 'Do you want to save your friends or not?' she snapped.

Ruth stared at the broom handle with distaste for a long moment. Then she asked, 'Are you sure this will do any good?'

'A few months back I would have said no. Now ... of course!'

Ruth grimaced. 'Okay. I suppose. What do I have to do?'

'Hold the handle.' She opened herself up. 'Now insert it gently.' Ruth steeled herself, but Nina didn't seem concerned. She relaxed on to it, then closed her eyes. After a moment she motioned to Ruth to remove it. 'Now it's your turn.'

Nina reapplied the salve to the handle, then positioned herself between Ruth's legs. Ruth's muscles were so tense she couldn't get the stick to penetrate, but whatever powerful drug was on it seemed to begin to affect her from even a cursory application. She gradually relaxed, allowing Nina to insert the handle. At first she felt a not-unpleasant burning sensation, but then it changed, so that she felt like warm syrup was slowly rising up her body from her groin. There was a definite sexual element to it; her clitoris engorged and she had a sudden, nearly overwhelming desire to bring herself to orgasm. But when Nina removed the handle, the edge was taken off her desire and she was able to look up and around. The quality of light in the room had changed; it was more diffuse and golden, as if it were being refracted through crystal. The edges of the furniture sparkled and shimmered and the crackling of the fire shushed and boomed like the sound of the sea.

Then there was the odd sensation of her retreating into her body, as if she were looking out at the world from the end of a long tunnel.

'Hold on,' she heard Nina say distantly. 'It's beginning.'

And then she was rushing out of herself, as if she had been

fired from a cannon. She rocketed up to the ceiling, where she briefly looked down at her naked body staring with glassy eyes up at her; Nina was slumped next to her, one hand draped across her thigh. And then she felt as if someone had yanked a rope attached to her neck and she was dragged wildly into the fire, which fizzed coldly around her, and then up into the yawning black hole of the chimney.

A second later she burst out into the night sky, swooping and swirling as if she were smoke caught in the wind. It took her a second to get her bearings and then she discovered that, with the right mental effort, she could begin to control her movements. Ruth twisted in practice and caught sight of Nina floating over the thatch waiting for her. She looked beautiful, years younger, with a firm, full body. She smiled and beckoned.

'Where are we going?' Ruth said, but no sound came out of her mouth. Nina seemed to understand nonetheless. She pointed along the valley, away from where the Baobhan Sith had attacked. Ruth looked at her curiously, but she acted as if she wanted to show her something important.

And then she was away, rushing on the night winds. Ruth launched herself behind her, lost in the wild, exciting sensation of flying. She could feel the breeze on her skin, feel her hair flow behind her, but although she was still naked, she didn't feel the cold. It was a wonderfully exhilarating feeling as she swooped and soared, remembering a score of similar dreams, wishing she could never come down; it was so powerful it almost made her want to cry.

The trees passed beneath her in a black carpet, the sweet scent of the pine floating up to fill her nostrils. With care, she could dive down and skim their gossamer-frail uppermost branches, leaving them waving in her passage. From her vantage point, she could see the landscape in its true form: alive; the sweep and swirl of the hillsides, the subtle gradation of colours in the grasses, the snake-twist of rivers, the mirror-glimmer of lakes, all linked into one awesome organism, each part affecting its neighbour. From there, it all made sense.

A long, low hoot made Ruth look round to see her owl-companion flying in circles nearby. She waved to him, but he continued spiralling on the thermals without any sign that he had any connection with her.

Nina's mad aerial dash slowed near Loadpot Hill. Ruth could read caution in her body language as she took advantage of the occasional treetop for cover. Eventually she came to a halt and pointed to something ahead, her face drained of the good nature Ruth had seen before; now she was fearful.

Ruth followed her guide and could instantly see why. Rising up out of the isolated green hillside was something that reminded Ruth of pictures of enormous African termites' nests. It was the first part of a tower that was still under construction, covering an area the size of ten football pitches. Although it was fundamentally black, she could make out crushed cars and trucks, washing machines, fridges, plastic, girders and broken masonry embedded in its walls as if the makers had plundered the local communities for the material. Above it, the stars were obscured by smoke from a hundred fires burning a dull red, visible through ragged openings all over the tower. And as she watched, Ruth could see movement around the base of the construction, up its walls, on its growing summit; the termites were swarming.

In her uneasy curiosity, Ruth flew a little closer, only to be disturbed by roars, shrieks and insane monkey chattering. She felt as if a terrible power had been turned on her, like a black ray projected from the tower; she suddenly became so cold her entire body shook, and an unbearable sense of despair began to gnaw at the pit of her stomach.

It was numbing, but then she felt Nina frantically tugging at her arm. Her terrified face left no doubt that they had been seen. The fear was infectious, and as Nina pirouetted in the air and sped away faster than Ruth could imagine, she felt instinctively that whatever was being built there would be too terrible to even imagine.

Nina's panic lessened only once they had put several miles between them and the black tower. They followed the landmarks back to the cottage, and then Nina took the route Ruth had first expected, up the hillside to the road above. As they neared where the van had been parked, they dipped down beneath the treetops and made their way cautiously among the upper branches until they found an eyrie where they could peer down on the stretch of road like two ghostly birds.

The van was still there, glowing white in the moonlight, but weaving in and out of the trees in a wide circle around it were the Baobhan Sith, no longer shrieking or as wild and predatory as they had been earlier. Tom was sitting a distance away, his head between his knees. Church, Shavi and Veitch were on the ground, slumped against the van. They weren't moving and blood stained their clothes and skin; Veitch, in particular, had a ragged wound in his neck where Ruth had seen the spectral creature prepare to bite. Her first thought was that they were dead. Her stomach knotted and she felt like bursting into tears; another part of her told her that wasn't the case. With an effort, she calmed herself and watched.

Not long after, the silence was broken by the drone of a car engine as twin beams splayed light over the trees. A nearly new BMW, but with deep, fresh scratches on its wing, screeched to a halt near the van. Callow's grinning skullface was behind the wheel; in the back seat an ominous form was sprawled with a car blanket pulled roughly over it. Ruth could tell from its shape that a man lay beneath it; she guessed it was the car's former owner.

Callow stepped out with a flamboyant flourish, leaving the headlights switched on so they spotlit Church and the others. 'Mister Churchill! So pleased to see you again!' he said, grinning superciliously.

At his voice, Church stirred and looked around. When he saw Callow, rage crossed his face and he forced himself to his feet. A second later the Baobhan Sith were around him, shrieking and gnashing their teeth, and they didn't retreat until he had fallen again.

'Nice little doggies!' Callow said after them.

'You bastard!' Church yelled.

Callow waved his finger and tut-tutted, but he didn't seem interested in engaging in conversation. Instead, he walked to the rear of the car and opened the boot. The Baobhan Sith looked towards it and hissed as one, moving away from it before resuming their weird circling dance.

As if in answer to the boot opening, Ruth realised she could just make out an odd, distant noise, like metal being dragged across gravel, and the kind of hideous animal sounds she had heard at the black tower. Callow turned in its direction and peered into the gloom. Slowly, his grin melted away.

Ruth could feel whatever was coming on some instinctual level. Her skin, however insubstantial, was crawling, and she felt like snakes were slithering through her intestines. The Baobhan Sith seemed to sense it too; for the first time she saw them motionless, facing in the same direction as Callow. The air seemed to swell with feverish anticipation.

Tensely, she watched the shadows that clustered around the bend in the road and within minutes the night seemed to come alive with a greater darkness. An insectile swarming broke free from the gloom and headed towards the van. Although her eyes told her there were individual shapes, she felt there was just one hideous, dark creature, radiating an evil power that made her feel sick. And in the mass, the shapes themselves were difficult to distinguish, although she knew they were Fomorii. They continued until they were teeming around the van, the car, Callow, Church and the others, so that the road now resembled a churning black river.

My God! Ruth thought. *I never realised there were so many of them!*

One of the forms separated from the others and walked

into the glaring circle of light thrown by Callow's car head-lamps. It was a man with golden skin, long hair and a frail, spindly body; there was an air of sickness and decay about him, and however stylishly he had dressed, his long, white silk tunic appeared dirty. Ruth recognised him as Fomorii, although he was closer to how she had imagined the Tuatha Dé Danann. She guessed, from Church's description of his captor in the mine, that it was Calatin.

Veitch and Shavi were also conscious now, and Church was muttering something to them, although Ruth couldn't hear what it was.

'Little rabbits!' Calatin said in a voice like breaking glass. 'You ran the course I mapped for you so perfectly. How you slipped from your cell remains a mystery, but it was only a matter of time before the doors were left ajar. And from that point you did everything I hoped. Reclaimed the Quadrillax – a remarkable achievement. Even as Brothers and Sisters of Dragons, I thought it beyond you. And turned back the Wild Hunt too, though there was more of chance in that. But then this frail creature . . .' – he motioned to Callow – '. . . served his purpose well. And now, for the first time, the Quadrillax are in Fomorii hands. We thought you too weak for the responsibilities laid upon you and we have been proven correct.'

Ruth winced at that and she could see it hit Church too.

'Tom—' Church began weakly.

Calatin's smile was so cold it froze the words in Church's throat. He turned and summoned something from the seething mass of Fomorii; a second later something glinting silver, small and scurrying like a spider ran out, up his legs and into his hands, where it formed itself into a dagger. Ruth recognised it: she had seen something like it before, at Heston Services when the Fomor had first tried to kidnap her.

'The Caraprix,' Calatin said, examining it. In his hand the dagger shifted its shape, became something indistinct but disgusting, then returned to its dagger form. Calatin showed

482

it to Church as if it was explanation in itself, but when he saw Church's blank look, he continued, 'Their fluidity and versatility makes them useful to us.'

'They are alive?' Shavi asked.

Calatin looked at him as if he didn't understand. 'They do our bidding in many different ways. Sometimes,' he mused to himself, 'they are almost companions.'

'What's this got to do with Tom?' Church looked at him, still slumped on the roadside nearby.

Calatin eyed him slyly. 'Oh, the pain of betrayal.'

Church winced, looked away.

'When the wanderer fell into my hands, I saw the opportunity to have a subtle hand on your wheel.' He held up the Caraprix, which wriggled in the light from the headlamps. 'One deep incision is all it takes. Painful, but he remained conscious until the last. The Caraprix slipped in through the wound, attached itself in here.' He tapped his temple. 'It sits there still, tormenting him, doing our will.'

At first Church couldn't grasp what Calatin was saying, but then he remembered the wounds on Tom's forehead when they first met him in the mine and he felt horror grow within him. 'He's got one of those in his head?' he said with disgust.

'Oh, it's not all bad.' Callow sidled up until he was near Calatin.

'You've got one too?'

'Mine was by choice, dear boy. I have a remarkable aptitude for seizing opportunities.'

'You call that an opportunity?' Church was disgusted. 'It's probably eating away at your brain.'

'It can be removed at any time, or I can simply live with it. If you think that's bad, you should try to get rid of lice.'

'Why did you do it?' Church asked.

'I told you, an opportunity. By declaring my allegiance early in the game, it gave me access to all the miracles and wonders that will rain down on us.'

'You sold us all out.' The intensity of hatred in Veitch's voice made Church feel almost uncomfortable.

'Now, now,' Callow cautioned. 'You must accept some responsibility. If young Mr Churchill had not been so indiscreet about what was happening to the world that night in the tavern, I would not have been prepared when I did encounter my good allies here.' He sighed theatrically. 'Oh, how strange fate is. I knew sooner or later you would involve yourself in something that would favour me, so after our evening's wassailing I resolved to follow you. I must admit, after the devastation you wreaked at the depot in Salisbury I thought things might be a little too hot even for me. But then I met my good friends!' Callow seemed about to clap Calatin on the shoulders, then thought twice about it. 'They made it easier for me to shadow you. But at a distance it was so hard to discern exactly what you had achieved; it required a little, shall we say, investigative skill on my behalf. Did you ever wonder who had gained access to your car? Your tents?'

'I'm going to kill you.' Veitch's voice was low and understated, but the words contained power.

'I don't think so,' Callow replied sneeringly, but Church could see a flicker of unease in his eyes.

Calatin lurched forward unsteadily, knocking Callow out of the way; he looked even sicker than he had in the mine. 'You still do not seem to understand exactly what has occurred. Your loss of the Quadrillax has destroyed more than merely your own feeble attempt to stop our advance. Through all time and all space, their significance has radiated: objects of such power that we never dared achieve our ultimate dream – the eradication of all light from the universe. Our victories were always tempered. We settled for control, in the certain knowledge that a step too far would rebound on us tenfold. Now, anything is possible.'

As he neared, Church's gorge rose at the hideous stink coming off him. Calatin bent down and lowered the living dagger until its tip was only an inch from Church's right eye.

Church tried not to blink, nor even to think about what Calatin was going to do next; the Fomor had revealed his sadism quite plainly in the mine's torture chamber. He thought for a moment, then lowered it to Church's cheek, where he pressed its razored edge into the soft flesh and made a slight downward cut. Church winced as the blood flowed.

'With the Quadrillax in our hands, everything has been lost. And you are responsible.' He showed a row of blackened teeth and released a blast of foul breath into Church's face.

'You're going to destroy them?' Church asked once he had recovered.

Calatin peered at him as if he were insane, then rose and limped away. 'They will be taken from here to our nearest retreat, where they will be encased in molten iron, then buried in the furthest reaches of the earth, never to be recovered—'

'What about Balor?' Shavi interrupted.

Calatin whirled, his eyes blazing, but slowly the insipid smile returned to his face. 'The Highfather will soon be back,' he said in a manner that made Church shiver, 'and the glory will be mine.'

Then he turned and yelled out something in the guttural Fomorii language before limping away. A second later Church, Shavi and Veitch were wrenched up in the black mass of bodies and swept away.

Ruth watched the scene in horror from the treetop branch, then turned to Nina, who motioned that they should return. The brief journey back to the cottage contained none of the awe and wonder Ruth had felt during her first flight, just a sense of impending doom and a feeling of utter futility. Nina led the way back down the chimney and as they emerged into the main room, Ruth had the same sensation of being fired from a cannon as she rushed back into her prone body. A second later, she stirred, feeling leaden and stupid, her thoughts no longer quicksilver; her mouth felt as if she had awoken after a night on the tiles; all her muscles were aching. The loss seemed so great her eyes filled with tears.

'I could have stayed like that for ever,' she said.

'And there lies the danger.' Nina levered herself to her feet, stumbling awkwardly. 'Spend too long in that form and your essence begins to break down, dissipate like smoke, until you return to the universe.'

Ruth rose and dressed dismally, trying to tell herself it was simply the effects of coming down off the drug. But as the initial edge of her experience began to fade, the threat facing them returned in force.

'I can't let them take Church and the others to that awful black tower. I can't let them take the talismans. But what can I do?'

Nina nodded sympathetically. 'There were so many of them—'

'They've got a way to go to reach the tower. We could head them off!'

'You're starting to sound like John Wayne.' Nina's faint humour underlined the futility of what Ruth was saying, but she wasn't going to be deterred.

'Will you come with me?'

Nina shook her head. 'I love my life too much. If there was a chance—'

'Then I'll have to try it alone. I can't give up.' She fastened her jacket and strode defiantly to the door.

'Wait.' Nina hurried to the dresser and returned with what appeared to be a piece of root with grass and vines wrapped around it. 'I laboured hard over that. Slip it in your pocket. It won't make you invisible to the things out there, but it should mask your presence enough to make it easier for you to travel through the countryside at night.'

Ruth thanked her, but her mind was already on what lay ahead. As she opened the door and slipped out, Nina called behind her, 'Be true to your destiny. Blessed be.' And then the door slammed shut and Ruth was alone in the night.

* * *

486

It was a real effort to scramble up the steep hillside amongst the trees, but soon she was at the road. It was deserted, with no sign that the Fomorii had ever been there. Callow's car had gone too, and Ruth presumed they were using it to transport the talismans because the Fomorii were unable to touch them.

She ran to the van, then swore angrily; she didn't have the keys. 'Laura!' she called out. 'It's Ruth.' At first there was no answer and Ruth feared the worst, then she heard what seemed to be a stream of abuse in a frail voice. 'Never mind that. Open the doors.'

It took an agonisingly long time, but finally the doors swung open. Laura hung on the handle, obviously in great pain, barely able to hold herself up. 'It's freezing,' she said hoarsely. 'I thought I was going to die in here.'

'There's still a chance for that.' Ruth clambered past her. 'God, I hope your shady past taught you how to hotwire an ignition system.'

'Yes, but if you think I'm going to crawl under a steering wheel—'

'Just tell me!' Ruth heaved herself over the back of the seats. 'I never thought I'd say this, but I'm glad it's you here and not someone who's law-abiding.' She paused. 'How come they left you here?'

'I guess they thought I was dead after what that bastard did. No one figured to look in the van.'

Laura guided Ruth through the process, laughing at Ruth's scream as she almost burned her fingers in the flash as the spark jumped between the two wires. Once the engine roared into life, Ruth slammed the van into first and pulled on to the road. While she powered through the gears, Laura told how she had listened to the attack of the Baobhan Sith and everything that happened after, while keeping as quiet as she could to avoid detection.

'How do you feel?' Ruth asked.

'Like I've been slashed into bloody chunks with a razor. How do you think I feel?'

'Just asking.'

There was a long pause and then Laura said, 'I could do with some more painkillers.'

'Hurts?'

'Like hell. I think some of the wounds have opened up.' Ruth heard Laura shift around under the pile of sleeping bags that were supposed to be keeping her warm. 'Sorry I'm not going to be much use.'

'Even if you were fighting fit, there wouldn't be much you could do.'

'No big plan, then?'

Ruth didn't answer. She didn't even know what she was doing. The thought of that mass of Fomorii filled her with dread. The only way she could avoid paralysis was to keep moving on instinct, ignoring the ringing alarms in her head that were saying her futile act was going to be the death of her.

She took the treacherous bends at breakneck speed, peering over the wheel for some sign of the Fomorii. She knew they couldn't have travelled far in the time since she had left the cottage, so she killed the lights and cruised by the light of the moon, using the central white lines for guidance. She had the window wound down a little, listening for the cacophany of grunts and shrieks, but the night was eerily still, just the rustling of the trees and the singing of the tyres on the road.

Then, as she rounded the next bend, she saw the seething mass ahead of her, moving in complete silence – which was somehow even more disturbing than the hideous sound they normally made. She slammed on the brakes and slewed to a halt, switching off the engine as quickly as she could and praying the Fomorii were singleminded enough to ignore the sound of her approach. Away up front she could make out the headlamps of Callow's car, moving slowly.

She turned to Laura, whose shock of blonde hair glowed like the moon where it stuck out of the sleeping bags. 'Hold tight,' she said softly.

* * *

Although Church could feel rough hands on him, he seemed to be floating in and out of consciousness. It was all he could do to maintain any rational thought among the overwhelming sense of evil which seemed to wrap around him in thick, black swathes. But he could feel movement as he was dragged or carried, smell the sickening stink that clouded all around, hear the rasp of inhuman breath. He had no idea where they were being taken, but he knew their lives wouldn't last long after their arrival, and he feared, in a way he didn't think possible, what tortures Calatin would inflict before his death.

Then, through all the turmoil, he became aware of a distant sound, slowly rippling closer like the rumbling of an approaching tidal wave. As it neared, he tried to clutch at his ears to keep it out; his stomach bucked and flipped, his gorge rose, his mind threatened to switch off completely. And only then did he guess what it was: the sound of the Fomorii in fear.

Suddenly there was chaos. The night was torn apart by ferocious cries as the Fomorii broke up in disarray. Church was dropped roughly to the ground, where he bounced around like a pinball as the beasts surged in all directions, tearing and bruising his flesh. But with the claustrophobic atmosphere of evil disrupted by the confusion, he found it easier to think. Somehow he got to his feet and looked around frantically for Veitch and Shavi. Instead, he saw what appeared to be a whirlpool in the dark sea of Fomorii ahead of him as they circled crazily in one spot. At first he watched in confusion, until he realised there was something at the heart of the maelstrom. Slashing sounds began to cut through the frenzied gibberings, and then the black wave parted and he saw what lay at the heart of the churning area. There was a group of creatures about five feet high, their skin a sickening green, scaled in part, with long black hair and monstrous features. They were moving through the Fomorii with some kind of weapons that Church couldn't quite make out, but he saw the aftermath: disembowellings, severed limbs, hacked heads. A slurry of blood and bone was beginning to mire the green grass. There was something about the creatures' heads that didn't appear right, but it was only when they drew closer that he could see what it was; they wore head-dresses made out of bloody human body parts – torsos, scalps, faces – and the grue from them matted the creatures' hair and bodies.

Church was transfixed by the sheer savagery of their attack. The manner in which they cut a swathe through the Fomorii was almost hypnotic in its brutality.

The spell was broken when someone grabbed his arm. Church whirled, ready to lash out. He caught himself when he saw it was Tom, then roughly pushed him away in disgust.

'They don't control me all the time!' Tom protested.

'I can't believe you!' Church began searching for Veitch and Shavi.

'Then don't. But heed me – don't let the Redcaps see you! They're being controlled to attack the Fomorii, but their natural enemy is man!'

Just as Tom spoke, one of the creatures broke off his dismemberment of a Fomor and stared in Church's direction. A second later it had broken away from the pack and was running towards him, its face contorted with rage.

Church moved at once, sprinting painfully off to one side, but the Redcap followed him unerringly. There were still Fomorii everywhere, though most of them had turned on the attacking Redcaps and were attempting to repel the intruders. He tried to weave among the Fomorii, who were too distracted to pay him any attention, but still the Redcap dogged his heels. And now he could hear the noise it was making – a roar like a big cat that set the hairs on the back of his neck rising.

Then, through the turmoil, he spotted Shavi curiously up high, waving to him frantically. He turned and ran in his direction.

Emerging through a pack of Fomorii, Church saw Shavi

standing on the top of Callow's car while the battle raged all about. Veitch was at the rear with the boot open, repeatedly smashing his fist into Callow's face, which had dissolved into a bloody pulp. But it was Veitch's expression that concerned him the most: he was lost to the violence and rage. Church barged past him, almost stumbling into the boot, and flicked open the crate. A shimmer of blue fire crackled through the talismans. As Church reached in to grab the sword, he was taken aback to feel it leap into his hand. He whirled round with the sword raised just as the Redcap thundered towards him, roaring like the wind, a strangely shaped, heavily chipped axe raised above its head.

As the axe came down, Church parried the blow, half-expecting his sword to shatter. But it held firm, although the force of the clash jarred every bone in his body. He stumbled backwards against the car, fighting to regain his equilibrium. Then, as the Redcap raised the axe for another blow, Church lashed out madly. The sword hacked into the creature's face like a knife slicing through butter. Greenish blood showered all over him, burning his skin where it landed, and the Redcap slumped to its knees, dead.

Church yanked the sword out with an effort, then turned and caught Veitch's arm mid-punch. 'Leave him. We've got to get out of here.'

Without waiting for an answer, he clambered atop the car alongside Shavi, to get a better view. 'Any way out?'

'I cannot see one,' Shavi replied.

Oddly, Church found himself unable to focus on the Fomorii fighting the battle. He could see movement, flying blood and limbs, could hear the terrible sounds they were making, but beyond that it was almost as if they had merged into one lake of darkness which was roiling in the grip of a furious storm.

But he could see what remained of the Redcaps hacking a path directly to the car. 'They want the talismans too,' he said with sudden certainty. And then it came to him. Scanning the vicinity, he soon spotted the unmistakable flurry of movement in a field picked out in silver by the moon's light. Mollecht and a small group of Fomorii waited patiently.

'Whoever wins the talismans, gains the power,' he muttered to himself. He turned to Shavi. 'Infighting. Suits me fine. Now how—'

He was cut off by a high-pitched, shrieking cry in the nerve-jarring Fomorii dialect. Calatin had spotted them and was trying to divert his troops from the Redcaps to a defence of the talismans. Church felt a gush of icy fear drench him as the entire ranks of Fomorii and Redcaps turned as one to face him.

Ruth watched the chaos break out from further up the road, but from that distance it was impossible to tell exactly what was happening. She watched anxiously, wishing she were confident enough to make a decision, batting away Laura's increasingly irritated calls for information. But then her attention was caught by the briefest shimmer of blue fire and she picked out Church and Shavi standing on the car roof.

'Hold tight,' she said as she spun the van around in the road.

'You can't leave them!' Laura yelled angrily.

'I'm not. I'm . . .' – she took a deep breath and slammed the van into reverse – '. . . ramraiding.' Then she popped the clutch and the van shot backwards with such force Laura screamed. 'I said hold tight!' Ruth shouted above the roar of the engine.

They thundered into the middle of the Fomorii as if they were crashing into a forest. Every time they hit one, something buckled; the nearside was so badly dented Ruth was sure it was going to cave in. The rear windows shattered, showering Laura with glass, then the doors burst open and the one that had been replaced at Glastonbury was torn off. Ruth kept her foot on the accelerator and her gaze on the wing mirror, although she was shaking from head to toe.

Even if they made it to Church, she wondered if the van would be in any condition to get them out.

But then she saw the car's headlamps loom up and she popped the brakes, stopping an inch or so from its bumper. Before she had thrust the gear stick into first, Veitch had launched himself into the back, with the crate under one arm and the spear in the other hand. Church and Shavi dived in after.

The Fomorii were already regrouping. Ruth revved the engine and prepared to drive.

'Wait!' Church called out. She saw him scramble to the back of the van and drag in a bedraggled figure. It was Tom.

'Leave him!' Veitch yelled. 'He's a fucking traitor!'

Church bundled the man towards the front of the van, then called for Ruth to go. The van shot forward just as a Fomor punched a hole through the offside. Others were ready to clamber through the open doors. Ruth swung the van from side to side to throw off any that might be clinging on, then ploughed through whatever was in her path. The van was tossed and turned as if it were in an earthquake; she lost the wing mirror; one headlamp exploded; a terrible whine started to come from the engine.

But somehow she managed to keep going. And when they rumbled over the last body and hit the open road, she was so overcome with relief her eyes filled with tears. She wiped them away before any of the others could see, then moved through the gears rapidly. Soon the dark, turbulent countryside was whizzing by and they were heading back in the direction of the motorway.

CHAPTER TWENTY

Revelations

'I still say we should have dumped him.' Veitch was squatting dangerously near the missing door, trying to tend to his neck wound with the van's depleted first aid kit.

'He had his flaws, but he was okay before those bastards stuck that parasite in his head.' Church watched Tom surreptitiously as he sat quietly with his back to the driver's seat, bound with the tow rope. He looked about a hundred years old; his skin was sallow, his grey hair matted, and there was a crack across one of the lenses of his wire-rimmed spectacles.

'I tried to fight it,' Tom said. 'Every time it attempted to make me do something against my will, I tried.'

Church recalled the blood that had been streaming from his nose, ears and eyes at the roadside before the Baobhan Sith attacked, and realised just how hard he had fought.

'It doesn't matter,' Veitch continued. 'He's still a liability. However much he *wants* to help us, that thing in his head means he could turn against us any time. If you don't want to just throw him out the back, we should at least leave him at the side of the road somewhere.'

'If you leave me, you'll never discover what you have to do with the talismans to summon the Tuatha Dé Danann,' Tom said pointedly.

Veitch bristled, and made to advance on him. 'You trying to blackmail us now?'

'Leave it, Ryan.' Church turned to Tom. 'Is this another of your great deceits, or can we get a kernel of truth out of you this time?'

'I know,' Tom stressed. 'You need me.'

'Perhaps that creature in his head could be removed,' Shavi suggested.

'What? We should kidnap a brain surgeon next?' Veitch said sarcastically.

'There might be a way,' Tom said.

Church eyed him suspiciously. 'Who could do a thing like that?'

'No one on this earth.' Tom gave a sickly cough. 'Just take me home.'

They debated the matter as they limped through the remaining hours of night towards the motorway. Veitch was adamant he didn't want to follow any advice from Tom in case they were led into another trap, but Church felt Tom was telling the truth. He finally extracted a promise from him that he would tell them everything if they helped him, and that was enough of a spur to convince the others; without his information they were lost anyway.

Home for Tom was near Melrose on the Scottish borders, not far in terms of distance, but it might as well have been a million miles. The engine's insistent whine told them the van wouldn't last much longer, and even if they managed to get it fixed, the damage to the body was so bad the police would pull them over the moment they got on to the motorway.

When dawn finally broke and the landscape was transformed into a place they all recognised, they stopped at a small farm not far from the M6. The farmer was pleasant enough to suggest the nightmares they had experienced at the heart of the Lake District hadn't yet touched his borders. Even at that time of day he was a canny negotiator though, and he offered to give up his own battered Transit – a second vehicle that was at least ten years old and looked like it barely moved – only for Laura's portable PC. But at least his Transit was whole, and although the exhaust rattled noisily, it allowed them to continue on their way.

The day was already turning fine, with just a few streaky clouds on the horizon to mar the blue sky, but the atmosphere in the van was depressive. Although they had regained the talismans, they had paid a huge price. Laura looked sicker than ever, and they were worried she had developed an infection in some of the wounds; Church was concerned that if they didn't get her to a doctor soon she could become fatally ill. Veitch, Shavi and Church himself were all weakened from their experience and bore numerous wounds inflicted by the Baobhan Sith, with Veitch's neck the worst. Church was convinced the Baobhan Sith had wanted to kill them, but whatever control Calatin exerted had somehow restrained them at the last. Only Ruth seemed to have the strength to continue, and Church could sense she had changed in some way he couldn't quite understand; she seemed far removed from the woman he had first encountered under Albert Bridge.

The journey up the M6 was uneventful, but their vigilance didn't waver; they knew either Calatin or Mollecht would be on their trail soon enough; however, their own little difficulties had been resolved, and with the Fomorii's shapeshifting abilities, everyone they encountered would have to be studied carefully.

Tom began to speak more freely as soon as he saw the others were behind him, even though Veitch appeared to be unable to forgive him. As they dissected their experiences in the Lake District, Tom chipped in with occasional pieces of information, about the Baobhan Sith, and about the Redcaps, whom he claimed used to stalk the Border counties in the days when man was first beginning to get a foothold on the island. The battles between the two were bloody, but the Redcaps were eventually driven back into the wildernesses, their numbers dwindling until they eventually retreated to Otherworld. He declined to answer any questions about how he came by the information.

They took the M6 past Carlisle and then crossed the border into Scotland and headed up to Galashiels. Heavy traffic on the motorway and the arterial road suggested an unshakable normality, which jarred with what they had witnessed in the Lakes. Tom told them to make the most of the façade; it would soon all change.

Melrose was a compact town below the Eildon Hills on the south bank of the Tweed, dominated by a twelfth century Cistercian abbey. They parked the van near the golf course and wearily stretched their legs; it seemed like weeks since they had slept. Tom claimed his original home had been in the nearby village of Earlston, but after his wanderings began he found a new and unspecified home in the hills.

Church surveyed the three volcanic peaks which seemed to rise to at least a thousand feet. 'You're expecting us to climb up there?' he said incredulously. 'Look at us – we're on our last legs. Laura can barely stand.'

'You could always carry me in your big, strong masculine arms, Church-dude,' Laura said ironically.

'Two of us could accompany Tom,' Shavi suggested, but Church instantly vetoed the idea.

'After what happened in the Lake District, nobody should be isolated. We ought to stay together, and carry the talismans with us at all times until we get a chance to use them.'

Laura levered herself into a sitting position. Her skin was so pale it was almost translucent and her hair was matted to her forehead. 'There's a real stink of testosterone round here. Listen, don't wrap me in cotton wool – I'm not some fragile girlie. You might have to take baby steps, but I'll keep up with you.' Church began to protest, but she pulled a tape measure from the tool box and threw it at his head. He ducked at the last moment, and when he saw her searching for more ammunition, he knew he would have to relent.

They took a path beside the golf course. Although the day was sunny, the air had a definite crispness. They passed slowly through gently inclining fields where cows grazed lazily before

497

reaching the wooded lower slopes of the rounded hills. True to her word, Laura kept pace, but Church could see the effort and pain played out on her face; she never complained, nor asked for help. Yet the weakness that occasionally consumed her when they broke for rests gave him cause for concern; he could almost see her health deteriorating before his eyes.

As the afternoon drew on, grey clouds swept in from the north-east and the chill in the air took on a sharp edge. They became increasingly worried about being caught out in the hills in a storm, or not making it back before night fell.

'There's not a house in sight,' Ruth said with breathless irritation as the steepness of the climb increased sharply. 'If you're not having us on, where the hell do you expect to get any help?'

'Nearly there,' Tom said without meeting her eye. He scanned the landscape before pointing to a hawthorn sapling thirty feet away. 'The old tree died,' he said cryptically, 'but hawthorn always marks the spot.'

When they got within ten feet, Tom broke into a run and dropped to his knees before the hawthorn, where he delicately bent forward and kissed the ground.

'It's eaten his brain,' Veitch said.

'Wait, he's saying something under his breath,' Ruth said anxiously. 'He could be tricking us again.'

Before they could move, there was a deep judder that reverberated deep within the hill and then the ground next to the hawthorn began to tear apart. They fell to their knees from the tremors and when next they looked there was a ragged slit in the earth big enough for them to walk through.

'Just like the tor!' Shavi said with wonder. 'A passage to Otherworld!'

'I don't like this.' Ruth plucked up the spear and held it ready for defence. 'Who knows where that leads?'

'Wait. Look at Tom.' Church ran to his side; he had fallen over backwards and was trying to crawl away from the doorway. Strain was etched on his face as he fought the urging

498

of his body and there was blood once more around his nose and ears. 'It's trying to stop him going in there!'

'Could be a double bluff,' Veitch pointed out.

'Remember what happened at the tor,' Ruth cautioned. 'Time moves differently over there. We might come back and find we've missed the deadline.'

Church ran back to the crate and took out the sword; it rang with inner vibrations as it touched his flesh. 'I don't reckon we've got any choice. Let's get him inside.'

Church grabbed one of Tom's arms while Veitch hooked the other and together they hauled him towards the rift. A wind howled out of it, carrying with it alien scents that made the hairs on their neck stand upright. For an instant they glanced at each other for support and then, without saying a word, they marched into the dark.

Church had expected a balmy summer landscape like the one they had encountered beneath the tor. Instead the passage brought them out on to a rocky mountainside shadowed by night, strewn with craggy boulders, thorny, windswept trees and bunches of gorse. A harsh wind howled around them and lightning flashed across the great arc of the sky, although there was no rain. They bunched together for security, searching for any sign of where they were supposed to be going.

'Blimey. This is a bit different,' Veitch said unsurely.

'Otherworld has as many different aspects as there are views.' Tom raised himself up to his full height and looked around, a faint smile on his lips. He seemed transformed, at ease. 'It's fluid. A world behind every doorway.'

'How are you?' Church asked.

'As well as can be expected. The Caraprix isn't comfortable in this particular part of Otherworld – that's why it attempted to prevent me entering. It will hibernate until we leave.'

'Where do we go?' Ruth asked. The mountainside disappeared down into darkness and it was impossible to make out anything of the landscape beyond.

Tom searched the night, then pointed just above the edge of a massive boulder which was keeping the worst of the wind off them. In the distance they could make out a flickering light.

'I hoped there would be someone here who escaped the Wish-Hex,' Tom said. 'If it were to happen anywhere, it would have been in this place. Come.' He set off down the mountainside, keeping a surefooted control as he slipped and slid on the pebbles and exposed rock.

Before they could follow, Laura suddenly keeled over; Church lunged for her before she hit the hard ground, swinging her round into his arms. Her breathing was shallow and he could see the whites of her rolled eyes beneath her half-closed lids.

Shavi took Laura's pulse at her neck. 'We need to get her to a doctor very quickly,' he said grimly.

Church looked round frantically, wishing someone else could take responsibility, hating his own ineptitude at leadership. 'We've got to get her back – find a doctor in Melrose!'

'It's a long way down that hill,' Veitch said doubtfully.

Tom stepped forward with an expression of surprising concern. 'Our only hope is to go on. Otherwise she'll die.'

'No!' Church tried to get a grip on her to carry her back to the doorway.

Tom placed a gentle hand on his forearm. 'Believe me, I *know* she'll die if you try to take her back.' There was an unnervingly confident insistence in his voice.

Church felt a sudden hopelessness sweep through him. 'If you're lying and she dies, I'll kill you myself,' he said quietly.

Veitch helped Church carry her, all of them hoping the light wasn't as far away as it looked, praying that Church had made the right decision; wondering whether Tom really was leading them into a trap. And all the while the strange electrical storm seemed to grow in intensity over their heads.

* * *

The light was coming from a torch in the front porch of an imposing building which resembled a mediaeval stone monastery, although one constructed into, and part of, the mountainside. Above the porch was a squat, three-storey tower topped by a weathervane in the shape of a dragon and a lightning rod. Behind it, the slate roof and the walls with the tall, arched, leaded windows went straight into the bedrock, almost as if the mountain had formed around it. Three steps led up to the porch, where they were confronted by a large oaken door, studded with black nails.

'Where is this place?' Church asked suspiciously.

Tom traced his fingers down one of the porch's stone columns. 'Using the name you would understand, it is the Library of Ogma, wisest of all the Old Ones.'

Church searched his memory for the dimly recollected reference. 'In the myths he was supposed to have invented Ogham.'

'That's the writing you thought was on the spear,' Ruth said.

'A runic writing system. There's not much of it about, but it's the earliest form discovered in Ireland.' Church looked at Tom, who was lost in thought. 'One of the Danann?'

'His store of knowledge is vast. Chamber upon chamber, filling the entire mountain. If he were at the heart of it when the Wish-Hex struck, it should have afforded him some protection.' Tom climbed the steps cautiously and hammered on the door.

'So he's good with words. How's he going to help us?' Veitch asked.

'Have respect,' Tom cautioned; his tone suggested it was an imperative. 'He bonded with Etain, daughter of the great healer Dian Cécht. In his constant search for great wisdom, he has archived all the knowledge they possess.'

'That's not all.' Church suddenly began to make connections. 'He was also supposed to ferry the souls of the dead to Otherworld for a period of rest before they were reborn in our world.' There was almost a prayer woven into his words. 'Are there souls here?'

'So they say.'

'Don't you *know*?' Church wanted to shake Tom, to stop his obfuscation; there was only one lost soul that mattered to him.

'I'm just human like you, Jack,' Tom replied with some exasperation. 'I'm not privy to the great scheme. I observe, I consider, but I'm not always correct in my assumptions. And the gods don't give up their wisdom freely, and certainly not any wisdom that matters.'

'Typical bosses,' Veitch muttered. 'Keep the menials in the dark.'

'Actually,' Tom said tartly, 'they presume, rightly, that we wouldn't be able to handle the truth.'

'How very patrician of them,' Ruth replied, just as acidly.

They were interrupted by the sound of heavy footsteps approaching the door. When it finally swung open silently, they all caught their breath at the figure revealed: for a second, different faces seemed to flicker across him, some almost too terrible to behold, before one settled that was kind and thoughtful. It reminded Church of Oscar Wilde; Ruth of Einstein; Veitch of the only teacher who ever tried to help him. He was wearing long flowing robes that were grey and almost metallic in the way they caught the light.

His gaze took them all in in a second, but a broad smile formed when it fell upon Tom. 'Thomas!' he said warmly, in a voice that didn't seem to come from his mouth.

Tom bowed his head deferentially. 'Wise One. We come to ask your help in these difficult times.'

'Difficult times indeed. You have heard my brothers and sisters are scattered to the wind?' Tom nodded gravely. 'The Night Walkers, you know.' A rumble of what seemed like hate formed deep in his throat. 'Only a few of us evaded the Wish-Hex. I have since heard murmurings of an attempt to locate my brethren and return them to me.'

Tom motioned to the others. 'And here are the searchers, Wise One. They need to be restored if they are to complete their task.'

'And you, Thomas. I see you too need my ministrations.'

Tom nodded, looked away uncomfortably.

Ogma turned to Laura, who was cold and still in Church's arms, her breathing barely noticeable. Gently, he ran his fingers over her face. His face grew a little darker. 'Her light is weak. I do not know if there is aught I can do for her.'

'Please try,' Church pleaded.

'It was always said Dian Cécht could bring even the dead to life,' Tom interceded.

'But I am not Dian Cécht. And healing is not simply knowledge.' There was a brief pause while Ogma seemed to consider the matter. Then: 'Come, bring her. I will see what I can do.'

The place smelled of candle wax and limes. They trailed behind Ogma as he led them through an endless maze of chambers filled from floor to ceiling with leatherbound books, some half as big as Church and as thick as his thigh, manuscripts and papyri tied with red ribbon as if they were legal briefs. But when Shavi held back to sneak a peek at one of the books, they appeared to contain only a brilliant white light.

Finally, after what seemed to them like an hour, they reached a series of chambers that were filled with rough wooden furniture, which Church guessed were Ogma's personal rooms. He laid Laura on a low bed and stroked the hair from her forehead.

As his fingers touched her flesh, her eyes flickered open and focused on him briefly. 'I don't want to die,' she said weakly. There was a sheen of panic in her eyes.

'Do something,' Church implored Ogma.

If the god heeded, it didn't register on his face. He opened a large cabinet in one corner which was filled with jars and phials of powders, liquids and dried herbs. He selected a few, then began to mix them with a mortar and pestle on a heavy oak table. After a few moments of introspection, he seemed satisfied with a thick, reddish-brown salve, which he smeared on Laura's lips. It remained there for only a second before it was rapidly absorbed.

'Will that work?' Church asked anxiously.

Ogma fixed his curious eyes on Church, like an adult looking at a child. 'We wait. If she has it within her, her light will shine again.'

Church had to turn away from her then, barely able to cope with the painful emotions flooding him after so many months of numbness.

Ogma seemed to comprehend what was going through his head, and after cursorily examining Veitch and Shavi from a distance, he said, 'Your own light wavers. You must all rest. Use my chambers as your own. There is food and drink—' Tom started, but said nothing. Ogma noted his concern and added, 'It is given freely, without obligation.'

This seemed to satisfy Tom. After Ogma left them to explore his rooms, Veitch asked, 'What was that all about?'

'Never take food or drink in Otherworld, from anyone, unless you have their promise that it is given freely and without obligation. Otherwise, when the first drop or crumb touches your lips, you fall under the control of whomever has given it.'

Veitch looked to the other three, puzzled. 'Is that right? Or is he bullshitting again?'

'In the old tales,' Shavi began, 'anyone who crossed over to Faeryland had to avoid eating the faery food or they'd fall under the spell of the Faerie Queen.'

'So is that where we are? Faeryland?' Veitch said incredulously.

'Get a grip, Ryan,' Church replied wearily. 'Let's find somewhere to crash.'

In a nearby chamber, they found a room filled with sumptuous cushions, the harsh stone walls disguised by intricate tapestries. On a low table in the centre was an array of bowls filled with apples and oranges, some berries, tomatoes, and a selection of dried, spiced meats. A jug of wine and four goblets stood nearby.

Relishing the chance to rest their exhausted bodies, they fell on to the cushions, which were so soft and warm it was like they were floating on air. It was a difficult choice between sleeping or assuaging their pangs of hunger, but in the end the subtle aromas of the food won out. Yet as they ate and drank, they discovered their tiredness sloughing off them, and by the time they had finished their meal they felt as fully rested as if they had slept for hours. It provoked an animated conversation for a while, but Church had other things on his mind.

'We got you here,' he said to Tom. 'Now you owe us some answers.'

'What do you want to know?'

'For a start, how you know everything you do. Why you called this place home. Why Ogma seems to know you so well.'

'And no lies,' Veitch said.

Tom turned to him, eyes ablaze. 'I have never lied. I may not have given all the facts, but no untruths have ever passed my lips. I cannot lie.'

'What do you mean?' Church asked.

'What I say, as always. It is physically impossible for me to lie. One of the *gifts* bestowed upon me for my time in Otherworld.' There was a note of bitterness in his voice.

Church's eyes narrowed. 'Who are you?'

'I told you my name. Thomas Learmont. But you may also know me as Thomas the Rhymer.'

Veitch looked from the confusion on Church's face to the others. 'You bastards better keep me in the loop.'

'Thomas the Rhymer,' Church began cautiously, 'was a real person who managed to cross over into mythology. He was a Scottish Nationalist during the war with England. In

505

a way, he's like Scotland's answer to King Arthur – a mythical hero who was supposed to sleep under a hill—'

'Under this hill,' Tom interrupted.

'—until there was a time of great need, when he would return. That's what the old prophecies said. But he lived in the thirteenth century.'

Veitch looked at Tom. 'Blimey, you've aged well.'

'I lived at Earlston, a short ride from Melrose,' Tom said. 'We were an old family, quite wealthy, with land hereabouts, although my estate was eventually gifted to the Church by my son.' The faint sadness in his face at the memory was amplified by the shadows cast by the flickering torches. 'Unlike my father, who worked hard, I was always too much of a dreamer. I was an elegant singer and I spent many an hour lazing in the countryside composing new works, usually just ditties about the people I knew and the women I loved. There was one girl in particular. To seek true inspiration for a song about her I rode up into the Hills of Eildon, where I settled myself beneath a hawthorn tree with a view of what seemed like, at that time, the entire world. I chose to ignore the old wives' tales linked to the hawthorn, that it signified death, that its blossom represented rebirth.' He sighed. 'That it was the chosen tree of the Faerie Queen. But I had no idea that an entire world existed under the hill, like all the fools used to say about the faery mounds. But I was the true fool, wasn't I? They were simply misremembering old wisdom. I was ignoring it.'

He took off his cracked glasses to clean them. Church searched his face for any sign that this was more dissembling, but he could only see honesty there.

'So the Faerie Queen got you?' Veitch asked; he was still having trouble grasping the truth of everything they had experienced. In numerous conversations he had exasperated Shavi with his apparent inability to see beneath the surface of the myths and legends.

'The Faerie Queen. The Great Goddess. Just names we give

to attempt to understand something unknowable. She was terrible to behold. Terrible. When I looked at her I swore I was looking into the face of God. I loved her and hated her, couldn't begin to understand her. I let her take me apart and put me back together, let her put me through the most unimaginable torments, to sample the wonder that came off her. It was a time of the most incredible experiences, of pain and pleasure, of being given a vista deep into the mystery of existence.' He blinked away tears and, for a second, Church thought he saw in his eyes something that looked disturbingly like madness. 'I was like a dog looking up at his mistress,' he added wistfully. 'And I was a hostage who came to depend upon his captor.'

'It sounds awful.' Ruth placed a sympathetic hand on the back of his. 'Is that how they see us – as playthings?'

Tom nodded. 'In the main. Some are close to us and have grown closer through contact down the ages. Others could strip the meat from our bones and leave the remains in a pile without giving it a second thought. They see themselves as fluid, as a true part of the universe. We are just some kind of bacteria, with no significant abilities, no wisdom.'

'Then how did you get out?' Ruth said.

He smiled coldly. 'She took a liking to her pet. At times I felt like I was in Otherworld for just a night, at other times all that I experienced made it feel like centuries. In truth, seven years had passed when I was allowed to return. I wandered down from the hill, crazed and gibbering, and was eventually returned to my home to recuperate. It was only later I discovered how much she had changed me.'

'What did she do?' Ruth's voice was hushed; the others watched Tom intently.

'During one of my torments I was given the power of prophecy and The Tongue That Cannot Lie.' His laugh made them all uncomfortable. 'In a world built on lies, that was bad enough. But being able to see into the future . . .' He shook his head, looked away.

'You know everything that's going to happen?' Church asked.

'Not at all. I see glimpses, images frozen as if they were seen from the window of a speeding car. That's how *they* see it. They know time isn't fixed.'

'It must have been impossible for you to adjust,' Ruth said.

He smiled sadly at her insight. 'After all I'd been through, how could I begin to associate with my old friends and neighbours, my family? I tried. I married, and my wife bore me my son, Thomas. But I no longer felt a part of humanity. No one could begin to understand the thoughts in my head. I looked around me and saw simple people living simple lives, people ignorant of the universe. Savages. I'd moved beyond them, but I could never be a part of Otherworld. I'd lost everything. And I knew, in one terrible moment, that I was always meant to be alone.'

There was power in the emotion of Tom's words. Church had never truly liked the man, certainly had never trusted him, but now he was overcome with respect; how many people could have survived all he had experienced?

'True Thomas, they called me!' Tom laughed; the others could barely look at him. 'Still, I did my best. I became involved in politics, as an agent for the Scots against the English, but politics isn't a place for a man who cannot lie. I wasn't successful, to say the least, and as my failures mounted I discovered the Earl Of March was plotting to have me murdered.'

Tom rummaged in his haversack for the tin containing his hash and made a joint with such laborious attention to detail that Church could tell it was merely to distract him from the full force of his memories. The others waited patiently until he had sucked in the fragrant smoke, then he continued.

'I fled into the Highlands briefly, eventually ending up at Callanish, and it was there I met one of the guardians of the old places and the old wisdom that stretched back to the days of the Celts.'

'The people of the Bone Inspector?' Church asked.

Tom nodded. 'It seemed we had much in common. *He* knew the true meaning of the hawthorn. After much pleading, and due in the main to my particular circumstances, he agreed to initiate me in the ancient natural knowledge that his people had practised in the sacred groves until the Romans had driven them out to become wanderers, hidden from the eyes of those who needed them.'

He sighed and took another long, deep drag. 'But it still didn't give me that sense of belonging which I so desperately needed. I was adrift in this world and eventually, as I knew in my heart I would, I wandered back to Otherworld. By then, of course, my patron had lost interest in me, but I was accorded some respect for my shaping at her hands, and for my singing voice and poetry, by many of the others in this place.'

'But you still couldn't feel a part of it,' Ruth said.

He nodded. 'For nearly four hundred years in the world's time I attempted to find a place for myself, although it only seemed a handful of years here. But eventually I grew homesick and I realised that all my suffering had brought me one thing – my freedom. I could come and go as I pleased. Every now and then I would spend some time in our world, and when I got bored I would wander back.'

'The best of all possible worlds,' Church said.

'No. The worst.'

'Is that how you got stuck in all that sixties stuff?' Veitch nodded disrespectfully at Tom's hair and clothes.

'That period marked my longest time away from Otherworld. It was closest in thought and deed to how I felt inside me and I thoroughly enjoyed every moment of it.'

Ruth put an arm around his shoulders. 'Tom, you really are an old hippie. Peace, love and self-indulgence!'

'You could have told us all this before,' Church said.

'I had to be sure I could trust you implicitly before I told you anything of significance. If I learned anything from my time as a spy, it was that knowledge is power, and I didn't want to have my true nature exposed and used against me too early in the game.'

'And you're sure now?' Veitch said tartly. 'That's a relief.'

'What about the Fomorii and Balor?' Church asked. 'Did they let you in on what was happening?'

Tom shook his head; a spasm of pain crossed his face. 'It still will not let me talk about that.' He rubbed at his nose furiously. 'After Ogma has done what he can, perhaps.'

With the final barrier of deceit removed, they felt they had been brought closer together. Perhaps it was the special qualities of the food and drink, or the sense of security offered by Ogma's library, but despite the pressures and secrets amongst them, they felt ready to face up to what lay ahead; their failures didn't seem so bad, their successes great in the face of monstrous odds. Church even ventured to say they had a chance.

While Tom smoked another joint and Veitch finished off the wine, Shavi decided to investigate the bookshelves again, although he seemed disturbed at what he had discovered before. Church slipped out quietly, and though he didn't say where he was going, they all knew he was checking on Laura. Ruth was sure in her heart she had more in common with him than Laura; that, if they allowed themselves, they could have the kind of relationship about which they both had dreamed.

These thoughts were preying on her as she wandered disconsolately through the chambers until, by chance, she entered a room where Ogma sat at a table, hunched over an enormous book. She was so deep inside herself she was half-way across the room before she saw him and by then it was too late to retreat. He raised his head and levelled his undecipherable gaze at her.

'You have the mark of one of the Golden Ones upon you,' he said, although she was sure he hadn't glimpsed the design scorched into her palm.

She described her experiences with Cernunnos and he nodded thoughtfully as he listened. 'The Wish-Hex caused great hardship for us all.'

'Do you hate them?' she asked. 'The Fomorii, I mean.'

He raised his eyebrows curiously, as if he couldn't grasp her question. 'The Fomorii are an infection to be eradicated.' He seemed to think it was answer enough.

'If you don't mind me saying,' Ruth continued, 'you seem very different to Cernunnos or whatever his true name is. More approachable.' *But not much*, she thought.

He thought about this for a moment, then said, 'We are not of a kind. Some of us are very close to you, barely a shimmer of difference. Others are so far removed that they are like distant suns burning in the vast reaches of space. We have our own mythologies, our own codes, our own hierarchies. There are those we look up to and those we look down upon.'

'You have a structured society like ours? But you're supposed to be gods, at least that's what the ancient people of my world thought.'

He smiled. 'Even the gods have gods. There is always something higher.'

'Are you gods?'

He raised his open hands, but gave nothing away.

Church watched Laura for a while, but could tell nothing from her face. The only relief he felt was that at last he had some time alone to deal with the mess he felt inside. It was as if the moment he had reached out to touch Laura's back at Manorbier, his emotions had split open like a ripe peach. He didn't know how to deal with any of them; every single thought and sensation was almost unbearable. He fumbled anxiously with Marianne's locket, but it seemed to have lost its magic; nothing could calm him.

Worse, he still couldn't shake off the sensation of cold which seemed to be eating into his marrow. There was a thin coating of frost on the Black Rose which he constantly dusted away, only to see it replaced every time he secretly inspected it. He wondered if the rose itself were actually the cause of the iciness, but he didn't seem able to let himself consider that too deeply. He certainly couldn't bring himself to throw the flower away,

About an hour later, Ogma was ready to deal with Tom. They gathered in a room that was bare, apart from a sturdy oaken table and a small desk on which lay a range of shining silver instruments of indefinable use; Church was instantly reminded of Calatin's torture rack. While Tom climbed on to the table, apparently unafraid of what lay ahead, the others gathered in one corner to watch the proceedings.

'How's Laura?' Ruth whispered to Church.

His weary head shake told her all she needed to know. She didn't probe further, but deep down she wondered how the five Brothers and Sisters of Dragons would fare if one of them were missing.

Ogma applied some thick, white salve to Tom's lips and while it didn't knock him out, it must have anaesthetised his nerve endings, for a second later the god began to slice into Tom's temple with a long, cruel knife; Tom didn't flinch at all, but Ruth closed her eyes.

The salve must have done something to the blood flow too, for despite the depth of the incision, there was little bleeding. Ogma followed in with a hand-powered drill which ground slowly into Tom's skull as the god rotated the handle; all the time Tom's eyes flickered as he stared implacably at the vaulted ceiling.

But then, as the judder of Ogma's hand showed the drill had broken through, a transformation came over Tom: his eyes appeared to fill with blood and his face contorted into an expression of such primal rage it made him unrecognisable. The salve had worked its power on his body too, for it was obvious he couldn't move his arms and legs, but he opened his mouth to yell and scream in the hideous Fomorii language. Ogma ignored him, but it was so disturbing to see that the others had to look away and even Veitch blanched.

Then, as they looked back, they saw the strangest thing. The drill hole must only have been a pencil-width, but somehow Ogma seemed to work the tips of two fingers in there, then three, then four, and then his entire hand was sliding into the side of Tom's forehead. Tom shrieked and raged impotently, but Ogma simply laid his other hand on his head to hold it still. Finally his hand was immersed right up to his forearm before he began to withdraw it.

Church winced; Ruth gagged and covered her mouth with her hand; Veitch and Shavi were transfixed.

And then, with a twist of his wrist, Ogma's hand came free. Clutched in his now-stained fingers was a wriggling thing which looked like a human organ, slick with blood and pulsating. But worst of all was that the shriek that had been coming from Tom's mouth was now emanating from the Caraprix. The cry soared higher and higher and they had to cover their ears to protect themselves. When it reached its climax, the thing began to mutate. At first it started taking on the hard form of a weapon, then something furry with needle teeth, but before it could fix its shape, Ogma dropped it on to the table and brought his enormous fist down on it hard. It burst like a balloon filled with blood.

In the silence that followed the insane shrieking, the room seemed to hang still; then Ruth turned away, coughing, and the others muttered various epithets of disgust.

Ogma turned to them. 'It is done,' he said redundantly. 'True Thomas will recover apace. The Caraprix is a parasite, but it causes no permanent damage to its victim.'

'They're hideous!' Ruth said, still refusing to look at the splattered mess on the table.

Ogma seemed uncomfortable at this. 'The Danann have their own Caraprix,' Tom interjected. He levered himself up from the table with remarkable sprightliness after what he had just been through; the hole in his head had already healed.

Ogma removed a clasp from his robes, which transformed itself into a shape like an egg with tendrils, glowing bright white. 'Tools, weapons, faithful companions,' he said.

Church eyed it suspiciously for a second, then helped Tom to his feet, although he didn't appear to need it. 'We have much to do,' Tom said with a vigour Church recognised from the first time they had met. 'A brief rest, a talk about what lies ahead, and then we must be away, for Beltane is now too close for any more delays.'

After the operation, Ogma had lost himself among the chambers, leaving them free to talk and plan. They gathered in a dark, echoing room which resembled a baronial hall. At one end a log fire blazed in a fireplace so big Church could easily have walked into it, and collected before it were several sturdy wooden chairs with studded leather seats and backs. For some reason, no torches burnt in that room so they pulled the chairs up closer to the fire.

Tom had centre stage, his newly repaired glasses glinting in the firelight, his eyes merely pits of shadow. 'I'll answer all your questions as best I can,' he said, 'but I caution you that I don't know all.' He took a sip of wine from a goblet rescued from the dining room.

'Tell us what you know about the Bastards,' Veitch said; it was how he had taken to describing the Fomorii.

Tom nodded. 'Some said their forefather was Ham, who was cursed by Noah, and that curse transformed every descendant into a misshapen monster. Others claimed they were born in the all-encompassing darkness before the universe began.' The fire cracked, spurting a shower of sparks up the chimney, and they all jumped. The shadows at their backs seemed uncomfortable and claustrophobic. 'They were led by Balor, the one-eyed god of death,' Tom continued, and for a second his voice wavered. Church looked round suddenly; he had the unnerving feeling someone was standing just behind his chair.

'Balor.' Shavi shifted uncomfortably. 'That is the name I heard in my trance.'

'The embodiment of evil,' Tom continued. 'Born of filth and corruption. So terrible that whoever he turned his one eye upon was destroyed.'

The room grew still; even the crackling of the fire seemed to retreat.

'In the first times, Balor led the Night Walkers across the land and all fell before them. After that we have only the myths to enable us to understand what happened. Before the Fomorii invasion, the Tuatha Dé Danann were led by Nuada, known as Nudd, known as Nuada Airgetlámh – Nuada of the Silver Arm – for the replacement created by Dian Cécht he wore for the hand he lost in the first battle of Magh Tuireadh. But because of his disability, the Danann deemed him not fit to lead them against the Fomorii and he was replaced by Breas, who was renowned for his great beauty.

'Except Breas was half-Fomorian and he allowed the Night Walkers to terrorise the land and enslave the Danann. Dian Cécht grew Nuada a new hand and he regained his position, but by then it was too late – he couldn't break the grip of the Fomorii.

'All seemed lost until Lugh presented himself to Nuada at Tara. Lugh, the god of the Sun, known as Lleu, or Lug, or Lugos, was a young, handsome warrior, but he, too, was part-Fomorii. Indeed, his grandfather was Balor. Lugh rallied the Danann and they rose against the Fomorii. All hung in the balance until the two sides faced each other at the second battle of Magh Tuireadh. It seemed that once again the battle would go the way of the Fomorii. But then Lugh, with the spear you recovered in Wales, fought his way through the lines and plunged it into Balor's eye. The Dark God was slain instantly and the Fomorii fell apart.' He sipped at the wine thoughtfully. 'Yes, Balor is a terrible threat. But the Danann

515

who helped defeat him still exist, locked in the place where the Wish-Hex banished them.'

'Then there is hope,' Church said.

'Is that how their original war really happened?' Ruth asked.

Tom shrugged. 'The Danann will no longer discuss that time. It was a period of great upheaval for them. At least now we know what the Fomorii are trying to do.' Veitch looked at him blankly. 'The truth was there in Shavi's vision, and Calatin confirmed it. They are attempting to bring back Balor.'

'How can they do that if he was destroyed?' Ruth asked apprehensively.

'The yellow drums you saw at the depot in Salisbury and which we found in vast quantities in the mine in Cornwall are the key.'

Ruth cast her mind back. 'That black gunge inside them—'

'A foul concoction distilled at one of the Fomorii warrens like the tower you saw being constructed in the Lake District. It will be the medium for the Dark God's rebirth.'

'Then that's why they haven't moved on the cities yet. They're waiting for Balor to lead them,' Veitch said.

The logs cracked and sputtered, but their thoughts were so leaden they barely registered it.

'Only the Tuatha Dé Danann could stand up to something like Balor,' Church said eventually.

'But take heed too. The Danann are not overtly predatory, nor do they act with malice unless provoked. But they have their own agenda and if we get in their way we will be destroyed without a second thought,' Tom warned.

'I thought they were angels,' Ruth said sadly.

'At times they *look* like angels. Perhaps they were responsible for our myths of angels. But they are so complex in thought and deed, so unknowable in every aspect, good is too simplistic a concept.'

They were suddenly disturbed by a movement in the dark

behind them. Veitch jumped to his feet, bristling alert, but the others watched cautiously as two figures emerged from the shadows.

'You never get treatment like this on the NHS.' Laura was walking with only the faintest sign of weakness, smiling apprehensively; everything about her body language suggested defensiveness, and the reason was plain to see. The patch of bandages had been removed from her face, revealing the mess Callow had made. Although the wounds appeared to have miraculously healed, the pink scars were still evident against her pale skin.

Ogma laid a heavy hand on her shoulder. 'She is strong of spirit. My attempts at healing merely gave her respite to fight back herself.'

She raised a hand to her face. 'Just let me know when you're opening the cosmetic surgery ward.'

She seemed afraid to come into the circle of light, so the others went to her. Shavi hugged her warmly and Veitch attempted to do the same, but she kept his show of emotion at arm's length. Tom's nod of support was restrained, but left her in no doubt of his feelings, while Ruth circled her before she gave in to her feelings as much as she could and clapped her on the arm.

And then Laura turned to Church, searching his face for any response to her scarring. She seemed pleased by what she saw.

'We were worried you might not be along for the last leg of this great road trip,' Church said, smiling.

'Somebody's got to keep an eye on you. Make sure you don't slip back into your moody, maudlin ways.'

They held each other's eyes for a moment, then shifted uncomfortably and moved away without any physical contact.

Ogma led them to a series of interconnecting chambers where he offered them beds for the night. After their conversation with Tom, they were all convinced they wouldn't sleep a wink, but within ten minutes most of them were resting peacefully.

For Church the thoughts and emotions were crashing around his head too turbulently and he lay with his hands behind his head, staring at the ceiling, trying to put them in order. When he heard Laura's whisper at the open door soon after, everything else was swept away in an instant.

'I couldn't sleep.' She snorted contemptuously. 'I'm getting good with the clichés. It's like some cheap romance novel.' The analogy seemed to surprise her, and then made her feel uneasy, but she sat on the edge of his bed nonetheless. She thought for a moment, then put a hand on his chest. He slid his own on the top of hers and she instantly folded against him, nestling into the undulations of his body, resting her face against his neck. 'Don't worry,' she said. 'I'm not going to say anything pathetic.'

'Then that's up to me.' His words seemed to float in the dark. 'I'm glad you're here.'

They held each other for a moment longer and then they turned to each other and kissed; there were so many complex emotions tied up in that simple act – affection and passion, guilt and loss, loneliness and fear – that they were both afraid it would swallow them up. Then the desperation that knotted them up faded for the first time in years, leaving a sense of simple contentment they had both convinced themselves they would never feel again.

They awoke wrapped together several hours later, although in Ogma's library it was almost impossible to mark any passage of time. Laura hurried back to her room before the others discovered them, but the glance she gave him at the door was enough to show a bond had been forged.

They gathered for a breakfast of bread, fruit and milk in the dining chamber where they were all, once more, astonished by how rested they felt.

'You promised to tell us what we need to do next,' Church

said to Tom as they finished up the last of the food.

Tom wiped the milk from his mouth and replied, 'The power of the talismans will act as a beacon for the Danann once they have been brought into contact with another sacred item which has been used as an article of communication with the gods for generations.'

'What, there's a big searchlight somewhere that shines the shape of a sword on the clouds?' Laura sniggered. 'Or is there a god-phone with a direct link—'

'In Dunvegan Castle on the Isle of Skye is the Fairy Flag, the Bratach Sith,' Tom said. 'It has the power we need.'

'If we drive hard we could reach it in a day,' Shavi said.

Veitch clapped his hands. 'Then we can wrap it up and be down the boozer for last orders!'

'You think the Fomorii aren't going to try to stop us?' Ruth asked caustically. 'It would be a big mistake to think it's all going to be plain sailing from here. They'll probably throw everything but the kitchen sink at us to stop us.'

'Ruth's right,' Church said. 'It's been tough so far, but this could be the worst part.'

They gathered up their things and Ogma led them through the maze of chambers to the entrance. They thanked him profusely for his hospitality and his aid for Tom and Laura, but it was so hard to read his emotions they felt uneasy and headed hastily back to the path up the mountainside.

Tom hung back on the steps of the porch to offer his private thanks to Ogma. Together they watched the others walking away, chatting and bickering.

Ruth's owl appeared suddenly from somewhere above their heads and swooped down until it was hovering a few feet away. Ogma spoke to it in a strange, keening voice.

'What is that?' Tom asked.

'A friend. An aide on your mission.'

The bird soared once over their heads, then shot up into the sky. Ogma watched it disappear into the clouds, then turned his attention back to the others as they made their way up the mountainside.

'You see clearly, True Thomas?' Ogma asked.

Tom nodded, his face suddenly dark and sad. 'We're going to hell and we won't all be coming back. How do I tell them that?'

'You offer the truth selectively, Thomas, as you always have.' For a second his eyes seemed to burn with fire, then he turned and went back to his books without another word.

Tom stood on the steps a moment longer, struggling to damp down the simmering emotions that threatened to consume him. Once he had regained his equilibrium, he hurried after the others, fervently wishing he had died the day before he had fallen asleep under that hawthorn tree.

CHAPTER TWENTY-ONE

Last Stand

The sun was only just rising as they passed through the rift back into the world and by the time they had trekked into Melrose, it was apparent it was going to be a fine spring day. The sky was blue and cloudless; in the sun it was beautifully warm, but with an exhilarating crispness from that faint underlying chill that was always present at that time of year that far north. But not even the fair weather could mitigate the desperate anticipation they all felt.

They picked up the van and drove to a 24-hour garage. 'Everything looks normal,' Church said. 'But here's the moment of truth.'

They all watched anxiously as Ruth darted inside to buy a paper. She picked one up, scanned the date, but her face gave nothing away. By the time she had clambered back into the van, the others couldn't contain themselves. 'Well?' Veitch almost shouted.

Ruth held out the paper. 'It's Mayday. Today's the day.'

There was a long moment of silence until Church said, 'Do we still have time to reach Dunvegan?'

'It is less than a day's drive,' Shavi replied. 'Unless we encounter any obstacles.'

His words hung in the air for a second or two, and then they launched themselves into frantic activity. Veitch ran back into the garage to load up with sandwiches and crisps while Church selected a cheap portable radio to replace the one they had lost with their old van.

Once they were on the road, he swept through the bands, but the radio could only tune into a disappointing handful of stations. There was one playing classical music, another with easy listening tracks and one which concentrated on old pop and rock back-to-back, punctuated by the occasional jingle, but with no DJ in evidence. The jaunty sound of The Turtles' 'So Happy Together' rang out.

'Spare us the sickening optimism,' Laura moaned. 'I could do with some jungle or techno or anything with a beat to clear my head out.'

'At least it's not Sinatra,' Ruth said.

'Bit of a coincidence that we emerged with just enough time to spare,' Church noted. He caught Tom's eye and mouthed, 'There are no coincidences,' just as Tom started to spout his mantra. The others laughed; Tom looked irritable.

'So what's this Beltane?' Veitch asked.

'The great festival of light in the Celtic world,' Tom replied moodily. 'It's the midpoint of the Celtic year. In the old days, the people used to offer tributes to Belenus, the god of sun, light and warmth, to mark the onset of summer, the return of the sun's heat and the fertility of the land.'

'But why's today so important as a deadline? It's just a day like any other one.'

Tom opened a bag of cheese and onion crisps and began to munch on them with irritating slowness. Out of the corner of his eye, Church could see Laura glancing around for something to throw at him. 'Imbolg, Beltane, Lughnasad and Samhain — the four great Celtic festivals — weren't just chosen at random,' he said with his mouth full. 'They were of vital importance to the gods, when all of reality was so aligned that power flowed back and forth between Otherworld and here. On those days it was like the whole of the universe was filled with a charge. Days when anything could happen.'

'So if we miss out today we've got to wait until the next festival?' Veitch asked.

Tom nodded. 'And by then it will be too late.'

* * *

Despite the momentous events that lay ahead, Church found himself feeling surprisingly bright. It wasn't hard to guess why: in just a few short hours he would finally get the answers he had prayed for during the bitter months when his life had seemed to be over, although the *why* had now been replaced by *who*. He could barely contain his anticipation, yet behind it he felt the cold, hard core which he knew was a desire for retribution just waiting to be unleashed. Closing his eyes, he drifted along with The Beach Boys singing 'Wouldn't it be Nice'. If only he could get warm.

They took the A72 out of Galashiels, then swung north to Edinburgh, crossing the Firth of Forth to pick up the M90. They selected the major routes, both for speed and to keep away from the more desolate areas, but as they hit Perth, where the map showed fewer and fewer signs of population, they knew they were drawing into dangerous territory.

After passing Dalwhinnie, they steeled themselves and set off across country. Up in the hills the air was crystal clear and filled with the scent of pines. They passed barely a car and any traffic they did see appeared to be local; farmers in beat-up old bangers splattered with primer, or old ladies taking the air, driving excruciatingly slow. An eerie stillness lay over the whole landscape.

As they progressed further into the Highlands, Church felt the biting coldness in his chest begin to grow more intense, as if someone were driving an icicle into his heart. A corresponding sweat sprang out on his forehead. Slipping his hand into his pocket and touching the Roisin Dubh, he felt as if he had plunged his hand into snow. When he drew it partly out, away from the eyes of the others, he saw its delicate petals were now obscured by hoar frost that sparkled when it caught the light; it was almost too cold to touch. And the iciness seemed to be spreading from the rose deep into his body; it felt like it was consuming him. He knew he should tell the others, but the cold seemed to have numbed his brain.

He fumbled with Marianne's locket, vaguely hoping it would make him feel better. Then he slipped the flower back into his pocket and tried to ignore the alarm bell that was starting to toll sonorously, deep in his mind.

They crossed the country without incident, and after following the placid, picturesque waters of Loch Lochy for a short spell, they picked up the A87 which would take them directly to Kyle of Lochalsh, the crossing point for Skye.

But as they trundled along the edge of Loch Cluanie, Shavi noticed a column of black smoke rising from an area beyond a steep bank just off the road. Although wary of stopping, once the acrid stink permeated the van it brought with it such an overwhelming sense of unease that they felt an obligation to pull over to investigate. While Veitch scrambled up the bank, the others watched from the van. They knew their worst fears had been confirmed when they saw him grow rigid at the summit. For several moments he stared at what lay beyond and then, without turning, he waved a hand for them to follow. Outside, the smell of oily smoke was choking and the air was filled with the screeching of birds. Cautiously they climbed the bank.

Stretched out in a large field was a scene of utter carnage. Scattered as far as the eye could see were the dead bodies of hundreds of soldiers, some of them mutilated beyond recognition, the churned turf of the field dyed red with their blood. It was like some horrific mediaeval battlefield. The carrion birds were already feeding on the remains with greedy shrieks and frenzied pecking. The smoke was billowing up from the remains of a burnt-out truck or troop carrier.

'They didn't stand a chance.' Veitch's voice trembled with emotion.

As they returned to the van in silence, Veitch pulled out his gun, examined it for a second, then tossed it away.

* * *

It was several miles before they could bring themselves to discuss what they had seen.

'At least we can be sure the Government knows. There's some kind of resistance,' Ruth ventured.

'For what it's worth.' Church hugged himself for warmth. 'All those modern weapons, all those experts in the art of warfare, they didn't mean a thing. There wasn't one enemy body there.'

'So what chance do we have if a bunch of professional killers can't cut the mustard?' Laura was wearing her sunglasses once again, hiding her true emotions from them all.

'You want to know what's worse?' Veitch said quietly. 'That they're obviously somewhere between us and where we're supposed to be going, settled in to a nice defensive position.'

'We have to keep going,' Ruth said. 'What else can we do?'

They fell silent once more.

They saw the smoke from fifteen miles away. They had probably noticed it earlier and mistaken it for a storm cloud, so large was the black column; it rose up thickly and rolled out to obscure the sun. At ten miles Shavi had to use the windscreen wipers and spray continuously to clear away the charred flakes caught in the wind.

'Black snow,' Laura said absently. 'Trippy.'

The atmosphere became unbearable as they neared the coast; even in the confines of the van they were coughing and covering their mouths. Then, as they crested a ridge and looked out over the sea, they saw the source. Kyle of Lochalsh, the tiny historic town that guarded the crossing to Skye, was burning. From their vantage point, they could see almost every building was ablaze, painting the lapping waves burnt orange and smoky red. It was almost deafening: the roaring of the flames caught by the wind, the sound of dropped milk crates as superheated windows erupted out, the thunder of crashing walls, every now and then punctuated by an explosion as a car petrol tank went up. There was no sign of life.

They stumbled from the van like drunks, intoxicated by the sheer horror of their vision. At least they could breathe a little easier as the wind took the worst of the smoke inland, but every breath was still filled with the stink of charcoal, rubber and plastic.

'God,' Ruth said in a voice so small it was almost lost beneath the noise of the inferno. 'Is this how the world is going to look?'

Through their daze, harsh truths began to seep; eventually Laura gave voice to them. 'Nobody's forcing us to do this. We could turn back, make the most of whatever time we've got left . . .' Her voice trailed off hopefully.

'How could we live with ourselves?' Church glanced at her briefly before staring back into the flickering light. 'Nobody wants to be here, but some responsibilities are too big to ignore. This is what we were *meant* to do—'

'Perhaps it is the only reason we are alive,' Shavi noted.

'We have to see it through to the end.' Laura nodded reluctantly at the resolution in Church's voice; in her heart she had known there was no other option.

'Should we search for any survivors?' Shavi suggested.

Church shook his head. 'I don't think there's any point. It looks like they went through the place systematically.'

'Look.' Veitch pointed beyond the flames to the short stretch of water that separated Skye from the mainland. The bridge that had been built at a cost of millions of pounds was shattered. The first section ended suddenly, as if it had been lopped off by an axe, and chunks of concrete and steel protruded from the swirling water. Nearby they could see the old ferries that had prospered before the bridge were burning or half-submerged in the tiny harbour.

'What are we going to do now?' Veitch continued. 'Swim?'

'I do not think so.' Shavi stood beside him and directed his gaze away from the harbour to the deep water in the middle of the channel. At first it just seemed to be a mass of chopping waves and odd little eddies and whirlpools, but then Veitch noticed a strange sinuous motion that was at odds with the movement of the water; it was like a black pipe rolling gently as it moved between the mainland and the island.

He was about to ask what Shavi was suggesting when there was a sudden churning of the water and something large rose up in a gush of white foam and sleek black skin cast ruddy in the light of the fire. Its head reached as high as a double-decker bus for just an instant before it ducked back beneath the waves.

'What the hell was that?' Veitch looked dumbfounded.

'The sea serpents have always been close to the Fomorii. They don't need to be coerced like the Fabulous Beasts.' Tom shuffled up beside them to watch the swirling water. 'Even when the doorways were supposed to be closed, the serpents swam back and forth, prefering neither here nor there, but somewhere in between.'

'Are they dangerous?' Veitch's eyes narrowed thoughtfully as he considered ways to reach the island.

'They have the teeth of sharks and their coils can crush bones and boats.'

'A watchdog,' Ruth said.

'Then how the hell are we going to get over there?' Veitch's frustration boiled over into impotent rage.

While the others threw ideas around, Laura watched from a distance, and she was the only one who saw the faint shadow cross Shavi's face. Quietly she tugged at his sleeve and drew him away from the rest.

'Spit it out,' she whispered.

When he looked at her she realised the expression had been one of fear. 'I cannot control these changes that are coming over me—'

'You should try being a twelve-year-old girl.'

'—the things I can do . . .' He struggled to find the correct words.

'I know it's scary. But everything's spinning out of control.'

He sighed and lowered his dark brown eyes. 'At first it seemed so wonderful, all these amazing new possibilities opening up to me. The trances, the dreams. But when I had that vision at Manorbier, it took nothing at all to get it started and it was so powerful it was almost as if I was really there. I could *smell* the blood on the wind . . .' He raised the back of his hand to his mouth in distaste. 'Now I am afraid. I wonder where it will all end.'

Surreptitiously, Laura took his hand; his fingers were cool and supple against her hot palm.

That subtlest of connections brought a smile to his lips. 'One should never shy away from new experiences, I suppose.'

'So what can you do?'

'When the change first came over me it was like I could almost understand what the birds were saying in their song. Then, as time progressed, I discovered it was more than that . . . it was as if I were in their heads, listening to their thoughts. And not just birds, but all animals.' He paused for a long time as he weighed his words. 'It is possible I could get into *that* creature's head, enough to subtly direct it. Perhaps enough to keep it away from a boat.'

'But?'

'But I am afraid if I truly try to enter its mind, I may never be able to get out again.' He watched her face closely for her reaction. When none was noticeable, he said, 'I am waiting for you to tell me not to be so ridiculous and to do my duty.'

'You're talking like I'm the responsible one. It's your call – I won't think any differently of you one way or the other.'

He smiled broadly. 'You are very mature. Why do you act like you are not?'

'We all know what happens to cheese when it gets mature.'

Veitch suddenly spotted them huddled together. 'Oi! What are you two plotting?'

Shavi lost himself in thought for a moment, then confidently strode over.

They headed back a couple of miles until they found a road which skirted the town; the fires were burning too hard to drive through it. On the north side there were plenty of little coves and they eventually chanced on one where a boat was moored at a private jetty. If the owner had survived the Fomorii attack, he was nowhere to be seen. Reluctantly they abandoned the van and transferred the talismans and what provisions they thought absolutely essential to the boat.

'This may seem a stupid question,' Church said once they were all aboard, 'but has anyone here sailed before?'

Veitch made a face. 'Been on the Thames Ferry. Didn't like it very much. And that boat in Wales.'

'I owned a small boat for fishing on the loch in my heyday,' Tom said. 'And I have even fished at sea, so I have enough knowledge to get us out there. But the currents between the mainland and island are rumoured to be strong and if the serpent gets angry, his backwash will capsize us. I presume we can all swim?'

They all nodded, apart from Veitch, who began to look a little wary.

'That's not an option,' Church said. 'How are we going to do anything if the talismans are at the bottom of the deep blue? You've got to get us out there and keep us steady so Shavi can do his bit.'

'*Try* to,' Shavi stressed.

They cast off and Tom steered the boat away from the shore. Although the water had appeared calm from dry land, they were soon bouncing across the waves in a queasy chopping motion. The wind had changed direction and now the thick, acrid smoke was being blown out across the bay; it was as if a thick fog had rolled between them and Skye.

'If we get past the serpent, we can take the boat around the north of the island to Dunvegan. It is built on a sea loch, so we can go right up to its walls.'

Church stood in the prow, tasting the salt as the spray stung his face, trying to ignore the icy cold that now permeated his entire body. Shavi rested on the wooden rail next to him to stare into the blue-green depths.

'How are you holding up?' Church asked.

'I think we are all holding up remarkably well, seeing that we are a mass of neuroses and contradictions wrapped up in skin and bone – in short, very human – being expected to do the job of heroes.'

Church shrugged. 'What's a hero? Some big muscular guy with a sword? Or some normal person who takes a swing for the greater good, despite everything?'

Shavi looked at him curiously.

'I'm just saying we're trying to do the best we can under the circumstances. Maybe the historians will come in with their whitewash brushes in a few years' time to turn us into heroes.'

'You are only a hero if you win.' Shavi looked up, his smile taking the edge off the bitter words. 'There is no place in Valhalla for those who simply tried hard.'

The smoke rolled in around them, choking, stinging their eyes. They all sat down in the bottom of the boat where the air was freshest, listening to the eerie echoes as the smoke muffled the lapping of the water and the sound of the town burning. They could have been hundreds of miles away, lost in the centre of the Atlantic.

Then Shavi's clear, sharp voice made them all start. 'It is coming.'

At first they could hear nothing. A few seconds later, from out of the smoke, came the almost mechanical sound of something breaking the water at regular intervals, growing louder as it drew closer. Church watched anxiously as Shavi closed his eyes, his face growing taut with concentration. The splashing, stitching sound came on relentlessly. Shavi's brow furrowed, his lips pulled back from his teeth.

At the last moment Church realised it wasn't going to work and he called out to the others to hold on. The serpent surged just past the prow and the boat lifted up at forty-five degrees. Church ground his eyes shut and gritted his teeth: someone cried out; he was convinced they were going under, dragged to the bottom in the backwash; a horrible way to die. But the boat poised on the cusp of tragedy like some terrible fairground ride and then went prow down just as steeply into the trough left by the serpent's passing. Waves crashed over them. Church sucked in a mouthful of seawater, but somehow held on. The boat righted itself jarringly, as if it were skidding across sand dunes. Church looked round; amazingly, everyone was still clinging on.

'If it hits us astern it'll shatter the boat,' he yelled to Shavi.

Shavi screwed up his face in anger at his failure before flinging himself upright and gripping on to the rail. 'Here!' he shouted. 'To me!'

'Get down!' Church cried. 'If it comes by again you'll be over the side!'

Shavi ignored him. A second or two later a shiver ran down Church's spine as he heard the serpent stitching water towards them. It was like a goods train; his breath grew as hard as stone in his chest. He braced himself for the impact. And waited, and waited.

There was a sound like a boulder being pitched into the water and then the drizzle of falling droplets as a shadow fell across him. The serpent had risen up out of the waves, as high as a lamppost, its flattened head swaying from side to side like a cobra. It had skin that was as shiny black and slick as a seal and eyes that seemed to glow a dull yellow; odd whiskers tufted out around its mouth like a catfish. And it seemed to be staring at Shavi.

Church was about to call out to his friend when he noticed the rigid posture and ghosted expression on Shavi's face, as if he were in a coma with his eyes open. They stayed that way for a long moment, two drunks staring each other out in a bar, and then, slowly, the serpent melted into the waves and swam languorously away.

Church heard Laura whisper, 'Good doggy.'

A spontaneous cheer arose from the others, just as Shavi pitched backwards alongside Church. His face was still locked tight. Church felt a sudden surge of panic when he looked into those glassy eyes; there was not even the slightest sign of Shavi within them. He scrambled forward and began to shake his shoulders.

The others' jubilation died away when they saw the edge of panic in his actions. 'Shavi,' he said. 'Come back!'

'Leave him!' Tom barked. 'If you disturb him now he could be lost for ever!'

'But what if he can't get back?' Church said. He stared again into those glassy eyes and couldn't control his desperation; the price they were paying was increasing constantly and he despaired at where it would end.

'Leave him!' Tom shouted again.

Reluctantly, Church stood back in the prow – then suddenly all thought of Shavi was gone. A gust of wind cleared the billowing smoke like a theatre curtain being rolled back, presenting a view of Skye that chilled him to the bone. At first details along the coast were blurred and he blinked twice to clear his vision. Then he realised the loss of distinction to the sharp edges of the green and grey coastline was caused by constant movement. Along the seafront, Skye was swarming; there was a sickening infestation of darkness as far as the eye could see, like ants on a dead rat.

'My God! How many are there?' Ruth was beside him, one hand on his shoulder.

They were mesmerised by the sheer enormity of what they were seeing, the malevolence that seemed to wash out across the water towards them. In that one moment, they knew: the world was ending and there was nothing they could do about it.

Church turned to Veitch, Laura and Tom, who were bickering at the rear of the boat, oblivious to the brief vision of hell that had been presented. 'Come on,' he ordered. 'We need to get a move on if we want to be there before sundown.'

It was a long, arduous journey up the Sound of Raasay, where the currents were as powerful as they had feared. Tom fought to keep the boat under control and eventually they rounded the north of the island as the afternoon began to draw on. They were all desperately aware of the hours running away from them, but no one gave voice to fears that there was not enough time left. At least they had left the massed ranks of the Fomorii behind, which gave Church a little more hope. Shavi's sacrifice had at least bought them that.

As the wild hills rose up grey and purple, brooding and mist-shrouded, away to their left, Tom steered the boat around to the west and eventually into the loch that led to Dunvegan Castle. The more they progressed inland, the more the choppy seas subsided, until they were sailing on water as smooth as polished black glass. Everywhere was still; no birds sang, the wind had dropped and the only sound was the gentle lapping of the water against the boat. Eventually the castle loomed up, a squat, forbidding presence perched on a rocky outcropping overlooking the loch. There were no signs of life around it.

Church and Veitch scanned the steep banks where gnarled, rugged trees clustered together in the face of the biting Atlantic winds. 'Do you think they're lying in wait?' Veitch asked.

'Could be.' But Church's instinct told him otherwise. 'We might be lucky. I don't think they expected us to get this far.'

'After all the hassle we've been through, wouldn't it be a laugh if we just waltzed into the castle, got the flag and did our business?' He snapped his fingers. 'Over. Just like that.'

'You love tempting fate, don't you, Ryan?'

They pulled the boat up on to the rocks at the foot of the

castle where there was an easy path among the boulders round to the front. Veitch and Church shouldered the talismans between them, every muscle taut, eyes never still. They hated having to leave Shavi behind, but he was too much of a burden and time was short; the sun was already slipping down the sky and Church was afraid the castle would be sealed and they would have to find some way to break in.

But they had gone barely twenty paces from the boat when they heard Shavi cry out. They ran back to find him near-delirious, foam flecking his mouth, his eyes roving, unseeing. 'The Fairy Bridge!' he called out to someone they couldn't see. 'They come across the Fairy Bridge!'

'What's he talking about?' Veitch said dismissively. He had half-turned away when Tom caught his arm.

'The Fairy Bridge lies not far from here. It's over a stream, near to one of the liminal zones. Some of the Fomorii may pass through Otherworld to appear there quicker than if they'd travelled over the land.'

Veitch looked puzzled. 'Yeah, but doesn't everything move slower over there?'

'Time is fluid. Slower, faster, there are no rules. If there is a chance, the Fomorii will take it.'

Church chewed on a nail for a moment. 'Ryan and I can go down there and do what we can to delay them while the rest of you get into the castle.' He hoped it didn't sound as futile as it did in his head. Veitch nodded his agreement; in one glance they both recognised that it was probably a suicide mission.

Leaving Shavi raving in the boat, they all hurried up the path to the front of the castle. It was open, but there was no one in the ticket booth, nor could they hear any sound coming from anywhere within.

While Veitch searched for some weapons, Church opened the crate to examine the sword one final time; it seemed comfortingly familiar, radiating strength and security, and he wished he could take it with him, but it was needed for the summoning ritual. As he reached in to caress the worn handle, a blue spark jumped out from it with such force it threw him across the floor. His fingers ached painfully and there was a dim burning sensation; it felt so powerful because his entire body was numb with cold.

'What was that?' Ruth said. 'It was like it didn't want you to touch it.'

Church shook his head, puzzled, but he had a nagging feeling he knew why. The Roisin Dubh continued to pulse coldly against his heart.

Veitch returned soon after with two swords which he had stolen from a display at the end of the entrance hall. Church examined them apprehensively. They would be as much use against the Fomorii as a pair of dinner knives, but there was no point stating the obvious.

They took directions for the bridge from Tom and had just set off when Ruth called Church back. She ran forward and gave him a hug of surprising warmth. 'Don't be stupid,' she said. 'I don't want to lose my best friend.'

'Don't I get a hug and a kiss?' Veitch called to Laura, who seemed to be avoiding Church's gaze.

She blew him one theatrically. 'Throw yourself at them. It might buy us a minute.'

He mumbled something, then they turned and hurried across the moat to the winding road that led away from the castle.

'Where's this flag, then?' Laura asked as they began to trawl through the castle's many rooms. Their footsteps echoed dismally in the empty chambers.

'It has always been kept in the drawing room,' Tom replied. 'Wherever that might be.'

'What I don't understand is why beings as terrifying as the Danann provided the basis for faery tales,' Ruth said. 'You know, cuddly, mischievous little men and women with wings sitting on toadstools.'

'In the old days faeries *were* frightening. Their reputation has been watered down over the years.' Tom paused at a junction in a corridor, irritated by the maze of rooms. 'People would not venture near sidh – the fairy mounds – at night and would not take their name in vain for fear of their reputation. Their memories of when the Danann walked the earth were too strong.' He chose the lefthand path at random and strode away without checking that they were behind him. 'When the Age of Reason came around, the fear generated by the gods was too much to bear in the brave new world, and so the people set about diminishing them – not only in stature – to make them less of a threat to their way of life.'

Ruth wondered if the others recognised that they were making small talk to avoid thinking about what might be happening to Church. 'And the Fairy Bridge has that name because the locals dimly recollected there was some doorway to Otherworld nearby?' she continued.

'Not so dimly recollected. The Danann had connections with the Celts long after they left other parts of the country alone. In Scotland, Wales, Cornwall and Ireland they are always felt strongly nearby. They may be unknowable in their actions, but they seem to feel loyalty for the people who first accepted them.' He cursed as they came to another dead end, then swung on his heel and carried on marching forcibly. 'The Fairy Bridge is so called because of an old tale about a MacLeod clan chieftain who married a woman of the Danann—'

'What? Inter-species romance?' Ruth exclaimed.

Tom sighed. 'You know very well some of the Danann are not so far removed from us. And those nearest seem to feel a kinship which isn't evident in the higher gods. May I continue?' She nodded. 'After twenty years of marriage, the Danann wife felt driven to return to Otherworld – she couldn't bear to be separated from her people for any longer. The husband was heartbroken, but as a gift to show her love for their long – in human terms – romance, she gave him the Bratach Sith, the Fairy Flag, so he could call on her people for help if the MacLeods ever faced defeat in battle. And the Fairy Bridge was the place of the giving and the place of the parting.'

'What a sad story.'

'Over here.' Laura was standing near an open doorway, motioning to them.

Once they entered, Ruth could tell it was the drawing room, but there was no sign of a flag. 'Where is it?'

Tom pointed to a picture on the wall. 'That's all that's left of it.' Behind the glass was the remnant of what once had been a proud flag of brown silk, intricately darned in red.

'It looks like it will fall apart if we touch it,' Ruth said, not knowing what she had expected.

'It isn't how it appears.' Tom dropped the crate on the floor and Laura carefully removed the talismans while he took the flag down. With trembling hands, he cracked the back from the frame, then laid the glass on one side. Once the flag was freed, he took a step back and bowed before it. Then, with an obsessive attention to angles and distances, he laid out the artefacts around the flag so they made the four points of a star.

From his breathing and his body language, Ruth could tell he was gripped with a curious anxiety, but it didn't seem the time to ask what was on his mind.

'Now,' he said tremulously, 'it is time for the ritual of summoning.'

Tom stood before the artefacts, head bowed, and muttered something under his breath. There was an instant change in the quality of the atmosphere in the room; Ruth and Laura backed anxiously to the wall.

Above the talismans, light appeared to be folding out of nowhere, like white cloth being forced through a hole. There was a sucking sound, a smell like cardamom, and then the air tore apart and they saw something terrible rushing towards them.

537

Ruth felt her head start to spin. 'Oh Lord,' she whispered.

The road from the castle was bleak, the trees disappearing the further they got from the loch to leave a heartless landscape of rock and sheep-clipped grass. They were thankful for the faint, late-afternoon sun which at least provided a vague patina of colour to the desolation.

Church and Veitch rarely spoke; the oppressive weight of what lay ahead made any conversation seem too trivial. And for Church, the cold had become almost more than he could bear. There was a part of him demanding that he throw away the flower, tell Veitch that he was far from his peak, but a stronger and more worrying part suppressed it easily. Worse, the cold now seemed to be affecting his vision; he could see what appeared to be little dustings of frost appearing round the edges of his sight, sparkling in the sunlight.

But the rose was a gift from Marianne, the suppressing part of him said. *How could it be anything but good?*

They heard the babbling of water before they saw the bridge, but once they crested a slight incline it was before them: just a single arch in a mediaeval construction of stone. Yet the moment Church took in its style and setting in the rocks and grassy banks, he felt like his heart was being crushed. It was exactly the image he had seen in the Watchtower when he had received the premonition of his death.

His sudden terror must have played out on his face, for Veitch turned to him with concern. 'What's wrong?'

'Nothing.' But he was transfixed by the sight and he couldn't have moved if he had wanted to.

The spell was broken when Veitch clapped a supportive hand on his shoulder. 'Yeah, I'm scared too. But we've just got to do our best. No point worrying about what's going to happen.'

Church sucked in a juddering breath to calm himself. 'You're right.' Before he drove all fatalistic thoughts from his head, he had one fleeting wish that he had properly said goodbye to Laura, and then it was replaced with the unsettling certainty that soon he would be with Marianne again.

They took up position on their side of the bridge, ready for their last stand. The sword felt awkward in Church's hand; more than useless after wielding the Otherworld weapon. He wondered how long they would last. A minute? Two?

For a long time there was nothing but the tinkling of the brook and the smell of damp grass, constants that made the subtle changes which came next seem like the blaring of an alarm. First there was a stink like a hot generator and burnt diesel, then a sound that reminded Church of a long-closed door being wrenched open. Then, some time between his eye blinking shut and opening again, the entire world slipped into horror.

They seemed to rise from the grass and heather like twisted blackthorn in time-lapse photography, filling the banks and road ahead of them, bristling with hatred, eyes burning in faces too terrible to consider, dark skin that seemed to suck up the sunlight and corrupt it. Eerily silent, motionless, a tidal wave poised at the moment before it suddenly crashed forward.

Veitch stifled some faint noise in his throat. Church was so frozen he had barely been able to feel anything, but even the iciness could not contain the hot blast of fear that roared through him.

'Is it like staring into the face of death?' The voice floated out from the serried ranks. Church recognised it instantly. A second later Calatin limped from the mass, a fey, malignant smile on his lips. He held a rusty sword with darkly stained teeth along one edge like a saw.

Church gripped his own sword tightly, though he could barely feel it in his grasp. Veitch was saying something to him, but the words seemed to be breaking up like a badly tuned radio. He turned, saw Veitch's concerned face through a haze of hoar frost. He realised the iciness was starting to reach his brain.

Calatin was facing him across the bridge now, smiling maliciously as though he knew exactly what was going through Church's mind. Behind him there seemed to be just a black wall. Strangely, when he spoke, his voice rang as clear as a bell.

'Do you feel the thorns in your heart?' He laughed like glass breaking. 'We have her, you know, at least that pitiful part of her that remains after the body withers. I love to hear her screams.'

Marianne, Church thought. His heart began to pound, the heat dispelling some of the cold.

'If you had not allowed death and the past to taint you so, there might have been the slimmest of chances that you might have snatched victory here.'

'The sword—' Church croaked.

'The power is not in the sword, Dragon Brother, it is in you. You are the host of the Pendragon Spirit. And you have proven yourself a betrayer of that tradition. Too weak, too trapped by guilt and doubt. We could not have given you the Kiss of Frost if you had not allowed us into your life.'

Slowly, the truth stirred in the depths of his frozen mind. The Fomorii had left nothing to chance, attacking with the Fabulous Beast and the Hunt, using Callow as backup; but most subtly of all, invading him from within, driving into his heart and soul. The Roisin Dubh – the Kiss of Frost – had been seeded into his presence right at the very start, lying dormant until releasing its cold bloom when most needed, when everything else had failed. And the worst thing was that Calatin was right: he had done it to himself; he had known in his heart he should have thrown the rose away, but he had been trapped in his obsession with Marianne and her death and that had driven him to his fate. He *had* been weak, pathetic; and he had doomed them all.

'Oh, the pain,' Calatin mocked. 'It hurts so to see oneself truly in the mirror of life. Sick little boy. Weak little boy.'

Church raised his sword, but the heat he was generating

from his emotions was not yet enough; the weapon shook violently in his hand. Veitch seemed to sense Church's inability to act and, with a growl of obscenities, he launched himself forward. It was an attack born more out of desperation than expertise, and as he swung his sword, Calatin parried easily and lashed out with a backhanded stroke. It caught Veitch a glancing blow across the forehead and he fell to the bridge, unconscious.

Calatin gave a sickly, supercilious grin at Church. 'We come with the night,' he hissed, 'and all fall before us. Our ways are the truth of existence. Everything you see is decaying, winding its way down into the dark. Why fight the natural order? Welcome it into your lives. Drink up the shadows, still the ticking of the clock, open your heart to the void.'

Church shook his head weakly.

'Now,' Calatin said sarcastically, 'let us see how well you fight.'

Ironically, by focusing on Marianne and her torment, Church found he could move a little easier, although it was still not enough. Calatin came at him lazily, swinging his sword like a father fencing with a child. Church blocked and almost dropped his sword. Calatin nipped in and brought the serrated edge of his weapon across Church's arm; the blood burned on his frozen skin.

And then the strangest thing happened. Church felt as if a bright, white light had suddenly burst through his body; just a flash, and then gone in an instant. And somehow he knew it had emanated from Marianne's locket, which he kept hidden in the same pocket as the Black Rose.

Whatever had caused it, it was enough to give him a burst of energy. With a skill that seemed to come from somewhere else, he brought his sword up sharply. The tip caught Calatin's cheek, raising a line of insipid blood. The Fomor whipped his head back in shock, and when he next levelled his gaze at Church, another eyelid appeared to have opened vertically in the eyeball itself, revealing a piercing yellow slit-iris. There was no mistaking the fury in his face. In a frenzy of chopping and hacking, he moved forward. One blow raked open Church's chest. The next bit deeply into his neck. Blood flowed freely.

Church staggered sideways from the bridge and fell on to the bank. The hoar frost in his vision was turning black. Calatin jumped beside him, still wielding the sword venomously. Another blow, more blood.

Church fell on to his back and slithered down to the water's edge. He knew he was dying. As Calatin bore down on him, his sword wet with Church's blood, Church thought of Marianne as a painful swell of bitter emotions washed the ice from him, then Laura, then Ruth and all the others.

Calatin brought the sword down hard and Church had the fleeting impression of floating above himself, looking down on the vision he had had in the Watchtower. And then all became black.

Everything was golden and shimmering, like a river of sunlight, and Ruth felt herself drifting along at the heart of it. It was a far cry from the rush of terror she had felt when the doorway first opened and she had been presented with a vista on the terrible place where the Danann had been banished. But then they had burst out of it, like dawn breaking on a desolate world, and she had been swept up with them, along with Tom and Laura; quite how, she did not know, although she had images of stallions and mares and chariots. Everything was a blur of wonder and awe. Some of them seemed almost human, with beautiful faces, golden skin and flowing hair, but others seemed to be changing their shape constantly as they moved; a few appeared just as light and one or two made her eyes hurt so much she couldn't bear to look at them or attempt to give them any real shape.

We did it! she thought with a sweeping feeling of such relief and ecstatic joy it brought tears to her eyes. *We brought the angels down to earth.*

Within seconds they were out of the castle and on the road to the Fairy Bridge. Ruth caught glimpses of sky bluer than she had ever imagined, and grass so green and succulent she wanted to roll in it laughing. And there was music, although she had no idea where it was coming from, like strings and brass and voices mingling in one instrument. She closed her eyes and basked in the glory.

It didn't last long. Another sound, discordant and some-how stomach-turning, broke through the golden cocoon and she snapped her eyes open. She saw a wall of black, of mon-strous eyes, and deformed features, and she recognised the sound of the Fomorii shrieking in anger. As the Danann swept down the hillside towards them, they seemed to roll up, fold in on themselves and melt into the grass.

And then in the stillness that followed there was another sound, smaller and reedier, and she discovered Veitch kneel-ing on the bridge, yelling something at them. His face was filled with despair so acute it broke through her trance. With a terrible wrench she pulled herself from the golden mass and ran towards him.

There was blood on his temple, but that wasn't the cause of his dismay. He motioned over the side of the bridge, then looked away. She already knew what she would see. She told herself to turn away before she saw so the image would not be with her for ever, but she knew she couldn't be a coward. Her eyes brimming with tears, she looked down on Church's body half-submerged in the brook, his blood seeping away with the water. She didn't cry or shout or scream; it was as if all emotion had been torn out of her by a sucking vacuum.

By the time she skidded down the bank her tears were flowing freely and her throat burned from sobbing. She knelt next to the body and took his hand. Why should she feel so bad when it was someone she had met only a few weeks before?

A shadow fell across her and she looked up to see Laura silhouetted against the setting sun. She shifted her position to see Laura's face and it was as she had guessed: cold, dis-passionate. 'Don't you feel anything?' she said in a fractured voice.

But Laura didn't even seem to recognise she was there. She stared blankly at Church's staring eyes, cocking her head slightly to one side like she was examining a work of art. 'I knew you'd do this to me, you bastard,' she said softly.

Veitch slumped down on the edge of the bridge. 'At least we won,' he said wearily. 'We drove them off. Despite, you know . . . Despite us being a bunch of losers. We did it.'

They remained there for a painful moment, not knowing what bound them together any more, barely able even to recognise themselves. And then they heard a crunch of gravel and turned to see Tom and one of the Danann walking towards them. The god exuded power from every pore of his golden skin, and when they looked into his almond eyes they saw nothing they knew.

He stopped before them and rested his gaze on each one of them in turn, a faintly disturbing smile playing on his lips.

'Who are you?' Ruth asked faintly.

The smile grew even more enigmatic. 'Once my names were known to everyone in the land. So soon forgotten? It will change, it will change. Who am I? I am Nuada, known as Nuada Airgetlámh, known as Nudd, known as Lludd, known as Lud, founder of Londinium, wielder of Caledfwlch.' There was an unpleasant arrogance in the turn of his head. 'The Tuatha Dé Danann give you thanks for freeing us from our place of banishment. In return, the Allfather has given permission for the use of his cauldron.'

Tom held out the bowl they had found under Glastonbury Tor. Ruth looked at him blankly. 'The Cauldron of Dagda is the cornucopia, the Horn of Plenty,' he said softly. 'It is the Grail, the source of spiritual renewal. The taker of life and the giver of life. The crucible of rebirth.' He smiled. 'Take it.'

Ruth's hands trembled as she took it, barely able to believe what he was saying. The moment her fingers closed around it, she felt a subtle heat deep in her stomach, rising up through her arms to her hands. The moment it hit the bowl, it seemed to weep droplets of gold, which collected in the bottom. When it had partially filled, Tom motioned to Church.

Though uncomprehending, Veitch jumped from the bridge and dragged Church from the water, resting the body in his lap and the head in the crook of his arm. He looked up at Ruth with the simple belief of a child.

Ruth glanced at the golden liquid, which moved almost with a life of its own. A part of her could not bring herself to accept what was being suggested: the dead were dead, a machine switched off never to be restarted; there was no subtle spirit, no *beyond* or Happy Home fairytale for the religiously naive; everything she had seen could not shake that part of her. But still there was another part of her that accepted wonder and hope, that believed in the World Where Anything Can Happen. There was a time for cynicism and the restraining lessons of adulthood, but this was a time to be a child. She knelt down and placed the bowl to Church's lips, while Veitch manipulated his mouth so the liquid would flow in. And then the world seemed to hang in space.

There was darkness and warmth and a vertiginous, queasy plummet into something unpleasant. And then Church opened his eyes. Briefly, Veitch and Tom had to restrain him as he was overcome with convulsions; images of Calatin's attack, the agony of the serrated sword biting into his flesh, the smell of his own fear, passed through his uncomprehending mind in an instant. But the sensations of the changes coming over his body drove the disturbing thoughts from him; the golden liquid seemed to be seeping into every part of him, transforming him as it passed, although he had no idea what he was becoming; yet beneath it there was the numb antagonism of the Fomorii Kiss of Frost still within him; heat and cold, light and dark, battling for supremacy.

'You have been reborn.'

Church looked up into the face of Nuada. It took a second or two to recognise who he was and what he was doing there. Slowly he looked round at the vision of gold and silver, faces almost too beautiful, presences too divine, and the transcendental wonder he felt brought a shiver of deep emotion. Tears sprang to his eyes in relief at the miracle. 'The Danann!' His voice sounded like it was being ground out. 'The others freed you ... you drove away the Fomorii ...'

'The Night Walkers departed rather than face our anger at their betrayal of the Covenant.'

Church closed his eyes in relief, resting back against Veitch's arm. 'But you came. We won. Now you can face up to them ... drag them back ...'

In the long silence that followed, Church knew there was something wrong. He opened his eyes to see Nuada smiling dangerously. 'Now we are back,' he said, 'we will not be leaving.'

'What do you mean?' Church levered himself upright, suddenly afraid.

'We always coveted a return to this place. We staked our claim upon it in the time before your race. But the pact prevented it and the doors remained closed. Now the Night Walkers have broken the pact. And the doors are open.'

'But the Fomorii are your enemy!' Church protested.

'The fruits of this land are too succulent to ignore for unnecessary confrontation. We have co-existed before. Uneasily, certainly, but the pursuit of our will overrides all other concerns.'

'But they are going to bring back Balor!' There were tears of frustration in Ruth's eyes.

'Perhaps they will succeed,' he mused superciliously.

Tom knelt before Nuada and bowed his head in supplication. 'The Brothers and Sisters of Dragons sacrificed a great deal to free you from your place of banishment, my Lord.'

'And they have our thanks, True Thomas. But their work was not all as it seemed.' Tom looked up at him quizzically. 'We are not without foresight. The Fomorii betrayal was anticipated – after all, it was in their nature. We had our preparations. The Brothers and Sisters of Dragons were guided to this moment from the beginning.'

'How?' Church thought he was going to be sick; suddenly he could see all the answers, but he was afraid to examine them.

'The alchemy of death was necessary to change you, to spark the Pendragon Spirit, to start you down the road that would lead to this moment.'

They all looked blank. Tom turned to them, troubled, disorientated. 'In all your lives, someone had to die—'

'You killed Marianne!' Church raged suddenly.

Nuada fixed such a dark expression on him Church was shocked into silence. 'Our own hands were never raised. We set events in motion. We removed checks, moved balances.' He pointed at Veitch. 'He turned and used his weapon at the perfect moment, against his will. Other fragile creatures followed our guidance—'

'Then who killed her?' Church asked dismally.

Nuada turned from him; his smile was both patronising and frightening. 'There are many games we can play with this world.' Tom blanched at his words. 'The prize has been well worth the rigours.'

He began to walk back to the shimmering golden horde massed beyond the bridge. Church tried to scramble to his feet, but had to be helped up by Veitch. He choked back his emotion and said, as forcefully as he could muster, 'At least help us remove the Fomorii. We need you.'

Nuada turned coldly. 'Your voice might have carried more weight if it were not polluted by the taint of the Night Walkers. In times before, the Pendragon Spirit would not have occupied such a weak host.'

And then he had joined the rest of the Tuatha Dé Danann,

and Church, Veitch, Tom and Ruth could only watch as the shining host swept out across the countryside like a tidal wave of terrifying, alien force.

CHAPTER TWENTY-TWO

Beltane

Night fell quickly. Perhaps it was their mood, or the events of the day, but it seemed more preternatural than any they had so far experienced, alive with ancient terrors. They built a fire in the shelter of a grove on the top of a hill where they could see Skye spread out beneath the arc of stars. Ruth remarked they could easily have gone back in time to the Neolithic era. Church replied that in a way they had.

Before the sun set they had fetched Shavi from the boat. He had regained some of his equilibrium, but although he attempted to put on a brave face, they could all see that when his smile dropped, he had a look about him like something had been damaged inside; he was haunted, detached. He refused to talk about what had happened when he had linked with the serpent, but he was no longer the man he had been.

Since their individual journeys began, they had all gained new scars, some within, some external, but as their conversation slowly emerged from the atmosphere of desolation they were all secretly surprised to discover bonds of friendship had been forged among them which would not have been there in other circumstances. As Church looked at their faces around the fire, he found a surprising burst of hope at that revelation; it was such a tiny thing in the face of all that had happened, but somehow it seemed important.

Without it, he mused, the realisation that their lives had been manipulated and ruined by higher powers could have destroyed them. Even so, each of them, in their own way, felt broken. Veitch, who had been ruined by the guilt of the murder he had committed; Ruth, who had lost her uncle and father; Shavi, who had lost his boyfriend; and Laura, whose mother had died while she lay unconscious. And there he was, two years of his life wasted by a suffering that need never have happened, the one thing he valued most destroyed, his entire existence spoiled; Marianne had been so important to him, life itself, and she had been treated as if she mattered less than a weed in the garden. All of that misery had been carried out purely on a whim, by a race of beings who thought so little about humanity they couldn't even bring themselves to act with contempt. He would have felt rage if it hadn't been so terrible; instead there was just despair at the senselessness of it all.

He sat in silence with Laura for the first hour after twilight, both of them lost to their thoughts. 'Still, it could have been worse, right?' she said eventually. 'If the Danann hadn't returned, we wouldn't have been sitting here now. The Fomorii would have wiped the world clean. You did that.'

'*We* did it,' he corrected.

'So we live to fight another day. We don't give up, right? Right?' She wasn't going to back down until he agreed, and when he did, she smiled and kissed him gently on the cheek. 'Sinatra would be proud of you, boy.' She slipped away, trailing her hand across his shoulders and the back of his neck. It was a simple touch, but it filled him with strength.

The Danann's involvement in their tragedies had at least helped Ruth begin to come to terms with Veitch's murder of her uncle. The kind of person he had been prevented her absolving him of all guilt, but they were talking. As the fire began to die down, the two of them, together with Laura and Shavi, went in search of more wood while Tom and Church sat watching the glowing embers.

'We were supposed to be some kind of heroes,' Church began disconsolately. 'The defenders of humanity, of the world itself. What a laugh! Talk about fooling ourselves. We were so insignificant to the Danann they ran us like mice through a maze. We did all their dirty work for them *and* we suffered for it. And what did we get in return? Nothing.'

'You're blinding yourself to your achievements.' Tom rolled a joint and lit it. 'The Danann may still help us. They simply need to be won over. If you'd failed to release them by Beltane, everything truly would be lost. The Fomorii would have had no opposition.' He echoed Laura's words and Church wondered why he was the only one who failed to see anything positive. He began to protest, but Tom silenced him with a hand. 'No. This has been a setback, but your victory in freeing the Danann has bought us more time. And the recovery of the talismans was a remarkable thing – something that has never been achieved since the Danann hid them away.'

Church shook his head, unconvinced. 'You know the worst thing? We've brought about exactly what we were trying to stop. If the Danann are as dangerously unpredictable ... as alien ... as you described, if they can devastate our lives without a second thought in the way that they did, I'm afraid of what they're going to do now they're here.'

In Tom's silence, Church heard his worst fears confirmed.

'That's something to tell the grandchildren I'll probably never have,' he said with a bitter laugh. 'I was the man who helped bring about the end of the world.'

A shooting star rocketed breathtakingly across a sky unspoiled by light pollution. Tom followed its arc while taking the smoke deep into his lungs. 'When all this began I thought we were without hope,' he began quietly. 'You'll forgive me when I say, but when I looked at all of you I saw failure writ large. But you've torn the scales from my eyes. Through hardship you persevered and the Pendragon Spirit has truly awoken in you, in all of you. You carry within you the manifestation of all that is good in humanity, the strength, the true power, perhaps, of the highest force.' He nodded to himself thoughtfully. 'We must have faith.'

'Faith, right. I tell you what I've got faith in: that I'm going to find out who or what the Danann used to kill Marianne and the others and I'm going to make them pay. And if I had the power within me, I'd make the Danann pay too.'

Tom said nothing.

Church watched the others approaching through the gloom, laughing amongst themselves, despite everything. Slowly, deep within him, he began to feel the stirrings of that affirmation to which Tom had given voice. He was the one who had ruined everything; his weakness; but he could change. It would have been easy to give in to it, but that wasn't the kind of person he was. Somehow he had to dig down deep, learn from his terrible failure and move on. And hope that redemption lay somewhere in the future.

'What have you done with the Roisin Dubh?' Tom asked.

Church dipped in his pocket and pulled out the rose; it was withered and desiccated. Wrapped around the stem was Marianne's locket. 'We're living in strange times,' he began. 'Look at this – a little girl's piece of cheap jewellery. And now it's a thing of wonder.' As he carefully untangled the chain, he explained about the white light that had infused him during his battle with Calatin. 'We've seen a lot of terrible things, but this . . . this fills me with hope. I still don't know what it means, but I know what I'd *like* it to mean.' He flicked open the locket and glanced at the photo inside. 'A time of miracles,' he said under his breath. As his words disappeared in the wind, the rose finally crumbled into dust and was whisked away from his palm.

'Gone,' Tom said.

'But not completely. I can still feel some of its taint inside me. I don't know what that will mean.'

'The Danann will not heed you while it remains.'

They fell silent for a long minute, and then Tom said, 'I think you need to make some explanations to the others.'

'I know. I owe them that, certainly. And I hope I'll be able to make amends. I'll tell them later, after we've eaten.' He sighed.

'Just a few weeks ago I thought I was incapable of feeling anything again,' he went on, thoughtfully. 'Now I could be convinced I'm feeling too much.' He laughed ironically. 'In this new Dark Age, it's easy to think we've lost so much – a way of life, technology that works, logic. But is that true? We've still got all the things that truly matter. It might sound twee, but maybe the importance of life comes down to just a few simple things – friendship, love, trust, a belief in something better. Faith. And in the face of all this inhumanity, maybe those human things are all we really need.'

Tom laughed, a sound Church couldn't recall hearing before. 'And you call me the hippie.'

Church scanned his face, saw the suffering and the strengths that had overcome it. 'It's not over, you know.'

'I know.'

'You're right, we've done great things. Amazing things. We may not be much to look at, but . . .' He looked round at the others. 'Look at them. I wouldn't want anybody else by my side. We're going to fight back. Find some way to make a difference. And we'll do it, you know?'

'I know.'

'So what do we do now?'

'That,' Tom said, 'is a question for tomorrow.'

They stoked up the fire and dined on the last of the sandwiches and crisps they had brought from the van. Later, while the others sat quietly thinking, Laura took the radio Church had bought in Melrose and wandered off, trying to find some music. Not long after she came hurrying back with it.

'You'd better listen to this,' she said. 'I went right across the bands trying to find some music that wasn't from another century. But every station was playing the same recorded message – that there's about to be some kind of Government statement.'

They put the radio down and huddled round it. Soon after

there was a burst of sombre music, and then the clipped, precise tones of a BBC newsreader.

'This is the BBC, calling the country from London. We have a statement from the Prime Minister which will be repeated at intervals of thirty minutes.'

A recording of the Prime Minister rang out, the voice clear, unwavering, drained of any emotion at all. 'As of 10 p.m. on May 1, martial law has been declared throughout the United Kingdom. The activities of Parliament have been suspended until further notice. This difficult decision has been taken in the light of the crisis facing the country. I can give no further details at this moment. In the meantime, all media has been suspended and once the situation has been clarified, official announcements will made through the BBC radio and television channels. In this troubling time, I would urge you all to remain calm. This action has been forced upon us, and it has been adopted reluctantly, but it is for the protection of all. A curfew will be instigated during the hours of darkness. The Government offers the strongest advice to congregate in areas of human habitation. Stay away from open countryside. Avoid lakes and rivers. The National Parks are restricted areas until further notice. Do not venture into any area considered lonely or secluded. Remain in well-lit localities at all times. Do not travel alone. In rural areas our stringent gun laws are being relaxed for the protection of the populace.

'On a more personal note, I must say I am well aware of the strength of character that lies at the heart of this proud nation. In the days and weeks that lie ahead, we must all reach deep into that well of courage that we have exhibited so many times before in our glorious history. By standing together, we shall prevail.'

There was a brief pause and then the announcer said, 'That is all. This is the BBC, calling—'

Laura flicked off the radio. They remained silent for a long moment and then Veitch said, 'It's started, then.'

As if in response, a fire erupted magically on the hilltop

554

close by; there was no fuel anyone could see, and though it blazed powerfully, it didn't seem to scorch the surrounding grass. Then others burst like tiny fireflies on nearby hilltops, spreading out across the land as far as the eye could see.

'The Beltane fires,' Tom said quietly. 'The season has turned.'

They stood together looking out at the flickering beacons, feeling lonely and insignificant in the vast chamber of night. The world was no longer their own. The Age of Reason had died, and a new Dark Age had dawned.

BIbliography

Bently, Peter (ed.) *The Mystic Dawn: Celtic Europe* (Time-Life)

Bord, Janet and Colin *Mysterious Britain* (Thorsons)

Briggs, Katharine *An Encyclopedia of Fairies* (Penguin)

Bulfinch *Bulfinch's Mythology* (Spring)

Bushell, Rev William Done *Caldey: An Island of the Saints* (Lewis Printers)

Coghlan, Ronan *The Encyclopedia of Arthurian Legends* (Element)

Cope, Julian *The Modern Antiquarian* (Thorsons)

Cotterell, Arthur *Celtic Mythology* (Ultimate Editions)

Crisp, Roger *Ley Lines of Wessex* (Wessex Books)

Crossing, William *Folklore and Legends of Dartmoor* (Forest Publishing)

Davies, Margaret *The Story of Tenby* (Tenby Museum)

Dunning, R.W. *Arthur: The King in the West* (Grange Books)

Fitzpatrick, Jim *The Book of Conquests* (Paper Tiger)

Graves, Robert *The White Goddess* (Faber & Faber Ltd)

Hadingham, Evan *Circles and Standing Stones* (William Heinemann Ltd)

Hardcastle, F. *The Chalice Well* (The Chalice Well Trust)

Larousse *The Larousse Encyclopedia of Mythology*

Mann, Nicholas R. *The Isle of Avalon* (Llewellyn Publications, USA)

Matthews, John & Stead, Michael J. *King Arthur's Britain: A Photographic Odyssey* (Brockhampton Press)

Michell, John *New Light on the Ancient Mystery of Glastonbury* (Gothic Image)

Michell, John *Sacred England* (Gothic Image)

Miller, Hamish & Broadhurst, Paul *The Sun and the Serpent* (Pendragon Press)

Radford, Roy and Ursula *West Country Folklore* (Peninsula Press)

Richards, Julian *Beyond Stonehenge* (Trust for Wessex Archaeology)

Rutherford, Ward *Celtic Mythology* (Thorsons)

St Leger-Gordon, Ruth E. *The Witchcraft and Folklore of Dartmoor* (Peninsula Press)

Stewart, Bob & Matthews, John *Legendary Britain* (Blandford)

Various *Folklore, Myths and Legends of Britain* (Reader's Digest)

White, Richard (ed.) *King Arthur in Legend and History* (Dent)

Wilde, Lady *Ancient Legends of Ireland* (Ward & Downey)

Zink, David D. *The Ancient Stones Speak* (Paddington Press)